Goodbye, Columbus and Five Short Stories copyright © 1959 by
Philip Roth, copyright renewed © 1987 by Philip Roth. Published
by arrangement with Houghton Mifflin Company.

Letting Go copyright © 1961, 1962 by Philip Roth. Published by
arrangement with Random House Trade Publishing,
a division of Random House, Inc.

The paper used in this publication meets the
minimum requirements of the American National Standard for
Information Sciences—Permanence of Paper for Printed
Library Materials, ANSI Z39.48—1984.

Distributed to the trade
in the United States by Penguin Putnam Inc.
and in Canada by Penguin Books Canada Ltd.

Library of Congress Catalog Number: 2005040916
For cataloging information, see end of Notes.
ISBN 1-931082-79-0

———

First Printing
The Library of America—157

PHILIP ROTH

Manufactured in the United States of America

PHILIP ROTH

NOVELS & STORIES 1959–1962

Goodbye, Columbus and Five Short Stories
Letting Go

THE LIBRARY OF AMERICA

ROSS MILLER
WROTE THE CHRONOLOGY AND NOTES
FOR THIS VOLUME

Philip Roth's
Novels & Stories 1959–1962
is published with support from
a friend of The Library of America

Philip Roth's
Novels & Stories 1959–1962
is kept in print by a gift from

JOEL CONARROE

to the Guardians of American Letters Fund,
established by The Library of America
to ensure that every volume in the series
will be permanently available.

Contents

GOODBYE, COLUMBUS

AND

FIVE SHORT STORIES

To my mother and father

"The heart is half a prophet."
Yiddish proverb

Contents

Goodbye, Columbus

THE FIRST TIME I saw Brenda she asked me to hold her glasses. Then she stepped out to the edge of the diving board and looked foggily into the pool; it could have been drained, myopic Brenda would never have known it. She dove beautifully, and a moment later she was swimming back to the side of the pool, her head of short-clipped auburn hair held up, straight ahead of her, as though it were a rose on a long stem. She glided to the edge and then was beside me. "Thank you," she said, her eyes watery though not from the water. She extended a hand for her glasses but did not put them on until she turned and headed away. I watched her move off. Her hands suddenly appeared behind her. She caught the bottom of her suit between thumb and index finger and flicked what flesh had been showing back where it belonged. My blood jumped.

That night, before dinner, I called her.

"Who are you calling?" my Aunt Gladys asked.

"Some girl I met today."

"Doris introduced you?"

"Doris wouldn't introduce me to the guy who drains the pool, Aunt Gladys."

"Don't criticize all the time. A cousin's a cousin. How did you meet her?"

"I didn't really meet her. I saw her."

"Who is she?"

"Her last name is Patimkin."

"Patimkin I don't know," Aunt Gladys said, as if she knew anybody who belonged to the Green Lane Country Club. "You're going to call her you don't know her?"

"Yes," I explained. "I'll introduce myself."

"Casanova," she said, and went back to preparing my uncle's dinner. None of us ate together: my Aunt Gladys ate at five o'clock, my cousin Susan at five-thirty, me at six, and my

7

uncle at six-thirty. There is nothing to explain this beyond the fact that my aunt is crazy.

"Where's the suburban phone book?" I asked after pulling out all the books tucked under the telephone table.

"What?"

"The suburban phone book. I want to call Short Hills."

"That skinny book? What, I gotta clutter my house with that, I never use it?"

"Where is it?"

"Under the dresser where the leg came off."

"For God's sake," I said.

"Call information better. You'll go yanking around there, you'll mess up my drawers. Don't bother me, you see your uncle'll be home soon. I haven't even fed *you* yet."

"Aunt Gladys, suppose tonight we all eat together. It's hot, it'll be easier for you."

"Sure, I should serve four different meals at once. You eat pot roast, Susan with the cottage cheese, Max has steak. Friday night is his steak night, I wouldn't deny him. And I'm having a little cold chicken. I should jump up and down twenty different times? What am I, a workhorse?"

"Why don't we all have steak, or cold chicken—"

"Twenty years I'm running a house. Go call your girl friend."

But when I called, Brenda Patimkin wasn't home. She's having dinner at the club, a woman's voice told me. Will she be home after (my voice was two octaves higher than a choirboy's)? I don't know, the voice said, she may go driving golf balls. Who is this? I mumbled some words—nobody she wouldn't know I'll call back no message thank you sorry to bother . . . I hung up somewhere along in there. Then my aunt called me and I steeled myself for dinner.

She pushed the black whirring fan up to *High* and that way it managed to stir the cord that hung from the kitchen light.

"What kind of soda you want? I got ginger ale, plain seltzer, black raspberry, and a bottle cream soda I could open up."

"None, thank you."

"You want water?"

"I don't drink with my meals. Aunt Gladys, I've told you that every day for a year already—"

"Max could drink a whole case with his chopped liver only. He works hard all day. If you worked hard you'd drink more."

At the stove she heaped up a plate with pot roast, gravy, boiled potatoes, and peas and carrots. She put it in front of me and I could feel the heat of the food in my face. Then she cut two pieces of rye bread and put that next to me, on the table.

I forked a potato in half and ate it, while Aunt Gladys, who had seated herself across from me, watched. "You don't want bread," she said, "I wouldn't cut it it should go stale."

"I *want* bread," I said.

"You don't like with seeds, do you?"

I tore a piece of bread in half and ate it.

"How's the meat?" she said.

"Okay. Good."

"You'll fill yourself with potatoes and bread, the meat you'll leave over I'll have to throw it out."

Suddenly she leaped up from the chair. "Salt!" When she returned to the table she plunked a salt shaker down in front of me—pepper wasn't served in her home: she'd heard on Galen Drake that it was not absorbed by the body, and it was disturbing to Aunt Gladys to think that anything she served might pass through a gullet, stomach, and bowel just for the pleasure of the trip.

"You're going to pick the peas out is all? You tell me that, I wouldn't buy with the carrots."

"I love carrots," I said, "I love them." And to prove it, I dumped half of them down my throat and the other half onto my trousers.

"Pig," she said.

Though I am very fond of desserts, especially fruit, I chose not to have any. I wanted, this hot night, to avoid the conversation that revolved around my choosing fresh fruit over canned fruit, or canned fruit over fresh fruit; whichever I preferred, Aunt Gladys always had an abundance of the other jamming her refrigerator like stolen diamonds. "He wants canned peaches, I have a refrigerator full of grapes I have to get rid of . . ." Life was a throwing off for poor Aunt Gladys, her greatest joys were taking out the garbage, emptying her pantry, and making threadbare bundles for what she still referred to as the Poor Jews in Palestine. I only hope she dies with an empty refrigerator, otherwise she'll ruin eternity for everyone else, what with her Velveeta turning green, and her navel oranges growing fuzzy jackets down below.

My Uncle Max came home and while I dialed Brenda's number once again, I could hear soda bottles being popped open in the kitchen. The voice that answered this time was high, curt, and tired. "Hullo."

I launched into my speech. "Hello-Brenda-Brenda-you-don't-know-me-that-is-you-don't-know-my-name-but-I-held-your-glasses-for-you-this-afternoon-at-the-club . . . You-asked-me-to-I'm-not-a-member-my-cousin-Doris-is-Doris-Klugman-I-asked-who-you-were . . ." I breathed, gave her a chance to speak, and then went ahead and answered the silence on the other end. "Doris? She's the one who's always reading *War and Peace*. That's how I know it's the summer, when Doris is reading *War and Peace*." Brenda didn't laugh; right from the start she was a practical girl.

"What's your name?" she said.

"Neil Klugman. I held your glasses at the board, remember?"

She answered me with a question of her own, one, I'm sure, that is an embarrassment to both the homely and the fair. "What do you look like?"

"I'm . . . dark."

"Are you a Negro?"

"No," I said.

"What *do* you look like?"

"May I come see you tonight and show you?"

"That's nice," she laughed. "I'm playing tennis tonight."

"I thought you were driving golf balls."

"I drove them already."

"How about after tennis?"

"I'll be sweaty after," Brenda said.

It was not to warn me to clothespin my nose and run in the opposite direction; it was a fact, it apparently didn't bother Brenda, but she wanted it recorded.

"I don't mind," I said, and hoped by my tone to earn a niche somewhere between the squeamish and the grubby. "Can I pick you up?"

She did not answer a minute; I heard her muttering, "Doris

Klugman, Doris Klugman . . ." Then she said, "Yes, Briarpath Hills, eight-fifteen."

"I'll be driving a—" I hung back with the year, "a tan Plymouth. So you'll know me. How will I know you?" I said with a sly, awful laugh.

"I'll be sweating," she said and hung up.

Once I'd driven out of Newark, past Irvington and the packed-in tangle of railroad crossings, switchmen shacks, lumberyards, Dairy Queens, and used-car lots, the night grew cooler. It was, in fact, as though the hundred and eighty feet that the suburbs rose in altitude above Newark brought one closer to heaven, for the sun itself became bigger, lower, and rounder, and soon I was driving past long lawns which seemed to be twirling water on themselves, and past houses where no one sat on stoops, where lights were on but no windows open, for those inside, refusing to share the very texture of life with those of us outside, regulated with a dial the amounts of moisture that were allowed access to their skin. It was only eight o'clock, and I did not want to be early, so I drove up and down the streets whose names were those of eastern colleges, as though the township, years ago, when things were named, had planned the destinies of the sons of its citizens. I thought of my Aunt Gladys and Uncle Max sharing a Mounds bar in the cindery darkness of their alley, on beach chairs, each cool breeze sweet to them as the promise of afterlife, and after a while I rolled onto the gravel roads of the small park where Brenda was playing tennis. Inside my glove compartment it was as though the map of *The City Streets of Newark* had metamorphosed into crickets, for those mile-long tarry streets did not exist for me any longer, and the night noises sounded loud as the blood whacking at my temples.

I parked the car under the black-green canopy of three oaks, and walked towards the sound of the tennis balls. I heard an exasperated voice say, "Deuce *again*." It was Brenda and she sounded as though she was sweating considerably. I crackled slowly up the gravel and heard Brenda once more. "My ad," and then just as I rounded the path, catching a cuff full of burrs, I heard, "Game!" Her racket went spinning up in the air and she caught it neatly as I came into sight.

"Hello," I called.

"Hello, Neil. One more game," she called. Brenda's words seemed to infuriate her opponent, a pretty brown-haired girl, not quite so tall as Brenda, who stopped searching for the ball that had been driven past her, and gave both Brenda and myself a dirty look. In a moment I learned the reason why: Brenda was ahead five games to four, and her cocksureness about there being just one game remaining aroused enough anger in her opponent for the two of us to share.

As it happened, Brenda finally won, though it took more games than she'd expected. The other girl, whose name sounded like Simp, seemed happy to end it at six all, but Brenda, shifting, running, up on her toes, would not stop, and finally all I could see moving in the darkness were her glasses, a glint of them, the clasp of her belt, her socks, her sneakers, and, on occasion, the ball. The darker it got the more savagely did Brenda rush the net, which seemed curious, for I had noticed that earlier, in the light, she had stayed back, and even when she had had to rush, after smashing back a lob, she didn't look entirely happy about being so close to her opponent's racket. Her passion for winning a point seemed outmatched by an even stronger passion for maintaining her beauty as it was. I suspected that the red print of a tennis ball on her cheek would pain her more than losing all the points in the world. Darkness pushed her in, however, and she stroked harder, and at last Simp seemed to be running on her ankles. When it was all over, Simp refused my offer of a ride home and indicated with a quality of speech borrowed from some old Katharine Hepburn movie that she could manage for herself; apparently her manor lay no further than the nearest briar patch. She did not like me and I her, though I worried it, I'm sure, more than she did.

"Who is *she*?"

"Laura Simpson Stolowitch."

"Why don't you call her Stolo?" I asked.

"Simp is her Bennington name. The ass."

"Is that where you go to school?" I asked.

She was pushing her shirt up against her skin to dry the perspiration. "No. I go to school in Boston."

I disliked her for the answer. Whenever anyone asks me where I went to school I come right out with it: Newark Colleges of Rutgers University. I may say it a bit too ringingly, too fast, too up-in-the-air, but I say it. For an instant Brenda reminded me of the pug-nosed little bastards from Montclair who come down to the library during vacations, and while I stamp out their books, they stand around tugging their elephantine scarves until they hang to their ankles, hinting all the while at "Boston" and "New Haven."

"Boston University?" I asked, looking off at the trees.

"Radcliffe."

We were still standing on the court, bounded on all sides by white lines. Around the bushes back of the court, fireflies were cutting figure eights in the thorny-smelling air and then, as the night suddenly came all the way in, the leaves on the trees shone for an instant, as though they'd just been rained upon. Brenda walked off the court, with me a step behind her. Now I had grown accustomed to the dark, and as she ceased being merely a voice and turned into a sight again, some of my anger at her "Boston" remark floated off and I let myself appreciate her. Her hands did not twitch at her bottom, but the form revealed itself, covered or not, under the closeness of her khaki Bermudas. There were two wet triangles on the back of her tiny-collared white polo shirt, right where her wings would have been if she'd had a pair. She wore, to complete the picture, a tartan belt, white socks, and white tennis sneakers.

As she walked she zipped the cover on her racket.

"Are you anxious to get home?" I said.

"No."

"Let's sit here. It's pleasant."

"Okay."

We sat down on a bank of grass slanted enough for us to lean back without really leaning; from the angle it seemed as though we were preparing to watch some celestial event, the christening of a new star, the inflation to full size of a half-ballooned moon. Brenda zipped and unzipped the cover while she spoke; for the first time she seemed edgy. Her edginess coaxed mine back, and so we were ready now for what, magically, it seemed we might be able to get by without: a meeting.

"What does your cousin Doris look like?" she asked.

"She's dark—"

"Is she—"

"No," I said. "She has freckles and dark hair and she's very tall."

"Where does she go to school?"

"Northampton."

She did not answer and I don't know how much of what I meant she had understood.

"I guess I don't know her," she said after a moment. "Is she a new member?"

"I think so. They moved to Livingston only a couple of years ago."

"Oh."

No new star appeared, at least for the next five minutes.

"Did you remember me from holding your glasses?" I said.

"Now I do," she said. "Do you live in Livingston too?"

"No. Newark."

"We lived in Newark when I was a baby," she offered.

"Would you like to go home?" I was suddenly angry.

"No. Let's walk though."

Brenda kicked a stone and walked a step ahead of me.

"Why is it you rush the net only after dark?" I said.

She turned to me and smiled. "You noticed? Old Simp the Simpleton doesn't."

"Why do you?"

"I don't like to be up too close, unless I'm sure she won't return it."

"Why?"

"My nose."

"What?"

"I'm afraid of my nose. I had it bobbed."

"What?"

"I had my nose fixed."

"What was the matter with it?"

"It was bumpy."

"A lot?"

"No," she said, "I was pretty. Now I'm prettier. My brother's having his fixed in the fall."

"Does he want to be prettier?"

She didn't answer and walked ahead of me again.

"I don't mean to sound facetious. I mean why's he doing it?"

"He *wants* to . . . unless he becomes a gym teacher . . . but he won't," she said. "We all look like my father."

"Is he having his fixed?"

"Why are you so nasty?"

"I'm not. I'm sorry." My next question was prompted by a desire to sound interested and thereby regain civility; it didn't quite come out as I'd expected—I said it too loud. "How much does it cost?"

Brenda waited a moment but then she answered. "A thousand dollars. Unless you go to a butcher."

"Let me see if you got your money's worth."

She turned again; she stood next to a bench and put the racket down on it. "If I let you kiss me would you stop being nasty?"

We had to take about two too many steps to keep the approach from being awkward, but we pursued the impulse and kissed. I felt her hand on the back of my neck and so I tugged her towards me, too violently perhaps, and slid my own hands across the side of her body and around to her back. I felt the wet spots on her shoulder blades, and beneath them, I'm sure of it, a faint fluttering, as though something stirred so deep in her breasts, so far back it could make itself felt through her shirt. It was like the fluttering of wings, tiny wings no bigger than her breasts. The smallness of the wings did not bother me—it would not take an eagle to carry me up those lousy hundred and eighty feet that make summer nights so much cooler in Short Hills than they are in Newark.

2

The next day I held Brenda's glasses for her once again, this time not as momentary servant but as afternoon guest; or perhaps as both, which still was an improvement. She wore a black tank suit and went barefooted, and among the other women, with their Cuban heels and boned-up breasts, their knuckle-sized rings, their straw hats, which resembled immense wicker pizza plates and had been purchased, as I heard one deeply tanned woman rasp, "from the cutest little *shvartze* when we docked at Barbados," Brenda among them was elegantly simple, like a sailor's dream of a Polynesian maiden, albeit one with prescription sun glasses and the last name of Patimkin. She brought a little slurp of water with her when she crawled back towards the pool's edge, and at the edge she grabbed up with her hands and held my ankles, tightly and wet.

"Come in," she said up to me, squinting. "We'll play."

"Your glasses," I said.

"Oh break the goddam things. I hate them."

"Why don't you have your eyes fixed?"

"There you go again."

"I'm sorry," I said. "I'll give them to Doris."

Doris, in the surprise of the summer, had gotten past Prince Andrey's departure from his wife, and now sat brooding, not, it turned out, over the lonely fate of poor Princess Liza, but at the skin which she had lately discovered to be peeling off her shoulders.

"Would you watch Brenda's glasses?" I said.

"Yes." She fluffed little scales of translucent flesh into the air. "Damn it."

I handed her the glasses.

"Well, for God's sake," she said, "I'm not going to hold them. Put them down. *I'm* not her slave."

"You're a pain in the ass, you know that, Doris?" Sitting there, she looked a little like Laura Simpson Stolowitch, who was, in fact, walking somewhere off at the far end of the pool, avoiding Brenda and me because (I liked to think) of the defeat Brenda had handed her the night before; or maybe (I didn't like to think) because of the strangeness of my presence. Regardless, Doris had to bear the weight of my indictment of both Simp and herself.

"Thank you," she said. "After I invite you up for the day."

"That was yesterday."

"What about last year?"

"That's right, your mother told you last year too—invite Esther's boy so when he writes his parents they won't complain we don't look after him. Every summer I get my day."

"You should have gone with them. That's not our fault.

You're not our charge," and when she said it, I could just tell it was something she'd heard at home, or received in a letter one Monday mail, after she'd returned to Northampton from Stowe, or Dartmouth, or perhaps from that weekend when she'd taken a shower with her boyfriend in Lowell House.

"Tell your father not to worry. Uncle Aaron, the sport. I'll take care of myself," and I ran on back to the pool, ran into a dive, in fact, and came up like a dolphin beside Brenda, whose legs I slid upon with my own.

"How's Doris?" she said.

"Peeling," I said. "She's going to have her skin fixed."

"*Stop* it," she said, and dove down beneath us till I felt her clamping her hands on the soles of my feet. I pulled back and then down too, and then, at the bottom, no more than six inches above the wiggling black lines that divided the pool into lanes for races, we bubbled a kiss into each other's lips. She was smiling there, at *me*, down at the bottom of the swimming pool of the Green Lane Country Club. Way above us, legs shimmied in the water and a pair of fins skimmed greenly by: my cousin Doris could peel away to nothing for all I cared, my Aunt Gladys have twenty feedings every night, my father and mother could roast away their asthma down in the furnace of Arizona, those penniless deserters—I didn't care for anything but Brenda. I went to pull her towards me just as she started fluttering up; my hand hooked on to the front of her suit and the cloth pulled away from her. Her breasts swam towards me like two pink-nosed fish and she let me hold them. Then, in a moment, it was the sun who kissed us both, and we were out of the water, too pleased with each other to smile. Brenda shook the wetness of her hair onto my face and with the drops that touched me I felt she had made a promise to me about the summer, and, I hoped, beyond.

"Do you want your sun glasses?"

"You're close enough to see," she said. We were under a big blue umbrella, side-by-side on two chaise longues, whose plastic covers sizzled against our suits and flesh; I turned my head to look at Brenda and smelled that pleasant little burning odor in the skin of my shoulders. I turned back up to the sun, as did she, and as we talked, and it grew hotter and brighter, the colors splintered under my closed eyelids.

"This is all very fast," she said.

"Nothing's happened," I said softly.

"No. I guess not. I sort of feel something has."

"In eighteen hours?"

"Yes. I feel . . . pursued," she said after a moment.

"*You* invited *me*, Brenda."

"Why do you always sound a little nasty to me?"

"Did I sound nasty? I don't mean to. Truly."

"You do! *You* invited *me*, Brenda. So what?" she said. "That isn't what I mean anyway."

"I'm sorry."

"Stop apologizing. You're so automatic about it, you don't even mean it."

"Now you're being nasty to me," I said.

"No. Just stating the facts. Let's not argue. I like you." She turned her head and looked as though she too paused a second to smell the summer on her own flesh. "I like the way you look." She saved it from embarrassing me with that factual tone of hers.

"Why?" I said.

"Where did you get those fine shoulders? Do you play something?"

"No," I said. "I just grew up and they came with me."

"I like your body. It's fine."

"I'm glad," I said.

"You like mine, don't you?"

"No," I said.

"Then it's denied you," she said.

I brushed her hair flat against her ear with the back of my hand and then we were silent a while.

"Brenda," I said, "you haven't asked me anything about me."

"How you feel? Do you want me to ask you how you feel?"

"Yes," I said, accepting the back door she gave me, though probably not for the same reasons she had offered it.

"How *do* you feel?"

"I want to swim."

"Okay," she said.

We spent the rest of the afternoon in the water. There were eight of those long lines painted down the length of the pool and by the end of the day I think we had parked for a while in every lane, close enough to the dark stripes to reach out and touch them. We came back to the chairs now and then and sang hesitant, clever, nervous, gentle dithyrambs about how we were beginning to feel towards one another. Actually we did not have the feelings we said we had until we spoke them —at least I didn't; to phrase them was to invent them and own them. We whipped our strangeness and newness into a froth that resembled love, and we dared not play too long with it, talk too much of it, or it would flatten and fizzle away. So we moved back and forth from chairs to water, from talk to silence, and considering my unshakable edginess with Brenda, and the high walls of ego that rose, buttresses and all, between her and her knowledge of herself, we managed pretty well.

At about four o'clock, at the bottom of the pool, Brenda suddenly wrenched away from me and shot up to the surface. I shot up after her.

"What's the matter?" I said.

First she whipped the hair off her forehead. Then she pointed a hand down towards the base of the pool. "My brother," she said, coughing some water free inside her.

And suddenly, like a crew-cut Proteus rising from the sea, Ron Patimkin emerged from the lower depths we'd just inhabited and his immensity was before us.

"Hey, Bren," he said, and pushed a palm flat into the water so that a small hurricane beat up against Brenda and me.

"What are you so happy about?" she said.

"The Yankees took two."

"Are we going to have Mickey Mantle for dinner?" she said. "When the Yankees win," she said to me, treading so easily she seemed to have turned the chlorine to marble beneath her, "we set an extra place for Mickey Mantle."

"You want to race?" Ron asked.

"No, Ronald. Go race alone."

Nobody had as yet said a word about me. I treaded unobtrusively as I could, as a third party, unintroduced, will step back and say nothing, awaiting the amenities. I was tired, however, from the afternoon's sport, and wished to hell brother and sister would not tease and chat much longer. Fortunately

Brenda introduced me. "Ronald, this is Neil Klugman. This is my brother, Ronald Patimkin."

Of all things there in the fifteen feet water, Ron reached out his hand to shake. I returned the shake, not quite as monumentally as he apparently expected; my chin slipped an inch into the water and all at once I was exhausted.

"Want to race?" Ron asked me good-naturedly.

"Go ahead, Neil, race with him. I want to call home and tell them you're coming to dinner."

"Am I? I'll have to call my aunt. You didn't say anything. My clothes—"

"We dine *au naturel*."

"What?" Ronald said.

"Swim, baby," Brenda said to him and it ached me some when she kissed him on the face.

I begged out of the race, saying I had to make a phone call myself, and once upon the tiled blue border of the pool, looked back to see Ron taking the length in sleek, immense strokes. He gave one the feeling that after swimming the length of the pool a half dozen times he would have earned the right to drink its contents; I imagined he had, like my Uncle Max, a colossal thirst and a gigantic bladder.

Aunt Gladys did not seem relieved when I told her she'd have only three feedings to prepare that night. "Fancy-shmancy" was all she said to me on the phone.

We did not eat in the kitchen; rather, the six of us—Brenda, myself, Ron, Mr. and Mrs. Patimkin, and Brenda's little sister, Julie—sat around the dining room table, while the maid, Carlota, a Navaho-faced Negro who had little holes in her ears but no earrings, served us the meal. I was seated next to Brenda, who was dressed in what was *au naturel* for her: Bermudas, the close ones, white polo shirt, tennis sneakers and white socks. Across from me was Julie, ten, round-faced, bright, who before dinner, while the other little girls on the street had been playing with jacks and boys and each other, had been on the back lawn putting golf balls with her father. Mr. Patimkin reminded me of my father, except that when he spoke he did not surround each syllable with a wheeze. He was tall, strong, ungrammatical, and a ferocious eater. When he attacked his salad—after drenching it in bottled French dressing—the veins swelled under the heavy skin of his forearm. He ate three helpings of salad, Ron had four, Brenda and Julie had two, and only Mrs. Patimkin and I had one each. I did not like Mrs. Patimkin, though she was certainly the handsomest of all of us at the table. She was disastrously polite to me, and with her purple eyes, her dark hair, and large, persuasive frame, she gave me the feeling of some captive beauty, some wild princess, who has been tamed and made the servant to the king's daughter— who was Brenda.

Outside, through the wide picture window, I could see the back lawn with its twin oak trees. I say oaks, though fancifully, one might call them sporting-goods trees. Beneath their branches, like fruit dropped from their limbs, were two irons, a golf ball, a tennis can, a baseball bat, basketball, a first-baseman's glove, and what was apparently a riding crop. Further back, near the scrubs that bounded the Patimkin property and in front of the small basketball court, a square red blanket, with a white O stitched in the center, looked to be on fire against the green grass. A breeze must have blown outside, for the net on the basket moved; inside we ate in the steady coolness of air by Westinghouse. It was a pleasure, except that eating among those Brobdingnags, I felt for quite a while as though four inches had been clipped from my shoulders, three inches from my height, and for good measure, someone had removed my ribs and my chest had settled meekly in towards my back.

There was not much dinner conversation; eating was heavy and methodical and serious, and it would be just as well to record all that was said in one swoop, rather than indicate the sentences lost in the passing of food, the words gurgled into mouthfuls, the syntax chopped and forgotten in heapings, spillings, and gorgings.

To Ron: When's Harriet calling?

Ron: Five o'clock.

Julie: It *was* five o'clock.

Ron: Their time.

Julie: Why is it that it's earlier in Milwaukee? Suppose you took a plane back and forth all day. You'd never get older.

Brenda: That's right, sweetheart.

Mrs. P.: What do you give the child misinformation for? Is that why she goes to school?

BRENDA: I don't know why she goes to school.

MR. P. (*lovingly*): College girl.

RON: Where's Carlota? Carlota!

MRS. P.: Carlota, give Ronald more.

CARLOTA (*calling*): More what?

RON: Everything.

MR. P.: Me too.

MRS. P.: They'll have to *roll* you on the links.

MR. P. (*pulling his shirt up and slapping his black, curved belly*): What are you talking about? Look at that?

RON (*yanking his T-shirt up*): Look at *this*.

BRENDA (*to me*): Would you care to bare your middle?

ME (*the choir boy again*): No.

MRS. P.: That's right, Neil.

ME: Yes. Thank you.

CARLOTA (*over my shoulder, like an unsummoned spirit*): Would *you* like more?

ME: No.

MR. P.: He eats like a bird.

JULIE: Certain birds eat a lot.

BRENDA: Which ones?

MRS. P.: Let's not talk about animals at the dinner table. Brenda, why do you encourage her?

RON: Where's Carlota, I gotta play tonight.

MR. P.: Tape your wrist, don't forget.

MRS. P.: Where do you live, Bill?

BRENDA: Neil.

MRS. P.: Didn't I say Neil?

JULIE: You said "Where do you live, *Bill*?"

MRS. P.: I must have been thinking of something else.

RON: I hate tape. How the hell can I play in tape?

JULIE: Don't curse.

MRS. P.: That's right.

MR. P.: What is Mantle batting now?

JULIE: Three twenty-eight.

RON: Three twenty-five.

JULIE: Eight!

RON: Five, jerk! He got three for four in the second game.

JULIE: *Four* for four.

RON: That was an error, Minoso should have had it.

JULIE: *I* didn't think so.

BRENDA (*to me*): See?

MRS. P.: See what?

BRENDA: I was talking to Bill.

JULIE: Neil.

MR. P.: Shut up and eat.

MRS. P.: A little less talking, young lady.

JULIE: *I* didn't say anything.

BRENDA: She was talking to me, sweetie.

MR. P.: What's this *she* business. Is that how you call your mother? What's dessert?

The phone rings, and though we are awaiting dessert, the meal seems at a formal end, for Ron breaks for his room, Julie shouts "Harriet!" and Mr. Patimkin is not wholly successful in stifling a belch, though the failure even more than the effort ingratiates him to me. Mrs. Patimkin is directing Carlota not to mix the milk silverware and the meat silverware again, and Carlota is eating a peach while she listens; under the table I feel Brenda's fingers tease my calf. I am full.

We sat under the biggest of the oak trees while out on the basketball court Mr. Patimkin played five and two with Julie. In the driveway Ron was racing the motor of the Volkswagen. "Will somebody *please* move the Chrysler out from behind me?" he called angrily. "I'm late as it is."

"Excuse me," Brenda said, getting up.

"I think I'm behind the Chrysler," I said.

"Let's go," she said.

We backed the cars out so that Ron could hasten on to his game. Then we reparked them and went back to watching Mr. Patimkin and Julie.

"I like your sister," I said.

"So do I," she said. "I wonder what she'll turn out to be."

"Like you," I said.

"I don't know," she said. "Better probably." And then she added, "or maybe worse. How can you tell? My father's nice to her, but I'll give her another three years with my mother . . . Bill," she said, musingly.

"I didn't mind that," I said. "She's very beautiful, your mother."

"I can't even think of her as my mother. She hates me. Other girls, when they pack in September, at least their mothers help them. Not mine. She'll be busy sharpening pencils for Julie's pencil box while I'm carrying my trunk around upstairs. And it's so obvious why. It's practically a case study."

"Why?"

"She's jealous. It's so corny I'm ashamed to say it. Do you know my mother had the best back-hand in New Jersey? Really, she was the best tennis player in the state, man or woman. You ought to see the pictures of her when she was a girl. She was so healthy-looking. But not chubby or anything. She was soulful, truly. I love her in those pictures. Sometimes I say to her how beautiful the pictures are. I even asked to have one blown up so I could have it at school. 'We have other things to do with our money, young lady, than spend it on old photographs.' Money! My father's up to here with it, but whenever I buy a coat you should hear her. 'You don't have to go to Bonwit's, young lady, Ohrbach's has the strongest fabrics of any of them.' Who *wants* a strong fabric! Finally I get what I want, but not till she's had a chance to aggravate me. Money is a waste for her. She doesn't even know how to enjoy it. She still thinks we live in Newark."

"But you get what you want," I said.

"Yes. Him," and she pointed out to Mr. Patimkin who had just swished his third straight set shot through the basket to the disgruntlement, apparently, of Julie, who stamped so hard at the ground that she raised a little dust storm around her perfect young legs.

"He's not too smart but he's sweet at least. He doesn't treat my brother the way she treats me. Thank God, for that. Oh, I'm tired of talking about them. Since my freshman year I think every conversation I've ever had has always wound up about my parents and how awful it is. It's universal. The only trouble is they don't know it."

From the way Julie and Mr. Patimkin were laughing now, out on the court, no problem could ever have seemed less universal; but, of course, it was universal for Brenda, more than that, cosmic—it made every cashmere sweater a battle with her mother, and her life, which, I was certain, consisted to a large part of cornering the market on fabrics that felt soft to the skin, took on the quality of a Hundred Years' War . . .

I did not intend to allow myself such unfaithful thoughts, to line up with Mrs. Patimkin while I sat beside Brenda, but I could not shake from my elephant's brain that she-still-thinks-we-live-in-Newark remark. I did not speak, however, fearful that my tone would shatter our post-dinner ease and intimacy. It had been so simple to be intimate with water pounding and securing all our pores, and later, with the sun heating them and drugging our senses, but now, in the shade and the open, cool and clothed on her own grounds, I did not want to voice a word that would lift the cover and reveal that hideous emotion I always felt for her, and is the underside of love. It will not always *stay* the underside—but I am skipping ahead.

Suddenly, little Julie was upon us. "Want to play?" she said to me. "Daddy's tired."

"C'mon," Mr. Patimkin called. "Finish for me."

I hesitated—I hadn't held a basketball since high school—but Julie was dragging at my hand, and Brenda said, "Go ahead."

Mr. Patimkin tossed the ball towards me while I wasn't looking and it bounced off my chest, leaving a round dust spot, like the shadow of a moon, on my shirt. I laughed, insanely.

"Can't you catch?" Julie said.

Like her sister, she seemed to have a knack for asking practical, infuriating questions.

"Yes."

"Your turn," she said. "Daddy's behind forty-seven to thirty-nine. Two hundred wins."

For an instant, as I placed my toes in the little groove that over the years had been nicked into a foul line, I had one of those instantaneous waking dreams that plague me from time to time, and send, my friends tell me, deadly cataracts over my eyes: the sun had sunk, crickets had come and gone, and leaves had blackened, and still Julie and I stood alone on the lawn, tossing the ball at the basket; "Five hundred wins," she called, and then when she beat me to five hundred she called, "Now *you* have to reach it," and I did, and the night lengthened, and she called, "*Eight* hundred wins," and we played on and then it was eleven hundred that won and we played on and it never was morning.

"Shoot," Mr. Patimkin said. "You're me."

That puzzled me, but I took my set shot and, of course, missed. With the Lord's blessing and a soft breeze, I made the lay-up.

"You have forty-one. I go," Julie said.

Mr. Patimkin sat on the grass at the far end of the court. He took his shirt off, and in his undershirt, and his whole day's growth of beard, looked like a trucker. Brenda's old nose fitted him well. There was a bump in it, all right; up at the bridge it seemed as though a small eight-sided diamond had been squeezed in under the skin. I knew Mr. Patimkin would never bother to have that stone cut from his face, and yet, with joy and pride, no doubt, had paid to have Brenda's diamond removed and dropped down some toilet in Fifth Avenue Hospital.

Julie missed her set shot, and I admit to a slight, gay, flutter of heart.

"Put a little spin on it," Mr. Patimkin told her.

"Can I take it again?" Julie asked me.

"Yes." What with paternal directions from the sidelines and my own grudging graciousness on the court, there did not seem much of a chance for me to catch up. And I wanted to, suddenly, I wanted to win, to run little Julie into the ground. Brenda was back on one elbow, under the tree, chewing on a leaf, watching. And up in the house, at the kitchen window, I could see that the curtain had swished back—the sun too low to glare off electrical appliances—and Mrs. Patimkin was looking steadily out at the game. And then Carlota appeared on the back steps, eating a peach and holding a pail of garbage in her free hand. She stopped to watch too.

It was my turn again. I missed the set shot and laughingly turned to Julie and said, "Can I take it again?"

"No!"

So I learned how the game was played. Over the years Mr. Patimkin had taught his daughters that free throws were theirs for the asking; he could afford to. However, with the strange eyes of Short Hills upon me, matrons, servants, and providers, I somehow felt I couldn't. But I had to and I did.

"Thanks a lot, Neil," Julie said when the game was ended— at 100—and the crickets had come.

"You're welcome."

Under the trees, Brenda smiled. "Did you let her win?"

"I think so," I said. "I'm not sure."

There was something in my voice that prompted Brenda to say, comfortingly, "Even Ron lets her win."

"It's all nice for Julie," I said.

3

The next morning I found a parking space on Washington Street directly across from the library. Since I was twenty minutes early I decided to stroll in the park rather than cross over to work; I didn't particularly care to join my colleagues, who I knew would be sipping early morning coffee in the binding room, smelling still of all the orange crush they'd drunk that weekend at Asbury Park. I sat on a bench and looked out towards Broad Street and the morning traffic. The Lackawanna commuter trains were rumbling in a few blocks to the north and I could hear them, I thought—the sunny green cars, old and clean, with windows that opened all the way. Some mornings, with time to kill before work, I would walk down to the tracks and watch the open windows roll in, on their sills the elbows of tropical suits and the edges of briefcases, the properties of businessmen arriving in town from Maplewood, the Oranges, and the suburbs beyond.

The park, bordered by Washington Street on the west and Broad on the east, was empty and shady and smelled of trees, night, and dog leavings; and there was a faint damp smell too, indicating that the huge rhino of a water cleaner had passed by already, soaking and whisking the downtown streets. Down Washington Street, behind me, was the Newark Museum—I could see it without even looking: two oriental vases in front like spittoons for a rajah, and next to it the little annex to which we had traveled on special buses as schoolchildren. The annex was a brick building, old and vine-covered, and always reminded me of New Jersey's link with the beginning of the country, with George Washington, who had trained his scrappy army—a little bronze tablet informed us children—in the very park where I now sat. At the far end of the park, beyond the Museum, was the bank building where I had gone to college. It had been converted some years before into an extension of Rutgers University; in fact, in what once had been the bank president's waiting room I had taken a course called Contemporary Moral Issues. Though it was summer now, and I was out of college three years, it was not hard for me to remember the other students, my friends, who had worked evenings in Bamberger's and Kresge's and had used the commissions they'd earned pushing ladies' out-of-season shoes to pay their laboratory fees. And then I looked out to Broad Street again. Jammed between a grimy-windowed bookstore and a cheesy luncheonette was the marquee of a tiny art theater—how many years had passed since I'd stood beneath that marquee, lying about the year of my birth so as to see Hedy Lamarr swim naked in *Ecstasy*; and then, having slipped the ticket taker an extra quarter, what disappointment I had felt at the frugality of her Slavic charm . . . Sitting there in the park, I felt a deep knowledge of Newark, an attachment so rooted that it could not help but branch out into affection.

Suddenly it was nine o'clock and everything was scurrying. Wobbly-heeled girls revolved through the doors of the telephone building across the way, traffic honked desperately, policemen barked, whistled, and waved motorists to and fro. Over at St. Vincent's Church the huge dark portals swung back and those bleary-eyes that had risen early for Mass now blinked at the light. Then the worshipers had stepped off the church steps and were racing down the streets towards desks, filing cabinets, secretaries, bosses, and—if the Lord had seen fit to remove a mite of harshness from their lives—to the comfort of air-conditioners pumping at their windows. I got up and crossed over to the library, wondering if Brenda was awake yet.

The pale cement lions stood unconvincing guard on the library steps, suffering their usual combination of elephantiasis and arteriosclerosis, and I was prepared to pay them as little attention as I had for the past eight months were it not for a small colored boy who stood in front of one of them. The lion had lost all of its toes the summer before to a safari of juvenile delinquents, and now a new tormentor stood before him, sagging a little in his knees, and growling. He would growl, low and long, drop back, wait, then growl again. Then he would straighten up, and, shaking his head, he would say to the lion, "Man, you's a coward . . ." Then, once again, he'd growl.

The day began the same as any other. From behind the desk on the main floor, I watched the hot high-breasted teen-age girls walk twitchingly up the wide flight of marble stairs that led to the main reading room. The stairs were an imitation of a staircase somewhere in Versailles, though in their toreador pants and sweaters these young daughters of Italian leatherworkers, Polish brewery hands, and Jewish furriers were hardly duchesses. They were not Brenda either, and any lust that sparked inside me through the dreary day was academic and time-passing. I looked at my watch occasionally, thought of Brenda, and waited for lunch and then for after lunch, when I would take over the Information Desk upstairs and John McKee, who was only twenty-one but wore elastic bands around his sleeves, would march starchily down the stairs to work assiduously at stamping books in and out. John McRubberbands was in his last year at Newark State Teachers College where he was studying at the Dewey Decimal System in preparation for his lifework. The library was not going to be my lifework, I knew it. Yet, there had been some talk—from Mr. Scapello, an old eunuch who had learned somehow to disguise his voice as a man's—that when I returned from my summer vacation I would be put in charge of the Reference Room, a position that had been empty ever since that morning when Martha Winney had fallen off a high stool in the Encyclopedia Room and shattered all those frail bones that come together to form what in a woman half her age we would call the hips.

I had strange fellows at the library and, in truth, there were many hours when I never quite knew how I'd gotten there or why I stayed. But I did stay and after a while waited patiently for that day when I would go into the men's room on the main floor for a cigarette and, studying myself as I expelled smoke into the mirror, would see that at some moment during the morning I had gone pale, and that under my skin, as under

McKee's and Scapello's and Miss Winney's, there was a thin cushion of air separating the blood from the flesh. Someone had pumped it there while I was stamping out a book, and so life from now on would be not a throwing off, as it was for Aunt Gladys, and not a gathering in, as it was for Brenda, but a bouncing off, a numbness. I began to fear this, and yet, in my muscleless devotion to my work, seemed edging towards it, silently, as Miss Winney used to edge up to the *Britannica*. Her stool was empty now and awaited me.

Just before lunch the lion tamer came wide-eyed into the library. He stood still for a moment, only his fingers moving, as though he were counting the number of marble stairs before him. Then he walked creepily about on the marble floor, snickering at the clink of his taps and the way his little noise swelled up to the vaulted ceiling. Otto, the guard at the door, told him to make less noise with his shoes, but that did not seem to bother the little boy. He clacked on his tiptoes, high, secretively, delighted at the opportunity Otto had given him to practice this posture. He tiptoed up to me.

"Hey," he said, "where's the heart section?"

"The what?" I said.

"The heart section. Ain't you got no heart section?"

He had the thickest sort of southern Negro dialect and the only word that came clear to me was the one that sounded like heart.

"How do you spell it?" I said.

"*Heart.* Man, pictures. Drawing books. Where you got them?"

"You mean art books? Reproductions?"

He took my polysyllabic word for it. "Yea, they's them."

"In a couple places," I told him. "Which artist are you interested in?"

The boy's eyes narrowed so that his whole face seemed black. He started backing away, as he had from the lion. "All of them . . ." he mumbled.

"That's okay," I said. "You go look at whichever ones you want. The next flight up. Follow the arrow to where it says Stack Three. You remember that? Stack Three. Ask somebody upstairs."

He did not move; he seemed to be taking my curiosity

about his taste as a kind of poll-tax investigation. "Go ahead," I said, slashing my face with a smile, "right up there . . ."

And like a shot he was scuffling and tapping up towards the heart section.

After lunch I came back to the in-and-out desk and there was John McKee, waiting, in his pale blue slacks, his black shoes, his barber-cloth shirt with the elastic bands, and a great knit tie, green, wrapped into a Windsor knot, that was huge and jumped when he talked. His breath smelled of hair oil and his hair of breath and when he spoke, spittle cobwebbed the corners of his mouth. I did not like him and at times had the urge to yank back on his armbands and slingshot him out past Otto and the lions into the street.

"Has a little Negro boy passed the desk? With a thick accent? He's been hiding in the art books all morning. You know what those boys *do* in there."

"I saw him come in, John."

"So did I. Has he gone *out* though."

"I haven't noticed. I guess so."

"Those are *very* expensive books."

"Don't be so nervous, John. People are supposed to touch them."

"There is touching," John said sententiously, "and there is touching. Someone should check on him. I was afraid to leave the desk here. You know the way they treat the housing projects we give them."

"*You* give them?"

"The city. Have you seen what they do at Seth Boyden? They threw *beer* bottles, those big ones, on the *lawn*. They're taking over the city."

"Just the Negro sections."

"It's easy to laugh, you don't live near them. I'm going to call Mr. Scapello's office to check the Art Section. Where did he ever find out about art?"

"You'll give Mr. Scapello an ulcer, so soon after his egg-and-pepper sandwich. I'll check, I have to go upstairs anyway."

"You know what they do in there," John warned me.

"Don't worry, Johnny, *they're* the ones who'll get warts on their dirty little hands."

"Ha ha. Those books happen to cost—"

So that Mr. Scapello would not descend upon the boy with his chalky fingers, I walked up the three flights to Stack Three, past the receiving room where rheumy-eyed Jimmy Boylen, our fifty-one-year-old boy, unloaded books from a cart; past the reading room, where bums off Mulberry Street slept over *Popular Mechanics*; past the smoking corridor where damp-browed summer students from the law school relaxed, some smoking, others trying to rub the colored dye from their tort texts off their fingertips; and finally, past the periodical room, where a few ancient ladies who'd been motored down from Upper Montclair now huddled in their chairs, pince-nezing over yellowed, fraying society pages in old old copies of the Newark *News*. Up on Stack Three I found the boy. He was seated on the glass-brick floor holding an open book in his lap, a book, in fact, that was bigger than his lap and had to be propped up by his knees. By the light of the window behind him I could see the hundreds of spaces between the hundreds of tiny black corkscrews that were his hair. He was very black and shiny, and the flesh of his lips did not so much appear to be a different color as it looked to be unfinished and awaiting another coat. The lips were parted, the eyes wide, and even the ears seemed to have a heightened receptivity. He looked ecstatic—until he saw me, that is. For all he knew I was John McKee.

"That's okay," I said before he could even move, "I'm just passing through. You read."

"Ain't nothing *to* read. They's pictures."

"Fine." I fished around the lowest shelves a moment, playing at work.

"Hey, mister," the boy said after a minute, "where is this?"

"Where is what?"

"Where is these pictures? These people, man, they sure does look cool. They ain't no yelling or shouting here, you could just see it."

He lifted the book so I could see. It was an expensive large-sized edition of Gauguin reproductions. The page he had been looking at showed an $8\frac{1}{2} \times 11$ print, in color, of three native women standing knee-high in a rose-colored stream. It *was* a silent picture, he was right.

"That's Tahiti. That's an island in the Pacific Ocean."

"That ain't no place you could go, is it? Like a ree-*sort*?"

"You could go there, I suppose. It's very far. People live there . . ."

"Hey, *look*, look here at this one." He flipped back to a page where a young brown-skinned maid was leaning forward on her knees, as though to dry her hair. "Man," the boy said, "that's the fuckin life." The euphoria of his diction would have earned him eternal banishment from the Newark Public Library and its branches had John or Mr. Scapello—or, God forbid, the hospitalized Miss Winney—come to investigate.

"Who took these pictures?" he asked me.

"Gauguin. He didn't take them, he painted them. Paul Gauguin. He was a Frenchman."

"Is he a white man or a colored man?"

"He's white."

"Man," the boy smiled, chuckled almost, "I knew that. He don't *take* pictures like no colored men would. He's a good picture taker . . . *Look*, *look*, look here at this one. Ain't that the fuckin *life*?"

I agreed it was and left.

Later I sent Jimmy Boylen hopping down the stairs to tell McKee that everything was all right. The rest of the day was uneventful. I sat at the Information Desk thinking about Brenda and reminding myself that that evening I would have to get gas before I started up to Short Hills, which I could see now, in my mind's eye, at dusk, rose-colored, like a Gauguin stream.

When I pulled up to the Patimkin house that night, everybody but Julie was waiting for me on the front porch: Mr. and Mrs., Ron, and Brenda, wearing a dress. I had not seen her in a dress before and for an instant she did not look like the same girl. But that was only half the surprise. So many of those Lincolnesque college girls turn out to be limbed for shorts alone. Not Brenda. She looked, in a dress, as though she'd gone through life so attired, as though she'd never worn shorts, or bathing suits, or pajamas, or anything but that pale linen dress. I walked rather bouncingly up the lawn, past the huge weeping willow, towards the waiting Patimkins, wishing all the while that I'd had my car washed. Before I'd even reached them, Ron stepped forward and shook my hand, vigorously, as though he hadn't seen me since the Diaspora. Mrs. Patimkin smiled and Mr. Patimkin grunted something and continued twitching his wrists before him, then raising an imaginary golf club and driving a ghost of a golf ball up and away towards the Orange Mountains, that are called Orange, I'm convinced, because in that various suburban light that's the *only* color they do not come dressed in.

"We'll be right back," Brenda said to me. "You have to sit with Julie. Carlota's off."

"Okay," I said.

"We're taking Ron to the airport."

"Okay."

"Julie doesn't want to go. She says Ron pushed her in the pool this afternoon. We've been waiting for you, so we don't miss Ron's plane. Okay?"

"*Okay.*"

Mr. and Mrs. Patimkin and Ron moved off, and I flashed Brenda just the hint of a glare. She reached out and took my hand a moment.

"How do you like me?" she said.

"You're great to baby-sit for. Am I allowed all the milk and cake I want?"

"Don't be angry, baby. We'll be right back." Then she waited a moment, and when I failed to deflate the pout from my mouth, she gave *me* a glare, no hints about it. "I *meant* how do you like me in a dress!" Then she ran off towards the Chrysler, trotting in her high heels like a colt.

When I walked into the house, I slammed the screen door behind me.

"Close the other door too," a little voice shouted. "The air-conditioning."

I closed the other door, obediently.

"Neil?" Julie called.

"Yes."

"Hi. Want to play five and two?"

"No."

"Why not?"

I did not answer.

"I'm in the television room," she called.

"Good."

"Are you supposed to stay with me?"

"Yes."

She appeared unexpectedly through the dining room. "Want to read a book report I wrote?"

"Not now."

"What do you want to do?" she said.

"Nothing, honey. Why don't you watch TV?"

"All right," she said disgustedly, and kicked her way back to the television room.

For a while I remained in the hall, bitten with the urge to slide quietly out of the house, into my car, and back to Newark, where I might even sit in the alley and break candy with my own. I felt like Carlota; no, not even as comfortable as that. At last I left the hall and began to stroll in and out of rooms on the first floor. Next to the living room was the study, a small knotty-pine room jammed with cater-cornered leather chairs and a complete set of *Information Please Almanacs*. On the wall hung three colored photo-paintings; they were the kind which, regardless of the subjects, be they vital or infirm, old or youthful, are characterized by bud-cheeks, wet lips, pearly teeth, and shiny, metallized hair. The subjects in this case were Ron, Brenda, and Julie at about ages fourteen, thirteen, and two. Brenda had long auburn hair, her diamond-studded nose, and no glasses; all combined to make her look a regal thirteen-year-old who'd just gotten smoke in her eyes. Ron was rounder and his hairline was lower, but that love of spherical objects and lined courts twinkled in his boyish eyes. Poor little Julie was lost in the photo-painter's Platonic idea of childhood; her tiny humanity was smothered somewhere back of gobs of pink and white.

There were other pictures about, smaller ones, taken with a Brownie Reflex before photo-paintings had become fashionable. There was a tiny picture of Brenda on a horse; another of Ron in bar mitzvah suit, *yamalkah*, and *tallas*; and two pictures framed together—one of a beautiful, faded woman, who must have been, from the eyes, Mrs. Patimkin's mother, and the other of Mrs. Patimkin herself, her hair in a halo, her eyes joyous and not those of a slowly aging mother with a quick and lovely daughter.

I walked through the archway into the dining room and stood a moment looking out at the sporting goods tree. From the television room that winged off the dining room, I could hear Julie listening to *This Is Your Life*. The kitchen, which winged off the other side, was empty, and apparently, with Carlota off, the Patimkins had had dinner at the club. Mr. and Mrs. Patimkin's bedroom was in the middle of the house, down the hall, next to Julie's, and for a moment I wanted to see what size bed those giants slept in—I imagined it wide and deep as a swimming pool—but I postponed my investigation while Julie was in the house, and instead opened the door in the kitchen that led down to the basement.

The basement had a different kind of coolness from the house, and it had a smell, which was something the upstairs was totally without. It felt cavernous down there, but in a comforting way, like the simulated caves children make for themselves on rainy days, in hall closets, under blankets, or in between the legs of dining room tables. I flipped on the light at the foot of the stairs and was not surprised at the pine paneling, the bamboo furniture, the ping-pong table, and the mirrored bar that was stocked with every kind and size of glass, ice bucket, decanter, mixer, swizzle stick, shot glass, pretzel bowl —all the bacchanalian paraphernalia, plentiful, orderly, and untouched, as it can be only in the bar of a wealthy man who never entertains drinking people, who himself does not drink, who, in fact, gets a fishy look from his wife when every several months he takes a shot of schnapps before dinner. I went behind the bar where there was an aluminum sink that had not seen a dirty glass, I'm sure, since Ron's bar mitzvah party, and would not see another, probably, until one of the Patimkin children was married or engaged. I would have poured myself a drink—just as a wicked wage for being forced into servantry —but I was uneasy about breaking the label on a bottle of whiskey. You had to break a label to get a drink. On the shelf back of the bar were two dozen bottles—twenty-three to be exact—of Jack Daniels, each with a little booklet tied to its collared neck informing patrons how patrician of them it was to drink the stuff. And over the Jack Daniels were more photos: there was a blown-up newspaper photo of Ron palming a basketball in one hand like a raisin; under the picture it said, "*Cen-*

ter, Ronald Patimkin, Millburn High School, 6'4", 217 pounds."
And there was another picture of Brenda on a horse, and next
to that, a velvet mounting board with ribbons and medals
clipped to it: Essex County Horse Show 1949, Union County
Horse Show 1950, Garden State Fair 1952, Morristown Horse
Show 1953, and so on—all for Brenda, for jumping and running
or galloping or whatever else young girls receive ribbons for.
In the entire house I hadn't seen one picture of Mr. Patimkin.

The rest of the basement, back of the wide pine-paneled
room, was gray cement walls and linoleum floor and contained innumerable electrical appliances, including a freezer
big enough to house a family of Eskimos. Beside the freezer,
incongruously, was a tall old refrigerator; its ancient presence
was a reminder to me of the Patimkin roots in Newark. This
same refrigerator had once stood in the kitchen of an apartment in some four-family house, probably in the same neighborhood where I had lived all my life, first with my parents and
then, when the two of them went wheezing off to Arizona, with
my aunt and uncle. After Pearl Harbor the refrigerator had
made the move up to Short Hills; Patimkin Kitchen and Bathroom Sinks had gone to war: no new barracks was complete
until it had a squad of Patimkin sinks lined up in its latrine.

I opened the door of the old refrigerator; it was not empty.
No longer did it hold butter, eggs, herring in cream sauce,
ginger ale, tuna fish salad, an occasional corsage—rather it was
heaped with fruit, shelves swelled with it, every color, every texture, and hidden within, every kind of pit. There were greengage plums, black plums, red plums, apricots, nectarines,
peaches, long horns of grapes, black, yellow, red, and cherries,
cherries flowing out of boxes and staining everything scarlet.
And there were melons—cantaloupes and honeydews—and on
the top shelf, half of a huge watermelon, a thin sheet of wax
paper clinging to its bare red face like a wet lip. Oh Patimkin!
Fruit grew in their refrigerator and sporting goods dropped
from their trees!

I grabbed a handful of cherries and then a nectarine, and I
bit right down to its pit.

"You better wash that or you'll get diarrhea."

Julie was standing behind me in the pine-paneled room. She
was wearing *her* Bermudas and *her* white polo shirt which was

unlike Brenda's only in that it had a little dietary history of its own.

"What?" I said.

"They're not washed yet," Julie said, and in such a way that it seemed to place the refrigerator itself out-of-bounds, if only for me.

"That's all right," I said, and devoured the nectarine and put the pit in my pocket and stepped out of the refrigerator room, all in one second. I still didn't know what to do with the cherries. "I was just looking around," I said.

Julie didn't answer.

"Where's Ron going?" I asked, dropping the cherries into my pocket, among my keys and change.

"Milwaukee."

"For long?"

"To see Harriet. They're in love."

We looked at each other for longer than I could bear. "Harriet?" I asked.

"Yes."

Julie was looking at me as though she were trying to look behind me, and then I realized that I was standing with my hands out of sight. I brought them around to the front, and, I swear it, she did peek to see if they were empty.

We confronted one another again; she seemed to have a threat in her face.

Then she spoke. "Want to play ping-pong?"

"God, yes," I said, and made for the table with two long, bounding steps. "You can serve."

Julie smiled and we began to play.

I have no excuses to offer for what happened next. I began to win and I liked it.

"Can I take that one over?" Julie said. "I hurt my finger yesterday and it just hurt when I served."

"No."

I continued to win.

"That wasn't fair, Neil. My shoelace came untied. Can I take it—"

"No."

We played, I ferociously.

"Neil, you leaned over the table. That's illegal—"

"I didn't lean and it's not illegal."

I felt the cherries hopping among my nickels and pennies.

"Neil, you gypped me out of a point. You have nineteen and I have eleven—"

"Twenty and *ten*," I said. "Serve!"

She did and I smashed my return past her—it zoomed off the table and skittered into the refrigerator room.

"You're a cheater!" she screamed at me. "You cheat!" Her jaw was trembling as though she carried a weight on top of her pretty head. "*I hate* you!" And she threw her racket across the room and it clanged off the bar, just as, outside, I heard the Chrysler crushing gravel in the driveway.

"The game isn't over," I said to her.

"You cheat! And you were stealing fruit!" she said, and ran away before I had my chance to win.

Later that night, Brenda and I made love, our first time. We were sitting on the sofa in the television room and for some ten minutes had not spoken a word to each other. Julie had long since gone to a weepy bed, and though no one had said anything to me about her crying, I did not know if the child had mentioned my fistful of cherries, which, some time before, I had flushed down the toilet.

The television set was on and though the sound was off and the house quiet, the gray pictures still wiggled at the far end of the room. Brenda was quiet and her dress circled her legs, which were tucked back beneath her. We sat there for some while and did not speak. Then she went into the kitchen and when she came back she said that it sounded as though everyone was asleep. We sat a while longer, watching the soundless bodies on the screen eating a silent dinner in someone's silent restaurant. When I began to unbutton her dress she resisted me, and I like to think it was because she knew how lovely she looked in it. But she looked lovely, my Brenda, anyway, and we folded it carefully and held each other close and soon there we were, Brenda falling, slowly but with a smile, and me rising.

How can I describe loving Brenda? It was so sweet, as though I'd finally scored that twenty-first point.

When I got home I dialed Brenda's number, but not before my aunt heard and rose from her bed.

"Who are you calling at this hour? The doctor?"

"No."

"What kind phone calls, one o'clock at night?"

"Shhh!" I said.

"He tells *me* shhh. Phone calls one o'clock at night, we haven't got a big enough bill," and then she dragged herself back into the bed, where with a martyr's heart and bleary eyes she had resisted the downward tug of sleep until she'd heard my key in the door.

Brenda answered the phone.

"Neil?" she said.

"Yes," I whispered. "You didn't get out of bed, did you?"

"No," she said, "the phone is next to the bed."

"Good. How is it in bed?"

"Good. Are you in bed?"

"Yes," I lied, and tried to right myself by dragging the phone by its cord as close as I could to my bedroom.

"I'm in bed with you," she said.

"That's right," I said, "and I'm with you."

"I have the shades down, so it's dark and I don't see you."

"I don't see you either."

"That was so nice, Neil."

"Yes. Go to sleep, sweet, I'm here," and we hung up without goodbyes. In the morning, as planned, I called again, but I could hardly hear Brenda or myself for that matter, for Aunt Gladys and Uncle Max were going on a Workmen's Circle picnic in the afternoon, and there was some trouble about grape juice that had dripped all night from a jug in the refrigerator and by morning had leaked out onto the floor. Brenda was still in bed and so could play our game with some success, but I had to pull down all the shades of my senses to imagine myself beside her. I could only pray our nights and mornings would come, and soon enough they did.

4

Over the next week and a half there seemed to be only two people in my life: Brenda and the little colored kid who liked Gauguin. Every morning before the library opened, the boy was waiting; sometimes he seated himself on the lion's back, sometimes under his belly, sometimes he just stood around throwing pebbles at his mane. Then he would come inside, tap around the main floor until Otto stared him up on tiptoes, and finally headed up the long marble stairs that led to Tahiti. He did not always stay to lunch time, but one very hot day he was there when I arrived in the morning and went through the door behind me when I left at night. The next morning, it was, that he did not show up, and as though in his place, a very old man appeared, white, smelling of Life Savers, his nose and jowls showing erupted veins beneath them. "Could you tell me where I'd find the art section?"

"Stack Three," I said.

In a few minutes, he returned with a big brown-covered book in his hand. He placed it on my desk, withdrew his card from a long moneyless billfold and waited for me to stamp out the book.

"Do you want to take this book *out*?" I said.

He smiled.

I took his card and jammed the metal edge into the machine; but I did not stamp down. "Just a minute," I said. I took a clipboard from under the desk and flipped through a few pages, upon which were games of battleship and tick-tacktoe that I'd been playing through the week with myself. "I'm afraid there's a hold on this book."

"A what?"

"A hold. Someone's called up and asked that we hold it for them. Can I take your name and address and drop a card when it's free . . ."

And so I was able, not without flushing once or twice, to get the book back in the stacks. When the colored kid showed up later in the day, it was just where he'd left it the afternoon before.

As for Brenda, I saw her every evening and when there was not a night game that kept Mr. Patimkin awake and in the TV room, or a Hadassah card party that sent Mrs. Patimkin out of the house and brought her in at unpredictable hours, we made love before the silent screen. One muggy, low-skied night Brenda took me swimming at the club. We were the only ones in the pool, and all the chairs, and cabañas, the lights, the diving boards, the very water seemed to exist only for our pleasure. She wore a blue suit that looked purple in the lights and down beneath the water it flashed sometimes green, sometimes black. Late in the evening a breeze came up off the golf course and we wrapped ourselves in one huge towel, pulled two chaise longues together, and despite the bartender, who was doing considerable pacing back and forth by the bar window, which overlooked the pool, we rested side by side on the chairs. Finally the bar light itself flipped off, and then, in a snap, the lights around the pool went down and out. My heart must have beat faster, or something, for Brenda seemed to guess my sudden doubt—*we should go*, I thought.

She said: "That's okay."

It was very dark, the sky was low and starless, and it took a while for me to see, once again, the diving board a shade lighter than the night, and to distinguish the water from the chairs that surrounded the far side of the pool.

I pushed the straps of her bathing suit down but she said no and rolled an inch away from me, and for the first time in the two weeks I'd known her she asked me a question about me.

"Where are your parents?" she said.

"Tucson," I said, "Why?"

"My mother asked me."

I could see the life guard's chair now, white almost.

"Why are you still here? Why aren't you with them?" she asked.

"I'm not a child any more, Brenda," I said, more sharply than I'd intended. "I just can't go wherever my parents are."

"But then why do you stay with your aunt and uncle?"

"They're not my parents."

"They're better?"

"No. Worse. I don't *know* why I stay with them."

"Why?" she said.

"Why don't I know?"

"Why do you stay? You do know, don't you?"

"My job, I suppose. It's convenient from there, and it's cheap, and it pleases my parents. My aunt's all right really . . . Do I really have to explain to your mother why I live where I do?"

"It's not for my mother. I want to know. I wondered why you weren't with your parents, that's all."

"Are you cold?" I asked.

"No."

"Do you want to go home?"

"No, not unless you do. Don't you feel well, Neil?"

"I feel all right," and to let her know that I was still me, I held her to me, though that moment I was without desire.

"Neil?"

"What?"

"What about the library?"

"Who wants to know that?"

"My father," she laughed.

"And you?"

She did not answer a moment. "And me," she said finally.

"Well, what about it? Do I like it? It's okay. I sold shoes once and like the library better. After the Army they tried me for a couple months at Uncle Aaron's real estate company—Doris' father—and I like the library better than that . . ."

"How did you get a job *there*?"

"I worked there for a little while when I was in college, then when I quit Uncle Aaron's, oh, I don't know . . ."

"What did you take in college?"

"At Newark Colleges of Rutgers University I majored in philosophy. I am twenty-three years old. I—"

"Why do you sound nasty again?"

"Do I?"

"Yes."

I didn't say I was sorry.

"Are you planning on making a career of the library?"

"Bren, I'm not planning anything. I haven't planned a thing in three years. At least for the year I've been out of the Army. In the Army I used to plan to go away weekends. I'm—I'm not a planner." After all the truth I'd suddenly given her, I shouldn't have ruined it for myself with that final lie. I added, "I'm a liver."

"I'm a pancreas," she said.

"I'm a—"

And she kissed the absurd game away; she wanted to be serious.

"Do you love me, Neil?"

I did not answer.

"I'll sleep with you whether you do or not, so tell me the truth."

"That was pretty crude."

"Don't be prissy," she said.

"No, I mean a crude thing to say about me."

"I don't understand," she said, and she didn't, and that she didn't pained me; I allowed myself the minor subterfuge, however, of forgiving Brenda her obtuseness. "Do you?" she said.

"No."

"I want you to."

"What about the library?"

"What about it?" she said.

Was it obtuseness again? I thought not—and it wasn't, for Brenda said, "When you love me, there'll be nothing to worry about."

"Then of course I'll love you." I smiled.

"I know you will," she said. "Why don't you go in the water, and I'll wait for you and close my eyes, and when you come back you'll surprise me with the wet. Go ahead."

"You like games, don't you?"

"Go ahead. I'll close my eyes."

I walked down to the edge of the pool and dove in. The water felt colder than it had earlier, and when I broke through and was headed blindly down I felt a touch of panic. At the top again, I started to swim the length of the pool and then turned at the end and started back, but suddenly I was sure that when I left the water Brenda would be gone. I'd be alone in this damn place. I started for the chairs and Brenda was there and I kissed her.

"God," she shivered. "You didn't stay long."

"I know."

"My turn," she said, and then she was up and a second later I heard a little crack of water and then nothing. Nothing for quite a while.

"Bren," I called softly, "are you all right?" but no one answered.

I found her glasses on the chair beside me and held them in my hands. "Brenda?"

Nothing.

"Brenda?"

"No fair calling," she said and gave me her drenched self. "Your turn," she said.

This time I stayed below the water for a long while and when I surfaced again my lungs were ready to pop. I threw my head back for air and above me saw the sky, low like a hand pushing down, and I began to swim as though to move out from under its pressure. I wanted to get back to Brenda, for I worried once again—and there was no evidence, was there?— that if I stayed away too long she would not be there when I returned. I wished that I had carried her glasses away with me, so she would have to wait for me to lead her back home. I was having crazy thoughts, I knew, and yet they did not seem un-called for in the darkness and strangeness of that place. Oh how I wanted to call out to her from the pool, but I knew she would not answer and I forced myself to swim the length a third time, and then a fourth, but midway through the fifth I felt a weird fright again, had momentary thoughts of my own extinction, and that time when I came back I held her tighter than either of us expected.

"Let go, let go," she laughed, "my turn—"

"But Brenda—"

But Brenda was gone and this time it seemed as though she'd never come back. I settled back and waited for the sun to dawn over the ninth hole, prayed it would if only for the comfort of its light, and when Brenda finally returned to me I would not let her go, and her cool wetness crept into me somehow and made me shiver. "That's it, Brenda. Please, no more games," I said, and then when I spoke again I held her so tightly I almost dug my body into hers, "I love you," I said, "I do."

So the summer went on. I saw Brenda every evening: we went swimming, we went for walks, we went for rides, up through the mountains so far and so long that by the time we started back the fog had begun to emerge from the trees and push out into the road, and I would tighten my hands on the wheel and Brenda would put on her glasses and watch the white line for me. And we would eat—a few nights after my discovery of the fruit refrigerator Brenda led me to it herself. We would fill huge soup bowls with cherries, and in serving dishes for roast beef we would heap slices of watermelon. Then we would go up and out the back doorway of the basement and onto the back lawn and sit under the sporting-goods tree, the light from the TV room the only brightness we had out there. All we would hear for a while were just the two of us spitting pits. "I wish they would take root overnight and in the morning there'd just be watermelons and cherries."

"If they took root in this yard, sweetie, they'd grow refrigerators and Westinghouse Preferred. I'm not being nasty," I'd add quickly, and Brenda would laugh, and say she felt like a greengage plum, and I would disappear down into the basement and the cherry bowl would now be a greengage plum bowl, and then a nectarine bowl, and then a peach bowl, until, I have to admit it, I cracked my frail bowel, and would have to spend the following night, sadly, on the wagon. And then too we went out for corned beef sandwiches, pizza, beer and shrimp, ice cream sodas, and hamburgers. We went to the Lions Club Fair one night and Brenda won a Lions Club ashtray by shooting three baskets in a row. And when Ron came home from Milwaukee we went from time to time to see him play basketball in the semi-pro summer league, and it was those evenings that I felt a stranger with Brenda, for she knew all the players' names, and though for the most part they were gawky-limbed and dull, there was one named Luther Ferrari who was neither, and whom Brenda had dated for a whole year in high school. He was Ron's closest friend and I remembered his name from the Newark *News*: he was one of the great Ferrari brothers, All State all of them in at least two sports. It was Ferrari who called Brenda Buck, a nickname which apparently went back to her ribbon-winning days. Like Ron, Ferrari was exceedingly polite, as though it were some affliction of those over six feet three; he was gentlemanly towards me and gentle towards Brenda, and after a while I balked when the suggestion was made that we go to see Ron play. And then one night we discovered that at eleven o'clock the cashier of the Hilltop Theatre went home and the manager disappeared into his office, and so that summer we saw the last quarter of at least fifteen movies, and then when we were driving home— driving Brenda home, that is—we would try to reconstruct the beginnings of the films. Our favorite last quarter of a movie was *Ma and Pa Kettle in the City*, our favorite fruit, greengage plums, and our favorite, our only, people, each other. Of course we ran into others from time to time, some of Brenda's friends, and occasionally, one or two of mine. One night in August we even went to a bar out on Route 6 with Laura Simpson Stolowitch and her fiancé, but it was a dreary evening. Brenda and I seemed untrained in talking to others, and so we danced a great deal, which we realized was one thing we'd never done before. Laura's boyfriend drank stingers pompously and Simp—Brenda wanted me to call her Stolo but I didn't—Simp drank a tepid combination of something like ginger ale and soda. Whenever we returned to the table, Simp would be talking about "the dance" and her fiancé about "the film," until finally Brenda asked him "Which film?" and then we danced till closing time. And when we went back to Brenda's we filled a bowl with cherries which we carried into the TV room and ate sloppily for a while; and later, on the sofa, we loved each other and when I moved from the darkened room to the bathroom I could always feel cherry pits against my bare soles. At home, undressing for the second time that night, I would find red marks on the undersides of my feet.

And how did her parents take all of this? Mrs. Patimkin continued to smile at me and Mr. Patimkin continued to think I ate like a bird. When invited to dinner I would, for his benefit, eat twice what I wanted, but the truth seemed to be that after he'd characterized my appetite that first time, he never really bothered to look again. I might have eaten ten times my normal amount, have finally killed myself with food, he would still have considered me not a man but a sparrow. No one seemed distressed by my presence, though Julie had cooled considerably; consequently, when Brenda suggested to her father that at the end of August I spend a week of my vacation at the Patimkin house, he pondered a moment, decided on the five iron, made his approach shot, and said yes. And when she passed on to her mother the decision of Patimkin Sink, there wasn't much Mrs. Patimkin could do. So, through Brenda's craftiness, I was invited.

On that Friday morning that was to be my last day of work,

my Aunt Gladys saw me packing my bag and she asked where I was going. I told her. She did not answer and I thought I saw awe in those red-rimmed hysterical eyes—I had come a long way since that day she'd said to me on the phone, "Fancy-shmancy."

"How long you going, I should know how to shop I wouldn't buy too much. You'll leave me with a refrigerator full of milk it'll go bad it'll stink up the refrigerator—"

"A week," I said.

"A *week*?" she said. "They got room for a week?"

"Aunt Gladys, they don't live over the store."

"I lived over a store I wasn't ashamed. Thank God we always had a roof. We never went begging in the streets," she told me as I packed the Bermudas I'd just bought, "and your cousin Susan we'll put through college, Uncle Max should live and be well. We didn't send her away to camp for August, she doesn't have shoes when she wants them, sweaters she doesn't have a drawerful—"

"I didn't say anything, Aunt Gladys."

"You don't get enough to eat here? You leave over sometimes I show your Uncle Max your plate it's a shame. A child in Europe could make a four-course meal from what you leave over."

"Aunt Gladys." I went over to her. "I get everything I want here. I'm just taking a vacation. Don't I deserve a vacation?"

She held herself to me and I could feel her trembling. "I told your mother I would take care of her Neil she shouldn't worry. And now you go running—"

I put my arms around her and kissed her on the top of her head. "C'mon," I said, "you're being silly. I'm not running away. I'm just going away for a week, on a vacation."

"You'll leave their telephone number God forbid you should get sick."

"Okay."

"Millburn they live?"

"Short Hills. I'll leave the number."

"Since when do Jewish people live in Short Hills? They couldn't be real Jews believe me."

"They're real Jews," I said.

"I'll see it I'll believe it." She wiped her eyes with the corner of her apron, just as I was zipping up the sides of the suitcase. "Don't close the bag yet. I'll make a little package with some fruit in it, you'll take with you."

"Okay, Aunt Gladys," and on the way to work that morning I ate the orange and the two peaches that she'd put in a bag for me.

A few hours later Mr. Scapello informed me that when I returned from my vacation after Labor Day, I would be hoisted up onto Martha Winney's stool. He himself, he said, had made the same move some twelve years ago, and so it appeared that if I could manage to maintain my balance I might someday be Mr. Scapello. I would also get an eight-dollar increase in salary which was five dollars more than the increase Mr. Scapello had received years before. He shook my hand and then started back up the long flight of marble stairs, his behind barging against his suit jacket like a hoop. No sooner had he left my side than I smelled spearmint and looked up to see the old man with veiny nose and jowls.

"Hello, young man," he said pleasantly. "Is the book back?"

"What book?"

"The Gauguin. I was shopping and I thought I'd stop by to ask. I haven't gotten the card yet. It's two weeks already."

"No," I said, and as I spoke I saw that Mr. Scapello had stopped midway up the stairs and turned as though he'd forgotten to tell me something. "Look," I said to the old man, "it should be back any day." I said it with a finality that bordered on rudeness, and I alarmed myself, for suddenly I saw what would happen: the old man making a fuss, Mr. Scapello gliding down the stairs, Mr. Scapello scampering up to the stacks, Scapello scandalized, Scapello profuse, Scapello presiding at the ascension of John McKee to Miss Winney's stool. I turned to the old man, "Why don't you leave your phone number and I'll try to get a hold of it this afternoon—" but my attempt at concern and courtesy came too late, and the man growled some words about public servants, a letter to the Mayor, snotty kids, and left the library, thank God, only a second before Mr. Scapello returned to my desk to remind me that everyone was chipping in for a present for Miss Winney and that if I liked I should leave a half dollar on his desk during the day.

After lunch the colored kid came in. When he headed past the desk for the stairs, I called over to him. "Come here," I said. "Where are you going?"

"The heart section."

"What book are you reading?"

"That Mr. Go-again's book. Look, man, I ain't doing nothing wrong. I didn't do *no* writing in *any*thing. You could search me—"

"I know you didn't. Listen, if you like that book so much why don't you please take it home? Do you have a library card?"

"No, sir, I didn't take *nothing*."

"No, a library card is what we give to you so you can take books home. Then you won't have to come down here every day. Do you go to school?"

"Yes, sir. Miller Street School. But this here's summertime. It's okay I'm not in school. I ain't *supposed* to be in school."

"I know. As long as you go to school you can *have* a library card. You could take the book home."

"What you keep telling me take that book home for? At home somebody dee-*stroy* it."

"You could hide it someplace, in a desk—"

"Man," he said, squinting at me, "why don't you want me to come round here?"

"I didn't say you shouldn't."

"I *likes* to come here. I likes them stairs."

"I like them too," I said. "But the trouble is that someday somebody's going to take that book out."

He smiled. "Don't you worry," he said to me. "Ain't nobody done that yet," and he tapped off to the stairs and Stack Three.

Did I perspire that day! It was the coolest of the summer, but when I left work in the evening my shirt was sticking to my back. In the car I opened my bag, and while the rush-hour traffic flowed down Washington Street, I huddled in the back and changed into a clean shirt so that when I reached Short Hills I'd look as though I was deserving of an interlude in the suburbs. But driving up Central Avenue I could not keep my mind on my vacation, or for that matter on my driving: to the distress of pedestrians and motorists, I ground gears, overshot crosswalks, hesitated at green and red lights alike. I kept thinking that while I was on vacation that jowly bastard would return to the library, that the colored kid's book would disappear, that my new job would be taken away from me, that, in fact my old job—but then why should I worry about all that: the library wasn't going to be *my* life.

5

"Ron's getting married!" Julie screamed at me when I came through the door. "Ron's getting married!"

"Now?" I said.

"Labor Day! He's marrying Harriet, he's marrying Harriet." She began to sing it like a jump-rope song, nasal and rhythmic. "I'm going to be a sister-in-law!"

"Hi," Brenda said, "I'm going to be a sister-in-law."

"So I hear. When did it happen?"

"This afternoon he told us. They spoke long distance for forty minutes last night. She's flying here next week, and there's going to be a *huge* wedding. My parents are flittering all over the place. They've got to arrange everything in about a day or two. And my father's taking Ron in the business—but he's going to have to start at two hundred a week and then work himself up. That'll take till October."

"I thought he was going to be a gym teacher."

"He was. But now he has responsibilities . . ."

And at dinner Ron expanded on the subject of responsibilities and the future.

"We're going to have a boy," he said, to his mother's delight, "and when he's about six months old I'm going to sit him down with a basketball in front of him, and a football, and a baseball, and then whichever one he reaches for, that's the one we're going to concentrate on."

"Suppose he doesn't reach for any of them," Brenda said.

"Don't be funny, young lady," Mrs. Patimkin said.

"I'm going to be an aunt," Julie sang, and she stuck her tongue out at Brenda.

"When is Harriet coming?" Mr. Patimkin breathed through a mouthful of potatoes.

"A week from yesterday."

"Can she sleep in my room?" Julie cried. "*Can* she?"

"No, the guest room—" Mrs. Patimkin began, but then she remembered me—with a crushing side glance from those purple eyes, and said, "Of course."

Well, I did eat like a bird. After dinner my bag was carried—by me—up to the guest room which was across from Ron's room and right down the hall from Brenda. Brenda came along to show me the way.

"Let me see your bed, Bren."

"Later," she said.

"Can we? Up here?"

"I think so," she said. "Ron sleeps like a log."

"Can I stay the night?"

"I don't know."

"I could get up early and come back in here. We'll set the alarm."

"It'll wake everybody up."

"I'll remember to get up. I can do it."

"I better not stay up here with you too long," she said. "My mother'll have a fit. I think she's nervous about your being here."

"So am I. I hardly know them. Do you think I should really stay a whole week?"

"A whole week? Once Harriet gets here it'll be so chaotic you can probably stay two months."

"You think so?"

"Yes."

"Do you want me to?"

"Yes," she said, and went down the stairs so as to ease her mother's conscience.

I unpacked my bag and dropped my clothes into a drawer that was empty except for a packet of dress shields and a high school yearbook. In the middle of my unpacking, Ron came clunking up the stairs.

"Hi," he called into my room.

"Congratulations," I called back. I should have realized that any word of ceremony would provoke a handshake from Ron;

he interrupted whatever it was he was about to do in his room, and came into mine.

"Thanks." He pumped me. "Thanks."

Then he sat down on my bed and watched me as I finished unpacking. I have one shirt with a Brooks Brothers label and I let it linger on the bed a while; the Arrows I heaped in the drawer. Ron sat there rubbing his forearm and grinning. After a while I was thoroughly unsettled by the silence.

"Well," I said, "that's something."

He agreed, to *what* I don't know.

"How does it feel?" I asked, after another longer silence.

"Better. Ferrari smacked it under the boards."

"Oh. Good," I said. "How does getting married feel?"

"Ah, okay, I guess."

I leaned against the bureau and counted stitches in the carpet.

Ron finally risked a journey into language. "Do you know anything about music?" he asked.

"Something, yes."

"You can listen to my phonograph if you want."

"Thanks, Ron. I didn't know you were interested in music."

"Sure. I got all the Andre Kostelanetz records ever made. You like Mantovani? I got all of him too. I like semi-classical a lot. You can hear my Columbus record if you want . . ." he dwindled off. Finally he shook my hand and left.

Downstairs I could hear Julie singing. "I'm going to be an a-a-aunt," and Mrs. Patimkin saying to her, "No, honey, you're going to be a sister-in-law. Sing that, sweetheart," but Julie continued to sing, "I'm going to be an a-a-aunt," and then I heard Brenda's voice joining hers, singing, "We're going to be an a-a-aunt," and then Julie joined that, and finally Mrs. Patimkin called to Mr. Patimkin, "Will you make her stop encouraging her . . ." and soon the duet ended.

And then I heard Mrs. Patimkin again. I couldn't make out the words but Brenda answered her. Their voices grew louder; finally I could hear perfectly. "I need a houseful of company at a time like this?" It was Mrs. Patimkin. "I asked you, Mother." "You asked your father. I'm the one you should have asked first. He doesn't know how much extra work this is for me . . ." "My God, Mother, you'd think we didn't have

Carlota and Jenny." "Carlota and Jenny can't do everything. This is not the Salvation Army!" "What the hell does that mean?" "Watch your tongue, young lady. That may be very well for your college friends." "Oh, *stop* it, Mother!" "Don't raise your voice to me. When's the last time you lifted a finger to help around here?" "I'm not a slave . . . I'm a daughter." "You ought to learn what a day's work means." "Why?" Brenda said. "*Why?*" "Because you're lazy," Mrs. Patimkin answered, "and you think the world owes you a living." "Whoever said *that?*" "You ought to earn some money and buy your own clothes." "Why? Good God, Mother, Daddy could live off the stocks alone, for God's sake. What are you complaining about?" "When's the last time you washed the dishes!" "Jesus Christ!" Brenda flared, "Carlota washes the dishes!" "Don't Jesus Christ me!" "Oh, Mother!" and Brenda was crying. "Why the hell are you like this!" "That's it," Mrs. Patimkin said, "cry in front of your company . . ." "My *company* . . ." Brenda wept, "why don't you go yell at him too . . . why is everyone so nasty to me . . ."

From across the hall I heard Andre Kostelanetz let several thousand singing violins loose on "Night and Day." Ron's door was open and I saw he was stretched out, colossal, on his bed; he was singing along with the record. The words belonged to "Night and Day," but I didn't recognize Ron's tune. In a minute he picked up the phone and asked the operator for a Milwaukee number. While she connected him, he rolled over and turned up the volume on the record player, so that it would carry the nine hundred miles west.

I heard Julie downstairs. "Ha ha, Brenda's crying, ha ha, Brenda's crying."

And then Brenda was running up the stairs. "Your day'll come, you little bastard!" she called.

"*Brenda!*" Mrs. Patimkin called.

"*Mommy!*" Julie cried. "Brenda cursed at me!"

"What's going *on* here!" Mr. Patimkin shouted.

"You call *me*, Mrs. P?" Carlota shouted.

And Ron, in the other room, said, "Hello, Har, I told them . . ."

I sat down on my Brooks Brothers shirt and pronounced my own name out loud.

—

"Goddam her!" Brenda said to me as she paced up and down my room.

"Bren, do you think I should go—"

"Shhh . . ." She went to the door of my room and listened. "They're going visiting, thank God."

"Brenda—"

"Shhh . . . They've gone."

"Julie too?"

"Yes," she said. "Is Ron in his room? His door is closed."

"He went out."

"You can't hear anybody move around here. They all creep around in *sneakers*. Oh Neil."

"Bren, I asked you, maybe I should just stay through tomorrow and then go."

"Oh, it isn't you she's angry about."

"I'm not helping any."

"It's Ron, really. That he's getting married just has her flipped. And me. Now with that goody-good Harriet around she'll just forget I ever exist."

"Isn't that okay with you?"

She walked off to the window and looked outside. It was dark and cool; the trees rustled and flapped as though they were sheets that had been hung out to dry. Everything outside hinted at September, and for the first time I realized how close we were to Brenda's departure for school.

"Is it, Bren?" but she was not listening to me.

She walked across the room to a door at the far end of the room. She opened it.

"I thought that was a closet," I said.

"Come here."

She held the door back and we leaned into the darkness and could hear the strange wind hissing in the eaves of the house.

"What's in here?" I said.

"Money."

Brenda went into the room. When the puny sixty-watt bulb was twisted on, I saw that the place was full of old furniture— two wing chairs with hair-oil lines at the back, a sofa with a paunch in its middle, a bridge table, two bridge chairs with their stuffing showing, a mirror whose backing had peeled off, shadeless lamps, lampless shades, a coffee table with a cracked glass top, and a pile of rolled up shades.

"What is this?" I said.

"A storeroom. Our old furniture."

"How old?"

"From Newark," she said. "Come here." She was on her hands and knees in front of the sofa and was holding up its paunch to peek beneath.

"Brenda, what the hell are we doing here? You're getting filthy."

"It's not here."

"*What?*"

"The money. I told you."

I sat down on a wing chair, raising some dust. It had begun to rain outside, and we could smell the fall dampness coming through the vent that was outlined at the far end of the store-room. Brenda got up from the floor and sat down on the sofa. Her knees and Bermudas were dirty and when she pushed her hair back she dirtied her forehead. There among the dis-arrangement and dirt I had the strange experience of seeing us, *both* of us, placed among disarrangement and dirt: we looked like a young couple who had just moved into a new apartment; we had suddenly taken stock of our furniture, finances, and future, and all we could feel any pleasure about was the clean smell of outside, which reminded us we were alive, but which, in a pinch, would not feed us.

"What money?" I said again.

"The hundred-dollar bills. From when I was a little girl . . ." and she breathed deeply. "When I was little and we'd just moved from Newark, my father took me up here one day. He took me into this room and told me that if anything should ever happen to him, he wanted me to know where there was some money that I should have. He said it wasn't for anybody else but me, and that I should never tell anyone about it, not even Ron. Or my mother."

"How much was it?"

"Three hundred-dollar bills. I'd never seen them before. I was nine, around Julie's age. I don't think we'd been living here a month. I remember I used to come up here about once a week, when no one was home but Carlota, and crawl under the sofa and make sure it was still here. And it always was. He never mentioned it once again. Never."

"Where is it? Maybe someone stole it."

"I don't know, Neil. I suppose he took it back."

"When it was gone," I said, "my God, didn't you tell him? Maybe Carlota—"

"I never knew it was gone, until just now. I guess I stopped looking at one time or another . . . And then I forgot about it. Or just didn't think about it. I mean I always had enough, I didn't need this. I guess one day *he* figured I wouldn't need it."

Brenda paced up to the narrow, dust-covered window and drew her initials on it.

"Why did you want it now?" I said.

"I don't know . . ." she said and went over and twisted the bulb off.

I didn't move from the chair and Brenda, in her tight shorts and shirt, seemed naked standing there a few feet away. Then I saw her shoulders shaking. "I wanted to find it and tear it up in little pieces and put the goddam pieces in her purse! If it was there, I swear it, I would have done it."

"I wouldn't have let you, Bren."

"Wouldn't you have?"

"No."

"Make love to me, Neil. Right now."

"Where?"

"Do it! *Here.* On this cruddy cruddy cruddy sofa."

And I obeyed her.

The next morning Brenda made breakfast for the two of us. Ron had gone off to his first day of work—I'd heard him singing in the shower only an hour after I'd returned to my own room; in fact, I had still been awake when the Chrysler had pulled out of the garage, carrying boss and son down to the Patimkin works in Newark. Mrs. Patimkin wasn't home either; she had taken her car and had gone off to the Temple to talk to Rabbi Kranitz about the wedding. Julie was on the back lawn playing at helping Carlota hang the clothes.

"You know what I want to do this morning?" Brenda said. We were eating a grapefruit, sharing it rather sloppily, for

Brenda couldn't find a paring knife, and so we'd decided to peel it down like an orange and eat the segments separately.

"What?" I said.

"Run," she said. "Do you ever run?"

"You mean on a track? God, yes. In high school we had to run a mile every month. So we wouldn't be Momma's boys. I think the bigger your lungs get the more you're supposed to hate your mother."

"I want to run," she said, "and I want you to run. Okay?"

"Oh, Brenda . . ."

But an hour later, after a breakfast that consisted of another grapefruit, which apparently is all a runner is supposed to eat in the morning, we had driven the Volkswagen over to the high school, behind which was a quarter-mile track. Some kids were playing with a dog out in the grassy center of the track, and at the far end, near the woods, a figure in white shorts with slits in the side, and no shirt, was twirling, twirling, and then flinging a shot put as far as he could. After it left his hand he did a little eagle-eyed tap dance while he watched it arch and bend and land in the distance.

"You know," Brenda said, "you look like me. Except bigger."

We were dressed similarly, sneakers, sweat socks, khaki Bermudas, and sweat shirts, but I had the feeling that Brenda was not talking about the accidents of our dress—if they were accidents. She meant, I was sure, that I was somehow beginning to look the way she wanted me to. Like herself.

"Let's see who's faster," she said, and then we started along the track. Within the first eighth of a mile the three little boys and their dog were following us. As we passed the corner where the shot putter was, he waved at us; Brenda called "Hi!" and I smiled, which, as you may or may not know, makes one engaged in serious running feel inordinately silly. At the quarter mile the kids dropped off and retired to the grass, the dog turned and started the other way, and I had a tiny knife in my side. Still I was abreast of Brenda, who as we started on the second lap, called "Hi!" once again to the lucky shot putter, who was reclining on the grass now, watching us, and rubbing his shot like a crystal ball. Ah, I thought, there's the sport.

"How about us throwing the shot put?" I panted.

"After," she said, and I saw beads of sweat clinging to the

last strands of hair that shagged off her ear. When we approached the half mile Brenda suddenly swerved off the track onto the grass and tumbled down; her departure surprised me and I was still running.

"Hey, Bob Mathias," she called, "let's lie in the sun . . ."

But I acted as though I didn't hear her and though my heart pounded in my throat and my mouth was dry as a drought, I made my legs move, and swore I would not stop until I'd finished one more lap. As I passed the shot putter for the third time, I called "Hi!"

She was excited when I finally pulled up alongside of her. "You're good," she said. My hands were on my hips and I was looking at the ground and sucking air—rather, air was sucking me, I didn't have much to say about it.

"Uh-huh," I breathed.

"Let's do this every morning," she said. "We'll get up and have two grapefruit, and then you'll come out here and run. I'll time you. In two weeks you'll break four minutes, won't you, sweetie? I'll get Ron's stop watch." She was so excited— she'd slid over on the grass and was pushing my socks up against my wet ankles and calves. She bit my kneecap.

"Okay," I said.

"Then we'll go back and have a real breakfast."

"Okay."

"You drive back," she said, and suddenly she was up and running ahead of me, and then we were headed back in the car.

And the next morning, my mouth still edgy from the grapefruit segments, we were at the track. We had Ron's stop watch and a towel for me, for when I was finished.

"My legs are a little sore," I said.

"Do some exercises," Brenda said. "I'll do them with you." She heaped the towel on the grass and together we did deep knee bends, and sit-ups, and push-ups, and some high-knee raising in place. I felt overwhelmingly happy.

"I'm just going to run a half today, Bren. We'll see what I do . . ." and I heard Brenda click the watch, and then when I was on the far side of the track, the clouds trailing above me like my own white, fleecy tail, I saw that Brenda was on the ground, hugging her knees, and alternately checking the watch and looking out at me. We were the only ones there, and it all reminded me of one of those scenes in race-horse movies, where an old trainer like Walter Brennan and a young handsome man clock the beautiful girl's horse in the early Kentucky morning, to see if it really is the fastest two-year-old alive. There were differences all right—one being simply that at the quarter mile Brenda shouted out to me, "A minute and fourteen seconds," but it was pleasant and exciting and clean and when I was finished Brenda was standing up and waiting for me. Instead of a tape to break I had Brenda's sweet flesh to meet, and I did, and it was the first time she said that she loved me.

We ran—I ran—every morning, and by the end of the week I was running a 7:02 mile, and always at the end there was the little click of the watch and Brenda's arms.

At night, I would read in my pajamas, while Brenda, in her room, read, and we would wait for Ron to go to sleep. Some nights we had to wait longer than others, and I would hear the leaves swishing outside, for it had grown cooler at the end of August, and the air-conditioning was turned off at night and we were all allowed to open our windows. Finally Ron would be ready for bed. He would stomp around his room and then he would come to the door in his shorts and T-shirt and go into the bathroom where he would urinate loudly and brush his teeth. After he brushed his teeth I would go in to brush mine. We would pass in the hall and I would give him a hearty and sincere "Good-night." Once in the bathroom, I would spend a moment admiring my tan in the mirror; behind me I could see Ron's jock straps hanging out to dry on the Hot and Cold knobs of the shower. Nobody ever questioned their tastefulness as adornment, and after a few nights I didn't even notice them.

While Ron brushed his teeth and I waited in my bed for my turn, I could hear the record player going in his room. Generally, after coming in from basketball, he would call Harriet —who was now only a few days away from us—and then would lock himself up with *Sports Illustrated* and Mantovani; however, when he emerged from his room for his evening toilet, it was not a Mantovani record I would hear playing, but something else, apparently what he'd once referred to as his

Columbus record. I *imagined* that was what I heard, for I
could not tell much from the last moments of sound. All I
heard were bells moaning evenly and soft patriotic music behind them, and riding over it all, a deep kind of Edward R.
Murrow gloomy voice: "*And so goodbye, Columbus,*" the voice
intoned, ". . . *goodbye, Columbus . . . goodbye . . .*" Then
there would be silence and Ron would be back in his room;
the light would switch off and in only a few minutes I would
hear him rumbling down into that exhilarating, restorative,
vitamin-packed sleep that I imagined athletes to enjoy.

One morning near sneaking-away time I had a dream and
when I awakened from it, there was just enough dawn coming
into the room for me to see the color of Brenda's hair. I
touched her in her sleep, for the dream had unsettled me: it
had taken place on a ship, an old sailing ship like those you see
in pirate movies. With me on the ship was the little colored kid
from the library—I was the captain and he my mate, and we
were the only crew members. For a while it was a pleasant
dream; we were anchored in the harbor of an island in the
Pacific and it was very sunny. Up on the beach there were
beautiful bare-skinned Negresses, and none of them moved;
but suddenly *we* were moving, our ship, out of the harbor, and
the Negresses moved slowly down to the shore and began to
throw leis at us and say "Goodbye, Columbus . . . goodbye,
Columbus . . . goodbye . . ." and though we did not want to
go, the little boy and I, the boat was moving and there was
nothing we could do about it, and he shouted at me that it was
my fault and I shouted it was his for not having a library card,
but we were wasting our breath, for we were further and further from the island, and soon the natives were nothing at all.
Space was all out of proportion in the dream, and things were
sized and squared in no way I'd ever seen before, and I think it
was that more than anything else that steered me into consciousness. I did not want to leave Brenda's side that morning,
and for a while I played with the little point at the nape of her
neck, where she'd had her hair cut. I stayed longer than I
should have, and when finally I returned to my room I almost
ran into Ron who was preparing for his day at Patimkin
Kitchen and Bathroom Sinks.

6

That morning was supposed to have been my last at the Patimkin house; however, when I began to throw my things into my bag late in the day, Brenda told me I could unpack—somehow she'd managed to inveigle another week out of her parents, and I would be able to stay right through till Labor Day, when Ron would be married; then, the following morning Brenda would be off to school and I would go back to work. So we would be with each other until the summer's last moment.

This should have made me overjoyed, but as Brenda trotted back down the stairs to accompany her family to the airport—where they were to pick up Harriet—I was not joyful but disturbed, as I had been more and more with the thought that when Brenda went back to Radcliffe, that would be the end for me. I was convinced that even Miss Winney's stool was not high enough for me to see clear up to Boston. Nevertheless, I tossed my clothing back into the drawer and was able, finally, to tell myself that there'd been no hints of ending our affair from Brenda, and any suspicions I had, any uneasiness, was spawned in my own uncertain heart. Then I went into Ron's room to call my aunt.

"Hello?" she said.

"Aunt Gladys," I said, "how are you?"

"You're sick."

"No, I'm having a fine time. I wanted to call you, I'm going to stay another week."

"Why?"

"I told you. I'm having a good time. Mrs. Patimkin asked me to stay until Labor Day."

"You've got clean underwear?"

"I'm washing it at night. I'm okay, Aunt Gladys."

"By hand you can't get it clean."

"It's clean enough. Look, Aunt Gladys, I'm having a wonderful time."

"*Shmutz* he lives in and I shouldn't worry."

"How's Uncle Max?" I asked.

"What should he be? Uncle Max is Uncle Max. You, I don't like the way your voice sounds."

"Why? Do I sound like I've got on dirty underwear?"

"Smart guy. Someday you'll learn."

"What?"

"What do you mean *what*? You'll find out. You'll stay there too long you'll be too good for us."

"Never, sweetheart," I said.

"I'll see it I'll believe it."

"Is it cool in Newark, Aunt Gladys?"

"It's snowing," she said.

"Hasn't it been cool all week?"

"You sit around all day it's cool. For me it's not February, believe me."

"Okay, Aunt Gladys. Say hello to everybody."

"You got a letter from your mother."

"Good. I'll read it when I get home."

"You couldn't take a ride down you'll read it?"

"It'll wait. I'll drop them a note. Be a good girl," I said.

"What about your socks?"

"I go barefoot. Goodbye, honey." And I hung up.

Down in the kitchen Carlota was getting dinner ready. I was always amazed at how Carlota's work never seemed to get in the way of her life. She made household chores seem like illustrative gestures of whatever it was she was singing, even if, as now, it was "I Get a Kick out of You." She moved from the oven to the automatic dishwasher—she pushed buttons, turned dials, peeked in the glass-doored oven, and from time to time picked a big black grape out of a bunch that lay on the sink. She chewed and chewed, humming all the time, and then, with a deliberated casualness, shot the skin and the pit directly into the garbage disposal unit. I said hello to her as I went out the back door, and though she did not return the greeting, I felt a kinship with one who, like me, had been partially wooed and won on Patimkin fruit.

Out on the lawn I shot baskets for a while; then I picked up an iron and drove a cotton golf ball limply up into the sunlight; then I kicked a soccer ball towards the oak tree; then I tried shooting foul shots again. Nothing diverted me—I felt open-stomached, as though I hadn't eaten for months, and though I went back inside and came out with my own handful of grapes, the feeling continued, and I knew it had nothing to

do with my caloric intake; it was only a rumor of the hollow-
ness that would come when Brenda was away. The fact of her
departure had, of course, been on my mind for a while, but
overnight it had taken on a darker hue. Curiously, the darkness
seemed to have something to do with Harriet, Ron's intended,
and I thought for a time that it was simply the reality of Harriet's arrival that had dramatized the passing of time: we had
been talking about it and now suddenly it was here—just as
Brenda's departure would be here before we knew it.

But it was more than that: the union of Harriet and Ron reminded me that separation need not be a permanent state.
People could marry each other, even if they were young! And
yet Brenda and I had never mentioned marriage, except perhaps for that night at the pool when she'd said, "When you
love me, everything will be all right." Well, I loved her, and she
me, and things didn't seem all right at all. Or was I inventing
troubles again? I supposed I should really have thought my lot
improved considerably; yet, there on the lawn, the August sky
seemed too beautiful and temporary to bear, and I wanted
Brenda to marry me. Marriage, though, was not what I proposed to her when she drove the car up the driveway, alone,
some fifteen minutes later. That proposal would have taken a
kind of courage that I did not think I had. I did not feel myself
prepared for any answer but "Hallelujah!" Any other kind of
yes wouldn't have satisfied me, and any kind of no, even one
masked behind the words, "Let's wait, sweetheart," would
have been my end. So I imagine that's why I proposed the sur-
rogate, which turned out finally to be far more daring than I
knew it to be at the time.

"Harriet's plane is late, so I drove home," Brenda called.

"Where's everyone else?"

"They're going to wait for her and have dinner at the airport. I have to tell Carlota," and she went inside.

In a few minutes she appeared on the porch. She wore a yellow dress that cut a wide-bottomed U across her shoulders
and neck, and showed where the tanned flesh began above her
breasts. On the lawn she stepped out of her heels and walked
barefoot over to where I was sitting under the oak tree.

"Women who wear high heels all the time get tipped
ovaries," she said.

"Who told you that?"

"I don't remember. I like to think everything's shipshape in there."

"Brenda, I want to ask you something . . ."

She yanked the blanket with the big O on it over to us and sat down.

"What?" she said.

"I know this is out of the blue, though really it's not . . . I want you to buy a diaphragm. To go to a doctor and get one."

She smiled. "Don't worry, sweetie, we're careful. Everything is okay."

"But that's the safest."

"We're safe. It'd be a waste."

"Why take chances?"

"But we *aren't*. How many things do you need."

"Honey, it isn't bulk I'm interested in. It's not even safety," I added.

"You just want me to own one, is that it? Like a walking stick, or a pith helmet—"

"Brenda, I want you to own one for . . . for the sake of pleasure."

"Pleasure? Whose? The doctor's?"

"Mine," I said.

She did not answer me, but rubbed her fingers along the ridge of her collarbone to wipe away the tiny globes of perspiration that had suddenly formed there.

"No, Neil, it's silly."

"Why?"

"Why? It just is."

"You know why it's silly, Brenda—because *I* asked you to do it?"

"That's sillier."

"If you asked *me* to buy a diaphragm we'd have to go straight to the Yellow Pages and find a gynecologist open on Saturday afternoon."

"I would never ask you to do that, baby."

"It's the truth," I said, though I was smiling. "It's the truth."

"It's not," she said, and got up and walked over to the basketball court, where she walked on the white lines that Mr. Patimkin had laid the day before.

"Come back here," I said.

"Neil, it's silly and I don't want to talk about it."

"Why are you being so selfish?"

"Selfish? You're the one who's being selfish. It's your pleasure . . ."

"That's right. My pleasure. Why not!"

"Don't raise your voice. Carlota."

"Then get the hell over here," I said.

She walked over to me, leaving white footprints on the grass. "I didn't think you were such a creature of the flesh," she said.

"Didn't you?" I said. "I'll tell you something that you ought to know. It's not even the pleasures of the flesh I'm talking about."

"Then frankly, I don't know *what* you're talking about. Why you're even bothering. Isn't what we use sufficient?"

"I'm bothering just because I want you to go to a doctor and get a diaphragm. That's all. No explanation. Just do it. Do it because I asked you to."

"You're not being reasonable—"

"Goddamit, Brenda!"

"Goddamit yourself!" she said and went up into the house.

I closed my eyes and leaned back and in fifteen minutes, or maybe less, I heard somebody stroking at the cotton golf ball. She had changed into shorts and a blouse and was still barefoot.

We didn't speak with each other, but I watched her bring the club back of her ear, and then swing through, her chin tilted up with the line of flight a regular golf ball would have taken.

"That's five hundred yards," I said.

She didn't answer but walked after the cotton ball and then readied for another swing.

"Brenda. Please come here."

She walked over, dragging the club over the grass.

"What?"

"I don't want to argue with you."

"Nor I with you," she said. "It was the first time."

"Was it such an awful thing for me to ask?"

She nodded.

"Bren, I know it was probably a surprise. It was for me. But we're not children."

"Neil, I just don't want to. It's not because you asked me to, either. I don't know where you get that from. That's not it."

"Then why is it?"

"Oh everything. I just don't feel *old* enough for all that equipment."

"What does age have to do with it?"

"I don't mean age. I just mean—well, *me*. I mean it's so conscious a thing to do."

"Of course it's conscious. That's exactly it. Don't you see? It would change us."

"It would change me."

"Us. Together."

"Neil, how do you think I'd feel lying to some doctor."

"You can go to Margaret Sanger, in New York. They don't ask any questions."

"You've done this before?"

"No," I said. "I just know. I read Mary McCarthy."

"That's exactly right. That's just what I'd feel like, somebody out of *her*."

"Don't be dramatic," I said.

"You're the one who's being dramatic. You think there would be something affairish about it, then. Last summer I went with this whore who I sent out to buy—"

"Oh, Brenda, you're a selfish egotistical bitch! You're the one who's thinking about 'last summer,' about an end for us. In fact, that's the whole thing, isn't it—"

"That's right, I'm a bitch. I want this to end. That's why I ask you to stay another week, that's why I let you sleep with me in my own house. What's the *matter* with you! Why don't you and my mother take turns—one day she can plague me, the next you—"

"Stop it!"

"Go to hell, all of you!" Brenda said, and now she was crying and I knew when she ran off I would not see her, as I didn't, for the rest of the afternoon.

Harriet Ehrlich impressed me as a young lady singularly unconscious of a motive in others or herself. All was surfaces, and she seemed a perfect match for Ron, and too for the Patimkins. Mrs. Patimkin, in fact, did just as Brenda prophesied: Harriet appeared, and Brenda's mother lifted one wing and pulled the girl in towards the warm underpart of her body, where Brenda herself would have liked to nestle. Harriet was built like Brenda, although a little chestier, and she nodded her head insistently whenever anyone spoke. Sometimes she would even say the last few words of your sentence with you, though that was infrequent; for the most part she nodded and kept her hands folded. All evening, as the Patimkins planned where the newlyweds should live, what furniture they should buy, how soon they should have a baby—all through this I kept thinking that Harriet was wearing white gloves, but she wasn't.

Brenda and I did not exchange a word or a glance; we sat, listening, Brenda somewhat more impatient than me. Near the end Harriet began calling Mrs. Patimkin "Mother," and once, "Mother Patimkin," and that was when Brenda went to sleep. I stayed behind, mesmerized almost by the dissection, analysis, reconsideration, and finally, the embracing of the trivial. At last Mr. and Mrs. Patimkin tumbled off to bed, and Julie, who had fallen asleep on her chair, was carried into her room by Ron. That left us two non-Patimkins together.

"Ron tells me you have a very interesting job."

"I work in the library."

"I've always liked reading."

"That'll be nice, married to Ron."

"Ron likes music."

"Yes," I said. What had I *said*?

"You must get first crack at the best-sellers," she said.

"Sometimes," I said.

"Well," she said, flapping her hands on her knees, "I'm sure we'll all have a good time together. Ron and I hope you and Brenda will double with us soon."

"Not tonight." I smiled. "Soon. Will you excuse me?"

"Good night. I like Brenda very much."

"Thank you," I said as I started up the stairs.

I knocked gently on Brenda's door.

"I'm sleeping."

"Can I come in?" I asked.

Her door opened an inch and she said, "Ron will be up soon."

"We'll leave the door open. I only want to talk."

She let me in and I sat in the chair that faced the bed.

"How do you like your sister-in-law?"

"I've met her before."

"Brenda, you don't have to sound so damn terse."

She didn't answer and I just sat there yanking the string on the shade up and down.

"Are you still angry?" I asked at last.

"Yes."

"Don't be," I said. "You can forget about my suggestion. It's not worth it if this is what's going to happen."

"What did you expect to happen?"

"Nothing. I didn't think it would be so horrendous."

"That's because you can't understand my side."

"Perhaps."

"No perhaps about it."

"*Okay*," I said. "I just wish you'd realize what it is you're getting angry about. It's not my suggestion, Brenda."

"No? What is it?"

"It's me."

"Oh don't start that again, will you? I can't win, no matter what I say."

"Yes, you can," I said. "You have."

I walked out of her room, closing the door behind me for the night.

When I got downstairs the following morning there was a great deal of activity. In the living room I heard Mrs. Patimkin reading a list to Harriet while Julie ran in and out of rooms in search of a skate key. Carlota was vacuuming the carpet; every appliance in the kitchen was bubbling, twisting, and shaking. Brenda greeted me with a perfectly pleasant smile and in the dining room, where I walked to look out at the back lawn and the weather, she kissed me on the shoulder.

"Hello," she said.

"Hello."

"I have to go with Harriet this morning," Brenda told me. "So we can't run. Unless you want to go alone."

"No. I'll read or something. Where are you going?"

"We're going to New York. Shopping. She's going to buy a wedding dress. For after the wedding. To go away in."

"What are *you* going to buy?"

"A dress to be maid of honor in. If I go with Harriet then I can go to Bergdorf's without all that Ohrbach's business with my mother."

"Get me something, will you?" I said.

"Oh, Neil, are you going to bring that up again!"

"I was only *fooling*. I wasn't even thinking about that."

"Then why did you say it?"

"Oh Jesus!" I said, and went outside and drove my car down into Millburn Center where I had some eggs and coffee.

When I came back, Brenda was gone, and there were only Carlota, Mrs. Patimkin, and myself in the house. I tried to stay out of whichever rooms they were in, but finally Mrs. Patimkin and I wound up sitting opposite each other in the TV room. She was checking off names on a long sheet of paper she held; next to her, on the table, were two thin phone books which she consulted from time to time.

"No rest for the weary," she said to me.

I smiled hugely, embracing the proverb as though Mrs. Patimkin had just then coined it. "Yes. Of course," I said. "Would you like some help? Maybe I could help you check something."

"Oh, no," she said with a little head-shaking dismissal, "it's for Hadassah."

"Oh," I said.

I sat and watched her until she asked, "Is your mother in Hadassah?"

"I don't know if she is now. She was in Newark."

"Was she an active member?"

"I guess so, she was always planting trees in Israel for someone."

"Really?" Mrs. Patimkin said. "What's her name?"

"Esther Klugman. She's in Arizona now. Do they have Hadassah there?"

"Wherever there are Jewish women."

"Then I guess she is. She's with my father. They went there for their asthma. I'm staying with my aunt in Newark. She's not in Hadassah. My Aunt Sylvia is, though. Do you know her, Aaron Klugman and Sylvia? They belong to your club. They have a daughter, my cousin Doris—" I couldn't stop myself "—They live in Livingston. Maybe it isn't Hadassah my Aunt Sylvia belongs to. I think it's some TB organization. Or cancer. Muscular dystrophy, maybe. I know she's interested in *some* disease."

"That's very nice," Mrs. Patimkin said.

"Oh yes."

"They do very good work."

"I know."

Mrs. Patimkin, I thought, had begun to warm to me; she let the purple eyes stop peering and just look out at the world for a while without judging. "Are you interested in B'nai Brith?" she asked me. "Ron is joining, you know, as soon as he gets married."

"I think I'll wait till then," I said.

Petulantly, Mrs. Patimkin went back to her lists, and I realized it had been foolish of me to risk lightheartedness with her about Jewish affairs. "You're active in the Temple, aren't you?" I asked with all the interest I could muster.

"Yes," she said.

"What Temple do *you* belong to?" she asked in a moment.

"We used to belong to Hudson Street Synagogue. Since my parents left, I haven't had much contact."

I didn't know whether Mrs. Patimkin caught a false tone in my voice. Personally I thought I had managed my rueful confession pretty well, especially when I recalled the decade of paganism prior to my parents' departure. Regardless, Mrs. Patimkin asked immediately—and strategically it seemed— "We're all going to Temple Friday night. Why don't you come with us? I mean, are you orthodox or conservative?"

I considered. "Well, I haven't gone in a long time . . . I sort of switch . . ." I smiled. "I'm just Jewish," I said, well-meaningly, but that too sent Mrs. Patimkin back to her Hadassah work. Desperately I tried to think of something that would convince her I wasn't an infidel. Finally I asked: "Do you know Martin Buber's work?"

"Buber . . . Buber," she said, looking at her Hadassah list. "Is he orthodox or conservative?" she asked.

". . . He's a philosopher."

"Is he *reformed*?" she asked, piqued either at my evasiveness or at the possibility that Buber attended Friday night services without a hat, and Mrs. Buber had only one set of dishes in her kitchen.

"Orthodox," I said faintly.

"That's very nice," she said.

"Yes."

"Isn't Hudson Street Synagogue orthodox?" she asked.

"I don't know."

"I thought you belonged."

"I was bar-mitzvahed there."

"And you don't know that it's orthodox?"

"Yes. I do. It is."

"Then *you* must be."

"Oh, yes, I am," I said. "What are you?" I popped, blushing.

"Orthodox. My husband is conservative," which meant, I took it, that he didn't care. "Brenda is nothing, as you probably know."

"Oh?" I said. "No, I didn't know that."

"She was the best Hebrew student I've ever seen," Mrs. Patimkin said, "but then, of course, she got too big for her britches."

Mrs. Patimkin looked at me, and I wondered whether courtesy demanded that I agree. "Oh, I don't know," I said at last, "I'd say Brenda is conservative. Maybe a little reformed . . ."

The phone rang, rescuing me, and I spoke a silent orthodox prayer to the Lord.

"Hello," Mrs. Patimkin said. ". . . no . . . I can *not*, I have all the Hadassah calls to make . . ."

I acted as though I were listening to the birds outside, though the closed windows let no natural noises in.

"Have Ronald drive them up . . . But we can't wait, not if we want it on time . . ."

Mrs. Patimkin glanced up at me; then she put one hand over the mouthpiece. "Would you ride down to Newark for me?"

I stood. "Yes. Surely."

"Dear?" she said back into the phone, "Neil will come for it . . . No, *Neil*, Brenda's friend . . . Yes . . . Goodbye.

"Mr. Patimkin has some silver patterns I have to see. Would you drive down to his place and pick them up?"

"Of course."

"Do you know where the shop is?"

"Yes."

"Here," she said, handing a key ring to me, "take the Volkswagen.

"My car is right outside."

"Take these," she said.

Patimkin Kitchen and Bathroom Sinks was in the heart of the Negro section of Newark. Years ago, at the time of the great immigration, it had been the Jewish section, and still one could see the little fish stores, the kosher delicatessens, the Turkish baths, where my grandparents had shopped and bathed at the beginning of the century. Even the smells had lingered: whitefish, corned beef, sour tomatoes—but now, on top of these, was the grander greasier smell of auto wrecking shops, the sour stink of a brewery, the burning odor from a leather factory; and on the streets, instead of Yiddish, one heard the shouts of Negro children playing at Willie Mays with a broom handle and half a rubber ball. The neighborhood had changed: the old Jews like my grandparents had struggled and died, and their offspring had struggled and prospered, and moved further and further west, towards the edge of Newark, then out of it, and up the slope of the Orange Mountains, until they had reached the crest and started down the other side, pouring into Gentile territory as the Scotch-Irish had poured through the Cumberland Gap. Now, in fact, the Negroes were making the same migration, following the steps of the Jews, and those who remained in the Third Ward lived the most squalid of lives and dreamed in their fetid mattresses of the piny smell of Georgia nights.

I wondered, for an instant only, if I would see the colored kid from the library on the streets here. I didn't, of course, though I was sure he lived in one of the scabby, peeling buildings out of which dogs, children, and aproned women moved continually. On the top floors, windows were open, and the very old, who could no longer creak down the long stairs to the street, sat where they had been put, in the screenless windows, their elbows resting on fluffless pillows, and their heads tipping forward on their necks, watching the push of the young and the pregnant and the unemployed. Who would come after the Negroes? Who was left? No one, I thought, and someday these streets, where my grandmother drank hot tea from an old *jahrzeit* glass, would be empty and we would all of us have moved to the crest of the Orange Mountains, and wouldn't the dead stop kicking at the slats in their coffins then?

I pulled the Volkswagen up in front of a huge garage door that said across the front of it:

PATIMKIN KITCHEN AND BATHROOM SINKS
"Any Size—Any Shape"

Inside I could see a glass-enclosed office; it was in the center of an immense warehouse. Two trucks were being loaded in the rear, and Mr. Patimkin, when I saw him, had a cigar in his mouth and was shouting at someone. It was Ron, who was wearing a white T-shirt that said Ohio State Athletic Association across the front. Though he was taller than Mr. Patimkin, and almost as stout, his hands hung weakly at his sides like a small boy's; Mr. Patimkin's cigar locomoted in his mouth. Six Negroes were loading one of the trucks feverishly, tossing— my stomach dropped—sink bowls at one another.

Ron left Mr. Patimkin's side and went back to directing the men. He thrashed his arms about a good deal, and though on the whole he seemed rather confused, he didn't appear to be at all concerned about anybody dropping a sink. Suddenly I could see myself directing the Negroes—I would have an ulcer in an hour. I could almost hear the enamel surfaces shattering on the floor. And I could hear myself: "Watch it, you guys. Be careful, will you? *Whoops!* Oh, please be—*watch* it! Watch! Oh!" Suppose Mr. Patimkin should come up to me and say, "Okay, boy, you want to marry my daughter, let's see what you can do." Well, he would see: in a moment that floor would be a shattered mosaic, a crunchy path of enamel. "Klugman, what kind of worker are you? You work like you eat!" "That's right, that's right, I'm a sparrow, let me go." "Don't you even know how to load and unload?" "Mr. Patimkin, even breathing gives me trouble, sleep tires me out, let me go, let me go . . ."

Mr. Patimkin was headed back to the fish bowl to answer a ringing phone, and I wrenched myself free of my reverie and headed towards the office too. When I entered, Mr. Patimkin looked up from the phone with his eyes; the sticky cigar was in his free hand—he moved it at me, a greeting. From outside I heard Ron call in a high voice, "You can't all go to lunch at the same time. We haven't got all day!"

"Sit down," Mr. Patimkin shot at me, though when he went back to his conversation I saw there was only one chair in the office, his. People did not sit at Patimkin Sink—here you earned your money the hard way, standing up. I busied myself looking at the several calendars that hung from filing cabinets; they showed illustrations of women so dreamy, so fantastically thighed and uddered, that one could not think of them as pornographic. The artist who had drawn the calendar girls for "Lewis Construction Company," and "Earl's Truck and Auto Repair," and "Grossman and Son, Paper Box" had been painting some third sex I had never seen.

"Sure, sure, sure," Mr. Patimkin said into the phone. "To-morrow, don't tell me tomorrow. Tomorrow the world could blow up."

At the other end someone spoke. Who was it? Lewis from the construction company? Earl from truck repair?

"I'm running a business, Grossman, not a charity."

So it was Grossman being browbeaten at the other end.

"Shit on that," Mr. Patimkin said. "You're not the only one in town, my good friend," and he winked at me.

Ah-ha, a conspiracy against Grossman. Me and Mr. Patimkin. I smiled as collusively as I knew how.

"All right then, we're here till five . . . No later."

He wrote something on a piece of paper. It was only a big X.

"My kid'll be here," he said. "Yes, he's in the business."

Whatever Grossman said on the other end, it made Mr. Patimkin laugh. Mr. Patimkin hung up without a goodbye.

He looked out the back to see how Ron was doing. "Four years in college he can't unload a truck."

I didn't know what to say but finally chose the truth. "I guess I couldn't either."

"You could learn. What am I, a genius? I learned. Hard work never killed anybody."

To that I agreed.

Mr. Patimkin looked at his cigar. "A man works hard he's got something. You don't get anywhere sitting on your behind, you know . . . The biggest men in the country worked hard, believe me. Even Rockefeller. Success don't come easy . . ." He did not say this so much as he mused it out while he surveyed his dominion. He was not a man enamored of words, and I had the feeling that what had tempted him into this barrage of universals was probably the combination of Ron's performance and my presence—me, the outsider who might one day be an insider. But did Mr. Patimkin even consider that possibility? I did not know; I only knew that these few words he did speak could hardly transmit all the satisfaction and surprise he felt about the life he had managed to build for himself and his family.

He looked out at Ron again. "Look at him, if he played basketball like that they'd throw him the hell off the court." But he was smiling when he said it.

He walked over to the door. "Ronald, let them go to lunch."

Ron shouted back, "I thought I'd let some go now, and some later."

"Why?"

"Then somebody'll always be—"

"No fancy deals here," Mr. Patimkin shouted. "We all go to lunch at once."

Ron turned back. "All right, boys, lunch!"

His father smiled at me. "Smart boy? Huh?" He tapped his head. "That took brains, huh? He ain't got the stomach for business. He's an idealist," and then I think Mr. Patimkin suddenly realized who *I* was, and eagerly corrected himself so as not to offend. "That's all right, you know, if you're a schoolteacher, or like you, you know, a student or something like that. Here you need a little of the *gonif* in you. You know what that means? *Gonif?*"

"Thief," I said.

"You know more than my own kids. They're *goyim*, my kids, that's how much they understand." He watched the Negro loading gang walk past the office and shouted out to them,

"You guys know how long an hour is? All right, you'll be back in an hour!"

Ron came into the office and of course shook my hand.

"Do you have that stuff for Mrs. Patimkin?" I asked.

"Ronald, get him the silver patterns." Ron turned away and Mr. Patimkin said, "When I got married we had forks and knives from the five and ten. This kid needs gold to eat off," but there was no anger; far from it.

I drove to the mountains in my own car that afternoon, and stood for a while at the wire fence watching the deer lightly prance, coyly feed, under the protection of signs that read, Do Not Feed the Deer, *By Order of South Mountain Reservation.* Alongside me at the fence were dozens of kids; they giggled and screamed when the deer licked the popcorn from their hands, and then were sad when their own excitement sent the young loping away towards the far end of the field where their tawny-skinned mothers stood regally watching the traffic curl up the mountain road. Young white-skinned mothers, hardly older than I, and in many instances younger, chatted in their convertibles behind me, and looked down from time to time to see what their children were about. I had seen them before, when Brenda and I had gone out for a bite in the afternoon, or had driven up here for lunch: in clotches of three and four they sat in the rustic hamburger joints that dotted the Reservation area while their children gobbled hamburgers and malteds and were given dimes to feed the jukebox. Though none of the little ones were old enough to read the song titles, almost all of them could holler out the words, and they did, while the mothers, a few of whom I recognized as high school mates of mine, compared suntans, supermarkets, and vacations. They looked immortal sitting there. Their hair would always stay the color they desired, their clothes the right texture and shade; in their homes they would have simple Swedish modern when that was fashionable, and if huge, ugly baroque ever came back, out would go the long, midget-legged marble coffee table and in would come Louis Quatorze. These were the goddesses, and if I were Paris I could not have been able to choose among them, so microscopic were the differences. Their fates had collapsed them into one. Only

Brenda shone. Money and comfort would not erase her single-ness—they hadn't yet, or had they? What was I loving, I won-dered, and since I am not one to stick scalpels into myself, I wiggled my hand in the fence and allowed a tiny-nosed buck to lick my thoughts away.

When I returned to the Patimkin house, Brenda was in the living room looking more beautiful than I had ever seen her. She was modeling her new dress for Harriet and her mother. Even Mrs. Patimkin seemed softened by the sight of her; it looked as though some sedative had been injected into her, and so relaxed the Brenda-hating muscles around her eyes and mouth.

Brenda, without glasses, modeled in place; when she looked at me it was a kind of groggy, half-waking look I got, and though others might have interpreted it as sleepiness it sounded in my veins as lust. Mrs. Patimkin told her finally that she'd bought a very nice dress and I told her she looked lovely and Harriet told her she was very beautiful and that *she* ought to be the bride, and then there was an uncomfortable silence while all of us wondered who ought to be the groom.

Then when Mrs. Patimkin had led Harriet out to the kitchen, Brenda came up to me and said, "I *ought* to be the bride."

"You ought, sweetheart." I kissed her, and suddenly she was crying.

"What is it, honey?" I said.

"Let's go outside."

On the lawn, Brenda was no longer crying but her voice sounded very tired.

"Neil, I called Margaret Sanger Clinic," she said. "When I was in New York."

I didn't answer.

"Neil, they *did* ask if I was married. God, the woman sounded like my mother . . ."

"What did you say?"

"I said *no*."

"What did she say?"

"I don't know. I hung up." She walked away and around the oak tree. When she appeared again she'd stepped out of her shoes and held one hand on the tree, as though it were a Maypole she were circling.

"You can call them back," I said.

She shook her head. "No, I can't. I don't even know why I called in the first place. We were shopping and I just walked away, looked up the number, and called."

"Then you can go to a doctor."

She shook again.

"Look, Bren," I said, rushing to her, "we'll go together, to a doctor. In New York—"

"I don't want to go to some dirty little office—"

"We won't. We'll go to the most posh gynecologist in New York. One who gets *Harper's Bazaar* for the reception room. How does that sound?"

She bit her lower lip.

"You'll come with me?" she asked.

"I'll come with you."

"To the office?"

"Sweetie, your husband wouldn't come to the office."

"No?"

"He'd be working."

"But you're not," she said.

"I'm on vacation," I said, but I had answered the wrong question. "Bren, I'll wait and when you're all done we'll buy a drink. We'll go out to dinner."

"Neil, I shouldn't have called Margaret Sanger—it's not right."

"It is, Brenda. It's the most right thing we can do." She walked away and I was exhausted from pleading. Somehow I felt I could have convinced her had I been a bit more crafty; and yet I did not want it to be craftiness that changed her mind. I was silent when she came back, and perhaps it was just that, my *not* saying anything, that prompted her finally to say, "I'll ask Mother Patimkin if she wants us to take Harriet too . . ."

7

I shall never forget the heat and mugginess of that afternoon we drove into New York. It was four days after the day she'd called Margaret Sanger—she put it off and put it off, but finally on Friday, three days before Ron's wedding and four before her departure, we were heading through the Lincoln

Tunnel, which seemed longer and fumier than ever, like Hell with tiled walls. Finally we were in New York and smothered again by the thick day. I pulled around the policeman who directed traffic in his shirt sleeves and up onto the Port Authority roof to park the car.

"Do you have cab fare?" I said.

"Aren't you going to come with me?"

"I thought I'd wait in the bar. Here, downstairs."

"You can wait in Central Park. His office is right across the street."

"Bren, what's the diff—" But when I saw the look that invaded her eyes I gave up the air-conditioned bar to accompany her across the city. There was a sudden shower while our cab went crosstown, and when the rain stopped the streets were sticky and shiny, and below the pavement was the rumble of the subways, and in all it was like entering the ear of a lion.

The doctor's office was in the Squibb Building, which is across from Bergdorf Goodman's and so was a perfect place for Brenda to add to her wardrobe. For some reason we have never once considered her going to a doctor in Newark, perhaps because it was too close to home and might allow for possibilities of discovery. When Brenda got to the revolving door she looked back at me; her eyes were very watery, even with her glasses, and I did not say a word, afraid what a word, any word, might do. I kissed her hair and motioned that I would be across the street by the Plaza fountain, and then I watched her revolve through the doors. Out on the street the traffic moved slowly as though the humidity were a wall holding everything back. Even the fountain seemed to be bubbling boiling water on the people who sat at its edge, and in an instant I decided against crossing the street, and turned south on Fifth and began to walk the steaming pavement towards St. Patrick's. On the north steps a crowd was gathered; everyone was watching a model being photographed. She was wearing a lemon-colored dress and had her feet pointed like a ballerina, and as I passed into the church I heard some lady say, "If I ate cottage cheese *ten* times a day, I couldn't be that skinny."

It wasn't much cooler inside the church, though the stillness and the flicker of the candles made me think it was. I took a seat at the rear and while I couldn't bring myself to kneel, I did lean forward onto the back of the bench before me, and held my hands together and closed my eyes. I wondered if I looked like a Catholic, and in my wonderment I began to make a little speech to myself. Can I call the self-conscious words I spoke prayer? At any rate, I called my audience God. God, I said, I am twenty-three years old. I want to make the best of things. Now the doctor is about to wed Brenda to me, and I am not entirely certain this is all for the best. What is it I love, Lord? Why have I chosen? Who is Brenda? The race is to the swift. Should I have stopped to think?

I was getting no answers, but I went on. If we meet You at all, God, it's that we're carnal, and acquisitive, and thereby partake of You. I am carnal, and I know You approve, I just know it. But how carnal can I get? I am acquisitive. Where do I turn now in my acquisitiveness? Where do we meet? Which prize is You?

It was an ingenious meditation, and suddenly I felt ashamed. I got up and walked outside, and the noise of Fifth Avenue met me with an answer:

Which prize do you think, *schmuck*? Gold dinnerware, sporting-goods trees, nectarines, garbage disposals, bumpless noses, Patimkin Sink, Bonwit Teller—

But damn it, God, that *is* You!

And God only laughed, that clown.

On the steps around the fountain I sat in a small arc of a rainbow that the sun had shot through the spray of the water. And then I saw Brenda coming out of the Squibb Building. She carried nothing with her, like a woman who's only been window shopping, and for a moment I was glad that in the end she had disobeyed my desire.

As she crossed the street, though, that little levity passed, and then I was myself again.

She walked up before me and looked down at where I sat; when she inhaled she filled her entire body, and then let her breath out with a "Whew!"

"Where is it?" I said.

My answer, at first, was merely that victorious look of hers, the one she'd given Simp the night she'd beaten her, the one I'd gotten the morning I finished the third lap alone. At last she said, "I'm wearing it."

"Oh, Bren."

"He said shall I wrap it or will you take it with you?"

"Oh, Brenda, I love you."

We slept together that night, and so nervous were we about our new toy that we performed like kindergartners, or (in the language of that country) like a lousy double-play combination. And then the next day we hardly saw one another at all, for with the last-minute wedding preparations came scurrying, telegramming, shouting, crying, rushing—in short, lunacy. Even the meals lost their Patimkin fullness, and were tortured out of Kraft cheese, stale onion rolls, dry salami, a little chopped liver, and fruit cocktail. It was hectic all weekend, and I tried as best I could to keep clear of the storm, at whose eye, Ron, clumsy and smiling, and Harriet, flittering and courteous, were being pulled closer and closer together. By Sunday night fatigue had arrested hysteria and all of the Patimkins, Brenda included, had gone off to an early sleep. When Ron went into the bathroom to brush his teeth I decided to go in and brush mine. While I stood over the sink he checked his supports for dampness; then he hung them on the shower knobs and asked me if I would like to listen to his records for a while. It was not out of boredom and loneliness that I accepted; rather a brief spark of lockerroom comradery had been struck there among the soap and the water and the tile, and I thought that perhaps Ron's invitation was prompted by a desire to spend his last moments as a Single Man with another Single Man. If I was right, then it was the first real attestation he'd given to my masculinity. How could I refuse?

I sat on the unused twin bed.

"You want to hear Mantovani?"

"Sure," I said.

"Who do you like better, him or Kostelanetz?"

"It's a toss-up."

Ron went to his cabinet. "Hey, how about the Columbus record? Brenda ever play it for you?"

"No. I don't think so."

He extracted a record from its case, and like a giant with a sea shell, placed it gingerly on the phonograph. Then he smiled at me and leaned back onto his bed. His arms were behind his head and his eyes fixed on the ceiling. "They give this to all the seniors. With the yearbook—" but he hushed as soon as the sound began. I watched Ron and listened to the record.

At first there was just a roll of drums, then silence, then another drum roll—and then softly, a marching song, the melody of which was very familiar. When the song ended, I heard the bells, soft, loud, then soft again. And finally there came a Voice, bowel-deep and historic, the kind one associates with documentaries about the rise of Fascism.

"The year, 1956. The season, fall. The place, Ohio State University . . ."

Blitzkrieg! Judgment Day! The Lord had lowered his baton, and the Ohio State Glee Club were lining out the Alma Mater as if their souls depended on it. After one desperate chorus, they fell, still screaming, into bottomless oblivion, and the Voice resumed:

"The leaves had begun to turn and redden on the trees. Smoky fires line Fraternity Row, as pledges rake the leaves and turn them to a misty haze. Old faces greet new ones, new faces meet old, and another year has begun . . ."

Music. Glee Club in great comeback. Then the Voice: "The place, the banks of the Olentangy. The event, Homecoming Game, 1956. The opponent, the ever dangerous Illini . . ."

Roar of crowd. New voice—Bill Stern: "Illini over the ball. The snap. Linday fading to pass, he finds a receiver, he passes long *long* down field—and IT'S INTERCEPTED BY NUMBER 43, HERB CLARK OF OHIO STATE! Clark evades one tackler, he evades another as he comes up to midfield. Now he's picking up blockers, he's down to the 45, the 40, the 35—"

And as Bill Stern egged on Clark, and Clark, Bill Stern, Ron, on his bed, with just a little body-english, eased Herb Clark over the goal.

"And it's the Buckeyes ahead now, 21 to 19. *What a game!*"

The Voice of History baritoned in again: "But the season was up and down, and by the time the first snow had covered the turf, it was the sound of dribbling and the cry *Up and In!* that echoed through the fieldhouse . . ."

Ron closed his eyes.

"The Minnesota game," a new, high voice announced, "and for some of our seniors, their last game for the red and white . . . The players are ready to come out on the floor and into the spotlight. There'll be a big hand of appreciation from this capacity crowd for some of the boys who won't be back next year. Here comes Larry Gardner, big Number 7, out onto the floor, Big Larry from Akron, Ohio . . ."

"Larry—" announced the P.A. system; "Larry," the crowd roared back.

"And here comes Ron Patimkin dribbling out. Ron, number 11, from Short Hills, New Jersey. Big Ron's last game, and it'll be some time before Buckeye fans forget him . . ."

Big Ron tightened on his bed as the loudspeaker called his name; his ovation must have set the nets to trembling. Then the rest of the players were announced, and then basketball season was over, and it was Religious Emphasis Week, the Senior Prom (Billy May blaring at the gymnasium roof), Fraternity Skit Night, E. E. Cummings reading to students (verse, silence, applause); and then, finally, commencement:

"The campus is hushed this day of days. For several thousand young men and women it is a joyous yet a solemn occasion. And for their parents a day of laughter and a day of tears. It is a bright green day, it is June the seventh of the year one thousand nine hundred and fifty-seven and for these young Americans the most stirring day of their lives. For many this will be their last glimpse of the campus, of Columbus, for many many years. Life calls us, and anxiously if not nervously we walk out into the world and away from the pleasures of these ivied walls. But not from its memories. They will be concomitant, if not the fundament, of our lives. We shall choose husbands and wives, we shall choose jobs and homes, we shall sire children and grandchildren, but we will not forget you, Ohio State. In the years ahead we will carry with us always memories of thee, Ohio State . . ."

Slowly, softly, the OSU band begins the Alma Mater, and then the bells chime that last hour. Soft, very soft, for it is spring.

There was goose flesh on Ron's veiny arms as the Voice continued. "We offer ourselves to you then, world, and come at you in search of Life. And to you, Ohio State, to you Columbus, we say thank you, thank you and goodbye. We will miss you, in the fall, in the winter, in the spring, but some day we shall return. Till then, goodbye, Ohio State, goodbye, red and white, goodbye, Columbus . . . goodbye, Columbus . . . goodbye . . ."

Ron's eyes were closed. The band was upending its last truckload of nostalgia, and I tiptoed from the room, in step with the 2163 members of the Class of '57.

I closed my door, but then opened it and looked back at Ron: he was still humming on his bed. Thee! I thought, my brother-in-law!

The wedding.

Let me begin with the relatives.

There was Mrs. Patimkin's side of the family: her sister Molly, a tiny buxom hen whose ankles swelled and ringed her shoes, and who would remember Ron's wedding if for no other reason than she'd martyred her feet in three-inch heels, and Molly's husband, the butter and egg man, Harry Grossbart, who had earned his fortune with barley and corn in the days of Prohibition. Now he was active in the Temple and whenever he saw Brenda he swatted her on the can; it was a kind of physical bootlegging that passed, I guess, for familial affection. Then there was Mrs. Patimkin's brother, Marty Kreiger, the Kosher Hot-Dog King, an immense man, as many stomachs as he had chins, and already, at fifty-five, with as many heart attacks as chins and stomachs combined. He had just come back from a health cure in the Catskills, where he said he'd eaten nothing but All-Bran and had won $1500 at gin rummy. When the photographer came by to take pictures, Marty put his hand on his wife's pancake breasts and said, "Hey, how about a picture of this!" His wife, Sylvia, was a frail, spindly woman with bones like a bird's. She had cried throughout the ceremony, and sobbed openly, in fact, when the rabbi had pronounced Ron and Harriet "man and wife in the eyes of God and the State of New Jersey." Later, at dinner, she had hardened enough to slap her husband's hand as it reached out for a cigar. However, when he reached across to hold her breast she just looked aghast and said nothing.

Also there were Mrs. Patimkin's twin sisters, Rose and Pearl, who both had white hair, the color of Lincoln convertibles, and nasal voices, and husbands who followed after them but talked only to each other, as though, in fact, sister had married sister, and husband had married husband. The husbands, named Earl Klein and Manny Kartzman, sat next to each other during the ceremony, then at dinner, and once, in fact, while the band was playing between courses, they rose, Klein and Kartzman, as though to dance, but instead walked to the far end of the hall where together they paced off the width of the floor. Earl, I learned later, was in the carpet business, and apparently he was trying to figure how much money he would make if the Hotel Pierre favored him with a sale.

On Mr. Patimkin's side there was only Leo, his half-brother. Leo was married to a woman named Bea whom nobody seemed to talk to. Bea kept hopping up and down during the meal and running over to the kiddie table to see if her little girl, Sharon, was being taken care of. "I told her not to take the kid. Get a baby-sitter, I said." Leo told me this while Brenda danced with Ron's best man, Ferrari. "She says what are we, millionaires? No, for Christ sake, but my brother's kids gets married, I can have a little celebration. No, we gotta *shlep* the kid with us. Aah, it gives her something to do! . . ." He looked around the hall. Up on the stage Harry Winters (né Weinberg) was leading his band in a medley from *My Fair Lady*; on the floor, all ages, all sizes, all shapes were dancing. Mr. Patimkin was dancing with Julie, whose dress had slipped down from her shoulders to reveal her soft small back, and long neck, like Brenda's. He danced in little squares and was making considerable effort not to step on Julie's toes. Harriet, who was, as everyone said, a beautiful bride, was dancing with her father. Ron danced with Harriet's mother, Brenda with Ferrari, and I had sat down for a while in the empty chair beside Leo so as not to get maneuvered into dancing with Mrs. Patimkin, which seemed to be the direction towards which things were moving.

"You're Brenda's boy friend? Huh?" Leo said.

I nodded—earlier in the evening I'd stopped giving blushing explanations. "You gotta deal there, boy," Leo said, "you don't louse it up."

"She's very beautiful," I said.

Leo poured himself a glass of champagne, and then waited as though he expected a head to form on it; when one didn't, he filled the glass to the brim.

"Beautiful, not beautiful, what's the difference. I'm a practical man. I'm on the bottom, so I gotta be. You're Aly Khan you worry about marrying movie stars. I wasn't born yesterday . . . You know how old I was when I got married? Thirty-five years old. I don't know what the hell kind of hurry I was in." He drained his glass and refilled it. "I'll tell you something, one good thing happened to me in my whole life. Two maybe. Before I came back from overseas I got a letter from my wife—she wasn't my wife then. My mother-in-law found an apartment for us in Queens. Sixty-two fifty a month it cost. That's the last good thing that happened."

"What was the first?"

"What first?"

"You said *two* things," I said.

"I don't remember. I say two because my wife tells me I'm sarcastic and a cynic. That way maybe she won't think I'm such a wise guy."

I saw Brenda and Ferrari separate, and so excused myself and started for Brenda, but just then Mr. Patimkin separated from Julie and it looked as though the two men were going to switch partners. Instead the four of them stood on the dance floor and when I reached them they were laughing and Julie was saying, "What's so funny!" Ferrari said "Hi" to me and whisked Julie away, which sent her into peals of laughter.

Mr. Patimkin had one hand on Brenda's back and suddenly the other one was on mine. "You kids having a good time?" he said.

We were sort of swaying, the three of us, to "Get Me to the Church on Time."

Brenda kissed her father. "Yes," she said. "I'm so drunk my head doesn't even need my neck."

"It's a fine wedding, Mr. Patimkin."

"You want anything just ask me . . ." he said, a little drunken himself. "You're two good kids . . . How do you like that brother of yours getting married? . . . Huh? . . . Is that a girl or is that a girl?"

Brenda smiled, and though she apparently thought her father had spoken of her, I was sure he'd been referring to Harriet.

"You like weddings, Daddy?" Brenda said.

"I like my kids' weddings . . ." He slapped me on the back.

"You two kids, you want anything? Go have a good time. Remember," he said to Brenda, "you're my honey . . ." Then he looked at me. "Whatever my Buck wants is good enough for me. There's no business too big it can't use another head."

I smiled, though not directly at him, and beyond I could see Leo sopping up champagne and watching the three of us; when he caught my eye he made a sign with his hand, a circle with his thumb and forefinger, indicating, "That a boy, that a boy!"

After Mr. Patimkin departed, Brenda and I danced closely, and we only sat down when the waiters began to circulate with the main course. The head table was noisy, particularly at our end where the men were almost all teammates of Ron's, in one sport or another; they ate a fantastic number of rolls. Tank Feldman, Ron's roommate who had flown in from Toledo, kept sending the waiter back for rolls, for celery, for olives, and always to the squealing delight of Gloria Feldman, his wife, a nervous, undernourished girl who continually looked down the front of her gown as though there was some sort of construction project going on under her clothes. Gloria and Tank, in fact, seemed to be self-appointed precinct captains at our end. They proposed toasts, burst into wild song, and continually referred to Brenda and me as "love birds." Brenda smiled at this with her eyeteeth and I brought up a cheery look from some fraudulent auricle of my heart.

And the night continued: we ate, we drank, we danced—Rose and Pearl did the Charleston with one another (while their husbands examined woodwork and chandeliers), and then I did the Charleston with none other than Gloria Feldman, who made coy, hideous faces at me all the time we danced. Near the end of the evening, Brenda, who'd been drinking champagne like her Uncle Leo, did a Rita Hayworth tango with herself, and Julie fell asleep on some ferns she'd whisked off the head table and made into a mattress at the far end of the hall. I felt a numbness creep into my hard palate, and by three o'clock people were dancing in their coats, shoeless ladies were wrapping hunks of wedding cake in napkins for their children's lunch, and finally Gloria Feldman made her way over to our end of the table and said, freshly, "Well, our little Radcliffe smarty, what have *you* been doing all summer?"

"Growing a penis."

Gloria smiled and left as quickly as she'd come, and Brenda without another word headed shakily away for the ladies' room and the rewards of overindulgence. No sooner had she left than Leo was beside me, a glass in one hand, a new bottle of champagne in the other.

"No sign of the bride and groom?" he said, leering. He'd lost most of his consonants by this time and was doing the best he could with long, wet vowels. "Well, you're next, kid, I see it in the cards . . . You're nobody's sucker . . ." And he stabbed me in the side with the top of the bottle, spilling champagne onto the side of my rented tux. He straightened up, poured more onto his hand and glass, but then suddenly he stopped. He was looking into the lights which were hidden beneath a long bank of flowers that adorned the front of the table. He shook the bottle in his hand as though to make it fizz. "The son of a bitch who invented the fluorescent bulb should drop dead!" He set the bottle down and drank.

Up on the stage Harry Winters brought his musicians to a halt. The drummer stood up, stretched, and they all began to open up cases and put their instruments away. On the floor, relatives, friends, associates, were holding each other around the waists and the shoulders, and small children huddled around their parents' legs. A couple of kids ran in and out of the crowd, screaming at tag, until one was grabbed by an adult and slapped soundly on the behind. He began to cry, and couple by couple the floor emptied. Our table was a tangle of squashed everything: napkins, fruits, flowers; there were empty whiskey bottles, droopy ferns, and dishes puddled with unfinished cherry jubilee, gone sticky with the hours. At the end of the table Mr. Patimkin was sitting next to his wife, holding her hand. Opposite them, on two bridge chairs that had been pulled up, sat Mr. and Mrs. Ehrlich. They spoke quietly and evenly, as though they had known each other for years and years. Everything had slowed down now, and from time to time people would come up to the Patimkins and Ehrlichs, wish them *mazel tov*, and then drag themselves and their families out into the September night, which was cool and windy, someone said, and reminded me that soon would come winter and snow.

"They never wear out, those things, you know that." Leo was pointing to the fluorescent lights that shone through the flowers. "They last for years. They could make a car like that if they wanted, that could never wear out. It would run on water in the summer and snow in the winter. But they wouldn't do it, the big boys . . . Look at me," Leo said, splashing his suit front with champagne, "I sell a good bulb. You can't get the kind of bulb I sell in the drugstores. It's a quality bulb. But I'm the little guy. I don't even own a car. His brother, and I don't even own an automobile. I take a train wherever I go. I'm the only guy I know who wears out three pairs of rubbers every winter. Most guys get new ones when they lose the old ones. I wear them out, like shoes. Look," he said, leaning into me, "I could sell a crappy bulb, it wouldn't break my heart. But it's not good business."

The Ehrlichs and Patimkins scraped back their chairs and headed away, all except Mr. Patimkin who came down the table towards Leo and me.

He slapped Leo on the back. "Well, how you doing, *shtarke*?"

"All right, Ben. All right . . ."

"You have a good time?"

"You had a nice affair, Ben, it must've cost a pretty penny, believe me . . ."

Mr. Patimkin laughed. "When I make out my income tax I go to see Leo. He knows just how much money I spent . . . You need a ride home?" he asked me.

"No, thanks. I'm waiting for Brenda. We have my car."

"Good night," Mr. Patimkin said.

I watched him step down off the platform that held the head table, and then start towards the exit. Now the only people in the hall—the shambles of a hall—were myself, Leo, and his wife and child who slept, both of them, with their heads pillowed on a crumpled tablecloth at a table down on the floor before us. Brenda still wasn't around.

"When you got it," Leo said, rubbing his fingers together, "you can afford to talk like a big shot. Who needs a guy like me any more. Salesmen, you spit on them. You can go to the supermarket and buy anything. Where my wife shops you can buy sheets and pillowcases. Imagine, a grocery store! Me, I sell to gas stations, factories, small businesses, all up and down the east coast. Sure, you can sell a guy in a gas station a crappy bulb that'll burn out in a week. For inside the pumps I'm talking, it takes a certain kind of bulb, and then a week later he puts in a new one, and while he's screwing it in he still remembers your name. Not me. I sell a quality bulb. It lasts a month, five weeks, before it even flickers, then it gives you another couple days, dim maybe, but so you shouldn't go blind. It hangs on, it's a quality bulb. Before it even burns out you notice it's getting darker, so you put a new one in. What people don't like is when one minute it's sunlight and the next dark. Let it glimmer a few days and they don't feel so bad. Nobody ever throws out my bulb—they figure they'll save them, can always use them in a pinch. Sometimes I say to a guy, you ever throw out a bulb you bought from Leo Patimkin? You gotta use psychology. That's why I'm sending my kid to college. You don't know a little psychology these days, you're licked . . ."

He lifted an arm and pointed out to his wife; then he slumped down in his seat. "Aaach!" he said, and drank off half a glass of champagne. "I'll tell you, I go as far as New London, Connecticut. That's as far as I'll go, and when I come home at night I stop first for a couple drinks. Martinis. Two I have, sometimes three. That seems fair, don't it? But to her a little sip or a bathtubful, it smells the same. She says it's bad for the kid if I come home smelling. The kid's a baby, for God's sake, she thinks that's the way I'm *supposed* to smell. A forty-eight-year-old man with a three-year-old kid! She'll give me a thrombosis that kid. My wife, she wants me to come home early and play with the kid before she goes to bed. Come home, she says, and *I'll* make you a drink. Hah! I spend all day sniffing gas, leaning under hoods and grimy *poilishehs* in New London, trying to force a lousy bulb into a socket—I'll screw it in myself, I tell them—and she thinks I want to come home and drink a martini from a jelly glass! How long are you going to stay in bars, she says. Till a Jewish girl is Miss Rheingold!

"Look," he went on after another drink, "I love my kid like Ben loves his Brenda. It's not that I don't want to play with her. But if I play with the kid and then at night get into bed with my wife, then she can't expect fancy things from me. It's one or the other. I'm no movie star."

Leo looked at his empty glass and put it on the table; he tilted the bottle up and drank the champagne like soda water. "How much do you think I make a week?" he said.

"I don't know."

"Take a guess."

"A hundred dollars."

"Sure, and tomorrow they're gonna let the lions out of the cage in Central Park. What do you think I make?"

"I can't tell."

"A cabdriver makes more than me. That's a fact. My wife's brother is a cabdriver, *he* lives in Kew Gardens. And he don't take no crap, no sir, not those cabbies. Last week it was raining one night and I said the hell with it, I'm taking a cab. I'd been all day in Newton, Mass. I don't usually go so far, but on the train in the morning I said to myself, stay on, go further, it'll be a change. And I know all the time I'm kidding myself. I wouldn't even make up the extra fare it cost me. But I stay on. And at night I still had a couple boxes with me, so when the guy pulls up at Grand Central there's like a genie inside me says get in. I even threw the bulbs in, not even caring if they broke. And this cabbie says, Whatya want to do, buddy, rip the leather? Those are brand new seats I got. No, I said. Jesus Christ, he says, some goddam people. I get in and give him a Queens address which ought to shut him up, but no, all the way up the Drive he was Jesus Christing me. It's hot in the cab, so I open a window and *then* he turns around and says, Whatya want to do, give me a cold in the neck? I just got over a goddam cold . . ." Leo looked at me, bleary-eyed. "This city is crazy! If I had a little money I'd get out of here in a minute. I'd go to California. They don't need bulbs out there it's so light. I went to New Guinea during the war from San Francisco. *There*," he burst, "there is the other good thing that happened to me, that night in San Francisco with this Hannah Schreiber. That's the both of them, you asked me I'm telling you—the apartment my mother-in-law got us, and this Hannah Schreiber. One night was all. I went to a B'nai Brith dance for servicemen in the basement of some big temple, and I met her. I wasn't married then, so don't make faces."

"I'm not."

"She had a nice little room by herself. She was going to

school to be a teacher. Already I knew something was up because she let me feel inside her slip in the cab. Listen to me, I sound like I'm always in cabs. Maybe two other times in my life. To tell the truth I don't even enjoy it. All the time I'm riding I'm watching the meter. Even the pleasures I can't enjoy!"

"What about Hannah Schreiber?"

He smiled, flashing some gold in his mouth. "How do you like that name? She was only a girl, but she had an old lady's name. In the room she says to me she believes in oral love. I can still hear her: Leo Patimkin, I believe in oral love. I don't know what the hell she means. I figure she was one of those Christian Scientists or some cult or something. So I said, But what about for soldiers, guys going overseas who may get killed, God forbid." He shrugged his shoulders. "The smartest guy in the world I wasn't. But that's twenty years almost, I was still wet behind the ears. I'll tell you, every once in a while my wife—you know, she does for me what Hannah Schreiber did. I don't like to force her, she works hard. That to her is like a cab to me. I wouldn't force her. I can remember every time, I'll bet. Once after a Seder, my mother was still living, she should rest in peace. My wife was up to here with Mogen David. In fact, *twice* after Seders. Aachhh! Everything good in my life I can count on my fingers! God forbid some one should leave me a million dollars, I wouldn't even have to take off my shoes. I got a whole other hand yet."

He pointed to the fluorescent bulbs with the nearly empty champagne bottle. "You call that a light? That's a light to *read* by? It's purple, for God's sake! Half the blind men in the world ruined themselves by those damn things. You know who's behind them? The optometrists! I'll tell you, if I could get a couple hundred for all my stock and the territory, I'd sell tomorrow. That's right, Leo A. Patimkin, one semester accounting, City College nights, will sell equipment, territory, good name. I'll buy two inches in the *Times*. The territory is from here to everywhere. I go where I want, my own boss, no one tells me what to do. You know the Bible? 'Let there be light—and there's Leo Patimkin!' That's my trademark, I'll sell that too. I tell them that slogan, the *poilishehs*, they think I'm making it up. What good is it to be smart unless you're in on the ground floor! I got more brains in my pinky than Ben got in his whole *head*. Why is it he's on top and I'm on the bottom! *Why!* Believe me, if you're born lucky, you're lucky!" And then he exploded into silence.

I had the feeling that he was going to cry, so I leaned over and whispered to him, "You better go home." He agreed, but I had to raise him out of his seat and steer him by one arm down to his wife and child. The little girl could not be awakened, and Leo and Bea asked me to watch her while they went out into the lobby to get their coats. When they returned, Leo seemed to have dragged himself back to the level of human communication. He shook my hand with real feeling. I was very touched.

"You'll go far," he said to me. "You're a smart boy, you'll play it safe. Don't louse things up."

"I won't."

"Next time we see you it'll be *your* wedding," and he winked at me. Bea stood alongside, muttering goodbye all the while he spoke. He shook my hand again and then picked the child out of her seat, and they turned towards the door. From the back, round-shouldered, burdened, child-carrying, they looked like people fleeing a captured city.

Brenda, I discovered, was asleep on a couch in the lobby. It was almost four o'clock and the two of us and the desk clerk were the only ones in the hotel lobby. At first I did not waken Brenda, for she was pale and wilted and I knew she had been sick. I sat beside her, smoothing her hair back off her ears. How would I ever come to know her, I wondered, for as she slept I felt I knew no more of her than what I could see in a photograph. I stirred her gently and in a half-sleep she walked beside me out to the car.

It was almost dawn when we came out of the Jersey side of the Lincoln Tunnel. I switched down to my parking lights, and drove on to the Turnpike, and there out before me I could see the swampy meadows that spread for miles and miles, watery, blotchy, smelly, like an oversight of God. I thought of that other oversight, Leo Patimkin, half-brother to Ben. In a few hours he would be on a train heading north, and as he passed Scarsdale and White Plains, he would belch and taste champagne and let the flavor linger in his mouth. Alongside him on the seat, like another passenger, would be cartons of bulbs. He would get off at New London, or maybe, inspired by the sight of his half-brother, he would stay on again, hoping for some new luck further north. For the world was Leo's territory, every city, every swamp, every road and highway. He could go on to Newfoundland if he wanted, Hudson Bay, and on up to Thule, and then slide down the other side of the globe and rap on frosted windows on the Russian steppes, if he wanted. But he wouldn't. Leo was forty-eight years old and he had learned. He pursued discomfort and sorrow, all right, but if you had a heartful by the time you reached New London, what new awfulness could you look forward to in Vladivostok?

The next day the wind was blowing the fall in and the branches of the weeping willow were fingering at the Patimkin front lawn. I drove Brenda to the train at noon, and she left me.

8

Autumn came quickly. It was cold and in Jersey the leaves turned and fell overnight. The following Saturday I took a ride up to see the deer, and did not even get out of the car, for it was too brisk to be standing at the wire fence, and so I watched the animals walk and run in the dimness of the late afternoon, and after a while everything, even the objects of nature, the trees, the clouds, the grass, the weeds, reminded me of Brenda, and I drove back down to Newark. Already we had sent our first letters and I had called her late one night, but in the mail and on the phone we had some difficulty discovering one another; we had not the style yet. That night I tried her again, and someone on her floor said she was out and would not be in till late.

Upon my return to the library I was questioned by Mr. Scapello about the Gauguin book. The jowly gentleman *had* sent a nasty letter about my discourtesy, and I was only able to extricate myself by offering a confused story in an indignant tone. In fact, I even managed to turn it around so that Mr. Scapello was apologizing to me as he led me up to my new post, there among the encyclopedias, the bibliographies, the indexes and guides. My bullying surprised me, and I wondered if some of it had not been learned from Mr. Patimkin that morning I'd heard him giving Grossman an earful on the phone. Perhaps I was more of a businessman than I thought. Maybe I could learn to become a Patimkin with ease . . .

Days passed slowly; I never did see the colored kid again, and when, one noon, I looked in the stacks, Gauguin was gone, apparently charged out finally by the jowly man. I wondered what it had been like that day the colored kid had discovered the book was gone. Had he cried? For some reason I imagined that he had blamed it on me, but then I realized that I was confusing the dream I'd had with reality. Chances were he had discovered someone else, Van Gogh, Vermeer . . . But no, they were not his kind of artists. What had probably happened was that he'd given up on the library and gone back to playing Willie Mays in the streets. He was better off, I thought. No sense carrying dreams of Tahiti in your head, if you can't afford the fare.

Let's see, what else did I do? I ate, I slept, I went to the movies, I sent broken-spined books to the bindery—I did everything I'd ever done before, but now each activity was surrounded by a fence, existed alone, and my life consisted of jumping from one fence to the next. There was no flow, for that had been Brenda.

And then Brenda wrote saying that she could be coming in for the Jewish holidays which were only a week away. I was so overjoyed I wanted to call Mr. and Mrs. Patimkin, just to tell them of my pleasure. However, when I got to the phone and had actually dialed the first two letters, I knew that at the other end there would be silence; if there was anything said, it would only be Mrs. Patimkin asking, "What is it you want?" Mr. Patimkin had probably forgotten my name.

That night, after dinner, I gave Aunt Gladys a kiss and told her she shouldn't work so hard.

"In less than a week it's Rosh Hashana and he thinks I should take a vacation. Ten people I'm having. What do you think, a chicken cleans itself? Thank God, the holidays come once a year, I'd be an old woman before my time."

But then it was only nine people Aunt Gladys was having, for only two days after her letter Brenda called.

"Oy, Gut!" Aunt Gladys called. "Long *distance*!"

"Hello?" I said.

"Hello, sweetie?"

"Yes," I said.

"What *is* it?" Aunt Gladys tugged at my shirt. "What is it?"

"It's for me."

"Who?" Aunt Gladys said, pointing into the receiver.

"Brenda," I said.

"Yes?" Brenda said.

"Brenda?" Aunt Gladys said. "What does she call long distance, I almost had a heart attack."

"Because she's in Boston," I said. "Please, Aunt Gladys . . ."

And Aunt Gladys walked off, mumbling, "These kids . . ."

"Hello," I said again into the phone.

"Neil, how are you?"

"I love you."

"Neil, I have bad news. I can't come in this week."

"But, honey, it's the Jewish holidays."

"Sweet*heart*," she laughed.

"Can't you say that, for an excuse?"

"I have a test Saturday, and a paper, and you know if I went home I wouldn't get anything done . . ."

"You would."

"Neil, I just *can't*. My mother'd make me go to Temple, and I wouldn't even have enough time to see *you*."

"Oh God, Brenda."

"Sweetie?"

"Yes?"

"Can't you come up here?" she asked.

"I'm working."

"The Jewish holidays," she said.

"Honey, I can't. Last year I didn't take them off, I can't all—"

"You can say you had a conversion."

"Besides, my aunt's having all the family for dinner, and you know what with my parents—"

"Come up, Neil."

"I can't just take two days off, Bren. I just got promoted and a raise—"

"The hell with the raise."

"Baby, it's my job."

"Forever?" she said.

"No."

"Then come. I've got a hotel room."

"For me?"

"For us."

"Can you do that?"

"No and yes. People do it."

"Brenda, you tempt me."

"Be tempted."

"I could take a train Wednesday right from work."

"You could stay till Sunday night."

"Bren, I can't. I still have to be back to work on Saturday."

"Don't you ever get a day *off*?" she said.

"Tuesdays," I said glumly.

"God."

"And Sunday," I added.

Brenda said something but I did not hear her, for Aunt Gladys called, "You talk all day long distance?"

"Quiet!" I shouted back to her.

"Neil, will you?"

"Damn it, yes," I said.

"Are you angry?"

"I don't think so. I'm going to come up."

"Till Sunday."

"We'll see."

"Don't feel upset, Neil. You sound upset. It is the Jewish holidays. I mean you *should* be off."

"That's right," I said. "I'm an orthodox Jew, for God's sake, I ought to take advantage of it."

"That's right," she said.

"Is there a train around six?"

"Every hour, I think."

"Then I'll be on the one that leaves at six."

"I'll be at the station," she said. "How will I know you?"

"I'll be disguised as an orthodox Jew."

"Me too," she said.

"Good night, love," I said.

Aunt Gladys cried when I told her I was going away for Rosh Hashana.

"And I was preparing a big meal," she said.

"You can still prepare it."

"What will I tell your mother?"

"I'll tell her, Aunt Gladys. Please. You have no right to get upset . . ."

"Someday you'll have a family you'll know what it's like."

"I have a family now."

"What's a matter," she said, blowing her nose, "That girl couldn't come home to see her family it's the holidays?"

"She's in school, she just can't—"

"If she loved her family she'd find time. We don't live six hundred years."

"She does love her family."

"Then one day a year you could break your heart and pay a visit."

"Aunt Gladys, you don't understand."

"Sure," she said, "when I'm twenty-three years old I'll understand everything."

I went to kiss her and she said, "Go away from me, go run to Boston . . ."

The next morning I discovered that Mr. Scapello didn't want me to leave on Rosh Hashana either, but I unnerved him, I think, by hinting that his coldness about my taking the two days off might just be so much veiled anti-Semitism, so on the whole he was easier to manage. At lunch time I took a walk down to Penn Station and picked up a train schedule to Boston. That was my bedtime reading for the next three nights.

She did not look like Brenda, at least for the first minute. And probably to her I did not look like me. But we kissed and held each other, and it was strange to feel the thickness of our coats between us.

"I'm letting my hair grow," she said in the cab, and that in fact was all she said. Not until I helped her out of the cab did I notice the thin gold band shining on her left hand.

She hung back, strolling casually about the lobby while I signed the register "Mr. and Mrs. Neil Klugman," and then in the room we kissed again.

"Your heart's pounding," I said to her.

"I know," she said.

"Are you nervous?"

"No."

"Have you done this before?" I said.

"I read Mary McCarthy."

She took off her coat and instead of putting it in the closet, she tossed it across the chair. I sat down on the bed; she didn't.

"What's the matter?"

Brenda took a deep breath and walked over to the window, and I thought that perhaps it would be best for me to ask nothing—for us to get used to each other's presence in quiet. I hung her coat and mine in the empty closet, and left the suitcases—mine and hers—standing by the bed.

Brenda was kneeling backwards in the chair, looking out the window as though out the window was where she'd rather be. I came up behind her and put my hands around her body and held her breasts, and when I felt the cool draft that swept under the sill, I realized how long it had been since the first warm night when I had put my arms around her and felt the tiny wings beating in her back. And then I realized why I'd really come to Boston—it had been long enough. It was time to stop kidding about marriage.

"Is something the matter?" I said.

"Yes."

It wasn't the answer I'd expected; I wanted no answer really, only to soothe her nervousness with my concern.

But I asked, "What is it? Why didn't you mention it on the phone?"

"It only happened today."

"School?"

"Home. They found out about us."

I turned her face up to mine. "That's okay. I told my aunt I was coming here too. What's the difference?"

"About the summer. About our sleeping together."

"Oh?"

"Yes."

". . . Ron?"

"No."

"That night, you mean, did Julie—"

"No," she said, "it wasn't *anybody*."

"I don't get it."

Brenda got up and walked over to the bed where she sat down on the edge. I sat in the chair.

"My mother found the thing."

"The diaphragm?"

She nodded.

"When?" I asked.

"The other day, I guess." She walked to the bureau and opened her purse. "Here, you can read them in the order I got them." She tossed an envelope at me; it was dirty-edged and crumpled, as though it had been in and out of her pockets a good many times. "I got this one this morning," she said. "Special delivery."

I took out the letter and read:

PATIMKIN KITCHEN AND BATHROOM SINKS
"Any Size—Any Shape"

Dear Brenda—

Don't pay any Attention to your Mother's Letter when you get it. I love you honey if you want a coat I'll buy You a coat. You could always have anything you wanted. We have every faith in you so you won't be too upset by what your mother says in her Letter. Of course she is a little hystericall because of the shock and she has been Working so hard for Hadassah. She is a Woman and it is hard for her to understand some of the Shocks in life. Of course I can't say We weren't all surprised because from the beginning I was nice to him and Thought he would appreciate the nice vacation we supplied for him. Some People never turn out the way you hope and pray but I am willing to forgive and call Buy Gones, Buy Gones, You have always up till now been a good Buck and got good scholastic Grades and Ron has always been what we wanted a Good Boy, most important, and a Nice boy. This late in my life believe me I am not going to start hating my own flesh and blood. As for your mistake it takes Two to make a mistake and now that you will be away at school and from him and what you got involved in you will probably do all right I have every faith you will. You have to have faith in your children like in a Business or any serious undertaking and there is nothing that is so bad that we can't forgive especially when Our own flesh and blood is involved. We have a nice close nitt family and why not????

Have a nice Holiday and in Temple I will say a Prayer for you as I do every year. On Monday I want you to go into Boston and buy a coat. Whatever you need because I know how Cold it gets up where you are . . . Give my regards to Linda and remember to bring her home with you on Thanksgiving like last year. You two had such a nice time. I have always never said bad things about any of your friends or Rons and that this should happen is only the exception that proves the rule. Have a Happy Holiday.

YOUR FATHER

And then it was signed BEN PATIMKIN, but that was crossed out and written beneath "Your Father" were again, like an echo, the words, "Your Father."

"Who's Linda?" I asked.

"My roommate, last year." She tossed another envelope to me. "Here. I got this one in the afternoon. Air Mail."

The letter was from Brenda's mother. I started to read it and then put it down a moment. "You got this *after*?"

"Yes," she said. "When I got his I didn't know what was happening. Read hers."

I began again.

Dear Brenda:

I don't even know how to begin. I have been crying all morning and have had to skip my board meeting this afternoon because my eyes are so red. I never thought this would happen to a daughter of mine. I wonder if you know what I mean, if it is at least on your conscience, so I won't have to degrade either of us with a description. All I can say is that this morning when I was cleaning out the drawers and putting away your summer clothing I came upon something in your bottom drawer, *under* some sweaters which you probably remember leaving there. I cried the minute I saw it and I haven't stopped crying yet. Your father called a while ago and now he is driving home because he heard how upset I was on the phone.

I don't know what we ever did that you should reward us this way. We gave you a nice home and all the love and respect a child needs. I always was proud when you were a little girl that you could take care of yourself so well. You took care of Julie so beautifully it was a treat to see, when you were only fourteen years old. But you drifted away from your family, even though we sent you to the best schools and gave you the best money could buy. Why you should reward us this way is a question I'll carry with me to the grave.

About your friend I have no words. He is his parents' responsibility and I cannot imagine what kind of home life he had that he could act that way. Certainly that was a fine way to repay us for the hospitality we were nice enough to show to him, a perfect stranger. That the two of you should be carrying on like that in our very house I will never in my life be able to understand. Times certainly have changed since I was a girl that this kind of thing could go on. I keep asking myself if at least you didn't think of us while you were doing that. If not for me, how could you do this to your father? God forbid Julie should ever learn of this.

God only knows what you have been doing all these years we put our trust in you.

You have broken your parents' hearts and you should know that. This is some thank you for all we gave you.

MOTHER

She only signed "Mother" once, and that was in an extraordinarily miniscule hand, like a whisper.

"Brenda," I said.

"What?"

"Are you starting to cry?"

"No. I cried already."

"Don't start again."

"I'm trying not to, for God's sake."

"Okay . . . Brenda, can I ask you one question?"

"What?"

"Why did you leave it home?"

"Because I didn't plan on using it here, that's why."

"Suppose I'd come up. I mean I have come up, what about that?"

"I thought I'd come down first."

"So then couldn't you have carried it down then? Like a toothbrush?"

"Are you trying to be funny?"

"No. I'm just asking you why you left it home."

"I told you," Brenda said. "I thought I'd come home."

"But, Brenda, that doesn't make any sense. Suppose you did come home, and then you came back again. Wouldn't you have taken it with you then?"

"I don't *know*."

"Don't get angry," I said.

"You're the one who's angry."

"I'm upset, I'm not angry."

"I'm upset then too."

I did not answer but walked to the window and looked out. The stars and moon were out, silver and hard, and from the window I could see over to the Harvard campus where lights burned and then seemed to flicker when the trees blew across them.

"Brenda . . ."

"What?"

"Knowing how your mother feels about you, wasn't it silly to leave it home? Risky?"

"What does how she feels about me have to do with it?"

"You can't trust her."

"Why can't I?"

"Don't you see. You *can't*."

"Neil, she was only cleaning out the drawers."

"Didn't you know she would?"

"She never did before. Or maybe she did. Neil, I couldn't think of everything. We slept together night after night and nobody heard or noticed—"

"Brenda, why the hell are you willfully confusing things?"

"I'm not!"

"Okay," I said softly. "All right."

"It's you who's confusing things," Brenda said. "You act as though I wanted her to find it."

I didn't answer.

"Do you believe *that*?" she said, after neither of us had spoken for a full minute.

"I don't know."

"Oh, Neil, you're *crazy*."

"What was crazier than leaving that damn thing around?"

"It was an oversight."

"Now it's an oversight, before it was deliberate."

"It was an oversight about the drawer. It wasn't an oversight about leaving it," she said.

"Brenda, sweetheart, wouldn't the safest, smartest, easiest, simplest thing been to have taken it with you? Wouldn't it?"

"It didn't make any difference either way."

"Brenda, this is the most frustrating argument of my life!"

"You keep making it seem as though I *wanted* her to find it. Do you think I need this? Do you? I can't even go home any more."

"Is that so?"

"Yes!"

"No," I said. "You can go home—your father will be waiting with two coats and a half-dozen dresses."

"What about my mother?"

"It'll be the same with her."

"Don't be absurd. How can I face them!"

"Why can't you face them? Did you do anything wrong?"

"Neil, look at the reality of the thing, will you?"

"*Did* you do anything wrong?"

"Neil, *they* think it's wrong. They're my parents."

"But do you think it's wrong—"

"That doesn't *matter*."

"It does to me, Brenda . . ."

"Neil, why are *you* confusing things? You keep accusing me of things."

"Damn it, Brenda, you're guilty of some things."

"*What?*"

"Of leaving that damn diaphragm there. How can you call it an oversight!"

"Oh, Neil, don't start any of that psychoanalytic crap!"

"Then why else did you do it? You wanted her to find it!"

"Why?"

"I don't know, Brenda, *why?*"

"Oh!" she said, and she picked up the pillow and threw it back on to the bed.

"What happens now, Bren?" I said.

"What does that mean?"

"Just that. What happens now?"

She rolled over on to the bed and buried her head in it.

"Don't start crying," I said.

"I'm *not.*"

I was still holding the letters and took Mr. Patimkin's from its envelope.

"Why does your father capitalize all these letters?"

She didn't answer.

"'As for your mistake,'" I read aloud to Brenda, "'it takes Two to make a mistake and now that you will be away at school and from him and what you got involved in you will probably do all right I have every faith you will. Your father. Your father.'"

She turned and looked at me; but silently.

"'I have always never said bad things about any of your friends or Rons and that this should happen is only the exception that proves the rule. Have a Happy Holiday.'" I stopped; in Brenda's face there was positively no threat of tears; she looked, suddenly, solid and decisive. "Well, what are you going to do?" I asked.

"Nothing."

"Who are you going to bring home Thanksgiving—Linda?" I said, "or me?"

"Who *can* I bring home, Neil?"

"I don't know, who can you?"

"Can I bring you home?"

"I don't know," I said, "can you?"

"Stop repeating the question!"

"I sure as hell can't give you the answer."

"Neil, be realistic. After this, can I bring you home? Can you see us all sitting around the table?"

"I can't if you can't, and I can if you can."

"Are you going to speak Zen, for God's sake!"

"Brenda, the choices aren't mine. You can bring Linda or me. You can go home or not go home. That's another choice. Then you don't even have to worry about choosing between me and Linda."

"Neil, you don't understand. They're still my parents. They

did send me to the best schools, didn't they? They have given me everything I've wanted, haven't they?"

"Yes."

"Then how can I not go home? I *have* to go home."

"Why?"

"You don't understand. Your parents don't bother you any more. You're lucky."

"Oh, sure. I live with my crazy aunt, that's a real bargain."

"Families are different. You don't understand."

"Goddamit, I understand more than you think. I understand why the hell you left that thing lying around. Don't you? Can't you put two and two together?"

"Neil, what are you talking about! You're the one who doesn't understand. You're the one who from the very beginning was accusing me of things! Remember? Isn't it so? Why don't you have your eyes fixed? Why don't you have this fixed, that fixed? As if it were my fault that I *could* have them fixed. You kept acting as if I was going to run away from you every minute. And now you're doing it again, telling me I planted that thing on purpose."

"I loved you, Brenda, so I cared."

"I loved *you*. That's why I got that damn thing in the first place."

And then we heard the tense in which we'd spoken and we settled back into ourselves and silence.

A few minutes later I picked up my bag and put on my coat. I think Brenda was crying too when I went out the door.

Instead of grabbing a cab immediately, I walked down the street and out towards Harvard Yard which I had never seen before. I entered one of the gates and then headed out along a path, under the tired autumn foliage and the dark sky. I wanted to be alone, in the dark; not because I wanted to think about anything, but rather because, for just a while, I wanted to think about nothing. I walked clear across the Yard and up a little hill and then I was standing in front of the Lamont Library, which, Brenda had once told me, had Patimkin Sinks in its rest rooms. From the light of the lamp on the path behind me I could see my reflection in the glass front of the building. Inside, it was dark and there were no students to be seen, no librarians. Suddenly, I wanted to set down my suitcase and pick up a rock and heave it right through the glass, but of course I didn't. I simply looked at myself in the mirror the light made of the window. I was only that substance, I thought, those limbs, that face that I saw in front of me. I looked, but the outside of me gave up little information about the inside of me. I wished I could scoot around to the other side of the window, faster than light or sound or Herb Clark on Homecoming Day, to get behind that image and catch whatever it was that looked through those eyes. What was it inside me that had turned pursuit and clutching into love, and then turned it inside out again? What was it that had turned winning into losing, and losing—who knows—into winning? I was sure I had loved Brenda, though standing there, I knew I couldn't any longer. And I knew it would be a long while before I made love to anyone the way I had made love to her. With anyone else, could I summon up such a passion? Whatever spawned my love for her, had that spawned such lust too? If she had only been slightly *not* Brenda . . . but then would I have loved her? I looked hard at the image of me, at that darkening of the glass, and then my gaze pushed through it, over the cool floor, to a broken wall of books, imperfectly shelved.

I did not look very much longer, but took a train that got me into Newark just as the sun was rising on the first day of the Jewish New Year. I was back in plenty of time for work.

The Conversion of the Jews

"Y OU'RE a real one for opening your mouth in the first
place," Itzie said. "What do you open your mouth all the
time for?"

"I didn't bring it up, Itz, I didn't," Ozzie said.

"What do you care about Jesus Christ for anyway?"

"I didn't bring up Jesus Christ. He did. I didn't even know
what he was talking about. Jesus is historical, he kept saying.
Jesus is historical." Ozzie mimicked the monumental voice of
Rabbi Binder.

"Jesus was a person that lived like you and me," Ozzie continued. "That's what Binder said—"

"Yeah? . . . So what! What do I give two cents whether he
lived or not. And what do you gotta open your mouth!" Itzie
Lieberman favored closed-mouthedness, especially when it
came to Ozzie Freedman's questions. Mrs. Freedman had to
see Rabbi Binder twice before about Ozzie's questions and
this Wednesday at four-thirty would be the third time. Itzie
preferred to keep *his* mother in the kitchen; he settled for
behind-the-back subtleties such as gestures, faces, snarls and
other less delicate barnyard noises.

"He was a real person, Jesus, but he wasn't like God, and we
don't believe he is God." Slowly, Ozzie was explaining Rabbi
Binder's position to Itzie, who had been absent from Hebrew
School the previous afternoon.

"The Catholics," Itzie said helpfully, "they believe in Jesus
Christ, that he's God." Itzie Lieberman used "the Catholics"
in its broadest sense—to include the Protestants.

Ozzie received Itzie's remark with a tiny head bob, as
though it were a footnote, and went on. "His mother was
Mary, and his father probably was Joseph," Ozzie said. "But
the New Testament says his real father was God."

"His *real* father?"

"Yeah," Ozzie said, "that's the big thing, his father's supposed to be God."

109

"Bull."

"That's what Rabbi Binder says, that it's impossible—"

"Sure it's impossible. That stuff's all bull. To have a baby you gotta get laid," Itzie theologized. "Mary hadda get laid."

"That's what Binder says: 'The only way a woman can have a baby is to have intercourse with a man.'"

"He said *that*, Ozz?" For a moment it appeared that Itzie had put the theological question aside. "He said that, intercourse?" A little curled smile shaped itself in the lower half of Itzie's face like a pink mustache. "What you guys do, Ozz, you laugh or something?"

"I raised my hand."

"Yeah? Whatja say?"

"That's when I asked the question."

Itzie's face lit up. "Whatja ask about—intercourse?"

"No, I asked the question about God, how if He could create the heaven and earth in six days, and make all the animals and the fish and the light in six days—the light especially, that's what always gets me, that He could make the light. Making fish and animals, that's pretty good—"

"That's damn good." Itzie's appreciation was honest but unimaginative: it was as though God had just pitched a one-hitter.

"But making light . . . I mean when you think about it, it's really something," Ozzie said. "Anyway, I asked Binder if He could make all that in six days, and He could *pick* the six days he wanted right out of nowhere, why couldn't He let a woman have a baby without having intercourse."

"You said intercourse, Ozz, to Binder?"

"Yeah."

"Right in class?"

"Yeah."

Itzie smacked the side of his head.

"I mean, no kidding around," Ozzie said, "that'd really be nothing. After all that other stuff, that'd practically be nothing."

Itzie considered a moment. "What'd Binder say?"

"He started all over again explaining how Jesus was historical and how he lived like you and me but he wasn't God. So I said I under*stood* that. What I wanted to know was different."

What Ozzie wanted to know was always different. The first

time he had wanted to know how Rabbi Binder could call the Jews "The Chosen People" if the Declaration of Independence claimed all men to be created equal. Rabbi Binder tried to distinguish for him between political equality and spiritual legitimacy, but what Ozzie wanted to know, he insisted vehemently, was different. That was the first time his mother had to come.

Then there was the plane crash. Fifty-eight people had been killed in a plane crash at La Guardia. In studying a casualty list in the newspaper his mother had discovered among the list of those dead eight Jewish names (his grandmother had nine but she counted Miller as a Jewish name); because of the eight she said the plane crash was "a tragedy." During free-discussion time on Wednesday Ozzie had brought to Rabbi Binder's attention this matter of "some of his relations" always picking out the Jewish names. Rabbi Binder had begun to explain cultural unity and some other things when Ozzie stood up at his seat and said that what he wanted to know was different. Rabbi Binder insisted that he sit down and it was then that Ozzie shouted that he wished all fifty-eight were Jews. That was the second time his mother came.

"And he kept explaining about Jesus being historical, and so I kept asking him. No kidding, Itz, he was trying to make me look stupid."

"So what he finally do?"

"Finally he starts screaming that I was deliberately simple-minded and a wise guy, and that my mother had to come, and this was the last time. And that I'd never get bar-mitzvahed if he could help it. Then, Itz, then he starts talking in that voice like a statue, real slow and deep, and he says that I better think over what I said about the Lord. He told me to go to his office and think it over." Ozzie leaned his body towards Itzie. "Itz, I thought it over for a solid hour, and now I'm convinced God could do it."

Ozzie had planned to confess his latest transgression to his mother as soon as she came home from work. But it was Friday night in November and already dark, and when Mrs. Freedman came through the door she tossed off her coat, kissed Ozzie quickly on the face, and went to the kitchen table to light the three yellow candles, two for the Sabbath and one for Ozzie's father.

When his mother lit the candles she would move her two arms slowly towards her, dragging them through the air, as though persuading people whose minds were half made up. And her eyes would get glassy with tears. Even when his father was alive Ozzie remembered that her eyes had gotten glassy, so it didn't have anything to do with his dying. It had something to do with lighting the candles.

As she touched the flaming match to the unlit wick of a Sabbath candle, the phone rang, and Ozzie, standing only a foot from it, plucked it off the receiver and held it muffled to his chest. When his mother lit candles Ozzie felt there should be no noise; even breathing, if you could manage it, should be softened. Ozzie pressed the phone to his breast and watched his mother dragging whatever she was dragging, and he felt his own eyes get glassy. His mother was a round, tired, gray-haired penguin of a woman whose gray skin had begun to feel the tug of gravity and the weight of her own history. Even when she was dressed up she didn't look like a chosen person. But when she lit candles she looked like something better; like a woman who knew momentarily that God could do anything.

After a few mysterious minutes she was finished. Ozzie hung up the phone and walked to the kitchen table where she was beginning to lay the two places for the four-course Sabbath meal. He told her that she would have to see Rabbi Binder next Wednesday at four-thirty, and then he told her why. For the first time in their life together she hit Ozzie across the face with her hand.

All through the chopped liver and chicken soup part of the dinner Ozzie cried; he didn't have any appetite for the rest.

On Wednesday, in the largest of the three basement class-rooms of the synagogue, Rabbi Marvin Binder, a tall, hand-some, broad-shouldered man of thirty with thick strong-fibered black hair, removed his watch from his pocket and saw that it was four o'clock. At the rear of the room Yakov Blotnik, the seventy-one-year-old custodian, slowly polished the large window, mumbling to himself, unaware that it was four o'clock or six o'clock, Monday or Wednesday. To most of the students

Yakov Blotnik's mumbling, along with his brown curly beard, scythe nose, and two heel-trailing black cats, made of him an object of wonder, a foreigner, a relic, towards whom they were alternately fearful and disrespectful. To Ozzie the mumbling had always seemed a monotonous, curious prayer; what made it curious was that old Blotnik had been mumbling so steadily for so many years, Ozzie suspected he had memorized the prayers and forgotten all about God.

"It is now free-discussion time," Rabbi Binder said. "Feel free to talk about any Jewish matter at all—religion, family, politics, sports—"

There was silence. It was a gusty, clouded November afternoon and it did not seem as though there ever was or could be a thing called baseball. So nobody this week said a word about that hero from the past, Hank Greenberg—which limited free discussion considerably.

And the soul-battering Ozzie Freedman had just received from Rabbi Binder had imposed its limitation. When it was Ozzie's turn to read aloud from the Hebrew book the rabbi had asked him petulantly why he didn't read more rapidly. He was showing no progress. Ozzie said he could read faster but that if he did he was sure not to understand what he was reading. Nevertheless, at the rabbi's repeated suggestion Ozzie tried, and showed a great talent, but in the midst of a long passage he stopped short and said he didn't understand a word he was reading, and started in again at a drag-footed pace. Then came the soul-battering.

Consequently when free-discussion time rolled around none of the students felt too free. The rabbi's invitation was answered only by the mumbling of feeble old Blotnik.

"Isn't there anything at all you would like to discuss?" Rabbi Binder asked again, looking at his watch. "No questions or comments?"

There was a small grumble from the third row. The rabbi requested that Ozzie rise and give the rest of the class the advantage of his thought.

Ozzie rose. "I forget it now," he said, and sat down in his place.

Rabbi Binder advanced a seat towards Ozzie and poised himself on the edge of the desk. It was Itzie's desk and the rabbi's frame only a dagger's-length away from his face snapped him to sitting attention.

"Stand up again, Oscar," Rabbi Binder said calmly, "and try to assemble your thoughts."

Ozzie stood up. All his classmates turned in their seats and watched as he gave an unconvincing scratch to his forehead.

"I can't assemble any," he announced, and plunked himself down.

"Stand up!" Rabbi Binder advanced from Itzie's desk to the one directly in front of Ozzie; when the rabbinical back was turned Itzie gave it five-fingers off the tip of his nose, causing a small titter in the room. Rabbi Binder was too absorbed in squelching Ozzie's nonsense once and for all to bother with titters. "Stand up, Oscar. What's your question about?"

Ozzie pulled a word out of the air. It was the handiest word. "Religion."

"Oh, now you remember?"

"Yes."

"What is it?"

Trapped, Ozzie blurted the first thing that came to him. "Why can't He make anything He wants to make!"

As Rabbi Binder prepared an answer, a final answer, Itzie, ten feet behind him, raised one finger on his left hand, gestured it meaningfully towards the rabbi's back, and brought the house down.

Binder twisted quickly to see what had happened and in the midst of the commotion Ozzie shouted into the rabbi's back what he couldn't have shouted to his face. It was a loud, toneless sound that had the timbre of something stored inside for about six days.

"You don't know! You don't know anything about God!"

The rabbi spun back towards Ozzie. "What?"

"You don't know—you don't—"

"Apologize, Oscar, apologize!" It was a threat.

"You don't—"

Rabbi Binder's hand flicked out at Ozzie's cheek. Perhaps it had only been meant to clamp the boy's mouth shut, but Ozzie ducked and the palm caught him squarely on the nose.

The blood came in a short, red spurt on to Ozzie's shirt front.

The next moment was all confusion. Ozzie screamed, "You bastard, you bastard!" and broke for the classroom door. Rabbi Binder lurched a step backwards, as though his own blood had started flowing violently in the opposite direction, then gave a clumsy lurch forward and bolted out the door after Ozzie. The class followed after the rabbi's huge blue-suited back, and before old Blotnik could turn from his window, the room was empty and everyone was headed full speed up the three flights leading to the roof.

If one should compare the light of day to the life of man: sunrise to birth; sunset—the dropping down over the edge— to death; then as Ozzie Freedman wiggled through the trapdoor of the synagogue roof, his feet kicking backwards bronco-style at Rabbi Binder's outstretched arms—at that moment the day was fifty years old. As a rule, fifty or fifty-five reflects accurately the age of late afternoons in November, for it is in that month, during those hours, that one's awareness of light seems no longer a matter of seeing, but of hearing: light begins clicking away. In fact, as Ozzie locked shut the trapdoor in the rabbi's face, the sharp click of the bolt into the lock might momentarily have been mistaken for the sound of the heavier gray that had just throbbed through the sky.

With all his weight Ozzie kneeled on the locked door; any instant he was certain that Rabbi Binder's shoulder would fling it open, splintering the wood into shrapnel and catapulting his body into the sky. But the door did not move and below him he heard only the rumble of feet, first loud then dim, like thunder rolling away.

A question shot through his brain. "Can this be *me*?" For a thirteen-year-old who had just labeled his religious leader a bastard, twice, it was not an improper question. Louder and louder the question came to him—"Is it me? Is it me?"—until he discovered himself no longer kneeling, but racing crazily towards the edge of the roof, his eyes crying, his throat screaming, and his arms flying everywhichway as though not his own.

"Is it me? Is it me Me ME ME ME! It has to be me—but is it!"

It is the question a thief must ask himself the night he

jimmies open his first window, and it is said to be the question with which bridegrooms quiz themselves before the altar.

In the few wild seconds it took Ozzie's body to propel him to the edge of the roof, his self-examination began to grow fuzzy. Gazing down at the street, he became confused as to the problem beneath the question: was it, is-it-me-who-called-Binder-a-bastard? or, is-it-me-prancing-around-on-the-roof? However, the scene below settled all, for there is an instant in any action when whether it is you or somebody else is academic. The thief crams the money in his pockets and scoots out the window. The bridegroom signs the hotel register for two. And the boy on the roof finds a streetful of people gaping at him, necks stretched backwards, faces up, as though he were the ceiling of the Hayden Planetarium. Suddenly you know it's you.

"Oscar! Oscar Freedman!" A voice rose from the center of the crowd, a voice that, could it have been seen, would have looked like the writing on scroll. "Oscar Freedman, get down from there. Immediately!" Rabbi Binder was pointing one arm stiffly up at him; and at the end of that arm, one finger aimed menacingly. It was the attitude of a dictator, but one—the eyes confessed all—whose personal valet had spit neatly in his face.

Ozzie didn't answer. Only for a blink's length did he look towards Rabbi Binder. Instead his eyes began to fit together the world beneath him, to sort out people from places, friends from enemies, participants from spectators. In little jagged starlike clusters his friends stood around Rabbi Binder, who was still pointing. The topmost point on a star compounded not of angels but of five adolescent boys was Itzie. What a world it was, with those stars below, Rabbi Binder below . . . Ozzie, who a moment earlier hadn't been able to control his own body, started to feel the meaning of the word control: he felt Peace and he felt Power.

"Oscar Freedman, I'll give you three to come down."

Few dictators give their subjects three to do anything; but, as always, Rabbi Binder only looked dictatorial.

"Are you ready, Oscar?"

Ozzie nodded his head yes, although he had no intention in the world—the lower one or the celestial one he'd just entered—of coming down even if Rabbi Binder should give him a million.

"All right then," said Rabbi Binder. He ran a hand through his black Samson hair as though it were the gesture prescribed for uttering the first digit. Then, with his other hand cutting a circle out of the small piece of sky around him, he spoke. "One!"

There was no thunder. On the contrary, at that moment, as though "one" was the cue for which he had been waiting, the world's least thunderous person appeared on the synagogue steps. He did not so much come out the synagogue door as lean out, onto the darkening air. He clutched at the doorknob with one hand and looked up at the roof.

"Oy!"

Yakov Blotnik's old mind hobbled slowly, as if on crutches, and though he couldn't decide precisely what the boy was doing on the roof, he knew it wasn't good—that is, it wasn't-good-for-the-Jews. For Yakov Blotnik life had fractionated itself simply: things were either good-for-the-Jews or no-good-for-the-Jews.

He smacked his free hand to his in-sucked cheek, gently. "Oy, Gut!" And then quickly as he was able, he jacked down his head and surveyed the street. There was Rabbi Binder (like a man at an auction with only three dollars in his pocket, he had just delivered a shaky "Two!"); there were the students, and that was all. So far it-wasn't-so-bad-for-the-Jews. But the boy had to come down immediately, before anybody saw. The problem: how to get the boy off the roof?

Anybody who has ever had a cat on the roof knows how to get him down. You call the fire department. Or first you call the operator and you ask her for the fire department. And the next thing there is great jamming of brakes and clanging of bells and shouting of instructions. And then the cat is off the roof. You do the same thing to get a boy off the roof.

That is, you do the same thing if you are Yakov Blotnik and you once had a cat on the roof.

When the engines, all four of them, arrived, Rabbi Binder had four times given Ozzie the count of three. The big hook-and-ladder swung around the corner and one of the firemen leaped from it, plunging headlong towards the yellow fire hydrant in front of the synagogue. With a huge wrench he began to unscrew the top nozzle. Rabbi Binder raced over to him and pulled at his shoulder.

"There's no fire . . ."

The fireman mumbled back over his shoulder and, heatedly, continued working at the nozzle.

"But there's no fire, there's no fire . . ." Binder shouted. When the fireman mumbled again, the rabbi grasped his face with both his hands and pointed it up at the roof.

To Ozzie it looked as though Rabbi Binder was trying to tug the fireman's head out of his body, like a cork from a bottle. He had to giggle at the picture they made: it was a family portrait—rabbi in black skullcap, fireman in red fire hat, and the little yellow hydrant squatting beside like a kid brother, bareheaded. From the edge of the roof Ozzie waved at the portrait, a one-handed, flapping, mocking wave; in doing it his right foot slipped from under him. Rabbi Binder covered his eyes with his hands.

Firemen work fast. Before Ozzie had even regained his balance, a big, round, yellowed net was being held on the synagogue lawn. The firemen who held it looked up at Ozzie with stern, feelingless faces.

One of the firemen turned his head towards Rabbi Binder. "What, is the kid nuts or something?"

Rabbi Binder unpeeled his hands from his eyes, slowly, painfully, as if they were tape. Then he checked: nothing on the sidewalk, no dents in the net.

"Is he gonna jump, or what?" the fireman shouted.

In a voice not at all like a statue, Rabbi Binder finally answered. "Yes. Yes, I think so . . . He's been threatening to . . ."

Threatening to? Why, the reason he was on the roof, Ozzie remembered, was to get away; he hadn't even thought about jumping. He had just run to get away, and the truth was that he hadn't really headed for the roof as much as he'd been chased there.

"What's his name, the kid?"

"Freedman," Rabbi Binder answered. "Oscar Freedman."

The fireman looked up at Ozzie. "What is it with you, Oscar? You gonna jump, or what?"

Ozzie did not answer. Frankly, the question had just arisen.

"Look, Oscar, if you're gonna jump, jump—and if you're not gonna jump, don't jump. But don't waste our time, willya?"

Ozzie looked at the fireman and then at Rabbi Binder. He wanted to see Rabbi Binder cover his eyes one more time.

"I'm going to jump."

And then he scampered around the edge of the roof to the corner, where there was no net below, and he flapped his arms at his sides, swishing the air and smacking his palms to his trousers on the downbeat. He began screaming like some kind of engine, "Wheeeee . . . wheeeeee," and leaning way out over the edge with the upper half of his body. The firemen whipped around to cover the ground with the net. Rabbi Binder mumbled a few words to Somebody and covered his eyes. Everything happened quickly, jerkily, as in a silent movie. The crowd, which had arrived with the fire engines, gave out a long, Fourth-of-July fireworks oooh-aahhh. In the excitement no one had paid the crowd much heed, except, of course, Yakov Blotnik, who swung from the doorknob counting heads. "Fier und tsvansik . . . finf und tsvantsik . . . Oy, Gut!" It wasn't like this with the cat.

Rabbi Binder peeked through his fingers, checked the sidewalk and net. Empty. But there was Ozzie racing to the other corner. The firemen raced with him but were unable to keep up. Whenever Ozzie wanted to he might jump and splatter himself upon the sidewalk, and by the time the firemen scooted to the spot all they could do with their net would be to cover the mess.

"Wheeeee . . . wheeeee . . ."

"Hey, Oscar," the winded fireman yelled, "What the hell is this, a game or something?"

"Wheeeee . . . wheeeee . . ."

"Hey, Oscar—"

But he was off now to the other corner, flapping his wings fiercely. Rabbi Binder couldn't take it any longer—the fire engines from nowhere, the screaming suicidal boy, the net. He fell to his knees, exhausted, and with his hands curled together in front of his chest like a little dome, he pleaded, "Oscar, stop it, Oscar. Don't jump, Oscar. Please come down . . . Please don't jump."

And further back in the crowd a single voice, a single young voice, shouted a lone word to the boy on the roof.

"Jump!"

It was Itzie. Ozzie momentarily stopped flapping.

"Go ahead, Ozz—jump!" Itzie broke off his point of the star and courageously, with the inspiration not of a wise-guy but of a disciple, stood alone. "Jump, Ozz, jump!"

Still on his knees, his hands still curled, Rabbi Binder twisted his body back. He looked at Itzie, then, agonizingly, back to Ozzie.

"OSCAR, DON'T JUMP! PLEASE, DON'T JUMP . . . please please . . ."

"Jump!" This time it wasn't Itzie but another point of the star. By the time Mrs. Freedman arrived to keep her four-thirty appointment with Rabbi Binder, the whole little upside down heaven was shouting and pleading for Ozzie to jump, and Rabbi Binder no longer was pleading with him not to jump, but was crying into the dome of his hands.

Understandably, Mrs. Freedman couldn't figure out what her son was doing on the roof. So she asked.

"Ozzie, my Ozzie, what are you doing? My Ozzie, what is it?"

Ozzie stopped wheeeeeing and slowed his arms down to a cruising flap, the kind birds use in soft winds, but he did not answer. He stood against the low, clouded, darkening sky—light clicked down swiftly now, as on a small gear—flapping softly and gazing down at the small bundle of a woman who was his mother.

"What are you doing, Ozzie?" She turned towards the kneeling Rabbi Binder and rushed so close that only a paper-thickness of dusk lay between her stomach and his shoulders.

"What is my baby doing?"

Rabbi Binder gaped up at her but he too was mute. All that moved was the dome of his hands; it shook back and forth like a weak pulse.

"Rabbi, get him down! He'll kill himself. Get him down, my only baby . . ."

"I can't," Rabbi Binder said, "I can't . . ." and he turned his handsome head towards the crowd of boys behind him. "It's them. Listen to them."

And for the first time Mrs. Freedman saw the crowd of boys, and she heard what they were yelling.

"He's doing it for them. He won't listen to me. It's them." Rabbi Binder spoke like one in a trance.

"For them?"

"Yes."

"Why for them?"

"They want him to . . ."

Mrs. Freedman raised her two arms upward as though she were conducting the sky. "For them he's doing it!" And then in a gesture older than pyramids, older than prophets and floods, her arms came slapping down to her sides. "A martyr I have. Look!" She tilted her head to the roof. Ozzie was still flapping softly. "My martyr."

"Oscar, come down, *please*," Rabbi Binder groaned.

In a startlingly even voice Mrs. Freedman called to the boy on the roof. "Ozzie, come down, Ozzie. Don't be a martyr, my baby."

As though it were a litany, Rabbi Binder repeated her words. "Don't be a martyr, my baby. Don't be a martyr."

"Gawhead, Ozz—*be* a Martin!" It was Itzie. "Be a Martin, be a Martin," and all the voices joined in singing for Martin-dom, whatever *it* was. "Be a Martin, be a Martin . . ."

Somehow when you're on a roof the darker it gets the less you can hear. All Ozzie knew was that two groups wanted two new things: his friends were spirited and musical about what they wanted; his mother and the rabbi were even-toned, chanting, about what they didn't want. The rabbi's voice was without tears now and so was his mother's.

The big net stared up at Ozzie like a sightless eye. The big, clouded sky pushed down. From beneath it looked like a gray corrugated board. Suddenly, looking up into that unsympathetic sky, Ozzie realized all the strangeness of what these people, his friends, were asking: they wanted him to jump, to kill himself; they were singing about it now—it made them that happy. And there was an even greater strangeness: Rabbi Binder was on his knees, trembling. If there was a question to be asked now it was not "Is it me?" but rather "Is it us? . . . Is it us?"

Being on the roof, it turned out, was a serious thing. If he jumped would the singing become dancing? Would it? What would jumping stop? Yearningly, Ozzie wished he could rip open the sky, plunge his hands through, and pull out the sun; and on the sun, like a coin, would be stamped JUMP or DON'T JUMP.

Ozzie's knees rocked and sagged a little under him as though they were setting him for a dive. His arms tightened, stiffened, froze, from shoulders to fingernails. He felt as if each part of his body were going to vote as to whether he should kill himself or not—and each part as though it were independent of *him*.

The light took an unexpected click down and the new darkness, like a gag, hushed the friends singing for this and the mother and rabbi chanting for that.

Ozzie stopped counting votes, and in a curiously high voice, like one who wasn't prepared for speech, he spoke.

"Mamma?"

"Yes, Oscar."

"Mamma, get down on your knees, like Rabbi Binder."

"Oscar—"

"Get down on your knees," he said, "or I'll jump."

Ozzie heard a whimper, then a quick rustling, and when he looked down where his mother had stood he saw the top of a head and beneath that a circle of dress. She was kneeling beside Rabbi Binder.

He spoke again. "Everybody kneel." There was the sound of everybody kneeling.

Ozzie looked around. With one hand he pointed towards the synagogue entrance. "Make *him* kneel."

There was a noise, not of kneeling, but of body-and-cloth stretching. Ozzie could hear Rabbi Binder saying in a gruff whisper, ". . . or he'll *kill* himself," and when next he looked there was Yakov Blotnik off the doorknob and for the first time in his life upon his knees in the Gentile posture of prayer.

As for the firemen—it is not as difficult as one might imagine to hold a net taut while you are kneeling.

Ozzie looked around again; and then he called to Rabbi Binder.

"Rabbi?"

"Yes, Oscar."

"Rabbi Binder, do you believe in God."

"Yes."

"Do you believe God can do Anything?" Ozzie leaned his head out into the darkness. "Anything?"

"Oscar, I think—"

"Tell me you believe God can do Anything."

There was a second's hesitation. Then: "God can do Anything."

"Tell me you believe God can make a child without intercourse."

"He can."

"Tell me!"

"God," Rabbi Binder admitted, "can make a child without intercourse."

"Mamma, you tell me."

"God can make a child without intercourse," his mother said.

"Make *him* tell me." There was no doubt who *him* was.

In a few moments Ozzie heard an old comical voice say something to the increasing darkness about God.

Next, Ozzie made everybody say it. And then he made them all say they believed in Jesus Christ—first one at a time, then all together.

When the catechizing was through it was the beginning of evening. From the street it sounded as if the boy on the roof might have sighed.

"Ozzie?" A woman's voiced dared to speak. "You'll come down now?"

There was no answer, but the woman waited, and when a voice finally did speak it was thin and crying, and exhausted as that of an old man who had just finished pulling the bells.

"Mamma, don't you see—you shouldn't hit me. He shouldn't hit me. You shouldn't hit me about God, Mamma. You should never hit anybody about God—"

"Ozzie, please come down now."

"Promise me, promise me you'll never hit anybody about God."

He had asked only his mother, but for some reason everyone kneeling in the street promised he would never hit anybody about God.

Once again there was silence.

"I can come down now, Mamma," the boy on the roof
finally said. He turned his head both ways as though checking
the traffic lights. "Now I can come down . . ."

And he did, right into the center of the yellow net that
glowed in the evening's edge like an overgrown halo.

Defender of the Faith

I N MAY of 1945, only a few weeks after the fighting had ended in Europe, I was rotated back to the States, where I spent the remainder of the war in a training company at Camp Crowder, Missouri. Along with the rest of the Ninth Army, I had been racing across Germany so swiftly during the late winter and spring that when I boarded the plane, I couldn't believe its destination lay to the west. My mind might inform me otherwise, but there was an inertia of the spirit that told me we were flying to a new front, where we would disembark and continue our push eastward—eastward until we'd circled the globe, marching through villages along whose twisting, cobbled streets crowds of the enemy would watch us take possession of what, up till then, they'd considered their own. I had changed enough in two years not to mind the trembling of the old people, the crying of the very young, the uncertainty and fear in the eyes of the once arrogant. I had been fortunate enough to develop an infantryman's heart, which, like his feet, at first aches and swells but finally grows horny enough for him to travel the weirdest paths without feeling a thing.

Captain Paul Barrett was my C.O. in Camp Crowder. The day I reported for duty, he came out of his office to shake my hand. He was short, gruff, and fiery, and—indoors or out—he wore his polished helmet liner pulled down to his little eyes. In Europe, he had received a battlefield commission and a serious chest wound, and he'd been returned to the States only a few months before. He spoke easily to me, and at the evening formation he introduced me to the troops. "Gentlemen," he said, "Sergeant Thurston, as you know, is no longer with this company. Your new first sergeant is Sergeant Nathan Marx, here. He is a veteran of the European theater, and consequently will expect to find a company of soldiers here, and not a company of *boys*."

I sat up late in the orderly room that evening, trying half-heartedly to solve the riddle of duty rosters, personnel forms, and morning reports. The Charge of Quarters slept with his mouth open on a mattress on the floor. A trainee stood reading the next day's duty roster, which was posted on the bulletin board just inside the screen door. It was a warm evening, and I could hear radios playing dance music over in the barracks. The trainee, who had been staring at me whenever he thought I wouldn't notice, finally took a step in my direction.

"Hey, Sarge—we having a G.I. party tomorrow night?" he asked. A G.I. party is a barracks cleaning.

"You usually have them on Friday nights?" I asked him.

"Yes," he said, and then he added, mysteriously, "that's the whole thing."

"Then you'll have a G.I. party."

He turned away, and I heard him mumbling. His shoulders were moving, and I wondered if he was crying.

"What's your name, soldier?" I asked.

He turned, not crying at all. Instead, his green-speckled eyes, long and narrow, flashed like fish in the sun. He walked over to me and sat on the edge of my desk. He reached out a hand. "Sheldon," he said.

"Stand on your feet, Sheldon."

Getting off the desk, he said, "Sheldon Grossbart." He smiled at the familiarity into which he'd led me.

"You against cleaning the barracks Friday night, Grossbart?" I said. "Maybe we shouldn't have G.I. parties. Maybe we should get a maid." My tone startled me. I felt I sounded like every top sergeant I had ever known.

"No, Sergeant." He grew serious, but with a seriousness that seemed to be only the stifling of a smile. "It's just—G.I. parties on Friday night, of all nights."

He slipped up onto the corner of the desk again—not quite sitting, but not quite standing, either. He looked at me with those speckled eyes flashing, and then made a gesture with his hand. It was very slight—no more than a movement back and forth of the wrist—and yet it managed to exclude from our affairs everything else in the orderly room, to make the two of us the center of the world. It seemed, in fact, to exclude everything even about the two of us except our hearts.

"Sergeant Thurston was one thing," he whispered, glancing

at the sleeping C.Q., "but we thought that with you here things might be a little different."

"We?"

"The Jewish personnel."

"Why?" I asked, harshly. "What's on your mind?" Whether I was still angry at the "Sheldon" business, or now at something else, I hadn't time to tell, but clearly I was angry.

"We thought you—Marx, you know, like Karl Marx. The Marx Brothers. Those guys are all— M-a-r-x. Isn't that how *you* spell it, Sergeant?"

"M-a-r-x."

"Fishbein said—" He stopped. "What I mean to say, Sergeant—" His face and neck were red, and his mouth moved but no words came out. In a moment, he raised himself to attention, gazing down at me. It was as though he had suddenly decided he could expect no more sympathy from me than from Thurston, the reason being that I was of Thurston's faith, and not his. The young man had managed to confuse himself as to what my faith really was, but I felt no desire to straighten him out. Very simply, I didn't like him.

When I did nothing but return his gaze, he spoke, in an altered tone. "You see, Sergeant," he explained to me, "Friday nights, Jews are supposed to go to services."

"Did Sergeant Thurston tell you you couldn't go to them when there was a G.I. party?"

"No."

"Did he say you had to stay and scrub the floors?"

"No, Sergeant."

"Did the Captain say you had to stay and scrub the floors?"

"That isn't it, Sergeant. It's the other guys in the barracks." He leaned toward me. "They think we're goofing off. But we're not. That's when Jews go to services, Friday night. We have to."

"Then go."

"But the other guys make accusations. They have no right."

"That's not the Army's problem, Grossbart. It's a personal problem you'll have to work out yourself."

"But it's un*fair*."

I got up to leave. "There's nothing I can do about it," I said.

Grossbart stiffened and stood in front of me. "But this is a matter of *religion*, sir."

"Sergeant," I said.

"I mean 'Sergeant,'" he said, almost snarling.

"Look, go see the chaplain. You want to see Captain Barrett, I'll arrange an appointment."

"No, no. I don't want to make trouble, Sergeant. That's the first thing they throw up to you. I just want my rights!"

"Damn it, Grossbart, stop whining. You have your rights. You can stay and scrub floors or you can go to shul—"

The smile swam in again. Spittle gleamed at the corners of his mouth. "You mean church, Sergeant."

"I mean shul, Grossbart!"

I walked past him and went outside. Near me, I heard the scrunching of a guard's boots on gravel. Beyond the lighted windows of the barracks, young men in T shirts and fatigue pants were sitting on their bunks, polishing their rifles. Suddenly there was a light rustling behind me. I turned and saw Grossbart's dark frame fleeing back to the barracks, racing to tell his Jewish friends that they were right—that, like Karl and Harpo, I was one of them.

The next morning, while chatting with Captain Barrett, I recounted the incident of the previous evening. Somehow, in the telling, it must have seemed to the Captain that I was not so much explaining Grossbart's position as defending it. "Marx, I'd fight side by side with a nigger if the fella proved to me he was a man. I pride myself," he said, looking out the window, "that I've got an open mind. Consequently, Sergeant, nobody gets special treatment here, for the good *or* the bad. All a man's got to do is prove himself. A man fires well on the range, I give him a weekend pass. He scores high in P.T., he gets a weekend pass. He *earns* it." He turned from the window and pointed a finger at me. "You're a Jewish fella, am I right, Marx?"

"Yes, sir."

"And I admire you. I admire you because of the ribbons on your chest. I judge a man by what he shows me on the field of battle, Sergeant. It's what he's got *here*," he said, and then, though I expected he would point to his chest, he jerked a thumb toward the buttons straining to hold his blouse across his belly. "Guts," he said.

"O.K., sir. I only wanted to pass on to you how the men felt."

"Mr. Marx, you're going to be old before your time if you worry about how the men feel. Leave that stuff to the chaplain—that's his business, not yours. Let's us train these fellas to shoot straight. If the Jewish personnel feels the other men are accusing them of goldbricking—well, I just don't know. Seems awful funny that suddenly the Lord is calling so loud in Private Grossman's ear he's just got to run to church."

"Synagogue," I said.

"Synagogue is right, Sergeant. I'll write that down for handy reference. Thank you for stopping by."

That evening, a few minutes before the company gathered outside the orderly room for the chow formation, I called the C.Q., Corporal Robert LaHill, in to see me. LaHill was a dark, burly fellow whose hair curled out of his clothes wherever it could. He had a glaze in his eyes that made one think of caves and dinosaurs. "LaHill," I said, "when you take the formation, remind the men that they're free to attend church services *whenever* they are held, provided they report to the orderly room before they leave the area."

LaHill scratched his wrist, but gave no indication that he'd heard or understood.

"LaHill," I said, "*church*. You remember? Church, priest, Mass, confession."

He curled one lip into a kind of smile; I took it for a signal that for a second he had flickered back up into the human race.

"Jewish personnel who want to attend services this evening are to fall out in front of the orderly room at 1900," I said. Then, as an afterthought, I added, "By order of Captain Barrett."

A little while later, as the day's last light—softer than any I had seen that year—began to drop over Camp Crowder, I heard LaHill's thick, inflectionless voice outside my window: "Give me your ears, troopers. Toppie says for me to tell you that at 1900 hours all Jewish personnel is to fall out in front, here, if they want to attend the Jewish Mass."

—

At seven o'clock, I looked out the orderly-room window and saw three soldiers in starched khakis standing on the dusty quadrangle. They looked at their watches and fidgeted while they whispered back and forth. It was getting dimmer, and, alone on the otherwise deserted field, they looked tiny. When I opened the door, I heard the noises of the G.I. party coming from the surrounding barracks—bunks being pushed to the walls, faucets pounding water into buckets, brooms whisking at the wooden floors, cleaning the dirt away for Saturday's inspection. Big puffs of cloth moved round and round on the windowpanes. I walked outside, and the moment my foot hit the ground I thought I heard Grossbart call to the others, "'Ten-*hut*!" Or maybe, when they all three jumped to attention, I imagined I heard the command.

Grossbart stepped forward. "Thank you, sir," he said.

"'Sergeant,' Grossbart," I reminded him. "You call officers 'sir.' I'm not an officer. You've been in the Army three weeks—you know that."

He turned his palms out at his sides to indicate that, in truth, he and I lived beyond convention. "Thank you, anyway," he said.

"Yes," a tall boy behind him said. "Thanks a lot."

And the third boy whispered, "Thank you," but his mouth barely fluttered, so that he did not alter by more than a lip's movement his posture of attention.

"For what?" I asked.

Grossbart snorted happily. "For the announcement. The Corporal's announcement. It helped. It made it—"

"Fancier." The tall boy finished Grossbart's sentence.

Grossbart smiled. "He means formal, sir. Public," he said to me. "Now it won't seem as though we're just taking off—goldbricking because the work has begun."

"It was by order of Captain Barrett," I said.

"Aaah, but you pull a little weight," Grossbart said. "So we thank you." Then he turned to his companions. "Sergeant Marx, I want you to meet Larry Fishbein."

The tall boy stepped forward and extended his hand. I shook it. "You from New York?" he asked.

"Yes."

"Me, too." He had a cadaverous face that collapsed inward

from his cheekbone to his jaw, and when he smiled—as he did at the news of our communal attachment—revealed a mouthful of bad teeth. He was blinking his eyes a good deal, as though he were fighting back tears. "What borough?" he asked.

I turned to Grossbart. "It's five after seven. What time are services?"

"Shul," he said, smiling, "is in ten minutes. I want you to meet Mickey Halpern. This is Nathan Marx, our sergeant."

The third boy hopped forward. "Private Michael Halpern." He saluted.

"Salute officers, Halpern," I said. The boy dropped his hand, and, on its way down, in his nervousness, checked to see if his shirt pockets were buttoned.

"Shall I march them over, sir?" Grossbart asked. "Or are you coming along?"

From behind Grossbart, Fishbein piped up. "Afterward, they're having refreshments. A ladies' auxiliary from St. Louis, the rabbi told us last week."

"The chaplain," Halpern whispered.

"You're welcome to come along," Grossbart said.

To avoid his plea, I looked away, and saw, in the windows of the barracks, a cloud of faces staring out at the four of us. "Hurry along, Grossbart," I said.

"O.K., then," he said. He turned to the others. "Double time, *march!*"

They started off, but ten feet away Grossbart spun around and, running backward, called to me, "Good *shabbus*, sir!" And then the three of them were swallowed into the alien Missouri dusk.

Even after they had disappeared over the parade ground, whose green was now a deep blue, I could hear Grossbart singing the double-time cadence, and as it grew dimmer and dimmer, it suddenly touched a deep memory—as did the slant of the light—and I was remembering the shrill sounds of a Bronx playground where, years ago, beside the Grand Concourse, I had played on long spring evenings such as this. It was a pleasant memory for a young man so far from peace and home, and it brought so many recollections with it that I began to grow exceedingly tender about myself. In fact, I indulged myself in a reverie so strong that I felt as though a hand were reaching down inside me. It had to reach so very far to touch me! It had to reach past those days in the forests of Belgium, and past the dying I'd refused to weep over; past the nights in German farmhouses whose books we'd burned to warm us; past endless stretches when I had shut off all softness I might feel for my fellows, and had managed even to deny myself the posture of a conqueror—the swagger that I, as a Jew, might well have worn as my boots whacked against the rubble of Wesel, Münster, and Braunschweig.

But now one night noise, one rumor of home and time past, and memory plunged down through all I had anesthetized, and came to what I suddenly remembered was myself. So it was not altogether curious that, in search of more of me, I found myself following Grossbart's tracks to Chapel No. 3, where the Jewish services were being held.

I took a seat in the last row, which was empty. Two rows in front of me sat Grossbart, Fishbein, and Halpern, holding little white Dixie cups. Each row of seats was raised higher than the one in front of it, and I could see clearly what was going on. Fishbein was pouring the contents of his cup into Grossbart's, and Grossbart looked mirthful as the liquid made a purple arc between Fishbein's hand and his. In the glaring yellow light, I saw the chaplain standing on the platform at the front; he was chanting the first line of the responsive reading. Grossbart's prayer book remained closed on his lap; he was swishing the cup around. Only Halpern responded to the chant by praying. The fingers of his right hand were spread wide across the cover of his open book. His cap was pulled down low onto his brow, which made it round, like a yarmulke. From time to time, Grossbart wet his lips at the cup's edge; Fishbein, his long yellow face a dying light bulb, looked from here to there, craning forward to catch sight of the faces down the row, then of those in front of him, then behind. He saw me, and his eyelids beat a tattoo. His elbow slid into Grossbart's side, his neck inclined toward his friend, he whispered something, and then, when the congregation next responded to the chant, Grossbart's voice was among the others. Fishbein looked into his book now, too; his lips, however, didn't move.

Finally, it was time to drink the wine. The chaplain smiled down at them as Grossbart swigged his in one long gulp,

Halpern sipped, meditating, and Fishbein faked devotion with an empty cup. "As I look down amongst the congregation"— the chaplain grinned at the word—"this night, I see many new faces, and I want to welcome you to Friday-night services here at Camp Crowder. I am Major Leo Ben Ezra, your chaplain." Though an American, the chaplain spoke deliberately—syllable by syllable, almost—as though to communicate, above all, with the lip readers in his audience. "I have only a few words to say before we adjourn to the refreshment room, where the kind ladies of the Temple Sinai, St. Louis, Missouri, have a nice setting for you."

Applause and whistling broke out. After another momentary grin, the chaplain raised his hands, palms out, his eyes flicking upward a moment, as if to remind the troops where they were and Who Else might be in attendance. In the sudden silence that followed, I thought I heard Grossbart cackle, "Let the goyim clean the floors!" Were those the words? I wasn't sure, but Fishbein, grinning, nudged Halpern. Halpern looked dumbly at him, then went back to his prayer book, which had been occupying him all through the rabbi's talk. One hand tugged at the black kinky hair that stuck out under his cap. His lips moved.

The rabbi continued. "It is about the food that I want to speak to you for a moment. I know, I know, I know," he intoned, wearily, "how in the mouths of most of you the *trafe* food tastes like ashes. I know how you gag, some of you, and how your parents suffer to think of their children eating foods unclean and offensive to the palate. What can I tell you? I can only say, close your eyes and swallow as best you can. Eat what you must to live, and throw away the rest. I wish I could help more. For those of you who find this impossible, may I ask that you try and try, but then come to see me in private. If your revulsion is so great, we will have to seek aid from those higher up."

A round of chatter rose and subsided. Then everyone sang "Ain Kelohainu"; after all those years, I discovered I still knew the words. Then, suddenly, the service over, Grossbart was upon me. "Higher up? He means the General?"

"Hey, Shelly," Fishbein said, "he means God." He smacked his face and looked at Halpern. "How high can you go!"

"Sh-h-h!" Grossbart said. "What do you think, Sergeant?"

"I don't know," I said. "You better ask the chaplain."

"I'm going to. I'm making an appointment to see him in private. So is Mickey."

Halpern shook his head. "No, no, Sheldon—"

"You have rights, Mickey," Grossbart said. "They can't push us around."

"It's O.K.," said Halpern. "It bothers my mother, not me."

Grossbart looked at me. "Yesterday he threw up. From the hash. It was all ham and God knows what else."

"I have a cold—that was why," Halpern said. He pushed his yarmulke back into a cap.

"What about you, Fishbein?" I asked. "You kosher, too?"

He flushed. "A little. But I'll let it ride. I have a very strong stomach, and I don't eat a lot anyway." I continued to look at him, and he held up his wrist to reinforce what he'd just said; his watch strap was tightened to the last hole, and he pointed that out to me.

"But services are important to you?" I asked him.

He looked at Grossbart. "Sure, sir."

"'Sergeant.'"

"Not so much at home," said Grossbart, stepping between us, "but away from home it gives one a sense of his Jewishness."

"We have to stick together," Fishbein said.

I started to walk toward the door; Halpern stepped back to make way for me.

"That's what happened in Germany," Grossbart was saying, loud enough for me to hear. "They didn't stick together. They let themselves get pushed around."

I turned. "Look, Grossbart. This is the Army, not summer camp."

He smiled. "So?"

Halpern tried to sneak off, but Grossbart held his arm.

"Grossbart, how old are you?" I asked.

"Nineteen."

"And you?" I said to Fishbein.

"The same. The same month, even."

"And what about him?" I pointed to Halpern, who had by now made it safely to the door.

"Eighteen," Grossbart whispered. "But like he can't tie his shoes or brush his teeth himself. I feel sorry for him."

"I feel sorry for all of us, Grossbart," I said, "but just act like a man. Just don't overdo it."

"Overdo what, sir?"

"The 'sir' business, for one thing. Don't overdo that," I said.

I left him standing there. I passed by Halpern, but he did not look at me. Then I was outside, but, behind, I heard Grossbart call, "Hey, Mickey, my *leben*, come on back. Refreshments!"

"*Leben!*" My grandmother's word for me!

One morning a week later, while I was working at my desk, Captain Barrett shouted for me to come into his office. When I entered, he had his helmet liner squashed down so far on his head that I couldn't even see his eyes. He was on the phone, and when he spoke to me, he cupped one hand over the mouthpiece. "Who the hell is Grossbart?"

"Third platoon, Captain," I said. "A trainee."

"What's all this stink about food? His mother called a goddam congressman about the food." He uncovered the mouthpiece and slid his helmet up until I could see his bottom eyelashes. "Yes, sir," he said into the phone. "Yes, sir. I'm still here, sir. I'm asking Marx, here, right now—"

He covered the mouthpiece again and turned his head back toward me. "Lightfoot Harry's on the phone," he said, between his teeth. "This congressman calls General Lyman, who calls Colonel Sousa, who calls the Major, who calls me. They're just dying to stick this thing on me. Whatsa matter?" He shook the phone at me. "I don't feed the troops? What is this?"

"Sir, Grossbart is strange—" Barrett greeted that with a mockingly indulgent smile. I altered my approach. "Captain, he's a very orthodox Jew, and so he's only allowed to eat certain foods."

"He throws up, the congressman said. Every time he eats something, his mother says, he throws up!"

"He's accustomed to observing the dietary laws, Captain."

"So why's his old lady have to call the White House?"

"Jewish parents, sir—they're apt to be more protective than you expect. I mean, Jews have a very close family life. A boy goes away from home, sometimes the mother is liable to get very upset. Probably the boy mentioned something in a letter, and his mother misinterpreted."

"I'd like to punch him one right in the mouth," the Captain said. "There's a war on, and he wants a silver platter!"

"I don't think the boy's to blame, sir. I'm sure we can straighten it out by just asking him. Jewish parents worry—"

"*All* parents worry, for Christ's sake. But they don't get on their high horse and start pulling strings—"

I interrupted, my voice higher, tighter than before. "The home life, Captain, is very important—but you're right, it may sometimes get out of hand. It's a very wonderful thing, Captain, but because it's so close, this kind of thing . . ."

He didn't listen any longer to my attempt to present both myself and Lightfoot Harry with an explanation for the letter. He turned back to the phone. "Sir?" he said. "Sir—Marx, here, tells me Jews have a tendency to be pushy. He says he thinks we can settle it right here in the company. . . . Yes, sir. . . . I *will* call back, sir, soon as I can." He hung up. "Where are the men, Sergeant?"

"On the range."

With a whack on the top of his helmet, he crushed it down over his eyes again, and charged out of his chair. "We're going for a ride," he said.

The Captain drove, and I sat beside him. It was a hot spring day, and under my newly starched fatigues I felt as though my armpits were melting down onto my sides and chest. The roads were dry, and by the time we reached the firing range, my teeth felt gritty with dust, though my mouth had been shut the whole trip. The Captain slammed the brakes on and told me to get the hell out and find Grossbart.

I found him on his belly, firing wildly at the five-hundred-feet target. Waiting their turns behind him were Halpern and Fishbein. Fishbein, wearing a pair of steel-rimmed G.I. glasses I hadn't seen on him before, had the appearance of an old peddler who would gladly have sold you his rifle and the cartridges that were slung all over him. I stood back by the ammo boxes, waiting for Grossbart to finish spraying the distant targets. Fishbein straggled back to stand near me.

"Hello, Sergeant Marx," he said.

"How are you?" I mumbled.

"Fine, thank you. Sheldon's really a good shot."

"I didn't notice."

"I'm not so good, but I think I'm getting the hang of it now. Sergeant, I don't mean to, you know, ask what I shouldn't—" The boy stopped. He was trying to speak intimately, but the noise of the shooting forced him to shout at me.

"What is it?" I asked. Down the range, I saw Captain Barrett standing up in the jeep, scanning the line for me and Grossbart.

"My parents keep asking and asking where we're going," Fishbein said. "Everybody says the Pacific. I don't care, but my parents— If I could relieve their minds, I think I could concentrate more on my shooting."

"I don't know where, Fishbein. Try to concentrate anyway."

"Sheldon says you might be able to find out."

"I don't know a thing, Fishbein. You just take it easy, and don't let Sheldon—"

"*I'm* taking it easy, Sergeant. It's at home—"

Grossbart had finished on the line, and was dusting his fatigues with one hand. I called to him. "Grossbart, the Captain wants to see you."

He came toward us. His eyes blazed and twinkled. "Hi!"

"Don't point that rifle!" I said.

"I wouldn't shoot you, Sarge." He gave me a smile as wide as a pumpkin, and turned the barrel aside.

"Damn you, Grossbart, this is no joke! Follow me."

I walked ahead of him, and had the awful suspicion that, behind me, Grossbart was *marching*, his rifle on his shoulder, as though he were a one-man detachment. At the jeep, he gave the Captain a rifle salute. "Private Sheldon Grossbart, sir."

"At ease, Grossman." The Captain sat down, slid over into the empty seat, and, crooking his finger, invited Grossbart closer.

"Bart, sir. Sheldon Gross*bart*. It's a common error." Grossbart nodded at me; *I* understood, he indicated. I looked away just as the mess truck pulled up to the range, disgorging a half-dozen K.P.s with rolled-up sleeves. The mess sergeant screamed at them while they set up the chow-line equipment.

"Grossbart, your mama wrote some congressman that we don't feed you right. Do you know that?" the Captain said.

"It was my father, sir. He wrote to Representative Franconi that my religion forbids me to eat certain foods."

"What religion is that, Grossbart?"

"Jewish."

"'Jewish, *sir*,'" I said to Grossbart.

"Excuse me, sir. Jewish, sir."

"What have you been living on?" the Captain asked. "You've been in the Army a month already. You don't look to me like you're falling to pieces."

"I eat because I have to, sir. But Sergeant Marx will testify to the fact that I don't eat one mouthful more than I need to in order to survive."

"Is that so, Marx?" Barrett asked.

"I've never seen Grossbart eat, sir," I said.

"But you heard the rabbi," Grossbart said. "He told us what to do, and I listened."

The Captain looked at me. "Well, Marx?"

"I still don't know what he eats and doesn't eat, sir."

Grossbart raised his arms to plead with me, and it looked for a moment as though he were going to hand me his weapon to hold. "But, Sergeant—"

"Look, Grossbart, just answer the Captain's questions," I said sharply.

Barrett smiled at me, and I resented it. "All right, Grossbart," he said. "What is it you want? The little piece of paper? You want out?"

"No, sir. Only to be allowed to live as a Jew. And for the others, too."

"What others?"

"Fishbein, sir, and Halpern."

"They don't like the way we serve, either?"

"Halpern throws up, sir. I've seen it."

"I thought *you* throw up."

"Just once, sir. I didn't know the sausage was sausage."

"We'll give menus, Grossbart. We'll show training films

about the food, so you can identify when we're trying to poison you."

Grossbart did not answer. The men had been organized into two long chow lines. At the tail of one, I spotted Fishbein—or, rather, his glasses spotted me. They winked sunlight back at me. Halpern stood next to him, patting the inside of his collar with a khaki handkerchief. They moved with the line as it began to edge up toward the food. The mess sergeant was still screaming at the K.P.s. For a moment, I was actually terrified by the thought that somehow the mess sergeant was going to become involved in Grossbart's problem.

"Marx," the Captain said, "you're a Jewish fella—am I right?"

I played straight man. "Yes, sir."

"How long have you been in the Army? Tell this boy."

"Three years and two months."

"A year in combat, Grossbart. Twelve goddam months in combat all through Europe. I admire this man." The Captain snapped a wrist against my chest. "Do you hear him peeping about the food? Do you? I want an answer, Grossbart. Yes or no."

"No, sir."

"And why not? He's a Jewish fella."

"Some things are more important to some Jews than other things to other Jews."

Barrett blew up. "Look, Grossbart. Marx, here, is a good man—a goddam hero. When you were in high school, Sergeant Marx was killing Germans. Who does more for the Jews—you, by throwing up over a lousy piece of sausage, a piece of first-cut meat, or Marx, by killing those Nazi bastards? If I was a Jew, Grossbart, I'd kiss this man's feet. He's a goddam hero, and *he* eats what we give him. Why do you have to cause trouble is what I want to know! What is it you're buckin' for—a discharge?"

"No, sir."

"I'm talking to a wall! Sergeant, get him out of my way." Barrett swung himself back into the driver's seat. "I'm going to see the chaplain." The engine roared, the jeep spun around in a whirl of dust, and the Captain was headed back to camp.

For a moment, Grossbart and I stood side by side, watching the jeep. Then he looked at me and said, "I don't want to start trouble. That's the first thing they toss up to us."

When he spoke, I saw that his teeth were white and straight, and the sight of them suddenly made me understand that Grossbart actually did have parents—that once upon a time someone had taken little Sheldon to the dentist. He was their son. Despite all the talk about his parents, it was hard to believe in Grossbart as a child, an heir—as related by blood to anyone, mother, father, or, above all, to me. This realization led me to another.

"What does your father do, Grossbart?" I asked as we started to walk back toward the chow line.

"He's a tailor."

"An American?"

"Now, yes. A son in the Army," he said, jokingly.

"And your mother?" I asked.

He winked. "A *ballabusta*. She practically sleeps with a dust-cloth in her hand."

"She's also an immigrant?"

"All she talks is Yiddish, still."

"And your father, too?"

"A little English. 'Clean,' 'Press,' 'Take the pants in.' That's the extent of it. But they're good to me."

"Then, Grossbart—" I reached out and stopped him. He turned toward me, and when our eyes met, his seemed to jump back, to shiver in their sockets. "Grossbart—you were the one who wrote that letter, weren't you?"

It took only a second or two for his eyes to flash happy again. "Yes." He walked on, and I kept pace. "It's what my father *would* have written if he had known how. It was his name, though. *He* signed it. He even mailed it. I sent it home. For the New York postmark."

I was astonished, and he saw it. With complete seriousness, he thrust his right arm in front of me. "Blood is blood, Sergeant," he said, pinching the blue vein in his wrist.

"What the hell *are* you trying to do, Grossbart?" I asked. "I've seen you eat. Do you know that? I told the Captain I don't know what you eat, but I've seen you eat like a hound at chow."

"We work hard, Sergeant. We're in training. For a furnace to work, you've got to feed it coal."

"Why did you say in the letter that you threw up all the time?"

"I was really talking about Mickey there. I was talking *for* him. He would never write, Sergeant, though I pleaded with him. He'll waste away to nothing if I don't help. Sergeant, I used my name—my father's name—but it's Mickey, and Fishbein, too, I'm watching out for."

"You're a regular Messiah, aren't you?"

We were at the chow line now.

"That's a good one, Sergeant," he said, smiling. "But who knows? Who can tell? Maybe you're the Messiah—a little bit. What Mickey says is the Messiah is a collective idea. He went to Yeshiva, Mickey, for a while. He says *together* we're the Messiah. Me a little bit, you a little bit. You should hear that kid talk, Sergeant, when he gets going."

"Me a little bit, you a little bit," I said. "You'd like to believe that, wouldn't you, Grossbart? That would make everything so clean for you."

"It doesn't seem too bad a thing to believe, Sergeant. It only means we should all *give* a little, is all."

I walked off to eat my rations with the other noncoms.

Two days later, a letter addressed to Captain Barrett passed over my desk. It had come through the chain of command—from the office of Congressman Franconi, where it had been received, to General Lyman, to Colonel Sousa, to Major Lamont, now to Captain Barrett. I read it over twice. It was dated May 14, the day Barrett had spoken with Grossbart on the rifle range.

Dear Congressman:

First let me thank you for your interest in behalf of my son, Private Sheldon Grossbart. Fortunately, I was able to speak with Sheldon on the phone the other night, and I think I've been able to solve our problem. He is, as I mentioned in my last letter, a very religious boy, and it was only with the greatest difficulty that I could persuade him that the religious thing to do—what God Himself would want Sheldon to do—would be to suffer the pangs of religious remorse for the good of his country and all mankind. It took some doing, Congressman, but finally he saw the light. In fact, what he said (and I wrote down the words on a scratch pad so as never to forget), what he said was "I guess you're right, Dad. So many millions of my fellow-Jews gave up their lives to the enemy, the least I can do is live for a while minus a bit of my heritage so as to help end this struggle and regain for all the children of God dignity and humanity." That, Congressman, would make any father proud.

By the way, Sheldon wanted me to know—and to pass on to you—the name of a soldier who helped him reach this decision: SERGEANT NATHAN MARX. Sergeant Marx is a combat veteran who is Sheldon's first sergeant. This man has helped Sheldon over some of the first hurdles he's had to face in the Army, and is in part responsible for Sheldon's changing his mind about the dietary laws. I know Sheldon would appreciate any recognition Marx could receive.

Thank you and good luck. I look forward to seeing your name on the next election ballot.

> Respectfully,
> Samuel E. Grossbart

Attached to the Grossbart communiqué was another, addressed to General Marshall Lyman, the post commander, and signed by Representative Charles E. Franconi, of the House of Representatives. The communiqué informed General Lyman that Sergeant Nathan Marx was a credit to the U.S. Army and the Jewish people.

What was Grossbart's motive in recanting? Did he feel he'd gone too far? Was the letter a strategic retreat—a crafty attempt to strengthen what he considered our alliance? Or had he actually changed his mind, via an imaginary dialogue between Grossbart *père* and Grossbart *fils?* I was puzzled, but only for a few days—that is, only until I realized that, whatever his reasons, he had actually decided to disappear from my life; he was going to allow himself to become just another trainee. I saw him at inspection, but he never winked; at chow formations, but he never flashed me a sign. On Sundays, with the other trainees, he would sit around watching the noncoms' softball team, for which I pitched, but not once did he speak an unnecessary word to me. Fishbein and Halpern retreated, too—at Grossbart's command, I was sure. Apparently he had seen that wisdom lay in turning back before he plunged over into the ugliness of privilege undeserved. Our separation allowed me to forgive him our past encounters, and, finally, to admire him for his good sense.

Meanwhile, free of Grossbart, I grew used to my job and my administrative tasks. I stepped on a scale one day, and discovered I had truly become a noncombatant; I had gained seven pounds. I found patience to get past the first three pages of a book. I thought about the future more and more, and wrote letters to girls I'd known before the war. I even got a few answers. I sent away to Columbia for a Law School catalogue. I continued to follow the war in the Pacific, but it was not my war. I thought I could see the end, and sometimes, at night, I dreamed that I was walking on the streets of Manhattan—Broadway, Third Avenue, 116th Street, where I had lived the three years I attended Columbia. I curled myself around these dreams and I began to be happy.

And then, one Sunday, when everybody was away and I was alone in the orderly room reading a month-old copy of the *Sporting News,* Grossbart reappeared.

"You a baseball fan, Sergeant?"

I looked up. "How are you?"

"Fine," Grossbart said. "They're making a soldier out of me."

"How are Fishbein and Halpern?"

"Coming along," he said. "We've got no training this afternoon. They're at the movies."

"How come you're not with them?"

"I wanted to come over and say hello."

He smiled—a shy, regular-guy smile, as though he and I well knew that our friendship drew its sustenance from unexpected visits, remembered birthdays, and borrowed lawnmowers. At first it offended me, and then the feeling was swallowed by the general uneasiness I felt at the thought that everyone on the post was locked away in a dark movie theater and I was here alone with Grossbart. I folded up my paper.

"Sergeant," he said, "I'd like to ask a favor. It is a favor, and I'm making no bones about it."

He stopped, allowing me to refuse him a hearing—which, of course, forced me into a courtesy I did not intend. "Go ahead."

"Well, actually it's two favors."

I said nothing.

"The first one's about these rumors. Everybody says we're going to the Pacific."

"As I told your friend Fishbein, I don't know," I said. "You'll just have to wait to find out. Like everybody else."

"You think there's a chance of any of us going East?"

"Germany?" I said. "Maybe."

"I meant New York."

"I don't think so, Grossbart. Offhand."

"Thanks for the information, Sergeant," he said.

"It's not information, Grossbart. Just what I surmise."

"It certainly would be good to be near home. My parents—you know." He took a step toward the door and then turned back. "Oh, the other thing. May I ask the other?"

"What is it?"

"The other thing is—I've got relatives in St. Louis, and they say they'll give me a whole Passover dinner if I can get down there. God, Sergeant, that'd mean an awful lot to me."

I stood up. "No passes during basic, Grossbart."

"But we're off from now till Monday morning, Sergeant. I could leave the post and no one would even know."

"I'd know. You'd know."

"But that's all. Just the two of us. Last night, I called my aunt, and you should have heard her. 'Come—come,' she said. 'I got gefilte fish, *chrain*—the works!' Just a day, Sergeant. I'd take the blame if anything happened."

"The Captain isn't here to sign a pass."

"You could sign."

"Look, Grossbart—"

"Sergeant, for two months, practically, I've been eating *trafe* till I want to die."

"I thought you'd made up your mind to live with it. To be minus a little bit of heritage."

He pointed a finger at me. "You!" he said. "That wasn't for you to read."

"I read it. So what?"

"That letter was addressed to a congressman."

"Grossbart, don't feed me any baloney. You *wanted* me to read it."

"Why are you persecuting me, Sergeant?"

"Are you kidding!"

"I've run into this before," he said, "but never from my own!"

"Get out of here, Grossbart! Get the hell out of my sight!"

He did not move. "Ashamed, that's what you are," he said. "So you take it out on the rest of us. They say Hitler himself was half a Jew. Hearing you, I wouldn't doubt it."

"What are you trying to do with me, Grossbart?" I asked him. "What are you after? You want me to give you special privileges, to change the food, to find out about your orders, to give you weekend passes."

"You even talk like a goy!" Grossbart shook his fist. "Is this just a weekend pass I'm asking for? Is a Seder sacred, or not?"

Seder! It suddenly occurred to me that Passover had been celebrated weeks before. I said so.

"That's right," he replied. "Who says no? A month ago— and I was in the field eating hash! And now all I ask is a simple favor. A Jewish boy I thought would understand. My aunt's willing to go out of her way—to make a Seder a month later. . . ." He turned to go, mumbling.

"Come back here!" I called. He stopped and looked at me. "Grossbart, why can't you be like the rest? Why do you have to stick out like a sore thumb?"

"Because I'm a Jew, Sergeant. I *am* different. Better, maybe not. But different."

"This is a war, Grossbart. For the time being *be* the same."

"I refuse."

"What?"

"I refuse. I can't stop being me, that's all there is to it." Tears came to his eyes. "It's a hard thing to be a Jew. But now I understand what Mickey says—it's a harder thing to stay one." He raised a hand sadly toward me. "Look at *you*."

"Stop crying!"

"Stop this, stop that, stop the other thing! *You* stop,

Sergeant. Stop closing your heart to your own!" And, wiping his face with his sleeve, he ran out the door. "The least we can do for one another—the least . . ."

An hour later, looking out of the window, I saw Grossbart headed across the field. He wore a pair of starched khakis and carried a little leather ditty bag. I went out into the heat of the day. It was quiet; not a soul was in sight except, over by the mess hall, four K.P.s sitting around a pan, sloped forward from their waists, gabbing and peeling potatoes in the sun.

"Grossbart!" I called.

He looked toward me and continued walking.

"Grossbart, get over here!"

He turned and came across the field. Finally, he stood before me.

"Where are you going?" I asked.

"St. Louis. I don't care."

"You'll get caught without a pass."

"So I'll get caught without a pass."

"You'll go to the stockade."

"I'm *in* the stockade." He made an about-face and headed off.

I let him go only a step or two. "Come back here," I said, and he followed me into the office, where I typed out a pass and signed the Captain's name, and my own initials after it.

He took the pass and then, a moment later, reached out and grabbed my hand. "Sergeant, you don't know how much this means to me."

"O.K.," I said. "Don't get in any trouble."

"I wish I could show you how much this means to me."

"Don't do me any favors. Don't write any more congressmen for citations."

He smiled. "You're right. I won't. But let me do something."

"Bring me a piece of that gefilte fish. Just get out of here."

"I will!" he said. "With a slice of carrot and a little horseradish. I won't forget."

"All right. Just show your pass at the gate. And don't tell *anybody*."

"I won't. It's a month late, but a good Yam Tov to you."

"Good Yom Tov, Grossbart," I said.

"You're a good Jew, Sergeant. You like to think you have a hard heart, but underneath you're a fine, decent man. I mean that."

Those last three words touched me more than any words from Grossbart's mouth had the right to. "All right, Grossbart," I said. "Now call me 'sir,' and get the hell out of here."

He ran out the door and was gone. I felt very pleased with myself; it was a great relief to stop fighting Grossbart, and it had cost me nothing. Barrett would never find out, and if he did, I could manage to invent some excuse. For a while, I sat at my desk, comfortable in my decision. Then the screen door flew back and Grossbart burst in again. "Sergeant!" he said. Behind him I saw Fishbein and Halpern, both in starched khakis, both carrying ditty bags like Grossbart's.

"Sergeant, I caught Mickey and Larry coming out of the movies. I almost missed them."

"Grossbart—did I say tell no one?" I said.

"But my aunt said I could bring friends. That I should, in fact."

"*I'm* the Sergeant, Grossbart—not your aunt!"

Grossbart looked at me in disbelief. He pulled Halpern up by his sleeve. "Mickey, tell the Sergeant what this would mean to you."

Halpern looked at me and, shrugging, said, "A lot."

Fishbein stepped forward without prompting. "This would mean a great deal to me and my parents, Sergeant Marx."

"No!" I shouted.

Grossbart was shaking his head. "Sergeant, I could see you denying me, but how you can deny Mickey, a Yeshiva boy—that's beyond me."

"I'm not denying Mickey anything," I said. "You just pushed a little too hard, Grossbart. *You* denied him."

"I'll give him my pass, then," Grossbart said. "I'll give him my aunt's address and a little note. At least let him go."

In a second, he had crammed the pass into Halpern's pants pocket. Halpern looked at me, and so did Fishbein. Grossbart was at the door, pushing it open. "Mickey, bring me a piece of gelfilte fish, at least," he said, and then he was outside again.

The three of us looked at one another, and then I said, "Halpern, hand that pass over."

He took it from his pocket and gave it to me. Fishbein had now moved to the doorway, where he lingered. He stood there for a moment with his mouth slightly open, and then he pointed to himself. "And me?" he asked.

His utter ridiculousness exhausted me. I slumped down in my seat and felt pulses knocking at the back of my eyes. "Fishbein," I said, "you understand I'm not trying to deny you anything, don't you? If it was my Army, I'd serve gefilte fish in the mess hall. I'd sell *kugel* in the PX, honest to God."

Halpern smiled.

"You understand, don't you, Halpern?"

"Yes, Sergeant."

"And you, Fishbein? I don't want enemies. I'm just like you —I want to serve my time and go home. I miss the same things you miss."

"Then, Sergeant," Fishbein said, "why don't you come, too?"

"Where?"

"To St. Louis. To Shelly's aunt. We'll have a regular Seder. Play hide-the-matzoh." He gave me a broad, black-toothed smile.

I saw Grossbart again, on the other side of the screen.

"Pst!" He waved a piece of paper. "Mickey, here's the address. Tell her I couldn't get away."

Halpern did not move. He looked at me, and I saw the shrug moving up his arms into his shoulders again. I took the cover off my typewriter and made out passes for him and Fishbein. "Go," I said. "The three of you."

I thought Halpern was going to kiss my hand.

That afternoon, in a bar in Joplin, I drank beer and listened with half an ear to the Cardinal game. I tried to look squarely at what I'd become involved in, and began to wonder if perhaps the struggle with Grossbart wasn't as much my fault as his. What was I that I had to *muster* generous feelings? Who was I to have been feeling so grudging, so tight-hearted? After all, I wasn't being asked to move the world. Had I a right, then, or a reason, to clamp down on Grossbart, when that meant clamping down on Halpern, too? And Fishbein—that ugly, agreeable soul? Out of the many recollections of my childhood that had tumbled over me these past few days I heard my grandmother's voice: "What are you making a *tsimmes?*" It was what she would ask my mother when, say, I had cut myself doing something I shouldn't have done, and her daughter was busy bawling me out. I needed a hug and a kiss, and my mother would moralize. But my grandmother knew—mercy overrides justice. I should have known it, too. Who was Nathan Marx to be such a penny pincher with kindness? Surely, I thought, the Messiah himself—if He should ever come—won't niggle over nickels and dimes. God willing, he'll hug and kiss.

The next day, while I was playing softball over on the parade ground, I decided to ask Bob Wright, who was noncom in charge of Classification and Assignment, where he thought our trainees would be sent when their cycle ended, in two weeks. I asked casually, between innings, and he said, "They're pushing them all into the Pacific. Shulman cut the orders on your boys the other day."

The news shocked me, as though I were the father of Halpern, Fishbein, and Grossbart.

That night, I was just sliding into sleep when someone tapped on my door. "Who is it?" I asked.

"Sheldon."

He opened the door and came in. For a moment, I felt his presence without being able to see him. "How was it?" I asked.

He popped into sight in the near-darkness before me. "Great, Sergeant." Then he was sitting on the edge of the bed. I sat up.

"How about you?" he asked. "Have a nice weekend?"

"Yes."

"The others went to sleep." He took a deep, paternal breath. We sat silent for a while, and a homey feeling invaded my ugly little cubicle; the door was locked, the cat was out, the children were safely in bed.

"Sergeant, can I tell you something? Personal?"

I did not answer, and he seemed to know why. "Not about me. About Mickey. Sergeant, I never felt for anybody like I feel for him. Last night I heard Mickey in the bed next to me. He was crying so, it could have broken your heart. Real sobs."

"I'm sorry to hear that."

"I had to talk to him to stop him. He held my hand, Sergeant—he wouldn't let it go. He was almost hysterical. He kept saying if he only knew where we were going. Even if he knew it *was* the Pacific, that would be better than nothing. Just to know."

Long ago, someone had taught Grossbart the sad rule that only lies can get the truth. Not that I couldn't believe in the fact of Halpern's crying; his eyes *always* seemed red-rimmed. But, fact or not, it became a lie when Grossbart uttered it. He was entirely strategic. But then—it came with the force of indictment—so was I! There are strategies of aggression, but there are strategies of retreat as well. And so, recognizing that I myself had not been without craft and guile, I told him what I knew. "It is the Pacific."

He let out a small gasp, which was not a lie. "I'll tell him. I wish it was otherwise."

"So do I."

He jumped on my words. "You mean you think you could do something? A change, maybe?"

"No, I couldn't do a thing."

"Don't you know anybody over at C. and A.?"

"Grossbart, there's nothing I can do," I said. "If your orders are for the Pacific, then it's the Pacific."

"But Mickey—"

"Mickey, you, me—everybody, Grossbart. There's nothing to be done. Maybe the war'll end before you go. Pray for a miracle."

"But—"

"Good night, Grossbart." I settled back, and was relieved to feel the springs unbend as Grossbart rose to leave. I could see him clearly now; his jaw had dropped, and he looked like a dazed prizefighter. I noticed for the first time a little paper bag in his hand.

"Grossbart." I smiled. "My gift?"

"Oh, yes, Sergeant. Here—from all of us." He handed me the bag. "It's egg roll."

"Egg roll?" I accepted the bag and felt a damp grease spot on the bottom. I opened it, sure that Grossbart was joking.

"We thought you'd probably like it. You know—Chinese egg roll. We thought you'd probably have a taste for—"

"Your aunt served egg roll?"

"She wasn't home."

"Grossbart, she invited you. You told me she invited you and your friends."

"I know," he said. "I just reread her letter. *Next* week."

I got out of bed and walked to the window. "Grossbart," I said. But I was not calling to him.

"What?"

"What are you, Grossbart? Honest to God, what are you?"

I think it was the first time I'd asked him a question for which he didn't have an immediate answer.

"How can you do this to people?" I went on.

"Sergeant, the day away did us all a world of good. Fishbein, you should see him, he *loves* Chinese food."

"But the Seder," I said.

"We took second best, Sergeant."

Rage came charging at me. I didn't sidestep. "Grossbart, you're a liar!" I said. "You're a schemer and a crook. You've got no respect for anything. Nothing at all. Not for me, for the truth—not even for poor Halpern! You use us all—"

"Sergeant, Sergeant, I feel for Mickey. Honest to God, I do. I *love* Mickey. I try—"

"You try! You feel!" I lurched toward him and grabbed his shirt front. I shook him furiously. "Grossbart, get out! Get out and stay the hell away from me. Because if I see you, I'll make your life miserable. *You understand that?*"

"Yes."

I let him free, and when he walked from the room, I wanted to spit on the floor where he had stood. I couldn't stop the fury. It engulfed me, owned me, till it seemed I could only rid myself of it with tears or an act of violence. I snatched from the bed the bag Grossbart had given me and, with all my strength, threw it out the window. And the next morning, as the men policed the area around the barracks, I heard a great cry go up from one of the trainees, who had been anticipating only his morning handful of cigarette butts and candy wrappers. "Egg roll!" he shouted. "Holy Christ, Chinese goddam egg roll!"

A week later, when I read the orders that had come down from C. and A., I couldn't believe my eyes. Every single trainee was to be shipped to Camp Stoneman, California, and from there to the Pacific—every trainee but one. Private Sheldon Grossbart. He was to be sent to Fort Monmouth, New Jersey. I read the mimeographed sheet several times. Dee, Farrell, Fishbein, Fuselli, Fylypowycz, Glinicki, Gromke, Gucwa, Halpern, Hardy, Helebrandt, right down to Anton Zygadlo— all were to be headed West before the month was out. All except Grossbart. He had pulled a string, and I wasn't it.

I lifted the phone and called C. and A.

The voice on the other end said smartly, "Corporal Shulman, sir."

"Let me speak to Sergeant Wright."

"Who is this calling, sir?"

"Sergeant Marx."

And, to my surprise, the voice said, "*Oh!*" Then, "Just a minute, Sergeant."

Shulman's "*Oh!*" stayed with me while I waited for Wright to come to the phone. Why "*Oh!*"? Who was Shulman? And then, so simply, I knew I'd discovered the string that Grossbart had pulled. In fact, I could hear Grossbart the day he'd discovered Shulman in the PX, or in the bowling alley, or maybe even at services. "Glad to meet you. Where you from? Bronx? Me, too. Do you know So-and-So? And So-and-So? Me, too! You work at C. and A.? Really? Hey, how's chances of getting East? Could you do something? Change something? Swindle, cheat, lie? We gotta help each other, you know. If the Jews in Germany . . ."

Bob Wright answered the phone. "How are you, Nate? How's the pitching arm?"

"Good. Bob, I wonder if you could do me a favor." I heard clearly my own words, and they so reminded me of Grossbart that I dropped more easily than I could have imagined into what I had planned. "This may sound crazy, Bob, but I got a kid here on orders to Monmouth who wants them changed. He had a brother killed in Europe, and he's hot to go to the

Pacific. Says he'd feel like a coward if he wound up Stateside. I don't know, Bob—can anything be done? Put somebody else in the Monmouth slot?"

"Who?" he asked cagily.

"Anybody. First guy in the alphabet. I don't care. The kid just asked if something could be done."

"What's his name?"

"Grossbart, Sheldon."

Wright didn't answer.

"Yeah," I said. "He's a Jewish kid, so he thought I could help him out. You know."

"I guess I can do something," he finally said. "The Major hasn't been around here for weeks. Temporary duty to the golf course. I'll try, Nate, that's all I can say."

"I'd appreciate it, Bob. See you Sunday." And I hung up, perspiring.

The following day, the corrected orders appeared: Fishbein, Fuselli, Fylypowycz, Glinicki, Gromke, Grossbart, Gucwa, Halpern, Hardy . . . Lucky Private Harley Alton was to go to Fort Monmouth, New Jersey, where, for some reason or other, they wanted an enlisted man with infantry training.

After chow that night, I stopped back at the orderly room to straighten out the guard-duty roster. Grossbart was waiting for me. He spoke first.

"You son of a bitch!"

I sat down at my desk, and while he glared at me, I began to make the necessary alterations in the duty roster.

"What do you have against me?" he cried. "Against my family? Would it kill you for me to be near my father, God knows how many months he has left to him?"

"Why so?"

"His heart," Grossbart said. "He hasn't had enough troubles in a lifetime, you've got to add to them. I curse the day I ever met you, Marx! Shulman told me what happened over there. There's no limit to your anti-Semitism, is there? The damage you've done here isn't enough. You have to make a special phone call! You really want me dead!"

I made the last few notations in the duty roster and got up to leave. "Good night, Grossbart."

"You owe me an explanation!" He stood in my path.

"Sheldon, you're the one who owes explanations."

He scowled. "To *you?*"

"To me, I think so—yes. Mostly to Fishbein and Halpern."

"That's right, twist things around. I owe nobody nothing, I've done all I could do for them. Now I think I've got the right to watch out for myself."

"For each other we have to learn to watch out, Sheldon. You told me yourself."

"You call this watching out for me—what you did?"

"No. For all of us."

I pushed him aside and started for the door. I heard his furious breathing behind me, and it sounded like steam rushing from an engine of terrible strength.

"*You'll* be all right," I said from the door. And, I thought, so would Fishbein and Halpern be all right, even in the Pacific, if only Grossbart continued to see—in the obsequiousness of the one, the soft spirituality of the other—some profit for himself.

I stood outside the orderly room, and I heard Grossbart weeping behind me. Over in the barracks, in the lighted windows, I could see the boys in their T shirts sitting on their bunks talking about their orders, as they'd been doing for the past two days. With a kind of quiet nervousness, they polished shoes, shined belt buckles, squared away underwear, trying as best they could to accept their fate. Behind me, Grossbart swallowed hard, accepting his. And then, resisting with all my will an impulse to turn and seek pardon for my vindictiveness, I accepted my own.

Epstein

Michael, the weekend guest, was to spend the night in one of the twin beds in Herbie's old room, where the baseball pictures still hung on the wall. Lou Epstein lay with his wife in the room with the bed pushed cater-corner. His daughter Sheila's bedroom was empty; she was at a meeting with her fiancé, the folk singer. In the corner of her room a childhood teddy bear balanced on its bottom, a VOTE SOCIALIST button pinned to its left ear; on her bookshelves, where volumes of Louisa May Alcott once gathered dust, were now collected the works of Howard Fast. The house was quiet. The only light burning was downstairs in the dining room where the *shabus* candles flickered in their tall golden holders and Herbie's *jahrzeit* candle trembled in its glass.

Epstein looked at the dark ceiling of his bedroom and let his head that had been bang-banging all day go blank for a moment. His wife Goldie breathed thickly beside him, as though she suffered from eternal bronchitis. Ten minutes before she had undressed and he had watched as she dropped her white nightdress over her head, over the breasts which had funneled down to her middle, over the behind like a bellows, the thighs and calves veined blue like a roadmap. What once could be pinched, what once was small and tight, now could be poked and pulled. Everything hung. He had shut his eyes while she had dressed for sleep and had tried to remember the Goldie of 1927, the Lou Epstein of 1927. Now he rolled his stomach against her backside, remembering, and reached around to hold her breasts. The nipples were dragged down like a cow's, long as his little finger. He rolled back to his own side.

A key turned in the front door—there was whispering, then the door gently shut. He tensed and waited for the noises—it didn't take those Socialists long. At night the noise from the zipping and the unzipping was enough to keep a man awake. "What are they doing down there?" he had screamed at his wife one Friday night, "trying on clothes?" Now, once again, he waited. It wasn't that he was against their playing. He was no puritan, he believed in young people enjoying themselves. Hadn't he been a young man himself? But in 1927 he and his wife were handsome people. Lou Epstein had never resembled that chinless, lazy smart aleck whose living was earned singing folk songs in a saloon, and who once had asked Epstein if it hadn't been "thrilling" to have lived through "a period of great social upheaval" like the thirties.

And his daughter, why couldn't she have grown up to be like—like the girl across the street whom Michael had the date with, the one whose father had died. Now there was a pretty girl. But not his Sheila. What happened, he wondered, what happened to that little pink-skinned baby? What year, what month did those skinny ankles grow thick as logs, the peaches-and-cream turn to pimples? That lovely child was now a twenty-three-year-old woman with "a social conscience"! Some conscience, he thought. She hunts all day for a picket line to march in so that at night she can come home and eat like a horse . . . For her and that guitar plucker to touch each other's unmentionables seemed worse than sinful—it was disgusting. When Epstein tossed in bed and heard their panting and the zipping it sounded in his ears like thunder.

Zip!

They were at it. He would ignore them, think of his other problems. The business . . . here he was a year away from the retirement he had planned but with no heir to Epstein Paper Bag Company. He had built the business from the ground, suffered and bled during the Depression and Roosevelt, only, finally, with the war and Eisenhower to see it succeed. The thought of a stranger taking it over made him sick. But what could be done? Herbie, who would have been twenty-eight, had died of polio, age eleven. And Sheila, his last hope, had chosen as her intended a lazy man. What could he do? Does a man of fifty-nine all of a sudden start producing heirs?

Zip! Pant-pant-pant! Ahh!

He shut his ears and mind, tighter. He tried to recollect things and drown himself in them. For instance, dinner . . .

He had been startled when he arrived home from the shop to find the soldier sitting at his dinner table. Surprised because the boy, whom he had not seen for ten or twelve years, had grown up with the Epstein face, as his son would have, the small bump in the nose, the strong chin, dark skin, and shock of shiny black hair that, one day, would turn gray as clouds.

"Look who's here," his wife shouted at him the moment he entered the door, the day's dirt still under his fingernails. "Sol's boy."

The soldier popped up from his chair and extended his hand. "How do you do, Uncle Louis?"

"A Gregory Peck," Epstein's wife said, "a Monty Clift your brother has. He's been here only three hours already he has a date. And a regular gentleman . . ."

Epstein did not answer.

The soldier stood at attention, square, as though he'd learned courtesy long before the Army. "I hope you don't mind my barging in, Uncle Louis. I was shipped to Monmouth last week and Dad said I should stop off to see you people. I've got the weekend off and Aunt Goldie said I should stay—" He waited.

"Look at him," Goldie was saying, "a Prince!"

"Of course," Epstein said at last, "stay. How is your father?" Epstein had not spoken to his brother Sol since 1945 when he had bought Sol's share of the business and his brother had moved to Detroit, with words.

"Dad's fine," Michael said. "He sends his regards."

"Sure, I send mine too. You'll tell him."

Michael sat down, and Epstein knew that the boy must think just as his father did: that Lou Epstein was a coarse man whose heart beat faster only when he was thinking of Epstein Paper Bag.

When Sheila came home they all sat down to eat, four, as in the old days. Goldie Epstein jumped up and down, up and down, slipping each course under their noses the instant they had finished the one before. "Michael," she said historically, "Michael, as a child you were a very poor eater. Your sister Ruthie, God bless her, was a nice eater. Not a good eater, but a nice eater."

For the first time Epstein remembered his little niece Ruthie, a little dark-haired beauty, a Bible Ruth. He looked at his own daughter and heard his wife go on, and on. "No, Ruthie wasn't such a good eater. But she wasn't a picky eater.

Our Herbie, he should rest in peace, was a picky eater . . ."
Goldie looked towards her husband as though he would remember precisely what category of eater his beloved son had
been; he stared into his pot roast.

"But," Goldie Epstein resumed, "you should live and be
well, Michael, you turned out to be a good eater . . ."

Ahhh! Ahhh!

The noises snapped Epstein's recollection in two.

Aaahhhh!

Enough was enough. He got out of bed, made certain that
he was tucked into his pajamas, and started down to the living
room. He would give them a piece of his mind. He would tell
them that—that 1927 was not 1957! No, that was what they
would tell him.

But in the living room it was not Sheila and the folk singer.
Epstein felt the cold from the floor rush up the loose legs of
his pajamas and chill his crotch, raising goose flesh on his
thighs. They did not see him. He retreated a step, back behind
the archway to the dining room. His eyes, however, remained
fixed on the living room floor, on Sol's boy and the girl from
across the street.

The girl had been wearing shorts and a sweater. Now they
were thrown over the arm of the sofa. The light from the candles was enough for Epstein to see that she was naked. Michael
lay beside her, squirming and potent, wearing only his army
shoes and khaki socks. The girl's breasts were like two small
white cups. Michael kissed them, and more. Epstein tingled;
he did not dare move, he did not want to move, until the two,
like cars in a railroad yard, slammed fiercely together, coupled,
shook. In their noise Epstein tiptoed, trembling, up the stairs
and back to his wife's bed.

He could not force himself to sleep for what seemed like
hours, not until the door had opened downstairs and the two
young people had left. When, a minute or so later, he heard
another key turn in the lock he did not know whether it was
Michael returning to go to sleep, or—

Zip!

Now it was Sheila and the folk singer! The whole world, he
thought, the whole young world, the ugly ones and the pretty
ones, the fat and the skinny ones, zipping and unzipping!

He grabbed his great shock of gray hair and pulled it till his scalp hurt. His wife shuffled, mumbled a noise. "Brrr . . . brrrrr . . ." She captured the blankets and pulled them over her. "Brrr . . ."

Butter! She's dreaming about butter. Recipes she dreams while the world zips. He closed his eyes and pounded himself down down into an old man's sleep.

2

How far back must you go to discover the beginning of trouble? Later, when Epstein had more time he would ask himself this question. When did it begin? That night he'd seen those two on the floor? Or the summer night seventeen years before when he had pushed the doctor away from the bed and put his lips to his Herbie's? Or, Epstein wondered, was it that night fifteen years ago when instead of smelling a woman between his sheets he smelled Bab-o? Or the time when his daughter had first called him "capitalist" as though it were a dirty name, as though it were a crime to be successful? Or was it none of these times? Maybe to look for a beginning was only to look for an excuse. Hadn't the trouble, the big trouble, begun simply when it appeared to, the morning he saw Ida Kaufman waiting for the bus?

And about Ida Kaufman, why in God's name was it a stranger, nobody he loved or ever could love, who had finally changed his life?—she, who had lived across the street for less than a year, and who (it was revealed by Mrs. Katz, the neighborhood Winchell) would probably sell her house now that Mr. Kaufman was dead and move all-year-round into their summer cottage at Barnegat? Until that morning Epstein had not more than noticed the woman: dark, good-looking, a big chest. She hardly spoke to the other housewives, but spent every moment, until a month ago, caring for her cancer-eaten husband. Once or twice Epstein had tipped his hat to her, but even then he had been more absorbed in the fate of Epstein Paper Bag than in the civility he was practicing. Actually then, on that Monday morning it would not have been unlikely for him to have driven right past the bus stop. It was a warm April day, certainly not a bad day to be waiting for a bus. Birds fussed and sang in the elm trees, and the sun glinted in the sky like a young athlete's trophy. But the woman at the bus stop wore a thin dress and no coat, and Epstein saw her waiting, and beneath the dress, the stockings, the imagined underthings he saw the body of the girl on his living room rug, for Ida Kaufman was the mother of Linda Kaufman, the girl Michael had befriended. So Epstein pulled slowly to the curb and, stopping for the daughter, picked up the mother.

"Thank you, Mr. Epstein," she said. "This is kind of you."

"It's nothing," Epstein said. "I'm going to Market Street."

"Market Street will be fine."

He pressed down too hard on the accelerator and the big Chrysler leaped away, noisy as a hot-rodder's Ford. Ida Kaufman rolled down her window and let the breeze waft in; she lit a cigarette. After a while she asked, "That was your nephew, wasn't it, that took Linda out Saturday night?"

"Michael? Yes." Epstein flushed, for reasons Ida Kaufman did not know. He felt the red on his neck and coughed to make it appear that some respiratory failure had caused the blood to rush up from his heart.

"He's a very nice boy, extremely polite," she said.

"My brother Sol's," Epstein said, "in Detroit." And he shifted his thoughts to Sol so that the flush might fade: if there had been no words with Sol it would be Michael who would be heir to Epstein Paper Bag. Would he have wanted that? Was it any better than a stranger . . . ?

While Epstein thought, Ida Kaufman smoked, and they drove on without speaking, under the elm trees, the choir of birds, and the new spring sky unfurled like a blue banner.

"He looks like you," she said.

"What? Who?"

"Michael."

"No," Epstein said, "him, he's the image of Sol."

"No, no, don't deny it—" and she exploded with laughter, smoke dragoning out of her mouth; she jerked her head back mightily, "No, no, no, he's got your face!"

Epstein looked at her, wondering: the lips, big and red, over her teeth, grinning. Why? Of course—your little boy looks like the iceman, she'd made that joke. He grinned, mostly at the thought of going to bed with his sister-in-law, whose everything had dropped even lower than his wife's.

Epstein's grin provoked Ida Kaufman into more extravagant mirth. What the hell, he decided, he would try a joke himself.

"Your Linda, who does *she* look like?"

Ida Kaufman's mouth straightened; her lids narrowed, killing the light in her eyes. Had he said the wrong thing? Stepped too far? Defiled the name of a dead man, a man who'd had cancer yet? But no, for suddenly she raised her arms in front of her, and shrugged her shoulders as though to say, "Who knows, Epstein, who knows?"

Epstein roared. It was so long since he had been with a woman who had a sense of humor; his wife took everything he said seriously. Not Ida Kaufman, though—she laughed so hard her breasts swelled over the top of her tan dress. They were not cups but pitchers. The next thing Epstein knew he was telling her another joke, and another, in the middle of which a cop screamed up alongside him and gave him a ticket for a red light which, in his joy, he had not seen. It was the first of three tickets he received that day; he earned a second racing down to Barnegat later that morning, and a third speeding up the Parkway at dusk, trying not to be late for dinner. The tickets cost him $32 in all, but, as he told Ida, when you're laughing so hard you have tears in your eyes, how can you tell the green lights from the red ones, fast from slow?

At seven o'clock that evening he returned Ida to the bus stop on the corner and squeezed a bill into her hands.

"Here," he said. "Here—buy something"; which brought the day's total to fifty-two.

Then he turned up the street, already prepared with a story for his wife: a man interested in buying Epstein Paper Bag had kept him away all day, a good prospect. As he pulled into his driveway he saw his wife's square shape back of the venetian blinds. She ran one hand across a slat, checking for dust while she awaited her husband's homecoming.

3

Prickly heat?

He clutched his pajama trousers around his knees and looked at himself in the bedroom mirror. Downstairs a key turned in the lock but he was too engaged to hear it. Prickly heat is what Herbie always had—a child's complaint. Was it possible for a grown man to have it? He shuffled closer to the mirror, tripping on his half-hoisted pajamas. Maybe it was a sand rash. Sure, he thought, for during those three warm, sunny weeks, he and Ida Kaufman, when they were through, would rest on the beach in front of the cottage. Sand must have gotten into his trousers and irritated him on the drive up the Parkway. He stepped back now and was squinting at himself in the mirror when Goldie walked into the bedroom. She had just emerged from a hot tub—her bones ached, she had said—and her flesh was boiled red. Her entrance startled Epstein, who had been contemplating his blemish with the intensity of a philosopher. When he turned swiftly from his reflection, his feet caught in his pants leg, he tripped, and the pajamas slipped to the floor. So there they were, naked as Adam and Eve, except that Goldie was red all over, and Epstein had prickly heat, or a sand rash, or—and it came to him as a first principle comes to a metaphysician. Of course! His hands shot down to cover his crotch.

Goldie looked at him, mystified, while Epstein searched for words appropriate to his posture.

At last: "You had a nice bath?"

"Nice, schmice, it was a bath," his wife mumbled.

"You'll catch a cold," Epstein said. "Put something on."

"I'll catch a cold? *You'll* catch a cold!" She looked at the hands laced across his crotch. "Something hurts?"

"It's a little chilly," he said.

"Where?" She motioned towards his protection. "There?"

"All over."

"Then cover all over."

He leaned over to pick up his pajama trousers; the instant he dropped the fig leaf of his hands Goldie let out a short airless gasp. "What is *that*?"

"What?"

"That!"

He could not look into the eyes of her face, so concentrated instead on the purple eyes of her droopy breasts. "A sand rash, I think."

"*Vus far* sand!"

"A rash then," he said.

She stepped up closer and reached out her hand, not to touch but to point. She drew a little circle of the area with her index finger. "A rash, there?"

"Why not there?" Epstein said. "It's like a rash on the hand or the chest. A rash is a rash."

"But how come all of a sudden?" his wife said.

"Look, I'm not a doctor," Epstein said. "It's there today, maybe tomorrow it'll be gone. How do I know! I probably got it from the toilet seat at the shop. The *shvartzes* are pigs—"

Goldie made a clicking sound with her tongue.

"You're calling me a liar?"

She looked up. "Who said liar?" And she gave her own form a swift looking-over, checked limbs, stomach, breasts, to see if she had perhaps caught the rash from him. She looked back at her husband, then at her own body again, and suddenly her eyes widened. "You!" she screamed.

"Shah," Epstein said, "you'll wake Michael."

"You pig! Who, who was it!"

"I told you, the *shvartzes*—"

"Liar! Pig!" Wheeling her way back to the bed, she flopped onto it so hard the springs squeaked. "Liar!" And then she was off the bed pulling the sheets from it. "I'll burn them, I'll burn every one!"

Epstein stepped out of the pajamas that roped his ankles and raced to the bed. "What are you doing—it's not catching. Only on the toilet seat. You'll buy a little ammonia—"

"Ammonia!" she yelled, "you should *drink* ammonia!"

"No," Epstein shouted, "no," and he grabbed the sheets from her and threw them back over the bed, tucking them in madly. "Leave it be—" He ran to the back of the bed but as he tucked there Goldie raced around and ripped up what he had tucked in the front; so he raced back to the front while Goldie raced around to the back. "Don't touch me," she screamed, "don't come near me, you filthy pig! Go touch some filthy whore!" Then she yanked the sheets off again in one swoop, held them in a ball before her and spat. Epstein grabbed them back and the tug-of-war began, back and forth, back and forth, until they had torn them to shreds. Then for the first time Goldie cried. With white strips looped over her arms she began to sob. "My sheets, my nice clean sheets—" and she threw herself on the bed.

Two faces appeared in the doorway of the bedroom. Sheila Epstein groaned, "Holy Christ!"; the folk singer peeped in, once, twice, and then bobbed out, his feet scuttling down the stairs. Epstein whipped some white strands about him to cover his privates. He did not say a word as his daughter entered.

"Mamma, what's the matter?"

"Your father," the voice groaned from the bed, "he has—a rash!" And so violently did she begin to sob that the flesh on her white buttocks rippled and jumped.

"That's right," Epstein said, "a rash. That's a crime? Get out of here! Let your mother and father get some sleep."

"Why is she crying?" Sheila demanded. "I want an answer!"

"How do I know! I'm a mind reader? This whole family is crazy, who knows what they think!"

"Don't call my mother crazy!"

"Don't you raise your voice to me! Respect your father!" He pulled the white strips tighter around him. "Now get out of here!"

"No!"

"Then I'll throw you out." He started for the door; his daughter did not move, and he could not bring himself to reach out and push her. Instead he threw back his head and addressed the ceiling. "She's picketing my bedroom! Get out, you lummox!" He took a step towards her and growled, as though to scare away a stray cat or dog. With all her one hundred and sixty pounds she pushed her father back; in his surprise and hurt he dropped the sheet. And the daughter looked on the father. Under her lipstick she turned white.

Epstein looked up at her. He pleaded, "I got it from the toilet seat. The *shvartzes*—"

Before he could finish, a new head had popped into the doorway, hair messed and lips swollen and red; it was Michael, home from Linda Kaufman, his regular weekend date. "I heard the noise, is any—" and he saw his aunt naked on the bed. When he turned his eyes away, there was Uncle Lou.

"All of you," Epstein shouted. "Get out!"

But no one obeyed. Sheila blocked the door, politically committed; Michael's legs were rooted, one with shame, the other with curiosity.

"Get out!"

Feet now came pounding up the stairs. "Sheila, should I call somebody—" And then the guitar plucker appeared in the doorway, eager, big-nosed. He surveyed the scene and his gaze, at last, landed on Epstein's crotch; the beak opened.

"What's he got? The syph?"

The words hung for a moment, bringing peace. Goldie Epstein stopped crying and raised herself off the bed. The young men in the doorway lowered their eyes. Goldie arched her back, flopped out her breasts, and began to move her lips. "I want . . ." she said. "I want . . ."

"What, Mamma?" Sheila demanded. "What is it?"

"I want . . . a divorce!" She looked amazed when she said it, though not as amazed as her husband; he smacked his palm to his head.

"Divorce! Are you crazy?" Epstein looked around; to Michael he said, "She's crazy!"

"I want one," she said, and then her eyes rolled up into her head and she passed out across the sheetless mattress.

After the smelling salts Epstein was ordered to bed in Herbie's room. He tossed and turned in the narrow bed which he was unused to; in the twin bed beside him he heard Michael breathing. Monday, he thought, Monday he would seek help. A lawyer. No, first a doctor. Surely in a minute a doctor could take a look and tell him what he already knew—that Ida Kaufman was a clean woman. Epstein would swear by it—he had smelled her flesh! The doctor would reassure him: his blemish resulted simply from their rubbing together. It was a temporary thing, produced by two, not transmitted by one. He was innocent! Unless what made him guilty had nothing to do with some dirty bug. But either way the doctor would prescribe for him. And then the lawyer would prescribe. And by then everyone would know, including, he suddenly realized, his brother Sol who would take special pleasure in thinking the worst. Epstein rolled over and looked to Michael's bed. Pinpoints of light gleamed in the boy's head; he was awake, and wearing the Epstein nose, chin, and brow.

"Michael?"

"Yes."

"You're awake?"

"Yes."

"Me too," Epstein said, and then apologetically, "all the excitement . . ."

He looked back to the ceiling. "Michael?"

"Yes?"

"Nothing . . ." But he was curious as well as concerned. "Michael, you haven't got a rash, have you?"

Michael sat up in bed; firmly he said, "No."

"I just thought," Epstein said quickly. "You know, I have this rash . . ." He dwindled off and looked away from the boy, who, it occurred to him again, might have been heir to the business if that stupid Sol hadn't . . . But what difference did the business make now. The business had never been for him, but for them. And there was no more them.

He put his hands over his eyes. "The change, the change," he said. "I don't even know when it began. Me, Lou Epstein, with a rash. I don't even feel any more like Lou Epstein. All of a sudden, pffft! and things are changed." He looked at Michael again, speaking slowly now, stressing every word, as though the boy were more than a nephew, more, in fact, than a single person. "All my life I tried. I swear it, I should drop dead on the spot, if all my life I didn't try to do right, to give my family what I didn't have . . ."

He stopped; it was not exactly what he wanted to say. He flipped on the bedside light and started again, a new way. "I was seven years old, Michael. I came here I was a boy seven years old, and that day, I can remember it like it was yesterday. Your grandparents and me—your father wasn't born yet, this stuff believe me he doesn't know. With your grandparents I stood on the dock, waiting for Charlie Goldstein to pick us up. He was your grandfather's partner in the old country, the thief. Anyway, we waited, and finally he came to pick us up, to take us where we would live. And when he came he had a big can in his hand. And you know what was in it? Kerosene. We stood there and Charlie Goldstein poured it on all our heads. He rubbed it in, to delouse us. It tasted awful. For a little boy it was awful . . ."

Michael shrugged his shoulder.

"Eh! How can you understand?" Epstein grumbled. "What do you know? Twenty years old . . ."

Michael shrugged again. "Twenty-two," he said softly.

There were more stories Epstein could tell, but he wondered if any of them would bring him closer to what it was he had on his mind but could not find the words for. He got out of bed and walked to the bedroom door. He opened it and stood there listening. On the downstairs sofa he could hear the folk singer snoring. Some night for guests! He shut the door and came back into the room, scratching his thigh. "Believe me, *she's* not losing any sleep . . . She doesn't deserve me. What, she cooks? That's a big deal? She cleans? That deserves a medal? One day I should come home and the house should be a *mess*. I should be able to write my initials in the dust, somewhere, in the basement at least. Michael, after all these years that would be a pleasure!" He grabbed at his gray hair. "How did this happen? My Goldie, that such a woman should become a cleaning machine. Impossible." He walked to the far wall and stared into Herbie's baseball pictures, the long jaw-muscled faces, faded technicolor now, with signatures at the bottom: Charlie Keller, Lou Gehrig, Red Ruffing . . . A long time. How Herbie had loved his Yankees.

"One night," Epstein started again, "it was before the Depression even . . . you know what we did, Goldie and me?" He was staring at Red Ruffing now, through him. "You didn't know my Goldie, what a beautiful beautiful woman she was. And that night we took pictures, photos. I set up the camera— it was in the old house—and we took pictures, in the bedroom." He stopped, remembered. "I wanted a picture of my wife naked, to carry with me. I admit it. The next morning I woke up and there was Goldie tearing up the negatives. She said God forbid I should get in an accident one day and the police would take out my wallet for identification, and then oy-oy-oy!" He smiled. "You know, a woman, she worries . . . But at least we took the pictures, even if we didn't develop them. How many people even do that?" He wondered, and then turned away from Red Ruffing to Michael, who was, faintly, at the corners of his mouth, smiling.

"What, the photos?"

Michael started to giggle.

"Huh?" Epstein smiled. "What, you never had that kind of idea? I admit it. Maybe to someone else it would seem wrong, a sin or something, but who's to say—"

Michael stiffened, at last his father's son. "Somebody's got to say. Some things just aren't right."

Epstein was willing to admit a youthful lapse. "Maybe," he said, "maybe she was even right to tear—"

Michael shook his head vehemently. "No! Some things aren't right. They're just not!"

And Epstein saw the finger pointing not at Uncle Lou the Photographer, but at Uncle Lou the Adulterer. Suddenly he was shouting. "Right, wrong! From you and your father that's all I ever hear. Who are you, what are you, King Solomon!" He gripped the bedposts. "Should I tell you what else happened the night we took pictures? That my Herbie was started that night, I'm sure of it. Over a year we tried and tried till I was *oysgamitched*, and that was the night. After the pictures, because of the pictures. Who knows!"

"But—"

"But what! But *this?*" He was pointing at his crotch. "You're a boy, you don't understand. When they start taking things away from you, you reach out, you *grab*—maybe like a pig even, but you grab. And right, wrong, who knows! With tears in your eyes, who can even see the difference!" His voice dropped now, but in a minor key the scolding grew more fierce. "Don't call *me* names. I didn't see you with Ida's girl, there's not a name for that? For *you* it's right?"

Michael was kneeling in his bed now. "*You—saw?*"

"I saw!"

"But it's different—"

"Different?" Epstein shouted.

"To be married is different!"

"What's different you don't know about. To have a wife, to be a father, twice a father—and then they start taking things away—" and he fell weak-kneed across Michael's bed. Michael leaned back and looked at his uncle, but he did not know what to do or how to chastise, for he had never seen anybody over fifteen years old cry before.

4

Usually Sunday morning went like this: at nine-thirty Goldie started the coffee and Epstein walked to the corner for the lox and the Sunday *News*. When the lox was on the table, the bagels in the oven, the rotogravure section of the *News* two inches from Goldie's nose, then Sheila would descend the stairs, yawning, in her toe-length housecoat. They would sit down to eat, Sheila cursing her father for buying the *News* and "putting money in a Fascist's pocket." Outside, the Gentiles would be walking to church. It had always been the same, except, of course, that over the years the *News* had come closer to Goldie's nose and further from Sheila's heart; she had the *Post* delivered.

This Sunday, when he awoke, Epstein smelled coffee bubbling in the kitchen. When he sneaked down the stairs, past the kitchen—he had been ordered to use the basement bathroom until he'd seen a doctor—he could smell lox. And, at last, when he entered the kitchen, shaved and dressed, he heard newspapers rattling. It was as if another Epstein, his ghost, had risen an hour earlier and performed his Sunday duties. Beneath the clock, around the table, sat Sheila, the folk singer, and Goldie. Bagels toasted in the oven, while the folk singer, sitting backwards in a chair, strummed his guitar and sang—

> *I've been down so long*
> *It look like up to me . . .*

Epstein clapped his hands and rubbed them together, preparatory to eating. "Sheila, you went out for this?" He gestured towards the paper and the lox. "Thank you."

The folk singer looked up, and in the same tune, improvised—

> *I went out for the lox . . .*

and grinned, a regular clown.

"Shut up!" Sheila told him.

He echoed her words, plunk! plunk!

"Thank *you*, then, young man," Epstein said.

"His name is Marvin," Sheila said, "for your information."

"Thank you, Martin."

"Mar*vin*," the young man said.

"I don't hear so good."

Goldie Epstein looked up from the paper. "Syphilis softens the brain."

"What!"

"Syphilis softens the brain . . ."

Epstein stood up, raging. "Did you tell her that?" he shouted at his daughter. "Who told her that?"

The folk singer stopped plucking his guitar. Nobody answered; a conspiracy. He grabbed his daughter by the shoulders. "You respect your father, you understand!"

She jerked her shoulder away. "You're not *my* father!"

And the words hurled him back—to the joke Ida Kaufman had made in the car, to her tan dress, the spring sky . . . He leaned across the table to his wife. "Goldie, Goldie, look at me! Look at *me*, Lou!"

She stared back into the newspaper, though she held it far enough from her nose for Epstein to know she could not see the print; with everything else, the optometrist said the muscles in her eyes had loosened. "Goldie," he said, "Goldie, I did the worst thing in the world? Look me in the eyes, Goldie. Tell me, since when do Jewish people get a divorce? Since when?"

She looked up at him, and then at Sheila. "Syphilis makes soft brains. I can't live with a pig!"

"We'll work it out. We'll go to the rabbi—"

"He wouldn't recognize you—"

"But the children, what about the children?"

"What children?"

Herbie was dead and Sheila a stranger; she was right.

"A grown-up child can take care of herself," Goldie said. "If she wants, she can come to Florida with me. I'm thinking I'll move to Miami Beach."

"Goldie!"

"Stop shouting," Sheila said, anxious to enter the brawl. "You'll wake Michael."

Painfully polite, Goldie addressed her daughter. "Michael left early this morning. He took his Linda to the beach for the day, to their place in Belmar."

"Barnegat," Epstein grumbled, retreating from the table.

"What did you say?" Sheila demanded.

"Barnegat." And he decided to leave the house before any further questions were asked.

At the corner luncheonette he bought his own paper and sat alone, drinking coffee and looking out the window beyond which the people walked to church. A pretty young *shiksa* walked by, holding her white round hat in her hand; she bent over to remove her shoe and shake a pebble from it. Epstein watched her bend, and he spilled some coffee on his shirt front. The girl's small behind was round as an apple beneath the close-fitting dress. He looked, and then as though he was praying, he struck himself on the chest with his fist, again and again. "What have I done! Oh, God!"

When he finished his coffee, he took his paper and started up the street. To home? What home? Across the street in her backyard he saw Ida Kaufman, who was wearing shorts and a halter, and was hanging her daughter's underwear on the clothesline. Epstein looked around and saw only the Gentiles walking to church. Ida saw him and smiled. Growing angry, he stepped off the curb and, passionately, began to jaywalk.

At noon in the Epstein house those present heard a siren go off. Sheila looked up from the *Post* and listened; she looked at her watch. "Noon? I'm fifteen minutes slow. This lousy watch, my father's present."

Goldie Epstein was leafing through the ads in the travel section of the *New York Times*, which Marvin had gone out to buy for her. She looked at her watch. "I'm fourteen minutes slow. Also," she said to her daughter, "a watch from him . . ."

The wail grew louder. "God," Sheila said, "it sounds like the end of the world."

And Marvin, who had been polishing his guitar with his red handkerchief, immediately broke into song, a high-pitched, shut-eyed Negro tune about the end of the world.

"Quiet!" Sheila said. She cocked her ear. "But it's Sunday. The sirens are Saturday—"

Goldie shot off the couch. "It's a real air raid? Oy, that's all we need!"

"It's the police," Sheila said, and fiery-eyed she raced to the front door, for she was politically opposed to police. "It's coming up the street—an ambulance!"

She raced out the door, followed by Marvin, whose guitar still hung around his neck. Goldie trailed behind, her feet slapping against her slippers. On the street she suddenly turned back to the house to make sure the door was shut against daytime burglars, bugs, and dust. When she turned again she had not far to run. The ambulance had pulled up across the street in Kaufman's driveway.

Already a crowd had gathered, neighbors in bathrobes, housecoats, carrying the comic sections with them; and too, churchgoers, *shiksas* in white hats. Goldie could not make her way to the front where her daughter and Marvin stood, but even from the rear of the crowd she could see a young doctor leap from the ambulance and race up to the porch, his stethoscope wiggling in his back pocket as he took two steps at a time.

Mrs. Katz arrived. A squat red-faced woman whose stomach seemed to start at her knees, she tugged at Goldie's arm. "Goldie, more trouble here?"

"I don't know, Pearl. All that racket. It sounded like an atomic bomb."

"When it's that, you'll know," Pearl Katz said. She surveyed the crowd, then looked at the house. "Poor woman," she said, remembering that only three months before, on a windy March morning an ambulance had arrived to take Mrs. Kaufman's husband to the nursing home, from which he never returned.

"Troubles, troubles . . ." Mrs. Katz was shaking her head, a pot of sympathy. "Everybody has their little bundle, believe me. I'll bet she had a nervous breakdown. That's not a good thing. Gallstones, you have them out and they're out. But a nervous breakdown, it's very bad . . . You think maybe it's the daughter who's sick?"

"The daughter isn't home," Goldie said. "She's away with my nephew, Michael."

Mrs. Katz saw that no one had emerged from the house yet; she had time to gather a little information. "He's who, Goldie?

The son of the brother-in-law that Lou doesn't talk to? That's his father?"

"Yes, Sol in Detroit—"

But she broke off, for the front door had opened, though still no one could be seen. A voice at the front of the crowd was commanding. "A little room here. Please! A little room, damn it!" It was Sheila. "A little room! Marvin, help me!"

"I can't put down my guitar—I can't find a place—"

"Get them back!" Sheila said.

"But my instrument—"

The doctor and his helper were now wiggling and tilting the stretcher through the front door. Behind them stood Mrs. Kaufman, a man's white shirt tucked into her shorts. Her eyes peered out of two red holes; she wore no make-up, Mrs. Katz noted.

"It must be the girl," said Pearl Katz, up on her toes. "Goldie, can you see, who is it—it's the girl?"

"The girl's *away*—"

"Stay back!" Sheila commanded. "Marvin, for crying out loud, help!"

The young doctor and his attendant held the stretcher steady as they walked sideways down the front steps.

Mrs. Katz jumped up and down. "Who *is* it?"

"I can't see," Goldie said. "I can't—" She pushed up on her toes, out of her slippers. "I—oh God! My God!" And she was racing forward, screaming, "Lou! Lou!"

"Mamma, stay back." Sheila found herself fighting off her mother. The stretcher was sliding into the ambulance now.

"Sheila, let me go, it's your father!" She pointed to the ambulance, whose red eye spun slowly on top. For a moment Goldie looked back to the steps. Ida Kaufman stood there yet, her fingers fidgeting at the buttons of the shirt. Then Goldie broke for the ambulance, her daughter beside her, propelling her by her elbows.

"Who are you?" the doctor said. He took a step towards them to stop their forward motion, for it seemed as if they intended to dive right into the ambulance on top of his patient.

"The wife—" Sheila shouted.

The doctor pointed to the porch. "Look, lady—"

"I'm the *wife*," Goldie cried. "Me!"

The doctor looked at her. "Get in."

Goldie wheezed as Sheila and the doctor helped her into the ambulance, and she let out a gigantic gasp when she saw the white face sticking up from the gray blanket; his eyes were closed, his skin grayer than his hair. The doctor pushed Sheila aside, climbed in, and then the ambulance was moving, the siren screaming. Sheila ran after the ambulance a moment, hammering on the door, but then she turned the other way and was headed back through the crowd and up the stairs to Ida Kaufman's house.

Goldie turned to the doctor. "He's dead?"

"No, he had a heart attack."

She smacked her face.

"He'll be all right," the doctor said.

"But a heart attack. Never in his life."

"A man sixty, sixty-five, it happens." The doctor snapped the answers back while he held Epstein's wrist.

"He's only fifty-nine."

"Some only," the doctor said.

The ambulance zoomed through a red light and made a sharp right turn that threw Goldie to the floor. She sat there and spoke. "But how does a healthy man—"

"Lady, don't ask questions. A grown man can't act like a boy."

She put her hands over her eyes as Epstein opened his.

"He's awake now," the doctor said. "Maybe he wants to hold your hand or something."

Goldie crawled to his side and looked at him. "Lou, you're all right? Does anything hurt?"

He did not answer. "He knows it's me?"

The doctor shrugged his shoulders. "Tell him."

"It's me, Lou."

"It's your wife, Lou," the doctor said. Epstein blinked his eyes. "He knows," the doctor said. "He'll be all right. All he's got to do is live a normal life, normal for sixty."

"You hear the doctor, Lou. All you got to do is live a normal life."

Epstein opened his mouth. His tongue hung over his teeth like a dead snake.

"Don't you talk," his wife said. "Don't you worry about

anything. Not even the business. That'll work out. Our Sheila will marry Marvin and that'll be that. You won't have to sell, Lou, it'll be in the family. You can retire, rest, and Marvin can take over. He's a smart boy, Marvin, a *mensch*."

Lou rolled his eyes in his head.

"Don't try to talk. I'll take care. You'll be better soon and we can go someplace. We can go to Saratoga, to the mineral baths, if you want. We'll just go, you and me—" Suddenly she gripped his hand. "Lou, you'll live normal, won't you? *Won't you?*" She was crying, "'Cause what'll happen, Lou, is you'll kill yourself! You'll keep this up and that'll be the end—"

"All right," the young doctor said, "you take it easy now. We don't want two patients on our hands."

The ambulance was pulling down and around into the side entrance of the hospital and the doctor knelt at the back door.

"I don't know why I'm crying." Goldie wiped her eyes. "He'll be all right? You say so, I believe you, you're a doctor." And as the young man swung open the door with the big red cross painted on the back, she asked, softly, "Doctor, you have something that will cure what else he's got—this rash?" She pointed.

The doctor looked at her. Then he lifted for a moment the blanket that covered Epstein's nakedness.

"Doctor, it's bad?"

Goldie's eyes and nose were running.

"An irritation," the doctor said.

She grabbed his wrist. "You can clean it up?"

"So it'll never come back," the doctor said, and hopped out of the ambulance.

You Can't Tell a Man by the Song He Sings

IT WAS in a freshman high school class called "Occupations" that, fifteen years ago, I first met the ex-con, Alberto Pelagutti. The first week my new classmates and I were given "a battery of tests" designed to reveal our skills, deficiencies, tendencies, and psyches. At the end of the week, Mr. Russo, the Occupations teacher, would add the skills, subtract the deficiencies, and tell us what jobs best suited our talents; it was all mysterious but scientific. I remember we first took a "Preference Test": "Which would you prefer to do, this, that, or the other thing . . ." Albie Pelagutti sat one seat behind me and to my left, and while this first day of high school I strolled happily through the test, examining ancient fossils here, defending criminals there, Albie, like the inside of Vesuvius, rose, fell, pitched, tossed, and swelled in his chair. When he finally made a decision, he made it. You could hear his pencil drive the *x* into the column opposite the activity in which he thought it wisest to prefer to engage. His agony reinforced the legend that had preceded him: he was seventeen; had just left Jamesburg Reformatory; this was his third high school, his third freshman year; but now—I heard another *x* driven home—he had decided "to go straight."

Halfway through the hour Mr. Russo left the room. "I'm going for a drink," he said. Russo was forever at pains to let us know what a square-shooter he was and that, unlike other teachers we might have had, he would not go out the front door of the classroom to sneak around to the back door and observe how responsible we were. And sure enough, when he returned after going for a drink, his lips were wet; when he came back from the men's room, you could smell the soap on his hands. "Take your time, boys," he said, and the door swung shut behind him.

His black wingtipped shoes beat down the marble corridor and five thick fingers dug into my shoulder. I turned around; it was Pelagutti. "What?" I said. "Number twenty-six," Pelagutti

said, "What's the answer?" I gave him the truth: "Anything."
Pelagutti rose halfway over his desk and glared at me. He was
a hippopotamus, big, black, and smelly; his short sleeves
squeezed tight around his monstrous arms as though they were
taking his own blood pressure—which at that moment was sky-
bound: "What's the answer!" Menaced, I flipped back three
pages in my question booklet and reread number twenty-six.
"Which would you prefer to do: (1) Attend a World Trade
Convention. (2) Pick cherries. (3) Stay with and read to a sick
friend. (4) Tinker with automobile engines." I looked blank-
faced back to Albie, and shrugged my shoulders. "It doesn't
matter—there's no right answer. Anything." He almost rock-
eted out of his seat. "Don't give me that crap! What's the answer!" Strange heads popped up all over the room—thin-eyed
glances, hissing lips, shaming grins—and I realized that any
minute Russo, wet-lipped, might come back and my first day
in high school I would be caught cheating. I looked again at
number twenty-six; then back to Albie; and then propelled—
as I always was towards him—by anger, pity, fear, love, ven-
geance, and an instinct for irony that was at the time delicate as
a mallet, I whispered, "Stay and read to a sick friend." The vol-
cano subsided, and Albie and I had met.

We became friends. He remained at my elbow throughout
the testing, then throughout lunch, then after school. I learned
that Albie, as a youth, had done all the things I, under direction, had not: he had eaten hamburgers in strange diners; he
had gone out after cold showers, wet-haired, into winter
weather; he had been cruel to animals; he had trafficked with
whores; he had stolen, he had been caught, and he had paid.
But now he told me, as I unwrapped my lunch in the candy
store across from school, "Now, I'm through crappin' around.
I'm gettin' an education. I'm gonna—" and I think he picked
up the figure from a movie musical he had seen the previous
afternoon while the rest of us were in English class— "I'm
gonna put my best foot forward." The following week when
Russo read the results of the testing it appeared that Albie's
feet were not only moving forward but finding strange, wonderful paths. Russo sat at his desk, piles of tests stacked before
him like ammunition, charts and diagrams mounted huge on

either side, and delivered our destinies. Albie and I were going to be lawyers.

Of all that Albie confessed to me that first week, one fact in particular fastened on my brain: I soon forgot the town in Sicily where he was born; the occupation of his father (he either made ice or delivered it); the year and model of the cars he had stolen. I did not forget though that Albie had apparently been the star of the Jamesburg Reformatory baseball team. When I was selected by the gym teacher, Mr. Hopper, to captain one of my gym class's softball teams (we played softball until the World Series was over, then switched to touch football), I knew that I had to get Pelagutti on my side. With those arms he could hit the ball a mile.

The day teams were to be selected Albie shuffled back and forth at my side, while in the lockerroom I changed into my gym uniform—jockstrap, khaki-colored shorts, T-shirt, sweat socks, and sneakers. Albie had already changed: beneath his khaki gym shorts he did not wear a support but retained his lavender undershorts; they hung down three inches below the outer shorts and looked like a long fancy hem. Instead of a T-shirt he wore a sleeveless undershirt; and beneath his high, tar-black sneakers he wore thin black silk socks with slender arrows embroidered up the sides. Naked he might, like some centuries-dead ancestor, have tossed lions to their death in the Colosseum; the outfit, though I didn't tell him, detracted from his dignity.

As we left the lockerroom and padded through the dark basement corridor and up onto the sunny September playing field, he talked continually, "I didn't play sports when I was a kid, but I played at Jamesburg and baseball came to me like nothing." I nodded my head. "What you think of Pete Reiser?" he asked. "He's a pretty good man," I said. "What you think of Tommy Henrich?" "I don't know," I answered, "he's dependable, I guess." As a Dodger fan I preferred Reiser to the Yankees' Henrich; and besides, my tastes have always been a bit baroque, and Reiser, who repeatedly bounced off outfield walls to save the day for Brooklyn, had won a special trophy in the Cooperstown of my heart. "Yeh," Albie said, "I like all them Yankees."

I didn't have a chance to ask Albie what he meant by that, for Mr. Hopper, bronzed, smiling, erect, was flipping a coin; I looked up, saw the glint in the sun, and I was calling "heads." It landed tails and the other captain had first choice. My heart flopped over when he looked at Albie's arms, but calmed when he passed on and chose first a tall, lean, first-baseman type. Immediately I said, "I'll take Pelagutti." You don't very often see smiles like the one that crossed Albie Pelagutti's face that moment: you would think I had paroled him from a life sentence.

The game began. I played shortstop—left-handed—and batted second; Albie was in center field and, at his wish, batted fourth. Their first man grounded out, me to the first baseman. The next batter hit a high, lofty fly ball to center field. The moment I saw Albie move after it I knew Tommy Henrich and Pete Reiser were only names to him; all he knew about baseball he'd boned up on the night before. While the ball hung in the air, Albie jumped up and down beneath it, his arms raised upward directly above his head; his wrists were glued together, and his two hands flapped open and closed like a butterfly's wings, begging the ball toward them.

"C'mon," he was screaming to the sky, "c'mon you bastard . . ." And his legs bicycle-pumped up and down, up and down. I hope the moment of my death does not take as long as it did for that damn ball to drop. It hung, it hung, Albie cavorting beneath like a Holy Roller. And then it landed, smack into Albie's chest. The runner was rounding second and heading for third while Albie twirled all around, looking, his arms down now, stretched out, as though he were playing ring-around-a-rosy with two invisible children. "Behind you, Pelagutti!" I screamed. He stopped moving. "What?" he called back to me. I ran halfway out to center field. "Behind you—relay it!" And then, as the runner rounded third, I had to stand there defining "relay" to him.

At the end of the first half of the first inning we came to bat behind, 8–0—eight home runs, all relayed in too late by Pelagutti.

Out of a masochistic delight I must describe Albie at the plate: first, he *faced* the pitcher; then, when he swung at the ball

—and he did, at every one—it was not to the side but down, as though he were driving a peg into the ground. Don't ask if he was right-handed or left-handed. I don't know.

While we changed out of our gym uniforms I was silent. I boiled as I watched Pelagutti from the corner of my eye. He kicked off those crazy black sneakers and pulled his pink gaucho shirt on over his undershirt—there was still a red spot above the U front of the undershirt where the first fly ball had hit him. Without removing his gym shorts he stuck his feet into his gray trousers—I watched as he hoisted the trousers over the red splotches where ground balls had banged off his shins, past the red splotches where pitched balls had smacked his knee caps and thighs.

Finally I spoke, "Damn you, Pelagutti, you wouldn't know Pete Reiser if you fell over him!" He was stuffing his sneakers into his locker; he didn't answer. I was talking to his mountainous pink shirt back. "Where do you come off telling me you played for that prison team?" He mumbled something. "What?" I said. "I did," he grumbled. "Bullshit!" I said. He turned and, black-eyed, glared at me: "I did!" "That must've been some team!" I said. We did not speak as we left the locker-room. As we passed the gym office on our way up to Occupations, Mr. Hopper looked up from his desk and winked at me. Then he motioned his head at Pelagutti to indicate that he knew I'd picked a lemon, but how could I have expected a bum like Pelagutti to be an All-American boy in the first place? Then Mr. Hopper turned his sun-lamped head back to his desk.

"Now," I said to Pelagutti as we turned at the second floor landing, "now I'm stuck with you for the rest of the term." He shuffled ahead of me without answering; his oxlike behind should have had a tail on it to flick the flies away—it infuriated me. "You goddam liar!" I said.

He spun around as fast as an ox can. "You ain't stuck with nobody." We were at the top of the landing headed into the locker-lined corridor; the kids who were piling up the stairs behind stopped, listened. "No you ain't, you snot-ass!" And I saw five hairy knuckles coming right at my mouth. I moved but not in time, and heard a crash inside the bridge of my nose. I felt my hips dip back, my legs and head come forward, and, curved like the letter c, I was swept fifteen feet backward before I felt cold marble beneath the palms of my hands. Albie stepped around me and into the Occupations room. Just then I looked up to see Mr. Russo's black wingtipped shoes enter the room. I'm almost sure he had seen Albie blast me but I'll never know. Nobody, including Albie and myself, ever mentioned it again. Perhaps it had been a mistake for me to call Albie a liar, but if he had starred at baseball, it was in some league I did not know.

By way of contrast I want to introduce Duke Scarpa, another ex-con who was with us that year. Neither Albie nor the Duke, incidentally, was a typical member of my high school community. Both lived at the other end of Newark, "down neck," and they had reached us only after the Board of Education had tried Albie at two other schools and the Duke at four. The Board hoped finally, like Marx, that the higher culture would absorb the lower.

Albie and Duke had no particular use for each other; where Albie had made up his mind to go straight, one always felt that the Duke, in his oily quietness, his boneless grace, was planning a job. Yet, though affection never lived between them, Duke wandered after Albie and me, aware, I suspect, that if Albie despised him it was because he was able to read his soul—and that such an associate was easier to abide than one who despises you because he does not know your soul at all. Where Albie was a hippopotamus, an ox, Duke was reptilian. Me? I don't know; it is easy to spot the animal in one's fellows.

During lunch hour, the Duke and I used to spar with each other in the hall outside the cafeteria. He did not know a hook from a jab and disliked having his dark skin roughened or his hair mussed; but he so delighted in moving, bobbing, coiling, and uncoiling, that I think he would have paid for the privilege of playing the serpent with me. He hypnotized me, the Duke; he pulled some slimy string inside me—where Albie Pelagutti sought and stretched a deeper and, I think, a nobler cord.

But I make Albie sound like peaches-and-cream. Let me tell you what he and I did to Mr. Russo.

Russo believed in his battery of tests as his immigrant parents (and Albie's, and maybe Albie himself) believed in papal infallibility. If the tests said Albie was going to be a lawyer then he was going to be a lawyer. As for Albie's past, it seemed only to increase Russo's devotion to the prophecy: he approached Albie with salvation in his eyes. In September, then, he gave Albie a biography to read, the life of Oliver Wendell Holmes; during October, once a week, he had the poor fellow speak impromptu before the class; in November he had him write a report on the Constitution, which I wrote; and then in December, the final indignity, he sent Albie and me (and two others who displayed a legal bent) to the Essex County Court House where we could see "real lawyers in action."

It was a cold, windy morning and as we flicked our cigarettes at the Lincoln statue on the courtyard plaza, and started up the long flight of white cement steps, Albie suddenly did an about-face and headed back across the plaza and out to Market Street. I called to him but he shouted back that he had seen it all before, and then he was not walking, but running towards the crowded downtown streets, pursued not by police, but by other days. It wasn't that he considered Russo an ass for having sent him to visit the Court House—Albie respected teachers too much for that; rather I think he felt Russo had tried to rub his nose in it.

No surprise, then, when the next day after gym Albie announced his assault on the Occupations teacher; it was the first crime he had planned since his decision to go straight back in September. He outlined the action to me and indicated that I should pass the details on to the other members of the class. As liaison between Albie and the well-behaved, healthy nonconvicts like myself who made up the rest of the class, I was stationed at the classroom door and as each member passed in I unfolded the plot into his ear: "As soon after ten-fifteen as Russo turns to the blackboard, you bend over to tie your shoelaces." If a classmate looked back at me puzzled, I would motion to Pelagutti hulking over his desk; the puzzled expression would vanish and another accomplice would enter the room. The only one who gave me any trouble was the Duke. He listened to the plan and then scowled back at me with the look of a man who's got his own syndicate, and, in fact, has never even heard of yours.

Finally the bell rang; I closed the door behind me and

moved noiselessly to my desk. I waited for the clock to move
to a quarter after; it did; and then Russo turned to the board
to write upon it the salary range of aluminum workers. I bent
to tie my shoelaces—beneath all the desks I saw other upside-
down grinning faces. To my left behind me I heard Albie
hissing; his hands fumbled about his black silk socks, and the
hiss grew and grew until it was a rush of Sicilian, muttered,
spewed, vicious. The exchange was strictly between Russo and
himself. I looked to the front of the classroom, my fingers
knotting and unknotting my shoelaces, the blood pumping
now to my face. I saw Russo's legs turn. What a sight he must
have seen—where there had been twenty-five faces, now there
was nothing. Just desks. "Okay," I heard Russo say, "okay."
And then he gave a little clap with his hands. "That's enough
now, fellas. The joke is over. Sit up." And then Albie's hiss
traveled to all the blood-pinked ears below the desks; it rushed
about us like a subterranean stream—"Stay down!"

While Russo asked us to get up we stayed down. And we did
not sit up until Albie told us to; and then under his direction
we were singing—

> *Don't sit under the apple tree*
> *With anyone else but me,*
> *Anyone else but me,*
> *Anyone else but me,*
> *Oh, no, no, don't sit under the apple tree . . .*

And then in time to the music we clapped. What a noise!

Mr. Russo stood motionless at the front of the class, listening, astonished. He wore a neatly pressed dark blue pin-
striped suit, a tan tie with a collie's head in the center, and a
tieclasp with the initials R.R. engraved upon it; he had on the
black wingtipped shoes; they glittered. Russo, who believed in
neatness, honesty, punctuality, planned destinies—who believed in the future, in Occupations! And next to me, behind
me, inside me, all over me—Albie! We looked at each other,
Albie and I, and my lungs split with joy: "*Don't sit under the
apple tree*—" Albie's monotone boomed out, and then a thick
liquid crooner's voice behind Albie bathed me in sound: it was
the Duke's; he clapped to a tango beat.

Russo leaned for a moment against a visual aids chart—

"Skilled Laborers: Salaries and Requirements" —and then scraped back his chair and plunged down into it, so far down it looked to have no bottom. He lowered his big head to the desk and his shoulders curled forward like the ends of wet paper; and that was when Albie pulled his coup. He stopped singing "Don't Sit Under the Apple Tree"; we all stopped. Russo looked up at the silence; his eyes black and baggy, he stared at our leader, Alberto Pelagutti. Slowly Russo began to shake his head from side to side: this was no Capone, this was a Garibaldi! Russo waited, I waited, we all waited. Albie slowly rose, and began to sing "*Oh, say can you see, by the dawn's early light, what so proudly we hailed—*" And we all stood and joined him. Tears sparkling on his long black lashes, Mr. Robert Russo dragged himself wearily up from his desk, beaten, and as the Pelagutti basso boomed disastrously behind me, I saw Russo's lips begin to move, "*the bombs bursting in air, gave proof—*" God, did we sing!

Albie left school in June of that year—he had passed only Occupations—but our comradeship, that strange vessel, was smashed to bits at noon one day a few months earlier. It was a lunch hour in March, the Duke and I were sparring in the hall outside the cafeteria, and Albie, who had been more hospitable to the Duke since the day his warm, liquid voice had joined the others—Albie had decided to act as our referee, jumping between us, separating our clinches, warning us about low blows, grabbing out for the Duke's droopy crotch, in general having a good time. I remember that the Duke and I were in a clinch; as I showered soft little punches to his kidneys he squirmed in my embrace. The sun shone through the window behind him, lighting up his hair like a nest of snakes. I fluttered his sides, he twisted, I breathed hard through my nose, my eyes registered on his snaky hair, and suddenly Albie wedged between and knocked us apart—the Duke plunged sideways, I plunged forward, and my fist crashed through the window that Scarpa had been using as his corner. Feet pounded; in a second a wisecracking, guiltless, chewing crowd was gathered around me, just me. Albie and the Duke were gone. I cursed them both, the honorless bastards! The crowd did not drift back to lunch until the head dietitian, a huge, varicose-veined matron in a laundry-stiff white uniform had written down my name and led me to the nurse's office to have the glass picked out of my knuckles. Later in the afternoon I was called for the first and only time to the office of Mr. Wendell, the Principal.

Fifteen years have passed since then and I do not know what has happened to Albie Pelagutti. If he is a gangster he was not one with notoriety or money enough for the Kefauver Committee to interest itself in several years ago. When the Crime Committee reached New Jersey I followed their investigations carefully but never did I read in the papers the name Alberto Pelagutti or even Duke Scarpa—though who can tell what name the Duke is known by now. I do know, however, what happened to the Occupations teacher, for when another Senate Committee swooped through the state a while back it was discovered that Robert Russo—among others—had been a Marxist while attending Montclair State Teachers' College circa 1935. Russo refused to answer some of the Committee's questions, and the Newark Board of Education met, chastised, and dismissed him. I read now and then in the Newark *News* that Civil Liberties Union attorneys are still trying to appeal his case, and I have even written a letter to the Board of Education swearing that if anything subversive was ever done to my character, it wasn't done by my ex-high school teacher, Russo; if he was a Communist I never knew it. I could not decide whether or not to include in the letter a report of the "Star-Spangled Banner" incident: who knows what is and is not proof to the crotchety ladies and chainstore owners who sit and die on Boards of Education?

And if (to alter an Ancient's text) a man's history is his fate, who knows whether the Newark Board of Education will ever attend to a letter written to them by me. I mean, have fifteen years buried that afternoon I was called to see the Principal?

. . . He was a tall, distinguished gentleman and as I entered his office he rose and extended his hand. The same sun that an hour earlier had lit up snakes in the Duke's hair now slanted through Mr. Wendell's blinds and warmed his deep green carpet. "How do you do?" he said. "Yes," I answered, non sequiturly, and ducked my bandaged hand under my unbandaged hand. Graciously he said, "Sit down, won't you?" Frightened, unpracticed, I performed an aborted curtsy and sat. I watched Mr. Wendell go to his metal filing cabinet, slide one drawer open, and take from it a large white index card. He set the card on his desk and motioned me over so I might read what was typed on the card. At the top, in caps, was my whole name—last, first, and middle; below the name was a Roman numeral one, and beside it, "Fighting in corridor; broke window (3/19/42)." Already documented. And on a big card with plenty of space.

I returned to my chair and sat back as Mr. Wendell told me that the card would follow me through life. At first I listened, but as he talked on and on the drama went out of what he said, and my attention wandered to his filing cabinet. I began to imagine the cards inside, Albie's card and the Duke's, and then I understood—just short of forgiveness—why the two of them had zoomed off and left me to pay penance for the window by myself. Albie, you see, had always known about the filing cabinet and these index cards; I hadn't; and Russo, poor Russo, has only recently found out.

Eli, the Fanatic

LEO TZUREF stepped out from back of a white column to welcome Eli Peck. Eli jumped back, surprised; then they shook hands and Tzuref gestured him into the sagging old mansion. At the door Eli turned, and down the slope of lawn, past the jungle of hedges, beyond the dark, untrampled horse path, he saw the street lights blink on in Woodenton. The stores along Coach House Road tossed up a burst of yellow—it came to Eli as a secret signal from his townsmen: "Tell this Tzuref where we stand, Eli. This is a modern community, Eli, we have our families, we pay taxes . . ." Eli, burdened by the message, gave Tzuref a dumb, weary stare.

"You must work a full day," Tzuref said, steering the attorney and his briefcase into the chilly hall.

Eli's heels made a racket on the cracked marble floor, and he spoke above it. "It's the commuting that's killing," he said, and entered the dim room Tzuref waved open for him. "Three hours a day . . . I came right from the train." He dwindled down into a harp-backed chair. He expected it would be deeper than it was and consequently jarred himself on the sharp bones of his seat. It woke him, this shiver of the behind, to his business. Tzuref, a bald shaggy-browed man who looked as if he'd once been very fat, sat back of an empty desk, halfway hidden, as though he were settled on the floor. Everything around him was empty. There were no books in the bookshelves, no rugs on the floor, no draperies in the big casement windows. As Eli began to speak Tzuref got up and swung a window back on one noisy hinge. "May and it's like August," he said, and with his back to Eli, he revealed the black circle on the back of his head. The crown of his head was missing! He returned through the dimness—the lamps had no bulbs—and Eli realized all he'd seen was a skullcap. Tzuref struck a match and lit a candle, just as the half-dying shouts of children at play rolled in through the open window. It was as though Tzuref had opened it so Eli could hear them.

"Aah, now," he said. "I received your letter."

Eli poised, waiting for Tzuref to swish open a drawer and remove the letter from his file. Instead the old man leaned forward onto his stomach, worked his hand into his pants pockets, and withdrew what appeared to be a week-old handkerchief. He uncrumpled it; he unfolded it; he ironed it on the desk with the side of his hand. "So," he said.

Eli pointed to the grimy sheet which he'd gone over word-by-word with his partners, Lewis and McDonnell. "I expected an answer," Eli said. "It's a week."

"It was so important, Mr. Peck, I knew you would come."

Some children ran under the open window and their mysterious babble—not mysterious to Tzuref, who smiled—entered the room like a third person. Their noise caught up against Eli's flesh and he was unable to restrain a shudder. He wished he had gone home, showered and eaten dinner, before calling on Tzuref. He was not feeling as professional as usual—the place was too dim, it was too late. But down in Woodenton they would be waiting, his clients and neighbors. He spoke for the Jews of Woodenton, not just himself and his wife.

"You understood?" Eli said.

"It's not hard."

"It's a matter of zoning . . ." and when Tzuref did not answer, but only drummed his fingers on his lips, Eli said, "We didn't make the laws . . ."

"You respect them."

"They protect us . . . the community."

"The law is the law," Tzuref said.

"Exactly!" Eli had the urge to rise and walk about the room.

"And then of course" —Tzuref made a pair of scales in the air with his hands— "The law is not the law. When is the law that is the law not the law?" He jiggled the scales. "And vice versa."

"Simply," Eli said sharply. "You can't have a boarding school in a residential area." He would not allow Tzuref to cloud the issue with issues. "We thought it better to tell you before any action is undertaken."

"But a house in a residential area?"

"Yes. That's what residential means." The DP's English was perhaps not as good as it seemed at first. Tzuref spoke slowly, but till then Eli had mistaken it for craft—or even wisdom. "Residence means home," he added.

"So this is my residence."

"But the children?"

"It is their residence."

"*Seventeen* children?"

"Eighteen," Tzuref said.

"But you *teach* them here."

"The Talmud. That's illegal?"

"That makes it school."

Tzuref hung the scales again, tipping slowly the balance.

"Look, Mr. Tzuref, in America we call such a place a boarding school."

"Where they teach the Talmud?"

"Where they teach period. You are the headmaster, they are the students."

Tzuref placed his scales on the desk. "Mr. Peck," he said, "I don't believe it . . ." but he did not seem to be referring to anything Eli had said.

"Mr. Tzuref, that is the law. I came to ask what you intend to do."

"What I *must* do?"

"I hope they are the same."

"They are." Tzuref brought his stomach into the desk. "We stay." He smiled. "We are tired. The headmaster is tired. The students are tired."

Eli rose and lifted his briefcase. It felt so heavy packed with the grievances, vengeances, and schemes of his clients. There were days when he carried it like a feather—in Tzuref's office it weighed a ton.

"Goodbye, Mr. Tzuref."

"Sholom," Tzuref said.

Eli opened the door to the office and walked carefully down the dark tomb of a corridor to the door. He stepped out on the porch and, leaning against a pillar, looked down across the lawn to the children at play. Their voices whooped and rose and dropped as they chased each other round the old house. The dusk made the children's game look like a tribal dance. Eli straightened up, started off the porch, and suddenly the dance was ended. A long piercing scream trailed after. It was the first time in his life anyone had run at the sight of him. Keeping his eyes on the lights of Woodenton, he headed down the path.

And then, seated on a bench beneath a tree, Eli saw him. At first it seemed only a deep hollow of blackness—then the figure emerged. Eli recognized him from the description. There he was, wearing the hat, that hat which was the very cause of Eli's mission, the source of Woodenton's upset. The town's lights flashed their message once again: "Get the one with the hat. What a nerve, what a nerve . . ."

Eli started towards the man. Perhaps he was less stubborn than Tzuref, more reasonable. After all, it was the law. But when he was close enough to call out, he didn't. He was stopped by the sight of the black coat that fell down below the man's knees, and the hands which held each other in his lap. By the round-topped, wide-brimmed Talmudic hat, pushed onto the back of his head. And by the beard, which hid his neck and was so soft and thin it fluttered away and back again with each heavy breath he took. He was asleep, his sidelocks curled loose on his cheeks. His face was no older than Eli's.

Eli hurried towards the lights.

The note on the kitchen table unsettled him. Scribblings on bits of paper had made history this past week. This one, however, was unsigned. "Sweetie," it said, "I went to sleep. I had a sort of Oedipal experience with the baby today. Call Ted Heller."

She had left him a cold soggy dinner in the refrigerator. He hated cold soggy dinners, but would take one gladly in place of Miriam's presence. He was ruffled, and she never helped that, not with her infernal analytic powers. He loved her when life was proceeding smoothly—and that was when she loved him. But sometimes Eli found being a lawyer surrounded him like quicksand—he couldn't get his breath. Too often he wished he were pleading for the other side; though if he were on the other side, then he'd wish he were on the side he was. The trouble was that sometimes the law didn't seem to be the answer, *law* didn't seem to have anything to do with what was aggravating everybody. And that, of course, made him feel foolish and unnecessary . . . Though that was not the situation here—the townsmen had a case. But not *exactly*, and if Miriam were awake to see Eli's upset, she would set about explaining his distress to him, understanding him, forgiving him, so as to get things back to Normal, for Normal was where they loved one another. The difficulty with Miriam's efforts was they only upset him more; not only did they explain little to him about himself or his predicament, but they convinced him of *her* weakness. Neither Eli nor Miriam, it turned out, was terribly strong. Twice before he'd faced this fact, and on both occasions had found solace in what his neighbors forgivingly referred to as "a nervous breakdown."

Eli ate his dinner with his briefcase beside him. Halfway through, he gave in to himself, removed Tzuref's notes, and put them on the table, beside Miriam's. From time to time he flipped through the notes, which had been carried into town by the one in the black hat. The first note, the incendiary:

To whom it may concern:

Please give this gentleman the following: Boys shoes with rubber heels and soles.

> 5 prs size 6c
> 3 prs size 5c
> 3 prs size 5b
> 2 prs size 4a
> 3 prs size 4c
> 1 pr size 7b
> 1 pr size 7c

Total 18 prs. boys shoes. This gentleman has a check already signed. Please fill in correct amount.

> L. TZUREF
> Director, Yeshivah of
> Woodenton, N.Y.
> (5/8/48)

"Eli, a regular greenhorn," Ted Heller had said. "He didn't say a word. Just handed me the note and stood there, like in the Bronx the old guys who used to come around selling Hebrew trinkets."

"A Yeshivah!" Artie Berg had said. "Eli, in Woodenton, a Yeshivah! If I want to live in Brownsville, Eli, I'll live in Brownsville."

"Eli," Harry Shaw speaking now, "the old Puddington place. Old man Puddington'll roll over in his grave. Eli, when I left the city, Eli, I didn't plan the city should come to me."

Note number two:

Dear Grocer:
Please give this gentleman ten pounds of sugar. Charge it to our account, Yeshivah of Woodenton, NY—which we will now open with you and expect a bill each month. The gentleman will be in to see you once or twice a week.

L. TZUREF, Director
(5/10/48)

P.S. Do you carry kosher meat?

"He walked right by my window, the greenie," Ted had said, "and he nodded, Eli. He's my *friend* now."

"Eli," Artie Berg had said, "he handed the damn thing to a *clerk* at Stop N' Shop—and in that hat yet!"

"Eli," Harry Shaw again, "it's not funny. Someday, Eli, it's going to be a hundred little kids with little *yamalkahs* chanting their Hebrew lessons on Coach House Road, and then it's not going to strike you funny."

"Eli, what goes on up there—my kids hear strange sounds."

"Eli, this is a modern community."

"Eli, we pay taxes."

"Eli."

"Eli!"

"*Eli!*"

At first it was only another townsman crying in his ear; but when he turned he saw Miriam, standing in the doorway, behind her belly.

"Eli, sweetheart, how was it?"

"He said no."

"Did you see the other one?" she asked.

"Sleeping, under a tree."

"Did you let him know how people feel?"

"He was sleeping."

"Why didn't you wake him up? Eli, this isn't an everyday thing."

"He was tired!"

"Don't shout, please," Miriam said.

"'Don't shout. I'm pregnant. The baby is heavy.'" Eli found he was getting angry at nothing she'd said yet; it was what she was going to say.

"He's a very heavy baby the doctor says," Miriam told him.

"Then sit *down* and make my dinner." Now he found himself angry about her not being present at the dinner which he'd just been relieved that she wasn't present at. It was as though he had a raw nerve for a tail, that he kept stepping on. At last Miriam herself stepped on it.

"Eli, you're upset. I understand."

"You *don't* understand."

She left the room. From the stairs she called, "I do, sweetheart."

It was a trap! He would grow angry knowing she would be "understanding." She would in turn grow more understanding seeing his anger. He would in turn grow angrier . . . The phone rang.

"Hello," Eli said.

"Eli, Ted. So?"

"So nothing."

"Who is Tzuref? He's an American guy?"

"No. A DP. German."

"And the kids?"

"DP's too. He teaches them."

"What? What subjects?" Ted asked.

"I don't know."

"And the guy with the hat, you saw the guy with the hat?"

"Yes. He was sleeping."

"Eli, he sleeps with the *hat*?"

"He sleeps with the hat."

"Goddam fanatics," Ted said. "This is the twentieth century, Eli. Now it's the guy with the hat. Pretty soon all the little Yeshivah boys'll be spilling down into town."

"Next thing they'll be after our daughters."

"Michele and Debbie wouldn't look at them."

"Then," Eli mumbled, "you've got nothing to worry about, Teddie," and he hung up.

In a moment the phone rang. "Eli? We got cut off. We've got nothing to worry about? You worked it out?"

"I have to see him again tomorrow. We can work something out."

"That's fine, Eli. I'll call Artie and Harry."

Eli hung up.

"I thought you said *nothing* worked out." It was Miriam.

"I did."

"Then why did you tell Ted *something* worked out?"

"It did."

"Eli, maybe you should get a little more therapy."

"That's enough of that, Miriam."

"You can't function as a lawyer by being neurotic. That's no answer."

"You're ingenious, Miriam."

She turned, frowning, and took her heavy baby to bed.

The phone rang.

"Eli, Artie. Ted called. You worked it out? No trouble?"

"Yes."

"When are they going?"

"Leave it to me, will you, Artie? I'm tired. I'm going to sleep."

In bed Eli kissed his wife's belly and laid his head upon it to think. He laid it lightly, for she was that day entering the second week of her ninth month. Still, when she slept, it was a good place to rest, to rise and fall with her breathing and figure things out. "If that guy would take off that crazy hat. I know it, what eats them. If he'd take off that crazy hat everything would be all right."

"What?" Miriam said.

"I'm talking to the baby."

Miriam pushed herself up in bed. "Eli, please, baby, shouldn't you maybe stop in to see Dr. Eckman, just for a little conversation?"

"I'm fine."

"Oh, sweetie!" she said, and put her head back on the pillow.

"You know what your mother brought to this marriage—a sling chair and a goddam New School enthusiasm for Sigmund Freud."

Miriam feigned sleep, he could tell by the breathing.

"I'm telling the kid the truth, aren't I, Miriam? A sling chair, three months to go on a *New Yorker* subscription, and *An Introduction to Psychoanalysis*. Isn't that right?"

"Eli, must you be aggressive?"

"That's all you worry about, is your insides. You stand in front of the mirror all day and look at yourself being pregnant."

"Pregnant mothers have a relationship with the fetus that fathers can't understand."

"Relationship my ass. What is my liver doing now? What is my small intestine doing now? Is my island of Langerhans on the blink?"

"Don't be jealous of a little fetus, Eli."

"I'm jealous of your island of Langerhans!"

"Eli, I can't argue with you when I know it's not me you're really angry with. Don't you see, sweetie, you're angry with yourself."

"You and Eckman."

"Maybe he could help, Eli."

"Maybe he could help you. You're practically lovers as it is."

"You're being hostile again," Miriam said.

"What do you care—it's only *me* I'm being hostile towards."

"Eli, we're going to have a beautiful baby, and I'm going to have a perfectly simple delivery, and you're going to make a fine father, and there's absolutely no reason to be obsessed with whatever is on your mind. All we have to worry about—" she smiled at him "—is a name."

Eli got out of bed and slid into his slippers. "We'll name the kid Eckman if it's a boy and Eckman if it's a girl."

"Eckman Peck sounds terrible."

"He'll have to live with it," Eli said, and he went down to his study where the latch on his briefcase glinted in the moonlight that came through the window.

He removed the Tzuref notes and read through them all again. It unnerved him to think of all the flashy reasons his wife could come up with for his reading and rereading the notes. "Eli, why are you so *preoccupied* with Tzuref?" "Eli, stop getting *involved*. Why do you think you're getting *involved*, Eli?" Sooner or later, everybody's wife finds their weak spot. His goddam luck he had to be neurotic! Why couldn't he have been born with a short leg.

He removed the cover from his typewriter, hating Miriam for the edge she had. All the time he wrote the letter, he could hear what she would be saying about his not being *able* to let the matter drop. Well, her trouble was that she wasn't *able* to face the matter. But he could hear her answer already: clearly, he was guilty of "a reaction formation." Still, all the fancy phrases didn't fool Eli: all she wanted really was for Eli to send Tzuref and family on their way, so that the community's temper would quiet, and the calm circumstances of their domestic happiness return. All she wanted were order and love in her private world. Was she so wrong? Let the world bat its brains out—in Woodenton there should be peace. He wrote the letter anyway:

Dear Mr. Tzuref:

Our meeting this evening seems to me inconclusive. I don't think there's any reason for us not to be able to come up with some sort of compromise that will satisfy the Jewish community of Woodenton and the Yeshivah and yourself. It seems to me that what most disturbs my neighbors are the visits to town by the gentleman in the black hat, suit, etc. Woodenton is a progressive suburban community whose members, both Jewish and Gentile, are anxious that their families live in comfort and beauty and serenity. This is, after all, the twentieth century, and we do not think it too much to ask that the members of our community dress in a manner appropriate to the time and place.

Woodenton, as you may not know, has long been the home of well-to-do Protestants. It is only since the war that Jews have been able to buy property here, and for Jews and Gentiles to live beside each other in amity. For this adjustment to be made, both Jews and Gentiles alike have had to give up some of their more extreme practices in order not to threaten or offend the other. Certainly such amity is to be desired. Perhaps if such conditions had existed in prewar Europe, the persecution of the Jewish people, of which you and those 18 children have been victims, could not have been carried out with such success—in fact, might not have been carried out at all.

Therefore, Mr. Tzuref, will you accept the following conditions? If you can, we will see fit not to carry out legal action against the Yeshivah for failure to comply with township Zoning ordinances No. 18 and No. 23. The conditions are simply:

1. The religious, educational, and social activities of the Yeshivah of Woodenton will be confined to the Yeshivah grounds.

2. Yeshivah personnel are welcomed in the streets and stores of Woodenton provided they are attired in clothing usually associated with American life in the 20th century.

If these conditions are met, we see no reason why the Yeshivah of Woodenton cannot live peacefully and satisfactorily with the Jews of Woodenton—as the Jews of Woodenton have come to live with the Gentiles of Woodenton. I would appreciate an immediate reply.

Sincerely,
ELI PECK, Attorney

Two days later Eli received his immediate reply:

Mr. Peck:

The suit the gentleman wears is all he's got.

Sincerely,
LEO TZUREF, Headmaster

Once again, as Eli swung around the dark trees and onto the lawn, the children fled. He reached out with his briefcase as if to stop them, but they were gone so fast all he saw moving was a flock of skullcaps.

"Come, come . . ." a voice called from the porch. Tzuref appeared from behind a pillar. Did he *live* behind those pillars? Was he just watching the children at play? Either way, when Eli appeared, Tzuref was ready, with no forewarning.

"Hello," Eli said.

"Sholom."

"I didn't mean to frighten them."

"They're scared, so they run."

"I didn't do anything."

Tzuref shrugged. The little movement seemed to Eli strong as an accusation. What he didn't get at home, he got here.

Inside the house they took their seats. Though it was lighter than a few evenings before, a bulb or two would have helped. Eli had to hold his briefcase towards the window for the last gleamings. He removed Tzuref's letter from a manila folder. Tzuref removed Eli's letter from his pants pocket. Eli removed the carbon of his own letter from another manila folder. Tzuref removed Eli's first letter from his back pocket. Eli removed the carbon from his briefcase. Tzuref raised his palms. ". . . It's all I've got . . ."

Those upraised palms, the mocking tone—another accusation. It was a crime to keep carbons! Everybody had an edge on him—Eli could do no right.

"I offered a compromise, Mr. Tzuref. You refused."

"Refused, Mr. Peck? What is, is."

"The man could get a new suit."

"That's all he's got."

"So you told me," Eli said.

"So I told you, so you know."

"It's not an insurmountable obstacle, Mr. Tzuref. We have stores."

"For that too?"

"On Route 12, a Robert Hall—"

"To take away the one thing a man's got?"

"Not take away, *replace*."

"But I tell you he has nothing. *Nothing*. You have that word in English? *Nicht? Gornisht?*"

"Yes, Mr. Tzuref, we have the word."

"A mother and a father?" Tzuref said. "No. A wife? No. A baby? A little ten-month-old baby? No! A village full of friends? A synagogue where you knew the feel of every seat under your pants? Where with your eyes closed you could smell the cloth of the Torah?" Tzuref pushed out of his chair, stirring a breeze that swept Eli's letter to the floor. At the window he leaned out, and looked, beyond Woodenton. When he turned he was shaking a finger at Eli. "And a medical experiment they performed on him yet! That leaves nothing, Mr. Peck. Absolutely nothing!"

"I misunderstood."

"No news reached Woodenton?"

"About the suit, Mr. Tzuref. I thought he couldn't afford another."

"He can't."

They were right where they'd begun. "Mr. Tzuref!" Eli demanded. "*Here?*" He smacked his hand to his billfold.

"Exactly!" Tzuref said, smacking his own breast.

"Then we'll buy him one!" Eli crossed to the window and taking Tzuref by the shoulders, pronounced each word slowly. "We-will-pay-for-it. All right?"

"Pay? What, diamonds!"

Eli raised a hand to his inside pocket, then let it drop. Oh stupid! Tzuref, father to eighteen, had smacked not what lay under his coat, but deeper, under his ribs.

"Oh . . ." Eli said. He moved away along the wall. "The suit is all he's got then."

"You got my letter," Tzuref said.

Eli stayed back in the shadow, and Tzuref turned to his chair. He swished Eli's letter from the floor, and held it up. "You say too much . . . all this reasoning . . . all these conditions . . ."

"What can I do?"

"You have the word 'suffer' in English?"

"We have the word suffer. We have the word law too."

"Stop with the law! You have the word suffer. Then try it. It's a little thing."

"They won't," Eli said.

"But you, Mr. Peck, how about you?"

"I am them, they are me, Mr. Tzuref."

"Aach! You are us, we are you!"

Eli shook and shook his head. In the dark he suddenly felt that Tzuref might put him under a spell. "Mr. Tzuref, a little light?"

Tzuref lit what tallow was left in the holders. Eli was afraid to ask if they couldn't afford electricity. Maybe candles were all they had left.

"Mr. Peck, who made the law, may I ask you that?"

"The people."

"No."

"Yes."

"Before the people."

"No one. Before the people there was no law." Eli didn't care for the conversation, but with only candlelight, he was being lulled into it.

"Wrong," Tzuref said.

"We make the law, Mr. Tzuref. It is our community. These are my neighbors. I am their attorney. They pay me. Without law there is chaos."

"What you call law, I call shame. The heart, Mr. Peck, the heart is law! God!" he announced.

"Look, Mr. Tzuref, I didn't come here to talk metaphysics. People use the law, it's a flexible thing. They protect what they value, their property, their well-being, their happiness—"

"Happiness? They hide their shame. And you, Mr. Peck, you are shameless?"

"We do it," Eli said, wearily, "for our children. This is the twentieth century . . ."

"For the goyim maybe. For me the Fifty-eighth." He pointed at Eli. "That is too old for shame."

Eli felt squashed. Everybody in the world had evil reasons for his actions. Everybody! With reasons so cheap, who buys bulbs. "Enough wisdom, Mr. Tzuref. Please. I'm exhausted."

"Who isn't?" Tzuref said.

He picked Eli's papers from his desk and reached up with them. "What do you intend for us to do?"

"What you must," Eli said. "I made the offer."

"So he must give up his suit?"

"Tzuref, Tzuref, leave me be with that suit! I'm not the only lawyer in the world. I'll drop the case, and you'll get some-body who won't talk compromise. Then you'll have no home, no children, nothing. Only a lousy black suit! Sacrifice what you want. I know what I would do."

To that Tzuref made no answer, but only handed Eli his letters.

"It's not me, Mr. Tzuref, it's them."

"They are you."

"No," Eli intoned, "I am me. They are them. You are you."

"You talk about leaves and branches. I'm dealing with under the dirt."

"Mr. Tzuref, you're driving me crazy with Talmudic wisdom. This is that, that is the other thing. Give me a straight answer."

"Only for straight questions."

"Oh, God!"

Eli returned to his chair and plunged his belongings into the case. "Then, that's all," he said angrily.

Tzuref gave him the shrug.

"Remember, Tzuref, you called this down on yourself."

"*I* did?"

Eli refused to be his victim again. Double-talk proved nothing.

"Goodbye," he said.

But as he opened the door leading to the hall, he heard Tzuref.

"And your wife, how is she?"

"Fine, just fine." Eli kept going.

"And the baby is due when, any day?"

Eli turned. "That's right."

"Well," Tzuref said, rising. "Good luck."

"You know?"

Tzuref pointed out the window—then, with his hands, he drew upon himself a beard, a hat, a long, long coat. When his fingers formed the hem they touched the floor. "He shops two, three times a week, he gets to know them."

"He *talks* to them?"

"He sees them."

"And he can tell which is my wife?"

"They shop at the same stores. He says she is beautiful. She has a kind face. A woman capable of love . . . though who can be sure."

"*He* talks about *us*, to *you*?" demanded Eli.

"You talk about us, to her?"

"Goodbye, Mr. Tzuref."

Tzuref said, "Sholom. And good luck—I know what it is to have children. Sholom," Tzuref whispered, and with the whisper the candles went out. But the instant before, the flames leaped into Tzuref's eyes, and Eli saw it was not luck Tzuref wished him at all.

Outside the door, Eli waited. Down the lawn the children were holding hands and whirling around in a circle. At first he did not move. But he could not hide in the shadows all night. Slowly he began to slip along the front of the house. Under his hands he felt where bricks were out. He moved in the shadows until he reached the side. And then, clutching his briefcase to his chest, he broke across the darkest spots of the lawn. He aimed for a distant glade of woods, and when he reached it he did not stop, but ran through until he was so dizzied that the trees seemed to be running beside him, fleeing not towards Woodenton but away. His lungs were nearly ripping their seams as he burst into the yellow glow of the Gulf station at the edge of town.

"Eli, I had pains today. Where were you?"

"I went to Tzuref."

"Why didn't you call? I was worried."

He tossed his hat past the sofa and onto the floor. "Where are my winter suits?"

"In the hall closet. Eli, it's May."

"I need a strong suit." He left the room, Miriam behind him.

"Eli, talk to me. Sit down. Have dinner. Eli, what are you doing? You're going to get moth balls all over the carpet."

He peered out from the hall closet. Then he peered in again —there was a zipping noise, and suddenly he swept a greenish tweed suit before his wife's eyes.

"Eli, I love you in that suit. But not now. Have something to eat. I made dinner tonight—I'll warm it."

"You've got a box big enough for this suit?"

"I got a Bonwit's box, the other day. Eli, *why?*"

"Miriam, you see me doing something, let me do it."

"You haven't eaten."

"I'm *doing* something." He started up the stairs to the bedroom.

"Eli, would you please tell me what it is you want, and why?"

He turned and looked down at her. "Suppose this time you give me the reasons *before* I tell you what I'm doing. It'll probably work out the same anyway."

"Eli, I want to help."

"It doesn't concern you."

"But I want to help *you*," Miriam said.

"Just be quiet, then."

"But you're upset," she said, and she followed him up the stairs, heavily, breathing for two.

"Eli, what now?"

"A shirt." He yanked open all the drawers of their new teak dresser. He extracted a shirt.

"Eli, batiste? With a tweed suit?" she inquired.

He was at the closet now, on his knees. "Where are my cordovans?"

"Eli, why are you doing this so compulsively? You look like you *have* to do something."

"Oh, Miriam, you're supersubtle."

"Eli, stop this and talk to me. Stop it or I'll call Dr. Eckman."

Eli was kicking off the shoes he was wearing. "Where's the Bonwit box?"

"Eli, do you want me to have the baby right *here*!"

Eli walked over and sat down on the bed. He was draped not only with his own clothing, but also with the greenish tweed suit, the batiste shirt, and under each arm a shoe. He raised his arms and let the shoes drop onto the bed. Then he undid his necktie with one hand and his teeth and added that to the booty.

"Underwear," he said. "He'll need underwear."

"Who!"

He was slipping out of his socks.

Miriam kneeled down and helped him ease his left foot out of the sock. She sat with it on the floor. "Eli, just lie back. Please."

"Plaza 9-3103."

"What?"

"Eckman's number," he said. "It'll save you the trouble."

"Eli—"

"You've got that goddam tender 'You need help' look in your eyes, Miriam, don't tell me you don't."

"I don't."

"I'm not flipping," Eli said.

"I know, Eli."

"Last time I sat in the bottom of the closet and chewed on my bedroom slippers. That's what I did."

"I know."

"And I'm not doing that. This is not a nervous breakdown, Miriam, let's get that straight."

"Okay," Miriam said. She kissed the foot she held. Then, softly, she asked, "What *are* you doing?"

"Getting clothes for the guy in the hat. Don't tell me why, Miriam. Just let me do it."

"That's all?" she asked.

"That's all."

"You're not leaving?"

"No."

"Sometimes I think it gets too much for you, and you'll just leave."

"What gets too much?"

"I don't *know*, Eli. Something gets too much. Whenever everything's peaceful for a long time, and things are nice and pleasant, and we're expecting to be even happier. Like now. It's as if you don't think we *deserve* to be happy."

"Damn it, Miriam! I'm giving this guy a new suit, is that all right? From now on he comes into Woodenton like everybody else, is that all right with you?"

"And Tzuref moves?"

"I don't even know if he'll take the suit, Miriam! What do you have to bring up moving!"

"Eli, I didn't bring up moving. Everybody did. That's what everybody wants. Why make everybody un*happy*. It's even a law, Eli."

"Don't tell me what's the law."

"All right, sweetie. I'll get the box."

"*I'll* get the box. Where is it?"

"In the basement."

When he came up from the basement, he found all the clothes neatly folded and squared away on the sofa: shirt, tie, shoes, socks, underwear, belt, and an old gray flannel suit. His wife sat on the end of the sofa, looking like an anchored balloon.

"Where's the green suit?" he said.

"Eli, it's your loveliest suit. It's my favorite suit. Whenever I think of you, Eli, it's in that suit."

"Get it out."

"Eli, it's a Brooks Brothers suit. You say yourself how much you love it."

"Get it out."

"But the gray flannel's more practical. For shopping."

"Get it out."

"You go overboard, Eli. That's your trouble. You won't do anything in moderation. That's how people destroy themselves."

"I do *everything* in moderation. That's my trouble. The suit's in the closet again?"

She nodded, and began to fill up with tears. "Why does it have to be *your* suit? Who are you even to decide to give a suit? What about the others?" She was crying openly, and holding her belly. "Eli, I'm going to have a baby. Do we need all *this*?" and she swept the clothes off the sofa to the floor.

At the closet Eli removed the green suit. "It's a J. Press," he said, looking at the lining.

"I hope to hell he's happy with it!" Miriam said, sobbing.

A half hour later the box was packed. The cord he'd found in the kitchen cabinet couldn't keep the outfit from popping through. The trouble was there was too much: the gray suit *and* the green suit, an oxford shirt as well as the batiste. But let him have two suits! Let him have three, four, if only this damn silliness would stop! And a hat—of course! God, he'd almost forgotten the hat. He took the stairs two at a time and in Miriam's closet yanked a hatbox from the top shelf. Scattering hat and tissue paper to the floor, he returned downstairs, where he packed away the hat he'd worn that day. Then he looked at his wife, who lay outstretched on the floor before the fireplace. For the third time in as many minutes she was saying, "Eli, this is the real thing."

"Where?"

"Right under the baby's head, like somebody's squeezing oranges."

Now that he'd stopped to listen he was stupefied. He said, "But you have two more weeks . . ." Somehow he'd really been expecting it was to go on not just another two weeks, but another nine months. This led him to suspect, suddenly, that his wife was feigning pain so as to get his mind off delivering the suit. And just as suddenly he resented himself for having such a thought. God, what had he become! He'd been an unending bastard towards her since this Tzuref business had come up—just when her pregnancy must have been most burdensome. He'd allowed her no access to him, but still, he was sure, for good reasons: she might tempt him out of his confusion with her easy answers. He could be tempted all right, it was why he fought so hard. But now a sweep of love came over him at the thought of her contracting womb, and his child. And yet he would not indicate it to her. Under such splendid martial conditions, who knows but she might extract some promise from him about his concern with the school on the hill.

Having packed his second bag of the evening, Eli sped his wife to Woodenton Memorial. There she proceeded not to have her baby, but to lie hour after hour through the night having at first oranges, then bowling balls, then basketballs, squeezed back of her pelvis. Eli sat in the waiting room, under the shattering African glare of a dozen rows of fluorescent bulbs, composing a letter to Tzuref.

Dear Mr. Tzuref:
    The clothes in this box are for the gentleman in the hat. In a life of sacrifice what is one more? But in a life of no sacrifices even one is impossible. Do you see what I'm saying, Mr. Tzuref? I am not a Nazi who would drive eighteen children, who are probably frightened at the sight of a firefly, into homelessness. But if you want a home here, you must accept what we have to offer. The world is the world, Mr. Tzuref. As you would say, what is, is. All we say to this man is change your clothes. Enclosed are two suits and two shirts, and everything else he'll need, including a new hat. When he needs new clothes let me know.
    We await his appearance in Woodenton, as we await friendly relations with the Yeshivah of Woodenton.

He signed his name and slid the note under a bursting flap and into the box. Then he went to the phone at the end of the room and dialed Ted Heller's number.

"Hello."

"Shirley, it's Eli."

"Eli, we've been calling all night. The lights are on in your place, but nobody answers. We thought it was burglars."

"Miriam's having the baby."

"At home?" Shirley said. "Oh, Eli, what a fun-idea!"

"Shirley, let me speak to Ted."

After the ear-shaking clatter of the phone whacking the floor, Eli heard footsteps, breathing, throat-clearing, then Ted. "A boy or a girl?"

"Nothing yet."

"You've given Shirley the bug, Eli. Now she's going to have *our* next one at home."

"Good."

"That's a terrific way to bring the family together, Eli."

"Look, Ted, I've settled with Tzuref."

"When are they going?"

"They're not exactly going, Teddie. I settled it—you won't even know they're there."

"A guy dressed like 1000 B.C. and I won't know it? What are you thinking about, pal?"

"He's changing his clothes."

"Yeah, to what? Another funeral suit?"

"Tzuref promised me, Ted. Next time he comes to town, he comes dressed like you and me."

"What! Somebody's kidding somebody, Eli."

Eli's voice shot up. "If he says he'll do it, he'll do it!"

"And, Eli," Ted asked, "he said it?"

"He said it." It cost him a sudden headache, this invention.

"And suppose he doesn't change, Eli. Just suppose. I mean that *might* happen, Eli. This might just be some kind of stall or something."

"No," Eli assured him.

The other end was quiet a moment. "Look, Eli," Ted said, finally, "he changes. Okay? All right? But they're still up there, aren't they? *That* doesn't change."

"The point is you won't know it."

Patiently Ted said, "Is this what we asked of you, Eli? When we put our faith and trust in you, is that what we were asking? We weren't concerned that this guy should become a Beau

Brummel, Eli, believe me. We just don't think this is the community for them. And, Eli, we isn't me. The Jewish members of the community appointed me, Artie, and Harry to see what could be done. And we appointed you. And what's happened?"

Eli heard himself say, "What happened, happened."

"Eli, you're talking in crossword puzzles."

"My wife's having a baby," Eli explained, defensively.

"I realize that, Eli. But this is a matter of zoning, isn't it? Isn't that what we discovered? You don't abide by the ordinance, you go. I mean I can't raise mountain goats, say, in my backyard—"

"This isn't so simple, Ted. People are involved—"

"People? Eli, we've been through this and through this. We're not just dealing with people—these are religious fanatics is what they are. Dressing like that. What I'd really like to find out is what goes on up there. I'm getting more and more skeptical, Eli, and I'm not afraid to admit it. It smells like a lot of hocus-pocus abracadabra stuff to me. Guys like Harry, you know, they think and they think and they're afraid to admit what they're thinking. I'll tell you. Look, I don't even know about this Sunday school business. Sundays I drive my oldest kid all the way to Scarsdale to learn Bible stories . . . and you know what she comes up with? This Abraham in the Bible was going to kill his own *kid* for a sacrifice. She gets nightmares from it, for God's sake! You call that religion? Today a guy like that they'd lock him up. This is an age of science, Eli. I size people's feet with an X-ray machine, for God's sake. They've disproved all that stuff, Eli, and I refuse to sit by and watch it happening on my own front lawn."

"Nothing's happening on your front lawn, Teddie. You're exaggerating, nobody's sacrificing their kid."

"You're damn right, Eli—I'm not sacrificing mine. You'll see when you have your own what it's like. All the place is, is a hideaway for people who can't face life. It's a matter of *needs.* They have all these superstitions, and why do you think? Because they can't face the world, because they can't take their place in society. That's no environment to bring kids up in, Eli."

"Look, Ted, see it from another angle. We can convert them," Eli said, with half a heart.

"What, make a bunch of Catholics out of them? Look, Eli—pal, there's a good healthy relationship in this town because it's modern Jews and Protestants. That's the point, isn't it, Eli? Let's not kid each other, I'm not Harry. The way things are now are fine—like human beings. There's going to be no pogroms in Woodenton. Right? 'Cause there's no fanatics, no crazy people—" Eli winced, and closed his eyes a second— "just people who respect each other, and leave each other be. Common sense is the ruling thing, Eli. I'm for common sense. Moderation."

"Exactly, exactly, Ted. I agree, but common sense, maybe, says make this guy change his clothes. Then maybe—"

"Common sense says that? Common sense says to me they go and find a nice place somewhere else, Eli. New York is the biggest city in the world, it only 30 miles away—why don't they go there?"

"Ted, give them a chance. Introduce them to common sense."

"Eli, your dealing with *fanatics*. Do they display common sense? Talking a dead language, that makes sense? Making a big thing out of suffering, so you're going oy-oy-oy all your life, that's common sense? Look, Eli, we've been through all this. I don't know if you know—but there's talk that *Life* magazine is sending a guy out to the Yeshivah for a story. With pictures."

"Look, Teddie, you're letting your imagination get inflamed. I don't think *Life*'s interested."

"But I'm interested, Eli. And we thought you were supposed to be."

"I am," Eli said, "I am. Let him just change the clothes, Ted. Let's see what happens."

"They live in the medieval ages, Eli—it's some superstition, some *rule*."

"Let's just *see*," Eli pleaded.

"Eli, every day—"

"One more day," Eli said. "If he doesn't change in one more day. . . ."

"What?"

"Then I get an injunction first thing Monday. That's that."

"Look, Eli—it's not up to me. Let me call Harry—"

"You're the spokesman, Teddie. I'm all wrapped up here with Miriam having a baby. Just give me the day—them the day."

"All right, Eli. I want to be fair. But tomorrow, that's all. Tomorrow's the judgment day, Eli, I'm telling you."

"I hear trumpets," Eli said, and hung up. He was shaking inside—Teddie's voice seemed to have separated his bones at the joints. He was still in the phone booth when the nurse came to tell him that Mrs. Peck would positively not be delivered of a child until the morning. He was to go home and get some rest, he looked like *he* was having the baby. The nurse winked and left.

But Eli did not go home. He carried the Bonwit box out into the street with him and put it in the car. The night was soft and starry, and he began to drive the streets of Woodenton. Square cool windows, apricot-colored, were all one could see beyond the long lawns that fronted the homes of the townsmen. The stars polished the permanent baggage carriers atop the station wagons in the driveways. He drove slowly, up, down, around. Only his tires could be heard taking the gentle curves in the road.

What peace. What incredible peace. Have children ever been so safe in their beds? Parents—Eli wondered—so full in their stomachs? Water so warm in its boilers? Never. Never in Rome, never in Greece. Never even did walled cities have it so good! No wonder then they would keep things just as they were. Here, after all, were peace and safety—what civilization had been working toward for centuries. For all his jerkiness, that was all Ted Heller was asking for, peace and safety. It was what his parents had asked for in the Bronx, and his grandparents in Poland, and theirs in Russia or Austria, or wherever else they'd fled to or from. It was what Miriam was asking for. And now they had it—the world was at last a place for families, even Jewish families. After all these centuries, maybe there just had to be this communal toughness—or numbness—to protect such a blessing. Maybe that was the trouble with the Jews all along—too soft. Sure, to live takes guts . . . Eli was thinking as he drove on beyond the train station, and parked his car at the darkened Gulf station. He stepped out, carrying the box.

At the top of the hill one window trembled with light. What *was* Tzuref doing up there in that office? Killing babies —probably not. But studying a language no one understood? Practicing customs with origins long forgotten? Suffering sufferings already suffered once too often? Teddie was right— why keep it up! However, if a man chose to be stubborn, then he couldn't expect to survive. The world is give-and-take. What sense to sit and brood over a suit. Eli would give him one last chance.

He stopped at the top. No one was around. He walked slowly up the lawn, setting each foot into the grass, listening to the shh shhh shhhh his shoes made as they bent the wetness into the sod. He looked around. Here there was nothing. Nothing! An old decaying house—and a suit.

On the porch he slid behind a pillar. He felt someone was watching him. But only the stars gleamed down. And at his feet, off and away, Woodenton glowed up. He set his package on the step of the great front door. Inside the cover of the box he felt to see if his letter was still there. When he touched it, he pushed it deeper into the green suit, which his fingers still remembered from winter. He should have included some light bulbs. Then he slid back by the pillar again, and this time there was something on the lawn. It was the second sight he had of him. He was facing Woodenton and barely moving across the open space towards the trees. His right fist was beating his chest. And then Eli heard a sound rising with each knock on the chest. What a moan! It could raise hair, stop hearts, water eyes. And it did all three to Eli, plus more. Some feeling crept into him for whose deepness he could find no word. It was strange. He listened—it did not hurt to hear this moan. But he wondered if it hurt to make it. And so, with only stars to hear, he tried. And it did hurt. Not the bumble-bee of noise that turned at the back of his throat and winged out his nostrils. What hurt buzzed down. It stung and stung inside him, and in turn the moan sharpened. It became a scream, louder, a song, a crazy song that whined through the pillars and blew out to the grass, until the strange hatted creature on the lawn turned and threw his arms wide, and looked in the night like a scarecrow.

Eli ran, and when he reached the car the pain was only a bloody scratch across his neck where a branch had whipped back as he fled the greenie's arms.

The following day his son was born. But not till one in the afternoon, and by then a great deal had happened.

First, at nine-thirty the phone rang. Eli leaped from the sofa—where he'd dropped the night before—and picked it screaming from the cradle. He could practically smell the hospital as he shouted into the phone, "Hello, yes!"

"Eli, it's Ted. Eli, he *did* it. He just walked by the store. I was opening the door, Eli, and I turned around and I swear I thought it was you. But it was him. He still walks like he did, but the clothes, Eli, the clothes."

"Who?"

"The greenie. He has on man's regular clothes. And the suit, it's a beauty."

The suit barreled back into Eli's consciousness, pushing all else aside. "What color suit?"

"Green. He's just strolling in the green suit like it's a holiday. Eli . . . is it a Jewish holiday?"

"Where is he now?"

"He's walking straight up Coach House Road, in this damn tweed job. Eli, it worked. You were right."

"We'll see."

"What next?"

"We'll see."

He took off the underwear in which he'd slept and went into the kitchen where he turned the light under the coffee. When it began to perk he held his head over the pot so it would steam loose the knot back of his eyes. It still hadn't when the phone rang.

"Eli, Ted again. Eli, the guy's walking up and down every street in town. Really, he's on a tour or something. Artie called me, Herb called me. Now Shirley calls that he just walked by our house. Eli, go out on the porch you'll see."

Eli went to the window and peered out. He couldn't see past the bend in the road, and there was no one in sight.

"Eli?" He heard Ted from where he dangled over the telephone table. He dropped the phone into the hook, as a few

last words floated up to him—"Eliyousawhim . . . ?" He threw
on the pants and shirt he'd worn the night before and walked
barefoot on to his front lawn. And sure enough, his apparition
appeared around the bend: in a brown hat a little too far down
on his head, a green suit too far back on the shoulders, an
unbuttoned-down button-down shirt, a tie knotted so as to
leave a two-inch tail, trousers that cascaded onto his shoes—
he was shorter than that black hat had made him seem. And
moving the clothes was that walk that was not a walk, the tiny-
stepped shlumpy gait. He came round the bend, and for all
his strangeness—it clung to his whiskers, signaled itself in his
locomotion—he looked as if he belonged. Eccentric, maybe,
but he belonged. He made no moan, nor did he invite Eli with
wide-flung arms. But he did stop when he saw him. He
stopped and put a hand to his hat. When he felt for its top, his
hand went up too high. Then it found the level and fiddled
with the brim. The fingers fiddled, fumbled, and when they'd
finally made their greeting, they traveled down the fellow's
face and in an instant seemed to have touched each one of his
features. They dabbed the eyes, ran the length of the nose,
swept over the hairy lip, until they found their home in the
hair that hid a little of his collar. To Eli the fingers said, *I have
a face, I have a face at least.* Then his hand came through the
beard and when it stopped at his chest it was like a pointer—
and the eyes asked a question as tides of water shifted over
them. *The face is all right, I can keep it?* Such a look was in
those eyes that Eli was still seeing them when he turned his
head away. They were the hearts of his jonquils, that only last
week had appeared—they were the leaves on his birch, the
bulbs in his coach lamp, the droppings on his lawn: those eyes
were the eyes in his head. They were his, he had made them.
He turned and went into his house and when he peeked out
the side of the window, between shade and molding, the green
suit was gone.

The phone.

"Eli, Shirley."

"I saw him, Shirley," and he hung up.

He sat frozen for a long time. The sun moved around the
windows. The coffee steam smelled up the house. The phone

began to ring, stopped, began again. The mailman came, the cleaner, the bakery man, the gardener, the ice cream man, the League of Women Voters lady. A Negro woman spreading some strange gospel calling for the revision of the Food and Drug Act knocked at the front, rapped the windows, and finally scraped a half-dozen pamphlets under the back door. But Eli only sat, without underwear, in last night's suit. He answered no one.

Given his condition, it was strange that the trip and crash at the back door reached his inner ear. But in an instant he seemed to melt down into the crevices of the chair, then to splash up and out to where the clatter had been. At the door he waited. It was silent, but for a fluttering of damp little leaves on the trees. When he finally opened the door, there was no one there. He'd expected to see green, green, green, big as the doorway, topped by his hat, waiting for him with those eyes. But there was no one out there, except for the Bonwit's box which lay bulging at his feet. No string tied it and the top rode high on the bottom.

The coward! He couldn't do it! He couldn't!

The very glee of that idea pumped fuel to his legs. He tore out across his back lawn, past his new spray of forsythia, to catch a glimpse of the bearded one fleeing naked through yards, over hedges and fences, to the safety of his hermitage. In the distance a pile of pink and white stones—which Harriet Knudson had painted the previous day—tricked him. "Run," he shouted to the rocks, "Run, you . . ." but he caught his error before anyone else did, and though he peered and craned there was no hint anywhere of a man about his own size, with white, white, terribly white skin (how white must be the skin of his body!) in cowardly retreat. He came slowly, curiously, back to the door. And while the trees shimmered in the light wind, he removed the top from the box. The shock at first was the shock of having daylight turned off all at once. Inside the box was an eclipse. But black soon sorted from black, and shortly there was the glassy black of lining, the coarse black of trousers, the dead black of fraying threads, and in the center the mountain of black: the hat. He picked the box from the doorstep and carried it inside. For the first time in his life he *smelled* the color of blackness: a little stale, a little sour, a little old, but nothing that could overwhelm you. Still, he held the package at arm's length and deposited it on the dining room table.

Twenty rooms on a hill and they store their old clothes with me! What am I supposed to do with them? Give them to charity? That's where they came from. He picked up the hat by the edges and looked inside. The crown was smooth as an egg, the brim practically threadbare. There is nothing else to do with a hat in one's hand but put it on, so Eli dropped the thing on his head. He opened the door to the hall closet and looked at himself in the full-length mirror. The hat gave him bags under the eyes. Or perhaps he had not slept well. He pushed the brim lower till a shadow touched his lips. Now the bags under his eyes had inflated to become his face. Before the mirror he unbuttoned his shirt, unzipped his trousers, and then, shedding his clothes, he studied what he was. What a silly disappointment to see yourself naked in a hat. Especially in that hat. He sighed, but could not rid himself of the great weakness that suddenly set on his muscles and joints, beneath the terrible weight of the stranger's strange hat.

He returned to the dining room table and emptied the box of its contents: jacket, trousers, and vest (*it* smelled deeper than blackness). And under it all, sticking between the shoes that looked chopped and bitten, came the first gleam of white. A little fringed serape, a gray piece of semi-underwear, was crumpled at the bottom, its thready border twisted into itself. Eli removed it and let it hang free. What is it? For warmth? To wear beneath underwear in the event of a chest cold? He held it to his nose but it did not smell from Vick's or mustard plaster. It was something special, some Jewish thing. Special food, special language, special prayers, why not special BVD's? So fearful was he that he would be tempted back into wearing his traditional clothes—reasoned Eli—that he had carried and buried in Woodenton everything, including the special underwear. For that was how Eli now understood the box of clothes. The greenie was saying, Here, I give up. I refuse even to be tempted. We surrender. And that was how Eli continued to understand it until he found he'd slipped the white fringy surrender flag over his hat and felt it clinging to his chest. And now, looking at himself in the mirror, he was momentarily uncertain as to who was tempting who into what. Why *did* the greenie leave his clothes? Was it even the greenie? Then who was it? And why? But, Eli, for Christ's sake, in an age of science things don't happen like that. Even the goddam pigs take drugs . . .

Regardless of who was the source of the temptation, what was its end, not to mention its beginning, Eli, some moments later, stood draped in black, with a little white underneath, before the full-length mirror. He had to pull down on the trousers so they would not show the hollow of his ankle. The greenie, didn't he wear socks? Or had he forgotten them? The mystery was solved when Eli mustered enough courage to investigate the trouser pockets. He had expected some damp awful thing to happen to his fingers should he slip them down and out of sight—but when at last he jammed bravely down he came up with a khaki army sock in each hand. As he slipped them over his toes, he invented a genesis: a G.I.'s present in 1945. Plus everything else lost between 1938 and 1945, he had also lost his socks. Not that he had lost the socks, but that he'd had to stoop to accepting these, made Eli almost cry. To calm himself he walked out the back door and stood looking at his lawn.

On the Knudson back lawn, Harriett Knudson was giving her stones a second coat of pink. She looked up just as Eli stepped out. Eli shot back in again and pressed himself against the back door. When he peeked between the curtain all he saw were paint bucket, brush, and rocks scattered on the Knudsons' pink-spattered grass. The phone rang. Who was it— Harriet Knudson? Eli, there's a Jew at your door. *That's me.* Nonsense, Eli, I saw him with my own eyes. *That's me, I saw you too, painting your rocks pink.* Eli, you're having a nervous breakdown again. Jimmy, Eli's having a nervous breakdown again. Eli, this is Jimmy, hear you're having a little breakdown, anything I can do, boy? Eli, this is Ted, Shirley says you need help. Eli, this is Artie, you need help. Eli, Harry, you need help you need help . . . The phone rattled its last and died.

"God helps them who help themselves," intoned Eli, and once again he stepped out the door. This time he walked to the center of his lawn and in full sight of the trees, the grass, the birds, and the sun, revealed that it was he, Eli, in the costume. But nature had nothing to say to him, and so stealthily he made his way to the hedge separating his property from the field beyond and he cut his way through, losing his hat twice in the underbrush. Then, clamping the hat to his head, he began to run, the threaded tassels jumping across his heart. He ran through the weeds and wild flowers, until on the old road that skirted the town he slowed up. He was walking when he approached the Gulf station from the back. He supported himself on a huge tireless truck rim, and among tubes, rusted engines, dozens of topless oil cans, he rested. With a kind of brainless cunning, he readied himself for the last mile of his journey.

"How are you, Pop?" It was the garage attendant, rubbing his greasy hands on his overalls, and hunting among the cans.

Eli's stomach lurched and he pulled the big black coat round his neck.

"Nice day," the attendant said and started around to the front.

"Sholom," Eli whispered and zoomed off towards the hill.

The sun was directly overhead when Eli reached the top. He had come by way of the woods, where it was cooler, but still he was perspiring beneath his new suit. The hat had no sweatband and the cloth clutched his head. The children were playing. The children were always playing, as if it was that alone that Tzuref had to teach them. In their shorts, they revealed such thin legs that beneath one could see the joints swiveling as they ran. Eli waited for them to disappear around a corner before he came into the open. But something would not let him wait—his green suit. It was on the porch, wrapped around the bearded fellow, who was painting the base of a pillar. His arm went up and down, up and down, and the pillar glowed like white fire. The very sight of him popped Eli out of the woods onto the lawn. He did not turn back, though his insides did. He walked up the lawn, but the children played on; tipping the black hat, he mumbled, "Shhh . . . shhhh," and they hardly seemed to notice.

At last he smelled paint.

He waited for the man to turn to him. He only painted. Eli

felt suddenly that if he could pull the black hat down over his eyes, over his chest and belly and legs, if he could shut out all light, then a moment later he would be home in bed. But the hat wouldn't go past his forehead. He couldn't kid himself—he was there. No one he could think of had forced him to do this.

The greenie's arm flailed up and down on the pillar. Eli breathed loudly, cleared his throat, but the greenie wouldn't make life easier for him. At last, Eli had to say "Hello."

The arm swished up and down; it stopped—two fingers went out after a brush hair stuck to the pillar.

"Good day," Eli said.

The hair came away; the swishing resumed.

"Sholom," Eli whispered and the fellow turned.

The recognition took some time. He looked at what Eli wore. Up close, Eli looked at what he wore. And then Eli had the strange notion that he was two people. Or that he was one person wearing two suits. The greenie looked to be suffering from a similar confusion. They stared long at one another. Eli's heart shivered, and his brain was momentarily in such a mixed-up condition that his hands went out to button down the collar of his shirt that somebody else was wearing. What a mess! The greenie flung his arms over his face.

"What's the matter . . ." Eli said. The fellow had picked up his bucket and brush and was running away. Eli ran after him.

"I wasn't going to hit . . ." Eli called. "Stop . . ." Eli caught up and grabbed his sleeve. Once again, the greenie's hand flew up to his face. This time, in the violence, white paint spattered both of them.

"I only want to . . ." But in that outfit Eli didn't really know what he wanted. "To talk . . ." he said finally. "For you to look at me. Please, just *look* at me . . ."

The hands stayed put, as paint rolled off the brush onto the cuff of Eli's green suit.

"Please . . . please," Eli said, but he did not know what to do. "Say something, speak *English*," he pleaded.

The fellow pulled back against the wall, back, back, as though some arm would finally reach out and yank him to safety. He refused to uncover his face.

"Look," Eli said, pointing to himself. "It's your suit. I'll take care of it."

No answer—only a little shaking under the hands, which led Eli to speak as gently as he knew how.

"We'll . . . we'll moth-proof it. There's a button missing" —Eli pointed— "I'll have it fixed. I'll have a zipper put in . . . Please, please—just look at me . . ." He was talking to himself, and yet how could he stop? Nothing he said made any sense—that alone made his heart swell. Yet somehow babbling on, he might babble something that would make things easier between them. "Look . . ." He reached inside his shirt to pull the frills of underwear into the light. "I'm wearing the special underwear, even . . . Please," he said, "*please, please, please*," he sang, as if it were some sacred word. "Oh, *please* . . ."

Nothing twitched under the tweed suit—and if the eyes watered, or twinkled, or hated, he couldn't tell. It was driving him crazy. He had dressed like a fool, and for what? For this? He reached up and yanked the hands away.

"There!" he said—and in that first instant all he saw of the greenie's face were two white droplets stuck to each cheek.

"Tell me—" Eli clutched his hands down to his sides— "Tell me, what can I do for you, I'll do it . . ."

Stiffly, the greenie stood there, sporting his two white tears.

"Whatever I can do . . . Look, look, what I've done *already*." He grabbed his black hat and shook it in the man's face.

And in exchange, the greenie gave him an answer. He raised one hand to his chest, and then jammed it, finger first, towards the horizon. And with what a pained look! As though the air were full of razors! Eli followed the finger and saw beyond the knuckle, out past the nail, Woodenton.

"What do you want?" Eli said. "I'll bring it!"

Suddenly the greenie made a run for it. But then he stopped, wheeled, and jabbed that finger at the air again. It pointed the same way. Then he was gone.

And then, all alone, Eli had the revelation. He did not question his understanding, the substance or the source. But with a strange, dreamy elation, he started away.

On Coach House Road, they were double-parked. The Mayor's wife pushed a grocery cart full of dog food from Stop N' Shop to her station wagon. The President of the Lions

Club, a napkin around his neck, was jamming pennies into the meter in front of the Bit-in-Teeth Restaurant. Ted Heller caught the sun as it glazed off the new Byzantine mosaic entrance to his shoe shop. In pinkened jeans, Mrs. Jimmy Knudson was leaving Halloway's Hardware, a paint bucket in each hand. Roger's Beauty Shoppe had its doors open—women's heads in silver bullets far as the eye could see. Over by the barbershop the pole spun, and Artie Berg's youngest sat on a red horse, having his hair cut; his mother flipped through *Look*, smiling: the greenie had changed his clothes.

And into this street, which seemed paved with chromium, came Eli Peck. It was not enough, he knew, to walk up one side of the street. That was not enough. Instead he walked ten paces up one side, then on an angle, crossed to the other side, where he walked ten more paces, and crossed back. Horns blew, traffic jerked, as Eli made his way up Coach House Road. He spun a moan high up in his nose as he walked. Outside no one could hear him, but he felt it vibrate the cartilage at the bridge of his nose.

Things slowed around him. The sun stopped rippling on spokes and hubcaps. It glowed steadily as everyone put on brakes to look at the man in black. They always paused and gaped, whenever he entered the town. Then in a minute, or two, or three, a light would change, a baby squawk, and the flow continue. Now, though lights changed, no one moved.

"He shaved his beard," Eric the barber said.

"Who?" asked Linda Berg.

"The . . . the guy in the suit. From the place there."

Linda looked out the window.

"It's Uncle Eli," little Kevin Berg said, spitting hair.

"Oh, God," Linda said, "Eli's having a nervous breakdown."

"A nervous breakdown!" Ted Heller said, but not immediately. Immediately he had said, "Hoooly . . ."

Shortly, everybody in Coach House Road was aware that Eli Peck, the nervous young attorney with the pretty wife, was having a breakdown. Everybody except Eli Peck. He knew what he did was not insane, though he felt every inch of its strangeness. He felt those black clothes as if they were the skin of his skin—the give and pull as they got used to where he bulged and buckled. And he felt eyes, every eye on Coach

House Road. He saw headlights screech to within an inch of him, and stop. He saw mouths: first the bottom jaw slides forward, then the tongue hits the teeth, the lips explode, a little thunder in the throat, and they've said it: Eli Peck Eli Peck Eli Peck Eli Peck. He began to walk slowly, shifting his weight down and forward with each syllable: E–li–Peck–E–li–Peck– E–li–Peck. Heavily he trod, and as his neighbors uttered each syllable of his name, he felt each syllable shaking all his bones. He knew who he was down to his marrow—they were telling him. Eli Peck. He wanted them to say it a thousand times, a million times, he would walk forever in that black suit, as adults whispered of his strangeness and children made "Shame . . . shame" with their fingers.

"It's going to be all right, pal . . ." Ted Heller was motioning to Eli from his doorway. "C'mon, pal, it's going to be all right . . ."

Eli saw him, past the brim of his hat. Ted did not move from his doorway, but leaned forward and spoke with his hand over his mouth. Behind him, three customers peered through the doorway. "Eli, it's Ted, remember Ted . . ."

Eli crossed the street and found he was heading directly towards Harriet Knudson. He lifted his neck so she could see his whole face.

He saw her forehead melt down on her lashes. "Good morning, Mr. Peck."

"Sholom," Eli said, and crossed the street where he saw the President of the Lions.

"Twice before . . ." he heard someone say, and then he crossed again, mounted the curb, and was before the bakery, where a delivery man charged past with a tray of powdered cakes twirling above him. "Pardon me, Father," he said, and scooted into his truck. But he could not move it. Eli Peck had stopped traffic.

He passed the Rivoli Theater, Beekman Cleaners, Harris' Westinghouse, the Unitarian Church, and soon he was passing only trees. At Ireland Road he turned right and started through Woodenton's winding streets. Baby carriages stopped whizzing and creaked— "Isn't that . . ." Gardeners held their clipping. Children stepped from the sidewalk and tried the curb. And Eli greeted no one, but raised his face to all. He wished passionately that he had white tears to show them . . . And not till he reached his own front lawn, saw his house, his shutters, his new jonquils, did he remember his wife. And the child that must have been born to him. And it was then and there he had the awful moment. He could go inside and put on his clothes and go to his wife in the hospital. It was not irrevocable, even the walk wasn't. In Woodenton memories are long but fury short. Apathy works like forgiveness. Besides, when you've flipped, you've flipped—it's Mother Nature.

What gave Eli the awful moment was that he turned away. He knew exactly what he could do but he chose not to. To go inside would be to go halfway. There was more . . . So he turned and walked towards the hospital and all the time he quaked an eighth of an inch beneath his skin to think that perhaps he'd chosen the crazy way. To think that he'd *chosen* to be crazy! But if you chose to be crazy, then you weren't crazy. It's when you didn't choose. No, he wasn't flipping. He had a child to see.

"Name?"

"Peck."

"Fourth floor." He was given a little blue card.

In the elevator everybody stared. Eli watched his black shoes rise four floors.

"Four."

He tipped his hat, but knew he couldn't take it off.

"Peck," he said. He showed the card.

"Congratulations," the nurse said. ". . . the grandfather?"

"The father. Which room?"

She led him to 412. "A joke on the Mrs.?" she said, but he slipped in the door without her.

"Miriam?"

"Yes?"

"Eli."

She rolled her white face towards her husband. "Oh, Eli . . . Oh, Eli."

He raised his arms. "What could I do?"

"You have a son. They called all morning."

"I came to see him."

"Like *that*!" she whispered harshly. "Eli, you can't go around like that."

"I have a son. I want to see him."

"Eli, why are you doing this to me!" Red seeped back into her lips. "*He's* not your fault," she explained. "Oh, Eli, sweetheart, why do you feel guilty about everything. Eli, change your clothes. I forgive you."

"Stop forgiving me. Stop understanding me."

"But I love you."

"That's something else."

"But, sweetie, you *don't* have to dress like that. You didn't do anything. You don't have to feel guilty because . . . because everything's all right. Eli, can't you see that?"

"Miriam, enough reasons. Where's my son?"

"Oh, please, Eli, don't flip now. I need you now. Is that why you're flipping—because I need you?"

"In your selfish way, Miriam, you're very generous. I want my son."

"Don't flip now. I'm afraid, now that he's out." She was beginning to whimper. "I don't know if I love him, now that he's out. When I look in the mirror, Eli, he won't be there . . . Eli, Eli, you look like you're going to your own funeral. Please, can't you leave well enough *alone*? Can't we just have a family?"

"No."

In the corridor he asked the nurse to lead him to his son. The nurse walked on one side of him, Ted Heller on the other.

"Eli, do you want some help? I thought you might want some help."

"No."

Ted whispered something to the nurse; then to Eli he whispered, "Should you be walking around like this?"

"Yes."

In his ear Ted said, "You'll . . . you'll frighten the kid . . ."

"There," the nurse said. She pointed to a bassinet in the second row and looked, puzzled, to Ted. "Do I go in?" Eli said.

"No," the nurse said. "She'll roll him over." She rapped on the enclosure full of babies. "Peck," she mouthed to the nurse on the inside.

Ted tapped Eli's arm. "You're not thinking of doing something you'll be sorry for . . . are you, Eli? Eli—I mean you know you're still Eli, don't you?"

In the enclosure, Eli saw a bassinet had been wheeled before the square window.

"Oh, Christ. . . ." Ted said. "You don't have this Bible stuff on the brain—" And suddenly he said, "You wait, pal." He started down the corridor, his heels tapping rapidly.

Eli felt relieved—he leaned forward. In the basket was what he'd come to see. Well, now that he was here, what did he think he was going to say to it? I'm your father, Eli, the Flipper? I am wearing a black hat, suit, and fancy underwear, all borrowed from a friend? How could he admit to this reddened ball—*his* reddened ball—the worst of all: that Eckman would shortly convince him he wanted to take off the whole business. He couldn't admit it! He wouldn't do it!

Past his hat brim, from the corner of his eye, he saw Ted had stopped in a doorway at the end of the corridor. Two interns stood there smoking, listening to Ted. Eli ignored it.

No, even Eckman wouldn't make him take it off! No! He'd wear it, if he chose to. He'd make the kid wear it! Sure! Cut it down when the time came. A smelly hand-me-down, whether the kid liked it or not!

Only Teddie's heels clacked; the interns wore rubber soles— for they were there, beside him, unexpectedly. Their white suits smelled, but not like Eli's.

"Eli," Ted said, softly, "visiting time's up, pal."

"How are you feeling, Mr. Peck? First child upsets everyone. . . ."

He'd just pay no attention; nevertheless, he began to perspire, thickly, and his hat crown clutched his hair.

"Excuse me—Mr. Peck. . . ." It was a new rich bass voice. "Excuse me, rabbi, but you're wanted . . . in the temple." A hand took his elbow, firmly; then another hand, the other elbow. Where they grabbed, his tendons were taut.

"Okay, rabbi. Okay okay okay okay okay okay. . . ." He listened; it was a very soothing word, that okay. "Okay okay everything's going to be okay." His feet seemed to have left the ground some, as he glided away from the window, the bassinet, the babies. "Okay easy does it everything's all right all right—"

But he rose, suddenly, as though up out of a dream, and flailing his arms, screamed: "*I'm the father!*"

But the window disappeared. In a moment they tore off his jacket—it gave so easily, in one yank. Then a needle slid under his skin. The drug calmed his soul, but did not touch it down where the blackness had reached.

LETTING GO

All actuality is deadly earnest; and it is mortality itself
that, one with life, forbids us to be true to the guileless
unrealism of our youth.

—Thomas Mann
A Sketch of My Life

Men owe us what we imagine they will give
us. We must forgive them this debt.
—Simone Weil
Gravity and Grace

It may be that one life is a punishment
For another, as the son's life for the father's.
But that concerns the secondary characters.
It is a fragmentary tragedy
Within the universal whole. The son
And the father alike and equally are spent,
Each one, by the necessity of being
Himself, the unalterable necessity
Of being this unalterable animal.
—Wallace Stevens
"Esthétique du Mal"

For Maggie

Contents

ONE

Debts and Sorrows

1

D^{*ear Gabe,*}
    *The drugs help me bend my fingers around a pen. Some
times the whole sickness feels located in my hands. I have wanted
to write but not by dictating to your father. Later I don't want to
whisper last-minute messages to him at the bedside. With all the
panic and breathlessness I'll have too much influence. Now your
father keeps leaning across my bed. He runs in after every patient
and tells me what the weather is outside. He never once admits
that I've done him an injustice being his wife. He holds my hand
fifty times a day. None of this changes what has happened—the
injustice is done. Whatever unhappiness has been in our family
springs from me. Please don't blame it on your father however I
may have encouraged you over the years. Since I was a little girl
I always wanted to be Very Decent to People. Other little girls
wanted to be nurses and pianists. They were less dissembling. I
was clever, I picked a virtue early and hung on to it. I was always
doing things for another's good. The rest of my life I could push
and pull at people with a clear conscience. All I want to say now
is that I don't want to say anything. I want to give up the prerogative allowed normal dying people. Why I'm writing is to say
that I have no instructions.*

   *Your father is coming in again. He's carrying three kinds of
fruit juices. Gabe, it's to him I should admit all this. He won't
condemn me until I do first. All through our marriage I've been
improving his life for him, pushing, pulling. Oh decent decent.
Dear, the pen keeps falling*

Her letter had never been signed. The pen fell, and when
the night nurse came on duty she was no longer needed.
Nevertheless my father, obedient to the last, put the letter in
an envelope and without examination mailed it. I was a second
lieutenant in the artillery corps at this time, stationed in an un-
regenerate dust bowl in Oklahoma, and my one connection

with the world of feeling was not the world itself but Henry
James, whom I had lately begun to read. Oklahoma nights and
southwestern radio stations had thrust me into an isolation
wherein my concentration was exact enough for me to attend
at last to the involutions of the old master. All day I listened to
the booming of cannons, and all night to the words of heroes
and heroines tempting one another into a complex and often
tragic fate. Early in the summer that I had been called into the
Army—which was the summer after I had finished college—I
had spent my last six civilian weeks touring Europe; one week
was spent visiting with a friend of my mother's who lived in
London, where her husband was connected with the U.S.
Embassy. I remember having to hear endless incidents from
my mother's childhood while sitting with her friend in a small
church in Chelsea; she had taken me there to see a little-known
plaque dedicated to James. It was not a particularly successful
day, for the woman really liked the idea of putting on long
white gloves and showing a Harvard boy around cultural
nooks and crannies a good deal more than she liked the nooks
and crannies. But I do remember the words engraved onto
that small gray oval tablet: it was written of James that he was
"lover and interpreter of the fine amenities of brave decisions."

So it happened that when I received the letter my mother
had written and my father had posted, I was reading *Portrait
of a Lady*, and it was into its pages that I slid the envelope
and its single sheet of barely legible prose. When I returned
from the funeral, and in the weeks following, I read and reread
the letter so often that I weakened the binding of the book.
In my grief and confusion, I promised myself that I would do
no violence to human life, not to another's, and not to my
own.

———

It was a year later that I loaned the book to Paul Herz, who
looked to be a harried young man rapidly losing contact with
his own feelings; he might have been hearing the boom of big
guns going off all day himself. This was the fall after I had left
the Army, the fall of 1953, when we were both enrolled as graduate students at the University of Iowa. Paul's costume at that
time was the same day in and day out: khaki trousers threadbare around the back pocket, a white T-shirt shapeless around

the arms, tennis sneakers and, occasionally, socks. He was forever running—it was this that brought him to my attention—
and forever barely making it. The point of his briefcase could
be seen edging through the classroom door just at the moment
that the first unlucky student in our Anglo-Saxon class was
called upon to read aloud from *Beowulf*. Leaving the library at
night, I would see him streaking up the stairs after some reserve book, even while the head librarian turned the key in the
lock. He would stand shivering in his T-shirt until she broke
down and let him in. He was a man who evoked sympathy
even if he did not come right out and ask for it; even if he
would not ask for it. No heart could remain unmoved by the
sight of that dark, kinky-haired black-eyed head racing toward
the closing doors, or into them. Once, shopping for some
bread and milk, I saw him nearly break several of the major
bones of his body at the entrance to a downtown grocery
store. The electric eye swung the door out at him just as he
had turned, arms laden with packages, to watch a cop stick a
ticket under the single wiper of his battered, green, double-
parked Dodge.

I lived alone at the time in a small apartment near the campus, and was having troubles of my own; I was about ready to
find somebody to complain to. One day in November, as Herz
was darting from Anglo-Saxon, I stuck myself in his path and
asked him over to the Union for a cup of coffee. He couldn't
make it as he was supposed to have been somewhere else five
minutes earlier, but on the parking lot, to which I accompanied him, and where he sat yanking and yanking at the throttle
of his car, I managed to put in something about James, and
the next time we had class together, I brought *Portrait* for him
to take home and read. I awoke that night remembering that
tucked in the pages of the book I had pressed upon him,
somewhere between the hopes of Isabel Archer and her disappointments, was my mother's letter. I couldn't immediately
get back to sleep.

The following morning, directly after Medieval Romances, I
called Herz from a campus phone booth. Mrs. Herz answered
sounding hurried and on edge—the family tone. She and her
husband lived in one of those gray shells on the far side of
the river, the married students' barracks, and I was sure that

directly behind her, or beneath her, there flailed a squalling infant. Herz looked harassed enough to be the father of three or four small, mean, colicky children. Mrs. Herz, in a very few words, informed me that her husband had driven over to Cedar Rapids and that she was herself about to rush off. I decided instantly not to ask if I might come over to remove something that I had left in a book I had loaned Paul. Probably neither of them had had a chance at the book anyway, and I could wait and later get to Herz himself. I explained nothing whatsoever to the wife, who struck me as more rude than chagrined; besides, it was daylight and autumn and I was no longer afflicted with thoughts of the dead. The November morning was dazzling, the dead were dead.

My father had called again the night before, and I was certain now that any judgments I had made in the dark about my mother's ghost had been induced by my father's presence. Two or three evenings a week my father and I had the same phone conversation, pointless on the surface, pleading beneath. The old man stood being familyless all day, what with having his patients' mouths to look into; it was alone with his avocado and lettuce dinner that he broke down. When he called his voice shook; when he hung up—or when I did—his vibrato passed directly into the few meager objects in the room. I moved one way, my chair another; I have never sat on my reading glasses so many times in my life. I am, for good or bad, in a few ways like my father, and so have never been the same person alone that I am with people. The trouble with the phone calls, in fact, was that all the time I felt it necessary to the preservation of my life and sanity to resist the old man, I understood how it was for him sitting in that huge Victorian living room all alone. However, if I am my father's child, I am my mother's too. I cannot trace out exactly the influences, nor deal in any scientific way with the chromosomes passed on to me. I sometimes believe I know what it is I got from him and what from her, and when I hung up on Mrs. Herz that morning, without having said one word about the letter, I suppose I was using the decorum and good sense that has sifted down from the maternal line. I told myself that there was nothing really to fret about. Why would they read it anyway? And what if they did?

At five o'clock I was sitting in my apartment drinking coffee and finding no pleasure whatsoever in memorizing Anglo-Saxon verb endings, when Mrs. Herz called me back.

"You spoke to me this morning," she said. "Paul Herz's wife."

"Is your husband home?"

"His car broke down."

It was the sort of news that is not news as soon as one hears it—though Mrs. Herz herself sounded surprised. "That's too bad," I said.

"He blew a piston or he keeps blowing pistons—"

"I'll call him some other time. It's not urgent."

"Well—" she said, "he asked me to call *you*. He wondered if you might have a car. He's on the highway outside of Cedar Rapids."

I put down the Old English grammar book. A long drive was just the inconvenience I wanted. "How do I get there?"

"Could you pick me up at the barracks?"

"I'm sure I could find it."

"I know the way. We live just at the edge of Finkbine Park—could you pick me up?" Cryptically, she added, "I'm dressed."

From the doorway the first thing I saw after seeing Libby Herz herself was my book set on the edge of the kitchen sink; I could not see what was or was not stuck between its pages. And Mrs. Herz gave me no time to check; she ran into the bedroom and then out again, her raincoat whipping around her. Then yanking a kerchief from her pocket, she rushed out the door without once looking directly at me—though she managed to let me hear her say, "Paul called again. I told him we were coming."

As we drove, her eyes stared rigidly out the car window, while beside me her limbs fidgeted in turn. My first impression of her had been clear and sharp: profession—student; inclinations—neurotic. She moved jerkily and had the high black stockings and the underfed look. She was thin, dark, intense, and I could not imagine that she had ever once gotten anything but pain from entering a room full of people. Still, in an eager hawky way she was not bad looking. Her head was carried forward on her neck, and the result was that her large sculpted nose sailed into the wind a little too defiantly—which

compromised the pride of the appendage, though not its fanci-
ness. Her eyes were a pure black, and her shiny hair, also black,
was drawn off her face in a manner so stark and exact that at
the sight of it one could begin guessing at the depth and number of her anxieties. The skin was classic and pale: white with a
touch of blue, making it ivory—and when she pulled off her
kerchief she even had a tiny purple vein tapping at her temple;
it seemed to me like an affect, something willed there to remind the rest of us how delicate and fragile is a woman. My
initial feeling toward her was suspicion.

Nevertheless, by way of conversation I asked if she had any
children.

"Oh, no," she said. The deep breath she drew was to inform
me that she was rushed and harried without children. She
added a few mumbled words: "Thank goodness . . . children
. . . burden. . . ." It was difficult to understand her because she
did not bother to look at me either when speaking or sighing.
I knew she was avoiding my eyes—and then I knew that she
had opened the book, removed the envelope, and read my
mother's letter. Since she did not strike me as a person casual
about private lives, her own or others, her self-consciousness
became mine too.

Darkness had dimmed my vision before either of us spoke
again. "Are you in the Writers' Workshop?" she asked.

"No. Just English. Are you?"

"Paul's the writer," she said. "I'm still getting my B.A."

"I see."

"I've been getting it for about a decade." There was a frank
and simple note of exasperation in her voice, and it engaged
me. I looked away from the highway and she gave off staring
into the countryside, and with a glance as distinct, as audible
as a camera snapping, we registered each other's features.

"Paul said you're interested in James," she quickly said,
flushing. Then, "I'm Libby."

"I'm Gabe Wallach—" I stopped as once again the words
flew out of her.

"Neither of us know anything really outside the Edmund
Wilson one—" she said, "the ghost story."

"*Turn of the Screw*," I said, a good half minute after she had
not resumed talking.

"*Portrait of a Lady* is much better." She spoke these words as though to please.

"You like it?"

"The first scene is wonderful."

"When they're all on the lawn."

"Yes," she said, "when Isabel comes. I've been living so long in barracks, elegance has an abnormal effect on me."

"The prose?"

"The rug on the lawn. You know, they're all sitting on chairs on that immense lawn outside the Touchetts' house. Ralph and his father and Lord Warburton. James says the place was furnished as though it were a room. There's a rug on the lawn. I don't know, perhaps it's just across somebody's legs, one of those kind of rugs. I've read it over several times, and since you can't be sure, I like to think of it the other way, *on* the lawn. That appeals to me." She stopped, violently—and I was left listening for the next few words. I looked over and saw that she was drawing on her top lip so that her nose bent a little at the bottom. All that was dark, her eyes and hair, came to dominate her face. "That sounds terribly private," she said. "Sometimes I miss the point, I know." The little forced laugh that followed admitted to fallibilities not solely literary. I was touched by her frailty, until I wondered if perhaps I was supposed to be. "The rug," she was saying, "knocked me over anyway." Whereupon her gaze dropped to the floorboard of the car.

"It knocked Isabel over," I said.

She received the remark blankly. "Yes," she said.

I tried to remember where in the book the letter was stuck. "How far have you read?" I asked.

"Up to where she meets Osmond. I think I can see what's coming. Though," she rushed to add, "perhaps I can't. I really shouldn't say that."

"You must . . . you must have read all night," was all I finally said.

She flushed again. "Almost," she told me. "Paul hasn't started the book yet—" I was looking ahead at the road; I heard her voice stop, and then I felt her move a little toward me. I believe she touched my arm. "Mr. Wallach, there was a letter in your book."

"Was there?"

"You must have forgotten it."

The quality of her voice had altered so as to make the whole occasion much too momentous; I heard myself saying that I didn't remember any letter.

"I brought it with me," she said, and from the pocket of her shabby raincoat she took the envelope; it must have been this she had raced back into her bedroom to fetch while I had waited at the doorstep. Now she handed it to me. "It was in the book."

"Thank you." I put the letter immediately into my own jacket pocket. Out of sight I fumbled with it, but there was no evidence either way—the flap was tucked in. Nevertheless, I drove ahead with only one hand on the wheel. Mrs. Herz pulled at her black stockings, then stuck a fist under each knee. For two miles neither of us said anything.

In the tone of one musing she finally spoke. "She marries and is miserable."

I had been musing myself, and so I misunderstood at first who exactly was the subject of her observation. My misunderstanding must have produced a very strange expression on my face, for when I turned to demand an explanation, Libby Herz seemed nearly to dissolve in her seat. "Isabel will marry Osmond," she said, "and be miserable. She's—she's a romantic . . . isn't she?" she asked shakily.

I had not meant to threaten her. I forgot my family as rapidly as I could, and tried hard to be graceful. "I guess so," I said. "She likes rugs on lawns."

"She likes rugs on lawns," Mrs. Herz said, grinning. "That's the least of it. She wants to put rugs on other people's lawns."

"Osmond?"

"Osmond—and more than Osmond." She raised her hands and opened them, slowly and expressively. "*Every*thing," she said, drawing the word out. "She wants to alter what can't be altered."

"She believes in change."

"Change? My God!" She put her hand to her forehead.

It was the first time I was amused by her. "You don't believe in change?"

Without warning she turned momentous on me again. "I

suppose I do." She stared a little tragically into her college girl's raincoat: change, alteration, was not so much the condition of all life as it was some sad and private principle of her own. The hands tugged again at the stockings, went under the knees, and she withdrew. I drove faster and hunted the highway for Paul Herz.

"Well, do you believe," Mrs. Herz suddenly put in, "in altering that way? Isabel's trouble is she wants to change others, but a man comes along who can alter her, Warburton or what's his name, Ramrod—"

"Goodwood. Caspar Goodwood."

"Caspar Goodwood—and what happens? She gets the shakes, she gets scared. She's practically frigid, at least that's what it looks like a case of to me. She's not much different finally from her friend, that newspaper lady. She's one of those powerful women, one of those pushers-around of men—"

Before she went off the deep end, I interrupted and said, "I've always found her virtuous and charming."

"Charming?" Incredulity rendered her helpless. Slumping down in her seat, as though konked on the head, she said, "For marrying *Osmond?*"

"For liking rugs on lawns," I said.

It was as though I had touched her. She pushed up into a dignified posture and raised her chin. Actually I had only mildly been trying to charm her—and with the truth no less; but in the diminished light, alone on the highway, it had had for her all the earmarks of a pass. And perhaps, after all, that's what it was; I remembered the seriousness with which we had looked at each other some ten miles back.

To inform me of the depths of her loyalty to her husband, she insulted me. "Perhaps you just like pushy women. Some men do." I didn't answer, which did not stop her. Since I had asked for the truth, I was going to get all of it. "That book, as a matter of fact, is really full of people pushing and pulling at each other, and most often with absolutely clear—"

She had been speaking passionately, and leaving off there was leaving off entirely too late. There was no need for her to speak that final word of my mother's: *conscience.* I was not sure whether to be offended or humiliated or relieved; for a moment I managed to be all three. It actually seemed as though she had deliberately challenged me with my secret—and at the bottom I did not know if I really minded. The worst part of certain secrets is their secrecy. There is a comfort to be derived from letting strangers in on our troubles, especially, if one is a man, strangers who happen also to be women. Perhaps offering the book to be read in the first place had been my way of offering the letter to be read as well. For I was beginning really to be exhausted with standing over my mother's memory, making sure the light didn't go out. I had never even been willing to believe that my mother had treated my father badly, until she had gone ahead and told me so. Much as I loved him, he had seemed to me, while she still lived, unworthy of her; it was her letter that had made me see her as unworthy of him. And that is a strange thing to have happen to you—to feel yourself, after death, turning on a person you have always cherished. I had come to feel it was true that she had not merely handled him all her life, as one had to, but that she had mishandled him . . . At least I believed this with part of my mind. I had, curiously, over a period of a year, come to distrust the woman of whom the letter spoke, all the while I continued to honor and admire the memory of the woman who could have written it. And now, when I had begun to have to handle her husband myself, the letter came accidentally back into my life, to decrease in no way my confusion as to what to do with my father's overwhelming love.

"I'm sorry," Libby Herz was saying. "It was habit. Which makes it even worse. I am sorry."

"It's okay."

"It's not. I had to open it. I'm the sort of person who does that."

Now I was irritated at the way she seemed to be glorifying herself by way of her weaknesses. "Other people do it too," I said.

"Paul doesn't." And that fact seemed to depress her most of all; she worried it while we passed a tall white farmhouse with gingerbread ornament hanging from the frame of every window and door.

After some time had passed, I felt it necessary to caution her. "It's rather an easy letter to misunderstand," I said.

"I suppose so, yes," she answered, in a whisper. "I don't

think—" But she said no more. Her disturbance was private and deep, and I could not help but feel that she was behaving terribly. If she was going to feel so bad about somebody's feelings, I believed they should at least have been mine. But she seemed unable to work up sympathy for anyone but herself: *she* was still getting her B.A., after "a decade"; *she* lived in barracks, so that elegance had a special poignancy for her . . . Her own condition occupied her totally, and I knew that she could no more appreciate my mother's dilemma than she could Isabel Archer's. I was, at last, fed up with her. "*Portrait of a Lady*," I said, "is an easy book to misunderstand too. You're too harsh with Isabel Archer."

"I only meant—"

"Why don't you wait until you read it all."

"I read half—"

"She shows herself to have a lot of guts in the end," I said, again not allowing her to finish. "It's one thing marrying the wrong person for the wrong reasons; it's another sticking it out with them."

To that she had no answer: I had not really permitted one, and perhaps she realized that I was not talking only about the book.

Crushed, she answered finally, "I didn't mean to be so flip. Or nosey."

"All right, let's forget it." Though I was myself unable to. "I don't usually leave letters in books," I said. "It was a peculiar time. I was in the Army—" I heard myself becoming, in front of this girl, as momentous about my life as she had been about her own, and I stopped talking.

"Mr. Wallach," she said, "I didn't show it to Paul, if that alleviates anything."

"We're making much too much of this. Let's do forget it."

The next time she spoke it was only to point up ahead and say, "There he is."

On the other side of the highway a figure in a long coat was leaning against the darkened headlamp of a car. I moved onto the shoulder at the right-hand side of the road just as Libby took my arm.

"Please forgive me. I'm a snoop, and I'm dumb about novels," she said. "About people."

It was supposed to have been a genuine admission, but once made I realized that it was not true; she was not so dumb finally about either.

"I'm sure you're right about everything," she said to me.

"Maybe we're both right," I answered, though not over-generously, and turned off the motor and headlights.

Before she reached for the door handle, she turned her face toward me once again. When people have much to say to you, and hardly any time in which to say it, their eyes are sometimes like Libby Herz's were that moment; above all, they were kind. "Mr. Wallach, I stayed up to read the book because I was very moved by the letter," and then, as though we were being watched, we both jumped from the car.

—

All that had to be removed from Paul Herz's Dodge was a briefcase stuffed with freshman themes, a flashlight, and an old army blanket that had been used to cover the torn uphol-stery in the front seat. We had to sit for half an hour in my car waiting for the wrecker; Herz had asked a state trooper to call one for him. There was little conversation: Libby discovered that her husband had ripped his new coat, and Herz said that he'd caught it on the hood, and from the back seat I thought I heard his wife begin to sob. Finally the wrecker arrived and the four of us gathered solemnly in the dark around the dam-aged hood. A sinewy little grease monkey, the wrecker flexed his knuckles and then stuck his hand down through the hole which the flying piston had made in the engine.

"Ten dollars," he said.

"For repairs?" Libby asked.

"For the car," the wrecker replied.

Headlights flashed by on the highway, illuminating on Libby Herz's face astonishment and woe. "Ten dollars! That's ridiculous. Paul, that's ridiculous."

The wrecker addressed the husband. "It's junk."

"It's a '47," Libby said feebly.

"Lady, it's got five pistons. It's junk."

"Five?"

"It's gotta have six to go," said the wrecker.

"Still." Then she looked toward her husband. "Paul . . ."

The wrecker stuck his hand in again, and Libby turned

quickly back to him as though perhaps he'd miscounted the first time. He only looked at me and shrugged his shoulders. Herz looked at none of us; I saw him shut his eyes.

"How much would it cost . . . to fix it?" Libby asked the question generally, as she had to; she was being ignored all around. The wrecker folded his arms and made me once again special witness to his exasperation. The two of us, thank God, were not married to this woman: he gave off a slow hiss for our side.

"We can't fix it," Herz said. "Please, Lib."

"Paul, ten dollars. The parts alone—the *heater* alone."

"Lady," the wrecker said, and he seemed to have summoned his patience for an explanation of engine dynamics. "Lady, it's junk," he said.

"Will you stop saying *junk*!" She was seeing through teary eyes, and talking with a full nose, and she turned her back to all of us and walked off toward the tow truck. Under the thick iron hook that swung off the crane, she stopped and blew her nose; she looked up, whether at the clear moony sky or the iron hook I didn't know, but one or the other must have made an ungenerous comment to her about her fate, for she shuddered, and holding her arms around her front like a sick woman, climbed into the back seat of my car.

Paul Herz took his hands out of his coat pockets. "She's upset," he explained.

I nodded; the wrecker said, "I haven't got all night."

Herz looked at him and then, by himself, took a little walk around his car, staring down at each of the tires as though above all else he hated losing those four old friends. When he came back to us he tried to smile at me. "Okay," he said.

The wrecker took a tight fat wad from his pocket; he flashed it a little at us college boys and peeled off two fives. He rubbed them a moment with his black fingers and handed the cash to Herz.

"Is that all?" Herz said.

The grease monkey was overcome suddenly with cheeriness. He lifted his arms in the air. "That's all, professor."

—

We drove back to Iowa City with Paul Herz sitting alongside me in the front. As soon as we got in the car Herz had said to me, "Thanks for being so patient. I'm sorry about all this."

"It's okay."

"The thief," Libby Herz said. In the rear-view mirror I saw she was sitting on her knees looking out the back window.

Herz seemed at first to decide not to be provoked, but at last he spoke. "Libby, the car blew a piston. It's junk."

"That's what the man said," his wife answered.

"Okay," Herz said.

"Ten dollars . . . the fenders alone—"

Herz glanced my way to see if I was listening. I tried my best to attend only to the black road, but of course there were my ears to contend with. "Libby," he said, "will you please? You don't know anything about cars, honey."

"I know about thieves."

"Damn it," Herz said, turning in his seat, "nobody cheated me!"

"I didn't say he cheated you—"

"What did you expect me to do? Bargain with him for a couple of dollars in the middle of the highway? I've been standing there for over an hour!"

"We're not millionaires!"

"You don't know anything about cars. Will you please be quiet!"

"Why did the piston come through like that?" she whined.

Herz turned to the front window again; he was fingering his coat where the cuff was torn. "I don't know."

"What are we going to do?"

"I don't *know*!"

By this time I was practically hunched behind the wheel, feeling the emotions of an eavesdropper—and having the thoughts of one too. Like most people with an ear to the wall, I had taken a side: the impossible one to live with, I could see now, was clearly the wife. Her husband's car had been raised on a hook and towed away; his briefcase was splitting with ungraded themes; his new coat, which looked to me to be a pretty old coat, was torn in the sleeve; and to top things off, his Anglo-Saxon verbs, like mine, had been waiting for centuries to be memorized, and waited still. And she wouldn't let the poor guy alone. Without being too obvious about it, I pushed the accelerator into the floor, though I realized that by outracing Paul Herz's temper, and avoiding what I could of his familial difficulty, I was of course racing back to familial problems of my own. I would walk through the door, the phone would ring, I would lift it, and my father would say: "Where were you—I've been calling all night?" I could race up the stairs and crash through the apartment and catch the phone on the second ring, and he still wouldn't be satisfied: What's the matter I wasn't there for the first? In short, why hadn't I called him? In short, why had I run off to Iowa for graduate work when Columbia was only two subway stops north? I could go back to Harvard, couldn't I? At least it wasn't six million miles away!

"Can't you get another section on the campus?" Libby Herz was asking her husband.

"Honey, I'm just not quitting Coe," Herz explained.

"How are you going to get there?"

"I'll work it out."

"Don't you have a class there tomorrow?"

"Yes."

"How are you going to get there?"

"Why don't you wait until we get home, all right?"

Small sounds of brooding followed. Someone crossed a limb, someone sniffed, someone tapped for several minutes against an ash tray. I felt pressed to say something, and finally, innocuously, asked Herz if he taught at Coe College.

"That's where I was coming from." He seemed almost relieved to answer my question. "I teach two sections of composition."

"I thought you taught on the campus," I said.

"Just one section."

"I don't understand," Libby butted in, leaning forward from the back seat, "how a piston just *explodes*. Out of nowhere."

No one answered her.

"Wasn't there enough oil? It was probably the what-do-you-call-its," she said, "the tappets. Didn't the man say something once about tappets?"

It's the little questions from women about tappets that finally push men over the edge. Herz practically rose in his seat. "Libby, what do you think has been knocking in the engine since

Michigan? A piston has been cracking or whatever the hell it's been doing for two years. Since Detroit. Why don't you consider us lucky—we've driven that car thousands of miles. Stop thinking of the bad—think of all the *use* we got out of it. Let's not worry about the car. I sold it. We don't have it. For*get* it!"

"I'm just upset," she said.

That seemed a good enough explanation for Herz; a patient and forgiving man, he said, "We'll work something out."

"How?"

"We'll work something out, please."

"Oh *how*," she burst out, "like in Michigan?"

"Will you please *shut up*!"

Three gas stations, two roadhouses, and no words later we were in Iowa City. Paul Herz instructed me with terse lefts and mumbled rights until we turned a corner and were rewarded with a panoramic view of the settlement of barracks. Lights were on in the undersized windows and smoke curled from all the metallic funnels, and I felt a little like the enemy sneaking up on the ambushed. It might have seemed that an army was encamped here, were it not for the tricycles tipped over on the gravel lawns, and the few pieces of clothing that had been forgotten, and still hung on the lines that crisscrossed from one gray rectangle to another. When the motor of the car was slowed down, I could hear a creaking and a straining and a clanging, as though the metal sides of the barracks and the concrete foundations were slowly sabotaging themselves in the dark.

"Thanks," Herz said to me. "Right here is fine."

I heard Libby stir in the back seat. Without turning, I said, "You're welcome. And good night."

Libby was opening the back door; Herz himself had a hand on the front door handle, where for a moment he hesitated. I felt he wanted to apologize to me for what I had had to see and hear. I only smiled as a signal of my sympathy, while his wife moved wordlessly out of the car.

After a moment he asked, "Have you had dinner?"

"That's all right," I said.

"Maybe you'd like to join us. What are we having?" he asked his wife.

"I don't know."

He looked back at me and asked quickly, "Would you care to have some spaghetti with us?"

"I don't really think I can . . . I'm expecting a phone call."

He reached out then and shook my hand; I saw him try to eradicate with a smile his rotten mood. He didn't begin to succeed.

Suddenly his wife was speaking. "We have plenty—" Libby Herz seemingly had risen out of twenty feet of water. She spoke with that desperate breathlessness of hers, a girl who'd just discovered air. "Spaghetti, with garlic and oil. We'd *love* to have you."

Paul Herz had already swung his briefcase through the door, and was stuck, half-in, half-out; he looked just as shabby and defeated as a man can who has been made a fool of by his wife. I imagined that even living with another, he was no less alone than I was.

"I don't want to inconvenience you," I said, looking at neither of them.

"It's no inconvenience," Libby Herz said. "Please come," she said. "We have plenty."

Plenty! From her mouth no word could have sounded more pathetic.

—

When I returned home I went directly to the phone, picked it up, and said hello.

"Hello, Gabe? Where were you?"

"I had dinner out."

"Since five in the afternoon?"

"I was out before that for something else."

"Well," he said, working at being cheerful, "you're a tough man to catch at home. I don't know why you pay rent on an apartment, you're hardly there."

"Well, I had a busy day. How are you? I didn't expect you'd call again," I said. "You called last night."

"I was thinking it was two or three nights already," he said. "What's new?"

"Nothing. How's New York?"

"I took a walk after dinner. Millie made me an early dinner. What are you doing, still eating in restaurants? They overcook vegetables, I'll tell you that."

"I had dinner with friends."

"Look, when is your vacation again? I've got a calendar right in front of me."

"Christmas."

"I thought Thanksgiving."

"I don't get off then," I said. "Only Thanksgiving Day. I'm really busy with work, you know."

"You have dinner with friends, maybe you can have dinner with your father sometimes."

"It isn't just dinner with you," I said firmly, trying to keep separate my emotions and the facts. "It's all the traveling. It wouldn't be worth it coming all the way East for one or two days."

"Worth it." He simply repeated my words; then, having made his point, went on. "It's not my fault you went a million miles away," he reminded me. "There's NYU, there's Columbia, there's City College. I could name them all night."

"Don't," I said. "Please."

"Do you think I call up to be insulted?"

"I'm sorry. I don't mean to insult you. But these phone calls, these phone calls are driving me nuts."

"Well, I'm sorry," he said, after a pause. "I don't mean to drive you nuts. I just thought a father had a right to call his son when he wanted to. Five minutes a couple times a week . . ."

"You're right," I said.

"Gabe—Gabe, I sit around here and I look at that orange sofa and I think of your mother. And I look at that Moroccan rug and I think of her. What am I supposed to do, get rid of all this furniture? We had it thirty years."

"I understand."

"Why don't you fly in Thanksgiving? I'll send you a check, get a ticket, come home for a little while. Millie will make a regular Thanksgiving dinner. We'll have Dr. Gruber here. We'll go down to the Penn-Cornell game. How does that strike you?"

"Why don't we wait until Christmas. It's only a few weeks later, and I'll have plenty of time—"

"But Thanksgiving is *traditional!*" he exploded. "What's

the matter with you?" he said, and I heard him trying not to cry at the other end.

"I know it's traditional," I said. "I only get the day off. Just Thanksgiving Day. It's just not enough time. But Christmas I'll be home for two weeks."

"Your mother's been gone *sixty*-two weeks!" His unreason was nothing to the shaking in his voice. Yet there were no longer any patient explanations for me to make. Here it was November, 1953, the funeral had been in September of 1952, and still he was spinning down and around, deeper in his morbid sea. When I had been released from the Army early in August I had only suspicions about what it would be like; but three weeks with a drowning roommate had been all that I could bear. I could not help him out with his loneliness: I could not prop him up, counsel him, direct him, run him. I could not be Anna Wallach. I had finally to tell him (it had been a cold and nasty scene) that I was not his wife or his mother, but his son. A son, he said, a son *exactly*! What he wanted to know was if all sons run off, leaving fathers to sink forever by themselves.

I gave him several seconds now to get control. "Why don't you call Dr. Gruber?" I asked. "Why don't you go to the theater with him? See a show, go skating at Rockefeller Plaza—"

"Gruber? Gruber's happy. He had a wife he hated. I sit around with him all night and all he does is grin. It's worse than being alone, being with Gruber. I went skating with him last week. All he does, Gabe, all afternoon, is little figure eights, and all the time, smiling. What kind of man is that?"

He was not laughing, but at least the worst was over; he was willing to tease himself.

"Dad," I said, "I don't know what to tell you."

"That's funny," he said softly, "because I know just what to tell you."

"I don't think I'd be a help." I felt myself losing control.

"I think you would. Look, what's wrong with going back to Harvard? At least I'll expect you Thanksgiving, huh?"

I knew he was wrong; everything in my experience told me he was wrong, and yet I said, "I'll see about Thanksgiving. I can't promise."

"I never asked for promises, Gabe. Just try. Just meet me halfway. I'll send you a check for the plane."

"Why don't you hold it off until I see—"

"It's only a check."

"I've got two checks I haven't even cashed yet."

"Cash them. You want to foul up my bank statements?" he asked gaily.

"I just don't need all that money, that's all. I've got the G.I. Bill. I've got Mother's money—"

"Will it kill you to cash them?" he asked. "I send them off, it makes me feel good. Will it kill you if I can balance up my account at the end of the month?"

"No."

"You cash those checks. Is that too big a favor to ask?"

I said no again, with as little conviction this time as before.

"And I'll see you Thanksgiving," he said.

"Please, Dad—please stop pushing me—about Thanksgiving—"

"Who's pushing? Let's get it straight, are you coming Thanksgiving or aren't you? You want me to have Millie buy a turkey or not?"

"I don't really see how I can make it, truly."

"You have time for other things, to eat dinner out—you have time to visit people—"

"That was involved. I was doing somebody a favor."

"Well, that's all I'm asking for."

"Please, stop pleading!"

"Don't shout at me!"

"Well, don't *beg* me!"

"Tell me, tell me, how else does one get through to you?"

"By making decent demands, that's how."

"I don't want to push your generosity too far."

"It's not even generosity we're dealing with."

"No, you're right. It's supposed to be love."

"I don't think I deserve all this," I said.

"Nobody told you to run away."

"I didn't run."

"Iowa. Why not Canada! That's farther."

"That's closer," I said, but he wouldn't laugh. "I don't

think either of us wants to have these kind of conversations. I don't think this is how either of us feels. Let's relax."

"Gabe, I'm sitting here with a calendar in front of me. I count days. I know how many days between now and Thanksgiving, between now and Christmas, from now to *Easter*. Maybe I'm going nuts, I don't know."

"You're just lonely."

"Yeah," he said, "some just."

"Please," I said, "I do understand. I'll do my best."

"All right, all right." He sounded suddenly very tired.

"You're feeling all right, aren't you?"

He laughed. "Terrific."

"Maybe you should go to sleep."

"It's all right, I'm watching a little television. Why aren't you in bed? It's midnight where you are. It's like wearing two watches; whenever I think what time it is here, I think what time it is there. What are *you* doing so late?"

"I'm going to study some Anglo-Saxon."

"That would impress your mother," he said, wisecracking. "It doesn't impress me."

"It doesn't impress me either. It bores hell out of me."

"Then," he began, "I don't know why you do it—"

"Let's go to sleep," I said.

"Okay, okay," he said, and when he yawned it was as though we were in the same room. "Take it easy, boy."

"Good night."

"See you Thanksgiving," he said, and hung up before I could answer.

When I finally got to bed that night, I found it impossible to get any solace from feeling sorry for myself. The irritation I generally felt toward my father—for things like hanging up as calculatingly as he had—I now felt for myself. Fresh from their drafty little house, I could not help comparing my condition with the Herzes': what I had learned at dinner was that all that my father would bless me with, the Herzes of Brooklyn and the DeWitts of Queens withheld from their struggling offspring. Once Jew had wed Gentile wounds were opened—in Brooklyn, in Queens—that were unhealable. And all that Paul and Libby could do to make matters better had apparently only made them worse. Conversion, for instance, had been a fiasco. "Switching loyalties," Libby Herz had said, "somehow proved to them I didn't have any to begin with. I read six thick books on the plights and flights of the Jews, I met with this cerebral rabbi in Ann Arbor once a week, and finally there was a laying on of hands. I was a daughter of Ruth, the rabbi told me. In Brooklyn," she said, pouring me a second glassful of tinny-tasting tomato juice, "no one was much moved by the news. Paul called and they hung up. I might be Ruth's daughter—that didn't make me theirs. A shikse once," she said, drinking a tomato juice toast to herself, "a shikse for all time." As for *her* parents, they hadn't even been notified. Over the spaghetti I learned that a priest and two nuns already graced Mrs. DeWitt's side of the family; no Jew was needed to round things out.

The two families, it seemed, had chosen to withdraw help just when it was needed most. The young couple had been married at Cornell, sometime near the end of Paul's senior year and Libby's junior year. Apparently, in the weeks afterward, there followed some very stern phone calls from Queens. "Still," as Libby said, "they were phone calls. Someone at least did some dialing." When they went on to Ann Arbor, Paul for his M.A., Libby still for her B.A., the phone had gone dead. Only occasionally was there a check for twenty-five dollars, and that was to be paid to the order of Elizabeth DeWitt. The Herzes quit school and moved three suitcases and a typewriter into a housekeeping room in Detroit in order to accrue some capital. "And then," Libby explained, ladling out the Bartlett pears, "the money stopped. Paul worked in an automobile plant, hinging trunks, and I was a waitress. And my father wrote us a little note to say that he had obligations to a daughter in school, but none to Jewish housewives in Detroit. We saved what we could, which turned out to be about half what we'd planned—" At this point a fierce look from her husband caught her up short; when she started in again it was clear that she had passed over a little of their history. "And we came to Iowa. Now we don't hear from them at all," she told me. "They're my parents; I suppose I like them for some things—but mostly I despise them."

Paul Herz had already looked down into his pears and so

did not see what it had cost his wife to speak those last words. And that was too bad, for she had said them for his benefit. Having doubtless realized how much she had irritated him by chronicling so thoroughly their bad luck, she had tried to square things with him by denouncing those people who had once fed and clothed her, and probably loved her too. Whatever had befallen them—she had decided to make clear at the very end—had not been the fault of her husband, but of those despised parents in the East.

I finished my dessert and went off to the bathroom, where I stood looking in the mirror for a long time, hoping that when I returned to the table the both of them would be better able to face me as a guest again. Paul Herz may have smiled from time to time during dinner, but I knew he was not happy with his wife's performance. So I took my time, but coming out of the bathroom I was probably more stealthy than I had intended. I had given them no signal—I neither flushed the toilet, nor did I slam the door, the last only to spare the beaverboard interior of the house, which looked as though a little too much force might well bring down the works. From the hallway I was able to see into the living room, where the two Herzes were standing beside the dining table. Paul's arms were around his wife's waist, and his chin rested on her black hair. I stood with my hand on the bathroom door, unable to move one way or the other; I saw what Libby could not: her husband's face. His eyes were closed like a man in prayer. I heard him say, "*Please* don't complain. All you've done all night is complain." Earlier Libby had changed into a black full skirt, and now her hands were held close up against it; her head was bowed and no part of her touched her husband that could be prevented from touching him. "I'm not complaining," she said. "Every time I tell a story *you* think I'm complaining." Herz took his hands from her. "Well, you *were* complaining." I did not know what might come next and did not want to know; at the risk of unhinging the whole place, I laid my shoulder into the door and came clomping down the hallway, a man with shoes and ears entirely too large for himself. For our separate reasons, we were all uncomfortable saying good night.

From this I had come home to hear myself indicted for

spitting on parental benevolence. Here was I (I had been reminded) with all that these Herzes were without. When my
mother died, in fact, she had left to me all that her family had
left to her, which, if not a fortune, was enough to spare me
from calamity for the rest of my life; on top of this there was
my father and his checks. Phone calls. Love. Money. It did not
seem very manly of me to be suffering over my abundance,
and I began to wonder, as I went to sleep that night, how I
would perform if I were Paul Herz.

—

The following morning, out in the sunlight, I got a good
look at Herz's new coat. It could have been handed down
from a beggar; it had, I'm afraid, that much class. A big brown
tent, it enveloped him; for all anyone knew, within it he might
be living a separate life. When he walked no knees were to be
seen anywhere. Cloth shuffled and he moved three feet closer
to wherever he was going. Standing still and seated he picked
up more dignity. Swimming brown eyes, good dark skin, and
hair that rose in tenacious kinky ridges off a marked brow gave
him a grim and cocky air. On the first of November he had had
to give up on the T-shirt; now in a dark brown shirt and a
frayed green tie he had the look about him of a dissatisfied
civil servant, a product of some nineteenth-century Russian
imagination. In class he inhabited not the room but just his
own chair. Where the others skittered on the syntax of their
Beowulf like a pack of amateur mountain climbers, Herz, when
asked to recite aloud, delivered Old English so that the black-
boards shook; the vowels were from Brooklyn, but the force
was strictly for meadhalls. Finished, he slid his books into a
crumpling tan briefcase—the smell of egg salad wafted up from
its bottom—and head down, left the room, silent as the North
Pole. The separate life lived under the new coat was dead
serious.

The morning after our evening together, this same coat—
whose cuff I noticed had already been sewn into one piece
again—was swinging to and fro beside me. No words came
from its owner, which made speech somewhat difficult for me.
Upon arising I had thought of how I might be able to help
Herz alleviate one of his problems; now his reticence made me

hesitate to say what was on my mind. I had the feeling that he was nettled at me for having been witness to all that had happened the night before. If I were to make my suggestion, it would probably seem to him that I was prying into his affairs.

I asked him how Libby was and he replied with the shortest answers: fine. I invited him to the Union for coffee, but by the time we reached the stairs I couldn't think of anything more to say that wouldn't really have been beside the point—so I went ahead and offered him my car to drive up to Cedar Rapids on the afternoons he taught there.

He turned and fastened on me a look whose penetration sent my own eyes up to the treetops for a moment. "That's very nice of you," he said, and in his voice, as in his gaze, there was something more than gratitude. Later I realized that what he'd been searching for was my motive.

"I don't need it in the afternoon," I said. "I'm usually at the library."

"I appreciate the offer," he said.

Thinking that perhaps he could not accept until I assured him that the arrangement would inconvenience me in no way, I added, "I live close enough to the library to walk—"

"Yes, but you see, my wife and I had a talk."

"Oh, yes?"

"We're changing our plans."

He smiled; but there was in his manner something stiff and withdrawn, particularly when he had referred to Libby as "my wife." I asked him, after a moment's silence, if perhaps they had decided to leave Iowa. I said that I hoped they had not.

"We've just worked something out," he answered, and started down the stairs. I followed, too confused as yet to believe that I was simply being rebuffed. While we drank our coffee there came a moment (at least for me) when I felt that one or the other of us could have said, "Look, all I meant . . ." and so on. But neither of us felt called upon to be the one to say it. After all, it was only a car I was offering him a few afternoons a week, not a new overcoat. Why so curt?

I waited, but he volunteered no further information. For someone whose clothing made such a strenuous appeal, it was a little silly of him, I thought, not to admit to his neediness out loud. Not that I expected him to come begging; I simply did not care for my offer to be written off as patronizing . . . unless of course he really did have a new plan, which made my car unnecessary. Perhaps it was prying of me, but I thought I had a right to an explanation somewhat more detailed than the one with which he had shut me up.

I never got it. Outside the Union he was abrupt but by no means discourteous; he extended a hand, I shook it, and we said goodbye. But as I walked off I said to myself, So much for Mrs. Herz and her silent husband. And though we had an acquaintanceship of only some twenty-four hours, and not a particularly gracious one at that, I was saddened. Whether Herz was more proud than wise was beside the point for me; I had awakened that morning positively elated that I could come to his aid. Denying my help, he'd managed to deny me my elation as well.

Finally I discovered myself piqued with him. However he chose to increase his discomfort, I realized, he chose to increase Libby Herz's discomfort as well. Clearly, she had not the talent for misery that he had. Were she to go out after a new coat, she would not come back, I was sure, with such a wailing piece of goods. It seemed to me that Herz actually found pleasure in saying to the world: Woe is me. There was a scale moving inside me, and as my irritation with Herz grew weightier, my sympathy rose for his wife. The remark she had made late in the afternoon of the day before sounded clear once again in my ear.

The stresses and strains of the previous day had allowed me to forget that this girl, whose husband wouldn't sit behind the wheel of my car, had said to me that she had been moved by my mother's words; doubtless, too, by my mother's circumstance. And by my own? I wanted all at once to sit down with Libby Herz and explain to her why it was that my poor father had to be manipulated by the people with whom he shared his life. I wanted to explain why I had had to desert him. And for my explanation I would not have minded receiving the balm of sympathy. Which might have been the reason—might it not? —for Paul Herz finding it necessary to turn down my offer. When there's trouble at home, why encourage a sympathy-hunting young man to hang around? One can never tell—if there happens to be a sympathy-hunting young wife at the other end—just how the balm may find expression. That deep gaze Herz had given me then was explained: he hadn't been looking for a motive, he'd come up with one. Perhaps he did not see what Libby might give to me quite so clearly as he saw what he thought I could give to Libby, and what she might accept. But that had been enough to force him to rule me out as a friend or aid. And it was enough, I decided, to persuade me to rule myself out. We would each have to work out the problems of family life within the confines of the family in which the problem had arisen. I only hoped for Herz's wife that she would come through her tribulations with her energy and her complexion undamaged. Both, I discovered, had touched me more than I had thought.

—

We come now to an interlude about which there is not too much that need be explained. The girl's name was Marjorie Howells and she was in revolt against Kenosha, Wisconsin. For several months she had been sitting beside me in Bibliography, and the morning that I was rejected by Paul Herz, I happened to run into her in the library. I was feeling at the time somewhat superfluous—and here was this girl, very pretty, albeit a little overhealthy. I did not know, when I asked her to have a beer with me that night, that she was in revolt against Kenosha, Wisconsin; I only believed that few complications could thrive behind such a perfect set of teeth. We had many beers, it turned out, and after a while she was looking across at me with flames flashing in her eyes, and asking me how it felt to be a Jew in America. I asked her how it felt to be a Protestant in America—and she told me. It was very dry and very typical. Jews, she explained, were different. Marge's father, a white-haired investor in Chicago, of whom she showed me a rather intimidating photograph (high tariff written all over his face)—her father thought Jews were different too, but Margie thought they were different from the way her father thought they were different. When I told her that in 1948 my own father had been chairman of an organization called New York City Professional Men for Wallace, I only fed the furnace. It wound up that I could not say anything that did not produce in her a larger and larger passion for me and my background:

even the fact that the living room of my family's apartment looked out over Central Park seemed to impress her disproportionately. Halvah and Harvard and Henry Wallace—I suppose I cut an exotic figure. We wound up back in my apartment with no lights on and my sense of reality—as happens in the dark—out the window. It was all as typical as Protestantism: I held the girl and kissed her and soon enough the two of us were revolting against Kenosha as though Caligula himself were city manager. Margie had spent four years at Northwestern and later in the night we got in our licks against that bourgeois institution too. When we spoke again I teased her about her image of me—me, a delicious specimen of Hebraic, Marxist exotica—which was not exactly my image of myself. But by then teasing was only another endearment.

Margie said, "I'd like to stay with you."

"You can stay," I said.

"Can I?"

"Yes."

"Shouldn't we go back and get some things?"

"I have eggs and orange juice," I assured her.

"I meant stay," she said. "Really stay."

I spoke then not only for Kenosha but for all small towns everywhere. "Marge, we hardly know each other."

"We can be happy as kings," she said, very sweetly.

"What do you need to get?"

"Do you have Breck shampoo?"

"No."

"I want to get my Breck and my Olivetti. I have an electric frying pan," she said, a little breathlessly.

"I have gas," I pointed out.

"Electric cooks perfect eggs," she told me. "Oh I want to eat so many breakfasts here."

So we drove to Margie's room and she packed a suitcase full of skirts and underwear, and in a large cardboard carton which I took from the shelf of her closet, I began to lay her frying pan and her Olivetti and her steam iron and her Breck and her *Oxford Book of Seventeenth-Century Verse*. And all the time I bent over the carton I wondered what I was doing. Some things—carrying George Herbert into a sinful union! Not till I felt fully the absurdity of what I was about did I realize how clutchy I had become of late: when I had seen Paul Herz in class, I had rushed to give him a book; when Libby called for a lift, I had dropped my studies and run right over. That very morning I had tried virtually to graft the Herzes to me by loaning them my car. That was an anxious way to interpret a simple act of kindness, but with all the evidence, with Marge Howell's soapy smell moving back and forth only a foot behind me, what else could I think about myself? I had not realized that I had been missing my father as much as he had been missing me.

She put her arms around me, this sweet empty-headed girl, and from behind me kissed my neck. With wryness, which never protected anyone from anything for very long, I said, "Oh, Margie, I am your Trotsky, your Einstein, your Moses Maimonides." And that foe of Luther and the Middle West asked, "Was that his last name?"

Was it a feeble joke or didn't she know? Either way, I continued to lose confidence in myself.

—

Mindlessly, mindlessly, mindlessly—pushing our shopping cart through the market, and late in the afternoon sipping cocoa in bed, and every few nights watching Marge let down her whirly blond hair to be washed. I would be sitting on the edge of the tub translating *Beowulf* to her while she leaned across the sink wearing her half slip and raising luxurious bubbles on her scalp. With her hair combed out straight, the wet strands just touching her back, she would turn to me with a look of perfect well-being and satisfaction. "And yet I don't feel I have to marry you. Isn't that something? I didn't think I could feel so liberated." There were nights when it was charming, but there were other nights too, and then the girl at the sink and I on the tub seemed no more facts of this life than those impossibilities, Hrothgar and Grendel, whose words and deeds I had just been trying to comprehend.

Margie soon came down with the grippe and was very hard to deal with. In bed she took to wearing my pajamas, and posing in them. She wanted to hear about all the girls I had made love to, and then I could hear about all the boys who had wanted to make love to her. She would not sleep with the lights out, and finally when she did sleep and I was alone, I had to face the fact that she was not much different sick from what she was well: the strain was simply purer, that was all. On the third day of her illness I was at last able to tear myself away from her by way of the necessities of shopping. Leaving our casino game, I drove to the supermarket under threatening winter skies. I knew that when Margie was fully recovered, strong and bouncy, we would have to arrange a parting; I was no gray-haired Chicago investor, no left-wing Jewish intellectual, and I could not continue to serve as either, or both. Nevertheless, because I was at the time as weak in the face of loneliness as in the face of pleasure, I shopped for two for the week, buying in the drug section of the market four bottles of Breck and three jars of the dainty underarm deodorant she used, and later the chocolate drink she was so fond of. Then as I was rounding an isle by the meat department, I saw Libby Herz pushing a cart toward my own. I ducked away, but a few minutes later we collided in front of Detergents.

"Hi," she said.

"Why, hello—how are you?"

"Better. How are you?"

"I'm fine. What's the matter?" I asked. "Were you sick? Or are you just feeling generally better?"

"I had a fever."

"There's one going around."

"It's gone now," she answered cheerily; too cheerily, for looking at her I saw the after-affects of illness still in her face.

"How's your husband?"

"He's fine."

We both did not know where to go from there. She must have heard, as I did, that I had not called Paul Paul.

"You must come see us some night," Libby suggested.

"I've been very busy."

A strand of hair that was swept away from the side of her head suddenly engaged her; she brushed it with her hand, and pulled everything tighter through the rubber band at the back. "I want to thank you," she said, "for the car offer. That was very nice. Paul told me."

"I'm sorry he couldn't use it."

With her hair out of the way, she began fiddling with the items in her cart; she had a great deal of oleo but no Breck.

"Thank you anyway," she said, and we both looked off at the shelves of Tide and Rinso.

"How do you get all those groceries home now?" I asked. She shrugged. "Walk."

"It's far."

"Not that far."

"Why don't you wait—" I found myself looking at a crease that extended from the edges of her nostrils to the edges of her mouth, barely visible, but still a mark on the skin. "Maybe you shouldn't walk . . ."

"Oh but I'm fine."

"I can drive you. I'm almost finished."

When she looked to see how finished I was, I realized that it was clear from my cartful that I was feeding and deodorizing more than one. It was also clear—to me—that the other person was not one toward whom I had a great deal of feeling. It was beginning to seem that toward those for whom I felt no strong sentiment, I gravitated; where sentiment existed, I ran. There was my father; there was even the girl before me. With her, of course, circumstances had combined with judgment to hold me back. But no circumstances had forced me, really, into a liaison with Margie Howells, whose sickroom behavior informed me that even if I had not developed feelings, I had at any rate initiated obligations. Standing there with Libby Herz, I found myself feeling rather shabby.

"Do let me drive you," I said.

"I'll wait just outside."

In the car I put my bundles out of sight on the back seat. I propped up Libby's bag in front, between us, and asked her how school was.

"I'm not in school any more."

"I didn't know that," I said.

"I decided to quit a couple of weeks ago. A few days after we saw you, I guess."

"I suppose it's less hectic."

She shrugged her shoulders again, and I saw that somehow I was making her nervous. "I'm working in the registrar's office," she said. "You're right, it is less hectic. I mean generally." And rather than explain, she raced ahead. "I finished your book. You don't mind if we keep it for a while, do you? Paul hasn't gotten around to it yet. He's just starting to get some time."

"That's all right."

"Isabel *has* a lot of courage in the end," she said. "You were right. Going back to Osmond, I mean. I don't know—I think some people might think it was stubbornness. Do you think it was?"

I thought she thought it was, so I said, yes, in a way it probably was. However, I said, stubbornness might be the other side of courage.

"That's very hard to figure out," she answered. "When you're being stubborn and when you're being courageous. I mean, if you were alone—but there are other people . . ." The conversation seemed suddenly to depress her. Whenever we talked principle it always wound up seeming as though we were talking about her. I could tell when she spoke next that she had told herself to stop brooding.

"Why don't you come visit us?" she asked.

I did not answer.

"Don't judge us by that night," Libby said. "Please don't. We, both of us, were preoccupied."

"It's not that," I said. "Actually I've just been busy."

"Paul . . ." she began slowly, "did appreciate your offering the car." She looked out the side window as she spoke, and I was reminded vividly of our first interview. "It simply wasn't a solution for us. I hope you didn't think he was ungrateful. He did appreciate the ride. He appreciated it very much. He's— very private. He's sweet, you know"—she toppled one word on the next—"and, I know, I know he can look a little rude, to strangers—"

"No, no. I didn't think him rude at all."

"We're much better off now, really. I thought it was awfully kind of you, considering what we'd been the night before. I realize," she said in a voice too loud for a two-door sedan, "that I must have complained all night."

"Oh no. I just thought you were telling some stories."

What I said confused me, and confused Libby too. Her voice was hardly natural when she said, "Paul was just over-worked. It's not nearly so bad as I must have made it seem."

"Doesn't he teach at Coe any more?" I asked.

"Well, he does—but he won't be, starting next semester. It's too much. And I don't mind working. Really, it's sort of a nice change. There's a bus, he found out, that goes up to Cedar Rapids and he's finishing out the semester taking that. It shoots a lot of his day—but that's okay anyway because he can read on it—and oh, I know it sounds involved, but now in fact it's less involved than it was. Before he couldn't write, and he was up every night marking papers, and he was too upset. We'll finish one education at a time. I think tempers are better all around."

"I'm glad everything is going well."

"Oh yes. You must come to see us."

"I will."

"I'm sure Paul would like it."

Then why the hell hadn't he asked me himself? I saw him three times a week, and got from him only a hello and good-bye . . . But his life had only just changed, I told myself, and perhaps it was true that as his several frustrations dropped away, he would come to feel less defensive about me.

"I will come," I said.

"Come tonight."

"I don't think I can make it tonight."

As we headed up toward the barracks, Libby said, "You're certainly welcome to bring somebody with you, if you like."

"Maybe some other night." Obviously I could not tell her that at the moment there was a sick girl home in my bed. "After Christmas," I said, hoping that by then there would be no girl in my bed at all.

"Paul will return the book soon," Libby said. She pointed up to the gray hut that was theirs. "Right here. There are a lot of things to talk about, about Isabel's character."

"There are, I know."

"I'd like to talk about them," she said. "And do, really, bring anyone you like. I think Paul would like you to bring someone." When I looked at her pulling the bundle from the car, she tried to avoid my eyes. I knew she did not want me to suggest that I carry the bundle for her.

2

WE TWO Wallach men, my father and I, stood in place on the tennis court, pushing dull lifeless shots back and forth at one another. Each of us had been trying for over an hour not to inconvenience his opponent by so much as a foot. For four days now, life—off the court as well as on—had consisted of just this sort of polite emotionless volleying. Running into one another in the bathroom, we bowed in our bathrobes. At dinner, eyes glued to utensils, we waited for Millie to serve, then dipped into our grapefruit as though one wrist controlled our separate hands. One of us couldn't sneeze without the other waving a clean handkerchief in his face.

Now, when a slight powder-puff shot of my father's twisted three feet to my left, his apology was endless. He didn't want to see me moving—three feet to the left and next thing I'd be off the courts, out of the club, gone from New York forever. For the rest of the afternoon he aimed at a dime; all I had to do, in turn, was close my eyes and bring my racket forward and I would meet the ball. See how easy life is in New York?

I chose, however, to keep my eyes open and on him. Across the court, in WSAC sweatshirt and white ducks that broke so low on his sneakers they nearly covered his toes, his undernourished figure, spidery and nervous, bounced in place awaiting my return. He had a stringy little body, a large head, and thick hair the color of iron. I am taller and heavier, like my mother, but his face, without the sags and wrinkles, could have been my own: gray eyes, flat nose, wide nostrils, and a big jaw which my father maintains has resulted in no wisdom-teeth trouble for two centuries. In his family they rise right up through the gums with room to spare. The aesthetic results of functionalism, however, are not always very satisfying; these abundant jaws of ours tend to make both my father and myself look a little like farmers. Or soldiers. You know we come from strong stock, but that's all you know; it was on my mother's side that all the nuance lay.

The steely Germanic strain in my father's features may not at first seem at one with his manner—particularly with his wisecracking, which he was allowing me that day to sample after each of my returns. In part, I suppose, this wisecracking is a watered-down version of my mother's wit; in part it arises from having lived his life in America, where he early came to admire the spirit of certain of our radio comedians. But mostly what one is witnessing when my father makes a joke, is the surface reaction of a gloomy northern disposition, the response of a man who would gush and weep if he did not kid around.

"Oh-ho," my father called, as I, out of boredom, gave the ball a little spin. "Oh-ho, a trickster. Is that what I've got on my hands? What are you doing, working out your Oedipus complex?"

Subsequently I hit the ball listlessly back, a simple easy return. "So what now—giving up? Letting an old man beat your pants off? Oh-ho, a push-over, Charlie," he called to the towel-and-soap attendant who was passing along the side of the court. "Strictly a push-over I'm up against today."

"How are you, Doctor?" Charlie asked. "He sure has grown up."

"Ah him, he's still a school kid," my father called. "Still wet behind the ears," he added, so that Charlie laughed, and I felt provoked to give a little vent to my Oedipus complex and slammed a wicked one past his backhand. Charlie moved off, counting towels; my father quieted a moment; and I had the usual filial remorse.

———

At home, what was there to do? It looked as though I might at last get a chance to go out on the streets alone. Millie, the woman who had cooked and cleaned for our family for years, came into the living room directly after our return and said that there had been a phone call for me from Iowa City. My father, who had been rubbing his hands together in an anticipatory way and looking out the window at the park, asked his question without turning.

"A woman?"

"I think so. Specifically, a girl."

"Well," he said, "you better go ahead and phone her." In a voice with a little edge to it, he added, "It doesn't take you too long, huh?"

"For what?"

He looked at me, trying to grin. "To get a foot in the door. Hey, I sound dirty. To get established. You going to call?"

"Not now. I thought I might take a walk."

"It's freezing out. You'll freeze to death."

"It's not too bad."

"How about giving me a look at your teeth?"

"I think you looked at them in August."

"August, September, October, November— it's the end of December already. January is six months. Come in the office. I've got new equipment you haven't even seen yet."

"I think I saw it in August. I thought I'd walk down—"

"Come on, it's your vacation."

"It's your vacation too," I said. "You ought to stay out of the office today. Millie says you work too hard."

"Oh does Millie? Maybe Millie should take a couple lessons from me. Come on, you'll get me at the top of my form. A good game of tennis makes my technique sharper. Spend an hour in the office," he said, coming past me to put a hand to my shoulder, "you used to love it." He started down the hallway, calling out to the maid, "Millie, we're going out to dinner tonight." He opened the door at the end of the apartment, and there was nothing to do but follow him into the reception room.

Up straight in the dental chair, everything was as it used to be. He whistled some tuneless collection of notes, while behind me faucets dripped and little drawers were opened and closed. Over in the park, around the slickly iced reservoir, the limbs of the trees were as black this December as they'd been fifteen and twenty Decembers before. I heard my father's rubber-soled sports shoes—his working shoes—move across the floor, just as a window at 93rd and Fifth took the sun at a wide angle and flamed out over Manhattan. A plastic bib slid past my eyes, the back rest dropped gently down, and swimming familiarly above me was my father's face, his hand, his silver pick. Crisp from his shower at the club, his hair looked fierce as a helmet under the bluish bulb. Commanded, the patient opened wider, *wider*, and the slow trek began, the hunt, along the gum line into the darkest regions of the mouth. He searched deep inside me: how far down had I hidden my heart?

"Ah yes ah yes—" He lingered a while at each molar, then went on to caress the next. "Ah, this one was something. We took good care of this mouth, all right. Not a hundred mouths in all of New York like this one. People pay me to build a mouth like this—no, no, keep it open. Wider."

Marge Howells had called. I allowed *that* business to occupy my mind while I obliged my father with my mouth. I closed my eyes, shutting out his gleeful face, and took stock. Just five days earlier I had repacked Marge's cardboard carton, and had had to pack her suitcase too, while she pounded at me from behind with her fists. "You're not folding my skirts right!" she wailed into my ear. "Stop it, you're getting everything wrinkled! Oh Gabe, *stop*! I love you I love you I love you" until at last she hurled a bottle of Breck against the bathroom wall. Nevertheless I had carried her belongings to the car and driven her, weeping, to her room. Then I drove alone to the airport, and late that night had rubbed unshaven cheeks with another weeper, my father, in the freezing rainy openness of Idlewild. Now Marge had called and I was sure it was from my own phone. I was weary with the knowledge that despite all I had determined to set right, she had managed to retain her key—which I had forgotten about in my determination just to get her out—and had probably engaged some taxi driver to carry her belongings back up the two flights to my apartment.

I would not call her back.

"I just want to take some pictures," my father was saying. He had rolled the black X-ray machine noiselessly up to my cheek and was taking aim at my back molars. "Let's just get the lay of the land," he said. "Remember, Gabe, how I used to carry an X-ray of your mouth in my wallet? Just for a gag—"

"Why don't you use that one?" I asked limply.

The prints, when developed, glowed with health. What more was there to do? I made a move to leave the chair, but my father touched his fingers to my chest. "You know," he said, "you always have to have a total picture to see the whole thing."

I sighed. "What whole thing?"

"The X-rays, a check-up," he said vaguely. "Hygiene aside, consider it a matter of curiosity. A matter of self-investigation.

Know thyself, you know? I'm acquainted with people who think of dentists as mechanics, carpenters, nobodies. Ridiculous. Dentists are astronomers—just let me go on—dentists are geologists. Gabe, when seen from the proper angle, dentistry is a romance. Take the stars. I see the fellow next door up on the roof charting stars. 'Charting' them, is that right? Looking, examining, and so forth. Now I want to put it this way: what's so different about dentistry? I'm serious now— what's so different about getting directly at what's in a man's head? Not millions of light years away, but right here—God Almighty, almost touching the *brain*. Now there are cases, documented cases of the tooth actually *piercing* the brain. Can you imagine? So galaxies, solar systems—believe me, a tooth is just as much a mystery as a star. A man's got to have a philosophy of life, why he works, and that's mine. You get older and you wonder why you do what you do. A man doesn't get along without reasons. To go through life, just putting on your garters and eating your food, alone, by myself, without sufficient reasons, day after day, how can a fellow do it? Unless he's got like Gruber, smiling sickness, smiling on the brain. For myself, Gabe, I need a little mystery in life. As I get older I haven't got a lot of the old concerns, you know. Well, I find much to think about in terms of the human mouth. The third molar alone could occupy a lifetime. Don't laugh—that's a fact. Just the why of it, I'm telling you . . . Life makes you stop and think, that's the thing. Life changes on a man, and then he's got to have a little something in reserve. I feel a little ashamed about what I didn't have in reserve." He had then to look off for a moment in another direction. "Look, I don't have to go on and on. It's nice to talk to someone who understands. Lean back again, I want to clean them."

"Dad, the cleaning isn't necessary. Everything is fine here. I'm not going anywhere. I haven't any plans. I'll be here until New Year's Eve."

"I thought New Year's Day."

"New Year's Day, right." I tried to maintain a composed expression even while I remembered how we had tussled over dates driving back from Idlewild with his wallet-sized calendar between us. "So you can relax. Take it easy. There's no need to clean my teeth right now. I'm sure they're fine."

"Have you had a chance lately to look at your last molar?" He measured off a good size fish with two hands. "Tartar," he said. "Let me be the dentist and you be the patient."

"Fine," I said, smiling. "If I'm the patient, I think I've really had enough for today."

"You don't care that your teeth are all furry?"

"I have to make a phone call."

"How long will this take, ten more minutes? You're going to have it done you might as well have it done right."

"Oh Christ, can't they clean teeth in Iowa?"

A hand rose up as though to find its target on my cheek. It swiped at the overhead lamp, which buzzed and died. My father reached behind him to unbutton his white jacket. "You've got an important phone call, go make it." He walked to the window, as his fingers, traveling down his back, broke off a button that rattled to the floor. "Go call Alaska, call Bangkok. Go ask the operator for the furthest place she can get you—then go dial it." His foot slammed down on the button, producing absolute quiet in the room.

"What do you expect me to do?" I began, softly. "Sit in this chair the rest of my life?"

"I happen to be a thirty-thousand-dollar-a-year dentist. People wait hours so I can reconstruct their mouths. Some of the leading stage stars in New York have sat in this chair for *weeks*. I change people's looks. I give them health and beauty, two of the most wonderful things in the world. I take an interest in teeth. You're my son, I take an interest in yours. Is that a crime these days?"

"Nobody's talking about crimes."

"I get the feeling somebody around here is."

"Please," I said, "turn around. I only meant you don't have to trap me in the chair. I'm sorry if I was snide. I only mean that you would be better off if you take it easy about me. Just relax, that's all."

"I am relaxed. I know how to relax. If you don't relax at my age you get bad pressure, sluggishness. I am relaxed."

"If you want to go ahead," I said, after a moment, "why don't you just go ahead."

"Go ahead where?"

"Clean my teeth," I said, finding it difficult to talk.

"You have to call some girl."

"I've got a mouthful of tartar. How can I talk to anybody? Go ahead, if you want to."

"No, no," he said, "you go ahead. You have a life in Iowa. Go conduct it."

"Why don't you clean my teeth? I'm *asking* you to clean my teeth."

"You'll sit there fidgeting. I don't do a rush job. I'm not a plumber."

"I won't fidget."

Without looking at me, he walked around the chair. "I just won't work with somebody fidgeting." A hand appeared over my head and I was in the glare of the light again. He spoke from behind, like Marge, "I don't know when *you* became so casual about your health. You used to love to have your teeth cleaned; you used to say your mouth tasted pink afterward. I still tell that to patients. I don't know where you suddenly picked up such bad habits." Behind me he was scratching together a sweet-smelling paste. "It's funny," he went on, "how a mouth doesn't change, how yours is the same mouth now it was then. I can remember it, you know that? I can remember your mother's mouth. I find that I can remember every single tooth in her head." Then his face appeared above my own. I could have reached up and pulled him down and kissed him. But would he understand that I was not prepared to surrender my life to his? He was a wholehearted man, and such people are hard to kiss half-heartedly.

—

My mouth *was* tasting pink when I asked the operator for Iowa. I waited to be connected while my father's tuneless peppy little whistle came from the bedroom. Removing my tartar had restored his belief in the future. He walked past me into the living room, a white terry-cloth bathrobe around his shoulders and oriental slippers on his feet. He was back to Yoga again. I should have guessed it.

At the other end of the line, Margie said hello.

"Marge—it's me."

"Oh sweetie," she said, "how are you?"

"I'm all right. How are you?"

"I'm a little tired. I've been scrubbing shampoo off the walls all afternoon."

"Have you moved back in?"

"Gabe, this disengagement policy wasn't working at all. I was so lonely. I love you, honey."

"Margie, we can't keep living together. It's bad for our characters."

"I love you. It's good for my character."

"Stop being kittenish."

"Is that kittenish *too*?" she whined.

"Marge, why don't you go to Kenosha for a week? It's a holiday. You're lonely because there's no one on the campus. You don't miss me as much as you think. Why don't you go home for a while?"

"Because those people bore me."

"Margie, you just have to move out."

"You come back, you'll see. We'll have fun."

"You have to move out."

"I miss you. Don't you miss anything? How can you live with someone for a month and not *miss* them?"

"Missing is just more indulgence for us. The whole thing was very indulgent of both of us."

"I feel," she said, "very used . . ."

"Please, honey, don't talk too much like a movie, all right?"

"You're cynical about love. I'm only telling you how I feel."

"The truth is we were both used. We used each other. Now let's stop it."

"I can't."

"Why?"

"I love you."

"You don't," I said.

"Gabe, I don't want to fight with you. I didn't call to fight. The campus is empty. It's depressing me."

"What have you been doing?" I asked.

"I'm trying to read Proust," she said. "I think the translation must be lousy. He just doesn't seem that great. Sweetheart, I've written nearly fifty letters. I think all I've done is wash my damn hair and mail letters. Gabe, you've *got* to come back—for New Year's at least. Oh Gabe, New Year's Eve?"

"Marge," I said, not really knowing where to go from here, "why don't you go out and talk to people?" It began to seem that I had found my Bartleby: I would have to go back to Iowa City and find a new apartment, leaving Marge behind in the old one. "Why don't you go to the movies, go swimming. Make a life for yourself, baby, *please?*"

"I don't like movies alone. I'm not being obstinate—I don't. I had coffee with a friend of yours in the Union today."

It depressed me considerably to hear her settling down to be chatty. "Who?"

"Paul Kurtz."

"Herz."

"He seemed very nice. A little lugubrious."

"I hardly know him. What did he have to say?"

"We just chatted. His wife's sick. I think she had what I had. She's in the hospital. Gabe, is she really his wife, or is he just living with her?"

"Oh, Marge—"

"Gabe, he's the only person I've spoken with in *five days.* Aren't you going to come back for New Year's Eve?"

"I'm visiting with my father. Look, you've got to move out. You just can't keep being indulgent like this."

"Hasn't indulgence turned *into* anything?" she demanded to know. "You just can't walk out!" she cried into the phone.

"We're both walking out."

"I'm not walking anywhere! Don't tell me what I'm doing!"

"All right, I won't. Just call a taxi, and take your stuff, and get out."

"You don't respond—that's your trouble! You're heartless!"

"I expect you to be gone when I get back."

"How can you say that to me if you love me!"

"But I don't love you. I never said I did."

"You *used* me, you bastard." And she began to weep.

"Oh, Margie, nobody uses anybody for four weeks."

"*Five* weeks!"

"Look, hang up now, pack your bags, and leave."

"I'll ruin this place, you," she screamed. "I really will!"

"You're hysterical—" I said, astounding nobody with the insight.

"I'll tear up all your books! I'll break all the rotten spines—you'll *have* to come back!"

"I'm coming back on the first of January."

"Oh—" she wept, "I never expected this of you."

"Margie, you romanticized—"

"*You* romanticized!" and at her end the phone slammed down.

—

When my mother was alive she had done everything possible to prevent my father from assuming the Cobra Posture on her prized living room rug. However, she was gone, and I did not live with the man, so after my phone call—determined to put out of my mind those long-distance protestations of love—I sat down on the orange raw silk of our scrolly Victorian sofa, and I watched. And for the first time since my arrival, I found my father oblivious to me. It pleased me to think that we two were occupants of the same room, and that he was not investigating my plans for next month, or fiddling around inside my mouth. Not me, but the Cobra Posture—Bhujangansa—was the object upon which he focused all his soul and all his body. Clad in a blue jockey bathing suit, he was stretched rigidly before me on the floor, his stomach down, his toes pointed back, his chest nobly arched. All that moved, while he held himself aloft on locked wrists and elbows, were the muscles in his forearms, which jiggled at a high speed against the thin pale shell of his skin. The features of his face moved around a bit too as he tried to work them into a picture of repose. It was all very familiar, even down to the hour of the day; over in the Park, everything was growing dim.

"That rug," my mother used to say, dying to kick one arm out from under him, but knitting instead, "was woven by an entire village in North Africa, Gabriel, so that your father could make a damn fool of himself on it." She had a strategy of making certain matters that were important to her sound unimportant; but she was, after all, a strenuous woman and I knew she wasn't kidding. She had disapproved of his Yoga, as she had disapproved of his Reichian analysis, his health foods, and his allegiance in 1948 to Henry Wallace. She was a dedicated opponent of the impossible, which my father happened to be for; but he was for her too, and that was what had weakened him. Even so, it was no easy job for her to restore him to reason. It had finally been necessary, where his orgone box was concerned, to shame him out of the thing by hinting of its existence one night to a group of his colleagues at a convention of the American Dental Association in Miami. What had forced her to such a cruel extreme was something my father had done with his box one afternoon in her absence: he had put me in it. After the ADA convention, a length of wooden rod was purchased, some nails driven in the right places, and the next thing Millie knew she had a zinc lined wardrobe closet in the corner of her room. The end result of my mother's maneuver was that it managed to bring my father back into his family living room in the evenings, the proper place, my mother told him, to be collecting sexual energy in the first place.

As for the avocado and fresh vegetable dinners, she had put up with them and put up with them, until finally she had forbidden Millie to set *anything* green and uncooked on our table. We all had to go without vitamin C until it was certain that my father was on the wagon. My mother claimed she would hold out until the entire family had scurvy, though my father gave in before the first symptoms of the disease made an appearance. Henry Wallace is a more complicated story. He had been entertained in the Wallach apartment, and treated graciously. My father, as I had told Marge, had been chairman of an organization of doctors and lawyers in New York City who had dedicated themselves to campaigning for the third party. One would imagine, of course, that my father would then have voted for Wallace, but he did not; election eve my mother had kept him up, feeding him coffee, until she had finally convinced him that a vote for Wallace was a vote for Dewey. What a moment it must have been for him in the booth, pulling down that Truman lever. How he must have hated the woman he loved.

It was Hatha Yoga that she had not been able to lick. Even when my father had ceased being a damned fool on her Moroccan rug, his nurse reported persistence after hours in the waiting room. The fact was that his wife could have as easily shamed him out of Yoga as out of dentistry. He was much too attached to the idea of healing. At least that was the way he might have thought of it himself. More likely, for all his belief in restitution, progress, reform, reconstruction—he *had* re-built some of the most talked-about mouths in New York—he was more attracted to ideas of disease. Wilhelm Reich, Henry Wallace, leafy green vegetables: all somehow were antibodies. And the disease? He apparently blamed some bug, some germ, for his perennially swollen heart. The disease was the doctor's feelings. Not that he ever said this to anyone; to the world, professional and lay, he claimed dedication only to science. To the upper Fifth Avenue rabbis who made their way through our apartment, he was open-faced about his atheism. I have myself heard him explain his high colonic Yogic enema to the biggest internist in New York, absolutely physiologically, no mention of the soul at all. And Bhujangansa, of course, stimu-lated the autonomous and sympathetic nervous systems.

Well, that all may or may not have been so. My own suspi-cion, even as a growing boy, was that my father's particular trouble wasn't with his sympathetic nervous system at all. It was, as a matter of fact, with his sympathies: his passions ached him. Whatever terror he saw in life, whatever turbulence gave him inward hell, he was unable to answer it with reason. So he took to magic.

My mother was a different kind of person, which may be obvious by now. She was the one in our family with the ex-pressive face—baggy eyes, long nose, wide clown's mouth—but she had controlled it like a master. On the surface she was neither overly affectionate nor overly retiring, and as for sur-face manners, people have said on occasion that I take after her. Love her as I did, I don't know how much that pleases me. What with my father's steely physiognomy and my mother's crafty rule over her responses, I don't suppose I look much like a young man giving things away. I don't believe I look out-and-out mean, so much perhaps as self-concerned. My mother was more fortunate: she looked self-aware. She gave one the feeling that she knew precisely what she was doing when she made her offer of reason to my father. It was that—reason—which she had given him. Since no marriage is so sim-ple, there were of course other offerings as well; but it was reason more than anything else, for that was what my father seemed most desperately in need of. And that may have been what she had an excess of herself.

She checked cockeyed enthusiasms left and right, and for those of us up close it was most impressive. During the early years, however, my father did not apparently understand fully the exchange he had entered into. From time to time he would try to model himself after the handsome woman he had chosen, and for two or three weeks would defect from Yoga and charge at life from a reasonable angle. It was a change his very essence deplored; exercising a painful self-control, he wound up constipating himself. It was clear even to me, the child in the house, that he was not a logical man; while I listened to his explanations I knew that truth, whatever it was, plunged deeper than what he was telling me. But the difference between reason and unreason was for a child nothing more than a distinction. In the beginning I had no favorites. It was eventually under my mother's tutelage—and that consisted primarily of just being around her—that I came to have attitudes toward the objects of my father's passions. But then all the young finally get sophistication and go around the house feeling themselves surrounded by second-rate minds; it is to first-rate hearts that they cling, with innocence and greed. Red twilights in the park, every last patient having taken home his reconstructed jaw, my father would toss his darling son up toward the branches of the trees. Miles below me the grass would twirl, so that even *I* knew it was too high for safety. My father, however, was a turbulent man, and since nine in the morning he'd been working in millimeters.

But one evening, which it seems I will not forget, I came down into his arms wailing not with joy, but with fright. Up near the trees I had looked still higher, and from our living-room window I had seen a pair of hands stretching out and down, toward me. The hands were my mother's. I came back to earth whimpering, and my father had to hold me and then to carry me home on his shoulders, chattering all the while of circuses we would go to and fun we would have. I quickly got over my fantasy, but that made it no less significant: there *had* always been a struggle for me in the Wallach household. Each apparently saw my chances in life diminished if I grew in the image of the other. So I was pulled and tugged between these two somewhat terrorized people—a woman who gripped at life with taste and reason and a powerful self-control, and a man who preferred the strange forces to grip him. And still, I managed to move up through adolescence and into manhood without biting my nails or wetting my bed or stealing hubcaps off parked cars. Whatever it was in that apartment on Central Park West that had been compounded out of the polar personalities of my parents, I myself experienced it as love.

Death upset everything. When my mother died in 1952 she was clearly no less dedicated to helping my father keep his footing in this world than she had been in 1942; that he could not keep his footing alone had been the cause of much of the grief she chose to keep to herself. Immediately after her death I found myself blaming my father for having been unworthy of her. But then her letter was sent on to me, and heartbroken as I was, awed as I was by what had been the circumstance of its composition, the confession it contained forced upon me a truth that I had never permitted myself to see. She had been so attractive a person in life that it had been hard to judge her. But in death she came to seem a kind of villain, and I left the Army willing to believe that it was she who had ruined my father's life. He was the worthy one, for he had accepted the woman he had married. Mordecai Wallach loved Anna Wallach; she had loved what he was to be alchemized into six months hence. A woman of moderate emotions and good sense, and yet she had apparently had *her* love affair with power. Her restraint hadn't been all it had looked to be.

Or had it? Was she not, finally, loyal and honest and good? She did the best she could in balancing the emotional budget in the house of an extravagant man. When I speak of her as having acted villainously, I wonder if I am not speaking as a member of that vast and treacherous populace that has lately come out for Compassion. We seem called upon more and more to make very pious, very public, demonstrations of our feelings. You turn a corner and there's a suburban lady in a pillbox hat, jingling a container full of coins at you, demanding, *give*. Watch television, and fifty entertainers and ten disc jockeys are staging "a marathon"; they lose sleep, take their meals on the run, sing, make jokes and display themselves, and none of this for their own benefit. It is a peculiar age indeed, when even the corrupt and the unfeeling are out collecting so as to beat down hardening of the arteries. It's the age to feel sorry—a bleeding heart is standard equipment.

And the fact is that there are few of us who can resist an appeal. After all, you could free the slaves and hang the tyrants by their heels, but as for the rest, the other horrors, what do you do after you've bought your Christmas seals? We feel a debt, I know, hearing of the other fellow's sorrows, but the question I want to raise here is, What *good* is the bleeding heart? What's to be done with all this pitying? Look, even my mother had it; she pitied my father. Isabel Archer pitied Osmond. I pity you, you may pity me. I don't know if it makes any of us behave better, or wiser. Terrible struggles go on in the heart, to which the heart itself will not admit, when pity is mistaken for love.

—

As I was traveling west, away from a cold glittery day in New York, a fierce snowstorm had been traveling east from the great plains, and we met on the evening of New Year's Day, the moment I stepped off the plane. By seven o'clock the storm had gotten the upper hand over the population; on the street there were few cars and no pedestrians, and behind living-room windows I could see people peering out from between the curtains, gauging the power of the enemy.

I raced for the front door, but once inside the hallway took my time mounting the stairs. There was nothing for me in the mailbox, and upstairs no envelope was thumbtacked to my door. I waited to hear music playing, or water running, and then I entered the kitchen, turned the light on, and saw something glitter on the sink. To the key was attached a note, a note written on pink stationery with scalloped edges.

> *I gave too much to you. I don't think anybody can ever hurt me the way you have. I don't know what I'll do.*

That was all: my extra key and these twenty-four words, no one of them too much influenced by her reading of Proust. I unpacked my bags and emptied my pockets of the dental floss my father had given me at the airport, and then walked around my three rooms, picking up seven hairpins, a copy of *Swann's Way*—the corner of page seven turned back—and a tube of neutral polish that I remembered Marge massaging into her buff pumps. The Proust went back on the shelf, and what she had left behind, including the note, went into the empty garbage pail.

That, of course, was not the end. I then paced from room to room, turning up three more of her hairpins; I suppose I was looking for them. If New York had turned out better, I probably would not have been so susceptible to Marge's indictment, but as always happened with my father, our final hours together were as strained as our first; the dental floss, in fact, had been something more than hygienic: it was a last-minute attempt to bind us together across some thousand miles of this vast republic. "Take care of your teeth, sonny," he had said to me, and I had looked back to see that the smile on his face, like the one on the face of the stewardess, involved none of the deeper muscles. "See you when, Washington's Birthday?" were the last gallant, murderous words he had called out to me as I stepped aboard the plane. That was the state to which I had reduced him, anticipating patriotic holidays.

But that was mild compared to the night before, when my father and Dr. Gruber and I had celebrated the coming of the New Year at the theater. While to my right Gruber howled every time some character on the stage said "Oh God *damn* you" to some other character on the stage, to my left my father cried. Not until the middle of the last act did I notice. Then I inched my hand over the chair arm that separated us, until I touched his sleeve. Under my *Playbill*—so that Gruber would not see—I took his hand and held it until the final curtain and the light. I told myself he was impossible and I told myself he was unfair, but in the darkness there was nothing I could tell myself that was able to make him less unhappy.

With all this in the very recent past, I had now to confront the final, condemnatory words of my late mistress. To defend myself I tried to work up defamatory thoughts about her. I had no trouble at all imagining her going around the apartment *planting* hairpins. But the knowledge that she had soap-opera passions and a moral fiber as soft as her skin only worked to soften my own melting sense of dignity. I went to the window and must have watched an inch of snow pile against the houses across the street. Twice I circled the phone before deciding I would call Marge's rooming house and explain to her, as calmly and exactly as I could, why it was to her benefit that we discontinue seeing one another.

"Miss Howells?" said Mr. Trumbull, husband of the land-lady. "Just a minute."

In a minute he was back. "Miss Howells don't live here, no sir." There was a great deal of television racket behind him, so that I could hardly hear what he was saying.

I tried to be polite. "But she does live there."

"Just a minute." When he returned, he said, "Nope. She don't."

"You mean she's left?"

"Just a minute." When he came back to the phone he told me yep, she'd left.

"Where? When?" I asked.

"None of *my* business."

"Look, did she leave a forwarding address?"

"Look, yourself," he said, "we don't give out that kind of personal information on the phone. Who is this?"

After I hung up I searched the apartment again, but found nothing that would serve as a clue to Marge's whereabouts. Had she run away? What was she up to? I fished the note out of the garbage can. *I don't know what I'll do.* I had dismissed the statement earlier as a generalized expression of her frustra-tion; it had not been for exactness that I had valued her. Now I tried to tell myself just exactly what Marge was and was not capable of, and thereby regain my composure. But *could* she have done something stupid, like kill herself? I thought to call the rooming house again and if possible get Mrs. Trumbull from the TV set to ask *her* some questions. I even thought for a second about calling Kenosha, or the police. Then I remem-bered that Marge had had coffee with Paul Herz. I hung back from involving him in what might turn out to be a very com-plicated matter; yet my anxiety was by this time a little greater than my shame, and so I looked up the Herz number and dialed it. The phone rang so long that I was ready to hang up when Libby Herz said hello.

"Libby? This is Gabe Wallach."

"My goodness, how are you?"

"I'm fine. How are you?"

"Oh, I'm okay."

"I heard you were in the hospital. Are you all right now?"

"I'm convalescing." Her tone informed me just how boring that could be. "How—how did you know?"

"Oh, a friend of Paul's. Is Paul around?"

"He's in the bathroom. He's taking a bath. I'm not even supposed to be out of bed," she whispered.

"Never mind then. You go back to bed."

"No, no, it's all right. The phone ringing is the most exciting thing that's happened here in a month. I'm all right."

"It's not important," I said.

"Paul will be out soon. Should I give him a message?"

"Would you— Look, I'll see him tomorrow. It's not important."

"Why don't you come over?" she asked. "Are you busy? Come over and tell us about New York."

"I'm not busy. But if you're resting . . ."

"That's just it. All I do is rest. Paul will be out of his bath in a few minutes. Uh-uh, he's *getting* out. I'd better hang up— I'm not supposed to be out of bed even for the *toilet*. It's awful. Hey, do come over!"

Driving through the storm, I realized how groundless were my fears about Marge. She had probably taken a room in the graduate dormitory. Perhaps she was skiing in Colorado, or had moved in with a friend. I realized as I crossed the bridge over the river that it is the futureless who are found buried under two feet of snow or twenty feet of icy water, not girls who put their underwear on the radiator at night so that it will be warm for them in the morning. By the time I had reached the Herzes' my motive for visiting had nearly disappeared. Nevertheless, while I waited for the front door to open, the wind blew a handful of snow down my coat collar: I closed my eyes and prayed that wherever Margie had decided to take her broken heart, it was warm and safe.

Paul Herz opened the front door wearing his beggar's overcoat and holding his briefcase.

"Libby's in the bedroom," he said.

"Are you going somewhere?"

"You're letting in the cold," he said, giving me an agreeable look that only mystified me more. "Come in."

I stepped in, asking, "Are you going out?"

He held up his briefcase. "I'm afraid I've got some work." He stepped around me and was out the door. "Good night," he said, "nice to see you." His head went into his collar, and the overcoat was swinging down the path like a bell.

"Can I drive you anywhere?" I called after him.

Herz turned, but continued walking backwards; the snow had caked instantly on his shoulders. "You better close the door," he said.

"Gabe?" Libby's voice called out to me from the other end of the little apartment.

"Yes?"

"Could you close the door? There's a draft."

I was still looking out after her husband, however. I wanted to shout for him to come back: I wanted to *demand* a reason for his leaving.

"I'm in the bedroom," Libby said, directing me.

Herz walked further into the white mist, until at last I couldn't see him any more.

Libby was sitting in bed, propped up by two pillows, her knees bent girlishly under the blankets. The bed was made of iron and painted silver and had an institutional air. There was not much more furniture in the room. A floor lamp threw a saucer of light up on the water-damaged ceiling; poor for reading, it was at first generous to the sick. From the doorway Libby looked, in that dim light, no more ravaged than she had in the supermarket early in December; the man's woolen muffler thrown over her greenish shetland sweater even gave her somewhat of a rakish air. Only after I pulled up to the bed a cracking wicker chair, the room's *only* chair, could I see where the fever had turned against her. The fine polished edge of her complexion had been altered; the hollows, the curves, the distinctive shape of her face had been consumed by fatigue. And when she spoke, it was with her voice as with her features: no vigor. There were spurts of pep, as there had been on the phone, but nothing sustaining, nothing to signal a strong will and solid feelings. She was without energy, and that almost made her seem without sweetness. But perhaps she was simply nervous—I know I was. What kind of joke, after all, was Herz's departure? I remembered the day he had turned down my car, and after all these weeks I was disliking him again. I saw myself being made a pawn in another domestic argument.

"I wish Paul could have stayed a few minutes," I said.

"I told him you wanted to ask him something. He said he'll be back. Your coming gave him a chance to get out. I went into the hospital Christmas Eve. He's been up twenty-four hours a day since."

"Where did he have to go? It's storming out."

"To do some work. To his office."

"Can't he work in the living room?"

"We'd be talking. He'd be distracted. He hasn't written in weeks, you see. He—well, I've been sick, and time—oh his time is just all fouled up. He'll be back soon." She blushed at this point and looked away.

By no means did I find this a satisfactory explanation of Herz's behavior—or my reaction to it—but I nodded my head.

Libby said, "It hasn't been easy for him."

"It's probably not been easy for you," I replied.

"I don't know. I think maybe it's easier sometimes being sick."

"Easier than what?"

Clearly, she was sorry now for having made the distinction in the first place. Most of what Libby was sorry for or about, one saw just that way—clearly. "Oh—being well." She took a deep breath and pushed her back into the pillows. "I complain too much. I must have had my development arrested somewhere. I'm twenty-two; I should know enough not to go around having expectations all the time. I should be able to get used to things." She appeared to be making her resolves right in front of me. "Paul's the one who should be complaining," she said.

"Oh, doesn't he?"

She looked at me with real surprise. Immediately I regretted having been so openly skeptical about her husband's character; it only increased her uneasiness.

Vaguely she said, "His attitude toward life is better, I think. In the situation."

"Well," I said, smiling, "I suppose you have some right to complain," and tried to end it with that.

She shook her head, defending her husband by annihilating herself.

I said, "Well," again, and looked over her head, where there hung a rather pedestrian Utrillo print. I examined it while she organized her thoughts. The picture encouraged me to reorganize my own, for it managed to make me overwhelmingly aware that Libby Herz and Paul Herz were married. In all that institutional and castoff furniture (the wicker chair must surely have been bought off some Iowan's back porch) it alone looked to have been really *chosen*. Together they had hung it over the bed they shared.

"What's Paul working on?" I asked, trying to appear more kindly disposed toward the pursuits of the man who was her husband.

"A novel. He does one for a degree. Instead of a dissertation."

"How's it going?"

"Fine, wonderful," she said. "It's just, well, as I said—time. I mean that's why I went to work, to give him a little time. Now I haven't been in that damn office for almost three weeks."

"You'll be better soon. The flu has been going around."

"Oh yes, I know." The rapidity with which she answered indicated that she didn't want me to think that she felt she didn't *deserve* to get the flu. What made talking to her almost impossible for me was this incredible pendulum action of hers, the swiftness with which she swung back and forth between valuing herself too much and then valuing herself not at all. I realized now that, having had no questions for Herz, I should have turned around and gone home. One did not idly enter the door of this house.

"It's actually ironic," Libby was telling me. "When I was a student I could have gone into the hospital free, under student health. But I quit so we could get the tuition back, and then I got sick, and already it's cost even more than the tuition we got back. You see, it's not the flu," she corrected me. "They don't know what it is, but I don't think it's flu or gripppe. It's just—it's just ironic was all I meant to point out. At least I call it ironic. Paul doesn't call it anything." She spoke her next words with some disbelief. "He calls it life."

"Well," I said, while she waited to hear what I would say, "I suppose people have to expect a little trouble."

"Oh I know that," she interrupted. "I'm not *that* under-developed. I know people get sick. It's better to have to struggle when you're young, I think, than when you're older," she platitudinized. "I expect trouble, of course, but . . . but this is such a funny sickness, you know? What do I have? Maybe it's something psychosomatic—I mean that's always a possibility. God, everything enters your mind when they can't diagnose the thing. You think about it, and you think that here Paul wants to write—so I get sick. Do you think maybe I don't *want* him to write? Does that make any sense?"

"No. Does it make any sense to you?"

"Well if it's my unconscious, how can *I* know? Does it look to you as though I'm giving up? Because I'm not giving up. At least I don't think I'm giving up. Not *consciously*, at least. But then I've got this thing and they can't diagnose it. I left all that blood there and all that pee—you'd think they could find something. It's not a joke either; I just give in to myself, damn it."

"Maybe you're anemic. Maybe you're not eating right. Maybe it's Iowa. Everybody gets sick some time without their knowing why. I'd worry about my psyche last of all."

"You're trying to make me feel better."

"You try to make yourself feel worse."

"You've really been very kind to us," she said. "Paul appreciates it—"

I don't believe I could have done anything to keep my face from again registering my skepticism.

"—probably more than you think," she finished.

"Yes." Though I went on to ask none of the obvious questions, she started in answering them anyway.

"You see," she said, "if he acted grateful—well, he just can't. Not now."

I said that I understood.

"He doesn't want to look needy. He doesn't think he *is* needy. You see, I've had it so easy. I never had to pay for anything in my life. And I had lots of brothers and sisters, and everybody looking after me—and Paul, well, Paul had to work for everything. It's not so bad really if you had things and then you have to give them up. It's better than sacrificing at the beginning and then *still* sacrificing later on. The worst thing about poverty is it's so boring. He—he has to give up so many things." She paused here to fix her blankets; when she went on, the sacrifice of Paul's which she chose to speak about did not strike me as the specific one she'd had in mind. "He was an only child and very attached to his family, and now they've really been hideous. Do you know what a *mikvah* is? A ritual bath? Well, I had one. The rabbi in Ann Arbor took me to the swimming pool at the Y, and in my old blue Jantzen I had this *mikvah*. And his parents *still* won't lift the phone when he calls. We call and they hang up. I could just kill them for that. Really take a knife and drive it right in them."

"It doesn't sound very pleasant."

"It isn't."

For her sake, I generalized again. "Everybody has some kind of trouble with their family," I said.

"I know. It's just that sometimes the accident of things gets you. If Paul had had another set of parents . . . Oh this is silly."

But only a little later she rode on in the same direction. "When—" she said, "when I read your mother's letter— Is this rude?" she asked, and answered herself with a surge of blood to the forehead. "But I did read the letter, Gabe, and I saw she was intelligent, and I thought, Oh what a relief if Paul's parents could just be a little like that. I didn't think anybody was going to act the way they did. I thought it would be *exciting* to have Jewish in-laws. I was all ready to be—well, Christ, I had that *mikvah* in my Jantzen, what else could I do? But not them. They don't want to be happy. They want to be miserable, *that* makes them happy. Well, it doesn't make anybody else happy."

"My mother," I said, taking a final stab at cheering her up, "might not have been much of a help, you know. She was a very willful woman."

"She was intelligent."

"All I'm saying is that she was no less firm in her opinions than the Herzes apparently are."

"Yes?" Libby said. "But suppose you had married a Gentile. You're Jewish, aren't you?"

"I am, but I don't think that particular thing would have made any difference to her."

"Ah, you see . . ."

What I saw I did not like. I pretended to be straightening her out about my mother while I worked to squelch a regret she seemed momentarily to have developed over marrying Paul and not me! "Libby, look, you read the letter. My mother was a woman of strong likes and dislikes. She liked her way. There were plenty of things she wouldn't put up with. That Gentile business just wasn't one of them."

"Well, it's one of them with the Herzes all right."

I did not like her for the remark. I experienced my first real fellow-feeling for Paul Herz since that night out on the highway when Libby had behaved so badly. "What about the DeWitts?" I asked.

"I don't care about them any more. Not a single one of them!"

It was a fierce remark, and courageous mostly because it was so clearly a lie. Libby leaned over toward the wicker table—also porch furniture—and took a pill. When she turned back to me she was almost pleading. "Paul's my husband," she said. "I prefer him to them. I have to. But Paul—" I had to wait a long time for her to decide whether to finish what she had begun to say, or perhaps to decide how to finish it. "Paul," she said finally, "was very attached to his family. I mean he wants us all—he'd like us all. Together."

There was no sense in my saying anything but, "It's too bad he can't have that."

She looked up at me gratefully. "It is."

"Maybe you should begin to have a family of your own."

"Oh no!"

Apparently I had gone too far, but I simply didn't care. What *was* intimacy for this girl and what wasn't? I was close to exasperation when, looking down and fingering the binding of the blanket, Libby said, "I had a miscarriage in Detroit."

I couldn't believe her. No well was so bottomless, no storm so unrelenting; even the worst rocks have a little greenery sticking to the bottom, not just bugs. I was convinced now that she was a liar and a nut.

I said that I was sorry to hear it.

"We weren't," she answered icily. "We—we don't want any children now. We didn't want that one actually. I had to go to the hospital—but truly it made me *happy*. It was a mistake, you see—we . . . I—oh I don't know *what* I want!"

She covered her tears with the tips of her fingers. "I worked myself into this," she said. "I think I've been trying for this." She dried her face with her muffler and then reached under the pillow for a handkerchief. "We just don't want any children now, that's all. How can we afford children? We can't even really *risk* having any . . ."

Her white hands and her handkerchief flitted about her face, and just when I was hoping she was at the edge of self-control, having only to step across, she fell back the other way. The lower half of her face became just mouth, and her body shook and shook.

I did not leave my seat or lean forward. Yet all my impulses were directing me toward movement, one way or another. The girl was not a nut and she was not a liar, and that knowledge produced in me a feeling of helplessness that was almost a presence in my limbs. I just couldn't *sit* there, being witness to Libby Herz's troubles. "Please," I said, "please, Lib . . . Please, try to relax. Libby, you're sick, you're a little upset . . . Libby, you were in school," I said, "you were busy, you didn't want children then. There'll always—"

"I don't want them now! I just want him to sleep with me! Oh, Christ, that's all!" She twisted herself away from me and toward the wall, carrying the blanket with her up over her head.

When she spoke next it was in a voice so breathless with humiliation I could hardly hear her. "I've overstated things. We just feel . . . we feel we have to be extra careful. We—could you get me another glass of water?"

I took her old full glass and poured it out in the kitchen sink, and then I let the faucet run a very long time. The little kitchen was really nothing more than the end of the living room. Over the sink was a small window, and outside I could see that the storm had lost most of its strength; it was simply snowing now. Down the street someone starved for exercise had already begun to scrape the sidewalks with a shovel, and the rasping of the metal hitting the concrete floated all the way up to the Herz barrack.

When I came back into the bedroom again, Libby was sitting in her bed just as I had found her when I'd entered earlier. Only now she looked even more completely the victim of her undiagnosed illness.

"I managed it," she said.

I looked at her from the doorway. "What?"

"To tell somebody everything."

I walked over and handed her the water. She took only a sip and then handed it back. I felt the touch of both the cool glass and her fingers. I sat down on the edge of the bed and without too much confusion, we kissed each other. We held together afterwards, but for only a second.

"I'll be all right, I think," she said.

I stood, and then I sat again, very upright in the wicker chair.

"I'll be fine," she said. "You don't have to stay until Paul gets back." Her husband's name gave her trouble.

"I think I'd rather stay," I said.

"But I don't mind being alone."

"That's all right."

"I just don't want you to think I expect anything."

"I don't think you expect anything!" I answered. "Jesus, Libby."

She raised her hands to her face again so that the fingers barely touched it, as though the bone beneath were sore and fragile. "I wormed that out of you too," she said.

Following our embrace I had been visited with a mess of emotions, no one of which I could clearly identify. It wasn't so much emotion, in fact, as emotionality: much strong feeling, no particular object. Now all I'd felt refined itself down into anger. "Listen, you didn't have to do any worming of anything out of anybody. I did what I wanted to do. Stop feeling guilty about everything, will you? I don't even believe it. You wanted me to kiss you, and I wanted to. I was glad I had, in fact, until you started talking. I'm not going to run off now, Libby, and I'm not sneaking out of any bedroom windows. I'll wait till Paul gets back—" The name, short and simple as it was, gave me some trouble too. "I came over here to ask him something anyway." I had difficulty, momentarily, remembering what it was.

"I'm sorry," she said meekly. "You're right."

Now, sitting straight in my wicker chair, I found it impossible to look at anything other than the Utrillo print. I saw that they had used thumb tacks to secure the two top corners to the wall, and two pieces of ragged Scotch tape to secure the bottom.

"I'm something," Libby said.

"Why don't you rest? Why don't you try to sleep?"

"That's a good idea . . . Oh Gabe, what am I? Am I awful or am I crazy?"

"Go to sleep."

She turned her head on the pillow, closed her eyes, and tried for thirty seconds to follow my directions. Then her eyes opened. "Excuse me, but I don't think I can with you sitting there."

"I'll sit in the other room."

"That might be a help," she said.

I got up and went to the door and behind me I heard her say, very softly, "I'll really be all right, you know. I mean you could go home."

"It was only a kiss, Libby," I said, turning to face her.

She looked up at me hopelessly. "Still," she said.

And then, along with her, I felt ashamed for our having turned out to be just about as unreliable as Paul Herz had given us the opportunity to be. I went out of her room and in the kitchen found my copy of *Portrait of a Lady.* I left, telling myself that I had no business in the lives of these people and that I would not come back, no matter who invited me. I got into my car and started away, and as I slowly took the first corner I saw Herz trudging home through the snow. He was no more innocent than any of us, and no braver, and yet he was Libby's husband, and I felt moved to pull the car over and confess to him that I had held his wife—and that my holding her was as good as saying to her that her husband gave her a rotten life. Which perhaps he did.

I passed snow banks and moved cautiously around stalled cars, and heard the trees creaking under the storm's weight. Soon I was worrying all over again as to the whereabouts of Marge Howells. I should have pulled over to Herz to ask . . . But what business of mine was she any more? If Marge Howells wanted to run, let her run! If my father wanted to pine, let him pine! If Libby Herz wanted to weep, let her weep!

When I had crossed the bridge and was turning into Dubuque Street, I had to slow up because of an accident ahead. A police car and an ambulance and half a dozen people were gathered under the street light. There was a tow truck on the scene too, the driver of which I recognized, and down on the icy street I saw a stretcher. I was ready to drive around the squad car and head up the next cross street when I saw that on the stretcher there was a blanket, and under the blanket a person. I stopped my car and got out and walked straight toward the center of the circle. I suppose the policemen must have thought I was a friend or relative who had been summoned, for the two of them stepped aside and let me through. What I saw surprised me. The face sticking up above the blanket belonged to nobody I knew.

3

Dear Gabe,

I have had so much time to correspond with old friends lately and it has been so long since either Paul or myself has had a chance to hear how you're doing, that I thought to write to you. When I mentioned it Paul thought it would be a good idea, and he wants to send along his good wishes. He is doing well in the department here, though the quality of the students isn't all one could ask for. The novel is coming along, despite interruptions and distractions and those omnipresent freshman essays. We are hoping, however, that he'll be able to finish it by the end of the year and get his degree and perhaps move on then to a college a little further from the coal fields. There's still the German to pass, but he's getting on top of that and with a little time will probably be able to pass it with ease. I had an excellent job here up until a few months ago when that old fever business started and I finally wound up in the hospital. It turns out I've got some kind of kidney disturbance, but now that it's been properly diagnosed, I've gotten the proper drugs and am out of the hospital and feel much better. I've had much time and even tried writing a story—which was awful—but have been able to read volumes and volumes. I finally got around to Wings of the Dove, *which I think is the best of them all. Didn't you do your dissertation on it? Kate Croy engaged me so very much—does that say bad things about my character? Aside from my almost dying—which I almost did and which I repeat merely for the romance of it—the next most exciting thing of the last six months was that we met a famous poet. Through some fluke, D—— came to the campus to read his poetry. (He'd been invited by the head of the dept.—the only man in the state of Pennsylvania who reads a little bit of the* Faerie Queene *at bedtime each night—and apparently thought it was some other school, because he showed up.)* He was older than I had thought, *but I was consoled by the fact that he was thin, had tight skin, and a youthful manner. He seems to me everything his poems indicate. After an evening reading in the chapel, D. and* his wife were given a party by the dept. head. The entire English staff was invited, along with other greater or lesser folks, so I got to see and hear him informally. I'd memorized a little speech beforehand, but I got too shy to say anything to him, so I stared instead. And I wasn't disappointed at all. Both D. and his very beautiful wife are all that you would like—kind, quiet in a shy way and not distant, deeply in love with each other (I could tell, of course) and naturally, most intelligent. When I saw them together, I kept thinking of how happy they are, and I loved her for being the inspiration of all those nice husbandly poems etc. The party went on, with people drinking nervously, talking nervously, and those younger ones of us feeling ill at ease and clinging to those we knew. After a while, bolstered by Scotch of course, I followed D. into another room and sat on a long chintzy couch opposite him and watched and listened to the general chatter which never got very profound about anything (including poetry) and glowed from my Scotch and my fever and the new red dress I had on—two dollars a week saved from my job here in the Dean's office, but beautiful I think anyway. So red dress and all, I was hardly inconspicuous, though most silent. But to get to the point, finally the Dean came to say goodnight to D. and noticed me sitting there and said, "Have you met my secretary yet?" And as I was walking across that long room to say hello (finally), D. replied, "Not officially, but we've been staring at each other all evening." And they all laughed, and I said in an exaggeratedly low voice I was happy to meet him and then thank God the Dean introduced our poet (published in the obscurest of quarterlies) Charlie Regan and I retreated awkwardly to my couch. Then after a confused while, D. and his wife decided to leave—the whole thing must have been awful for them—and again I followed, staring, and stood with the others waving goodbye. And I was desperately wishing to say something to him, when he noticed me, said "Oh," and came in again, walked over to me, took my hand and then KISSED me on the forehead and said something, but I don't know what, I was so stunned. And then I said, "Thank you for your poetry," and he looked pleased and bowed thank-you and left. And I went soaring up to the stars literally; I've never in my life had such a feeling. I thought at the time that it all was most symbolic, even though I realized that he thought I was a sweet silly girl, in love with the idea of a poet. Reading all *this over I see that it sounds just like that, like so much honey and roses. But I can't help it because it's all true. And I was very happy. I'm looking forward now to getting up and around, and even to getting back to the filing cabinets in the Dean's office, so you see that I must be well, having become so edgey. I've written letters to dozens of people, and since you helped us out so long ago, when we were both down in the dumps, I thought it might be pleasant to write to you. The sad thing in life is that we don't see friends and let small things separate us, and after a while you just think that even a greeting is insignificant. I know that Paul does send his best, and the two of us hope your life at Chicago and your job at the university is going well. It seems like a marvelous opportunity for you, and we would of course be interested in hearing how everything is going and how you like teaching there. It's time for me to take one of my pills, they're as big as stones and expensive as jewels, so I must close . . .*

Best,
Libby

I did not answer.

4

NEVERTHELESS, on a dull afternoon late in October of 1956, I was at Midway Airport watching for a plane coming toward Chicago out of the east. In that rippled gray sky I could not be sure which plane was which, but I saw one above me lurch off to the side, tremble in the air for a moment, and I took it to be the one I was waiting to meet. Other planes landed all around, swishing beautifully in, while this one circled and circled and circled. I counted landing gear, I checked the wings, I spotted a dismal little cloud and called it smoke out of the tail. The plane made several worried turns around the clock, and then was roaring down, its nose aiming for the swinging Shell sign across the road from the airport. I closed my eyes and waited. When I looked out again I found it had cleared the sign and was motionless, one safe colossal hulk on the runway.

After most of the passengers had disembarked, a dark under-nourished-looking couple stuck their heads through the door. The woman was bundled in a coat and wore a black hat that shadowed her face. The man's suit pinched his waist as suits were supposed to in 1928. He carried a typewriter and a brief-case; the woman's arms were filled with two brown paper bags. They whispered to one another and then peered out again at the banal geological dullness of Cook County, Illinois—they might have just made it out of some steamy Latin American country only a few hours before the regime had fallen. I called out to them several times, and finally had to run onto the field shouting their names. Only then, above their parcels and belongings, did I see Paul and Libby smile.

—

The character sketches which follow may help to explain the reappearance of the Herzes in my life.

John Spigliano.

Chairman of the Humanities II staff, my boss, at one time an undergraduate with me at Harvard. He is reputed now to be one of the most reasonable and scholarly young men in our midst. At staff meetings John explicates texts with the craftiest of understanding. Gibbon's sentences grow longer—explains

John, engraving the blackboard with graphs and charts—as he discusses the furthest outposts of the Empire, and shorter as he returns to the Imperial City itself. "I think we should point out to the student," John says, having compared the number of adjectival clauses in one paragraph with the number in the next, "how Gibbon impresses upon the reader the geography of the event with the geography, as it were, of the prose."

As it were, my ass. Spigliano is a member of that great horde of young anagramists and manure-spreaders who, finding a good deal more ambiguity in letters than in their own ambiguous lives, each year walk through classroom doors and lay siege to the minds of the young, revealing to them Zoroaster in Sam Clemens and the hidden phallus in the lines of our most timid lady poets. Structure and form are two words that pass from his lips as often as they do from any corset manufacturer's on New York's West Side. He is proprietary, too, about languages, knowing as he does six, or sixteen. Where a few measly syllables of some other tongue have been borrowed and absorbed into our own, John reveals the strictest loyalty to the provenance of the word. He, for instance, does not go to the Bijou Theater—he goes to the Bi*jou*. Only Don Quixote does he pronounce with the hard X, and he had to learn that in Cambridge, where, having been born poor and Italian, he felt it necessary for himself to swim a little with the fashion. At a party which he and his wife give once a year, John dances a jumpy peasant number that his parents brought over with them to the South End from the Abruzzi; he is not sober at the time, and afterwards those of us who cannot stand him get together, not very sober ourselves, and say that John really isn't such a bad fellow. He is a nuisance, though, to his more slothful colleagues, because he writes, as he will tell you, an article a month, and publishes pathologically. He was trained as a child to be a Catholic, and though he has now given all that up, he apparently feels it necessary to earn everything, tenure included, for eternity. I cannot believe that all that ambition is for this life alone.

John is only recently the chairman of our department. On October 12, 1956, Edna Auerbach was attacked and beaten on S. Maryland Avenue and forced to resign for the year as both chairman and teacher. At the age of thirty-one, John was selected by the Dean to be father to ten staff members (it is a small staff—we all teach two sections of freshman English and a section of Humanities on the side), a cranky secretary, and two mimeograph machines. It is not sour grapes to say that it is a finicky scissors-and-paste job after which nobody else on the staff had particularly been whoring. But where John is concerned, there needn't really be that much connection between the task and the promotion. If the next step up involved swabbing the latrines in Cobb Hall, John Spigliano might not have turned advancement aside without a thought. He was not considered a reasonable young man for nothing.

On October 18, after a week-long search for someone to teach Edna's sections, John asked if I knew of anybody he might be able to get hold of right away. His preference, he told me privately, was for another Harvard man.

—

Pat Spigliano.
They deserved one another. At those parties at which her Johnny let his hair down and danced for us, Mrs. Spigliano swished about in her taffeta dress, fiercely American Young Mother, and—soon enough—fiercely The Chairman's Wife. At a Spigliano party every contingency appeared to have been taken care of in advance. Over the door to the room where coats were to be deposited, was a handprinted sign to greet the first guest: COATS HERE. Above the table where one picked up one's watery cocktail was written, a little misleadingly: AND DRINKS HERE. And signed, P.&J. Even Pat's little party hors d'oeuvres were apparently prepared in the morning and refrigerated on the spot, so that by evening the bread, as I recall it, was particularly without tension. Oftentimes one's teeth had to make their first soggy journey down into a Liverwurst Delight, with Pat at one's elbow, waiting. Oh, we would all comment in barely audible voices, how does Pat manage to look so fresh, wondering just the opposite about the lettuce. She stays so thin, we would add—for it has come to seem that she will not move on until something like this is said—and so youthful. "Oh I'm thin, I suppose," admits Pat, fingering her front buttons as though they were little awards for virtue, "because I'm just busy all the time." Eleven different budgetary tins on her kitchen counter encouraged one to believe that

what she kept herself busy with most of the time was por-
tioning out pleasure to her family. A piece of adhesive tape
across one of the tins read—

JOHN
Tobacco, scholarly journals, foot powder

The night I ran into them having dinner at the Faculty
Club, Pat had just found a new apartment on Woodlawn into
which the family was to be moved the following week. After
dinner I was invited to their table for a drink, to celebrate their
good fortune. "We're so glad to be moving from Maryland,"
Pat told me, "especially after what happened—Edna's accident. And the new apartment is marvelous. I have a wonderful
kitchen, and John has a wonderful study, and really," she said,
"what with his promotion, we're having too much good luck.
I expect there'll be an earthquake or some terrible catastrophe
to even things up." What riled me was that she didn't even
expect rain. Though I had breakable possessions of my own
—a new car, in fact—I wouldn't that moment have minded
hearing a rumbling under the floor and seeing the trees go
sailing down outside the window on Fifty-seventh. "But our
Michelle—she's one of the twins—Michelle was bringing"—
she made a quick check of the waiters—"little colored boys
home from school with her. Well, that's when I thought I'd
better start looking. She was bringing them into the house for
cookies, which is perfectly sweet, except Michelle is an affectionate child—I suppose she's always *had* a lot of affection—
and she was kissing them. On the lips. Well, sweet as it was, it
was a problem. It's difficult to explain these things to children,
yet I feel you've got to be realists with them. They *want* you to
be a realist—especially Michelle and Stella, at their age. How
old is your little girl, Mrs. Reganhart?" She asked this of a
blond woman in a purple suit who had eaten dinner with them.
Mrs. Reganhart's long hair was braided high on her head, and
her features were large and Nordic and symmetrical. On no
one of them had I seen a sign of any emotion, save boredom.
"Seven," the woman said. "You know then," said Pat, "what
little realists they are. We have a boy, John Junior, the twins'
older brother—and so we explained to Michelle that she
couldn't kiss little colored children for the same reason that

she couldn't marry her brother. And I believe she understood. There is a Negro problem in the neighborhood," said Pat, "and I don't know what's to be gained by not recognizing it." "There's a Negro little-boy problem," said Mrs. Reganhart, looking into her brandy glass, and Pat agreed. I don't think you can insult this woman, by the way, because I don't think she listens. "Edna, for instance," she began, "well apparently it was a *giant* of a colored man. Harold came by tonight —that's her husband, the doctor," she explained to Mrs. Reganhart. "A chiropodist," said John, who had till then been busy constructing a personality around his pipe. "But a very nice fellow," Pat added. "He said Edna was badly shaken up—she's had a very serious emotional breakdown. Perhaps I'm wrong, but speaking personally I really do think that certain women are rape *prone*. Carriage, for instance, has a great deal to do with it. Your psychological make-up—" she told Mrs. Reganhart while John turned to me and asked if I had picked up the essays Edna's class had written. "I wonder if you could mark a pile of them," he said. "I've read a few myself, and I'm afraid it's not a pleasant job. Edna is an excellent grammarian, but I don't know how much she's able to get over to the students about structural principles—" Whenever he could, John used his pipe to enforce his meaning; it was clear he would be a maiden with it until he died. I couldn't really look at him without feeling a little ashamed for all our puny masculine disguises. "You haven't thought of anyone since this morning, have you?" he asked. "I'm just opposed to letting a graduate student onto the staff. Now, ideally a Harvard man was what I was thinking—"

—

Martha Reganhart.

The first words I ever heard her speak were, "There's a Negro little-boy problem"; the second: "What a dumb, silly, impossible bitch." The dry whistling autumn air outside seemed to give to Martha Reganhart's voice a special quality of exuberance; since she seemed to have no intention of being secretive in the first place, she ended up practically shouting. We had managed to escape from the club at the same time and had turned east toward Woodlawn together, under a perfectly beautiful evening sky. "What a thing—*rape* prone! Don't you feel like stamping her out? Don't you want to *grind* her into something? God, she makes me ferocious! She doesn't read contemporary novels, do you know that? And she thinks water should be fluoridated. And her little girl can't kiss her little brother for the same reason he can't marry Negroes. Oh, you were there for that. You should have stopped by a little earlier —you missed all the casserole recipes, my friend. Do you know John speaks sixty—oh, you *know* all this. You don't happen to be a pal of theirs . . . ? Did you think I was? I sat there thinking, This fellow is going to hang me by association. Not that I read many contemporary novels myself, but I'm not against it for others, you know? Which is probably my fluoridation opinion too. What *is* fluoridation exactly? What? Oh I don't even know how I got invited to dinner— Oh I do know. I'm a gay divorcée and Spigliano is in on the folklore."

"He made a pass? John?"

"It does sound pretty unstructured of him, doesn't it? I took a course from him downtown this summer. I was leaning over my Ibsen in his office and he snuck up from behind. He put his hands on my waist. My hips, I suppose. But that's really all. I guess he felt, given that, I ought to meet his wife. Look, I don't know what he thought. He invited me and since it's nice to get out of the house once in a while, I came."

"How did it end?"

"I said, Cut it out."

"And John?"

"He said something about my not understanding his passionate Latin soul and then pole-vaulted out of the room. Excuse me, really. That woman makes me want to talk bawdy just as a kind of declaration of humanity. He wasn't as silly as that. I shouldn't even have been in that class in the first place. As I said, I get interested from time to time in getting out of— Does this all seem a little too defensive? I know what night school sounds like for a grown woman. Hiking up your earning ability. Improving your word power. But for me it was different, truly. I wore all kinds of jazzy clothes, and heels—so I suppose poor John's not so much to blame. But tonight I didn't know whether to apologize to that fastidious Arid-soaked little ladies' magazine of his, or whether he had brought us all together to confess. She said he'd been talking about me all summer. I was one of his best students and so on, and I just sat there looking stony as I could. Did I look stony?"

"Bored."

"Really? I wasn't. After a while I thought maybe it was a joke. Go explain men's consciences . . . I'm sorry if I'm being loud. It was a trying experience. You just had brandy—I sat there for two and a half *hours*. I thought I acted pretty well, though, didn't you? Oh I said that thing about Negroes, but how could I help myself? And she doesn't hear anyway. But you were wonderful, by the way. You were really excellent. I mean you know how to be stony, kid. After a while I began to wonder if you were one of them. I live down on Fifty-third, I have to turn off here."

"Would you like to have a beer with me?"

"I have a baby-sitter waiting."

"A short beer. I'll explain fluoridation."

"Explain the conscience of John Spigliano, if you want to do some explaining. Now that's something, isn't it?" She stood for a moment with her hands on her substantial hips, just a little off balance, contemplating the problem. In heels she was my equal, and when she stopped meditating and looked straight on at me, it was directly in the eye. Right off I liked Martha Reganhart a good deal. "To make a pass and then invite me to dinner with her," she said. "Who in hell was he trying to prove what to? I mean it about men's consciences. I don't understand them. They can't let go, you know? If they know they're so guilty, then why do they keep acting like bastards? I'm sounding unladylike again, but a woman at least realizes there are certain rotten things she's got to do in life and she does them. Men want to be heroes. They want to be noble and responsible, but they're so soft about it. Do you agree with this or are you laughing at me?"

We had a beer and on the way home, crossing Kenwood, I took her hand to guide her onto the curb. And then, with only sidewalk ahead, I kept it. Her next remark left me feeling rather feeble. "It's only a hand," she said. I released it. "I was only holding it," I said. At the corner of Kimbark and Fifty-third she stopped. "The fifth ugly porch down is mine. I think I can make it alone. Thanks for walking me. Thanks for making everything clear about water fluoridation. I'd like to

be against it, what with Mrs. Spigliano being for it, but I'm as
cavity-oriented as the next parent. Good night, Gabe," she
said. I am of a forgiving nature, and if somebody wants to
charm me, I let them. For a moment Martha Reganhart looked
up at the white moon, showing the underside of what looked
to be—despite my hospitable feelings toward her—a very uncompromising chin. She made a slight but weary sound. She
was not so big, really, as she seemed.

"Maybe we could have dinner some night," I said. "Without the Spiglianos."

She looked from the heavens back to me with what I
thought was genuine interest. Then she turned formal and altogether strange. "That's very nice of you. Perhaps we can
work that out some time." Her smile didn't help matters any.
"I work, you know, at night. Tonight is—was—an exception.
Thanks again for the beer." As she was about to move off
finally, she said, "Please excuse me, will you, if I sounded like a
grande dame just now. It's just the handholding. I don't see
the . . . I was going to say I don't see the sense." She turned
here and hurried up the street. I saw that for the most part she
took the width of her hips and the breadth of her thighs without very much complaint; in walking she made no attempt to
be languorous or statuesque, nor did she hide her neck and
slouch off inches in the shoulders, or even give in to buxom-
ness and gyrate belly and can. She walked with an unquestion-
able solidity; not mannish, mind you, but not tinkley-tinkley
or snap-snap either. I imagine that women over five eight have
decisions to make that other women don't; there's no absolute
relaxing, and probably they know best whether to be snugglers
and handholders. On the stairway of her front stoop Martha
Reganhart suddenly disappeared, and I wondered if she had
fallen. But she had only bent over to pick up something from
one of the steps. Throwing a child's doll over her shoulder, she
proceeded into the house.

—

Gabe Wallach.

Knows only two languages, and one badly, so perhaps he is
snotty out of envy. Unlike his boss, he has no wife whom he
deserves. As for girl friends, he would not be willing to say
that he has actually deserved any of them. He is better, he be-

lieves, than anything that he has done in life has shown him
to be. Often upon parting from friends and acquaintances, he
has the suspicion that he has behaved badly; what may or
may not have really happened alters very little his attitude
toward himself. He has the malaise of many wealthy but ordinary young men: he does not exactly know what to do with
himself. Though subject to his share of depressions, nightmares and melancholy, he cannot enjoy any of it thoroughly
(and thereby feel his true and tragic worth) because of a nag-
ging doubt that he is very lucky and ought to be thankful
and shut up. It would help if he would imagine himself without hope. He has an income, he has perfect health, and he
believes not only in the pursuit, but the catching by the tail
and dragging down into the clover, of happiness. Unfortunately, all these beliefs don't get too much in the way of his actions. If his own good fortune were inevitable, he should not
have so much trouble making up his mind. For an optimist, he
is very nervous and indecisive. Suppose happiness should twitch
her butt and dance merrily off the side of a cliff—should he
follow?

Five times during the day he had walked up the stairs of Cobb
Hall to Spigliano's office, and five times turned and walked
back down again to his own. At the dinner table there had been
at least five more occasions when he had been tempted to
speak. In fact, all the while Pat congratulated herself on her
good fortune, he ruminated silently on the brandy that slides
down the throats of the undeserving, and the fevers, the
popped pistons, the ugly iron beds of those who deserve, if not
more, surely no less than the others. But when asked again by
John Spigliano, he only shook his head and took his leave. It
was walking home with Martha Reganhart—touching her
hand, actually—that he had cause to remind himself that Libby
Herz was not the only woman in the world who could engage
his feelings. Not that Mrs. Reganhart, in their manic hour together, had engaged feelings of a sustaining and vibrant sort.
The moon and stars, as much as she, had combined to prickle
his easiest sentiments. But he had liked her, and in her frame
and voice, her country stride, he had recognized something
open and direct to which he could respond. She might turn
out to be a little motherly and instructive, but if so he could

move on. After all, the decision was not whether he should or should not marry Martha Reganhart. All he cared to make clear to himself was that if the Herzes should come to Chicago he could manage to have an active life of his own, independent of theirs. There was Martha Reganhart, and there were dozens of others too. It was not changing his own life that was finally uppermost in his mind; it was changing theirs. It was much too easy to imagine Herz out there in Reading resigning himself to no money and depressing surroundings and calling it "life." A message from Chicago might well be what would lift the Herzes up *into* life. A job at the University would be an improvement for Herz in every way—and for his wife as well. And if that was so, then it had been dishonorable of him not to have suggested Paul right off.

He would have lifted the phone then, had it not been that he knew the situation was not nearly so black and white as that. He was not (let a truth be repeated that is probably known already) a strong man. He was prone to self-deceptions, and some of his impetuosities were rehearsed as much as two or three months in advance. He had reason to believe that he might have fallen in love with Libby Herz. He had reason to believe that she might have fallen in love with him. So for whom, for what end, was he doing favors?

He marked three unstructured freshman papers, took a bath —but finally, he called.

"Pat, is John home?"

She said he was out at the Dean's. "Gabe, we do hope you liked Mrs. Reganhart. It must be hard for her to find a man as tall as she is, but when you walked out John commented on how well you went together. She has to wear Tall Gals' shoes, you know, so she *is* a tall person."

"She seems very nice. I didn't get a good look at her shoes. Will you ask John to call me?"

"She's divorced and has children and works as a waitress to support them—*and* takes courses. We think that's quite admirable."

When the phone rang twenty minutes later, he told John that a fellow he had known at Iowa was now teaching in Pennsylvania, and from what he understood he might be willing to leave his job. "His name is Paul Herz," he said.

"Didn't he have something in *Modern Philology* recently? Herz?"

"I don't know," he said. "He's a writer."

"A creative writer?"

"A novelist."

"What's he published?"

"I don't believe anything yet. He's just finishing a book. He was finishing it last year."

"Then he hasn't his degree yet?" John asked.

"Everything but the dissertation—the novel."

"You mean—" The voice on the other end was Pat Spigliano's. "You mean they do some kind of creative writing instead of a work of scholarship?"

He waited patiently for Spigliano to tell his wife to get the hell off the extension.

"Isn't that something?" Still Patricia. "I had thought you did a dissertation on James."

"I did."

"Oh, one has a choice then. I suppose Harvard is a little more traditional, though that *is* very up to date. We wondered why you didn't stay on for graduate work at Cambridge, but I see now that you probably preferred the freedom—"

"John, are you still there?"

"I'm here. I'm thinking."

"Well, it's only a suggestion."

"This is very considerate of you, Gabe, but you know the difficulty with creative writers."

"What?"

"They're apt to be a little too personal about literature."

"Oh."

"Most of them are without any real critical system. I've never really known a writer who finally understood writing."

There was no sense, he knew, in bringing up old Henry James; there was no sense in bringing up anything.

He said, "Paul is a very bright guy. He's an excellent man."

An hour later, when he had already settled into a chair convinced that he had at least done the decent thing, the phone rang again.

"Look, do you think this Herz could come out here right away? Within a day or two?"

"You'd have to ask him. It would probably depend on whether he could get out of the job he has."

"Will you call him for us?"

"What?"

"Call him for us."

He found himself terribly unsettled by this very obvious suggestion. "Don't you think you'd better call, John? As chairman? I can give you his address. Just wait a minute."

He left the receiver hanging off the edge of the desk and hunted through the bookshelf for his copy of *Portrait of a Lady*. In its middle pages were two envelopes. He carried one back to the phone and read the return address to John Spigliano. After he hung up he read the letter itself. Then he settled into a chair and read the other letter too.

Paul Loves Libby

1

H E HAD uncles who had failed. He had a father who had
failed too, but that was in the world of commerce. Mr.
Herz bought and sold with little talent and saved where interest amounted to pennies; when he finally emerged from his
fourth failure—this last in frozen foods—he had nothing to
show for himself save a sinus condition and holy dread of heart
failure. He took to melting Vicks in a spoon under his nose
and arranged for a small bank loan so as to purchase, for his
heart's ease, a BarcaLounger; and then he settled down to wait
for the end. Still, there is a hierarchy of failures; better bankruptcy than tension in the kitchen and in the bed. There was a
man's home life to judge him by. Uncle Asher might have clear
nasal passages but he had a ruined life: he had never married.
Up close you could see and smell his single condition—suits
swollen at the knee, heels a disgrace, and as far as anyone could
tell, only one tie to his name. His sister, who was Paul Herz's
mother, said that from Asher's smell alone she didn't even
have to guess what shape his linens were in. One foul snowy
evening she had seen her baby brother emerge from Riker's
with a toothpick in his mouth. Riker's! For an Asher! She had
cried herself to sleep for a week.

Asher had begun life a genius, having begun to play Mozart
at just about the same age Mozart had begun to play Mozart.
At sixteen he had received free tuition to pose life models at
the Art Students League; he was allowed to touch and arrange
their bare limbs, so advanced for his years was his sense of
grace. When he brought home his charcoal drawings they
were tacked up in the living room. "You don't even think dirty
when you look at such pictures," Asher's mother had reassured
the neighbors. "Look how artistic he makes those fat girls."
A piano was brought into the house for Asher; later a violin

and a cello. He spent a summer in the Louvre, copying; he did his first commissioned portrait at eighteen—the captain of the Mauritania! But that captain was long dead, and other captains had come and gone, and in the meantime no girl had married Asher. Didn't he know girls were soft? asked Paul's father. Didn't he know they were nice to hold? Had he never kissed one? Was he a— Absolutely not! He wasn't a good mixer, that's all. He was just a little scholarly.

What his sister and brother-in-law decided was that it was necessary to *put* a young lady in Asher's path. They invited him to dinner, and they invited a secretary from Mr. Herz's office; they invited school teachers, colleagues of Mrs. Herz. Once they tried a distant cousin who was in town, and once even—for who knows what goes on in the head of an artist —once they even tried (all the dead should rest in peace!) a shikse, but a girl who hung around with Jews. They turned on the radio but Asher wouldn't dance. They brought out the cards but Asher wouldn't play. How could you put a girl in this fellow's path—he *had* no path! Though it brought tears to his sister's eyes and even a kind of tsk-tsk compassion to his brother-in-law's tongue, Asher's ruination was nevertheless of his own doing.

The other flop was Uncle Jerry. He had married, but only for twenty-five years. A quarter of a century with a woman and then he divorces her. So who could feel sorry for him? A beautiful twelve-room house in Mt. Kisco with grass all around and a pine-paneled basement; four beautiful daughters with beautiful builds—one married, two in college, and the fourth, Claire, the little *shaifele*, still in high school; and for a wife, a wonderful woman, a princess, a queen. What if she weighed 180 pounds? Did he expect that to change? Could he roll her out twenty-five years after the wedding night because she was still making the same dent in the mattress now as then? Who could feel any sorrow for *him*! Why, *why* did he do it? Did he have some tootsie on the side? No, no—it was his what-do-you-call-it, his psychoanalysis! His psycho*analyst* made him do it. *That* son of a bitch. What did that guy think life was, easy? A bowl of cherries? You love your wife, you don't love her; you fondle her, you can't stand to touch her—that happens! Does that mean you destroy a family? When a father dies it's a catastrophe. Here's a man who *walks* out!

Two years after he had walked out, Jerry married a twenty-seven-year-old, just the type everybody had been looking for for Asher for years. "What's he doing? *Another* big woman— what's the matter with him? A twenty-seven-year-old—what's he *thinking* about? When she's forty, when she's thirty-*five* even . . . What kind of business is this!"

"Then call him, Leonard. Stop getting upset and call him. Talk to him. He's your brother."

"It's his life. Let him ruin it. Would he call me? If I had a seizure tomorrow, would he so much as lift the phone off the hook?"

"Your heart is perfectly all right. The doctor listened to it. He checked everything. They have graphs, Leonard, that show. You've got a nice even line. Don't get overexcited because you'll give yourself trouble."

"I'm not overexcited. I'm practically lying down. He could marry a ten-year-old and I wouldn't turn a pinky. I told him when he married Selma, didn't I? Jerry, you're wet behind the ears. Jerry, you never even had a woman yet. Jerry, give yourself a chance. Jerry this, Jerry that, Jerry, she's a very big girl, Jerry—is that what you want? And now this one, also a horse. Why doesn't he at least *call* me, ask my advice. Say to me, Lenny, what do you think—Lenny, does this seem to you like I'm doing a sensible thing? No, him, he's smarter than the rest of the world."

Three weeks later ("to the day" as it later came to be reported) the girl telephoned. "He left! Your brother left! He walked out! What did I do? What will I do? All this new silverware," she cried. "Please come somebody. *Help me!*"

"Leonard, where are you going in your slippers?"

"I'm going! What—is he crazy? Is he a crackpot?"

"Leonard, don't get involved now."

"I am involved. The telephone rings, this girl is hysterical, I'm involved. She's a baby—she'll do something insane. How do I know?"

When Mr. Herz went out the door his wife grew hysterical herself. She knelt beside the BarcaLounger and wept into the still-warm leather. Who knew best whether a man's heart is weak, the doctor or the man himself? How could a machine tell a man he didn't have pains? In the night he couldn't even roll over, his ribs were so sore. And one morning she would wake up and he wouldn't. Oh God! God! He would get over-excited, involved, wrought up—and die! She wept and wept and finally she pulled herself to the telephone and looked up the analyst's name. She dialed, and when she had him on the phone, she cried, "You son of a bitch! My sister-in-law, you ruined her life, you son of a bitch! She had everything and you ruined it! What kind of ideas do you put in people's heads? What is he—a *boy*? A man fifty-two years old and he marries girls, *children*! You *quack*, you *fraud*—"

———

Yet when their son came down one Christmas from Cornell to drop the name Libby DeWitt into their lap, it was to Asher and Jerry that they referred him. Tears flowed from his parents for two reasons: there was grief over his marital decision, and grief too at their own impotence. They had somehow reared a boy whom they could not bludgeon or make hysterical. By way of ruination, selfishness and stupidity, Jerry and Asher seemed better equipped than themselves to deal with the dis-aster. There even seemed to the parents to be some affinity between the boy and his uncles, which was yet a third reason for tears. "I let him down," wept the father in bed, both hands over his ribs. "He won't listen to me. In my own house my voice don't carry from the kitchen to the toilet. All his life the boy has been filling in applications. You lift up a piece of paper in this house and underneath's an application. When did I ever see him? When did he learn to listen to a father? He was always running out to get somebody to recommend him for some-thing. A waiter in the mountains, a stock boy, a scholarship student. Once he should listen to me. Just once."

Paul's mother was crying too, but at least—to her credit—she tried to change the subject. "A scholarship is an honor," she sobbed, touching her husband's wet face. "We should be proud—"

"It's an honor for the son, not for me. Just once, *once* . . . Five years later and frozen foods was already a craze. This man

Birdseye is coining it, and my son, my son . . . A Catholic the
girl is, practically an invalid, nineteen years old and she ain't
had a healthy day in her life—"

"My baby," his mother wept. "He could read the mileage
off the speedometer before other kids could even talk. What's
happening to my baby?"

———

When Asher called to invite Paul for a walk, Paul saw no
need to be rude to someone essentially an outsider in the whole
affair. He went with Asher because he knew his parents had
asked Asher to phone; he went to make it easier on Asher, who
like himself must have felt obliged to comply with whatever
sad maneuverings these two helpless people could devise; he
went for the sake of everybody's dignity. It happened also that
he knew that Asher would be sympathetic, or at the least noncommittal. The values of a man who had studied art in New
York, in Chicago, in Europe, who had composed music, who
chose to live in a loft over a Third Avenue bar—these were not
the values of a washed-out bourgeois and his wife. Asher was a
free man; an eccentric perhaps, but free.

The day they met was windless and cold. They walked side
by side, two scrawny bareheaded men, one bald, the other
with kinky black ridges beginning only two fingers above his
eyebrows. One rounded his shoulders to stay warm; the other
had had round shoulders for years. Though this posture gave
Asher a thoughtful mien, the drop that formed and reformed
at the end of his spiritless nose was not nearly so pensive-
looking; it had the air of an oversight, as had his clothes and
his features. His misshapen lobes, for example, made his ears
look like accidents; on top of that, hair grew out of them.
Asher did not seem to believe that outside the skin there were
things to be taken care of. A full day of barbers, tailors, shoe-
makers, cleaners, and opticians would just about begin to put
him in order. His spectacles were a little storage bin of paper
clips and Scotch tape.

None of this run-downness depressed Paul, however. He
leaned closer to catch the soft, whispery words his uncle spoke,
while overhead the El trains broke metallically through the cold
steely air. He managed to hear ". . . oh . . . not . . . people

. . . parents—yes?" Asher turned his head in the raised collar of his overcoat and peered questioningly at his nephew.

"I'm sorry," Paul said. "I didn't—"

"Not bad people, do you think?" Asher swung his head, freeing his nose of its burden.

"No. I know, Asher."

"They have your interests in mind. That's so, isn't it?"

"*Their* interests." What with the noise overhead, Asher must not have understood what he'd been saying. "It would be in my interest to make me happy. It would be in my interest to give me a blessing."

"They'd love to give you a blessing. They're dying to give you a blessing," said Asher, raising his ungloved hands from his pockets.

"Let them go ahead then," Paul said.

Asher was peeling paint from under his nails. "They'd like to give me a blessing, they'd like to give everybody a blessing. How old are you, Paulie?"

"Twenty-one."

Asher made a face, as though he'd eaten something unpalatable. "So what's your hurry?"

"What hurry? Hurry for what?"

"You have a nice sweet life ahead of you, isn't that a fact?"

Where was this conversation drifting? "But I'm in love," said Paul, shrugging.

"Let's get out from this noise, and talk," Asher said, taking Paul by the elbow. As they crossed the street, he pulled his nephew close to him and with a sleepy closing of his swollen lids back of the tortured glasses, said, "I'm in love myself."

"Yes?"

"Absolutely."

"I didn't know that," Paul said, trying to remain composed.

"Sure. She comes to my studio every Wednesday afternoon. Today, this afternoon. It gets dark and she goes home. A girl twenty-five." He spoke as if each fact had to be remembered from the dim past. Though he did not want to, Paul suspected his uncle of lying.

"Is she married?" Paul asked.

"I know her four years, and every Wednesday . . . the most valuable thing in my life . . . She's married, sure. She has a baby." Asher took a frayed billfold from his coat and handed Paul a picture of a little girl. "A darling," Asher said.

"She's very nice."

"A darling child," Asher said. He stuffed the billfold back inside his coat. "Look, Paulie, I've loved a lot of women. Six years I lived with a Chinese woman, for example. Many different types and personalities. I've screwed all kinds, every imaginable variety of cunt, I've had it. I'm no amateur at this business."

"I didn't know that."

"What? What didn't you know?"

"For instance, the Chinese."

"Oh sure—well, I didn't make a point of it with your mother. I think she has a prejudice against non-Occidentals."

"That's giving her a break, but that's true."

"Is she pregnant?" Asher suddenly asked. "This girl? I'm trying to get to your motivation."

"Are we talking about me now?"

"About your girl friend," Asher said. "What's the story, Paulie?"

"My father told you she must be pregnant, is that it? Don't you think that shows how he doesn't begin to understand?"

"Don't worry about his understanding. Of course he's a dope. You didn't knock her up?"

He felt moved to deny even sleeping with Libby; the conversation had turned in a way he could not have imagined. But he had reasons stronger than pride for not wanting Asher to confuse himself about his experience. He had not come out on a below-freezing day for bad advice. "She's not intact, but she's not pregnant either."

"She's not intact by you or before you?"

"By me."

"Oh it clears up. And for that you're throwing out all your opportunities? For that small puncture you'll tie yourself down? How will you support this girl you ruined?"

"Asher, what are you talking about?"

"Money. Life."

"You sound like my old man."

"You haven't got good ears—I'm at the other end of the globe. I understand she's a little sickly."

"She gets *colds*, Asher. They met her twice and both times she had colds. It's winter. She's human—"

"Even nose drops cost money," Asher was explaining. "Kleenex can run you into a fortune, I mean paupers like you and me. You want to tie a stone around your neck?" Asher asked. "You'll fall in love all your life, in and out all your life. You can even find a lady with a wooden leg, I don't care. It isn't the colds, Paulie, it's the principle. You're twenty-one, you drew a little blood from her, so you think there's only one girl in the world for you. But you've got no obligations according to the date of entry, you understand me? If it wasn't you, it would be another smart fellow. Don't bind yourself round for having a little fun. Is it you who wants to marry or is it this girl?"

"We both want to. We arrived at the decision mutually." He made no effort to hide his anger.

"Which more mutually than the other?"

"Mutually mutually!"

"And how old is she that she's so in tune with you and life?"

"Nineteen."

"Nineteen and a Catholic. Splendid."

"Asher, I didn't expect this from you."

"So what am I supposed to do? Tell lies? You only take walks with right-minded people?"

"You can disagree, but why on this level?" Paul demanded.

"*What* level? You tell me you like shikse pussy, you're telling me something I don't know? I'm *you*, Paulie, I'm you. Jewish girls devour you. Haven't I seen my friends go under? The wives can't walk upstairs. They need maids. They need vacations— once in August, then in January all over again. They're sorry they laid anybody before they married you. They stop sanctioning looseness, bang, all of a sudden. One Friday you come in the door and they got the candles going, and then you're *really* home. I'm not saying I blame you, Paul. I'm only trying to get to the bottom."

"Getting to the bottom doesn't mean digging into sewers. How can you talk like this? You don't even know the girl. You never even saw her."

"I never even saw that baby I carry a picture of either. But I know what a baby is, so I can appreciate this one. This girl's got a background on her you don't even begin to understand. She's got a family that probably this minute is churning gall over you. True?"

"Like mine over her. Just as smart and sensible."

"You think happiness comes out of gall? You think that'll be nice, earning all those enemies? You think it's enough to squirm around in bed with her, to wake up with her hand on your vitals? What do you think that solves, Paulie, after the wad is popped?"

"Christ, Asher, you're a dunghole, a toilet!"

"We're talking man to man, right? Don't start crying. I'm not a charming man."

"All right, Asher, man to man. If you're a man, a human being, then why don't you talk about love? *I love Libby*. I'm giving it to you straight now, though not so flowery as you. I love Libby. She's alive, she's sweet, she has deep and generous instincts. She has feelings. She, unlike you, is charming."

"You like that?"

"Yes."

"Charm is shit."

"She's a woman, Asher, *listen* to me! She behaves like a woman. I want to stick with her, to live with her."

"Go ahead."

"I am. I'm marrying her."

"You're a circular reasoner," said Asher, "and I'm a cynic, but you're worse. Marriage kills love. Do me a favor, look around at all the loving happy couples. You count them for me, all right? I'll close my eyes, you tell me how many you come up with." He took off his glasses, blew into them, then wiped away the steam on a piece of cloth he extracted from his coat pocket. His lower lids were jeweled with tears from the cold. Hooking the rims back over his elaborate ears, he said, "How many? Once you get past the Duke and Duchess of Windsor it's slim pickings, no? Paulie, kiss the girl, caress her, stick it right up in her, but for Christ's sake do me a favor and wait a year. You're an artistic type, a serious observer of life, why kill your talent? You'll sap yourself with worry, you'll die of a hard-on in the streets. Other women will tantalize you some day and you and your conscience will wrestle till you choke. Artists and artistic types must go it alone. If a year elapses and the urge remains, then go ahead, hang yourself, there's nothing anybody can do. Is a year too much to ask?"

"I'm graduating, Asher," Paul said, speaking with the patience of a wronged man. "She has a year to go, this girl you have so little regard for. When I leave Ithaca she'll stay. Because I am so hard up, you see, so controlled by my hot pants and this guilt I feel at having deflowered her, I feel I want to marry her. It's as simple as that."

"Precisely."

"Asher! Asher! When I leave, you shmuck, I *lose* her. That'll be that."

"I wouldn't myself, if I were you, stand in the way of an ending."

"But the plain and simple fact is, Asher, I don't *want* it to end! Does that mean nothing?"

"Don't you read history in your school? Don't you study *anything?*" Asher demanded. He ran his sleeve roughly under his nose so that the whole ungristled last inch of it moved back toward his face. The amazing thing was that Asher Buckner seemed to be angry. He swallowed; he looked as though he'd been weeping and wailing for an hour. "Listen to Uncle Shmuck, will you? Things come and go, and you have got to be a receptacle, let them pass right through. Otherwise death will be a misery for you, boy; I'd hate to see it. What are you going to grow up to be, a canner of experience? You going to stick plugs in at either end of your life? Let it flow, let it go. Wait and accept and learn to pull the hand away. *Don't clutch!* What is marriage, what is it but a pissy form of greed, a terrible, disgusting ambitiousness. Do you know what I do now, Paulie, for a living? I paint gangsters, petty thieves, the lousiest of rats, way way up there in the unions and the garment trade. They come in with their henchmen and they spit tangerine pits on my floor and they make fun of me while I paint the boss. They're rich and lord it over whole precincts, and I'm a sloppy-ass bohemian. They're the big shots and I'm the nothing. All right, I take it. I accept. The boss's got warts, I lop them off. He's got murder in his eyes, I put doves instead. He sends his wife, and I fill up her brassiere for her. I take out scowls, boils, wrinkles, bags, pores—everything goes. I give out only peaches and cream. Please, I don't want to be the greatest painter in the world. I don't want to be a maker of beauty, a religious personage. I don't bottle experience. I'm interested in the flow. I'll take the shape the world gives me. Fuck the rest. Let me buy you a drink. It's a hell of a day for a walk. You could freeze."

In the bar, a no man's land where Madison Avenue and the Bowery met and embraced, a drunken youngster in a tight suit and tight hair had his arm draped around a seventy-year-old alcoholic—somebody's mother. "Nothing in the world is irretrievable," said the young man to the old woman, his head lolling down on his shirt front. "Nothing. If you'd just go back to County Cork and start all over again you'd be amazed—"

The woman was shaking her head. "Ah, you just don't know what it's like, having to take all that crap day in and day out . . ."

The uncle and the nephew sipped whiskey and said nothing; Asher looked at his watch, then began to whistle to himself between his teeth. He didn't look much less ravaged to Paul than the old lady next to him. So was this girl friend of his a dream? Asher had bad breath—wouldn't a twenty-five-year-old girl mind? Had there ever really been a Chinese who had drawn with her lips at that skin of his, wrinkly like a dying old flower? Asher was a total surprise, not at all the kind of monk Paul had imagined. All his renunciations—family, children, food, clothes—hadn't been for his art at all. He had no art left. He was a tube with no plugs at either end. A receptacle. And that was what—courage or cowardice?

Paul was serious beyond his twenty-one years, and once an idea had been planted he could not easily discard it. He could not help asking himself if it made any sense at all to let Libby go. He was too purposive a young man—applying always in January for scholarships in September had given him a strong sense of consequence—to be casual about his decisions. However, his plan to marry was, he knew, no simple revolt against family, no simple sexual bite. As an adolescent busing tables in mountain resorts, he had been well enough tipped by vacationing housewives and lonely widows; from beneath him they had stroked his hair: "Oh, how nice and serious. You'll be something in life. I'm not worried about your future." As for the family, there was no sense talking about revolutions at this point; he had revolted at birth and lived a separate life under his own flag from infancy on. His kind of independence had not even allowed for the usual complaints; nobody had to stand and shout at him to get into his bedroom and study—he had always gotten A's and never once in his life had he been in trouble. If his father was prickled by his own failures, it was not because his son had insulted him by bringing them up. Something had tipped off the boy early not to expect anything of the man, and he had gone ahead to respect his father, if only on the strength of his office. When he had not known the spelling of a word, he had taken down the dictionary—this at age seven. His mother claimed it made her proud, though secretly it gave her the shivers. She was a normal-school graduate, a major in arithmetic, and she could have helped him with his long division. But he did everything himself, even fractions. When he was between the years one and four his father had failed in haberdashery; four to six it was hardware; six to eleven real estate; and then eleven to twelve—the blinding, total crash—he lost his shirt in quick-frozen foods. One day, creditors calling at every door, he got into the cab of a truckful of his frozen rhubarb and took a ride out to Long Island to think; the refrigeration failed just beyond Mineola, and by the time he got home his life was a zero, a ruined man. Now, in his reclining years, he got up once in a while to collect rents for an old friend.

And during all this, through all the bank notes and bewilderment, Paul had learned to read and write and reason, and above all to use his will. He had even willed Libby Herz herself into a seriousness she had not possessed when he had first met her. So complete a job had he done, in fact, that it had been she who had first suggested marriage. Though it was none of Asher's business, it was nevertheless so. How could she go back to the other boys after Paul?

His own decision was not, however, out of anything so simple, so unemotional, as obligation. If there *was* a sense of obligation it was to himself; he would unite with her not to make Libby a better woman, but to make himself a better man. He would place a constant demand upon his spirit, solidify his finest intentions by keeping beside him this mixture of frailty, gravity, spontaneity, and passion. He would serve another with the same sense of worthiness he served himself. Surely that was love, where duty and passion (and lust too, to swallow Asher's argument) mingled.

"Paulie, I have to leave," said Asher. "First let me go to the toilet." In a few minutes he came out of the men's room wiping his hands on his coat. "Look, how about you come back with me? I want Patricia Ann and you to meet. She'll make some tea. I won't say anything more. You're too smart for me to flood you with my personal philosophy. Just come back for an hour or two. I'm past fifty, nearing the end. Every emotion you've felt, multiply it by a thousand and that's how often I felt it. It gives me a little edge, don't it, Paulie? Till forty you think you've got bad emotions, you know, real killers—and then you find out they're only little flowers compared with what's coming. I'm not going to bombard you with any more wisdom of the aged. I only say you shouldn't consider yourself a special case. Look at the hag next to you—her mistakes," he said, not lowering his voice, "crawling over her like bugs. I'm not selling you my life, Paulie. Just maybe you should wait."

Asher paid for the both of them on the bus they took downtown. He dropped thirty pennies into the driver's hand. "What's your problem, buddy, a wise guy?" the driver said. "Pennies are money," Asher said. "Shut your ass and drive." He seemed in a very depressed state.

—

After Asher's mother had died, her son had taken all of her potted plants to live with him in Manhattan. For the two years she was ill he had gone over to Brooklyn every other day to water them; the old lady claimed that the day nurse was an anti-Semite and would either drown her plants, or leave them to dry up and crack. Some of them were now higher than Asher himself, and the pots, spread around three of his walls, weighed up to seventy-five pounds. What furniture there was in the room was beyond description. Before a row of tall windows at the front of the studio stood Asher's easel, and outside was the El. They had walked up to the building past a row of bars, all of them full of bums.

When Paul and his uncle entered the room, Patricia Ann was wiping the leaves of the plants with an old piece of her lover's undershorts; she immediately stuffed the dustrag under a pillow on the sofa.

"It's all right," Asher told her. "Patricia Ann Keller—my nephew, Paul Herz."

She shook Paul's hand. "I never think of Asher having relatives. What do you call him? Uncle Asher?" The laugh this produced in her seemed to have directly to do with her very small bones—as though a wind had blown through them. She was not really very much taller or heavier than Libby. Her gold ballet slippers had an inward, tomboyish turn, and her skirt and sweater left no doubt as to how high and how round were her various parts. Where run-of-the-mill people have the small of their back, she carried a little cannonball of a behind. Her breasts too, packed up nearly on a line with her shoulders, had the suggestion of small metallic spheres. Her face was a not very arresting, meager thing, pretty on the style of high school baton twirlers; the mouth a bow, the chin a point, the eyes blue beads, the nose hardly big enough to support its freckles. Her hair fell onto her shoulders in ringlets, naturally curly.

Asher ran a finger over a philodendron leaf and then dropped into a ratty leather club chair, where he proceeded to kick off his shoes. He dropped his glasses into his left shoe and rolled his thumb and forefinger deep into his closed eyes. His mouth was open and Paul could see his tongue. "Make a little tea, dearie," he said, very weary.

What a sloppy man, thought Paul. What an unattractive played-out old lecher. How many dearies over the years had dusted his leaves, carried him his tea? Why did they come, what enticed them—the greenery? When they left on Wednesday evenings, what feelings washed up from Asher's chest into his throat and mouth?"

Patricia Ann brought Paul his cup. "You go to college?"

"Yes," he said.

"I have a stepbrother—*Virgil*," she called over to Asher. Then to Paul, "Virgil Cooper—he used to play basketball for City."

"Yes?"

"Yeah, but that's about ten years ago already. Even more." She carried a cup to Asher. He directed her to put it at his feet and leave him be. "You have a headache, Puss?" she asked him.

"Uh-uh."

"The plants really got all dusty," she told him.

"Okay."

"It's from the windows being open," she said to Paul.

"I gotta breathe," Asher said, more sleepy than rude, and the girl left his side.

A long silence followed.

"Excuse me for being informal." She pointed to her slippers. "It's for comfort around the house." She sat down on a stool beside Asher's easel and lifted a pair of pumps from the floor. "Would you care for me to put these on?"

"No," Paul said. "That's fine."

"Well," she said, sighing.

Asher mumbled. Then he mumbled again, in sleep. The day grew darker and darker, and across the room the man's outline became less distinct.

"It's cold out," Patricia Ann said. "You can feel it right through the window. Is it still cold out?"

"Very," Paul said.

"What college?" she asked.

"Cornell."

"Oh. In California."

"No. New York," Paul said.

"Really?"

"New York *State*."

"*Oh.*" She broke out laughing again, high, anxious, joyless.

Paul couldn't believe it. He was nervous for himself and ashamed for his uncle and overcome with pathos for the girl. She crossed and uncrossed her legs, she examined and re-examined her nails, and finally she shrugged, as though resigning herself to some tragedy having to do with her cuticles. The El train made five trips down below the window, and in that time nobody spoke. Paul's curiosity finally went dead under his disbelief. What—*what* had Asher wanted him to see? Was he missing something? Was this happiness, saintliness, the serenity of which men dream? Was he witnessing a rejection of the baser things, the ambitions, the quests, the greeds? Look, was this or was this not human waste?

It was. And, curiously, the sight of his uncle's condition brought palpitations to Paul's heart. The messiness surrounding him, the indignity of it all, suddenly shook his own faith in himself. He experienced dread at the thought of his own life going wrong. He actually allowed himself to wonder if there might not be a less stern path he might take . . . for just a little while longer. Could he not chase butterflies again in Prospect Park, catch them fluttering in his cheesecloth and coat hanger? Couldn't he wait outside the showers at Ebbets Field for a glimpse of Pee Wee Reese? Couldn't he rise and fall, just for a while again, over those sun-tanned ladies in South Fallsburg, New York? Diligent Paul, hopeful Paul, penniless Paul—couldn't he sit alone in his room composing one thousand heartfelt words for the scholarship committee, promising that he would be a good boy, that he would study if awarded the eight hundred dollars? No! Absolutely not! He was fed up with being a boy. That's why Asher looked so pathetic; fifty and bald and still wearing his Eton suit. Asher could not confront the world a full-sized man; he could never take a wife, accept the burden. He mistook the gifts for the penalties, the penalties for the gifts, and backed away from life—so life backed away from him. And now look: a receptacle all right, a garbage can, full of dirty talk and volcanic regrets. Paul could not believe in Asher not having regrets; to do so upset his picture of the world.

A light went on. Patricia Ann looked at her watch and then at her Asher, and gave out a soft moan. She tried to turn a smile on the nephew but only revealed impatience and loss. Her Wednesday afternoon was going, going—

"Do you have the time?" she asked.

His kindness went out to her. "I think I'll leave," Paul said. Almost instantly she was at the door.

"It was nice meeting you," Paul said. "Don't wake him."

"I never met a person from Asher's family before," she whispered, and then gave the crumpled-up, sleeping figure across the room a loving glance. "It's very nice," she said, and took Paul's hand to shake it. "Asher's a terrific painter. He's the most wonderful person I ever met. He's not like anybody."

"I know," Paul said. "I'm very fond of Asher."

"Me too," she said. "Are you interested in art very much?"

"Yes."

"He's doing me. You know? For—our anniversary. Do you really appreciate art?"

"Well, yes."

"If you appreciate art, you wouldn't be embarrassed . . ."

"I don't understand."

"Would you like to see it? Me. Our fifth anniversary."

"If you think I should—"

On her toes she walked slowly to the corner behind the stool. "Here," she said, motioning for him to follow. She flipped through several canvases piled against the wall and then reached in to take one out. First she only looked at it herself; then, somewhat uncertainly, she put it on the easel and twisted a bulb on above them.

"It's not done," she said immediately. Then she laughed. Then she shrugged. Then she was dead serious. "Like it?"

The idea was not original with Asher. The figure in the painting was reclining unclothed on a sofa, one arm back of her hair, the other down beside her. But, unlike other women who had been posed in the position, Patricia Ann was not a particularly languorous specimen. She looked as though she'd just heard a knock at the door and was about to fly up after her clothes. The hand at her side was rolled into a fist, and her knees were together, discouraging entrance. The Woman Who Gets and Gives No Pleasure.

"Is it finished?" These were the only words that seemed available to him.

"I think he has to do more coloring," she said. But he had her shade already; Asher knew exactly the depth and tone of his mistress. "It's nice, isn't it?" the girl asked the college boy, and then did not wait for an answer. "My girl friends and me once made a record—singing?—and when we heard it, we were hysterical. I mean laughing. But after a while, you know, we started to think it was kind of good and we were even going to send it to some disc jockey, with a photograph of us. But at first it seemed just real funny."

"I know," Paul said, hearing his uncle behind him release a desperate, froggy snore. "I've heard myself on a tape recorder. It's a surprise."

"It's a surprise, all right . . . And," she added gravely, "my husband Charlie, you know, don't know anything about this. I had a whole picture painted, and Charlie don't know. I even have a daughter, a little darling child."

They both looked at the painting. At the door she smiled at him. "Good luck at Cordell."

"Thank you."

Pushing the door shut, she said, "Have a nice time at college."

The stairs were unlit and he did not descend for a moment. He groped for a handrail, but there wasn't any. Behind the door Paul heard, "Asher, Asher, oh wake up, pussy cat, it's after five already."

———

Uncle Jerry sent a note. If Paul felt inclined to, he could call Jerry at his office. If he chose to ignore the note, that was his prerogative as well.

"How are you holding up?" Jerry inquired when Paul telephoned.

"I think I'm all right. I've lost two pounds but I've got all my faculties."

"How are things at home?"

"Just as you can imagine," Paul said. "My mother keeps breaking down and my father keeps wanting to talk to me, but he gets all filled up too. I've explained several times, Jerry, but I've stopped. I'm not going to make a dent. They just say, Please don't marry that girl. At least not now. At least put it off. And so forth, on and on and on. Honest to God, they're going to make me hate them!"

He had not realized how menacing he had sounded until he heard Jerry protecting himself. "Paul, I feel obliged, you know —your father called me, he was in tears. I told him I would contact you. That's why I dropped you the note. I don't know what to say to you. I don't want to advise you. I don't believe in interfering."

The intervention of Paul's family in Jerry's affairs lent a particular weightiness, a certain melancholy strain, to this remark. Paul felt a strong kinship with his uncle then—but it did not make him especially happy. It had not been his plan or his hope to line up, finally, against his family. He had decided to tell them about Libby in December so that their protests might wither with the months and they would come around to the idea of a wedding just after graduation. He had a sense of propriety about his parents, a realization of their responsibilities that perhaps they themselves had not. He had never given in, he thought, to any impulse to be cruel to them, and even if he had worked hard independently of them, it had been in part so as not to increase in any way their disappointments. He felt it now a filial duty to give them every chance; it humbled him not to, in the great world beyond the family to which he aspired, a world of order and decency, which, if he had not as yet experienced, he had fully imagined. Nevertheless, it began to appear that perhaps he had called Jerry for reasons no more elevated than those which had sent him on his walk with Asher: to be reassured.

"I told your father I would contact you," Jerry said. "But of course I can't say anything. I don't even know the girl. Paul, *we* hardly know each other. I didn't complicate matters explaining any of this to Leonard. It wouldn't have interested him. I understand," he said to Paul, softly, intimately. "Paul, you tell me, all right. What do *you* think?"

The young man's voice was sharp when he answered. "What do I think? I think I'll marry Libby! I don't think any of this hysteria has anything to do with us. They hardly know her. In fact, they *don't* know her." Then his own chagrin swallowed him up; he had no reason whatsoever to be short-tempered with this particular uncle.

"Your father says they met her?" Jerry inquired, still delicate.

"I brought her here Thanksgiving. I wanted to please them." Those words, like the rest of his familial generosity, suddenly turned a little sour on him. If his family wouldn't please him, why must he be trying so hard to please them? "They knew I was going with a girl—I let them see her. She came for half an hour last week too, before I told them our plans."

"Your father said something about her being a sickly girl. I'm only repeating him, believe me."

"Jerry, she gets *colds*," he answered wearily. "Jerry, let's even say she's a frail girl. But she's not going to be a farmer. She's going to be my wife. This is all very silly. Jerry, you know what they object to?"

"She's Catholic."

"She's Catholic." He himself knew that to be, however, only a strand in the whole tapestry of rejection. It was not just one crime they wanted to hang the girl on—there was her faith, plus her health, her youth, their son's youth, and a dozen things more. If they had known the word they would have claimed that their sense of Paul's error was intuitive; it was the word with which he had begun to argue with himself in *favor* of his decision. "Jerry, she's a Catholic like I'm a Jew. It's not the kind of thing that'll have much to do with our lives. It hasn't to do with us. It's another ruse."

"Paul, I'm put in a position where I'm asking questions I don't even want to ask. How could I hope to reason with you, anyway, one way or the other? Even if I had the foolish impulse to. We're not dealing with the mind, with the practical senses anyway. This is the mysterious, spontaneous choice—the choice of the heart. The unencumbered heart," Jerry said.

"Yes," Paul answered, unhinged slightly by his uncle's reverent tones.

"The heart, Paul, *knows*. It cost me half a lifetime to learn such a simple fact. I had such neuroses pressing in upon me, they were the size of mountains. Tremendous pathetic pressures building and building, cutting me off from what you think of as your inside self. Paul, I didn't do a spontaneous thing in twenty-seven years. Because the heart was under this terrific pressure. But what the heart decides, Paul, *must be*. I'm telling you, it won't give you peace if it's defied Love!" Jerry cried.

And Paul cried back, "Jerry, I love her."

And his uncle replied sweetly, "That's all then. That's all that counts."

Then, for having provoked such wholesale approval, Paul felt wave upon wave of indecency wash over him. True as they may have been, his words had been spoken out of nothing less than design. And why had he to convince Jerry? So Jerry could turn around and convince him? It was an unavoidable fact that, ever since his afternoon on Third Avenue, certainty had somehow been seeping away. He could not believe that Asher and his bird-brained mistress had demonstrated anything other than what everybody knew about squandered lives, yet he had begun to think of himself as being not so courageous as fearful. Fear began to seem the springboard of much that he had done in his short life. He was a scholarship holder all right, a planner, a young man investing emotions one day to accumulate love and admiration the next. He had come to see his marrying Libby in two distinct ways, both of which, unfortunately, cast doubt on his manliness and dignity.

On the one hand, it all seemed so safe. Husband, wage-earner, father—right on down the line, all the duties and offices laid out for him. From home to college to a wife, no chances taken. Without much effort, he could recall from his past more than a few risks he had worked a little hard at avoiding. Even recently with his parents: he knocked against the walls of their house in December, hoping that somehow by May they would find a way to prevent the roof from falling in. He wanted to remain the good son. Even to himself he seemed to be working strenuously at being upright.

Otherwise he would tell them to go to hell. Run off, marry the girl and leave them to drip tears till their eyes fell out. It was what Asher would have done, he thought. And because he saw it as being a choice that Asher might have made, it too caused him discomfort. If marrying Libby was taking no risks, it was also taking every risk. Asher's life had unnerved him deeply; with a little twisting and turning he could think of it as his own. Way down, he had begun to bend an ear toward his parents' objections. He was no longer so sure that he was seeing Libby as clearly as his uncle saw Patricia Ann, at least as he saw her in paint, if not in life. He did not know that he *wanted* to see that clearly. He only knew that he did not want merely to stick it right up in Libby; he wanted to love her.

Feeling something less than a daredevil, he listened to Uncle Jerry on the other end comforting him. "Paul, good luck then. I think that's the only proper thing for any of us to say."

"Thank you."

"Tell Libby good luck too." Jerry pronounced her name easily, and Paul knew they would like each other right off. "When will you be married?"

"Not till May. Around graduation."

"Will I get to see you before you go back? I'd like to take you to dinner. I'll invite Claire and her husband. She'd love to see you."

"That's very kind, Jerry. I'll call Libby. I think tomorrow night, if you could, would be best for us. We were going to meet with news from both fronts."

"How is she bearing up?"

"Fine," Paul said, lying, as if he had to spare that two-time loser from any further knowledge of the hardships of loving.

—

"I know I've got character in my face, but won't someone say I'm pretty?" Well, on the steps of the Plaza, with all that swank hurrying by, she had her wish. Character had been bled from her for the evening, and in its place was prettiness. She had made up her eyes heavily, and managed even to reduce the proud leap of her nose—its sailing proportions were lost beneath the great mast of her black hair, which was piled atop her head, revealing a slender boyish back of the head. The doorman bowed and opened the door for both the lady and her escort, who even in dark suit and tie made a slightly seedy appearance—seedy perhaps only by comparison to the glitter and chic of the slender girl beside him.

At the sight of Libby, Paul had been visited with a definite burst of pleasure. Gradually, however, he became irritated because she had decked herself out. *Why?* Actually she was wearing only a simple black suit with a tight jacket and a full skirt, but its fetchingness—acknowledged by its owner in her very gait—was in the way it made so apparent the delicacy of her shoulders and neck. Despite her dripping nose and the weather, she had worn no blouse, so that one was of course touched by the wistful fragility revealed in the wide neck of the jacket. The wad of Kleenex in her white glove (there to inform his parents of sanitoriums and hospital bills) only made more glamorous her tiny garnet earrings and bracelet. They proceeded through the lobby to the entrance of the Oak Room, and when Paul looked at her again, he looked deeply, intently, for some sign of the college girl he had planned to marry: the straight shoulder-length black hair, the pale lips, the over-used eyes, the winterized, libraryized, studentized Libby. What he found instead was something that bothered him, something he could only think of as aspiration.

Yet as they spotted Uncle Jerry, and moved into the dining room, Paul put his mouth to her hair. He explained her little display of prosperity and polish to himself as an attempt to impress *some* Herz. That his mother and father dreaded her so for their son, led her, he knew, to begin to wonder what kind of ogre she might actually be. He knew this, and he knew how much protection his intended needed. He said into her ear, "My wife," feeling a little ripple of well-being as the word passed from his lips.

"Husband," Libby whispered, and that thrilled him too. Oh Libby had come a long long way from being a sorority sister to being a woman. He, Paul, had lifted her up from childhood with him. Now—the thought had a peculiar forcefulness as Libby swished up to Uncle Jerry—now she was all his!

—

Uncle Jerry's daughter Claire was Paul's age. It had always been expected in the family that because they had been born within a month of each other they should like each other. But even during the flirtation they had carried on in the closing months of their seventeenth year, there had been little affection between them. Following an evening when they had taken off their clothes and stood glaring, breathlessly, at one another, Paul had gone on to college and high literature, and Claire to a promiscuity at Syracuse, stories of which had reached Paul's ears every Monday morning, sixty miles away at Cornell. But with dinner at the Plaza—snow fell on the carriages out the window, beyond Libby's hair—all was changed. Claire seemed to be taking a special delight in showing Paul how matronly she had become, and how human. With her whole being she listened to the remarks of her husband, an average crew-cut sort of I.B.M. machine, who had taken away from Syracuse an M.A. in Business Administration, and hot Claire Herz. The firm he was with was splitting stock or changing hands, or something that Paul was not following; whatever, Claire responded as though he was singing exquisite tenor. Once Paul thought he saw her eyes shut when her husband spoke about a large loan a Mr. Richmond was floating. She might have been visualizing it aloft. Finally she discovered Libby and her clothes; and Libby, it seemed, discovered herself.

"I never usually go to Carita," Libby said, measuring Claire's response, "because you have to wait so long."

"They do do a wonderful job," Claire said. "It's so lovely."

"It's only the second time I've been there."

Claire lifted a finger as though to touch Libby's crown, and Paul realized that they were *not* talking about Libby's clothes; Carita was where she had had her hair set. He had imagined that she had fixed it herself before the bathroom mirror in Queens. His astonishment led him into a grave contemplation of the future. All his thinking of the last few days had been grave in tone, and large in scope. He was no longer thinking ahead strictly in terms of semesters and summers.

In the meantime the young women had proceeded into a discussion of Delman's shoes. Finally, Libby excused herself and went off to the powder room—doubtless, thought Paul, to work her eyes up a little more.

Claire put her hand on her cousin's. "She's wonderful, Paul. I think she's the most wonderful thing that could have happened to you. She's so charming, and so alive, and so pretty. Her skin, her hair . . ."

"We wish you all the luck," Claire's husband said, and he snapped his head at Paul, meaning it. "I think we have to go home, hon," he said to his stout, good-looking young wife.

"Baby-sitters," Claire said. She spoke wearily, but it was an affect; she was obviously charmed by her own maternal obligations. She rose, a matron at twenty-one. She went around to her father, who pushed back his chair and rose too. At fifty-five Uncle Jerry might have been her beau; he stood straight and was dressed like his son-in-law in a narrow suit and a narrow tie. All that marred his crisp good looks was a distressing willingness in the eyes.

When Claire and her husband had left, he said, "Harold is a fine boy. A very solid boy."

"He seems very nice." Paul tried to concentrate on his uncle instead of himself; he was divided in his feelings about Libby's return to the table. When she had gotten up to leave he had actually felt relief, so uncertain was he about what she might say next. And he seemed to have *become* uncertain on the basis of her not setting her hair at home! He waited for her to return with a conscious ambivalence.

"He's especially fine for Claire," Jerry said. "He holds her in check. You may not have known it, but she had an exuberant streak in her in college."

"Yes?"

"Paul, she was a very promiscuous girl at Syracuse. She could have made a mess of herself. When I left Selma," Jerry said, "she lost a father image, there's no doubt about that. But had I stayed longer, she would have lost it anyway. Worse things might have happened." Paul wondered, until Jerry told him. "None of us," his uncle said, "are without incestuous feelings. And it isn't the feelings, you see—it's how you act them out."

Jerry seemed to feel that he had explained something; Paul only felt the desperate sordid decency of admitting to such motives. "This young man," Jerry was saying, "he's no whiz, no spectacular ball of fire. But he's steady and he's a *mensch*, and he's done wonders for Claire. You ought to see her with that baby. She relates so beautifully it could make you cry."

"I'll bet she's fine."

"She's become an outstanding mother."

"Yes," Paul said, "I'm glad we all had a chance to be together."

"I'm glad we all had a chance to meet Libby. I think you've got a fine girl."

"Thank you."

"Thank yourself. It's not often young people know what they want. It's not often you find a young person who's discovered the essentials. They run around and play around—like Claire—trying each other out. It's not a healthy thing, what's happening with this generation. They 'get laid,' they 'screw,'" he said, "and those expressions express just about what they do. A lot of grabbing and pawing, Paul, but very little touching. But I see your Libby and I see Claire now, and they look like two girls who know what that means, to touch." Uncle Jerry's eyes were wet suddenly. In the cultivated atmosphere of the dining room, with a steak sizzling at the next table and the candlelight shimmering on the long curtains, and outside the white flakes falling on the park, Jerry was not able to prevent the tears from sliding down his face. After he dried them, Paul expected he might see a pale spot where his uncle's coloring had been rubbed off by the napkin. Uncle Jerry, forever struggling up for air in the dark sea of maladjustment and poor mental health, had shed two tears for Love. *Love* was the name painted on the ship that would come along and pull him safely to shore. It had rescued his daughter, and now he was telling Paul it had rescued him, and one sunny day perhaps it would come along and rescue Jerry too. He would find a woman who was not a mother-figure, like the oversized Selma, nor a daughter-figure, like the short-lived twenty-seven-year-old; just a woman who could touch him.

Paul realized that since dinner had begun he had been looking at his uncle through Asher's eyes. Now he tried looking at himself through Asher's eyes. Just then Libby came back to the table, and so she was seen through Asher's eyes too. When Paul tried to look at her through Jerry's eyes, it occurred to him that that may have been how he had been looking all along. It was no longer clear in his mind whether he could consider himself a realist or a romantic.

"Are you all right?" Paul whispered, as he pulled her chair out for her.

"I just put some nose drops in to get some air," she said, but he smelled a perfume on her that he had never smelled before. "I was talking to Claire and Jack in the lobby," she said to Jerry.

"All this time?" asked Paul.

"Yes. They're *awfully* nice," she said to Jerry.

"They're all a father could hope for," Jerry answered, and from there he and Libby proceeded, for the rest of the evening, to discuss the theater. Jerry sat there, awed and charmed and won, while Libby's fingers waved above her water glass, and her eyes in turn grew grave and puzzled and gay. In the hour that followed, Paul heard her say *art*, and he heard her say *beauty*, and he heard her say *truth* three times. Twice she said *objective correlative*. But, of course, it did not matter that she echoed him; of course she was still learning. She had come a long way already from the Pi Phi house, on whose steps he had found her a little less than a year ago. In courting her he had changed her, he had *worked* at changing her; but now he wondered if she would ever be the genuine article. Was she bright? Was she true? Would she grow? Trying to improve her had he only made a monkey of her? What a time to be asking himself such questions!

He tried to admire her for winning so completely the affection of his uncle, but he was not able to.

—

On the subway back to Queens he asked her how much it cost to have one's hair set at the Carita Salon.

"Eight dollars."

"Just to heap it up like that?"

"They wash it and they set it—and then there's the tip. They have to tease my hair, it's so straight."

"Is the teasing figured into the bill, or is that free?"

"Did I behave badly?" Libby demanded. "Did I talk too much? I realized I was talking a lot. Oh Paul, what's the matter?"

"Nothing."

"You're not happy with me."

"Don't you think eight dollars is a lot to spend on hair?"

". . . Yes."

"Do you really, or is that to please me?"

"Both."

"And don't charm me, will you? I'm not Jerry."

"Paul, what's the matter? I *did* talk too much."

"No."

"Then what? Because I went to Carita? Because I talked about it with Claire? Please tell me." She was a self-improver, and that strain in her character (which once he had loved and now suddenly it seemed he loathed) showed through her request. "Please, Paul, tell me," she said.

"I didn't know you had such extravagant tastes. My haircuts cost me a buck."

"It was a special occasion." She began to cry. "I'm sorry I did it. I am . . ."

"I can't afford stuff like that, Libby. We're going to have to live a frugal life. A sensible life. I'm beginning to wonder if we're in agreement. I begin to wonder if you understand—"

"Oh honey," she said, and put her head into his shoulder. "I'm stupid." And she reached up for her mound of hair and pulled it down.

His heart lurched, but he kept his mouth shut; some pins clattered to the floor of the subway car, and she became the old Libby, hair to her shoulders.

"I'm sorry, Paul. Oh truly—I was putting on a performance to *please* everybody," she moaned. "I feel like a windmill. I feel running and pursued and just like I'm bouncing all over the place. I'm just exhausted, and this cold won't go away, and all I tasted all night were *nose* drops. Everybody said the wine was excellent and so I said so too." She had buried her head in his chest and he was stroking her hair. He did it to comfort her; he got no pleasure from the spongy resilient quality of that black hair whose crowy smoothness had always expressed something to him about the simple desires, the solid yearnings of the girl he had discovered, and who had so quickly and so passionately become dedicated to him.

After a while she took his hand and held it in her lap. "Paul?"

"Yes."

"—I don't think I can wait until May, or June. If I'm going to marry you I think it better be now. We'll move into your room and we'll be married and all this will be over. I can't *stand* it any more. Oh sweetheart, I'm sorry about my hair." She kissed his five fingers to prove it. "I knew you were upset about it. I knew it was that."

A Puerto Rican at the end of the car was reading a newspaper. He had looked up to watch the girl cry; now that she had pulled herself together he looked back into the paper again.

"Your uncle," she was saying, "is so nice and everybody else is so awful, and he's so unhappy."

"And so are you."

"And so am I, and so are you, and we're perfectly nice people *too*. He hasn't got anybody—"

"He's got Claire."

"Oh she's a phoney!" Libby cried, softly. "And so am I," she said. "I saw it in your eyes. Oh, you phoney, you were saying, why don't you cut it out. And I couldn't, Paul. I tried but I couldn't. I hate your Uncle Asher!" she announced. "I hate him! He's a disgusting man!"

"All right, Lib, calm down. Nobody's paying any attention to him at all."

She might have been hesitating, or she might have been calculating, but finally she whispered into his scarf, "You are."

"I am what?" he demanded.

"I can't talk without you getting some sour little look on your face. You're not you."

"You're imagining it." He sat up very straight, so that it became necessary for her to pull her face away. "You're just upset."

She was willing to be convinced. "Am I?"

"I think so."

"Because he doesn't even *know* me! Paul, Paul—what's wrong with me? What does everybody have against *me!*"

"I shouldn't have told you about him. Everything is all right."

"Paul, let's get married and go back to school tomorrow . . . Let's go back married. *Please.*"

His immediate vision was of the two of them trying to live in his tiny room. Libby's father would cut off next semester's tuition; his own family would refuse to be present at graduation . . . But more pleasant visions followed. For it would only continue to be as it had been before: they would study together in the library and sleep together in his room. Only now Libby could move in the rest of her clothes and stay clear through till morning. They wouldn't have to meet for breakfast; they would already be there, together. As for the families, they had obligations that they would finally admit to. And next year he would get some sort of graduate fellowship for himself; he had already sent off applications to Columbia, Penn, Michigan, and Chicago, well in advance of the closing date. Probably Libby's father would continue to pay *her* tuition through her senior year—

Or would he?

It was not the first time the question had occurred to him. To whom would the registrar address Mrs. Herz's bills? But even if it was to himself, they had already figured out on a blank page at the back of Libby's American Literature notebook that, what with summer jobs, fellowships, and part-time work, they would have enough to pay their bills, and maybe even some left over to buy an old car. They had worked out a budget in the library one idyllic night before the vacation, when the gorges and the trees were heavy with snow, and the moon was nearly full. Now on the empty subway, the overhead bulbs went black a moment, and he wondered if their estimates could have been right. They had figured up food, rent, tuition, laundry, amusements . . . He could think of no item they had overlooked; there was actually no *reason* he could think of not to marry tomorrow instead of in May. But it was with a distinct sensation of being torn apart that he agreed.

"Oh Paul . . ." She wept now in a different key.

"We'll get a license tomorrow and the blood business, and then we'll get married at City Hall. Only a few days." He kissed her hand. "Cheer up," he instructed them both.

But she didn't cheer up. By the time they left the subway there was a scattering of Kleenex around her shoes; she gave an especially heartening sob as they emerged into the raw, slushy night. He steered her across the street into a coffee shop, and not until she had drunk half a cup did he attempt conversation; he waited until her chest and throat noises had subsided, and only an occasional tear made an appearance beneath her murky eyes.

"What is it?" he asked. "What now?"

"Paul . . . I don't think—this may sound silly . . . I don't think I could *survive* City Hall." She even amused *herself* by the sheer torpor of the remark. But her smile, curling around two fresh tears, lifted him little.

"It takes five minutes," he said, closing his eyes.

"But I'm no orphan! I'm no culprit!" she said vehemently. "People get married at City Hall when they want to *hide* something. When they're running somewhere. When girls are pregnant they get married at City Hall. I'm not pregnant —I was spared that particular tragedy—why must I act like I wasn't! I'm not pregnant, damn it!" She dragged some grains of mascara across her nose with her Kleenex. Moral outrage was now sweeping hysteria away: she expelled a powerful breath, having thought probably of five more things she wasn't and wouldn't be compromised into being. "I'm not letting people —*parents*—force me to—to act as though I'm ashamed. To take away my dignity," she said, his student—his own words. "I'm not, Paul. You know we shouldn't *allow* them . . ."

He heard the conviction rush out of her like wind; she had looked up to see that he was holding his forehead in his hands.

"Paul? What do you think?"

"I don't know." He did not show her his eyes. "What do *you* think?"

"I don't know . . ."

"That's too bad," he said. "I've run out of suggestions."

"How about," Libby said, after a moment, "what do you think—of a rabbi?"

"Why?"

"Oh Paul, wouldn't he be more official, more everything we want? Wouldn't it show them something if we decided to be married by a rabbi? I'm not being defiant, I just won't cower in some corner when I get married! What kind of thing is that? You get married once. I think it should have some *weight* to it."

When he looked up it was because he had regained his control. "It should have weight. *We* give it the weight. You're not Jewish, Libby."

"But you are!"

He said nothing.

She blew her nose. "But . . . but we *are* basically religious people. Our values—oh stop giving me that sour look!"

"Well stop *talking* like that. I'm not Jerry."

"Why do you think I'm so stupid!"

"Libby, I don't. Don't cry, please. Lib, I'm sorry. It's just"— he tried it slowly—"we're not, honey, basically *Jewish* people."

"Paul, they're not going to make me into a nothing. I refuse to let them force me to be married in City Hall! I'll go to a priest then. Anything!"

"I couldn't go to a priest. I couldn't be married by a priest, that's all there is to it."

"Because you *are* Jewish finally! Sweetie, just be a *little* Jewish, will you? Just till we're married? After that—oh I don't want to sound so silly. I only want this one thing—"

And then never my own way again.

He heard these last words like an echo. At nineteen she had already given him whatever she had; now she would promise him the rest forever. All she wanted satisfied was her sense of decency, which was what he had cared for and nurtured in her. She had a knowledge, this frail girl, of what her rights were in love, and for that too he was thankful and proud. They need not crawl along the ground because others wanted them to.

—

But they were married in Yonkers by a Justice of the Peace they found in the Yellow Pages. No rabbi would handle their case, which came as a surprise to both of them. Their astonishment did not, however, keep them above having dirty feelings about themselves for very long. In the study of the third rabbi they visited, Paul rose up out of his seat and cursed him.

"Isn't there a hot rabbi who performs marriages on kitchen tables? In all of this city is there no man low enough to unite two people who want to be united?"

"Try City Hall," the rabbi said, a heavy dark-jowled man who hadn't liked him from the start. "Get united civilly."

"We can try City Hall without your advice!"

"Paul," Libby pleaded, stretching out a hand to him. But he didn't even want to see her face. Was he to compromise himself forever, honoring this girl's weaknesses? Attending to her wishes, did he not dissolve into a spineless ass! A hypocrite! A softie!

"I marry Jew and Jew," scowled Lichtman, the rabbi. "That's all."

"We're Jew and Gentile."

"The ceremony doesn't fit such occasions."

"God damn you!" Paul shouted.

"Don't raise your voice in this office! This isn't the street! Next, you don't know anything! A twenty-year-old snotnose! You should be as wise as you are loud, then come around here! If you believe, believe; if no, turn your back! Otherwise look other places! Go be religious your own way! Don't run here to make it all right with Mama! I'm no moral out for you. I'm not here to be amiable. That's a disgusting thought!"

"I'm not asking for my mama, Lichtman, I'm asking for my wife."

"Some improvement! You should be ashamed! Are you Catholic?" he demanded of Libby, a kind of agony suddenly in his face.

"Yes."

"So why not ask a priest? Why not ask *him* to unite you and this Jew? They have City Hall for mixtures like this."

"You don't have to be so nasty to her!"

"Shut up! You're a secular, *be* secular! Don't come tramping your muddy feet in my synagogue for sentimental reasons! I wouldn't marry you if you were *two* Jews! Now get out! You're stupid and you curse and you're a coward! Get out!"

The Justice of the Peace displayed no such force; for one thing, he had the gout. It was necessary for him to remain seated while he married them, though he compensated for his posture with a clear, loud, nondenominational voice. It was a Sunday afternoon and when Paul and Libby entered, they found the JP pulled up close to an old cabinet-model radio, a large scrolly piece with WEAF WJZ WOR WABC marked on the yellowed station selector. The JP's wife turned off the radio during the ceremony. She was an elderly lady who wore glasses and a print dress that was a little longer in back than in front; below were nurse's white oxfords. She touched the bride ten times at least, then removed some artificial flowers from the closet and put them in a blue vase behind her husband, whose bandage was in need of a change. She called him "the Judge," and she called his gout "the Judge's difficulty." "I hope you won't mind the Judge's difficulty," she whispered, and then raised his bandaged foot up onto a cushioned chair. It stared at them throughout the proceedings.

When it was all over the Judge's wife put the flowers back in the closet and turned on the radio. The couple from next door, who had been called in to serve as witnesses, hugged the newlyweds; the woman hugged Paul, the man Libby. The Judge's wife looked from Libby's ring to Paul's ring and said all there actually was to say about them; she managed more excitement than one really even had the right to expect from the wife of an old sick Yonkers JP. "They match," she said. The Judge said, "Elizabeth, Paul, will you step up here, please?" After a quick glance at each other, they approached and stood on either side of his difficulty, expecting his blessing. He said, "Now you know how to get back into the city, don't you?"

"Yes," they said.

"That'll be ten," said the Judge.

He preferred not to take a check on Paul's Ithaca bank. "We're dealing with strangers all the time," the Judge's wife reminded the young couple. Libby had to give them the cash.

Two buses and a subway carried them back to New York in an hour and a half; Libby got out before Paul in order to change trains for Queens—husband and wife would meet at Grand Central with their suitcases at six that night. When they parted, so preoccupied were they, that they forgot to embrace. Paul traveled the rest of the way alone, back to Brooklyn to tell his family what he had done.

He got off the subway at Atlantic Avenue, where he was struck with how familiar he was with every trash can, every last signpost and pillar. On the way up the street to his family's apartment he slipped the ring off his finger and into his coat pocket. He would begin his accounting slowly, give them a chance to . . . But then he saw the insults and the pain, and he put the ring that matched his wife's back on his finger and entered with his news.

And his father threw him out of the house. Mr. Herz had not summoned up so much courage since he had invested his life's savings in frozen foods and gone under for the fourth time. But he wouldn't go under again! In one life, how many times can a man fail?

On the train back to Ithaca, Paul wept.

"We don't need them," Libby said, cradling his head in the dark car. "We don't need anybody."

"That isn't it," her husband replied. "That isn't it . . ." And it was and it wasn't.

2

"How?"

"Paul, I don't know how. Maybe it's not even so."

"Well, it is so, isn't it? If it's not, what are we getting upset about?"

"Well—I think it is so, then."

"You haven't gone to a doctor, have you? By yourself?"

"Paul, I'm just always very regular—you could set your watch by me."

"Maybe you're upset. Maybe it's working at that place, all the running around you have to do. Maybe you should take a day off."

"I practically just started."

"That's all right. That's why you're upset."

"I've been upset before. I get a tight colon or a runny nose —but never this."

"But *how?*"

"I don't *know* how."

"You don't use that thing right."

"I do use it right."

"On the little booklet that comes with the grease it shows how you should lie down when you put it in. I've told you a hundred times, lie down the way it shows in the booklet. No— you've got to stand up. You've got to do it like you're putting on your shoes!"

"Either way—"

"Why can't you do it the way it says to do it? Why do we have to take chances?"

"Paul, that's not a chance. A doctor showed me how, standing up. It's perfectly all right."

"If it's so all right why are you ten days late?"

"That hasn't anything to do with it."

"What does?"

"I don't know what does. Please, let's not fight about it."

"What are we going to do if you're pregnant, Libby? What are we going to do with a baby now?"

"I'll menstruate. I've had pains—I had some this morning."

"I thought you didn't get pains."

"Maybe I will this time. Maybe that's why I'm irregular."

"Why?"

"*I don't know!* Leave me alone. I'll menstruate for you. Just leave me be!"

"Don't menstruate for *me*, Libby. Oh, don't start any crap like that. You came running to me, didn't you? 'Paul, I think I'm pregnant—oh what'll we do!'"

"I was upset. We quit school, we came here to make money, we got jobs, and now suddenly *this*!"

"All right, Libby, all right."

"All right what?"

"Arguing is stupid."

"Honey, I'll go to the bathroom. I'll check."

———

"You know how? That first day, right after your last period—"

"But it's *safe* then."

"No time is safe. I said use the damn thing. Take a minute out and use it."

"It's so unaesthetic—it's such a pain in the neck. It's so unspon*taneous*."

"And she romanticized them into a family of ten."

"Maybe I'm not pregnant. People miss whole months sometimes. If we can't figure out how, then I'm probably just missing a whole month. Maybe it's from working at a new job—"

"We can figure out how. I can figure out how."

"It's safe then! Four days at the beginning, four at the end. We *always* did that."

"We were lucky."

"It's biologically impossible—"

"They swim, Libby. They hide in nooks and crannies, waiting."

"I just know I'm not. I can't be. We *are* careful."

"Libby, you're careful when you use that thing the way it's supposed to be used, when you don't skimp on the goddam jelly."

"The jelly's expensive. The jelly costs two dollars a tube!"

"So what! Did I ever say anything? Did I ever say *don't* buy more jelly? Buy it! Use it! *Squander* it! That's what it's for!"

"But the diaphragm does all the work."

"Oh Libby."

"Well, I can't stand it! *I* have to put it in *me*! Right in the midst of everything and I have to stop and fill that plunger! I hate it!"

"And what do you prefer—this?"

"They don't have anything to do with one another. I mean I do use the goo and I do use the thing and we *are* careful."

"Go in the bathroom. Go take a look. Let's not argue."

"I just looked."

"Anything?"

"Not really."

"What's not really mean?"

"Well—nothing. But I'm sure tomorrow. I have a pimple on my forehead and one starting under my chin. I break out—"

"Do you?"

"Well, I used to."

"Libby, what are we going to do?"

"I'll be all right. I know I will."

"It was that first day, Libby."

"But it's so wonderful when I don't have to worry about anything, when we just do it whenever we want, without all that crap."

"How are we going to afford you pregnant? How are we going to afford a baby?"

"But people miss whole *months*—"

—

"I don't see what *good* it'll do."

"The good is we'll know, one way or another."

"We'll know anyway, if I miss another month. I don't see what's to be gained."

"What's to be gained is we'll know. Am I making myself clear, Lib, or do I have to say it again? We'll know."

"The test costs ten dollars."

"That's all right."

"It's *not* all right. This room costs that much a week. I may menstruate tomorrow and then it would just be ten bucks out the window."

"So let it be out the window."

"But, Paul, suppose I *am* pregnant. For ten dollars you can probably buy diapers—we'll *need* the ten dollars. Can't we wait? Can't we forget it for a while? We come home from work and that's all we talk about. I don't see you all day and that's all we ever talk about."

"We'll have the test and we'll know and then we can talk about other things."

"So we'll know. Then what! When we know it'll be worse!"

"It'll be better."

"It'll be worse, Paul. It'll be much worse."

———

"Paul, that's not so. You misunderstood."

"Don't please be a blockhead. We've got other things to think about."

"Honey, look up at me. Honey, positive means the rabbits responded *positively*. That I'm not pregnant."

"Libby, the guy on the phone said positive."

"And that's what I mean. Positive. Negative would mean I'm pregnant. Doesn't that make sense?"

"Negative means no."

"No I'm pregnant, or no I'm not pregnant?"

"No you're pregnant."

"That's right. No would mean I *was* pregnant. The test is to see whether you're not pregnant. No means you are. Yes you're not. The result is positive, though. Positive is good."

"Libby, you're getting things hopelessly confused."

"You are. Paul, I'm sure. It's negative you *don't* want. I knew I wasn't pregnant, honey. I just knew I couldn't be."

"But you are. You're negative—"

"No, no, Paul, positive. You see, *you're* confused."

"Well, stop *jabbering* a minute! You're positive, right? They take your urine, they shoot it in the rabbit—"

"Rabbits."

"Rabbits! All *right*. Then they wait for some kind of reaction. If the reaction is positive, you're pregnant. If it's negative, you're not. You were positive."

"Paul, they give the shot to the rabbits. If I'm all right, normal, then they react positively. Doesn't that make sense to you? If I want to see if you're all right, and I give you a shot and get a negative reaction, well, that's bad."

"Libby, you can't even add a column of figures. You're being illogical."

"You are. You're not thinking. Positive is good."

"Lib . . . Lib, I'll call the guy again. If you want me to I'll call him and ask."

"I just know it's so."

"I'll call him."

———

His job on the assembly line was to unite the half of the hinge on the trunk with the half of the hinge on the body. He had dreaded it all beforehand; whenever he had had to contemplate the change coming up in his life, he had to breathe deeply to keep control. During the week before he had dropped out of graduate school—while he and Libby were preparing to leave Ann Arbor—he had had claustrophobic dreams about being locked in small rooms, about submarines and strangulation. Beside him, Libby had moaned in deep dreams of her own. But now during the eight endless hours on the line, he was visited with an unexpected solemnity and calm. The submarine quality was there all right, the underwater lifeless feeling, as though none of this was happening in time; nevertheless the actual experience worked on him like a tonic. In place of dread came a sense of righteousness. He had at last raised a hand to the cruel world. Hinging a trunk to a car was not much, but it was something; he was earning a living. It did not even upset him—as he had been sure it would —to have Libby waiting on tables over in the executive dining room of the Chevrolet plant. At first she had been dumbstruck at having had to leave school in the middle of her senior year; but now each night when she came home from work she soaked her feet with a very gallant smile on her face. Truly, she inspired him—which did not necessarily mean that he had developed a sentimental attachment to their circumstances. Out of his hatred for their clammy basement room on West Grand Street, he had developed a hatred for all Detroit.

In the room itself, the lights had to be turned on even during the day. The yellow from the bulbs penetrated their furniture and curtains so as to bring out every inch of ugliness. Only old people moved about in the other rooms of the three-story house, and when they hawked up mucus into the sinks, the sounds carried through the thin walls. Ancient men urinated in the bathroom down the hall, leaving the door

open, leaning on their canes; often they were sick in the night,
and those noises carried too. Surely if Paul had had a rich
uncle and that uncle had died leaving him a fortune, he would
have quit on the spot and moved the two of them back to
Ann Arbor, where he had left two term papers half-written.
But since no such uncle was alive even to expire, since even his
possessionless father had dispossessed him, he accepted his
fate, and seemed to derive from it a feeling of resiliency. If such
lousy circumstances as these couldn't humble him, what could?
For all the beans they prepared on the hot plate, and for all the
movies they decided they couldn't afford to see, he felt his love
for Libby flowering again. They did not argue as often as they
had in Ann Arbor when they had begun to feel the financial
squeeze. Perhaps they were only too exhausted now at night
to sink their teeth in one another—but even the exhaustion
proved something.

But when Paul called him back, the pharmacist assured him
that positive meant only one thing: Libby was positively pregnant. Immediately Paul's trunk-hinging stopped soothing him
because it stopped engaging him. Cars fled past him as he
added and subtracted in his head. The doctor plus the hospital
plus the circumcision plus diapers, powders, formulas . . .

In how many months would she have to stop work?

How much are maternity clothes? Are they necessary?

How much would an apartment cost? Could they possibly
stay on in the room? Instead of two years servitude in Detroit
as planned, would they now be stuck here forever? A baby carriage plus a bassinet—

In the midst of his calculations, a passing auto frame nearly
chopped off his left hand. He was spurting blood from the wrist
when they rushed him to the infirmary. The doctor there, a
curly-haired dark Italian, gave him the name of the abortionist.

———

He was home by noon. He had wanted to stay on for the
afternoon, but the doctor said that considering everything
(they had discussed everything for some fifteen minutes) he
should go home, if only to pull himself together. With the
light off he lay in bed and turned over and over his hands the
small slip of paper upon which the doctor had written a very
few words. Paul studied the name: Dr. Thomas Smith. An

alias? With his picture in the Post Office? He fell asleep finally, having first imagined various unsavory faces over Dr. Smith's blood-stained white jacket.

Levy awakened him. Mr. Levy never smiled but was very friendly; it was only out of Libby's softness for all those with canes and crutches that he had become an acquaintance of theirs. Paul had to admit that being able to say hello to somebody in the corridors did make the place less depressing. However, Levy—sunburned, bald, hawk-nosed—did not strike Paul as someone to particularly feel sorry for; he was too peppy, and furthermore they suspected that he tried to peek at Libby in the toilet.

Now Levy's face was in the doorway. "How come you're home? I thought something was up."

"I cut my hand. They gave me the afternoon off."

"Whew! What a cut!" said Levy, advancing. "You got a bandage like a mummy."

"I'm all right." He sat up, shaking the grogginess out of his head; the doctor had given him some numbing drug. "I'll be fine."

"Want me to make you a little Lipton's tea?"

"No, thanks."

"It don't cost extra to boil water," Levi said, spreading his fingers across the chest of his oversized, monogrammed shirt. "The teabag is a treat from me. You got a pretty wife."

The remark irritated him. Levy was forever dropping his cane outside the bathroom keyhole in the morning, while Libby was brushing her teeth; sometimes it took him up to five minutes to retrieve it. So far they had been willing to believe the old man the victim of stiff knees and an arthritic back; if they did not jump to accuse him, it was because they felt sorely how unused they were to the inconveniences of rooming house living, of which Levy was only one. When Levy complimented him, Paul tried to smile—and the old man went off for the tea.

It seemed for a while that he would not return; when he did, carrying a tray with cups and kettle, he was accompanied by a pal.

"This is Korngold. Lives next door."

Korngold shook his head as though he were not Korngold and lived in India. But his hands shook too; everything shook, poor man. Where he wasn't brownish liver spots he was white as ashes. And his weight was not in keeping with his height; he was underfed, and leaning on his cane (not gold-headed like Levy's) he looked stretched and dried. It was truly pathetic to hear him get out, "Don't rise, please. It's a pleasure, my deep pleasure."

Paul moved off the bed, feeling invaded. There was a type-writer on the little oilcloth-covered table, and a pile of papers; recently he had begun to try writing stories. Levy lifted type-writer and papers and set them on the floor. In their place he set down his afternoon tea.

"Let's pull ourselves up here," he said. "Korngold, take off your coat. No wonder you cough up phlegm left and right."

"I cough up phlegm 'cause that Nazi hands out heat in a teaspoon. My chest kills me night and day."

"Then move. This room is a gem, was empty a whole month. I told you, Move in, Korngold."

"I was thinking. It's a ten-dollar place. I don't have to live fancy. Next door is seven fifty."

"You was thinking, all right. Now these lovely people moved in and you still live by that son of a bitch." Levy turned and almost bowed to Paul. "Sugar?"

Still groggy, with the feeling that he had mislaid something —that *he* was, in fact, the thing mislaid—Paul said yes, please.

"I take plain," Korngold said.

Levy said, "I know how you take."

"Lemon sticks in my heart," explained Korngold.

They each pulled a chair up to the table. It was too late to remove a slip of Libby's that was draped on the back of Levy's chair; Levy sank heavily down onto the white silky cloth. Korngold in the meantime was lifting his cup to his mouth. Three sips, and his shirt front and chin were soaked.

Levy said, "Mr. Herz, Korngold would like a word with you."

"It's a long story," Korngold said slowly. "It involves a lot of son of a bitches, a lot of crooks and bastards. Let me finish my tea."

"He had a wife," said Levy, "was nobody's business."

"Only half of it," Korngold murmured. "A son, tell him about my son."

"And a son to boot." Levy caught a glimpse of the slip over his shoulder.

"And," said Korngold, swallowing hard, "a daughter-in-law. A bastard like that you shouldn't leave out."

"Three such people picking at one man's insides," Levy said. "The son is on the inside with the Nike missile, coining it, we understand. Lives like a pagan, everything fancy. Korngold freezes by that Heinie son of a bitch, counting pennies, and the son has houses, we understand, all over Florida. Plus a daughter in Smith College."

"Europe he's been to *twice*."

"Europe twice," Levi repeated. "I'm coming to Europe under waste." He opened and closed his palms. "Korngold's life has been ruined by the serpent's tongue. Disappreciation from all sides. Seventy years in January."

"Aaach," said Korngold, "and its worse than that. Even going to the toilet is a terrible production."

"Korngold's plan is a letter."

"Two letters," said Korngold softly, "is the plan . . ."

"A letter first to the son," said Levy, very businesslike. "What kind of son are you and so forth."

"Maybe a photograph," Korngold said, his empty cup in his gaunt hand rattling in the saucer. "Let him see my condition," he said, a little proudly.

Levy considered the suggestion for hardly a moment. "That depends," he said. "But a sharp note, you know?"

"Then the other letter . . ." Korngold reminded him, touching Levy's sleeve.

"Then a letter to the Senate. What kind of man is this who we put secrets in his hands, should guide and steer our country, and has no respect for his father."

"Let them do an investigation," said Korngold, "he thinks he's such a foolproof big shot."

"Give him the works where it hurts," Levy said, and rose halfway out of the chair, his hands on Libby's slip. "But the second letter we don't send right off now. Give him a chance to make an offer."

"He don't deserve it."

"Korngold, turn the other cheek to the son of a bitch. I'm telling you what's practical. I'm talking about keeping a hot iron for striking over his head!" He sat back down and leaned toward Paul. "Korngold is a sick man in need of help. Has got one suit this fellow, and for a dry cleaning sits around for a week in his bathrobe, which also ain't particularly brand new. What kind of son is that when Russia has a smash head-on program in science?" He did not even wait to be understood; self-righteously he said, "I think us and the Senate may see eye to eye!"

"Exactly right," said Korngold, almost weeping.

"Korngold is in need of a companion."

The needy man looked at Paul for some word. When none came, he smiled. "A man like Levy can run two lives. A first-rate business head. A sharp wonderful man."

Levy hooked his fingers into his belt buckle, monogrammed ALL. "So you'll write the letter?" he asked.

"To whom?" Paul said. "What?"

"The son. I brought paper what's got my name on it. Typed," said Levy, "would be very impressive."

"I don't get exactly what you want," Paul said.

Levy extracted a folded paper from his coat pocket. "Here's a facsimile. Just fix my contractions is probably all that's needed." Though addressing Paul, he had spoken his last words toward Korngold, who seemed to brighten.

"He was some attorney in his day," Korngold told Paul. "Got gangsters off the hook. How can we miss?"

The letter in his hand—Levy over his shoulder—Korngold begging solace directly in his eyes—how could he protect himself? He read.

Dear Mr. Korngold:

Mr. Max Korngold, your father, has asked for me to contact you on the subject: his condition. What kind of son could leave a man seventy in January to live so? For twenty-five a week life would improve for him by way of a companion. He needs looking after for such simple incidents as toilets and meals even bed sheets are a problem. I am active with the Senator from Michigan and could pull strings by a full scale investigation of what you are up to in your private life—your spending for one thing. My secretary has ready in her hands a letter that the Senate will see eye to eye with me on when I send it special delivery. Why not be a good son and spare us all a mess? If not you will pull down your world out of selfishness and greed. Gone will be your homes up and down Florida. What is twenty-five a week to a man like you? Answer right now or my secretary will call the Senate in the morning long distance no expense spared.

"Do I make myself clear?" asked Levy. "Needs polishing?"

Korngold plucked at Levy's sleeve. "Maybe we should enclose a snapshot. Let him see what condition I live in."

"Why plead?" Levy reasoned, making a fist. "He should know I mean business. A wrong move and he's through. You could type it up, adding here and there a comma?" he asked Paul.

Paul had heard most, but not all, of what the old men had been saying since they had come into his room. He did not have enough strength—given what had happened that day—to attend totally to these two characters. However, as much as they confused him, they touched him, and he was ready to say something helpful when he saw Levy's hand come to rest again on the lace of Libby's slip. "I'm not feeling well, Mr. Levy. Maybe you and Mr. Korngold better go out." Then he smiled, for by choice and breeding he was not rude to elderly people.

"What?" asked Korngold. "A youngster like you with failing health?"

"Dummy, he's got a bad cut."

Levy pointed, and Korngold cringed at the sight of the bandage. Levy proceeded to assemble on the tray his cups and saucers. "I'll leave you a facsimile, Mr. Herz, for when you have the time. That's all right, not an intrusion?"

"No," Paul said, wearily.

"So I'll pick it up tomorrow. Don't feel you gotta rush. The afternoon is fine. You could slip it under the door. I'd appreciate you wouldn't knock—of an afternoon I take a little siesta."

"Me, I can't even sleep at night," Korngold put in, holding his forehead. "Up with the birds. Awake all the time with that Nazi. For a radio he's got a public address hookup. I wouldn't tell you what he does in the sink—I should turn him in to the public health commission. In his room he's got shortwave, direct to Berlin." Korngold pushed back his chair; long and spineless as a sagging candle, he limped from the room. Levy moved after him, and, gesturing with his tray at Korngold's back, he whispered over his shoulder to Paul, "Senility, a simple case. When the arteries go, you can call it quits."

———

Libby's face was over his. He heard her asking about his wrist before he was fully alive to the hour and the circumstance. Coming out of sleep was like climbing up a ladder. And for a moment he did not want to climb.

"I'm home," Libby said. "What happened?"

He saw her pale-blue waitress uniform, then her. "I cut my hand at work."

"Baby, are you all right?" She moved down beside him on the bed. "The bandage is so big." She held him, careful of the wrist, and he did not know whether she was on the edge of passion or panic. He was hoping for neither.

"I'm all right. I was home for the afternoon, that's all." He sat up. "I'm fine."

She turned on the bedside lamp. "How did it happen?"

"I don't know. I was daydreaming."

She touched the fingers of his bandaged arm. "Will it be all right? Can you work?"

"Tomorrow."

"Did you lose this afternoon's pay?"

He controlled his temper and said he didn't know.

"Didn't you ask?"

"No, Libby. I was bleeding. I could have bled to death." Not happy over his histrionics, he got up and went to the sink to wash his face.

"I only wanted to know," she said. "Your typewriter is on the floor." She rose from the bed. "Mail?"

"What?"

She was unfolding the letter Levy had left behind.

"No," he said.

Disappointed, she asked, "What is this?"

"Mr. Levy wants me to type a letter for him."

She let the paper float out of her hands onto the floor. "He dropped his cane again this morning."

"Look, Libby, do you want me to say something to him or don't you?"

"He's such a poor old man—" Libby began.

"Crap, Libby. We're poorer than he is."

"What kind of letter is it?" she asked.

"He brought a friend over with him. The man with the shakes next door. With the limp. Korngold. Korngold's son has ruined Korngold's life. Disappreciation—"

"Who's Dr. Smith?"

"Who?"

She was holding up the little white piece of paper. "Dr. Thomas Smith. BA 3-3349."

"Where was that?"

"On the table. Who is he?"

"He bandaged my hand. I have to call him."

"Are you all right, sweetheart?" she asked. "Are you very upset?"

"It's nothing."

"I mean the other thing. Me."

"You are," he said. "You're depressed."

"I'm not depressed, I'm just nauseous. Is that possible? So soon? I couldn't eat my lunch."

"Maybe you should go to a doctor."

"It's not necessary."

"If you're feeling nauseous you ought to go to a doctor. You've got to eat."

"We don't have to start with doctors already," she said. "I'm not going to pay anybody five dollars to tell me I *should* be nauseous."

"Then go to a clinic. Go to the City Hospital."

The suggestion visibly shocked her. "It's not necessary."

"Lib, you're going to have to see a doctor eventually. Not doing anything isn't going to make it not so."

"Don't lecture me, please. I'm quite aware of my condition and what to do about it."

Her words confused him—though within the confusion was a strain of relief. "What do you mean?"

"That you don't have to run to doctors in the second month. *Please*, Paul." She picked up Levy's letter from the floor; after looking at it for only a second, she buried her head in her arms on the table.

"Put something over your shoulders, Libby."

"I'm all right," she mumbled.

"Libby . . ."

She answered only with a tired sound.

"Dr. Smith is an abortionist," he said.

Her arms remained crossed on the table, and she raised her head very slowly. She had nothing to say.

"He does abortions," Paul said.

"I see."

He got up from the edge of the bed and moved toward her. "You don't see anything."

"I don't see anything," she repeated. "You just made me numb, saying that."

"I made myself numb."

"He bandages hands too?"

"The doctor at the plant bandaged my hand. I just said that. The plant doctor gave me Smith's name."

She hammered on the table. "I don't understand."

"What?"

"I don't understand how people give out *names* like that! I don't think I understand what you're talking about!"

He decided to say no more; he sat back down on the bed.

"I said I don't think I understand everything," Libby shouted. "Would you please tell me? I'd be interested to know how my condition was bandied about in some doctor's office."

"Nobody bandied anything."

"Then what happened?"

"Let's forget it. I've been stupid. I'm sorry."

"Let's not forget it till I know what I'm supposed to forget!"

"Libby, let's do forget it." He did not give in to his impulse to pretend that his wrist was hurting. But Libby fierce, Libby pounding on tables and shouting, made him very uncertain; this was the girl he had married to take care of. Sternly he said, "Forget it."

"Maybe I'm interested!" she said, pointing a finger at him. "Maybe I'm interested! All right?"

"Maybe I'm not."

He did not realize that she still had the piece of paper in her hand until he saw it being waved in his face. "Then why did you bring this home? Why did you bring it up in the first place?"

"The doctor did."

"But you brought it home, you wrote it down—"

"*He* wrote it down. Calm yourself. He asked me why I was so preoccupied. I told him. He took out a piece of paper and wrote this name down. He gave it to me, and I was in a daze, and I took it—and that's all."

"He didn't say anything."

"Nothing. It was all very . . . decent."

"So then how do you know it's an abortionist? Why do you come home and even say that?"

"Because I know. Because it is. He was trying to be kind."

At last she sat down beside him, helpless. "Do *you* think it was kind?"

"I don't know." He pulled her head down into his lap, and ran a finger along the hard bone of her nose. "Stop shouting abortionist around here," he said. "Levy's behind every door."

"All right."

After a few silent minutes, he asked, "What do you think?"

"How . . ." She held his hand over her mouth as she spoke. "How much is it? Is it too much?"

———

Around the corner from them was a little delicatessen with a neon Star of David in the window, and tile floors, and the usual smells. They ate dinner there often because it was cheap and the counterman was kind, especially to Libby. Jewish store owners were always taking her for a nice Jewish girl and giving her extra portions to fatten her up.

"What kind of dinner is that?" Solly called from behind the cold-cut slicer. "Consommé and tea, you'll dwindle away to nothing. We'll have to give you an anchor for outside in the wind." He had a concentration camp number on his forearm and had bought the store with Nazi reparation money; the Herzes respected him fiercely.

"I'm not hungry," Libby called back to him.

"You're not hungry, what's wrong with a piece of boiled chicken?"

"No thank you, Solly."

"Are you still nauseous?" Paul asked her.

She nodded and broke a slice of rye bread into small pieces; she touched a crust to her lips, but couldn't push it any further.

"Lib, I'm going to call him."

"From here?"

"From the booth. I'll just call. I'll inquire."

He waited, but she gave him no answer. A couple of teen-age boys came into the store and ordered knishes.

"Does that seem all right?" Paul asked.

". . . I think so."

"That doesn't sound like conviction, Lib. Should I or shouldn't I? What do you want me to do?"

"Whatever you want . . ." She collected all the little pieces of bread and put them in the ash tray.

He sat a moment longer and then got up and went to the phone booth. Solly passed him, carrying two bowls of soup. "It'll get cold," Solly said. Paul smiled and shut the door of the booth behind him. He looked at the piece of paper but could not read the number. *I drank tea with Levy . . . I kibitz with Solly . . . At the plant I eat my lunch with Harry Black, LeRoy Holmes . . .*

If no one knew my face or name—

"Hurry up," Solly called as he passed the booth again. Paul turned his back to the store; hunched on a corner of the seat, he dialed. The underwater feeling he had lately experienced returned. He waited until he heard a hello from the other end.

"Is Dr. Smith in?"

"He's eating—" a woman replied. "I said he's eating."

He did not know where to go from there.

"Hello—is this an emergency?" the woman shouted. "Is this Mr. Motta?"

"No."

"Well, the doctor is eating his dinner. You want him to call you back? Is this Mr. Motta?"

"No, no. I'm in a booth."

"Look, you call when he's finished eating. You hear me?"

When he got back to the table, the steam still rose off their bowls of soup. Libby had not disturbed the oily surface with her spoon.

"Are you sick again?" he asked.

"Still."

"Do you want a soft-boiled egg or something?"

"What did he say?"

"He was eating. I didn't talk to him. Lib, this is a mistake. I think we should go ahead and let what happens happen."

She picked up her spoon and stirred the soup at the edge of the dish.

"Does that make you feel better?" He covered one of her hands with his own.

"I think so," she said.

"All right. Let's just eat. It'll get cold."

Solly was trying to get their attention from behind the counter. "Go ahead," he said, pointing to their food, "give it a try."

Libby took two spoonfuls. "Who did you talk to, then?" she asked.

"A woman."

"His secretary?"

"I don't know."

"What did she sound like?"

"She sounded all right. She sounded fine. She just said he was eating."

"Are you going to call him back?"

"I thought you didn't want me to."

"I didn't say that."

"I said I wouldn't, and you said it made you feel better."

She dropped her spoon—deliberately, he thought—to the table. "I don't know *what* makes me feel better."

He looked quickly around: Solly was back in the kitchen joking with the cook. "Don't raise your voice, will you? Stop clanging your silverware. It's nobody's business. How do you feel now? Why don't you eat your soup?"

"I don't want it."

"You've got to eat something. You can't work all day and not eat anything. You'll get sick. Do you want some toast?"

"Paul, maybe we ought to . . ."

"What?"

"Maybe we ought to talk to somebody."

"You want me to call again? I don't want to pressure you. I don't want to decide without you."

"Well, *you* have to make up your mind, though, whether you want it or not."

"Want the baby or the other?"

"Want the other . . . A baby," she said, "a baby might be a pleasure.

"You want it then?"

"Don't you? Don't you think a little baby might be a pleasure for us?"

"Lib, it's just *now*. It's just how long can we keep being the victims of everything. I'm starting to think there's some conspiracy going."

"A lot of people look forward to having a baby."

"I look forward to it too. Don't accuse me, sweetheart. It's just not *now* . . . Why aren't you eating?"

"I told you a hundred times already. I'm nauseous! Don't you believe me?"

"You want a baby, Libby, we'll have a baby."

"I don't want anything you don't want."

"I'm not *saying* I don't want it. I'm only saying *now*. I feel like a snowball being pushed downhill. Things are getting out of hand."

"Every day somebody has a baby they hadn't planned on."

"All right then. We'll just let it ride."

"I mean what kind of way is that to have a family? To just let it *ride*."

"Don't raise your voice, I said."

"Well, what kind of way is it?"

"It's no way."

"Then you want to call him back?"

"I think maybe we ought to think about it."

"We can't think about it forever," Libby whined. "If you have a thing like that done it has to be soon."

"What are you talking about having it done? I just thought you didn't want to have it done. I thought now you *wanted* to have a baby."

"But *you* don't."

"It isn't that I don't—"

Solly rapped with a knuckle on the counter. "What's a matter, you kids can't decide what movie? See *Ten Commandments* —it's got a beautiful message."

"Thanks, Solly, no," Paul said. "Libby's got a cold."

"How about a piece of boiled chicken?" Solly asked.

"No, thank you," Libby said.

"Lib," Paul said, "let's save this conversation. Let's talk at home."

She agreed. But while eating his stuffed peppers, he couldn't prevent his mind from working. "If I call, Libby, I've got to call from here. I can't talk from the hall."

"Then you're going to call."

"Drink your tea at least."

As he pulled back his chair once again, Solly addressed the salami he was slicing: "There's a kid likes cold food."

This time his control was much better; he had no trouble making out the number, and his mouth moved into the mouthpiece at just the moment he wanted it to. His voice was his own when he asked for the doctor.

"He's eating," the woman said. "Didn't you call before?"

"This is an emergency. You better let me talk to him."

There was no response. Was he supposed to say he was Mr. Motta? "Hello—hello?" he said.

The voice from the other end was now a man's. "Doctor Tom speaking."

"Dr. Smith?"

"Who's calling?"

"Doctor, I'm calling about my wife. She's been having some menstrual trouble. I wondered if you might have a look at her."

"Think it's a matter of structural derangement, do you? Has she been to an osteopath before? Someone suggest to you that the fundamental condition was a lesion?"

"I don't understand, Doctor." The mumbo jumbo was making him perspire. "She's not menstruating properly. She's not menstruating on time. We're a little concerned."

"I see."

"Dr. Esposito gave me your name."

"Maybe you'd better bring her over for a checkup. Give her a once-over."

"Do you understand me, Doctor?"

"Why don't you get her over here in half an hour, all right?"

"Just for a checkup though . . ."

"I'll take care of her. What's your name, son?"

After he told him—his name and his wife's too—he could have cut out his tongue.

—

On the bus they sat in the last two seats in the back. Paul did all the talking. "We're not obliged to do anything, Lib. Don't be glum, please. We'll let him look at you. The worst it'll be is a checkup. I want you to make up your own mind. We don't have to tell him anything, we're not involved in any way. There's no reason, though, why we shouldn't investigate all the possibilities. If it sounds complicated, if there's anything you don't like about it, then we forget it. I'm sure it's a very simple procedure. People go back to work the next day. You could stay at home a week, though—that isn't what I mean. What I mean is you don't have to worry, you don't have to feel that we're helplessly entangled in anything. You say no and it's no. We have the name, we have the address—we'll just go. Most people who want to do it and don't, don't because they can't even find out who to go to. It goes on all the time, Lib. There are probably I don't know how many every day of the year. People like us, in our circumstances, unprepared for a child. There's no reason why we shouldn't at least inquire about a way out. I don't see why every rotten thing that falls our way has to be accepted. Don't you agree? You don't have to say a word, Lib. You don't have to say a thing. When we come out, you say yes or no, and that's that. You say no, that's fine with me. All right? Is that all right?"

"This is the stop," she said.

The office was in a ten-story apartment building near Grand Circus Park. In the entryway downstairs there was a brass plate:

THOMAS SMITH

DOCTOR OF OSTEOPATHY

ROOM 307

Passing the plate, Paul thought for the first time about the police.

The nurse said, "Herz?" when they walked into the waiting room, and then disappeared into the doctor's office; she wore glasses and had fat red peasant cheeks. Libby picked up a copy of *Look* and held it in her lap. Paul flipped sightlessly through an osteopathic journal. A close-shaven, gray-at-the-temples corporation executive came out of the doctor's office. "Hello there. I'm Doctor Tom," he said. "Come on in."

In the examination room both Herzes stood at attention before his desk. When he motioned for them to sit down, only Libby obliged. The doctor himself—chiseled features, leathery skin, a large brown mustache—placed himself on the edge of his desk, one leg swinging athletically. Paul noticed his hands: large and sculpted.

"Well," the doctor said, "what's the fundamental condition here?"

"We think my wife is pregnant. We want an abortion."

The only noise in the room was made by Libby—a small sound, neither of denial or agreement. Following a moment of blinding fatigue, Paul took command. "We had a rabbit test," he said. "The result was positive."

"Uh-huh." The doctor stood up, cracked his knuckles and furrowed his brow, thoroughly professional. "When was your last period?" he asked Libby.

They had themselves been over and over this ground; she answered instantly. "January sixth to January eleventh."

"Young man," said Dr. Smith, "why don't you step out of the room?"

He hung back for only a second, then did not look at Libby as he left. The nurse was stretched out on a leather chair in the waiting room. Above her hung a painting of two men duck hunting. One of her shoes dangled from either hand, and from her feet rose an appalling but universal odor. Not the doctor, but the nurse, was along the lines of what he had been expecting. In all her pores, all he saw was dirt, dirt and germs. He began to read in one of the osteopathic magazines about Dr. Selwyn Sales of Des Moines, the Osteopath of the Month.

"Don't be nervous," the nurse said. "Doctor Tom does beautiful work."

"I'm sure."

"His whole life is osteopathy. No family, no outside clubs, don't even pick up a book unless it's osteopathy. He wouldn't tell you himself, but he's a power in the field. People come to him from all over the world. He's already been asked to talk in Missouri twice."

"What's in Missouri?"

All at once, he had an enemy. She narrowed her eyes at him —or brought her great cheeks up to cover the bottom lids. "What do you think, it's a picnic for a doctor like Doctor Tom? This here is a dedicated man. Women tumble at his feet —but his whole life is osteopathy. He has a rotten foe in that

AMA. Think they own everything. You know an osteopath is better trained than a medical doctor, you know that, don't you?"

"I don't know much about osteopathy," he said apologetically, but too late.

"You know who controls the AMA, don't you? A man comes along like Doctor Tom, a man with an American background like his, six generations of Smith Smith Smith, and then you see them putting their noses together, turning the pressure on."

He flipped through the osteopathic magazine to the editorial page. Somewhere down the column he spotted the name: Dr. Thomas Smith.

"We have a woman comes in here with an allergy condition. MDs have been taking her for a ride for years. Dr. Goldberg's wife got six minks already, and this poor lady still can't breathe. She can't sleep, can't eat, and I'll tell you, she was growing poor from the way those country-club doctors was bleeding her. She finally saw Doctor Tom, and what was it but a problem of manipulation. A lesion in the joints of the neck. Right here. And this is the kind of thing the AMA is against, this is the kind of battle Doctor Tom has on his hands. You don't make a mistake when you come to an osteopath. I'll tell you where medicine comes from—it comes from Europe! Osteopathy is American, through and through. Someday, you wait, the osteopath will have his day. It's a damn shame—all that training, and they make our boys go into the service as privates. You know who's pulling the strings down in Washington, don't you? You know who's got the influence—"

Doctor Tom's head came through the door. "Mr. Herz?"

Libby was sitting up on the examination table, fully dressed except for her shoes. Doctor Tom was standing by the calendar on the wall. "When's best for you?" he asked. "Tomorrow night all right? About eight?"

"She's definitely pregnant?" Paul asked, for he had stepped back into the office hoping for a miracle.

"Uterus is enlarged, breasts tender, a little swollen—the morning sickness, the rabbit test . . ." He smiled, cracking his knuckles. He looked over at Libby; she said nothing.

"Doctor—" Paul asked, "how much?"

"For a D and C, four hundred dollars. For the anesthetic, fifty more. We do it right here in the office, Mrs. Kuzmyak assists me. You'll be in and out in an hour." The time element seemed to fill him with pride.

"Who administers the anesthetic?"

"Mrs. Kuzmyak."

"She's—" But he left off, and fortunately the doctor seemed not to have guessed what he was going to say.

"She's fine right away," Doctor Tom said. "You go home from here, and she can go back to work next day."

At last, Paul looked directly at his wife. Immediately she directed her attention to the calendar pinned on the wall. "It's safe?" he asked.

The doctor smiled. "Two hundred percent."

"The police—"

"As far as I'm concerned," said Doctor Tom, bringing a giant fist down into his palm, "a D and C is not illegal. What the AMA and that crowd thinks is their business."

"I meant about the law."

"You come in here at eight, Mr. Herz, I'll have you out by nine. You go home, your wife here gets a good night's sleep— if you want, let her stay off her feet the next day, and that's it. You have nothing to worry about." He crossed his arms and raised his chin. His lower lip came out, reaching up for his mustache. Was *he* nervous? Hadn't he ever done this before? Why didn't he answer the questions?

All Paul said was, "Four fifty is a little high."

"Listen, young man"—the voice was gentle and chastising —"you can find somebody for a hundred and fifty if you want to look down dark alleys. But this is your wife we're dealing with. I should think you would want the best."

"Yes, yes, absolutely."

"Tomorrow night at eight?"

"Lib?" Paul asked.

But Libby said nothing. While he waited for her to speak, his mind traveled all the way back—to Lichtman, to Uncle Asher, to his own parents. In a fit of defiance he shook the doctor's hand.

"Have a light lunch," said Doctor Tom, coming over and putting just a finger on Libby's clenched hand. "No dinner, an enema at five, and I'll see you at eight."

The anesthetist, Mrs. Kuzmyak, was gone from the waiting room when they left. Either it was Paul's strong imagination or the odor of Kuzmyak's feet, but something of her managed to cling to the place even in her absence. He found himself cursing her. The smelly pig! The fat frustrated bitch!

Oh God!

—

From the street, through the leafless hedge, they could see that a light was on behind the stained shade in their room.

"I turned them all off," Paul said. "Did you turn them on?"

"No."

"You must have, Lib—"

"I didn't," she said. "Oh Paul . . ."

"What?"

"I don't know. Everything."

"I probably left it on. It's all right." But he was suddenly so full of his own thoughts that he did not even take her hand. He opened the outside door with his key, and they walked down the narrow stairway to the basement. Outside their door he could not find his other key on his chain; as in the phone booth, his eyes blurred over. He remembered having seen a squad car on the corner when they had alighted from the bus. Earlier there had been a man in a hat outside Dr. Smith's apartment building—and he had looked too long at Libby, hadn't he? Had they been followed? *Caught?* He saw the life which he had so earnestly and diligently constructed falling away to nothing. He should have known . . . all the crumbling that had been going on over the months. He should have been stronger, *wiser*! Now the scandal, jail, poor poor pale Libby—

When he pushed open the door, Korngold made an effort to rise from the edge of the bed, but gave in to his arteries and only sat there, half raising his cane. "You was open . . ." the old man said, pointing at the door. "The hallways gets chilly. I was getting a pain in the lungs."

"Jesus, Korngold!" Paul said. "You frightened us."

Korngold made a joke, which did not for a moment transform the skeletal look of his face. "Consider it an honor. First one in thirty years. How do you do?" he said, feebly, to Libby. "Oh, you're pretty as Levy says. A *yiddishe maydele.*" For a moment the old man sat there loving her with his eyes.

Libby sat down at the table and looked kindly across at Korngold. "Thank you."

"What is it, Mr. Korngold?" Paul asked. "We're both very tired."

"I only need a minute."

"What is it?"

"I want to ask a little advise. You're a young man. You know about modern times. I ain't got all my perspectives. Please sit down too, would you? I get dizzy looking up."

Paul took off his coat but held it in a bundle on his lap when he sat. He could not hate this feeble old man, but still there was a momentum in his life that Korngold's presence was interrupting. He knew, of course, that this police business was only in his imagination. If he could just drive forward without stopping, without thinking, and get this done, then everything —he thought vaguely—would be all right.

"Does this seem like cheating to you?" Korngold was asking. "If my son gives me twenty a week, why do I need a Levy? This is a scheme—what do you think? Do you get the feeling Levy is a real friend? Or do you get another feeling? What does he care, a man was once a topnotch criminal lawyer, with little fish like me. First off I think he is strictly interested in my underwear. I got twenty-six cases, tops and bottoms, a nice close-knit cotton like you can't get no more. Levy comes in my room, sees all this goods, and he's my friend. So I tell him about that son of a bitch, my son, and all of a sudden Levy is a first-class chum, an old school-tie buddy. I'm asking you, Mr. Herz, as a young fellow, is this a genuine interest in my life, or is this a crook I got myself involved in?"

"Mr. Korngold, I can't give you any advice. I'm going to type the letter tonight."

"Yes?" Korngold paled, if such were possible. "So soon?"

"Look, why don't I type it, and you and Levy can decide what to do with it. Does that sound reasonable?"

Korngold was forced to admit that it was not; he shook his head, making his mouth a round black hole. "You type, then next thing it's in the U.S. mail, and I'm married to Levy. Somebody does you a favor, you can't suddenly take a walk across the street."

"What do you want me to do, then? I've had a very rough day. My wife and I are very tired."

"Oh, excuse me," the old man said; he bowed his head to the tired girl, then with his eyes drank her in again, unLevy-like, fatherly.

"What is it you want, Mr. Korngold?" Libby asked. Her voice surprised Paul. She sounded confident that she could give whatever Korngold might want. She was probably so much stronger than her husband ever allowed her to be . . . Here again, hadn't he bossed her into something? Hadn't her silence in the doctor's office been a negative vote, one he had not even bothered to count?

"A direct appeal," Korngold said. "I'm not proud, believe me. A plea. Tell the boy for Christ sake to send *money*. I don't need no Levy. I need a simple letter somebody should write for me. I can't even tie my shoes with these shakes."

"Then," Libby said, "maybe Mr. Levy would be a help."

"This is a crook, *lebele*, something tells me. He'll tie the laces and steal the shoes. He's got an eye already on an easy dollar via my underwear."

"Why don't you sell it?" Libby asked, coming over to him on the bed. "Is it all in your room?"

"You don't sell to robbers. I drag a box of briefs all over Detroit, they wouldn't give me enough to pay my bus fare. I don't sell nothing when the market stinks. If you don't specu-late, you don't accumulate—always my motto. Now is a buyer's market. Let them come begging, that's when Max Korngold does business!" he shouted.

"How did you come by all this underwear?" Paul asked.

"A three-way split with two partners, they should both go live in hell."

"When was that?"

"Seven years already. That kind of underwear they don't knit no more. Don't think Levy don't know that either . . ." But his mind suddenly was elsewhere. "Here," he said. He took a wallet from his inside coat pocket; the photograph he finally coaxed out of one of the folds was of himself, from a

Take Your Own Photo booth. There was Korngold, and there was his right hand, raised up beside his ear—and in it he was gripping his cane. He might have been shaking the cane at the camera; he might merely have been showing that he had one. At the bottom of the picture were written some words that Paul could just about decipher: *Your Old Father, Feb. 3, 1951.*

"You could enclose this with the letter?" he wanted to know.

Paul looked to Libby to speak for them both, but she seemed near tears. Korngold waited, then spoke again. "You see, just a few facts of my health I'm sure could make an impression. Here, take a look, please." He pulled up his trouser legs to show a pair of knees that were not wholly unexpected but were nevertheless shocking. "Undernourishment. Bad ventilation. Improper rest. Worry. Aloneliness. Let me tell you about a wife, gets a spurt of energy one day, aged sixty-one years old, hides my cane, steals my checkbook, runs off to Florida with an eighty-year-old *shmekele*, can't even pee straight cause he can't see what's doing under his belly. Excuse me. The facts are dirty and disgusting so I can't talk clean if I want"—this last to Libby, with a tender plea in his lips and eyes. "I got myself a lawyer, a young fellow with short hair, and he takes me for a ride—three times he's got to fly to Miami—and I got cleaned out. Now Levy keeps one eye on my underwear, another on my son, and what do you think I feel? Contented? Foolproof? Please, you write a simple note— here, I got the postage even." He removed some crumpled three-cent stamps from his watch pocket and counted them into Libby's hand. "One, two, three—go all-out. Don't worry about weight. I'm a desperate man." He patted Libby's arm. She helped him off the bed. "And how are you?" he asked Paul. "The wrist's improved?"

"Much better."

"You two kiddies look tired." He turned back once again, unable to keep his eyes from Libby's face. "My son, my own son, why couldn't he find a nice *yiddishe maydele*, a little dark darling. That girl—she poisoned his opinions of me!" He dragged his bad legs to the door.

"*Help* him," Libby whispered tearfully to Paul.

"Here," Paul said, and he was up from his chair at last and

reaching after the old man's elbow. So immune had he been feeling to anyone's suffering but his own, so lacking in tenderness and interest, that he wondered if he had left his heart for good in that doctor's office. "Here." He took hold of Korngold and led him out the door and up the stairs to the front entryway. As they emerged into the hall, the bathroom door slammed shut.

———

In bed, neither one touching the other, Libby said, "You decided. You said yes. You never so much as asked me."

"We can change our minds."

"We made an appointment already. We discussed money."

"That doesn't bind me to a thing."

"Where are we going to get all that money?"

"It's in the bank."

"Paul, that's all we've got. Everything!"

"Money," he said firmly, as though it were a truth he had known for more than a few hours, "is to get you out of trouble with."

"You've decided."

"I've decided." Quickly he added. "So did you."

"I didn't decide anything!"

"All afternoon you were on a seesaw, Libby. If you said no, it would have been no. I wouldn't have gone against you."

Limply, she held out for herself. "I did say no."

"No, then yes, then no. When you went to the doctor's office—"

"*You tricked me!*"

"Lower your voice!"

"It's my body! It's my body he's going to operate on!"

At last they touched: he clamped a hand over her mouth. "Libby, Libby," he said through his teeth, "it's been a difficult day. These old men, my hand, everything." When he removed his hand, allowing her to breathe again, she rolled away from him. "You want to think the decision is mine," he said, "then it's mine."

"It is yours."

"All right, you think that."

"Stop trying to get the upper hand!" she said. "I'm thinking it because it's *so.*"

"Libby, you're twenty years old. We came down here to make some money. We want to go back to school. We're married a year, we're broke—"

"We're not broke if we've got four hundred and fifty dollars in the bank to throw out!"

"In the end, a baby will cost more, much, much more. It'll change our lives altogether. Honey, I'm only trying to protect us from even more crap. If there's a baby, we have to move out of this room, you have to stop working. And we'll never get caught up, Libby. I know it, we'll just flounder along."

She turned back toward him, covering her face with her hands. "You think you shouldn't even have married me. I made you marry me."

"Don't talk stupidly, please."

"When I think of all the stuff I said I'm just so ashamed. You've changed me, now you've got to marry me—how can I ever go out with other boys—"

"Lib," Paul said, not sure that he wasn't lying, "you never said any of that."

"I thought it."

"I wanted to marry you. I went out of my way to marry you."

"I made you want to."

"Go to sleep. Nobody's talking sense at this hour."

"I can't go to sleep. My mind's a whirlpool . . . What does an osteopath know about uteruses?"

"Osteopaths are like doctors. Smith is very well known."

"They're bone-crackers."

"The man's been doing this for years."

"What about infection?"

"This is a doctor, Libby, not just anybody. Would he do it if it was risky?"

"Paul?"

"Yes."

"Give me your hand. Feel my breasts. Do they feel bigger?"

"I think so, honey."

She brought his hand up to her mouth and kissed it; she tried to be funny. "It's what I've always wanted." Then, as he knew she would, she wept. "And it's going to last one day. Oh Paul . . ." She lay still, holding his hand to her, and then because she was exhausted she soon fell asleep.

He himself had no such luck. His own whirlpool went round and round and round . . . Infection was Libby's worry; his own mind turned and turned now on a single word: jail. Korngold had been showing his pathetic photograph, and all he had been thinking was *jail!* Suppose the police should come in before Libby was in the operating room. Couldn't he simply say she was there for an examination? Couldn't they deny everything? Unless she were already on the table—then what? Whom do they put in jail? After all, he was her husband, not just a man who had got a girl into trouble. But what weight, if any, did that carry? Did that not make it seem worse? He tried to remember accounts of cases reported in the newspapers. Was the boy friend or husband an accomplice? The girl? Surely they didn't throw *her* in jail! But in the headlines she was always dead.

Through the hectic night, at the center of his imaginings, stood the police. You're an accomplice to an abortion. No, my wife said she had to come here to have a cyst removed. All right, says the Captain, ask the wife . . . Libby, if anything should happen, if anybody should question you, say I didn't know, say you told me it was a cyst—

—

In the morning neither of them heard the alarm clock. They dressed in a frenzy, couldn't get into the bathroom, and had no time for coffee on the hot plate. They parted at the bus stop without even a kiss. Only a few hours earlier, Paul had tried to force his way into sleep by telling himself that all this preoccupation with the police was only his super-ego asserting itself. But that had in no way been able to increase his self-respect; he felt lucky then to have avoided a morning conversation with his wife, for he might have confessed to her the nature of his fears and so shaken her even further. He was aware of his momentum again, carrying him forward.

The bus started away from the corner, then stopped; someone was hammering on the side. The driver swung back the doors and Mr. Levy charged up the stairs, eyebrows floating and sinking, cane swinging disastrously near the driver's head. "Don't be disrespectful! I'll take your number!" He started up the aisle, a little eager old man, sun-tanned from the ultraviolet bulb in his room. He snapped a sharp look into each seat until he spotted Paul. "Ah, nice morning," he said; refining himself down into an oily friendliness, he slid in beside the young man. "A little chilly, but bracing."

"Good morning," Paul said. He had to free his coat from Levy's backside.

"Heigh ho, heigh ho, off to work you go?"

"Yes," Paul said. "Yourself?"

"Enterprises, enterprises. I'm moving some gloves for a friend. You wrote the letter?"

He found himself looking out the window as he said, "I haven't gotten around to it yet."

"I thought maybe Korngold picked it up last night."

"No."

"I thought maybe it was his limp I heard dragging down the hall. Must be some mistake."

Paul's eyes fixed on the dull two-storied rooming houses along the street.

"You look a little underneath the weather," commented Levy. "Up too late at night, no?"

"No."

"Funny."

"What's funny?"

"Over sixty-five you can't trust your senses. My hearing is a tricky item where I'm concerned." Levy made a quick survey of the ads posted in the bus, checking the competition. He said, "Korngold, of course, is an old old friend, but senility will rob him of his sense of fair play, I'm afraid."

Paul at last forced himself to engage Levy's excited glittery eyes. "He doesn't seem senile. Maybe a little fatigued. He seems to have had a lot of trouble."

"Oh, nobody's taking his troubles away from him. A sad case, that man. Fleeced all his life, then health goes, whew! No wonder he's such a suspicious specimen. It's pathetic how he doesn't know the best road no longer. Needs help. Good thing you and me are around, because drowning would be his end. Starvation probably."

They rode on a little further. Paul's growing discomfort with Levy arose in part from a sense of incongruity; it was not simply that he did not like the fellow—it was that here was a crisis in his life, *the* crisis perhaps, and these two old men had somehow gotten tied up in it. It was all he could do not to get up and change his seat.

"So," said Levy, with a flourish of his cane, "you'll have it typed up this afternoon, righto?"

"I've got to work all day."

"So tonight?"

"Tonight I'm busy."

"More doctors?"

"What?"

"I didn't say nothing."

"What is it, Mr. Levy? What are you following me around this morning for?"

"My boy, my boy, don't be paranoyal. I got kid gloves I'm moving for a friend."

But when Paul rose to leave, Levy followed. The bus pulled away and the two of them were alone on the corner, within sight of the gate to the plant. "What is it, Levy? What do you want to tell me?"

Levy only sniffed in some of the bracing air. "We're going the same way," he said. "Smells like pine trees in the vicinity."

"What are you getting at? What's on your mind?"

"That question I'm saving for you." With Paul on his heels, Levy started to cross the street. A car came roaring down on them, and Paul couldn't believe his impulse: he wanted to push the old bastard in front of it.

"Look," he began, helping the elderly man up the opposite curb, "Korngold—"

"Korngold is senile. Korngold shouldn't go in the dark streets at night. He'll lose his footing and crack a hip. Then death. Korngold shouldn't be encouraged along foolish lines."

Paul was no longer helping Levy up the curb; nevertheless, he kept his fingers wrapped around the stringy arm. "Korngold asked me to write to his son for him," Paul said, spinning the old man around. "All right? So he came in our room. He spilled his old sick heart out. I listened, my wife listened. I don't have to hide anything from you, Mr. Levy. What the hell is going on here? Korngold has some rights in this thing."

"For rights," said Levy, shaking free his coat and smoothing out the cloth, "a legal mind is called for. Which I got, not you."

"Mr. Levy, this whole thing," said Paul, calming himself as best he could, "is very foolish. None of it is my business."

Levy suddenly took a strangle hold on that admission; in anger he said, "Leave it to the parties of the first and second part to judge the wisdom of Mr. Korngold's family problem. You just type neat the letter I gave you. Or"—he shook his cane—"give it back and go your way. Understand? *Clear?* This is in the shape of a warning, my young Mr. Herz. Keep your nose poked out of my professional life—"

But Paul could not bear for another moment to be in the company of meanness, his own or anybody else's. "Look, I don't care about your professional life, Levy. I don't care about your letter—" And then, because Levy had the nerve to give him a menacing glance, he added, "you presumptuous little bastard!" It felt so good to say it—he had taken too much already, from everybody. "What kind of Senate investigation! What kind of petty thief are you, screwing poor Korngold!"

Levy's eyes became tiny coin slots, big enough for dimes. "You want to pay for the label *bastard*, or you want to pay for that disgusting word *screw? Which?*"

"Don't threaten me."

"Dr. Thomas Smith. BA three dash three three four nine." For the first time Paul could remember, Levy proceeded to smile. He walked on then, Paul grabbing after his coat.

"What business is that of yours!"

"Don't hit an old man on the streets. Let go."

In absolute confusion, Paul dropped his hands to his sides.

"I'm interested in the law," said Levy. "When it gets busted, I feel a pain."

"You little thief! You eavesdropping little son of a bitch! You sneak looks at my wife in the john, you disgusting old fart!"

"Libel is a crime, Mr. Herz, even if only the other party is a witness. It's a crime against my feelings. Also illegal medical proceeding is a crime in a great state like Michigan. Watch your step!" With that, Levy turned back the way they had come, smashing at the pavement with his cane.

—

Late in the afternoon Paul complained to the foreman that his left wrist was throbbing, and managed to see the doctor. In the infirmary Dr. Esposito undid the bandage. "You called and took care of your business?"

"Everything is all right," Paul said.

The doctor smeared a cool ointment onto the wrist. "Well. Good. It's your business."

"You see, it worked out. She menstruated this morning."

"Is that so?" Esposito asked, smiling.

"No," Paul said. "No—look, is he all right, this Smith? Is he a quack?"

"Topnotch for what he does," Esposito said softly.

"I didn't like the looks of the nurse."

"You're overnervous. Who does the scraping, the nurse or Smitty?"

"Look, I appreciate everything. Please, call the foreman, will you? Tell him I'm sick. I've got to get home."

Esposito continued to be the most decent person around. He made the call, adding that Herz might not be able to come in for work the next day either.

From the bus Paul raced past his own house, flung open the little iron gate next door, and two at a time took the stairs of Korngold's red-sided rooming house. A rotund man was eating potato chips out of a bag and listening to the radio in the sitting room, a dark place where everything, floor, tables, chairs, seemed knee-deep in rugs and coverlets. "What!" the man boomed, before anything was said.

"Korngold."

"Next to the sink," said the man in a heavy accent. "Upstairs. What are you to him?" As Paul moved away, he shouted after him, "He owes his rent!"

Paul mounted the stairs. He knocked at the door to which a business card was thumbtacked:

MAX KORNGOLD

Haberdashery　　　*Kiddies Wear*

Waiting for some word from the other side, he looked in the sink. There was a Bab-o can on the ledge and he shook it and shook it over the filth; nothing, unfortunately, sprinkled forth.

"Who?" Korngold moaned.

"Paul Herz. From next door. Open up, please."

Minutes passed before Korngold—long underwear beneath his robe, his stained fedora back on his head—appeared in the doorway. "All right. Come in."

The tiny room was squeezed into an angle of the house, and so had five cracking walls. Around three of the walls cartons were piled; beside the bed, under whose covers Korngold had been laid out, was an end table with a flashlight, a glass, a paper-covered book, and a milk bottle half full of urine. In the grip of sadness and disgust, Paul looked away from Korngold's possessions. The old man, with some oow-ing and ahh-ing, had taken his place back in the bed.

"I got the shivers," Korngold explained. "Sit, why don't you."

"I'm in a hurry. I want to say to you that I had a talk with your friend Mr. Levy this morning. I think he has your interests at heart. What good would money be to you without a helper, somebody to give you a hand going up and down stairs, to sit across from you at meals? He has your interests at heart." He had gotten through it on just one breath.

"This," Korngold asked, "is something he told you?"

"I observed him. I listened to him, yes. Why don't you let him go through with his plan? See what happens."

Korngold stretched his neck up on his pillows, crossing his arms for protection. "You told him I came talking to you?"

"He knew it. He heard you."

"Oy, he's got six ears that guy! I thought he was asleep by eight. He says that, see, for propaganda. See how he tricks you out on things?" He seemed ready for tears.

"No, no. It's all right. I said you just wanted to give me your son's address."

Korngold put his head in his hands, and he let out some air with a high flutey sound. "Oh, nice thinking," he said.

"So you'll just go along, all right?"

"You saved my life, believe me."

"Your life's not in jeopardy, Mr. Korngold. What's the matter with you?"

"It's no good crossing Levy, I'm sure. Not when a fellow offers you so much."

"Don't be so nervous, please. I'm only saying that this is to your advantage."

"Of course it is. Sure. You're right. See what a wreck I turned into? Someone offers a helping hand, I give him for a reward suspicion. I could have made a bad mistake."

"You'll just go along then?"

Korngold raised a hand and waved it. "Of course. Lucky break," he said, as though to himself. Then: "What size?"

"What?"

Korngold considered Paul's physique. "What size in a jockey brief?"

"I don't wear jockeys."

"Foolish. Plus comfort, it protects from strains and hazards. Go take yourself a pair for a present. What—a thirty-two?"

"In the waist I'm thirty."

"Three boxes down, to the left by the window. Go ahead, take a pair. A pair," he added a little shyly, "is one. Two days wearing will change your whole attitude toward underwear. Please, for saving my life."

When Paul had removed the shorts from a box, Korngold said, "Give me a look, would you?" The old haberdasher and outfitter of kiddies fingered the briefs in his hand. "Once I thought, I'll build myself an empire. Now the *gonifs* want for nothing. Levy—sure, Levy—of course—you're right. With him is my last hopes. What good are cartons sitting in my room, huh? Wear it, enjoy it. And how is that little *maydele*, your wife? I could see right away all the sweetness in that face."

———

First the bathroom was occupied. Paul had to go out and hammer on the door.

"Please don't disturb," came Levy's voice from within.

"Somebody else wants to get in there," Paul shouted.

"Please don't *disturb* please," Levy sang out.

Back in the room Libby gnawed on her fingers. "The doctor said to do it by five. It's almost six," she said.

"He'll be right out."

"*You're* nervous now."

"Just be patient, please."

He went out into the hall and knocked again on the bathroom door.

"Please, Mr. Levy—my wife has to use the bathroom."

"I don't like carrying on conversations in such circumstances. Will you, please?"

"I'm giving you five minutes."

"The doctor will wait," whispered Levy.

"Shut up! Shut your mouth!"

"Please, this is not my cup of tea. Move away, all right?"

Paul pressed himself against the door, his body, his mouth. "I spoke to Korngold. He wants you to represent him. To write the letter, to be his companion."

"This is fact or fiction?"

"A fact. An hour ago. All right?"

"If true, all right."

"You understand me . . . ?"

"Please, I'm finishing up now."

"You understand me, don't you?"

"Understood," answered Levy, rattling paper.

While in the bathroom Libby readied herself for Dr. Smith, Paul collapsed onto the bed. All at once he remembered what he had forgotten. He jumped up, tied his shoelaces in knots, and without a coat—though it was the worst of winter in Detroit—ran all the way to the corner delicatessen. He dialed the doctor's number so fast he got no connection. Woozy, he dialed again. Solly kept wanting to kibitz through the phone-booth door.

"Dr. Smith, this is Paul Herz."

"This is Mrs. Kuzmyak, for Christ's sake."

"I want to speak to the doctor."

"He's not in. What is it?"

"Mrs. Kuzmyak, look, today was very hectic for me. I couldn't get to the bank. I don't have the money."

"What do you expect, something for nothing?" She seemed to be trying to talk in some sort of dialect.

"Can't I pay you tomorrow?"

She found now what it was she had wanted to say. "What do you think, my name is Fink, I do your clothes for nothing?"

"But, Mrs. Kuzmyak, we're both ready. It's been one hell of a day. My wife's taking an enema. I forgot all about the bank. She hasn't eaten—look, let me talk to the doctor, will you?"

"We've got books to keep straight," she said, sternly. "The doctor's got expenses to meet."

"Well," he said hopelessly, "what'll we *do*?"

"Hang on there, Herzie." She left the phone; then was back. "Doctor says tomorrow's no good. Make it Thursday. Same time. Bring cash."

———

Lunch hour the next day was spent waiting in line at the bank. After the withdrawal—a red stain on the left side of the little friendly green booklet—the balance was eleven dollars and some pennies. To brighten matters, the clerk warned him that he would lose out on his interest for the quarter.

It was not until Paul walked past the toothless, smiling guard at the bank door that he saw his error. He should have taken the money in bits and pieces over a period of time, rather than in five large unforgettable bills. Now the clerk would . . . But right in his hands was enough evidence to put him in jail for life: the bank book. How could he claim innocence with some histrionic D.A. waving withdrawal slips in the jury's angry face? His moment of fantasy drew out of him all his strength, and he was left with only a fear, a silly dreamlike overblown fear of little Levy. Had Levy understood? Had Korngold emerged from his sleepless night willing to stick by his new decision? He slapped all his pockets and turned them inside out—this, right in front of the guard!—searching for the slip of paper with Dr. Smith's name and number. Panic seized him—the paper was nowhere. It was not in the wallet with the five crisp bills. Had Libby—?

Levy!

His watch showed that twenty minutes of lunch hour remained. He signaled a cab, and with a sick stomach—for sometimes nickels eat away one's insides more than hundreds of dollars—watched every turn of the meter until the taxi deposited him in front of his house. Up the stairs, through the hallway, down to the basement, and along the corridor to Levy's door. He heard murmurs from inside and boldly knocked. No response; the whispers within were shushed. He hammered on the door till the molding creaked.

"Levy, I heard you talking. I want to speak with you. This is Herz, Levy, open up!"

Something—a shoe?—scraped along the floor. Hot-water pipes sizzled over his head; perspiring and furious, he slammed his shoulder into the door. It gave way and a piece of plaster floated down. Inside the room was no one. He moved down the hall to their own room; under their door he found a letter addressed to Libby. It did not even astonish him to think that something new was about to happen to him. He had never opened another's mail, but now he felt nothing initiating about the act. The return address affected him as would the stabbing of a knife: surprise—then nothing—then pain. He read:

Dear Mrs. Herz:

You possess, indeed, a phenomenal and singular sense of obligation. I do not know from whence it springs, your studies, your fancies, your greed, or perhaps from the man with whom you are cohabiting, and from whom you had drawn, I recall, other ideas, opinions, and manners of equal merit. I had thought that along with defiance you might at least have developed fortitude; in fact, however, you prove yourself in possession of more energy than character, which is of course the signature of the devil. Surely to one with an inspiration so inhuman, I can only reiterate that neither aid nor good wishes can be expected, now or in the days to come, from this quarter. Obligations are reciprocal, and when one party has failed another, the cessation of obligatory feelings from the injured can be designated with no word other than Justice; certainly with none of the words you suggest. My obligations, Mrs. Herz, are to sons and daughters, family and Church, Christ and country, and not to Jewish housewives in Detroit. On close examination you shall find this last statement not altogether villainous; the villainy you attribute to it may well arise from an excess in yourself. You have defied your father, your faith, and every law of decency, from the most sacred to the most ordinary. I should imagine that those who defy are subject to interesting feelings when they must beg. It remains to be seen whether you shall ever have the character to defy what all good people have always had to defy—their own sinfulness—and seek an annulment through the offices of the Church. The obligation of the sinner is to rectify his sins; and since that path which leads to rectification and glory is one of humiliation and pain, I shall have no choice but to continue myself with a course of action that

*shall render the life you have chosen unrelieved of privation. For
it is privation that shall lead you to The Shining Light.*

He sat on the bed, then floated, fell, died on the pillow. At
first he did not ask himself why or how or when she had written;
there was only the fact: *she had.* The letter rested on his chest,
and for a moment he wondered if perhaps now he could rest.
But even with the wind knocked out of him, it seemed he could
not; breathless, he was up off the mattress suddenly, hunting.
He poured out the contents of the trash can, sorting through
wads of Kleenex; on the damp floor he crawled halfway under
the bed; he looked through his wallet again. But he could not
find the paper with Smith's name. Then, with nothing better to
do, he counted out the money—he ruffled and snapped each of
the bills like a businessman, but they gave him none of what
they gave the businessman. It seemed that he did not so much
hate giving away this money as he hated himself for having it
to give in the first place. Confusion. Terrible confusion. He returned to the bed and lay there face down, clutching the
money in his hand. How easy, how soft and easy, he thought,
was the solution in his hand. How easy, how soft and easy, he
thought, was the solution: let go, give up, have a baby . . .

Okay then: consequences . . .

But for the first time he was not afflicted with visions of
dancing dollar signs. His visions were not of loss and chaos.
His family, for instance. Would not a baby's coo soften their
hearts? How could they resist a little dark-eyed child? This
would be different from Libby's conversion; this was nature,
not design. The conversion, which he had masterminded, he
knew now to have been a mistake, the real low point in his life.
He was almost glad that his parents had not been fooled by it.
Nobody else had, not even (most wretched of all) the convert
herself. Yet he had still been dazed enough at the time to figure that something dramatic would knock them all back to
their senses. After all, he was Paul, their son . . . it would forever remain a painful mystery to him that those parents whom
he had never needed could shake him so by deserting him and
his young wife.

It was easier understanding Libby and her parents. The protected child, the sheltered little girl, the baby sister. He could

almost bring himself to forgive her for writing that father of hers. A girl with a past full of Gloriful Heaven and Sweet Jesus could not believe that anything as innocent as their marriage could provoke in others such monstrousness. The values from which their union had grown were the values the world had smiled upon for centuries. Not for a moment was either of them irresponsible; they had not been able to sleep with one another for more than a night without serious and profound feelings. And once they had rushed to confess these feelings to each other, how could they ever part? Oh love—was that the seed from which dragons grew? It was disbelief not greed, wonder not stupidity, that had led Mr. DeWitt's loyal little girl to write to him.

But why had she to *plead* with him? Why ask for, of all things, *money*? How that sanctimonious bastard must have licked his chops! Privation, debts, hunger, fear! And up ahead, ah yes, there she glows, The Shining Light. The miserable sadist! The heartless Christ-kissing son of a bitch! Why should either of them have to plead with him, or anybody? Why must he suck around a dog like Levy? Suddenly he, Paul Herz, was a partner in the screwing of Korngold! And what, *what* was the best, the honorable, the manly course? He could put the four fifty back in the bank. He could give in to nature, let life—his, his wife's, his child's, roll on . . .

At work in the afternoon he knew he had changed his mind out of nothing noble. His decision not to go ahead with the abortion had little to do with any discovery of his own manliness. It was simple. How to avoid going to jail? Have the baby. How to get out from under Levy? Have the baby. How to win back his parents' love? How to make DeWitt eat his words? Simple—have the baby, but deprive that pious louse of any rights to it. If they threw out the daughter, he could give them the heave-ho too! But what machinations—*what cowardice!* The hand he had lifted against the cruel world was now a fist striking against his own heart.

—

Libby arrived home that night before he did. He heard her singing inside, and hesitated with his key; he still did not know what to do with the letter from her father. With no plan at all, he opened the door.

Matters were further confused by the kiss. "I've got control of myself," she said, brushing the side of his head with her lips. "I want to tell you that. I want you to know. I'm glad we had this extra day. I've got control of myself now."

"Good."

"I want to go to bed with you."

"Lib, my wrist—"

"Right now. Let's take advantage, Paul—" She still held him so that he could only feel her body and hear her voice. "We don't have to use anything. Nothing—just the two of us—"

"I'm just a little tired . . ."

"What is it? What's the matter now?"

"Nothing."

"Didn't you go to the bank again?"

"Everything's taken care of."

"What's the matter? I've gotten myself all ready for it. I've changed my attitude. I decided to be a woman about this thing. What's wrong now?"

Taking a deep breath, aware of how impossible he was being, he said, "Let's go to bed, Lib. Let's get in bed."

"Don't oblige me."

"I'm not obliging you. Don't you oblige me."

"I wasn't obliging you. I changed my *mind*."

"From what? I didn't know it needed changing. I thought you had agreed—"

"I can't stand any more of this!" she shouted. "Everything I do is wrong!"

He was shaking the letter at her. "Writing your father was wrong, damn it!"

She snatched it from him, crying, "Do I open *your* mail!"

"That isn't the point! The point is that you can't go crying back to your family!"

"I wasn't crying to him—as a matter of fact I was bawling him out. I was telling him what I thought of him!"

"How much did you say we needed?"

At the last moment, on the point of breaking down and sobbing an apology, she shouted, "Plenty! I said we needed plenty! What's wrong with that? Do you know when I wrote that letter?" She was crying, but not with any loss of force.

"The day we moved in here. That night, that terrible awful night. I wanted him to know, God damn him—I wanted him to know what his selfish mean stupid Catholic crap had driven us to—"

"He didn't drive us here, Libby. We chose to come here."

"I didn't choose it."

"You agreed, damn it! Don't start that. In Ann Arbor—"

"But I didn't *choose* it! I'm agreeing to this abortion, but I didn't *choose* to get pregnant. Oh Paul, I didn't *choose* any of this."

"Are you blaming me for dragging you down in the mud?"

"*I'm blaming him!* That's why I wrote the letter!"

"But he has nothing to do with it, Libby."

She wept. "Then who does?"

There was only one thing that remained to be said. His impulses were all confessional; he almost came to his knees when he admitted, "I do."

She misunderstood; or perhaps she would not allow herself to hear of his weakness. He heard her say, "Are you telling me you're sorry you married me again?"

"For Christ sake, *stop* that! Nobody said anything like that. My blood is like water from all this squabbling. Let's stop it!" But the moment to which he felt he had every right had been denied him. Caring for Libby, he could not be what perhaps he really was. They were—the word came at him with every ounce of its meaning—*married*.

And Libby was whining. "I don't know what to decide any more. Every time I decide to get that thing done to me, you decide I shouldn't."

"I didn't decide anything. I got the money out of the bank, didn't I? I called the doctor last night, didn't I?"

"But your heart isn't in it."

"Oh Libby, Libby, what a dopey statement . . ." He flopped onto the bed.

She kneeled on the floor, holding his legs. "I'm not anything you thought I'd be, am I? I turned out to be really dumb, didn't I?"

"No, Libby." She would confess and confess, and when would there ever be time for his confessions? Couldn't he just relax and be a rat?

"I'm not good enough for you," his wife said. "I know it. I'm just a goddam dope."

"Shhh," he told her. "Get off the floor, Lib. Get off your knees, please. Come up here."

"Paul," she said, beside him, "do it to me. Just the two of us. Nothing in between. Oh," she wept, "at least let's get pleasure out of this. *Some*thing—"

Later, curled in the arc between his knees and shoulders, she said, "I looked up osteopathy in the *Britannica*. I went to the library for lunch."

For the first time in the whole affair, Paul shed tears.

"The American Osteopathic Association," she said, "was organized in 1897. Did you ever hear of Still? He founded osteopathy. Discovered it."

"Never."

"They believe the body heals itself so long as it's mechanically adjusted. There are lesions, and they correct them by manipulation. It's not at all like chiropractors. It's sort of Eastern, in a certain way—Oriental. They study everything, just like MDs. Obstetrics—everything. The American Osteopathic Association was organized—"

"In 1897."

"It sticks in my mind . . ."

He thought she had fallen asleep, but a few minutes later she spoke again. "I looked up abortion."

"Libby—"

"Abortions contributed to sixteen percent of maternal deaths in America in 1943. Or '44."

"Look, Lib—"

"That's nothing, sweetie. When you sit down and figure it out it's a misleading fact. How many maternal deaths *are* there? Say it's as much as three percent. Well, sixteen percent of *that*. That makes it probably one in a hundred thousand. It's safer," she said, reaching back to touch him, "than crossing the street."

"Are you laughing?" he asked, burying his head in her hair.

"I'm smiling, baby. I'm trying to—"

"Shhh—" Paul said. He moved quickly to the edge of the bed, tiptoed to the door and put his ear to it; after a minute he threw it open. All that fell into the bedroom was the dim light from the corridor.

—

So that each minute would not be an hour, he had brought a book with him to read. He carried it in his hand while he paced, just like the expectant fathers in the movies. He sat down and opened an osteopathic magazine. Again he came upon the picture of Dr. Selwyn Sales of Des Moines. His hobbies were reading and his family. His wife was a Canadian. He had taught at Kirksville, Missouri. Missouri! Paul began to search, with no success, for the editorial in which he had seen Dr. Tom Smith's name. He flipped through magazine after magazine until he was nearly frantic. Finally he forced himself to put down the magazines, and started pacing again. The elevator door opened in the hallway. It slammed shut. A figure moved in the pebbled glass of Dr. Smith's outer doorway. Thank God—it moved on. He heard Mrs. Kuzmyak say something. He heard metallic clinking. Had Kuzmyak administered the pentothal? With those oversized brutish pumpkin hands, had she pushed too deep, too hard? He did not even know how many minutes the whole thing should take. Shouldn't it be over *soon*? When she hemorrhaged, what would they do? If there is a body to dispose of—

The door opened and Kuzmyak appeared. "Over," she said, yanking off her gloves. She hadn't even worn a mask! She had breathed her fat greasy germs right into Libby! Over? *What's over?*

"*What?*"

Kuzmyak did not like his tone or volume. "Just let Doctor Tom cover her up," she said abruptly.

"For Christ sake!" Paul rushed through the door just as the doctor's hands were pulling Libby's skirt down around her knees. She had worn the old skirt with the oversized girlish safety pin in front, to make it easier; twice before they had left the apartment she had put on fresh underwear. Her eyes were closed now, but she was breathing.

"It takes a few minutes," Dr. Tom said. But he would not look at Paul. Was he worried? What was going on? "Mrs. Kuzmyak will make some coffee."

Paul took his wife's hand—her blouse was unbuttoned. What had her blouse to do with anything? Asleep, anesthetized, what exactly had happened to her? All those women dropping at Smith's feet—

"Honey? Libby?"

"It takes a while," said Dr. Tom, washing his hands.

"She's all right?"

"Like new."

"Look—is she all right?" He only wanted the doctor to turn and talk to him. "Did you get it all out? Is she bleeding—"

"Control yourself."

"Just yes or no!"

"Just you don't be too snippy!" Kuzmyak was standing in the doorway with a kettle. "Poor Doctor Tom," she said, shaking her head.

"Libby?" Paul rubbed her hand. "C'mon, Lib."

"That one like Nescafé?" asked Kuzmyak.

"Anything." He was rubbing and rubbing her hand, to no avail. "Come on, honey, you're fine, just fine—"

Kuzmyak was standing beside him. "Come on there, Libby." With one hand she rolled Libby's head around, the girl's cheeks jelly between her thumb and forefinger. "Come on, Libbele—wake up, dahling, breakfast is ready."

"Her name is Libby."

"Just trying out my accent," Kuzmyak said, and she went over and poured hot water in the doctor's cup.

"Prop her up a little," said Doctor Tom, sitting in his leather chair.

Kuzmyak came back and pulled the girl up by her armpits. "Okay, let's snap out of it now, huh?"

Libby opened her eyes. She made some sounds. It took her three minutes before she said her husband's name, another three before she began to cry. She drank her coffee through white lips and took an unsteady practice walk around the office.

Downstairs a taxi was waiting that drove them home. "Are you all right? Did it go all right? Nothing hurts, does it?"

The cab turned through the dark streets. "I'm still sleepy," she answered. "Very sleepy."

"I love you, Libby. I love you. I do love you."

"I'm very tired. My arms are just sleepy."

"I love you. I want you to know I love you. I do love you, Libby. I love you. I'll do anything for you. Everything for you, Lib. I love you. Don't ever forget, Libby, that I love you. Please, please, that I love you."

At home he put her to bed, and then with all the lights out he sat beside her. "Was it all right? Did you feel anything? Did you go right to sleep?"

"Yes . . ."

"Don't you want to talk? Do you want to go to sleep?"

"I think so."

"All right. Just go to sleep."

"Paul?" She spoke with hardly any strength.

"What is it, honey? Yes?"

"When I walked in," she said, crying very softly now, "she took off my skirt and slip. I had to stand around in my stockings and blouse—"

He waited for more, but that was it; he heard her weeping, and then after a while he heard her asleep.

Thirty minutes must have passed before the scuffling began in the hall. In that time he had not moved.

First he heard a voice cry out, "Son of a bitch! No good rat! *Louse!*"

"Caaaaalm yourself," Levy was intoning in the meantime. "Caaaalm yourself down."

"Let go, cock sucker! Let me be! I'm going where I'm going!"

There was an unearthly banging on the door, a sound larger than he could have imagined two, three, or four old men making. "Herz! I'm Korngold!" Then: "Hands *off*, you bastard!"

Paul knocked over a chair running to the door; behind him, Libby stirred and mumbled.

The door opened, and before Paul could slam it shut, Korngold fell like a sack in his arms—simply toppled in. Levy was left standing in the hallway in furry slippers and a red satin robe initialed in gold ALL. All *what!* Wheedlingly he said, "Korngold, straighten up, act a man. Step back over here."

"Shush you cock sucker you! Herz, *help* me from him." Korngold struggled up straight in Paul's arms, then freed himself and turned on Levy. "Go! Wait! The authorities will

drag you screaming away! Close the door on him!" he said to
Paul.

"Uh-uh," said Levy, and his cane came poking through the
door. "You wait up a second—"

"Paul . . . ?" All three men turned and looked at her. Libby
had flipped on the reading lamp. Her cheeks were drawn; her
eyes were clouds of black. "Paul—Paul, what?"

"Sick?" asked Levy. "Or recovering?"

"Quiet!" Paul whispered. "Both of you! Now, please, let's
all of us step outside—"

"This son of a bitch—" began Korngold in a trembling
voice.

"Korngold." Paul grabbed the man's arm. "Korngold, please,
be still—now come on—"

Almost crying, Korngold raised his arms and said, "He stole
my underwear. Seven years," he moaned, "and along comes
this cock sucker—"

"*Korngold!*" Paul shouted, and shook him.

"That's the story . . ." the man said. Released by Paul, he
fell, in tears, into a chair.

"Look, gentlemen," said Paul. "My wife is sick. She has to
sleep. This is an outright invasion—"

"You hear him?" said Levy to Korngold. "Come along."

"Oh-oh," Korngold wailed, "thief, *mamza*, rat!"

"He's in hysterics, almost a fit," Levy explained, for now
Libby was propped up in bed, and her bewilderment seemed
to demand a reason, a word.

Paul went to Korngold and laid a hand, a friendly hand, on
his arm. Korngold instantly put out both of his hands, sand-
wiching Paul's. "Help," he whispered. "I'm fleeced still again."

"Mr. Korngold . . ." Paul knelt beside him, aware that now
Levy had moved all the way into the room and was circling
behind them. "Mr. Korngold, tonight you have to pull yourself together. We're going to go out into the hall now. My wife
is very sick—"

"Recovering . . ." he heard, and saw the rubber tip of
Levy's cane near his foot. In the bed, Libby was reddening,
not with health but with helplessness. She kept saying, "Paul,"
while he went on convincing Korngold.

"You've got to go home now," Paul said. "Get some sleep."

"What a life," exclaimed Korngold, bringing the three-hand sandwich up to rest his cheek upon. "I can't go to the toilet, I ain't stolen blind."

"What?" Paul said.

But Levy's cane was as good as in his ear. "We split—is that robbery?" asked Levy. "I moved them jockeys for him before they rot and mildew. A wet spring and he was finished. Is that a thing to throw a fit on? You understand?"

"Twenty dollars is a split?" cried Korngold. "On first-rate shorts? On a quality T-shirt? Die, you bastard, die you son of a bitch—"

"Control, Korngold. Control. You're in the room of a convalescent. Right, Paul?"

Still squatting at Korngold's knees, he looked up at Levy. The lawyer held his caneless hand to his chest, protecting his respiratory system with the plushy satin robe. "Paul," Levy said again—and saying that little word, it was as though he owned the world. "Senile," he whispered. "Don't be foolish, Paul. They would sit in that room till he passes on. Twenty dollars is not nothing. For him almost a month's rent."

"How much did you get, Levy?"

"Add twenty and twenty, what else? A split." He looked over at Libby as though perhaps she was the member of the family with the mathematical head.

"Paul," Libby said, "what *happened*?"

"Please," Paul said. "Please"—he controlled himself so, that tears were squeezed from his eyes—"let's go out into the hall. Let's go into Levy's room." But he could not drag Korngold from his chair.

He said please again, and then he said it one final time. In the moment that followed all sense fled, all plans; all the rules of his life deserted him, and he expelled a confused, immense groan.

Korngold looked at him in fright and awe. "*What*—" he cried.

Before it even happened Levy began backing away. But Paul had already grabbed him by the throat with two aching hands.

"Stop *pinching*!" screamed Levy.

"How much! How much was it! How much!" He was foaming, actually foaming at the mouth.

"I'm suffocating to death," Levy cried. He wheeled his cane, striking out at the madman who was whirling him into a corner. "Let go, abortionist! Let go—I'm having you incarcerated—"

Korngold was at last out of his chair, on Paul's heels. "Don't hurt him—just ask—"

"*Give him the money!*" Paul cried. "Give it up, you son of a bitch!"

"Aaaaaaacchhh . . ." went Levy, his eyes showing a sudden belief that the end was really at hand.

"Hey, Herz—" yelled Korngold. "Herz, you'll strangle him dead! *Herz!*"

"I give, I give—" Levy was screaming, his arms collapsing as though broken. "All right, I give!"

"He admits it!" Korngold triumphantly addressed the ceiling.

And then Paul felt Libby's arms pulling him back. Under his fingers he still had Levy's quaking chicken neck, still felt the disgusting bristly hairs. "*Paul,*" came Libby's voice. "Paul, oh honey, you're going crazy—"

"Get in bed!" He turned and took her by the hair. "Get in bed! Are *you* crazy! *Get in bed!*"

Her expression was incredulous, as though having leapt from a window, she had her first acute premonition of the pavement below. She winced, she wilted, and then she took two steps backwards and gave herself up, sobbing, to the bed.

But Levy was now in the doorway, slicing the air with his cane. Everyone jumped back as he made a vicious X with his weapon. "Disgusting! Killer!" he cried, slashing away. "Scraping life down sewers! I only make my way in the world, an old shit-on old man. I only want to live, but a murderer, *never!* This is your friend, Korngold," announced Levy. "This is your friend and accomplice, takes a seventeen-year-old girl and cuts her *life* out! Risks her life! Commits abortions! Commits *horrors!*" He gagged, clutched his heart, and ran from the room.

Breathless, Paul approached Korngold and took his arm. "Now you get out too—"

"The money—"

"That's your business."

"But I need—"

"Just get *out*!"

Libby still sobbed on the bed. Korngold, a man with all chances gone but one, looked wildly about him and, in a crazy imitation of his attorney, suddenly rose up and waved his cane at Paul's head. Paul only snarled, and Korngold dropped it; he fled then, not to the door, but to the girl on the bed. He took her head in his arms. "Oh a darling *yiddishe maydele*, a frail fish. Come, darling, tell me who I should call. I'll dial your good family, let them come take you—"

"I *have* no family," Libby sobbed.

"Libby! What is this! What's going on here! Korngold, get out! *Get out!*"

"Paul . . ." Libby begged. "*Paul*—"

"*Shut up!*"

"A monster," said Korngold, and he hid his face when Paul raised his hand.

"I give you three, Korngold!" And Korngold, looking once at the girl—his heart, his soul, his very being, in his eyes— Korngold disappeared.

"God damn you, Libby! God damn you!"

"This is the most horrible night of my *life*," his young wife cried.

—

He sat up all night in the chair. Near four—or perhaps later, for the buses were running—he walked into the hall. He hammered twice on Levy's door.

"Levy!"

No answer.

"Levy, do you hear me?" He kicked five distinct times on the door. He started to turn the knob but, at the last moment, decided not to. From the darkness behind the door might not Levy bring down a cane on his head?

"Levy—listen to me, Levy. You never open your mouth. You never in your life say one word to anybody. Never! I'll kill you, Levy. I'll strangle you to death! Never—understand, you filthy son of a bitch! I'll kill you and leave you for the rats! You filth!"

And that last word did not leave him; it hung suspended within the hollow of his being through the rest of the night, until at last it was white cold daylight.

—

Had everything worked out? Wife all right? Satisfied? Fine—
he did not mean to pry. Only one had to check on Smitty. He
fed the osteopath patients—almost one a month—but still it
was wise to keep an eye on the fellow. Every once in a while
Doctor Tom seemed to forget about slipping Dr. Esposito his
few bucks. You know what I mean? Not an entirely professional group, osteopaths. And how's the wrist?

3

The rottenest moment of all. All the lies and errors, but now these thoughts. Get up and go—he wrote, snow piling on his office window, on Iowa City, the river, the prairie, on all his brave plans and principles. *Stay here. Stay. Give them what time it takes. He'll crawl into our bed and free poor Libby. Am I crazy? No, let her go, let Wallach be the answer, this soft rich boyish boy, not-a-care-in-the-world boy. I only envy him all that free-and-easy business, not the money. But it's not my nature. Anything can be your nature. Make it your nature! Impossible. I should just write everything out. 1,2,3, et cetera. An outline, what I want and don't. What I'm not and am.*

1. (Face it.) Let them kiss in our bed, let him devour her, caress her, absolutely drive a wedge right through her loyalty to me. Take her loyalty away! Wheedle her, urge her, greet me at the door (fly unzipped, why not), say: Your wife spread everything for me mouth legs heart. Now we leave you. We leave you! *Then leave! Wallach will make her happy. But what couldn't? The normal progression of life, a fearless approach, an honest unselfish open loving, and the girl would blossom, come back to life again. Squabbling, bickering, fighting is all we do. Honey forgive me baby I'm sorry. Squirm. Beg. Grovel. Where was my mistake? The first mistake. This is devious and I know it. Something is simply missing in me. All that has happened doesn't just happen. Go ahead, progress. Wallach carries her away. Now 2. Face 2.*

2. Marge. A stranger. A different face, is that all? How long can I hold to the story that I was seduced? Not long. Plaintive and moping, sad, inviting, she knew what she was up to. But I knew what she was up to. Crying. Calling Wallach names. Her calling Wallach heartless perked me up! Is that seduction by any stretch of the imagination? Who tore whose clothes? How different— not since the beginning, with virginal Libby. My wife. I did the tearing. Me. Endlessly me. When she phoned, when we were just drinking coffee, didn't I already know? All her loneliness talk, all the talk of betrayal and subterfuge, and on my face what splendid concern. What sympathy. All the time I shook my head yes yes, poor girl.

3. Marge. Write it again. Margie. Margie. Marjorie. Say my name, she said—and I said it. Now say what we're doing—and I obliged. Screwing games. I could have carried those boxes and suitcases down the stairs and put her in a taxi for the station and then gone home. I knew the minute we began to talk. And did I need it? For ten minutes thrashing on Wallach's bed? But there was nothing to worry over. Just plain sweet coming, without Libby underneath. Libby underneath! Libby. My wife Libby. Libby and Paul Herz. What next? Next is this. Urging on another to fuck my wife. Say what we're doing. Say it, Paul. Libby. My Libby. Fuck my Libby. Take Libby. Take Libby away!

4. She leaned; I did not deliver. I could never stop organizing anything. I couldn't leave well enough—bad enough—alone. Pay my way, take my lumps, have my baby. Circumstances. No, me. No! I married her with ideals, all right. Hopes. Love. Caring. I cared for her into the ground. To elevate our lives. To be happy. To be good. What causes pain is that I still want the same. Nothing I do gets it. I fuck Marge, you fuck my wife. All right. Stop saying it.

5. What else? Biding time? Taking my time while Wallach is making his pass. Waiting for Libby to throw off her dedication. She will. He will. Unless I discouraged him. Take your car and shove it! I probably frightened him away. I frighten her. They all think what I am is what I'm not. I said to him stay out of my life when I meant come in. Make the girl a decent offer—an indecent offer. Relieve us, please. Everything is out of hand. Though not entirely—until one week ago. No, out of hand with the abortion. No, just one week ago with Marge Howells. A silly stupid girl, and that was more ruinous than what happened in Detroit. This very minute feeling has run out of me. More ruinous and so on. Do I mean a word of this? When I feel pain am I really even feeling pain? What am I doing here, Iowa? This writing business. Who am I trying to emulate? Asher? No. I'll come to understand my mess. Keep writing.

6. Why not have a baby now?

7. Start over. Make love to her. Be kind. Be soft-spoken. But it's she who bitches all the time. Don't let her. Take control again. But I have no force left.

8. Get force. Pull yourself together. Get force.

9. Suppose Marge tells Wallach. He tells Libby. Then tell her myself. Confess. Admit. Start over. We're young. I had guts turning down Wallach's car. But sense? I was trying to muster strength. I knew what I was. Not going to tempt Libby, because I saw her being tempted. I even made up my mind: make perfect love to her. Touch her. I cannot touch her. *Do it! Reach out a finger and do it! Once, then twice, and then life will come rushing back again. I know this is not insane. Perfectly natural, a mountain slide in my life. Only start up the other side. But I ruined it.*

10. Tenth commandment. Nothing. It's up to them. I have stayed away. Gabe and Libby. Libby and Gabe. Paul Herz. Do they know? Does Libby? Can she see that I want for her only the best? Do believe me, Lib! Right from the beginning. The first day, and still. Am I only stupid?

—

Midnight. *Libby* confessed. Wallach kissed her. She sobbed for an hour. Nothing more happened. Nothing. A precious girl. A precious girl. I'm ripping all this up. Every word. Start over. Try!

THREE

The Power of Thanksgiving

1

"Is it still baseball season?" frail Mrs. Norton was saying, trying—despite the inclinations of her frame to gaunt melancholy —to be jolly. With an unconvincing display of live-liness, she threw some jeweled fingers toward the bellowing TV set. Everybody around her turned for a moment to show a mouthful of toothy kindness. All her recent tragedies had made the rounds.

Dr. Gruber, sensitive as a bag of oats (which he resembled), wrapped an arm around her waist, and she whitened. "That's football, my dear girl," he cried, lipping his spiky mustache. "This is my alma mater, preparing to knock the tar out of that Cornell bunch. Anybody here for Cornell be prepared to shed tears!" he shouted, almost directly into her small ear.

Unspinning herself from the doctor, Mrs. Norton explained to anyone who would listen, "My goodness, it's as loud as baseball. I only know the world of sport through my husband. He had a box at Sportsman's Park—" She was all filled up but no one seemed to know she was speaking. She crept off to have her tomato juice iced by the silent, appreciative colored man who was tending bar in the dining room.

I went over to the set and turned down the volume knob. Settled into the two velvet-covered love seats that had been dragged in front of the machine were several of the paunchier, more afflicted men present. For the moment I only recognized and greeted Dr. Strauss, who had arthritis, and Sam Kirsch, my father's diabetic accountant. My father himself was gliding about on black patent-leather shoes he'd bought in Germany; he was endearing himself to J. F. and Hannah Golden, but soon he slipped away from them and released his high spirits on poker-faced Henny Sokoloff, widower and diamond king. When he finally came around to the TV screen, Dr. Strauss raised the toe of his shoe toward my father's seat. I heard my old man cackle, and, in his exuberant mood, he turned the sound up again. "Any score?" he asked. "Nothing nothing, it hasn't started—get the hell out of the way," Strauss scolded him. In the meantime, Mrs. Norton was standing beside the orange sofa, stirring her cube around. With the set blaring away again, carrying to all ears the measurements of the Penn linemen, she raced in tears for the nearest bathroom. Two startled people spilled drinks, and a silence drifted for a moment over the rest of the widows, widowers, and aging couples.

Later I saw my father stroking Cecilia Norton's hand, while she tried several gallant, coughy little smiles. Mrs. Norton had been a college friend of my mother's; after her marriage she had moved to St. Louis, where her husband was in the beer business. There he had made millions, suffered four heart attacks, and then died of pneumonia brought on by a case of the mumps. A week later she had had a breast removed. When she came on home to New York, having finished up in St. Louis by paying three doctors, two hospitals, and a funeral home, she telephoned my father. It is an indication of all his thoughtfulness and all his blindness that he tried to interest Gruber in her. But if anybody should have wooed Cecilia Norton, if anybody should have unfurled a soft palm for that small lame bird to rest in, it should have been himself. He didn't, however, and it probably did not even occur to him; all that had happened to him was drawing him now in another direction. He went off to Europe . . . But let me take things up in order, at least the order of that day.

A buffet dinner was laid out during the third quarter of the game. There were bottles and bottles of liquor (aside from Mrs. Norton's juice, and club soda for Sam Kirsch) and much of it had already been consumed when the appetizer was carried in. By the fourth quarter what appeared to be mouselike portions of turkey, candied sweets, and salad decorated my mother's Moroccan rug. Its dull green was bleeding a little red with cranberries, and ice cubes melted at a slow pace under chairs. Millie went starchily to and fro—for she had memories of other Thanksgivings too—and knelt between people with her dust pan and a damp cloth. "They should know better," she informed me, and then carried our slops back to her kitchen.

The purpose of the party was to celebrate not only the

national holiday, but the triumphant return to these shores of
my father and Dr. Gruber. This accounted for much of the levity and a good deal of the whiskey; imbibing had never been
important in our family Thanksgivings in the past. But for four
months the two widowers had been gone from us, and now all
the strays and waifs in New York had been gathered together
to see that they were alive, kicking, and full of information as a
consequence of their lengthy educational experience. They
had drunk the water from Oslo to Tel Aviv, they had slept in
forty-eight different beds, traveled in twelve countries, and
snapped several thousand pictures—and now they were ours
once again.

The air of celebration hung on for a good long time, and
even when the holiday spirit waned, the semihysteria of several
of the women kept a decidedly Dionysian mood about the
place. Then around half-past three came the first dying of spirits. Women stared for brief, deep moments over the shoulders
of their companions; well-dressed, not too faded, sparkling
women drifted away from us for seconds at a time, as though
having visions of the past, of Thanksgivings clear back to Gov-
ernor Winthrop of Massachusetts. Photographs began to appear; mince pie was balanced on laps, while little boys and girls
growing up in distant corners of the world made their debut.
"My daughter Sheila's little girl in Los Angeles . . ." "Mark's
son in Albany . . ." "My Howard's twins in Boulder, Colorado . . ." "Geraldine in Baltimore, Adam in Tennessee,
Susanna and Debby in Ontario." "Canada?" "Yes, Canada."
"That's nothing," said Dr. Strauss; he extended one arm back
over the love seat and handed around a snapshot of Michael
Strauss, age six months, in a baby carriage in Juneau, Alaska.
Alaska! Sure, my son's a metallurgist. But Alaska—how far is it
by plane? Far, says Strauss, turning back to the football game.

Suddenly there was traffic, most of it to the two bathrooms.
Women repaired their eyes in all the mirrors of the house.
Men blew their noses into expensive handkerchiefs. One's son,
one's grandchild, one's own flesh and blood, miles and miles
away . . . For a short while well-fleshed backs were all one
could see in the room. But through some miracle—the miracle of alcohol, companionship, of everybody feeling his obligation to the Pilgrim fathers—the party did not dissolve into old

people collapsing on the floor and beating their hearts with their fists. For a suspenseful few minutes it hung just above that—Mrs. Norton almost turned purple with sadness right in the center of the emptying room—but then feet began to ache, stomachs became gassy, and a little heartburn had to be taken care of. Groans and sighs took precedence over the deeper pains, and full bellies rose and fell in exhaustion. The women sat with heads back and arms folded; the men slept. A general mellowing took place, and the knowledge spread—silent, but electric—that there were thousands and thousands in the world in exactly the same fix as those aged gathered here. With the food moving through the system, the blood thickening, there came the hour of philosophy; outside the window the day turned purple and gold. This was the way of life—separation and loss. To be eating, drinking, to be warm, to be *left*, that was something. At least those who remained, remained.

I saw my father's iron-gray hair dart down to a woman's hand. This happened in the corner of the room near the spindly little Jane Austen desk, where the gas-and-electric bills had always been filed by my mother. The hand was not Cecilia Norton's; she had departed fifteen minutes earlier, a slice of pie—for her maid—clutched in wax paper to her mink. Goodbye, goodbye, Mordecai. Goodbye, Cecilia, poor Cecilia . . .

No, the hand to which my father had placed his lips had arrived draped on the arm of Dr. Gruber's vicuña coat. At first I had taken her for a visiting relative of Gruber's. Her name was Silberman, but *Fay* was the little word, the only word, that left my father's lips after he had raised his head to speak. Fay was obviously tight, and tight a shade beyond the others. Every hair of her bluish-gray coiffure, piled and elegant, was in place, but she was not so lucky with her eyes, whose lids obscured half the bleary pupils, nor with her mouth, nor with her jaw which, set off by a splendid pearl necklace, hung down just a little.

Dr. Gruber had already plugged in the slide projector. Millie was pulling shut the curtains, a little wearily, like a seaman running up the sail for the twentieth time that day. Shut out gradually was the grapy, wistful, end-of-holiday sky. The bartender was unrolling the white screen, and Millie heaved to the last inch of curtain, and I was left with a last inch of sky, streaky and somber and unforgettable. I had then one of those moments that one feels he will possess till death, but are somehow gone by morning. My most poetic emotions took hold of me—as a result, I think, of a general giving in, an uncomplicated and unconditional surrender I allowed myself after all the genial, good-natured crap I had been handing out through the day, since the previous night, in fact, when I had stepped off the plane. I caught that last inch of sky, and if skies have messages that one did; it told me lives go on.

A slide flashed; color, various and make-believe, came back into the living room.

"This is Venice," Dr. Gruber announced.

"*Florence!*" cried a woman behind him.

"Listen, Fay, all you saw was the vino."

"It's Florence, lover-boy," came Fay's voice, "nevertheless."

Dr. Gruber cleared his throat. "This is Florence," he said. "The water got me confused. That's the Arnold. It's very beautiful at night. And that's their old bridge. The Germans blew up the other ones. The Italians hate the Germans."

Next slide. The bartender peered around at the screen, while running a dishtowel over some glasses.

"The Bubbly Gardens," Dr. Gruber said. He raised his hand, making a shadow across the picture. "Also Florence. It was too hot to walk around there, though. Very famous gardens. Right in the center of Florence there." He changed the slide.

"What's *that*?" Everyone was laughing.

"Ah, *that's* cannelloni! Good old cannelloni! I ate it morning, noon, night, every day. That's my hand, see, with the fork in it? Cannelloni! Mother's milk!"

He turned to show everyone his mouth, curled up, raising the ends of his mustache. He changed to the next slide and we were back in the Boboli.

"We *saw* that," called Fay. "Get to the ones with *me* in it—"

"That's only a thousand, sweetie-pie," answered Dr. Gruber.

"Ah, *there* I am," explained Mrs. Silberman. And there she was, in her orange life jacket, one elbow resting on the ship railing, the whole great gorgeous Atlantic sky a backdrop of her blue rinse.

"This is Madame Pompadour in her evening gown," Dr.

Gruber informed us. "This is where the lovers met—our first life drill there on the Queen Elizabeth. Terrific service. And that's her, you see, Queen Elizabeth herself, caught by Mordecai in an unguarded moment. We had to wait ten minutes for her to comb out her eyelashes."

"Not funny," moaned Mrs. Silberman, Greta Garbo now in the dark reaches of the room. "Next slide, Dr. Gillespie."

"Mordecai in the market. He bargained that fellow there down to fifteen dollars for a straw hat for our companion. Mordecai's the guy with all his teeth. Ah—there's Queen Liz in her straw hat. Behind her is the Official Gallery there in Florence, which we didn't get a chance to get inside. Queen Elizabeth was shopping."

"Where's Queen Elizabeth?" asked some confused man, coming up out of a nap.

"What?" I heard the Queen herself whispering; and then she broke into laughter, laughter that for a moment shocked me, so much did it sound like tears.

"Rome!" a voice shouted.

"That's all of us"—Gruber threw a shadow again across the picture—"in the Roman Forum."

"Get your hand out of the way."

"That's all of us in the Roman Forum," he said. "Ain't a helluva lot of it left, you see, but that's where it all happened thousands of years ago. Caesar's buried there—"

"That's Venice!" Mrs. Silberman announced.

"Shhhhh." My father was trying to quiet her giggling.

"That's Vienna, Stanley," she called to Dr. Gruber. "Right outside Cannelloni—"

"Quiet in the rear," Dr. Gruber said over his shoulder. "That's the Forum." The slide flipped on.

"That's—oh, that's that little town right outside Florence. That's where we ate lunch. You see, there I've got it again, that's me eating my cannelloni." Gayly, Gruber moved ahead. "That's . . . oh, Christ, that's *Oslo*. Turn the lights on, will you? Mordecai, you got these all mixed up."

"That's Australia," Fay was saying. "That's Cannelloni, Australia." But now the lamps on two end tables were aglow, and everyone was sitting up and blinking.

As I rose to leave the room, I looked back to see my father glaring down at his companion. She was sleeping—or pretending to—with her mouth open and her cheek resting on his shoulder. He did not see me look, but he must have seen me leave, for in a moment he was standing next to me in the hall.

He said, "What's the matter?"

"Nothing. Nothing at all."

"Your face looks different. Where are you off to?"

"Nowhere. I have to run an errand later." I had made certain to keep the errand—which I wasn't even certain I *would* run—out of my mind all day. Now it came to my lips spontaneously, as unnecessary excuses are apt to. Adding mistake to mistake I said, "I was going to use the phone."

"Go right ahead."

"You don't mind—"

"Not at all—"

"—if I call Chicago."

"Call Cannelloni, Australia," he said, giving me a smile brimming with uncertainty. More soberly he said, "Just don't run off there on the next plane."

I touched his shoulder. "What are you talking about? I'm here for the whole weekend. I just want to say Happy Thanksgiving to a friend."

"A woman," he said, taking my hand.

"A woman who invited me for Thanksgiving dinner. What do you think of that? I gave her up for you."

"That's my boy," he said, rapping me on the arm with soft knuckles. "That's fine. That's terrific." Then he moved so close that he stepped on my toes. In a conspiratorial voice he said, "Fay Silberman, Gabe, is a very nice woman. A very fine person. She's had a lot of tragedy in her life. One sunny day she goes outside her place in South Orange and her husband is being driven all over the lawn in their power mower. He's dead in his seat. It was a horrible thing. He crashed into a tree with that damn machine. She's had a hell of a time. She's a good companion. You didn't think I could get around a whole continent with just Gruber, did you?"

"She seems very nice."

"Give her a chance, Gabe."

"I didn't say anything, honestly."

"You don't seem to be having a good time all of a sudden."

"I ate too much," I said, trying to smile. "I'm fine."

"Thanksgiving is a very hard day for all of us. She just drank too much. This was a great shock to her. It's not even a year. What do you think, Penn whipped Cornell like that?"

"Knew it all the time."

"Ah, the hell you did," he said. Then he hugged me; and he hung on. He rubbed his bristly cheek against mine and started to say something, but had to stop and deal with a little trouble in his throat. At last he said, "Everything's going to be all right. I'm a young man, I'm going to be all right. Knock on wood, I've got my health. I'm not going to be a burden to you any more."

"You're no burden," I said, but already he was moving back into the dark living room, where I heard Gruber holding forth. "That's Lady Godiva and a bottle of Chianti wine in front of the Leaning Tower of Pisa. I wouldn't go up in that thing for a million dollars. I've got news for you, if they're not careful—"

———

The phone in Chicago was answered by a small girl with a mouthful of food. The operator said that New York was calling for Mrs. Reganhart; would the little girl please stop clicking the receiver and call her mother to the phone. The phone dropped and the child screamed, "Oh, Mommy! It's Daddy!"

My confusion did not really become full-scale until the mother answered with a timid and uncharacteristic "Yes? . . . Operator? This is Martha Reganhart."

"It's not Daddy, however," I said.

"Oh, for Christ's sake!"

"Shall I hang up?"

"Certainly not—my child's drunk on Mott's apple juice. How are you?"

"Fine."

"*Where* are you?"

"Daddyland. New York."

"Oh, do excuse her. She gets overexcited when she's not in school. I think she's reacting to the company," she whispered.

"Who's there?"

"An old friend. He stimulates the children."

"And you?"

"No, no. No—that's true. Listen, I'm sounding tragic." But she wasn't; only forlorn. "How's Thanksgiving? How's your father's party? Is there really a father and a party or is some tootsie nestled beside you in her underwear?"

"I call in the absence of the latter."

"It's very sweet of you to call. Happy Thanksgiving."

"I'm having a nice unhappy one."

"Just a minute, will you?" She left the phone, but nevertheless I could hear her voice. "No, it is *not* Daddy! I *am* telling you the truth, Cynthia! Go talk to Sid, he's all alone. Cynthia!" She sighed into my ear. "I'm back."

"Good."

Why it was good I couldn't say; neither of us spoke.

"Well," she admitted finally. "What else is there to say?"

She was right, of course, for we hardly knew each other; I had not realized how strange it was for me to be calling her long distance until I was in the middle of the call. I had taken her to dinner some weeks back, and we had laughed and joked until the waiters stared, but that had not increased our knowledge of each other very much. Then she had called to ask me—and a nervous little exchange it had been—to come to Thanksgiving dinner. And now this. Strangely, I found myself waiting to believe that I had some rights to her total concern and attention.

I said, "I just wanted to say Merry Thanksgiving to you."

"Thank you."

I was preparing to hang up when she asked, "Shall I go ahead and invite you to another meal? Will you eat leftovers when you come back?"

"I'll be back Monday."

"Come then for dinner."

"Thank you, I will." Then I said, "Who's Sid?"

"He's a man who just asked me to marry him."

"I see."

"You'll come Monday night."

"As long as you're still single, I suppose so."

"Single as ever," she said.

"Does that upset you?"

"Specifically no; generally I'm not sure. This is some long-distance conversation."

"Long distance should be outlawed anyway. Were you expecting a call from your husband?"

"My *ex*-husband—from whom I have no expectations whatsoever." I heard a loud noise rise up behind her. "Oh God, my
son just hit my daughter with a chair or something. Give my
love to the girl in her underwear."

"You give my love to Sidney."

"We can't possibly be jealous over anything," she said, "so
we shouldn't really play at it. Should we?"

"I'm a little deranged today, Martha. I wonder if we'll ever
manage to be level with one another."

"You come Monday, Gabe. I'll be single." Then, all at once,
she did level with me. "They shouldn't outlaw long distance. I
feel you've saved my life." It was the sort of statement I had
come to expect her to qualify with irony; she didn't, however,
and so neither did I.

Instead I said, as though it were some revelation of character, "There is a father and a party, you know. And I look forward to seeing you."

But even while I spoke, she was explaining, "Sid is Sid
Jaffe—he was my lawyer. He got me my divorce half-price, and
I'm very indebted to him, Gabe, and the children are crazy
about him, as crazy as they can be about anybody, anyway. And
I have to stop talking on your money. Forgive me, please."

I remained seated at the phone table. There were some
eight hundred miles between us, and yet our acquaintanceship
had taken a sharp and serious turn. And when I had come out
into the hallway I hadn't even been intending to call her! She
had been the escape hatch, to put it crudely, through which I
could crawl from that new and startling image of my father.
During the previous spring he had gone to see a psycho-
therapist; he had been advised to travel; he had been advised
to spend large quantities of money, to enjoy the company of
women, and if possible to give up all mystical activities for a
period of six months. He had even asked me to take his long
trip with him, and when I offered my job as an excuse, he had
settled upon Gruber. And now, face to face with the results of
that trip, I had called Chicago.

I reached down and brought out the big Brooklyn telephone directory, mostly out of a feeling that if there was any

call I should have made, it was the one I had been asked to make. Millie was charging past me, still starchy and angry and efficient. "You call this an American Thanksgiving?" she asked. "Smells to me like New Year's Eve. Your father's become ultra-European, you know," she said, turning up her nose.

"Times change, Millie."

"Thanksgiving is Thanksgiving, young man!"

Light fell into the hallway from the living room, dull, apricot light, very comforting to find creeping along the rug and up your toes. The conversations I could hear from the lighted room sounded revitalized; aside from Mrs. Norton, nobody had made a move for the exit, though it was nearly four thirty. All their houses were empty; they stayed on.

I opened the Brooklyn directory and found the name I was after. I marked it, realizing that if I had turned to Martha Reganhart to escape my father, I had also called her so as to escape an old friend as well. Libby Herz had asked me to call—to call upon—her husband's parents. I have found in my life that I often phone one person when I expect myself, or others expect me, to be phoning someone else; it is what the telephone company calls displacement.

Libby and I had managed well enough, respectably enough, since her arrival in Chicago. Though I had discovered that the feeling we had for one another had not changed after three years and one letter, I nevertheless got through the early fall without doing anything I can think of to make the feeling concrete. Then, just before leaving Chicago for Thanksgiving, I had run into her quite accidentally on Madison Street. I was going into Brooks Brothers, and she was headed for Goldblatt's and then the Downtown College, where she was taking a course. My shopping expedition happened to have been of no significance, for I was after a hat. A real man's hat, you know—brim, crown, the works. It was to be my first; I was full with the knowledge that my father was waiting for me in New York, fresh from his world travels ("with a surprise" he had guaranteed me on the phone), and I had somehow reasoned that it would be to my advantage to confront him behatted. I felt at once gay and doubtful about the venture, and when I ran into Libby I asked her to come in with me to give her opinion.

Even to myself I do not think of it as an invitation innocent of charm, nor do I think of her acceptance as so innocent either.

My taste in personal effects is conventional, running to a kind of quiet fussiness, and marked by a decided Anglomania, common enough to my profession, I think, as well as my class and generation. That afternoon, however, I indulged my cabinet-minister inclinations with the wantonness of a Turk. Actually it was only of late that I had begun appreciating the pleasures to be derived from spending money on myself; as a child and youth, others for the most part had spent it on me. But with Libby, during those two solid hours of accumulation in Brooks, I unearthed new possibilities in capitalism, I saw that things are not going to be so easy for the Russians as they may think. There is something life-giving and religious in out-fitting yourself.

Back on the street we surrendered ourselves to shame. The Balboic, the Columbian emotions I had first experienced upon discovering myself in the full-length mirror, now washed right by me. And that absolute delight and sparkle in Libby's eyes—for it was she who had egged me on, past the fedora to the homburg, and on then to the puce gloves, the tight-rolled umbrella, the long lisle stockings, the garters, the ties, and finally to the glowing, noble scarlet smoking jacket—the sparkle that had given to Libby's face such incredible life, that had won envy for me from every man in the store, ran out of her eyes now in two barely visible tears. I knew I should never again be able to kid myself, even if I returned the smoking jacket the following day, into feeling lofty or virginal about our relationship.

"I have to run off—I have a class at six—I have to have a bite. I'm going, Gabe."

"I don't feel very splendid, Libby, about this whole silly in-dulgence."

"You . . ." She almost laughed, crying. "You look splendid. You look terribly splendid."

"I'm walking toward the train," I said.

"I'm going to have one of those dollar-seven steaks." She went off in the opposite direction, toward State Street.

And so there I was, under sunny skies, tapping the pavement

with the tip of my umbrella. I caught a glimpse of myself in a shop window. What a dandy! How weak and feeble! Some match for my father and his surprise! And then hurtling at me from behind, practically flying, came Libby's reflection. I turned to catch her, and she reached out with her hands to my new—our new—gloves. There on Madison Street, just within earshot of Michigan Boulevard, we came the closest we had come to each other in Chicago.

"In New York," she said, breathless from running, "go see Paul's family, will you? Oh, Gabe, just tell them, will you, about his job, that I'm working, that I'm going to school, that everything is working out? Will you, *please?*"

"Yes, sure, Lib—"

"Just tell them."

On the train back to the South Side I could not work out in my head exactly how the lines and angles of our triangle had altered; nor could I begin to see what my visiting the elder Herzes would do for everybody's well-being that it might not do to their detriment. I did not care either for the tone the mission had of a soldier paying a call on the family of a dead buddy. Despite definite feelings of obligation, I had a very imprecise sense of who I was feeling obliged *to*. In Chicago that day (and once again, sitting at the little phone table in my father's apartment), Martha Reganhart began to loom in my head—and subsequently in my heart too—as a green, watery spot in a dry land; I felt in her something solid to which I could anchor my wandering and strained affections.

Why I had called her now seemed perfectly clear. I slipped the Brooklyn directory back into the table and went into the kitchen, ostensibly because my mouth had gone dry, but actually, I think, to come close as I could to the pure, unspoiled realities of the holiday—the greasy turkey pan, the dirty dishes, the still-warm oven, the aromas of a happy and spontaneous American family life.

Fay Silberman was there, her head over a coffee cup.

Since I couldn't simply turn and walk out, I went to the sink and ran some cold water into a glass. Mrs. Silberman rose and smoothed her shaky hands over her smart velvet suit. My admiration for the fight she was trying to put up against her condition did not particularly alter my attitude toward the condition itself. She had made a silly fool of herself in the living room.

"We haven't had a chance to talk," she said. "You resemble your father remarkably."

The father, I realized, was about to be courted through the son. All the desperation I had been witness to during the long afternoon suddenly centered for me on this hungover, handsome, game, miserable woman, who had been beauty-parlored nearly to death. Her hair floated and glowed like a sky, and her face had been lifted and was too tight; her nails, ten roses, were long enough to sink deep, to hang on, tenaciously. She was heartbreaking, finally, but I wasn't in the mood.

"I look a little like my mother too."

"I haven't seen any pictures of her," she said.

"There are several in the living room."

She smiled hard, the end of round one. I summoned up whatever good sense I had accumulated over the years and came out like a small, affectionate dog for round two. "My father looks fine—he hasn't looked this well in years. The trip seems to have done him a lot of good."

"All he did was laugh. He laughed all the way through Europe."

"He can be a very happy man," I said.

Her answer confused me a moment. "Thank you," she said. "Nobody . . ." She swayed, tilting in some private breeze, but found strength against the sink. "Nobody should miss it. Europe. It's just another culture."

"Are you feeling all right?"

"I feel fine!" Then, focusing her eyes on the wall clock, she added, "I had too much to eat."

"So did I—"

"Don't hate me, young man. You have no right to hate me!" She slumped down into a kitchen chair and covered her eyes. I did not know now what to say or do, and only prayed that no one would come into the kitchen. "I have children of my own in California," she said, as though that were some threat against our home.

"Excuse me, Mrs. Silberman. I have to be going."

"Your father said you were here for the weekend." She spoke almost with alarm.

"I have to go to Brooklyn."

"I've never been to Brooklyn in my life." I wondered if that was supposed to have been a gay remark. Was she soused, or stupid, or both? "You better stay," said Mrs. Silberman, turning regal before my eyes. "After coffee, your father is going to announce our engagement." She stood up, quite steady now —the weather in the kitchen having calmed for her purposes— and turned to face me. I took a sip of water, waiting for my own responses (which were slow, very slow), and when I looked up again what I saw was that her face had gone all to pieces. "This is a wonderful thing in everybody's life. Don't you go throw a monkey wrench," she begged. "You're *supposed* to be an educated person!" Her whole body stiffened with that last plea.

"Maybe you better calm yourself."

"I'm not an invalid. I'm a very young woman. I'm fifty-four. What's wrong with that? I've had a shock in my life. I chose your father, after all, not Dr. Gruber."

I had to admit that her choice was meritorious, and whatever she might have thought, I had no intention of being caustic, nor anything to gain thereby; in fact, I wanted for personal reasons to give her all the credit her selection deserved. Unfortunately for all our futures, I chose the wrong words. "You did well for yourself."

"I make him laugh. It's more than anybody else in his family ever did! I make him feel important!"

"You don't know a great deal about what's happened, Mrs. Silberman. Lives are complicated and private."

"I know more than you think," she answered; and then with the wildness, the unbuttonedness of someone who has lost most of his perspective and a few of his faculties, she added irrelevantly, "Don't *you* worry about that!"

Fifteen minutes later we all stood at attention in the living room and drank a toast to the affianced. Mrs. Silberman's champagne ran down her chin, cutting a trail through her powder.

—

As soon as I pushed the buzzer to Paul Herz's parents' apartment, I knew I should have called in advance—perhaps simply called and left it at that. I pulled myself up to my full height, dropped my gloves into my hat and rang again, this time with a premonition that when I left this building, in fifteen or twenty minutes, I would not be the same man I had been when I entered. The boundaries of my own personality seemed as blurry and indefinite, as hazy, as the damp blowy mist above the river I had crossed from Manhattan.

A wide blubbery man with a jovial, self-pitying face answered the door; I had never seen a man so young so fat. Drifting between his voluminous trouser legs, sweeping past his thinning brown hair, came the sounds of television and talk. Friendly enough, he said, "This is four-C."

"Do the Herzes live here?"

"Sure, sure, come on in. I'm sorry—" He raised his arms to signal some mix-up and smiled helpfully over nothing.

"I didn't mean to interrupt anything."

"No-no-no." He was a very helpful person.

"Who is it, Maury?" a voice called.

"Come on in," Maury said to me. "We're just leaving. We live in the building."

I followed him down a long narrow corridor that was lit by three little bulbs meant to resemble candles; along the hallway at waist level hung a row of tiny framed documents. Before entering the living room, I bent over and took a close look at one of them: it was a grammar school report card made out to Paul Herz.

A woman in her early twenties was standing before a logless fireplace, one hand on her hip and the other out in front of her, making a point to a bathrobed man in a BarcaLounger. A shiny black pump stood beside each of her feet; the lines of her cocktail dress, a close-fitting black crepe number yoked daringly in front and fitted tightly at the knee, were the lines of her almost lovely figure—unfortunately her posture and the lines were not in exact accord. All she needed, however, was to suck in her little paunch and heave backwards with her shoulders to make perfect the whole works. But it was almost as though she didn't care to be perfect; tall and erect and exquisite, she might not have known what to make of herself. "So my sister-in-law said," the girl was explaining, the borough of her birth winding down through the faint arch of her nose, "this is my sister-in-law Ruthie from Roslyn. 'Look,' she said, 'if the child is *not* happy there, what's the sense? All that money, it's ridiculous. The child's happiness is what's uppermost, certainly, but if the child is not *happy*, if the child is not having herself a good time,' she said, 'then the money is money wasted.' And personally, Ruthie, to my way of thinking, is *right!*" The final dentalized *t* in *right* buzzed once around the room and then flew up the chimney. "I don't believe in that kind of money being wasted on a child. My brother-in-law Harvey doesn't find it growing on trees, believe me. The child can be perfectly happy at home."

The bathrobed man she was addressing glanced across the room at a tired-looking woman seated in an armchair, who I took to be his wife, and Paul's mother. "Absolutely," he said, as if it were a forgone conclusion that everyone was better off at home. "What's wrong with Brooklyn College?"

"Absolutely . . ." And then my presence was all at once recorded. Maury had been blocking me out, and now I was past him, into the living room, where despite the animated conversation, the TV set was on. The screen showed three men dressed as Pilgrims, scanning the horizon from the railing of a ship. "It looks to be land, sir," said one of them in an Anglo-Irish accent—while I said, "How do you do, my name is Gabe Wallach."

"Yes?" replied the man in the BarcaLounger.

"I'm a friend of your son's," I said. "Of Paul's. How do you do?" I looked away from the astonished face of Mr. Herz to the face of the young woman; it had not actually collapsed into horror, but considering the stiff, pretty, frozen face it was, it did display, all at once, some marked change.

"Maury," the girl said, stepping into her shoes. "I really think we have to run, doll." The heels gave her legs their final touch of beauty. "I keep tasting turkey," she said, half-smiling at me. I smiled back, with understanding; it was not that I had brought the plague into the room, it was simply that she had eaten too much.

Maury came up now to Mr. Herz, and smoothing for him the collar of his white terry cloth robe, said, "Look, take it easy, kiddo. Give yourself a couple more days rest. Stay off your feet, you'll wear the carpet out, huh?"

"Don't run on my account—" I said to Maury, who seemed a kind of bulwark to me against the worst. "Please don't," I said, and my eyes settled at last on Mrs. Herz, whose own eyes had been settled on me since I had come in and announced whose friend I was.

"No-no-no." Maury's meaty comforting hands moved away from Mr. Herz and onto my shoulders. "We had Thanksgiving out in Great Neck, and I'm telling you, kid, we're exhausted. We left the kids out there with their grandparents, and now we're going to enjoy a little peace and quiet. Look, take it easy, Leonard," he said, turning back to Mr. Herz, "stay off the carpet, will you, for a few days—"

"Leonard, I'll lend you *Marjorie Morningstar*."

"Look, Doris, I'll be all right."

I heard a sigh of hope rise from Mrs. Herz. Her husband went on. "It was indigestion. Something stuck in my chest, overexcitement. I'm fine." But he became vague even while he spoke.

"Just don't rush back," Maury said. "I've got everything under control, Leonard. Harry is taking care of yours." Now he strode to the club chair where Mrs. Herz was sitting and he placed one hand on either of the plastic coverlets that protected the arms. I could see only his back, but I heard lips smack together, and Mrs. Herz's hand came up onto his neck. "God bless you, Maury," she said.

Maury stood up and ran his thumb across her cheek. "How are you? Are you all right, sweetheart?"

"Look," said Mrs. Herz. "I'm all right if he's all right." And the voice of the martyr was heard in the land.

Just then Doris approached me. My heart went out to something in her that was simple and bored and satisfied; I actually had an impulse to take her hand as she went past me, and felt a personal sense of loss when she and her husband slammed the door of the Herzes' apartment behind them.

"I hope I haven't interrupted," I said. "I should have called." But behind me—a sound sweet as a rescue plane buzzing a life raft—a key turned in the lock and a hinge squeaked. There was a whispered exchange, then Maury's voice. "Mr. Wallach," he called, "I think you dropped something out here in the hall."

Dutifully, unthinkingly, Mrs. Herz rose from her chair to serve my needs.

"No, please, I'll get it," I said. "Excuse me."

In the doorway, Maury's tiny hooked nose, droopy cheeks, fleshy lips, and round little gray eyes all tried to come together in a smile, but mostly worry was written on his face. Doris took my hand and whispered, "Stop on the way out, *please.* Six-D. Horvitz."

"Okay."

"Be careful, kid, will you?" Maury said. Doris still held one of my hands; Maury took the other. "I'm Paul's oldest friend," he told me, and then the two of them turned down the hallway, past everybody's milk bottles. They went the first few feet on their toes.

When I came back into the living room I was met by the image of a united front. Mrs. Herz, with something of the pioneer woman about her, was standing beside her husband. I smiled at her, making believe that I was returning to my pocket something that I had dropped outside. But the woman had a bitter, drawn face that would not respond. She was tall, like Paul, but not skinny; rather she was hefty, large in the hips and feet and shoulders. Her hair had thinned on either side of the part and it bushed out from her head around the ears and neck—the genetic source of Paul's black kinks. Her coloring was spiritless, a brownish-gray. Mr. Herz was also old and worn. Coming directly from scenes of middle-age rejuvenation, the sight of them was uncomfortably shocking; I had almost forgotten that most of those within earshot of eternity look as if they hear just what they hear. Not everyone can afford a mask, or wants one.

"Take a seat," said Mr. Herz, for I was the soul of politeness, and that finally got to him. "Would you like a glass of soda?"

"No, thank you. I only dropped in."

"Darling," he addressed his wife, "get me a little seltzer."

"Are you all right?"

"Sure, sure, I'm fine. I'm excellent. Only my mouth tastes bad."

No sooner had Mrs. Herz left the room than her husband

shot straight up in the BarcaLounger, almost as though he'd been ripped down the center with the electric pains of a stroke. His face like a piece of crumpled white paper against the ruddy leather of the chair, he turned his palms down and supplicated with them, up and down—the motion of the umpire when the runner has slid in under the tag. "Please, please," he whispered, "she's having a very bad day. *Please*." A fizzing sound approached from the kitchen, and he settled back into a posture that struck me as an open invitation to death. In that one moment he appeared to have used up a week's energy.

His wife handed him a little glass on a coaster. "The glass is warm," he said. "It's practically hot."

"I put it in a warm glass. Cold is a shock to the system."

"Who likes warm seltzer, for God's sake."

"Drink it, please." It was as though now that he didn't like it, it would do him some good. While he drank, his hand went up to his chest and he performed various stretching gestures with his neck. Having thus coped successfully with the carbonation, he turned back to cope with me. Mrs. Herz returned to her chair—the edge of it—and her husband cupped his glass on his belly and took a businesslike but civil approach.

"Very nice to meet a friend of Paul's."

"I'm pleased to meet you. Paul asked that I stop in to say hello."

Nobody responded; was it so blatantly a lie?

"You live here?" Mrs. Herz demanded, putting the question not so much to me as to the puce gloves. "In Brooklyn?"

"My father lives in Manhattan," I said.

"What are you, a lawyer?" I was numbed by her particular brand of naïveté: it seemed a cross between xenophobia and plain old hate.

"I teach English at the University of Chicago. Paul is a colleague of mine."

"A colleague already." She made a face of mock awe toward her husband. "Next thing we know he'll be president of the college."

"He's doing very well. It's a very good university."

She put me quickly in my place. "Schools are wonderful things wherever they are," she said. "I was a teacher myself."

"He teaches English?" Mr. Herz asked. "What is that, spelling, grammar, that business?"

"One course is Freshman Composition. Then he also teaches Humanities."

"I see," they both said. Mrs. Herz seemed pressed to add something knowledgeable about the humanities but gave up and only grunted general disapproval of whatever that title encompassed.

"Libby works for the Dean of the College, you know."

No one knew; no one cared. "She's one of my favorite people," I said, and was rewarded for that complicated extravagance with a flush that took minutes to subside. Fortunately, the Herzes were now immune to anyone's feelings but their own. "She also takes courses in the evenings. She's a very hardworking girl."

"Sure, sure, sure," mumbled Mr. Herz, but the object of his certainty did not seem to be the subject of my conversation.

"I was visiting in Manhattan for the holiday, and so I came over here. I hope I haven't interrupted anything," I said, limp with my own repetitiveness.

"Mr. Herz has been sick," his wife informed me, having actually stared me into silence. "We decided to stay home for the day. Who wants to get tied up in all that traffic?"

"Yeah, we decided to stay home," Mr. Herz said. "We were going to go to Rio de Janeiro for the weekend, but we decided to stay home. Look, I think maybe I can move my bowels," he told his wife, and instantly she was out of her chair and freeing him from the languorous curves of the BarcaLounger. He insisted on walking under his own steam to the bathroom.

"Leave the door open a little," she said to him.

"All right, all right." Newspapers covered the floor at the entrance to the kitchen, and he crossed over them as though they were ice. Some seconds later the bathroom door shut. Mrs. Herz left the room hastily; I heard her call, "Are you all right?"

"I'm all right."

"Don't strain," she said. "Leave the door open."

Back in the living room those eyes that had so examined my habit and person now were kept carefully averted; she fussed about, straightening things.

"Is he very sick?" I asked.

"He has a terrible heart." She folded and refolded the afghan that had lain across her husband's feet.

"I'm sorry to hear that."

"What kind of courses—" she asked suddenly though her back was all she would show me. "She's going to school forever?"

"Who? What?"

"Her."

"Libby," I said, and waited for Mrs. Herz herself to repeat the name. I waited; then I said that Libby had not yet finished with her A.B.

"Sure—she was in a big rush." She came back to her chair, acting as though we hadn't been conversing at all. "You all right?" she called into the other room.

We both hung now on the reply, which was not forthcoming.

"Leonard, is everything all right in there?" And again she was up and off to the bathroom.

"I'm all right," her husband called. "I'm all right."

"Don't strain. If nothing happens, nothing happens. You're not engaged in some contest, Leonard." When she returned to the living room, she said, "He's having the worst day he's had in years."

"That's too bad. I'm sorry." I was sure that now I was in for some lecture from her. But I did not depart; I felt bound to wait for Mr. Herz's ascension back into his easeful chair.

"You teach what—law?" she asked.

My garb, my prosperity, my Harvard tones—and Mrs. Herz's colossal disappointment. I had not suspected that what she had always wanted her little Paul to be was an attorney. "No. I teach English, too."

"And what's humanities? What does Paul know about humanities?"

There was an intention in her words that I did not understand immediately. "It's a kind of literature course," I explained. "It's an introduction to literature. Paul teaches it very well. He's a very good critic, very sharp."

"He was always critical." She acknowledged the painful truth with a slow wagging of her head. "Suddenly nobody was good enough for him. In his whole life we never asked him to do one thing, one favor. He came home and told us he was going to Cornell—that was good enough for us. He was going to work in South Fallsburg, we wouldn't see him for a whole summer—we never said a word. We gave him all the independence he wanted. Maury Horvitz—his mother was always running his life. Maury drink this, Maury drink that—she used to run to school with his rubbers if it was only a little sun shower. Paul never had to put up with that. We always recognized his independence." She was picking threads from her apron while she spoke and depositing them in the pocket of her house dress. "But he wounded his father in such a way," she said, coming down with a fist on her knee, "you can never imagine it. He made that man an old man. One thing we asked him in his whole life. One thing." She held up a finger to convince me of the tininess of their request in the face of the vast universe. "He gave his father a wound that man will never forget. His father worked like a slave for him all his life, took every chance, and all he got was bad luck and a terrible slap in the face. Some Thanksgiving," she said, and with her lip trembling, she removed herself from the room.

Minutes went by, and then I heard her ask, "You finished?"

"I'm finished."

"You feel all right?"

"A little tired."

"I told you don't strain. The doctor told you—"

"I didn't!"

"You just let Mother Nature do the job."

I rose and waited for them to enter the living room. In my mind I ran over what had happened and what had been said. Had I done less than I believed Libby had intended for me to do? What more was it possible to do? I was no magician; her marriage to Paul was going to have to heal itself or finally rot away without my intervention. As I heard the forlorn sound of Mr. Herz's slippers cautiously crossing into the living room, I was moved to sorrow for him—and then to suspicion toward his adversary. At that moment, in fact, Libby seemed to be *my* adversary; I recognized how much craftiness there was in her behavior toward me. What craftiness there happened to be in my behavior toward her, seemed to me a craftiness of reservation and restraint, a decorousness on the side of virtue. If I was at fault, it was because I had actually permitted myself to be a good deal less crafty at times than it was my obligation to be. I felt a little abused by her, a little made a convenience of, and I shared momentarily in that suspiciousness toward her that this heart victim and his wife had allowed to ruin the last years of their lives. There must be some weakness in men, I thought, (in Paul and myself, I later thought) that Libby wormed her way into. Of course I had no business distrusting her because of *my* weakness—and yet women have a certain historical advantage (all those years of being downtrodden and innocent and sexually compromised) which at times can turn even the most faithful of us against them. I turned slightly at that moment myself, and was repelled by the sex toward which at bottom I have a considerable attachment.

I took my leave with soft words; I did not feel the shame of the intruder so much as his misguidedness and self-deception.

"Good luck in your new career," Mr. Herz called after me.

Though I could not locate the inspiration for his congratulatory remark, I thanked him. He lifted one hand as though to wave, then only rubbed it softly, with a sense of surrender, across his delicate chest.

I was halfway down the street when I remembered Doris and Maury Horvitz waiting for me in 6D. I turned and came back along the treeless block and entered the red-brick Tudorized apartment building where only one thing had been asked of Paul Herz in his entire life. The building was called "The Liverpool Arms."

When Doris whisked open her door and whisked me in, I felt as though I'd been followed. Once I was safely over the apartment threshold, she relaxed inside her toreador pants and white blouse and directed me to the living room with a copy of *Harper's* which she was holding in her hand. We were surrounded on all sides by pale blue carpeting and very low furniture. The room appeared to have been decorated with a special eye out for the comfort of aerial creatures. There was a lot of flying space over our heads, but if you happened to be a simple biped you had to chance it with your ankles through a Scandinavian jungle of coffee tables, throw cushions, and potted avocados. Maury's figure hogged a blond Swedish chair that cradled his behind no more than three inches off the carpet;

like Doris, he had changed into home attire, and was now sporting a pair of trousers the watery pastel color of some fruit-flavored Popsicle. They were cotton and baggy, and in place of a belt they had a three-inch band of elastic that could be stretched to accommodate the wearer. In the spectrum I would place them at cherry-raspberry. He had tiny, multi-colored slippers on, and I noticed how thin his calves and ankles were; there was a kind of buoyancy about him, in fact, as though once out of the low chair, he would rise to the ceiling and bump helplessly along it. Tapering down as he did, he reminded me of a Daumier barrister. He greeted me with a tremendously appreciative smile, and I realized that all that fat made him think of himself as a good guy. His lithe and sexy wife begged me to settle down on a cushion, and offered me a cup of Medaglio d'Oro. I accepted, and her black toreadored behind moved westward into the kitchen.

"Talk *loud*," she called, "so I can hear."

"We'll wait for you, Dor," her husband answered. While we waited, I noticed a photograph on the hi-fi cabinet; Maury noticed me noticing it. It was a large framed picture of Doris in a bathing suit. Maury said, "We'll be going down there again in a few weeks. Right after Christmas. It's terrific. It's fabulous."

"I'll bet," I said affably.

"You get a terrific sense of a good time down there. Everything they've got there is to make you comfortable and to give you a good time. Even the lobbies. After all, what do you do in a lobby? You wait for somebody, you kill time. But even there they've got your sense of beauty, of restfulness, in mind. Doris is crazy about it. All she talks about before we go to Miami is Miami, and all she talks about when we come back from Miami is Miami."

It left one with the impression that Miami was all Doris ever talked about, but I only showed her husband my admiration for his good luck. He did not, however, need my admiration; Maury seemed to be convinced that he had some moral edge over the rest of his generation simply by way of having taken his wife to spend their winter vacations in Miami Beach. I wondered what kind of advice Maury was going to give me to take back to Paul. What word was I to carry to Chicago

from the world of heavy food and unbroken family relations?
Maury's flashy up-to-date possessions crowed their master's
satisfaction and contentment. How did he do it? What was the
solution? I was asking not just for Paul, but for myself as well.
How do you love girls like Doris? How do you keep life going
exactly as it was when you were ten years old? That day I
wouldn't have minded arranging such a life for myself. I began
—or perhaps continued—in Maury's living room, to miss my
mother and to miss the past.

"Just a minute," Maury suddenly said. "I want to show you
something . . ."

When he returned he was holding a baseball in his right
hand. He gave the ball to me and I turned it slowly around so
as to read the inscription.

> *To that Great Battery*
> *Much Horvitz and*
> *Paul Herz—*
> *Your pal*
> *Kirby Higbe*

"Mush was my nickname," Maury said. "Higbe spelled it
wrong. Everybody was screaming at him anyway." He placed
before me next a photograph that he'd been holding in his
other hand. I took it just as Doris came back into the room,
carrying a tray. I felt Maury's fingers on my shoulder. "That's
Paul, there. That's me, with my arm around him. Christ," he
said, "we were like this," and he showed me with two fingers,
one twisted around the other.

In the picture Paul looked at twelve or thirteen pretty much
what he was now, except that his kinky hair came down in an
even line almost to his eyebrows. Maury was a round-faced bar
mitzvah boy, all cream sodas and smiles and surprises. "That's
Heshy Lerner," Maury said. "He was killed in Korea, and the
rest of the guys are everywhere. A lot of the guys have moved
to the suburbs, but I don't know, I love this block. To me
there's nothing like the city. Does Paul ever mention Heshy?"
he asked, making the ball roll up his forearm and bounce off
his elbow. "I wonder if he even knows he's dead."

"Heshy dead is just impossible to believe. Just thinking

about it," Doris said, setting out some frozen strudel she had heated for us, "is something. He was a terrific dancer, remember, Maur?"

"Heshy was a terrific everything. He was going to be a commercial artist. He used to draw caricatures of everybody, and Paul used to write little captions for them. They were the two talented guys, all right. Boy, I'm telling you . . ." He shook his head—a man of eighty walking through his small-town graveyard.

Now all three of us were on cushions around the coffee table; I was the only one still wearing shoes. We all drank out of demitasse cups that the Horvitzes had picked up on a cruise to St. Thomas, and every time Maury finished one of the tiny portions, Doris—with one hand on his leg—poured him another. I envied him his wife, nearly to the point of covetousness; and curiously, the envy did not diminish, the muscles in my chest only tightened another notch when Doris said, in the purest Brooklynese I'd ever heard, "Oy am I really tired. I mean I'm really beat, Maur."

But Maury brooded, even while he ate his strudel; he seemed occupied with the disappearance of the past. Then back in the present, he asked, "How did it go?"

"Mr. Herz seems sick," I said. "They both seemed very tired."

"He looked awful today, Maur." Doris was resting her head on her husband's knee and she tipped her throat back so as to look up at him when she spoke. "They both make me feel sad. They both have no life at all. Maury tried to get them interested at least in books, you know? We get Book of the Month, we get *Harper's* and *Look*, we belong to Play of the Month—" She threw an arm toward the wall behind me, to which I turned to find half a dozen framed *Playbills*. "We go to the Temple lectures, and we volunteer, we'll drive them there, right to the door. Last week we heard Dore Schary, and they wouldn't even go. They won't do *anything!* They sit, they mope, they worry, they live in the dead past. Personally, to my way of thinking, I don't know what the end is going to be for them."

"How come Paul didn't come himself?" Maury asked.

"What?"

"How come Paul asked you to come?" He reminded me of my father's accountant trying to get to the bottom of some tax problem.

"Paul didn't ask me," I said. "Libby did."

"We never met her. Neither did the folks, you know."

"The Herzes?"

"Never met her," Doris said.

"They did, though," I said. "They met her twice."

"I mean Paul never had her for dinner or anything," Maury said.

I agreed, though I knew I had been taken advantage of—rather, Paul had.

"What is she like?" The question was Doris's.

"I'm very fond of her," I said. "She's sweet and fragile and a very loving girl."

I had the feeling that not one word I had spoken had sunk in.

"I used to go out with Paul myself," Doris informed me. "Then he went away, you know, and I don't know, he came back, and we just didn't have the same interests. He was very gloomy to talk to. Remember, Maur?"

"He became an intellectual," Maury explained.

"I see," I said, and I suppose that at that moment I began really to tire of them and that damn leaning over the coffee table. Maury, however, was not nearly so insensitive as I thought; he caught whatever small flicker of boredom and resentment had crossed my face.

He said, "Paul just carried it too far there for a while, that was all. I mean he was all right," he added, cuing his wife, "he was always *Paul*."

"Oh he was a terrific *fella*," Doris chimed in. "Nobody ever said anything about that. You know, *my* interests must have changed too. I'm not saying it was strictly one-sided."

Here Maury decided to direct us all to the heart of the matter. "But the tragedy," he said, "is his folks. That's what you've got to face."

"They seemed very unhappy," I said.

"They're losing out on a lot of fun in their late years. This could be a terrific time for them, but they've just given up. They live like hermits."

"Hermits is right," Doris said. "It's terrible." She offered me more coffee.

"No thanks," I said.

"I'll just have to throw it out," she said. "I can't reheat espresso, it loses something." To pour she had to lean her face very close to mine; meanwhile, Maury did some serious thinking. It was clear that there was a good deal of satisfaction for these two in caring for Paul Herz's parents, if not his memory. But the way I had heard it, the tragedy the elder Herzes were suffering was a tragedy they had themselves constructed.

I said, "Don't you think, somehow, his parents might call Paul?"

I went no further; Maury looked at Doris, Doris at Maury. "*Please*," Doris said.

What seemed a solution to me was a cut-and-dried impossibility to those in the know. No, no, absolutely not! However, if there was something that *Paul* wanted to do at long last, if there was any humanity left in him (the humanities!), then perhaps what he should begin to think about was getting to work—that was Maury's phrase, getting to work—and bringing into the world a child for his mother and father to cherish as once they had cherished him.

"When they have a baby," said Doris, the last word on the struggle of the generations, "then that'll be that. What else?" she asked, showing me her palms. "We have two, and my parents, believe me, are having a whole new life through the grandchildren."

"Gabe," Maury said, frank and serious, "you know Paul probably better now than I do." But with his practical business head, I knew he did not believe I knew anything better than he did, except perhaps how to parse a sentence. "Gabe, would you do me a favor, do us all a favor? When you go back there to the University, when you see Paul and his wife, would you tell them that Maury Horvitz, Mushie, sends his regards? As far as I'm concerned, personally, I mean, whatever Paul did was all right with me—"

"Look, nobody's objecting to *that*," Doris announced. "Whatever he thought he wanted to do, he should have done. Nobody's denying him that."

"But his father is a sick man, we *see* how sick he is every day. This is something Paul doesn't see. And his mother is giving herself up to that man, she waits on him hand and foot. Just like she always waited on Paul. That woman has aged in three years in a most terrific way. As far as I'm concerned there's only one thing that can keep those two from just drying up and dying—"

"Maury—" said Doris.

"A baby!" declared Maury. "A baby would heal that rift, I *know* it. Gabe, I would write to Paul myself, I would tell him my feelings on this whole thing—but to Paul I'm probably just an old friend he doesn't even remember. But you could tell him. Somebody *has* to tell him. You can't be selfish all your life. Paul was my best friend, but he always had a tendency to be a little selfish. Not to think of the other guy. Just a tendency, but still . . ."

"I'll tell him," I said, as the phone rang.

"Thanks, kiddo," Maury said, taking my arm. Then he was on his sprightly elfin feet and had picked up the phone, which was pale blue to go with the carpet. I really couldn't stand him.

"Hello? What . . . No-no-no. Just chatting . . ."

"Who?" Doris whispered, and for an answer Maury merely had to close his eyes.

Doris nodded. She said, sotto voce, "They call three times a day."

When Maury hung up, he said, "I have to go down for a few minutes. Leonard says she's hysterical. She keeps crying about Thanksgiving."

"I hope I didn't do it," I said. "I probably shouldn't have come."

"How could *you* know?" Doris demanded in her singsong voice. "She's been like this for a week already."

"I'll be right back," Maury said.

"Take *Marjorie Morningstar*," Doris said. "Maybe they'll read it. If he'll just start it," she explained to me, "I'm sure he'll be gripped. Have you read it?"

"Not yet," I said, and began to get up.

"Wait a minute," Maury said to me. "I'll be right back."

"I have to run on home myself."

"Why don't you wait until I talk to the folks? I'd appreciate that."

"Sure. Okay." I sat down on the cushions.

When we were alone, Doris lost a little of her composure, or whatever you may choose to call it, and began to hum. She said finally, "You don't look Jewish, you know?"

"No?"

"You look Irish."

"Not really. Not Irish."

"Well, you know what I mean. Paul always looked very Jewish."

"I suppose so."

"You ought to read *Marjorie Morningstar*," she said. "It's about a girl who one of her problems is, I don't think she wants to be Jewish. I think maybe Paul ought to read it."

"You think I ought to recommend it to him?"

She did not know what to make of my response. She said, "Look, it's just funny when a boy you went out with marries a Gentile girl. I mean I always thought of Paul as a very Jewish fella. He worked in the *mountains*, he never got in any *trouble*, he went to *college*, he had a good sense of *humor*—and then he turns around and does a thing like that. I don't think those things generally work out, do you? Most divorces are intermarried, you know. Maybe Paul's will work out, I'm not saying that. I'm sure if Paul picked her she's a very nice girl. Certainly I have nothing *against* her. I don't even *know* her. It's just, I don't know, none of us expected it. Do you get what I'm talking about?"

"I think so. Yes, I do."

"Let me give you an example. Maury—now Maury, I mean you just know Maury wouldn't do it. Maury is a very Jewish fella. He's a very *haymishe* fella. To him a family is very *important*, a nice place to live is very *important*, he has a good sense of *humor*—" She got up off the floor and went to the piano, where there was another framed photograph. "This is Maury," she said, carrying it back to me, "with Ted Mack. Ted Mack from the Amateur Hour. You know Ted Mack, don't you?"

When I told her I did, she seemed somewhat relieved about my chances in the world.

"Now, Maury could have been a singer. Maury could have been a terrific singer on the style of Frankie Laine. Maury is a very interpretive fella with a song. He won two weeks in a row on Ted Mack, and when he lost, it was only to that little Rhonda whatever her name; you know, the one who had polio and overcame it. I mean that's very nice, but it certainly didn't have very much to do with talent. Maury was very unfortunate with that whole thing. Still, two weeks is definitely not nothing, and Arthur Godfrey was very interested in Maury, and the phone calls were coming in from agents for a week. In fact, we had a friend whose cousin was Ed Sullivan, so I mean anything could have happened. I mean Eddie Fisher just happened to meet Eddie Cantor and that was the whole thing. What I'm getting at is that Maury is a very different fella from Paul." Her point—some point—made, she took the picture back to the piano. I stood up to stretch my legs.

"When I met Maury," Doris was saying, "I had only really stopped seeing Paul because he went away to Cornell. Otherwise I don't know, I probably would still have been dating Paul. I was in NYU and I personally did not even know Maury was a friend of Paul's, can you imagine? And I was in this psychology class, and the first day in walks this very attractive fella, and it was Maury. And I knew how he had been on Ted Mack already, and what a terrific showman he was, and Maury asked me out, and then we just saw each other right on through, and then we got married. And that's it."

"And that's it," I said.

"Yeah," she said mousily, and shrugged her shoulders. "That was all really. We met each other and we liked each other and that was all." She put one hand on her hip; she seemed almost to have become angry with me. "I mean I never put out for Paul, you know. I mean I knew I would marry Maury very early."

"In life?"

"You remind me of a guy in *Marjorie Morningstar*," she said. "Noel Airman. He's an intellectual, you know, and also a wise guy. When I was reading the book, in fact, I was thinking of Paul. I'll bet he turned out a little bit that way too."

At this point I kissed her. I closed my eyes, dreaming of the simplest, the very simplest of lives.

For a second she looked nothing more than irritated, as though out on a picnic the weather had taken an unexpected turn. But then she bit her lip, and life became, even for Doris, a very threatening affair. Then that passed, too. She turned her back on me. I took my place on the cushion, and for the next five minutes neither of us said anything. She broke down at last and began to file her nails.

Maury came back shortly after. "I calmed her down," he said. "I told them Paul was thinking of having a baby. Even the old man got some blood in his face."

On that note I left.

—

The lights were out at home and I took it that everything had been cleared away and all were asleep. It was after midnight—I had come back from Brooklyn by way of the Village, where I had stopped off at several bars I used to habituate as a young man (a younger man) down from Cambridge. But the girls were the same and the boys were the same and so were the jazz musicians. I had enough beer to make me feel exactly as uncomfortable as the same amount had made me feel years ago, and then, whistling "Linda," the hit song of 1947, I had taken the Eighth Avenue subway home, the end of an atavistic day. I had spent much of the day looking for some door that would lead me back into the simple life, but I had not found one. On the subway I had a vision of dopey Doris Horvitz in bed snuggling up to Maury; then I had a vision of myself, spinning further and further from my youth, and kissing as I went all the women who had ever entered Paul Herz's life.

I sobered quickly at the entrance to the apartment. Though the lights were out not everyone was asleep. Gruber was in the living room showing himself slides, while in a posture of abandon—or rather in the posture of one abandoned—Mrs. Silberman was flung across a love seat. Her head lolled over one end, and one arm hung to the floor, dripping fingers. Over the further end, her hooked knees were weighted in place by two exhausted, earthbound legs. My father was rolled up on the sofa, his big jaw cradled on his knees. I stood in the doorway unnoticed as all the world flicked by. I watched them ride a gondola in Venice and mount the Acropolis in Greece; in the doorways of cathedrals in Paris, Chartres, and Milan, they all stood grinning. Beside the river Seine, my father took a woman's hand.

Gruber, thinking himself unobserved, made various noises; some were necessary to the maintenance of his body, the rest were appreciative, recollective. I came into the room and whispered hello, though it would have taken a cannon to awaken the two sleepers.

"Sit down. Want to see Europe? Want to see how the other half lives?" he asked. "Ten countries in fifteen minutes. England, Scotland, Belgium, Holland, France, Andorra—"

I plunged down into the deepest chair I could find and groaned like a man twice my age. "I've been to Europe," I said.

"Not in style, boy," the doctor said. "Bet you've never seen little Andorra. Look at that, that's me eating cannelloni in Sorrento."

"I think I saw you eating cannelloni in Fiesole."

"I ate it everywhere. Do you know the three smallest countries in Europe?"

"Andorra," I said, "and two others."

The wind leaving his sails came whistling by my ears. "Okay," he said, "a wise guy like your old man," and clicked off the machine. And then the room was dark, except for what light came up from the street below. We both burrowed into our chairs, witnesses only to our own thoughts and the deep sleep of the others.

"Look . . ." Dr. Gruber began.

Well, at least I would not have to bring it up myself; he too knew a mistake when he saw one.

"Yes?" I said, inviting him not to be shy.

"Look, who's this E. E. Cunningham? What's he trying to do, put something over on the public?"

"What? Who?"

"E. E. Cunningham. He writes poems. Does he think he's going to put something over on the public?"

"I don't think so. I don't know."

"What is that stuff supposed to be anyway? A *poem*?"

I had been willing to raise my mind out of grogginess for a discussion of the crisis in my home, but I could not manage to drag it higher, to manage Gruberian literary criticism. I remembered that when he had read Hemingway in *Life*, it had been me to whom he had come directly with his complaint: "What is this guy supposed to be, great?" Now, I supposed, Cummings had been quoted in *Time*, or, who knows, the *ADA Journal*. Culture is everywhere.

"I don't think the guy's going to put anything over on anybody. People," Gruber said, "have got a lot of native sense."

At that moment I couldn't think of anybody I knew who had a drop, but I only nodded my head. I said, "Dr. Gruber, I hate to change the subject, but don't you think she drinks a good deal?"

"Who?"

"Mrs. S."

"Fay? She's a good-time Charley! She's a terrific gal!"

"But she drinks a lot. Is my father drunk?"

"He had the time of his life—he's a new man. Christ, he was a melancholy specimen. Now he's topnotch."

"Do you think he's going to be happy, Doc?"

"What's the matter with you, boy? He *is* happy. Look at him now—he's smiling, for God's sake, in his sleep. We had the time of our *lives*." He suddenly leaped up. "Here," he said, "I want you to see some happy faces."

He flipped on the machine. "Switzerland! Just before we left. Skating in November, can you imagine?"

Alas, we were on a lake, cupped between two white peaks. Dr. Gruber was holding up Mrs. Silberman under the arms; the two of them were laughing, their heads thrown back, their mouths open. Over at the left-hand edge of the picture, stood my father, wearing a feathered Alpine hat and his gray pin-striped suit. Like the others, he was on skates, but his attention didn't seem to be on the sport.

"Look at her *ankles*!" Dr. Gruber said, but I was looking at those two eyes that were the color of my own. They were directed toward the distant mountains, fastened forever on the impossible.

———

In the morning, of course, neither Millie nor I, nor either of the lovers, commented on the fact that once again at our breakfast table sat three.

2

SARAH VAUGHAN awakened Martha Reganhart. She twisted around until she had plugged "Tenderly" out of her ears with her sheet and pillow—but then Markie was in bed beside her.

"Where's the turkey?"

"Honey, it's too early. Go color, go back to bed—"

"Sissy's playing records."

"Go tell Sissy to turn them off."

"I don't know how."

"Tell Cynthia to. Markie baby, Mother's beat. Will you just give her five more minutes? Tell Cynthia to tell Sissy to turn down the volume."

"What?"

"The volume. Tell her . . ." She caught sight of the whole family's dirty laundry heaped up in a corner of the gray room, and she almost went under. "Tell her to turn down the phonograph." A bleary eye fell on the electric clock. "It's seven, honey—it's a holiday. Tell Cynthia—"

"Cynthia's talking on the phone."

"What phone?"

"She called the weather."

"Oh Christ, Mark, tell your sister to hang up! Tell Sissy to lower the phonograph. Oh baby, your pants are wet—"

"It's going to be clouds all day," Mark said.

"Markie—"

> *You took my lips,*
> *You took my love,*
> *Soooooooooo—*

"Sissy! Lower that thing!"

"I can't *hear* you," Sissy shouted back; and a good forty minutes before it was supposed to, Mrs. Reganhart's day began.

Sissy was in her room, wearing a gossamer shorty nightgown and painting her toenails.

"Sissy, where are the oranges? How do you expect my kids to have breakfast without orange juice?"

"I thought they were my oranges."

"How could your oranges be on the top shelf, Sister? Where's your head?"

"I'm sorry."

"Sissy, yesterday I found a bunch of bananas in the refrigerator. My bananas. Ten million dollars' worth of advertising, and it goes right over your head. I'm on the edge with you, Sissy, I really am. Can't you keep that box off in the morning?"

"Jesus, you just got up. What are you coming on so salty for?"

"Please, do me a favor. Let's make a rule. No Sarah Vaughan until ten. There are two kids here, plus me, right? Either let's make this place a house, keep it a house, or else—I don't know. Can't you even close the door when you take a bath?"

"What's eating you, for God's sake? What are you so prissy about all of a sudden? The kid's four years old—"

"Just do me a favor," Martha Reganhart said, "and close the door."

"I'm claustrophobic."

"You're a goddam exhibitionist."

"For four-year-olds?"

"I'm not even talking about Mark. I'm talking about Cynthia. She's a big girl."

"Christ, we're all one sex."

"There's something about the sight of you shaving your legs in the bathtub that I think has a deleterious effect on her. All right?"

"You think she tends to be a little dykey?"

"That's a bad joke—" Martha Reganhart said. "Why don't you take it back?"

"I will. I'm sorry, Martha. I am."

Martha looked out past the window sill full of cigarette butts into the holiday sky: clouds all day. Oh God. In the room, Sissy's underwear was hanging over chair backs, on doorknobs, and on the two end posts of the bed; one brassiere was hooked over an andiron in the unused fireplace. Sissy herself sat on Martha's Mexican rug (the one she had moved into this back bedroom as a come-on for prospective roomers) painting her toenails. Martha decided not to express the whole new rush of irritation she felt toward the girl. The only roomer Martha could put up with anyway was no roomer at all; besides, Sissy's forty a month helped pay the rent. So she smiled at Sissy—who had, after all, behind those pendulous boobs, a big pendulous heart—and slingshotted a brassiere off the bedstead into Sissy's curly brown hair. It collapsed around her ears.

"It loves you," Martha said.

"You know, I think you're a little dykey too."

"Oh you're a hard girl to fool, Sis." She left the room wondering not how to dispossess Sissy, but simply how to get the Mexican rug back into the children's bedroom.

In the kitchen, she slid the turkey from the refrigerator and found that it had only just begun to unfreeze; she had been so tired when she got home last night that she had gone directly to bed, forgetting to leave the turkey out. "Why do they let these birds get so *hard*?" she said.

"Who?" Mark said.

"Markie, don't you have anything to do. Do you have to walk directly under my feet?"

"Why does that thing have a big hole in it like that?" he demanded.

"Get your arm out of there. Come on, Markie, take your arm out of there, will you?"

"Why does that turkey have a big hole in it?"

She carried it to the sink and turned the cold water on. She rapped on the breast with her knuckle, asking herself why November couldn't have sneaked by without causing a fuss. Holidays were even worse than work days. Couldn't everything, birthdays, Fourth of July, be celebrated at Christmas?

"Why does that turkey have a big—"

"I don't know."

"It's for the sexual organs," Cynthia said.

"Drink your prune juice."

"I don't like prune juice," Cynthia answered. "I like oranges."

"Sissy drank the oranges this morning."

"They weren't hers anyway."

"Yes they were," Martha said.

"You said so yourself," Cynthia replied.

"I made a mistake. I jumped to conclusions." Since her daughter's normal response to people seemed to be distrust, she saw no need to feed her inclinations; perhaps if everybody ignored the trait she would grow out of it. Martha told herself to be more motherly. "Cynthia, are you going to help me with dinner? You want to help stuff the turkey?"

"What's stuff it?" Markie asked.

"Stuffing," Cynthia said.

"*How?*" he pleaded.

"In the sexual organs."

"Cynthia, what's this sexual organs business?" Martha looked almost instinctively to Sissy's door, which closed (when Martha could convince Sissy to keep it closed) onto the kitchen. Behind it Sissy was singing a duet with Sarah Vaughan and dressing; that is, heavy objects were bouncing off the floor, so if she was not dressing she was bowling.

"That," Cynthia was saying, pointing toward the opening in the turkey.

"No it's not, honey."

"Yes it is, Mother."

"It's where they removed the insides of the turkey. This is a Tom, sweetie," Martha began to explain.

"It's the sexual organs," Cynthia said.

Markie looked from one to the other, with intermittent glances at the bird's posterior, and waited for the outcome; he seemed to be rooting for his mother.

"It *was* the sexual organs," Martha said. "It's where they remove the intestines—"

"Who?" Mark asked.

"Dears, it's very involved and mysterious and not terribly crucial. It's one of those things that one day is very complicated and the next day is very simple. Why don't you wait?"

"Okay," Mark said, but Cynthia complained again about her prune juice.

"Cynthia, why don't you run down to Wilson's and buy the paper for me?"

"Can I stop in the playground to see if Stephanie's there?"

"Stephanie's mother is sick."

"—sexual organs," Mark was saying.

"Markie, forget that, all right? Why don't you go color? Go with Cynthia—"

"I don't want him along!"

"Who cares!" Mark said, and left the kitchen.

"Please don't fight, will you, Cynthia? It's a holiday. Go get the *Times.*"

"Can I stop at Hildreth's?"

"For what? For candy, no."

"To talk to Blair."

"Blair isn't there."

"Blair's always there," said Cynthia, and Sissy laughed behind the door.

"Isn't it enough, honey, to take a walk? Cyn, I'd love to take a walk. I'd just love to take a nice leisurely walk and get the newspaper and bring it home and sit down for about six hours and read it. Can't you do that?"

"No!"

"Then go get the paper and keep quiet."

"Christ!"

"And enough of that," Martha said.

"*You* say it."

"I also work as a waitress—does that interest you?"

"I can't do *any*thing."

Martha took the dime for the paper out of her slacks pocket with wet hands. "Do you know what day this is?" she asked, wrapping her daughter's fingers around the coin.

Cynthia made a bored admission. "It's Thanksgiving."

"Thanksgiving is a very terrific holiday. How about we have a pleasurable day, all right? We're going to have a guest. Well, don't you want to know who?"

"Who?"

She mustered up an air of excitement, a good deal more than she felt. "Sidney Jaffe!"

And all at once the child, thank God, became a child, a little seven-year-old girl. "Goodie! Terrific!" She skipped out of the house after the paper.

—

There was one wall of the kids' room—before Sissy's arrival it had been Cynthia's alone—that Martha had given up on and

come to consider the coloring wall. Now Mark was laying purple on it with considerable force and violence.

"Markie, what is it you want to do?"

"Yes," the boy said, and continued hammering the crayons
against the wall.

"What's the trouble?"

He looked up. "Nothing."

"Are you happy?"

"Uh-huh."

She made Cynthia's bed and changed Mark's wet sheets.
Crumpling them into a sour wad, she bit her tongue and said
nothing. Finally, as though it was simple curiosity that moved
her to ask, she said, "Did you have any bad dreams, my friend?"

He looked up at her again. "Who?"

Why did he always say *who* to everything? All the frustrations
of the morning—the missing oranges, the frozen bird, Sarah
Vaughan—nearly came out on poor defenseless Mark. Everything: Sissy's stupidity and Cynthia's indefatigable opposition
and Markie's bed-wetting and her own unconquerable tired-
ness . . . She was twenty-six and tired right down to the bone.
And she was putting on weight. Twenty-six and becoming a
cow! Somehow the whole general situation would improve, she
thought hazily, if she could only get Sissy to pick up her underwear and put it in a drawer. Or move out. Or shut up. But
the truth was that she had been dying for a little companionship. When she dragged in from the Hawaiian House at one in
the morning, it gave her a small warm rush of pleasure to find
Sissy in the kitchen, drinking hot milk—more than likely laced
with Martha's brandy—and listening to Gerry Mulligan. Sissy
was silly and gossipy and she did not bother to vote, but it
seemed better coming home to her than coming home to
nothing. Still, why did she have to be a nut? Martha seemed
always to be latching onto people just as they were going
through some treacherous maturing period in their lives. Her
next roomer, she told herself, would not be under eighty—
better they should die in her spare room than grow up in it.

She planted a kiss on her son's neck and he drew a purple
line across the bridge of her nose. "Bang! Bang!" he shouted
into her ear, and she left him to his drawing.

"What's the matter with your nose?" Sissy asked. "You look like you've just been shat upon."

"Could you control your language in my house?"

"What are you coming on so salty again for?"

"I don't want my children saying shat, do you mind? And put on a bathrobe. My son's earliest memory is going to be of your ass."

"Now who's filthy?"

"I happen to be their mother. I support them. Please, Sissy, *don't* walk around here half-naked, will you?"

"Well, you don't have to be so defensive about it." Sissy went into her room, and came out again, robed, and dribbling ashes off her cigarette. Martha turned to the wall above the sink where the wallpaper was trying to crawl down; she gave it a swat, with the result that it unpeeled a little further. And for this, she thought, they raise the rent. During the last six months—since everybody had had the mumps—life had just been zipping along; then they raised the rent, she brought in Sissy, and things were down to normal again. She turned to her roomer and said, "Sissy, I want to ask you a question."

"What?"

"Stop plucking your face and listen to me."

Sissy lowered her mirror and tweezers. "All right, crab, what is it?"

"Do you smoke pot in there?"

The girl crossed her arms over her chest. "Never."

"Because don't. I don't ever want Blair sleeping over here again, *ever*—and I don't want any pot-smoking within ten feet of the kitchen table, where my children happen to eat their breakfast."

"It was Blair, Martha. He won't do it again."

"You're damn right he won't do it again. Why did I rent that room to you, Sister? I keep forgetting."

"I *applied*, you know, like everybody else. I answered the ad. Don't start shifting blame on me."

Martha returned to the turkey; she had popped a seam in the left side of her slacks, and when she bent over the sink it popped open further. "They're going to put me in a circus," she said. "Five nine and six hundred pounds."

"You eat too much. You could knock people's eyes out. You just eat too much."

"I don't eat too much," she said, running scalding water over the leaden turkey, "I'm just turning into a cow. A horse."

"You know what your trouble is?"

"What? What news do you bring from the far-out world? I'm dying to hear a capsule analysis of my character this morning."

"You're horny."

"You sound about as far out as *McCall's*, Sissy."

"Well, when *I'm* horny I'm a bitch."

"Your needs are more complicated than mine. I'm just tired."

"When I was married to old Curtis, I was practically flippy. You say *boo*, and I was halfway out the window. He was the creepiest, gentlest guy, and I was snapping at him all the time."

The tragedy in Sissy's young life was that she had been married for eleven months to a man who was impotent; she had married him, she said, because he struck her right off as being different. Now—in her continuing search for the exotic—she was involved with Blair Scott, who was a Negro about one and a half neuroses away from heroin, but coming up strong; and if he wasn't impotent, he was a flagellator or something in that general area.

"What about that Ivy League guy?" Sissy asked. "Joe Brummel."

"*Beau* Brummel, Sissy—what about him?"

"Don't you dig him or what?"

"He's in New York," Martha said.

"I thought he was coming for dinner."

"Sid is."

"Oh Jesus. That very buttoned-down guy, I mean he's not bad. He could be turned on with a little work. But old Sidney, I mean like what he digs is *law*."

"Sissy, how do you talk at the hospital? How do you address people when you're not at home?"

"What?"

"Forget it."

"I hate that God damn hospital. Blair says—" And she proceeded to repeat Blair's words in Blair's dialect, "I'm going to get desexized from the X-ray rays."

"Blair's a genius."

"Martha—" Sissy said, leaning forward and setting down her mirror.

"What?"

"I almost did the most far out thing of my life last night. I was like *close*."

"To what?"

"Turning tricks."

Martha felt the homey familiar enamel of the sink under her hands, and took a good grip on it. "*Here?*" she demanded. "You were going to be a prostitute in *my house*? *Are you crazy?*"

"No! No—what do you think I am!"

With relief—though by no means total relief—Martha said, "At Suey's."

"At Suey's," Sissy admitted. "Isn't that something? Suey was out getting her hair set, and this guy called to come over for a fast one. I told him Suey was out, and so he said what about you, sweetheart? And I said okay, come on over, you jerk. I told him to come over."

In a vague way, Suey O'Day was tied up with Martha's own past, but that was not sufficient explanation for the emotions —shame, fear, vulnerability—that Martha felt while Sissy was speaking. Martha and Suey had been freshmen together at the University. Suey had run off one day with a jockey from Washington Park, and Martha had run off and married Dick, and they had gone to Mexico and then she had come back from Mexico with the kids, and Suey was twenty-four and back in town too—as a call girl. Now Suey's future was said to be very bright; at one A.M., with background music by Gerry Mulligan, Sissy had informed Martha that there was a LaSalle Street broker whom Suey was tempted to marry for loot, and there was an instructor in math at the University who was crazy about her and whom she was tempted to marry for love. (The problem here was whether Suey should tell him The Truth About Herself, which the LaSalle Street broker already knew.) Of course Suey was worlds away from Martha, but Sissy wasn't: Sissy was in her house, Sissy was sleeping on her muslin sheets, and it was Sissy's dumb wildness, her endless temptations, that struck in Martha a painful remembered chord.

"What happened?" Martha said.

"I took off. I came home. I got in bed. That's how I was up so early—I was in bed at nine-thirty."

Martha sat down at the kitchen table and lit a cigarette; she caught sight of her hair in Sissy's mirror—another mess to be cleaned up before one o'clock. "Sissy, you're really going to screw up everything. Why don't you wise up? Dump Blair and dump all this hipster crap and do something with yourself. Honey, you can still dig Gerry Mulligan, but you don't have to *kill* yourself."

"Look, I was just going to turn a lousy trick to see what it was like. I wasn't going to jump off a bridge."

"But, Sissy, you don't want to be a call girl. Do you know what's very square, Sis? To want to be a call girl. Honestly, it's like wanting to be an airline stewardess or a nurse."

"Do you think I love being a stinking X-ray technician? Is that a noble calling? Sixty-five bucks a week?"

"Ah-ha, it's a matter of honor. I didn't know. The culture's crowding you in. We ought to set up an interview for you, Sissy, with Erich Fromm."

"Don't come on so motherly with me, Martha. You're about two years older—"

"True—"

"—and your life isn't exactly a model of order."

"You're going to get kicked in the teeth, Sister, so why don't you shut up." Martha pressed out her cigarette just as the janitor came up the back porch, waved at her, tried to catch a peek of some bare corner of Sissy's anatomy, and emptied—very, very slowly—the garbage.

At the sink she held the turkey submerged in hot water. Behind her Sissy began to apologize. "I just *thought* about it, Martha—"

"Who cares what you thought or what you did! Maybe what you ought to think about is moving out."

"I only just moved *in*."

"That'll make packing easier. Just roll up all your brassieres, scatter those cigarette butts to the wind, and move the hell out."

"You going to throw me out on a morals charge? Because I don't happen to be compulsively neat?"

"I don't want my kids lifting up the phone when your clients start to call—" Yet even as she spoke the whole business tired her. Everything tired her—even thinking about what she would have to do now. Take another ad, answer phone calls, arrange appointments, show the place to dozens of girls and ladies . . . Just the knowledge that after Sissy left she would have to scrub the place again from top to bottom weakened her resolve. Why hadn't she rented to some eager little physics major in the first place? What insanity it had been to think that this jerk was going to be sweet, fun, *laughs*! All she wanted now, really, was for Sissy to crawl back into her grubby room and close the door and ruin her life however she wanted. She said nothing, but there must have been some sagging in her posture that inspired Sissy to be nasty.

"Just because you have sex problems, Martha, don't call somebody who doesn't a nymphomaniac, all right? If you're frigid, or whatever the hell is bugging you, I don't say I'm not going to live in your *house* because of it. You, you're a regular sexual Senator McCarthy, honest to God you are."

"I'm trying to fix a traditional Thanksgiving Day turkey. Why don't you go play records."

"Actually, I think what it is that bugs you is that like Blair's a dinge."

"As far as I'm concerned, friend, you can go down for the whole Nigerian Army and the Belgian Congo Marines. Just leave me alone, all right?"

Sissy picked up her mirror and tweezers and left the room. And Martha Reganhart was sure that never before had she been so compromised and shat upon; never had she been so soft and expedient and unprincipled. Worst of all, never could it have bothered her less. If she had had the energy to be disgusted with herself, the object of her disgust would have been her inability to *care* any more. For nearly four years now she had been pretending to be two parents, and not half a set. Even the strict observance of national holidays had been a conscious noble decision, something she felt the divorced owed their offspring. Three and a half years ago she had made a whole potful of conscious noble decisions: if Cynthia had long legs, she would have ballet lessons; if she had a good head, she would go to the very best schools; Markie was going to learn to be as crazy over the White Sox as any Chicago kid with a full-time father . . . and so on and so on. Today, however, the whole fatuous lie, all that she had *not* done, screamed at her from every wall, door, and closet. With that granite turkey to roast and cranberries to boil and silverware to polish, she felt as though she had run her course. If she had been allowed one more hour of sleep she could doubtless have faced the next four years with an upper lip as stiff as ever. Now, everything foretold her doom—even the popped seam in her slacks through which anyone who cared to look could see that Martha Reganhart was wearing no underwear.

But what was she supposed to have done? The dilemma she had had to face at seven A.M., before brushing her teeth or drinking her coffee, was whether or not she would be less of a slob, or more of a hundred-percent-American mother, with no pants under her slacks, or dirty ones—for it turned out there were none clean. She had made her choice in a stupor, and was now suffering dismal emotions as a result. Feeling bedraggled made her feel unworthy, and over her sink she closed her eyes to the near and distant future. She thought it might give her some little solace if she could squeeze her hands around the neck of whoever it was who had raised her rent. But it wasn't a person—it was an agency. There wasn't even anybody to shout at really—they only worked here, lady—when you called up to complain.

Shortly thereafter, her daughter came racing through the front door, impervious to the scab on her right knee that was leaking blood down her shin.

"Mommy! Daddy's picture!"

"Daddy's *what*? Cynthia, look at your *knee*—"

"Daddy's picture. A *painting!*"

"Cynthia, what happened to your knee?"

"Nothing. I slipped. Look!" Cynthia had the paper folded to the art column. She jerked it back and forth in front of Martha's face, but did not relinquish it.

"Calm down," Martha said. "I can't see it if you keep moving it, can I? Go wash your knee. Please—do you want to get an infection and turn blue?"

"Daddy's picture—"

"Go wash your knee!"

Cynthia threw the paper on the floor and, crestfallen, went hobbling off to the bathroom; if the knee was going to use her, she would use the knee. "Christ!" she howled, limping down the hallway. "Christ and Jesus!"

With Cynthia gone, it was easier to take a look; she had not wanted a child around to witness whatever shock there might be. She picked up the paper from the floor and sat down with it at the kitchen table. Her heart slowly resumed its normal beat, though it was true, as Cynthia said, that a painting of her father's was actually printed in the *Times*. She recognized it immediately; only the title had been changed. What had once been "Ripe Wife" was now labeled "Mexico." The bastard. She allowed herself the pleasure of a few spiteful moments. Juvenilia. A steal from de Staël. Punk. Derivative. Corny. Literal. Indulgent. She repeated to herself all the words she would like to repeat to him, but all the incantation served to do was to bring back so vividly all that had been: all the awful quarrels, all the breakfasts he had thrown against the kitchen wall, all the times he had walked out, all the times he had come back, the times he had smacked her, the times he had wept, saying he was really a good and decent man . . . All of it lived at the unanesthetized edge of her memory. *Mexico!* Couldn't he have changed it to Yugoslavia? Bowl of Fruit? Anything but rotten Mexico!

Her eye ran up and down the column; she was unable to read it in any orderly way. It was captioned, *Tenth St. Show Uninspired; Reganhart Exception.*

> . . . except for Richard Reganhart. A resident of Arizona and Mexico, Reganhart, in his four paintings, reveals a talent . . .

> . . . manages a rigidity of space, a kind of compulsion to order, that makes one think of a fretful housekeeper . . .

> . . . especially "Mexico." The dull gold rectangles are played off against a lust and violence of savage purples, blacks, and scarlets that continually break in through the rigid . . .

> . . . will alone emerge of the seven young people

Crap! Fretful housekeeper, *crap!* House*breaker!* Weakling!

Selfish! Destroyer of her life! She hated him—she would never forgive him. Some day when it suited her purpose, she would get that son of a bitch. It was nearly three years since he had sent a penny to support their children. Three very long years.

She read the article over again from beginning to end.

When Cynthia came out of the bathroom, a bandage over half her leg, the child asked, "Remember when we were in Mexico?"

"Yes," Martha said.

"Can I remember it?"

"I think you were too small."

"I think I can remember it," Cynthia said. "Wasn't it very warm there?"

"Cyn, you know it's warm there. You learned that in school."

Cynthia reached out and Martha handed her back the paper. "See Daddy's name?" Cynthia asked.

"Uh-huh. I didn't mean to take it away from you, sweetie. I only wanted you to wash your knee—"

"I like that picture, don't you?" Cynthia asked.

"I think it's terrific," Martha said. "I think it's very beautiful."

"Can I cut it out and keep it?"

"Sure."

"Can I hang it up?"

"Absolutely."

"Oh boy! Hey Markie—look what Mommy gave *me!*"

"Oh Cynthia, don't start that, will you? Cynthia—" But the little girl was skipping off toward the living room; she met her brother halfway.

"Look what Mommy gave me. I'm going to hang it up!"

"I want it!" he shouted. "What is it?"

"Daddy's picture. Here. Don't touch. Don't *touch.*"

"I want it. Where—where's Daddy's picture?"

"Here, dope. Can't you see?"

"Cynthia—" Martha said, from the doorway to the living room. "Cynthia . . ." But she found herself unable to attach a command, an instruction, a warning, to her child's name. Cynthia, Cynthia, born of sin.

"Who—?" Markie was asking.

"This—" Cynthia said. "It's Daddy's picture!"

Mark didn't get it; his jaw only hung lower and lower. Would he ever learn to read? Lately she had begun to wonder if he might not be retarded. Should she take him in for tests?

"And it's mine. I'm hanging it over *my bed*!" Cynthia cried.

"*My* bed—" howled Mark, but his sister had already fled on one bare, one bandaged leg—both willowy, both more perfect every day—carrying her prize to some private corner of the house.

—

It might have been Christmas, and Sid, Saint Nick. He arrived with bottles of Pouilly Fuissé, Beefeater's, Noilly Prat dry vermouth, and a fifth of Courvoisier. "That's for the kids," he said, placing a row of liquor cartons at Markie's feet. "And now for you," and he unwrapped a doll almost three feet tall and a portable basketball set, both of which he deposited in Martha's arms.

"What's for us?" Cynthia demanded.

The sandpapery voice in which Cynthia had addressed him nearly flattened the man on the spot, but, hanging on courageously to what he had doubtless been planning for the last half hour, he said, "Whiskey."

"It's sour!" Markie cried. "It's beer!"

"Oh Mommy," cried Cynthia, "Mommy we didn't get anything—"

And then, just as Sid's good intentions and his bad judgment threatened to plunge all present into despair, Martha swooped into the center of the room, gathered her children in with the armful of presents, and went spinning around in a circle. "Dummies, dummies, this is for *you*!" Spinning, they fell onto the rug, and the two children came up clutching their rightful gifts to their chests. And Sid was down on the floor with them too, clutching Martha's wrist with his hand—and all the laughter and noise seemed to her only a mockery of a real and natural domesticity. Nevertheless, propelled by a seething desire to make the afternoon work, she kissed the faces of her two children and the brow of her gentleman caller. The skirt of her purple suit—an extravagance of her first winter back in Chicago—was above her knees. Sid Jaffe's weighty brown eyes, those pleading, generous orbs, turned liquidy and hot; he tried to engage her in a significant glance, but she quickly began to explain to Markie the rules of basketball, as she understood them.

There had been a scene with Sid the last time, which neither of them could have forgotten. Martha had rushed away from the sofa, trembling, but acting tough: "Stop persevering, will you! What are you—a schoolboy?" "Just the opposite, Martha!" he had said. "I want to sleep with you!" "I don't care *what* you want—*stop trying to cop feels!*" And he had left, she knew, feeling more abusive than abused, an unfair state to have produced in a man forty-one years old. But then Sid could never think of himself as having been in the right for very long anyway. Forceful as he may have been in court, out of it he defended himself with only the rawness of his needs—he seemed so badly willing to protect others and not himself. Much as this willingness of his sometimes discomfited her, in the end it was for sexual reasons that Martha had sworn she would let him drift out of her life, just as five or six men had had to drift out previously.

It was almost immediately after Sid had left last time that she had called Gabe Wallach and asked *him*—whom she hardly knew—to join her and hers for Thanksgiving dinner. He was a smoothy, though, and had given some excuse about a party for his father in New York. She, whose parents were of an entirely different chapter of her life, had accepted his refusal graciously, if disbelievingly. Since she suspected Wallach of a kind of polished lechery anyway, she almost felt relieved afterward—she might only have been throwing herself back into the struggle from which she had been trying to extricate herself. Yet she knew that Thanksgiving alone with the kids would be a hollow day. You might as well spend Thanksgiving in China if there wasn't a man around to carve. So some days later she had called Sid's office. And the first thing he said to her was that he was sorry, which only re-enforced a belief she had in her ability to emasculate when she put her mind to it. He said he had missed her; he said he had thought about her; he said he had thought about the kids; he said of course that he would come.

In a way Martha had missed him too, or missed the chance he had given her; she almost regretted now not having submitted to his passion and her own stifled, immeasurable itch.

Sid was a vigorous man with a bald head and a broken nose, both of which gave him a kind of athletic, trampled-on good looks. His body was exercised and a little thick, like a weight-lifter's, though he was two inches taller than Martha. He was a little too prissy about not running to seed, but that was a minor quibble and hardly the sort that soured lust. Which was fortunate, for it was lust (plus a natural instinct for sharing pleasure, an inability even to see a movie alone) that she would finally have to rely on with Sid. Well of decency that he was, she did not love him and never could. The affection he did inspire made her feel sorry for him, and sorrow had never for a moment produced a single quiver in her loins. Early in life she had allowed herself the luxury of many men, but she had never been swept backwards into bed out of feelings of pity or pathos. For all her genuine humanity the plight that touched her most was her own. She looked up fiercely and demandingly into men's faces, and some of them—those with more staying power than perception—had circulated stories of nymphomania, when what they had witnessed was only simple selfishness, the grinding out of one's own daily bread.

Sid gazed once again into her eyes; thinking to herself, *why not? what's lost?* she gazed back. Then she saw him soften, saw his eyes saying to her that he demanded no more than he deserved. Ah, he was *too* just, *too* kind. It seemed that almost as great as his desire to sleep with her was his desire to pay her bills and get her a steady maid; something he had once said led her to believe that he had already talked over the possibility with his own cleaning lady.

But despite the feelings which washed over and over her through the afternoon, she carried on with the festivities. After Markie had broken the hoop on the basketball set, and Cynthia had spilled Sid's martini—burrowing into his lap whenever he conversed with her mother—they had their dinner.

—

Martha Reganhart was sure you could tell something about a man's character from the way he carved a turkey. If he twittered and made excuses and finally hacked the bird to bits, he was Oedipal, wilted under responsibility, and considered himself a kind of aristocrat in the first place—*voilà*, Dick Reganhart. If he made a big production out of it, clanging armor and sharpening knives, performing the ritual and *commenting* on it at the same time, he was either egomaniacal or alcoholic, or in certain spectacular cases—her father's, for instance—both. Of course if the man just answered the need, if he stood up, executed his historical function, and then sat down and ate, chances were he was dutiful, steady, and boring. That was her grandfather, who had had to carve through many bleak Oregon Thanksgivings, after her father had packed his valise, looted the liquor cabinet, and left that eloquent, fateful note: "I am going to California or some God damned place where they make the stuff and you can at least sit in the sun and drink it with nobody looking out for your health." He had bequeathed his office and utensils to his father-in-law, a hard-working railroad engineer, and he had left forever.

Grandpa had filled the gap all right—and so too did Sid Jaffe, who freed both drumsticks from their sockets and laid them, one each, on the children's plates. Martha tried not to take any notice of the sinking in her stomach, which she knew to be a sure signal that self-deception is rampant in the body. She tried to ignore the fact the she had not her grandmother's taste: she tried with all her heart to look over at Sid Jaffe, carving away so efficiently there, and melt with love for him. She imagined all the good it would do them if she could only fall for him. She considered the $54 owed these many months to Marshall Fields, and the $300 loan from the co-op; she thought of the $36 bled from her by that thief, Dr. Slimmer. (Those she hated in this world and would never forgive were Dick Reganhart, her father, and Dr. Slimmer, the last for knowing nothing and charging double.) She thought of Sissy and the messy room—she heard Sissy, in fact, singing in the bathtub—and she knew that the only sensible thing was to close her eyes, tip forward, and dive down into an easy love. So she went under three times, but each time came bobbing back up to the surface.

"But what's a lawyer *do?*" Markie was asking. "I don't want to be a lawyer."

"There are laws," Sid was explaining, "like not crossing the street when the light is red. That's a law, right?"

"Of course," Cynthia said.

Mark nodded in agreement. He was hoisting a candied

sweet potato to his mouth, not with his fork, but wrapped in the center of his fist. Martha waited for the inevitable to happen: sure as hell he would stick it in his eye. But through luck, or instinct, he managed to locate his lips; he had, however, borne down too heavily on the frail potato, and just as it was to slide safely within, most of it made an appearance along the edges of his fingers. Totally absorbed, and confused, by Sid's explanation—"and the lawyer is the person, Markie, who explains to the judge why he thinks the other person, the person who crossed against the light, say"—floundering in the labyrinths of jurisprudence, Markie cleaned his hand on the front of his white shirt.

"*Mark!*"

Sid stopped short with his lecture; Markie looked up. "Who?"

"Don't you have a napkin?" Martha asked.

He showed her that he did. Sid said, "Markie, when you want to wipe your hands off, use your napkin."

"It's no use. I think he's part Eskimo," Martha said. "I think he's going to grow up and just head north and find a nice Eskimo girl and the two of them are going to sit around for the rest of their lives asking each other *Who?* and ripping blubber apart with their hands. Markie, my baby-love, pay attention to your food, all right?"

After speaking her last words she saw how she had hurt the feelings of her guest. He was being educational—his way of being fatherly—and she had directed the pupil away from his lessons and back to his plate and napkin. She tried to add some joke, but it was limp, and suddenly she felt unable to bear up much longer under Sid Jaffe's good intentions. Why must he feel obliged to try so hard with her children? It made her angry that, as much as he wanted to visit with her, he seemed to want to visit with Cynthia and Mark.

Sissy now traipsed through in her sheer robe. "Excuse me," she said, leaving water prints across the fringe of the floor. "What do you say, counselor? *Comment ça va?*"

Sid, who still could not understand Sissy's presence in the house, mumbled a greeting. Martha had not told him that her rent had gone up for fear he would volunteer to take the case to the Rent Control Board. She felt pre-defeated in the face of administrative bodies, which seemed to her to work in mad ways of their own; and besides, she owed Sid too much that was not money already. She wanted really to work herself free of this lawyer and of those legal maneuverings which she had once believed might get her more just treatment in the world. At a very early point in her misery she had believed in a kind of parliamentarian approach to confusion; now she understood things better.

"Sissy's feet are wet," Cynthia pointed out. "She's leaving a mess again."

"It's only dew, baby," said Martha. After Sissy had departed, she said, "She's part girl, part stripper—" But Sid was wiping his mouth and saying, "Sometimes I don't understand you, honey."

Cynthia leaned over to whisper into Mark's ear, "He called her honey again."

"Who?"

———

Since Martha had to be at work by five, they had begun dinner early. Now it was not quite three, but with the meal finished and the dishes stacked, though not washed, it seemed to Martha as though it were time for dusk to settle in. In Oregon at this time—or later, at the real dusk—they would be coming back from their tramp in the woods. She would have pebbles in her Girl Scout shoes, and the dust from the red leaves would have caked around her ankles, to be discovered later when she took off her socks for sleep. Her grandfather would be whistling, her grandmother clearing her throat (forever clearing her throat), and her father would be pinching the behind of her mother—poor baffled beautiful woman—and tripping over every rock on the path. "It's hot *toddy* time!" "Oh Floyd, you've had—" "For God's sake, where's your American spirit, Belle? Your old lady here is a matron of the DAR, and where is your American spirit residing, anyway?" "Why don't you go in and nibble on some turkey; why don't you—" "I'll tell you what I want to nibble on, old sweetheart!" "Floyd, the child—" "Martha Lee, who wants a hot toddy, my baby-love? Who's my baby-love? Who's got a collection of women around him could make a sheik's eyes pop? Is that right, Belle, isn't a sheik one of those fellas with the harems? Baby-love, you're in the sixth grade—haven't they mentioned harems?" It was that Thanksgiving, some long, long-gone holiday, when for the first time she had become dreadfully and unexplainably nervous in his presence.

Mark was taking his nap, Sissy had glided out in flat Capezios and black tights, and Cynthia's voice caroled up from the back yard, where she was jumping rope with Barbara, the janitor's daughter.

Sid kissed her. Following the old saw, she leaned back and tried, at least, to enjoy it. His hands were a great comfort, a regular joy—there was a nice easy stirring in her breasts that moved inward through her, picking up speed and power, until it produced at last a kind of groan in her bones down in the lowest regions of her torso. Then she was off the sofa.

"No," she said.

"Martha," Sid said calmly, "this is getting ridiculous. I'm a grown man, you're a grown woman—"

"It's one of those things that's ridiculous and is going to have to be, Sidney."

Sid swam an hour a day at the Chicago Athletic Club; he had been a Marine Corps officer in two wars; at forty-one he wore the same size belt he had at twenty-one—and now he asked, with a nervous display of bravado, if perhaps it was simply that she found him physically repellent.

"I find you nothing of the sort," she said, touched, but not of course impassioned, by the question. "A lot of traffic has moved across this sofa, Sid. I've been living here going on four years, and a lot of men have come through, you know, on their way home from work. I think there's a bus stop in front of our steps, I don't know. Anyway, if I let everybody's hands go traveling down my blouse, what kind of mother would I be?"

"I'd appreciate it, Martha, if you could just be serious for a minute."

He was dead serious, which caused her to feel all the strain of being a joker. She felt dumb and inconsequential and foolish. Here was a man with a hard-on (and all the seriousness that implied) and she wouldn't give him a straight answer. But there she went *again*! She just couldn't sneak out of things by turning phrases all the time. She addressed herself in a stern voice: *Be serious . . .* But if she were to become serious about

old Sidney, she knew—why not face it—that she would marry
him. Once they had stripped down together, and she had realized that aside from being a father to her children, he could
also give her about as much bedroom excitement as any other
girl she knew was getting—once she let him prove this,
wouldn't she be a goner? Wed once more for wrong and expedient reasons . . . No, there was only one bag to put your
marbles in, one basket for your eggs, and that was love. Nobody was going to marry her again out of necessity; nobody
was going to marry her for her breasts, her troubles, or her
kids. Nor was she going to miss the mark herself. This time she
would do it for love.

At bottom, her demands were no more complicated or original than any other girl's.

Sid walked to where she stood running her hand over the
bindings of her small and eclectic collection of paperbacks. He
said, "I didn't mean that, Martha," whereupon she thought:
What! What are you apologizing for now! "I understand," he
said. "You're in a tricky position. I'm not trying to make things
more difficult for you at all. I care for you so much, Martha.
You've got a lot of guts, and you've been remarkable, really, in
a very awkward situation. I do appreciate just how complicated
it's been for you. But, honey, there's such a simple solution. It
doesn't have to go on like this at all. I'm going to get you
down on the sofa, and you're going to jump up, and there's
such a simple and obvious solution."

"And what's that?"

He took her hand, as was appropriate. "Marry me."

Since her return to Chicago, two other proposals had come
Martha's way. One was from Andy Ratten, a Rush Street musician much admired by co-eds and their dates, who pretended
to be Paul Hindemith to one set of friends and Dizzy Gillespie
to another; when Martha turned him down, he had sent in the
mail—the measure of his crew-cutted wit and marijuanaed
charm—a Sammy Kaye LP. "Your fate, baby," was all the enclosed card had said. The second proposal had come from Billy
Parrino, who at the time was the husband of her best friend.
On the playground, while soft-faced, bug-eyed exhausted Billy
was watching his three kids—his wife was home cracking up,
a phenomenon only recently completed—and Martha was

watching her two, he had come right out with it. "Martha, let's just take off." "I think you have a wife named Beverly." "She's so wacked-up it's driving *me* crazy." "Well, I'd love to, Billy, but the kids—" "We'll take them; we'll take them all, and we'll just go somewhere. Paris." "It all sounds too glamorous —you, me, five kids, Paris." "Oh," wailed Billy, "how this life does stink," and he went home.

So a full-hearted, unqualified, sensible proposal from a man as substantial as Sid Jaffe—which now that it was here melted the cartilage in her knees—was a considerable achievement. Sid made $15,000 a year, was neat and clean, and, God knew, his heart was in the right place. Just three weeks before, they had sat by her TV set, and while poor Adlai Stevenson had conceded defeat in measured eighteenth-century sentences, tears had rolled from Sid's eyes. Sid Jaffe was for all the right things; he was decent and just and kind (she would always have her way; she would be in a marriage, imagine it, where she would always have her way) and he was good to children, if somewhat plodding. And even that was mostly eagerness, and would surely have disappeared by the time of their first anniversary—to be celebrated, no doubt, with ten days in the Bahamas . . .

She had really to search for some switch to throw, some-thing to divert the current that was building up to carry her toward an affirmative reply. "My kids, you know, are little Protestant kids. Markie's circumcision was strictly pragmatic, I don't want you to be tricked by that. He's a slow learner, Sid, and it may take him fifteen years to figure out what a Jew *is*. And Cynthia may turn out to be an anti-Semite; she comes home with something new every day. My grandmother, you know, is a flying buttress still of the DAR—" Yet even as her mouth released all this feeble chatter, she remembered her old grandmother's balanced judgment on the men of Zion: "They're tight-fisted ugly little fellas, Martha Lee, but they're good to their wives and children."

"Martha, you don't have to give me an answer in the next sixty seconds."

When it came to honoring the other person's surface emo-tions, Sid Jaffe was a very sweet considerate man. "Let me think about it, Sid—all right?"

But he had suggested she wait, apparently, not expecting she would choose to; he had to turn away to hide the fact that he was crushed. Suddenly Martha had a vision of Sid proposing to girls ever since high school.

And then he was pressing her to him. She was wearing her one other extravagance, her white silk V-neck blouse, and Sid had buried his head in the V. His mouth sent through her an arc, a spasm of passion, and if Markie was not sleeping in the other room, if Cynthia's jump-rope song had not ceased, if the phone had not all at once begun to ring, Martha Reganhart might have had a far different future.

"Martha, we can just have the most wonderful—" His mouth went down and down and she closed her eyes.

"Wonderful wonderful—"

"—The phone."

"Let it ring."

But it stopped ringing.

"Mommy! It's Daddy!"

"What!" She was racing for the kitchen—racing away, not toward. "What is it, Cynthia? *What?*"

"It's Daddy from New York! For Mrs. Reganhart! You, Mommy! The operator!"

She took the receiver from Cynthia's hands, wondering— among other things—how long the child had been in the kitchen. Couldn't she even get felt up in private? And now this—Dick Reganhart! From where! "Yes? . . . Operator? This is Martha Reganhart."

"It's not Daddy, however," said the voice at the other end. She sank down in a chair. "Oh, for Christ's sake."

"Shall I hang up?"

"Certainly not—my child's drunk on Mott's apple juice. How are you?"

"Fine."

"*Where* are you?"

"Daddyland," Gabe Wallach answered. "New York."

"Oh do excuse her. She gets overexcited when she's not in school. I think she's reacting to the company." She lowered her voice, for she saw the company pacing back and forth in the living room. Was he trying to overhear, or was he walking off lust? How unnatural everything was.

Gabe Wallach asked, "Who's there?" He sounded a little demanding, but Thanksgiving was doubtless a strain on everybody.

"An old friend," Martha said. "He stimulates the children."

"And you?"

More demanding yet. She would have been annoyed were it not as though some hand had reached down to pull her out of the fire. "No, no. No—that's true. Listen, I'm sounding tragic. How's your father's party? Is there really a father and a party, or is some tootsie nestled beside you in her underwear?"

"I call in the absence of the latter."

"It's very sweet of you to call. Happy Thanksgiving."

"I'm having a nice unhappy one."

"Mommy!" Cynthia said. "I want to talk to him—I want to—"

"Just a minute, will you?" Martha said into the phone. Then, away from it, "Cynthia, it is not Daddy!"

"It is!"

"It is not! I'm telling you the truth, Cynthia. Go talk to Sid, he's all alone. "Cynthia!" The child was threatening to throw a lollipop at her. "Cynthia!"

In tears, the little girl went toward the room where Markie was napping.

"I'm back," Martha said.

"Good," Wallach said.

Good for what? What kind of weak-kneed out was she going to make this into? Surely she couldn't reject a man who had been so good to her through all these rotten years for another with whom she'd eaten one lousy dinner two weeks before? What right had she to use this flukey phone call against Sid—in fact, to use Sid?

She could tell instantly from the voice on the other end that she had hurt the feelings of still another gentleman. "I just wanted to say Merry Thanksgiving to you."

"Thank you . . ." Then she realized that he was about to hang up. "Shall I go ahead," she asked, "and invite you to another meal? Will you eat leftovers when you come back?"

"I'll be back Monday."

"Come then," Martha Reganhart said, "for dinner."

"Yes, I will . . . Who's Sid?"

"He's a man who just asked me to marry him."

"I see."

"You'll come Monday night."

"As long as you're still single," he answered. "I suppose so."

"Single as ever," she said.

"Does that upset you?" Wallach asked.

"Specifically, no; generally, I'm not sure. This is some long-distance conversation."

"Long distance should be outlawed anyway," he said. "Were you expecting a phone call from your husband?"

"My *ex*-husband—from whom I have no expectations whatsoever." A cry went up from Markie's room. "Oh God, my son just hit my daughter with a chair or something. Give my love to the girl in her underwear."

"You give my love to Sidney."

She felt, when he said that, all the strangeness of their conversation; she wouldn't have minded being angry with him. "We can't possibly be jealous over anything," she said, "so we shouldn't really play at it. Should we?"

"I'm a little deranged today, Martha. I'm wondering," he said, in a very forlorn voice, "if we'll ever manage to level with one another."

And then she wanted really *only* to be level—she wanted to be serious, to be normal; she wanted to be soft and feminine; she wanted a love affair that was no jokes, just intensity; and because the man on the other end was practically a stranger, she led herself into thinking that he could service her in just that way. She wanted to be out of what she was inextricably a part of—her own life. "You come Monday, Gabe. I'll be single. They shouldn't outlaw long distance," she said, holding the phone very close to her. "I feel you've saved my life."

And on the other end he was saying, "There is a father and a party, you know. And I look forward to seeing you."

And she was explaining, "Sid is Sid Jaffe—he was my lawyer. He got me my divorce half-price, and I'm very indebted to him, Gabe, and the children are crazy about him, as crazy as they can be about anybody, anyway. And I have to stop talking on your money. Forgive me, please." She hung up, thinking herself her own woman.

But while she changed into her waitress uniform, she heard

laughing and chatter from the kitchen. The uproar in the kid's room had been a false alarm, and Markie had gone back to sleep; the two people having such a good time were her daughter and her lawyer. When she emerged in her starchy blue waitress uniform—her Renoir proportions having taken on the angles of a coffin—she saw that Sid had his sleeves rolled up and was washing the dishes. And Cynthia—complainer, beggar, favor-monger, liar, fatherless baby—Cynthia wiped, and wore upon her face the very sweetest of smiles.

Martha leaned against the door to her bedroom and let the tears come.

"My father painted a picture of me that was in the paper," Cynthia was saying.

"Did he?" Sid asked.

"We used to live in Mexico and he drew it down there. It's very hot down there, even in the winters."

"Can I see the picture? Did he make you as pretty as you are? Did he get those blue eyes in it?"

Cynthia, after a quick look around the kitchen, said, "Well, it's not exactly me. It's really all of us in Mexico."

"Martha too, you mean?"

"Everything. All of us."

"I certainly would like to see it," Sid said.

"Would you?"

"Sure, why not?"

"Just a minute!" she dropped her dishtowel where she stood, and took off for the bedroom, which was beside her mother's. "Hi, Mommy!" she said, and skipped into her own room. Instantly, all hell broke loose.

"Christ, Markie," roared Cynthia, "what's the matter with you? Are you nuts?"

"Whaaa? Whooo? Mommy!"

"Mark*ie*," Cynthia howled. She rushed back into the hall and began to stamp her feet. "That damn kid," she told her mother, "was sleeping with my picture! He wrinkled my whole picture!"

"It's not just your picture, sweetheart," Martha began.

"If he wants a paper," Cynthia shouted, "let him *buy* one!"

At this point the childless couple who lived above them began to hammer on the floor.

"Oh—" Martha cried, grabbing her hair. "What the fuck do they expect! *It's a holiday!*"

She screamed her words in Sid's direction, as though she *wanted* to frighten him; he paled, and dove back into the dishes. While she calmed herself and calmed the children, he finished the silverware—and then, in plain sight of her, he reached up into a cabinet and took down the Bon Ami. Oh the Bon Ami—the Bon Ami was just too much. What right had he to twist her arm so? What right had he to be so perfect? She would have sold her soul to the devil, were he able to make her love the man who stood in an apron in her kitchen, shaking the beautiful white cleanser down into the dirty sink.

—

It is difficult to be casual about the power of Thanksgiving; it produces expectations, and starts ordering around our emotions, and, above all, it takes unfair advantage of our memories. Though Martha Reganhart did not consider herself particularly reverent about celebrations, she nevertheless could not become accustomed to having to earn a living on Thanksgiving Day by waiting on tables. She could work without too much pain on Sundays, Labor Day, Memorial Day, and even the days of Christ's birth, crucifixion, and ascension; but that she had to spend eight hours on the next-to-last Thursday in November taking orders for fried jumbo shrimp was proof that her life had not turned out as she had hoped. She attempted to pay no attention to the direction in which they were headed. Instead of proceeding directly to the Hawaiian House, she suggested they stop first at the playground and let the kids run around.

Mark and Cynthia—and here was one of the mysteries that held their mother's world together—were strolling twenty feet in front, holding hands. Mark was wearing long pants and his blue coat, and Cynthia her red jacket with the hood; above them the sun was a dull light behind the clouds. Cynthia was helping Markie across the street and seeing to it that he did not toss his cap up into the branches of the bare trees. For twenty minutes she had been as well-behaved a child as one could ask for; outside the apartment building she had taken her brother aside and silently buttoned his fly.

"It comes over her," Martha said, "every once in a while. I

think she's going to take flight and join God's angels. Maybe it's fresh air that does it."

"She's going to be a knockout," Sid said. "She has those blue eyes, and then she *rolls* them . . ."

"She's a sweet child," Martha said. "She's just a little frantic."

"She'll be all right. They're perfectly decent, lively, charming kids," Sid told her. "Stop worrying."

They were inspiring words, upon which she was willing to lean. Sid himself was looking like something to lean upon—husky in his raglan coat, jaunty in his tweed hat with the green feather. She would have kissed him for his dependability, except that she was supposed to be deciding, even while they walked, whether to marry him for it; she had thought she had already made up her mind, but it appeared—to her own surprise—that she hadn't.

"It looks," Sid said, "as though Dick is coming up in the world." It looked, too, as though he were changing the subject, though he wasn't.

"Yes, doesn't it?" She took his arm as they crossed the street. Memory carried her all the way back to Oregon. "It's a lovely time of day," she said.

"What do you think he's going to do? Will he start sending money?"

She breathed in a good supply of the autumn air. "I don't think he could have made an awful lot from four or five pictures."

"I don't think that's our business. How much is he behind?"

She shrugged.

"Martha, I've asked you to simply keep a record—"

"He's probably going back to Arizona. He's probably as broke as ever."

"Then maybe he ought to stay in New York and get a job."

All she wanted to do now was to point out a house that reminded her of her family's big frame house back in Oregon; she did not care to dilute the day's pleasure any further with talk of her former husband. In 1953, when he had disappeared into the canyons of the Southwest, she had given up on chasing after him for the support payments. It was not only because she could not find him that she chose not to have any papers served. Dick's running off had told her what she had always wanted to know: paying all the bills, every nickel, dime, and quarter, had permitted her to stop condemning herself. She was not mean, bitchy, immoral, selfish, stupid and dishonest—all the words he had hurled at her when she had fled finally from Mexico with the children; it could not be she who was the betrayer of their children—not so long as she was harried and unhappy as she was.

Martha said, "He has a job. He's a painter."

"I meant a real job, to meet his obligations."

All she knew about painting was what Dick had taught her; still, it was no pleasure to see the Philistine in Sid oozing out. "It's not important," she said. "Please."

"Well, I'll tell you, that painting looked like hell to me, I'll tell you that."

"In black and white it's hard to know."

"Oh, yes? Did you like it? Would you like to tell me what it was supposed to be?"

". . . Cynthia had it—it's all of us in Mexico, I suppose. Look, it's a kind of painting I guess you're not in sympathy with. You've got to see a lot of it"—and the voice she heard was not her own, but her ex-instructor's—"before you start to get it."

"What am I supposed to *get*? That's what I'd like to find out."

"Oh, Sid, are you asking me to defend that whole God damn bunch of phonies? The guy doesn't have any money— what am I supposed to do, bleed him? He's a pathetic neurotic whom we should really all pity, except that he happens to be a son of a bitch. Sid, he couldn't *get* a regular job. If he worked in a factory or had to pump gas, well, he just couldn't. He's a painter—that's actually what he is, for some unfathomable reason, and there's nothing we can do to make him not one. So let's forget it for today, please."

"What are you so pigheaded for, Martha?"

"I'm not pigheaded. I don't need him." Sharply she added, "They're my children."

But Sid went right on, not figuring her anger to be directed in any way to him. "He's having a success, right? He's obviously made a little money, isn't that so? Then now is the time to open up correspondence. Honestly, honey, now is the time to slap him in court—"

"Why don't we wait? Why don't we just wait and see what he does, all right?" But when she squeezed his hand, it made it even more obvious that she had trampled once again on his concern for her. "Sid, I appreciate everything you've done—"

He stopped her. "Do you?"

There was no further conversation until they reached the playground, where Stephanie Parrino and her two little brothers were playing on the seesaw while their grandmother, Mrs. Baker, watched over them.

"My father sent me a picture," Cynthia told Stephanie's grandmother, and then went off with Mark to the swings.

Stephanie's grandmother had once been the mother-in-law of Billy Parrino, the man who had sat in this very playground and asked Martha to run off to Paris with five children and himself. Billy had finally divorced Bev, and Bev had tried to drown herself in the toilet. She was now on the ninth floor of Billings receiving shock treatment, though all discussion of her condition was carried on as though she were down with a bad cold.

"How is she feeling?" Martha asked.

"Oh not perfect yet, of course, but coming right along," said Mrs. Baker.

"That's fine."

"She's responding beautifully," Mrs. Baker said, and they all looked off at the children, rising on swings into the gray rough sky, a sky aching to plunge them directly from November to January. On the apartment-house wall directly behind them, some waggish University student had scrawled:

> *John Keats*
> *½ loves*
> *Easeful Death*

The words were enclosed in a heart. It did not strike her (as it might have on a day when there was a little sun in the sky) as witty at all. Keats had been dropped into his grave at the age of twenty-six. Thinking of the death of Keats, she thought of her own: for three years she had been meaning to scrape together enough to take out $10,000 worth of insurance on her life . . . She suddenly plunged headlong into gloom. Twenty-six.

Mrs. Baker, meanwhile, was saying that every day another kind mother invited Bev's children for lunch. A friend of Mrs. Baker's had sent a basket of fruit from Florida directly to the hospital, and though Bev wasn't quite up to peeling things yet, her mother had brought the oranges home and marked them with nail polish and put them in the refrigerator so Bev could have them when she got out. Tomorrow, Mrs. Baker said, she was taking all the youngsters bright and early down to see Don McNeill's "Breakfast Club."

Martha reached out for Sid's hand. She sat stone still, wondering how much worse off Bev Parrino would be if some doctor up in Billings shot too much juice through her one day and sent her from this impossible life. As they left the little park, silent but for the creaking of the swings, she managed to put down a strange noise that wanted to make itself heard in her throat. Then Markie began to cry that all he had done was push.

Her watch showed twenty-five minutes of holiday remaining; she tried to think of what they could do until five. The kids were moving—had moved—into their late-afternoon crabbiness, and Sid, she knew, was still waiting for her reply to his proposal. Patient, ever-ready, faithful, waiting. Only ten minutes had elapsed since he had thrown his most solid punch of the day. Do you? Do you appreciate me, Martha, your situation—do you see what I can do for you . . . And yes, she saw—she had reached out for his hand, and he had been there to give it to her, even if he did not understand for a moment the panic she had found herself enclosed in.

"I didn't swing! I always push!" Mark was crying. "I want something!"

"You'll swing next time, Markie—"

"I want a Coca-Cola! I want to go to Hildreth's! I want—"

For reasons of her own Martha did not want to go to Hildreth's; but she could not go back to the playground either, to confront Mrs. Baker's stiff inhuman smile and consider further Beverly Parrino's condition. So she stood in the middle of Fifty-seventh Street, while Markie screamed and Cynthia joined in with him, and she might have stood there for the full twenty-five minutes she had coming to her had not Sid taken her hand once again and led the three of them to Hildreth's for a Coke. And fortunately the place was empty; all the students had gone home for the holiday, and the hangers-on—the strays, the outcasts, all the purposeless people she had come to know during the last few years, who could only have put the final depressing touch to her afternoon—were either sleeping or hiding, or, in private and questionable ways, paying homage somewhere to the day.

The four of them sat at one of the booths along the window, Martha and Sid drinking coffee, and the children over their Cokes, stifling and giving in to gaseous burpings. Behind the lunch counter the Negro girl who ladled out the food was preparing an elaborate turkey sandwich for herself; inside the store dreamy dance music came from a radio, and outside a pleasant, gray, Sunday deadness hung over the street. Everything combined to lull Martha backwards—the music, the coffee, the plasticized smell of the booth itself, and of course the street. Aside from Pacific Avenue in Salem, where she had been born and raised, Chicago's Fifty-seventh Street, was the thoroughfare of her life. Looking at it, blowy and deserted, touched now by dusk, was like seeing the set of a familiar play without seeing the performers or hearing the lines. But in the dark theater of memory all the old scenes could easily be recollected, all the old heroes and heroines. She could remember this one long store-lined, tree-lined, University-lined street, and so very many Marthas. There, plain as day, was Martha Lee Kraft, buying her Modern Library books in Woodworth's. And there was Martha Kraft taking the I.C. train to the Loop, and having absolutely the most perfect and adult day in Carson's—a solid hour trying on dark cloche hats, and narrowing her eyes at herself in the mirror when the saleslady wasn't around. And there was Martha Kraft, saying to herself *Why can't I do anything?* and taking her first lover. And Martha Kraft carrying a placard: VOTE FOR HENRY WALLACE. It weaved above her head as she marched clear from Cottage to the Lake, and beside her, carrying his own sign—who was that anyway? Who was that sweet boy with the social consciousness and practically no hips at all? What was his name, the one into whose basement room she moved her guitar and her Greek sandals and her brilliant full skirts and her uncombed extravagant hair? And there was Martha being wooed and won, right in Hildreth's. Richard M. Reganhart of Cleveland, blue-eyed, dark-haired, fierce, wild, a painter, an ex-G.I.—he had not even to cajole her . . . And there was one morning when Martha was sitting in a booth opposite him, the two of them eating that skimpy, sufficient lover's breakfast of juice and coffee and jelly doughnuts, one morning when at the tip of Martha's uterus, Cynthia Reganhart was the size of a pinhead, when Cynthia (who is presently dredging at the bottom of her glass through a straw) was hardly bigger than nothing at all.

But—all those prayers and tears to the contrary—she was not nothing at all, and everything that had then to begin, began, and everything that had to end, ended. For five months Fifty-seventh Street was hardly seen, it was only walked upon, blindly; and then there was sunny Mexico, and Dick Reganhart was ripping the shirt off his own back—his fried eggs, lately heaved against the white stucco wall, sliding relentlessly toward the floor.

"I didn't marry you, you gutless bitch—*you* married *me*!"

"I thought you *love*d me—"

"You thought! You were hot, baby, and you itched for it and you got it! *And you made me marry you*, don't you forget that, *ever*! Four years in the Army, four years—and now *this*! I'm in prison. I can't paint! I have nightmares—"

"Then why can't you just *love* me—"

"You are a sly bitch, Martha Lee. You don't love me—you *know* you don't! Oh someday I'll find your ass down in Our Holy Mother of Guadalupe and you'll be crying out to Jesus for help—why did you get such a sonofabitching husband, why-yyy are you afflicted with such a sinful man! Well, you tell Our Holy Mother, the only sin, you conniving bitch, is this fucking prison of a marriage! Why don't you *listen* to me! *Leave that God damn egg alone!*"

"You miserable coward—don't tell me what to do! Everybody in the *world* loves each other! Every rotten secretary loves her boss! Guys fell off our front porch just from loving me, you bastard—*what's the matter with you!*"

"Let's keep it straight, America's Sweetheart—you used my cock! That's the why and wherefore, Martha—"

"*Shut up! We have a baby, you filthy beast!*"

"I told you, didn't I? I said get a God damn abortion—"

"I'd like to cut your tongue out, you mean pricky bastard! I'll ruin your life like you've ruined—"

"You *hooked* me is what happened, Martha—you hooked me and now you ought to be happy, you selfish, stupid—"

The train moved north, taking almost two whole days to get through Texas, five impossible meals in the State of Texas and innumerable voyages down the car to the toilet; tiny Mark cried and little Cynthia gloomed out at the never-ending brush, and then there was Oklahoma City, there was St. Louis and then Peoria, and now we are back in Chicago, we are back on Fifty-seventh Street, we are in Hildreth's once again, perhaps in that same historic booth. Dick Reganhart is destined to make a fortune painting rectangles, for he is a child of our times, but for Martha Reganhart life is a circle. And if it ends where it begins, where is that? What's next? Where was she going? This was not what she had envisioned for herself while she tweeked her brand new little nipples and stared up at the ceiling on those rainy, windy, winter nights in Salem, Oregon.

"Blair!" Cynthia screamed. "Hi!"

"My ofay baby! Honey chile! Cynthiapia!"

Cynthia dissolved, not entirely spontaneously, into laughter, and Mark, always a willing victim, doubled up in ecstasy, and hit his head on the table top.

Blair reached into the booth and plucked Markie out of his seat. "Hey, Daddy," he said, jiggling Markie in the air, "you will have dehydration of the ductual glands which corroborate the factation of the tears. Is this the reactionary reaction cogetary to the stimuli, or is you pulling our leg?"

Mark squelched his tears instantly and stared into the mysterious continent of Blair's skin; the man was brown and rangy and undernourished, with Caucasian lips and nose, dark glasses, and a manic potential that could turn Martha's mouth dry. Cynthia went flying out of her seat toward the visitor, and her Coke wobbled across the table; her mother, years of practice behind her, caught it just before it tipped over into Sid's lap. She looked at her companion and found him trying to throw a smile into this big pot of merriment. But then she heard him groan when Blair slid into the seat opposite them, a child in each of his arms.

"Where's your friend?" Martha asked, conversationally.

"She's buying her mayonnaise."

Several seconds passed before either man publicly acknowledged the presence of the other; then Blair peered over the top rim of his sunglasses. "How's the crime business, Your Honor? What's swinging in the underworld?"

"How are you?" Sid asked.

"Oh me, I'm toeing the ethical norm."

"That's fine."

"Man, I make *nothin'* but the super-ego scene."

Mark found the remark very funny; Cynthia curled up in Blair's arms. Sid sat upright in his chair. There was no question about his being a hundred times the man Blair Scott was, and yet Martha discovered she could not stand him at that moment for being so proper and protective; it seemed a crushing limitation on her life.

Partly out of pique with Sid, she cued Blair. "And how's the hipster movement in North America? What's new?" The children looked at her with wide eyes—she was drawing out the funny man for their enjoyment.

"Well, Mrs. Reganhart," said Blair, whose father was a highway commissioner in Pennsylvania, whose mother was a big shot in the NAACP, and whose masks were two: Alabama Nigger and Uppity Nigger, "well, to tell you the facts, we is all of us taking a deserved rest, for we expended a prodigious, a fantastic, a burdensomely amount of laboriousness and energy, as you might have been reading in the various organs, in placing in the White House that Supreme Hipster of them all, the Grand Potentate and Paragon of What Have You, the good general, DDE. It was a uphill battle and a mighty venture, and mightily did we deliver unto it. We are pushing presently for a hipster for Secretary of the State, and, of course, for Secretary of the Bread. What we are anxious to see primarily is one of our lad's names on all them dollar bills. You know, This here bill is legal tender, signed, Baudelaire. Of course, in our moment of spiritual need and necessitation— which we is regularly having biweekly, you know—we are also turning our fond and prodigious efforts and attentions to the Holy Roman Church, and praying on our bended knees, with much whooping and wailing, that it is from amongst our ranks that the next Pontiff-to-be will be selectified. As may be within the ken of your knowledge, sugar, up till the present hour there has been an unquestioning dearth of hipster Popes—one must go a considerable way back down the road to find hisself one. Like since Peter, *nothin'*. The Pope we got now, the thin fella with the glasses—now in my opinion this is a very square Pope, though on the other hand I learn from our sources in Vatican that this same cat was very hip as a cardinal. What we is looking for with fervor and prodigiosity, not to mention piety and love, is someone we can call 'Daddy' and look up to. How many years has it been now since Rutherford B. Hayes?"

"Coolidge," Martha suggested, fearing for the dryness of her children's underwear; both of them were slithering about in fits of laughter.

"Hip, my dear blond bombshell, but no hipster. Markie, do you agree here with the predilections of my predigitation, or what? You sit so silent, man"—Mark was nearly on the floor—"have you no thriving interest in the life political and the heavenly bodies, or is you numb, Dad, with Coca-Colorama?"

"Coke!" Mark erupted, as Sissy made her entrance, swinging within her clinging black tights her healthy behind, and unscrewing the cap on a jar of Hellmann's mayonnaise. She sat down at the booth and offered the jar around; then she dug in while Mark, awe-struck, watched every trip the spoon made from the jar to her mouth. For Martha, his absorption opened up a whole new world of agonies. Sid looked at her. Pleadingly he said, "It's getting late."

She heard herself answer, "It's only five to."

And Cynthia was shouting, "Blair! Blair!"

Oh father-starved child, modulate your voice! But Martha said not a word. Let them enjoy every last Thanksgiving minute.

"Blair! Tell an army story!"

"A story!" Mark joined in.

"Well, there I was—" Blair said, and the children hushed. "Up to here—no, higher—with dirty dishes and pots and pans laden and encrustated with an umbilicus of grease and various and sundry remnants and remains. I'm speaking of garbage, Markie—do you get the picture?"

"Picture."

"All right, you got it. I don't want no faking now. All right, up to here in muck. It was my duty, you understand, not only to native land, but to the ethical norm and the powers that am and was, to alleviate these crockeries of the burdensome load under which they was yoked by virtue of this delirious scum and dirt which so hid their splendor. Well, cheerily then, I am approaching the task when, coming from another part of the edifice, I smell upon my nostril's entrance there, some sort of conflagration, and I think unto myself, I think: Slime, Scum, Private Lowlife, where there is conflagration there is smoke. Erstwhile, says I, this here mess hall is perhaps out to be victimized by the dreadness of fire. *Alors!* I am alarmed when into my area I behold a white-glove inspection is moving itself. Great Scott, says I to myself in my characteristic manner, it is a full colonel, a veritable bastion of democracy and he is headed my way, seeking out signs of filth and dirt and thereby disrespectability and so forth. He is followed up upon, lapped up after, in a manner of speaking, by two captains and a major, and several noncommissioned bastions, patriotic and knowledgeable men one and all. Well, I snap to, heave forth, I take the extreme attitude of attention, sucking in even on my hair, while I continue preparing my hot sudsy water—and yet, in the meantime, this distinct aroma of a conflagration is sweeping up into my olfactory system and presenting to me the idea that we is all in a pericolous state of danger. This idea mushrooms in my head, and at last—for I am myself a kind of bastion of our way of life; I always eat Dolly Madison ice cream whenever there is the choice—and so I say, 'Your Colonelhood, pardon my humble ass—'"

"Blair!" Sissy said.

"'Pardon my humble bones, suh, my low condition, my dribbilafaction—' you seem puzzled, Cynthia honey—you ain't heard of that?"

"Yes. Oh yes."

"'Well, pardon all that then, Colonel, my de facto status and all, but I smell—' But I am cut off in the prime of life—from

my larynx and general voice box region my warning is un-
timely ripped—and all the bastions is shouting at me at once
and in unison. What we call A Capella. 'Shut your bones, man.
Do not address till you is yourself addressed, sealed, and
dropped down the slot there.' Me, I suspect them of high wisdom right off, so I sluk off, and cleave unto myself, and oh yes
rightly so, for his name's sake. And they too, in a huff, dealt
me a parting glance not deficient in informing me of just who
I was and why and what for, yes sir, and they were off to the
sagitary, a very snappy group could make your eyes water just
the sparkle alone. I was left alone—hang on now, Markie, we is
edging up on the end—and all alone it was I who had the glorious and untrammeled experience, the delirious and delectafa-
catory happiness, the supreme and pleasurable moment—I had
for myself, young 'uns, a little life-arama and the last laugh,
when that there edifice, all that government wood, and all
them government nails and shingles, all them dishes and
greasy-faced pots and pans, the whole works, my children,
came burning right on down and into the good earth. Thanks
go to the Wise Old Lord, too, for I fortunately escaped with
my life, and I stood out there on that little ol' company street,
and I watched that there mess hall expire and groan and puff
itself right out. It burned right on down to the ground, children, and into it, Amen."

"What did?" Cynthia asked.

"Who?"

"The edifice. Don't you listen when I'm talking here?"

It had been a long tiring day, and Cynthia's bafflement
brought her right to the edge of tears, with Mark only a step
behind.

"It's a *joke*, sweethearts!" Martha cried. "A funny story!"
And the little girl and her brother, relieved of their confusion,
were swept away on waves of laughter, far away from the cares
and conditions of their lives.

Necessity aside, it took an effort of the will for Martha to
leave Hildreth's. She was having a good time; she was liking
Blair Scott; by extension, she was even liking Sissy. She remembered now how much she had liked her on that quiet
afternoon she had come to look at the room—carefree and
silly and, for all her experience, innocent. Now, both Blair and

Sissy seemed to her very happy people. From the doorway, Martha turned back to them and waved a fluttery and uncharacteristic farewell. Sissy threw a kiss and Blair called after her, "*Au revoir*, blondie."

Outside Sid was already at the curb, crossing the children. He had warned and warned her about being late, until finally he had stopped whispering his warnings and gotten up and gone ahead. She watched him now as he looked both ways up the street. She started to follow him, but she couldn't. At first it was only that she wanted to turn back into Hildreth's and have one last cup of coffee. But then she wanted more; she wanted him to take her children not just across the street, but as far as he liked. She wanted all three of them to continue walking, right out of her life. She wanted to be as mindless as a high school sophomore. She wanted to be taken on a date in somebody's father's car. What she wanted were all those years back. She had never had the simple pleasure of being able to think of herself as a girl in her twenties. One day she had been nineteen; tomorrow she would be thirty. For a moment, she wanted time to stop. *I want to paint my toenails and worry about my hair. I want—*

She looked back over her shoulder into Hildreth's window and saw Sissy eating her mayonnaise. Suddenly it was as though her old Fifty-seventh Street had been pulled from beneath her: she was floating, nothing above or below. All her life seemed an emptiness, a loss.

At the door to the Hawaiian House, Sid stood holding Markie's hand. Cynthia was asking him, "Were you in the Army?"

"The Marines," he told her.

"Were you in a war?"

"Two." And he looked at Martha with his most open appeal of the day: *Two. All those years. I have no wife, no child. Don't deny me.*

"Tell us a story," Mark said.

"Children," Martha said, "Sid has to go home. He has some work to do."

"That's okay." His annoyance with her had disappeared. He spoke softly, setting the scene. It was here and now that she was supposed to say *yes*, kiss him, fall into his arms. He stood waiting in his big raglan coat, a solid and decent man. "I'll stay with them," he said.

"They can stay alone. It's all right, really."

"I don't mind," he said.

"As long as I'm in by one, Cynthia likes to stay alone." She touched her first baby's cheek. "Don't you, lovey? She's the best baby-sitter in Chicago. Barbie's mother looks in every hour or so."

"I can dial the police," Cynthia said, "the fire, the ambulance, Doctor Slimmer, I can dial Mother, I can dial Aunt Bev, I can find out the weather, the time—"

Martha bent down to kiss the children good night; it was four minutes after five. Kissing Cynthia, she said, "You're a very good brave girl. But, baby-love, *don't* call the weather any more, will you? It's tragically expensive. If you want to know how it is just look out the window. Good night, Markie. Are you happy, honeybunch?"

"Uh-huh," he said, yawning.

"Good night, Sid. Thank you for a merry Thanksgiving."

"Martha, if you want me to sit with them—"

"You have work to do."

"I can work at your place, honey."

Cynthia looked at Markie: *honey*. Martha put her cheek to Sid's and, for a second, kept it there.

"Martha—" he began. However, she chose to misunderstand him; no, no, they could stay alone; it was good for them, it developed character; it destroyed silly fears. But Cynthia, don't forget, you don't open the door for anybody. Then, feeling no compulsion to say any more, she left the three of them—it was dusk—and went into the Hawaiian House to feed a bunch of strangers their Thanksgiving dinner.

3

I SUPPOSE I have certain advantages over my colleagues (and 99 percent of the world's population) in not needing my job. I am alone in the world, and self-sufficient—economically, that is—while they, on pay checks that are slipped bimonthly into their boxes at Faculty Exchange, must buy provisions for wives, children, and in a few instances, psychoanalysts. Worse, they have aspirations, visions of tenure and professorships, and all of this combines to make them jittery on other scores as well. I teach out of neither spiritual nor financial urgency. Perhaps I could receive my share of satisfaction from some other job, but at present I prefer not to. I have never had any pressing interest in buying or selling, and I possess neither the demonic genius nor the duodenum necessary for mass persuasion. There are occupations outside the University that have interested me, but they are, to be frank, tasks that play footsy with the arts; whenever I think of them, I think of all those girls I used to know in Cambridge who, the day after graduation from Radcliffe, zoomed down to New York to be copyreaders in the text-book departments of vast publishing houses, or script girls for Elia Kazan, or secretaries at twenty a week for perennially collapsing, perennially sprouting, little magazines. Perhaps the other sex can afford such lapses into fetishism, but the rest of us are wise to take our places as men in the world as early as we can possibly make arrangements to.

So, for myself, I taught classes as diligently as I could, straining daily at being Socratic and serious; I marked all those weekly compositions with the wrath of the Old Testament God and the mercy of the New; I emerged bored but uncomplaining from endless, fruitless staff meetings; and every six months or so, I plunged into my grimy dissertation and mined from it another Jamesian nugget to be exhibited, for the sake of the bosses and their system, in some scholarly journal. But in the end I knew it was not from my students or my colleagues or my publications, but from my private life, my secret life, that I would extract whatever joy—or whatever misery—was going to be mine.

—

I reached Chicago so late on Sunday night, feeling so broken and foggy, that it was not until I awakened the following day that I realized that the taxi I had taken from the airport had skidded me home to my apartment through a snowstorm. My limbs and mind had been fatigued from both my journey and my visit, and that distant corner where consciousness still burned was fed with recollections of the weekend—of my father, his fiancée, the Horvitzes, the old Herzes, Martha Reganhart, and of myself, what I had and had not done. When I am about to die the last sound you hear will be that of conscience cracking its whip. I am not claiming that this makes me a better man or a worse man; it is merely what happens with me.

At seven-thirty the next morning, the alarm sang out one stiff brassy note. Beyond my frosted window, it was a lithographer's dream of winter; such Decembers they have in the Holland of children's books. The snow covered the ground, and the sun the snow. With a happiness so intense that I saw no reason to question it, I rose from my blankets. Just living, sheer delightful breathing, had, in earlier periods of my life, convinced me that a man, like a dog, is most himself wagging his tail. This truth now asserted itself again, and it was with genuine pleasure that I shaved my face, selected my clothes, and prepared my breakfast. Four inches of snow, and life had changed back to what it once had been, what it should be forever.

I walked to the University through the crackling weather and the virgin snows, and arrived at Cobb Hall feeling as righteous, as American, as inner-directed as a young Abe Lincoln. Ears tingling, I taught two consecutive classes with such passion and good spirits that one of my students—a kittenish girl who never read the assignments but had a strong desire to please—carried her pouty lips down the corridor after me and, before my office door, allowed them to part. "Mr. Wallach, I think that was the most important hour of my life. It opened up whole new worlds." We did not touch, but I went into my office thinking we had. My spirits remained untrammeled. I decided that before I began to mark papers I would call Martha Reganhart and verify our dinner date. By mistake I dialed the Herzes' number. Paul answered; following a moment of dumb silence, I hung up.

The moral: Don't be fooled by the weather. Beneath the lovely exteriors, life beats on.

—

Later, because it was four o'clock and because it was Monday, there was the usual meeting of the staff; so life is ordered in academe. I arrived early, chose a seat near the window, and made myself comfortable at the round meeting table. I had with me mimeographed copies of four student essays which had been handed out to us the Monday before; they were to have been graded and mulled over preparatory to today's meeting. A quarterly examination was coming up, and the object of evaluating these essays was to make sure that we were all in agreement about standards of judgment. We lived forever on the edge of a deep abyss: there was a chance that one of us might give an A to an essay to which another of us had given a B. And, intoned our more pious members, it was the student who paid the penalty. But it was we who paid the penalty, these grading sessions being nothing less than the student's last revenge on his teacher. If the phenomenon we all engaged in that afternoon were ever to be staged in the theater, I would suggest that a chorus of freshman be placed behind a gauze screen, visible to the audience but not to those playing the part of teachers; rhythmically, while the meeting progresses, the chorus is to chant *ha ha ha*.

My colleagues drifted in, alone and in pairs. First—always first, with a clean pad of lined yellow paper and a cartridge-belt arrangement of sharpened pencils around his middle—Sam McDougall, a man whose dedication to the principles of grammar could actually cover you with sorrow. Sam had written a long work on the history of punctuation, and though he looked to be the world's foremost authority on hayseed, he was in fact one of its foremost authorities on the semicolon and the dash. A year ago he had unearthed two comma faults in an article of mine in *American Studies*, and ever since had chosen to sit next to me at staff meetings to show me the light.

After Sam came our young ladies: Peggy Moberly, everybody's friend, plain and oval-faced, a girl who in certain sections of our land would probably be considered the prettiest in town; and Charleen Carlisle, with whom—a year and a half before—I had fallen in love for five minutes. She was tall, purple-eyed, and stunning in a haughty way, and the day the Dean had introduced the two of us I had thought he had said her *first* name was Carlisle. Flustered by her complacent beauty, I melted in the romance of her appellation. But she turned out to be called Charleen and was engaged to an intern at Billings, with whom she bowled twice a week.

Then entered Frank Tozier, about whose sexual persuasion I am to this day in doubt; and Walker Friedland, our glamour boy, who jumped up on desks in the classroom whenever he taught *Moby Dick*. Walker had made honest men of us all by marrying a student with a spectacular pair of legs. We had all hung around, yawning, waiting for her to swell up with Walker Jr., but a year had passed and now she was a slender sophomore, still locomoting herself with those legs, and Walker was probably swinging out over his class from the light fixture: he had gotten away with it. He was a peppy and amusing fellow, rumored to be our most popular member—though it was rumored that I was myself a little in contention, having been invited the previous year to partake of lunch once a week in the dining hall of one of the girls' dormitories—"Mr. Wallach, do you really believe Thomas Wolfe is *over*written?" "Mr. Wallach, don't *you* think Frannie is pregnant?" "Mr. Wallach, someone said that you said in class—" "Could you give a little talk to the girls, Mr. Wallach?"

There were two other bachelors engaged in this baleful competition: Larry Morgan, a petulant young fellow who sported a beret and a cane, and our madman, Bill Lake. Bill had been connected with the University of Chicago since before puberty; rumor had it that one day he had been seen slipping a note to Enrico Fermi—and from that it all began. In fact, Bill had been a Quiz Kid; I remember him from my own youth as the one with the noseful, who was always converting a hundred and sixty-four dollars and thirty-two cents into its equivalent in francs, marks, lire, and what have you. Now, wrapped in his red wool scarf, he stormed through the hallways leaking freshman compositions after him, bound for the sloppy smoky hell of his office, where it was his pleasure to reduce coeds to tears because of their lifeless prose styles. Next came Bill's buddy, Mona Meyerling, a bull-dyke, I'm afraid, but awfully sweet, though always a little too anxious, I thought, to give other people's cars a push with her Morris Minor. She had been an officer in the WACs and still wore the shoes. In a way, she always struck me as our most solid member, which may reveal some secret as to my own sexuality, or lack thereof.

Trotting on the heels of Mona was Cyril Houghton, who had confided to me once that he had invented most of the footnotes in his dissertation, which nevertheless was reputed, by Cyril, to be the last word on the poet Barnaby Googe. Also our New Critic, Victor Honingfeld, forever off to Breadloaf or the Indiana School of Letters, forever flashing at me rejection slips signed in John Crowe Ransom's own hand. And our Old Critic—our tired critic—the victim (willing, I believe) of two opinionated wives and college politics, gentle Ben Harnap. Next was Swanson, a blond, wide-faced boy from Minnesota who had a blond, wide-faced wife from Minnesota. He had been hired at the same time as I, and obviously some kind of scale-balancing was supposed to be going on. Prior to her retirement, Edna Auerbach had referred to me as "a playboy in academic clothing," and perhaps that helps to explain the presence of our silent, serious Lutheran.

Lastly, there was John Spigliano, and my contribution to the staff, Paul Herz.

I do not see that there is much to be gained by chronicling all that was said that afternoon. Since it is already clear that I have neither great love nor admiration for certain of my colleagues, it might seem that I was taking the opportunity of recording their words to make them appear silly. Teaching is a noble profession with a noble history, and it may simply be that we are living through a slack time.

I was not really giving the meeting all my attention anyway. No sooner had I sat down at the table than Paul Herz sat down across from me. The sight of him stimulated my memory; I was reminded of my recent encounter with his family, and with his wife . . . And an idea came to me then that seemed the most daring and spectacular of my life. All through the afternoon (Paul across from me) I tried to dismiss it, and yet it hung on—and not at all because it made sense. Perhaps it hung on because I wanted something to hang on—to hang on *to*—that didn't make sense. What I'd like to call my spirit, what I'd like to consider the most human part of me, was like some vapor that I couldn't get my hands on; it evaded all expression, it wouldn't leap out and shape my life. I wished I could just *push* it a little, and perhaps it was in an attempt to push it that I deliberately thought to myself all through the long afternoon: *Run off with Libby. Run off and marry Libby.*

Sense . . . nonsense—how one judges it is unimportant. It simply seemed like the next step. At least, I began to think, the next step someone else might have taken.

———

When I came out of the meeting, I stood in the doorway of Cobb Hall a moment, expelling from my lungs the stale fumes of the afternoon. I watched the last few windows blacken, one by one, in the laboratories and classrooms that faced out onto the quadrangle. It was nearly six, and the white tennis courts had a simple geometric grace under the dark sky. The Gothic archways attested to the serious purpose of the place and made me want to believe that we were all better people than one would suppose from the argument we had just had. Just before our session had ended, there had been a short, fierce combat between two of our members. Paul Herz had given an A-minus to a paper John Spigliano had marked D. It was the first time since his arrival that Paul had spoken up, and, provoked by John, he had unfortunately lost his temper. On the way out, Ben Harnap had said to me, shaking his head, "Well, your friend's one of those angry young men, all right," while Paul had simply charged by all of us, not saying good night. Earlier John had referred with little reverence to Paul as "a creative writer," and Paul finally had hit the table and said that John Spigliano must hate literature—otherwise why would he want to strangle it so? "At least there's a little *life* in this essay," Paul had said, his fury riding out of him at last, leaving him a little crumpled-looking in his chair. "The presence of life, or liveliness," John had replied, "by which I take it you mean a few turned phrases, may be a winning quality in the daily newspaper, but I don't know if it's what we're trying to teach students in this course." "What *are* we trying to teach them?" "We're not educating their souls," said John; to which Paul replied, loudly, "*Why not?*" Just before the end of the meeting —just before I had spoken my piece—John had said to all of us, charmingly almost, "We take up style in the last quarter, and perhaps Paul could lead the discussion for us then. If we have a creative writer on the staff, I certainly hope we'll be able to take advantage of his specialty." Paul Herz had mumbled as an answer, "I wasn't talking about style."

There had been nothing elevated about the exchange, and during it the rest of us had remained silent. Two opposite natures had met and collided before us, and so quickly had it happened that I did not even know what to think or to do. In fact, at the very moment it broke out, my mind had been spinning and spinning in its own direction. I was hearing Libby speak. She was telling me again what she had told me that afternoon a week before, just prior to our entering Brooks. She was saying that Paul was happier, and so she was happier too. Her husband was able to write through the afternoon (when staff meetings didn't intervene), and when she got in from work at five-fifteen, she found that he had set the water to boil for the vegetables and seasoned the meat. Eyes swelling with tears, she had told me that a change had taken place in Paul; ever since Reading and her stay in the hospital, he had been both a doctor and a servant to her. In the mornings he rose and squeezed orange juice and brought it to her bed. He walked with her to the I.C. station, and home again on the evenings when she had a class downtown. Order, said Libby, method, plan, accomplishment—all this gave meaning now to their days. There was this and there was that, but whether there was passion, whether there was pleasure and love, she had not made entirely clear. What was clear was simply that after our visit to Brooks, what had once existed between us seemed to exist again. As for the impassioned plea that I visit Paul's parents, and my decision to do so, what else was that but a last-ditch effort at hiding from the truth?

Marry Libby? I asked myself, while across the table it seemed as though her husband had just launched a campaign to lose his job. It was at this point that Peggy Moberly had nervously raised her hand and said that perhaps Paul and John were both right; she proposed that the student be given two grades, one for content, another for form. Victor Honingfeld instantly rose in his chair to say that he did not see how anybody could fail to understand that content-and-form, like good-and-evil, were one. Mona Meyerling, mother and father to us all, said that she for one did value liveliness, and felt it should influence the grade, but that she was not really certain that this particular paper was that lively—to give the student an A would perhaps only encourage him in his grammatical abuses. Most everyone had a go at the paper by then—as the tension in the room decreased—except Bill Lake, whose temperament and history made him a kind of open city in our midst, someone who need enter no battles. And except for me.

Sam McDougall, who had come out strongly for Spigliano —and had that personal interest in my grammatical education —now turned in his seat and looked in my direction. Paul was looking at me too; so was John. I opened my mouth, and after making a rather long-winded and dull introductory statement, I wound up hearing myself say that though I had originally given the paper a C, I thought that what Paul had said made a good deal of sense. I said I didn't mind a dozen misspellings ("Thirteen," Sam whispered to me, as he watched my ship drift out to sea) or that the dash was overused. I reminded everyone of *Tristram Shandy*. I said I disagreed with John in not finding the structure quite so primitive as he had argued it to be. I wanted to change my mark, I added, pointing to the board where the grades were tallied; I would come up to a B or a B-plus. "Actually," I heard Charleen Carlisle say, a moment later, "I'd come up to a B." And Swanson, with a look of great seriousness on his face, said he might see his way clear to a B-minus. At this point John stepped in to quiet the revolt, while beside me, his face drained of blood, Sam McDougall was suffering one of the crises of his life. Shortly thereafter— John having made his final reference to Paul as a creative writer —the meeting disbanded.

In my office, a few minutes later, while snow fell outside the window, I sat down at the desk with my coat on and removed the paper from my briefcase. Mona Meyerling poked her head into my cubicle to ask if my car was stuck. I said no, and she went off, leaving me to read the essay a second time. When I had finished it I knew it was no better than a C, just as I had known it at the meeting.

As I moved off the steps of Cobb and onto the snow-covered walk, I saw a man, bareheaded and bundled up, sitting on a wooden bench some twenty feet along the path. I was feeling limp—as a result of feeling misguided once again—and I was anxious now to get home and change and be off to Martha Reganhart's; then I saw that it was Paul Herz. I wondered if he had been watching me as I stood, thinking, on the steps of Cobb Hall. It made me feel vulnerable, as though just from seeing me there without my knowing, he could have divined the secrets of my life. I could not convince myself that he did not somehow know it was I who had called in the morning and hung up. Nor could I logically explain why I had not at least answered him after he had picked up the phone and said hello.

"How are you?" I asked, walking up to him. "Enjoying the night air? It's a relief, isn't it—after that?"

Paul removed one hand from his pocket and looked at his watch. "It's a relief," he said.

"Spigliano's mission in life is to burn out the guts of better people than himself. Don't take him to heart. I once overheard him say to someone on the phone, 'Gabe is probably a nice fellow, but I wouldn't say he has too many ideas.'" Snowflakes fell onto Paul's thinning hair, and I had the urge—the kind of silly urge one can so easily give in to—to brush them loose. "You made perfect sense," I said. "But he's unbeatable. He doesn't believe he can rise in the world unless everyone else falls."

He nodded his head, then checked the time again.

"Well, I won't keep you . . ." I said, though he hadn't moved.

"I shouldn't have lost my temper." He looked up at me, speaking in a very soft voice. "It was a bad outburst to show those pricks." The light from a nearby lamp revealed the creases in his thin face; at that moment he looked nothing at all like the boy in the picture with Maury Horvitz. "Don't you think so?"

I sat down next to him. "I don't think much of some of them," I said. "Do you mind if I sit down? I've got a few minutes before dinner."

"You liked that paper—it had a little something, didn't it?"

"I thought it was pretty good," I said. "It was lively, you were right."

A girl emerged from Goodspeed Hall, and Paul leaned forward and looked her way; then he leaned back again, saying nothing.

"Do you know the student who wrote the paper?" I asked.

"No. But that's the point . . ." he said.

I wondered if perhaps he had planned some elaborate hoax; I really didn't know very much about Paul Herz, and so it was possible to think any number of things. "You didn't write it, did you?" I asked, kiddingly.

"Who do *you* think—a boy or a girl?"

"I don't know."

"I've been thinking a boy. A kid I've seen in the halls."

"A student of yours?"

"No," he said, "I just picked him out. I saw him whining one day in the halls to a friend of his. He's got an awful face. He was making a terrible scene. Bad posture. Picking at his shorts all the time. He probably has some nasty habit like not flushing after himself."

The clock in Mitchell Tower struck six gongs, and I realized that I might be late for dinner. Still, across from me Paul Herz had smiled. He was talking, no small thing.

"Why this paper?" I asked. "Why this kid?"

"Just a joke. I'm reasoning after the fact," he said gloomily. "I don't know who wrote it."

"Oh," I said, mystified.

"Look, what *is* Spigliano?"

"What?"

"Spigliano. Harvard too?"

"Harvard too," I said.

"Who fires people around here?" he asked, after a moment.

"There's a committee. Spigliano's one. So is Sam, and the Dean—I don't know, three or four others. It's depressing, I know. Sometimes I wonder why I don't go downtown and get a job pushing toothpaste for five times the salary." I hadn't meant, of course, to indicate that I was in any need of cash; nevertheless, Paul sensed an irony I didn't intend, and gave me a fishy look. "But in the end," I said, meaning it, "it's a healthier life, this one. You go into class and you can do as you please. It's not a bad life."

Solemnly, suddenly, he said to me, "I appreciate, of course, what you were able to do . . ."

"Look," I jumped in, as his voice trailed off, "why do you think this kid who doesn't flush after himself wrote this paper? You may have developed a whole new technique of psychological testing."

He smiled. "Oh—here's this disgusting unimportant kid being a first-rate bastard to his roommate in public. And here's this sweet very excited little essay. That's all. It's nice to think it happens. I'd like to kick Spigliano right in the ass for filling their heads with all that *form* crap."

Hating the same people usually turns out to be a weak basis for friendship; nevertheless, I allowed myself to feel considerable fondness for Paul Herz. He seemed to me nothing less than a genuine and capable man. At any rate, I was willing to believe this as the snow fell and we sat together in the dignified environs of the University. I was even willing to believe that he was not Libby's misfortune, but that she was his. Perhaps the truth was that Libby was a girl with desires *nobody* could satisfy; perhaps they weren't even "desires" but the manifestation of some cellular disorder, some physiochemical imbalance that fated her to a life of agonized yearning in our particular world of flora and fauna, amongst our breed of humanity. I was willing to believe that Libby either did not need to be rescued, or was impossible to rescue. The more involved I became in her life, I told myself—repeating a lesson learned several times already—the more anguish we would all have. No one had to marry Libby; she was already married!

"Why don't you come over to the club with me?" I suggested. "We'll have a drink. Warm up—"

He checked his watch again and told me he was waiting for his wife.

"She's still working?" I asked.

". . . I suppose so."

"Well," I said, "we can all three have a drink."

"I'm afraid she'll be too tired. It's better not to tire her. The weather . . ." His mood had changed, and so had his voice. Leaving his sentence unfinished, he huddled in his coat.

"What is it?" I asked. "Is she ill?"

"No," he said. "She only gave it up because the doctors don't think she should be out at night. Not in this kind of climate."

"Gave what up? I'm sorry."

He peered over at me. "School. Classes."

"I haven't seen Libby, so I didn't know. I'm sorry."

"She said, I think, she met you in the Loop."

"I meant I haven't seen her to talk with. I was shopping."

He chose not to reply. Instantly I imagined scenes in his home where my name was introduced as evidence of duplicity and crime. The little trust that had seemed to have sprung up between us disappeared, and I began to wonder just how disloyal Libby was to *me*. It was clearly time for me to be moving off, by myself.

I said, "Well, I'm sorry about that."

"She can go back in the spring and summer, you see," Paul was telling me. "It'll be all right. When it's warm again, she can start in again." I felt as though I were a parent being given an explanation by a child; there was suddenly that in Paul Herz's tone. "Right now, getting to the train, getting off the train, walking to the Downtown College—" he said. "The doctors—" he began, and the plural of the noun seemed to depress both of us. "The doctors think she should build up resistance first."

"Yes. That sounds like a sensible solution."

However there was an even better one. Doubtless it came to me as quickly as it did because it had been hiding all these years only a little way under the surface. It made me feel both old and giddy: they could borrow my car. Warmed by my heater, Libby could drive back and forth to her classes; I could park it near Goodspeed on the days she would be needing it; an extra key could easily—

"Well," I said to Paul, "I'll be seeing you."

"Okay," he said.

The formal nature of our relationship immediately reasserted itself; more often than not, when Paul Herz and I came together or parted, we shook hands. It seemed to me always to combine a measure of distrust and a measure of hope. Now when we shook hands I felt a rush of words move up, and what I finally said had to stand for all that I had decided to keep to myself. "By the way, I was in a funk this morning. I dialed your number by mistake. I didn't realize it until I hung up. I hope it didn't ruin your day, the mystery of it."

Though I am twenty pounds heavier than Paul, we are the same height, and when he rose, suddenly, holding onto my hand, I found myself looking into his worried eyes. I couldn't imagine precisely what it was he was going to say—though I thought for a moment that we had at last reached our particular crisis. I was instantly unnerved, and also, melancholy. Though I tell myself I value passion, I must admit that I do not value scenes of it; though I try to live an honest life, I do not like to see honesty stripped of civility and care. I was prepared, all at once, to be humiliated. But all Paul said, with a painful look of determination, was, "Why don't we have that drink?"

"Why don't we," I said.

"We'll go. Libby too," he added.

"If she's tired, Paul—"

"Libby would like to see the club," he said. "Libby needs . . ." But that sentence was not finished either; just the simple subject and that simple verb. With gravity, with tenderness—all this in his dark eyes—he said, "It would be good for Libby."

I don't think it would have shocked either of us then if we had embraced. It was the kind of emotional moment that one knows is being shared.

We tramped together through the snow to Goodspeed, and we did not speak. I believed it was crucial for me to stay with him, even though my watch showed that I was going to be late for Martha Reganhart. I believed something was being settled.

Paul stopped some fifteen feet from the entryway. A light from a second floor window spread around us where we stood in the snow. My companion made a megaphone of his hands and whistled two notes up toward the window. Then, softly, he called, "Lib-by . . . Lib-byyy."

He actually sang her name. As though he loved her. "Lib-byyyy . . ." After a moment passed and no one had appeared, he called through his hands, "Hey, arise, fair sun, and kill the envious moon!" But when nothing happened, he turned to me and said, "We better go in."

I walked behind him thinking only one thought. *She is this man's wife.* I followed him up the stairs to the second floor and we turned down the corridor, by the water fountain, and then we stepped into the open doorway of Libby's office. And there she was, smashing away at the typewriter. Neither Paul nor I moved any further, and neither of us could speak.

Libby was hunched over the machine, wearing—for all that the radiator was bubbling and steaming away across the room—her polo coat and her red earmuffs; her face was scarlet and her hair was limp, and moving in and out of her mouth was the end of her kerchief, upon which she was chewing. Stencils were strewn over the desk and wadded on the floor, and from her throat came a noise so strange and eerie that it struck me as prehistoric, the noise of an adult who knows no words. Yearning and misery and impotence . . . She was like something in a cage or a cell—that was my first impression. It did not seem as though her own will or her own strength would be enough to remove her from this desk. I watched her first come down upon the spacer—clump! A stencil was torn free of the carriage with a loud whining that could have come either from the typist or the machine. She threw it onto the floor and then looked up and saw the two of us.

She gasped, she brushed her kerchief over her cheeks, she touched her fingers to her hair, and from behind a mass of clouds, she pretended to be that fair sun her husband had sung out to from beneath the window.

"I'm"—she drew in through her nostrils—"just finishing." She picked up a fresh stencil. "I'll only be a minute . . . Hello," she finally said.

Paul moved into the office. "Libby—"

But Libby was bending over now, sorting through the papers on the floor. Then, giving up, she raised her body, centered herself on her chair, centered the stencil, lifted her fingers, and her mouth began to widen across her face. Her eyes swam out of focus for a moment, as she turned to say, "I'm just having a little trouble. The typewriter"—she brought herself under control—"sticks." She looked down and made the smallest of sounds: she whimpered. "Another minute."

I remained in the doorway, while Paul's long figure inclined toward his wife. "Are you feeling all right? Are you feeling sick, you're so flushed—"

She picked her ratty, lifeless kerchief out of her lap, where it had dropped, and blew her nose into it. "I'm fine," she said. "I'm not used to stencils, that's all . . ."

"Libby, we're going to have a drink at the Quadrangle Club. Why don't you save the stencil for tomorrow?"

"I have to finish."

"You can finish tomorrow. You can't sit in here with your coat on. Take off your earmuffs, Libby, and we'll get the place in order and we'll all go have—"

She was shaking her head. "The Dean needs it. Paul, please, just sit down."

"Why do you have your coat on? Are you cold? It's hot in here. Libby, come on now, please."

"I'm fine—one more—"

"The Dean can wait," he said. "You're letting yourself get upset—it's not important."

But she was shifting herself around in her chair until she was in the posture prescribed for efficient typists.

"Please, Libby. It's after six. You're weak. You've been here since eight-thirty."

"I'm fine! I'm perfectly fine!" She looked over at me, and she exclaimed, as though I doubted the fact too: "I am!"

"Yes," I said, though not very forcefully.

"Now." She centered the stencil in the carriage once again, turned to the manuscript she was copying, and struck the first key. "Ooohhh," she moaned.

"What, honey? What is it?" Paul asked.

"Why do I keep hitting the *half*? I keep wanting the p and getting the half! Oh Paulie—" she bawled, ripping the stencil violently from the machine, "*I can't even type!*"

He kneeled beside her and tried to quiet her the way a conductor quiets a symphony orchestra; raising and lowering his palms, he said, "Okay now, okay. You can type, you can type just as well as anybody. Come on now—try to hang on. You can hang on now."

"I am hanging on."

"I know. Just keep it up—"

"Paul, I've made about—honestly, about thirty-five stencils. I just can't do it! What's the trouble with me? Haven't I got any coordination either? Can't I do *anything*?"

"Did the Dean make you stay? Doesn't he know you've been sick?"

"I want to stay." Her voice now was without passion. "I wanted to stay and finish. But I can't even do a paragraph. I can't type one lousy sentence through to the end."

"You can type," he said. "You can type perfectly well." Slowly he began to gather all the discarded papers and deposit them in the waste basket. "The machine sticks. It's not your fault."

"It just sticks a little."

"All right, calm down now." He rose and offered her his hands to help her from the chair. But Libby crossed her arms over the typewriter, lowered her head onto it, and wept.

Till then I had remained because I knew it would only doubly embarrass Herz if I were to disappear; I was sure that he was as determined as I that we should go ahead with our plans—he too, I thought, had felt that something was being settled. Now I stepped out of the doorway and around into the corridor. I did not even consider how late I was going to be for my engagement. I leaned against the wall and shut my eyes, and I remember saying to myself: *I don't understand.*

"You don't have to work in any office," Paul was saying. "You just stay at home and rest."

"I don't want to rest. I'm only twenty-five. I don't want to rest all the time."

"Maybe you could take some classes during the day—"

"It's one horrible mess after another, isn't it?" Her hysteria was almost completely run down now; she had simply asked a question. "I think"—I heard her taking deep breaths—"I think I need a glass of water, Paul, and a pill."

Without moving, I called into the room, "You stay, Paul. I'll get it." For when Libby had spoken, I had had the vision of Paul leaving the room, and Libby stepping to the window, and then Libby sailing, sweeping down through the air. I filled a cup at the water fountain and brought it back to the Dean's office.

Libby was by the window, it turned out, but she was using it as a mirror in which to comb her hair. Paul was twirling her earmuffs slowly around his fingers; he signaled for me to put the cup down on the desk.

"Libby says she'd like to have that drink at the club," he said.

"Fine," I answered.

Libby turned from the window, her face no longer tinged scarlet, but a chalky white. She sighed and blinked ruefully. I was surprised to see that she had a reserve of strength in her, and grateful that the incident was over.

"I'm terribly sorry," she said. "I've been so damn silly. I'd like to go to the club, if you still want me. I've never been there before."

"It's all right," I said. "Anybody who's after the p and keeps getting the half . . ." I smiled.

She pointed at the machine. "It's a ridiculous business, but I felt like one of those old movies—tied to the railroad tracks with the train coming."

"I understand."

"It sticks," Paul explained, picking up his briefcase. "It could frustrate anybody."

"Sure," I put in. "You ought to have them fix it."

"I will," Libby said. She blew her nose again into the kerchief and took a last look around the office.

"Now," Paul asked, "what are you going to put on your head?"

She pointed to the earmuffs.

"Your head," he said. "Not your ears. Didn't you have a handkerchief—did you have to use your kerchief?"

"I'll be all right."

"It's snowing out, Libby. It's freezing out."

"Wait a minute," Libby said, ignoring him, and turned back to the typewriter to put the plastic cover over it.

"Libby," Herz said, practically begging, "don't you have *any*thing to put on your head?"

Standing over the typewriter she began to cry. "You'd think," she sobbed, "a snowflake would *kill* me."

Paul moved toward her, offering the handkerchief from his own pocket. "Here," he whispered, "just till we get there. Just put this on your head, please. Look, Libby, if you don't like office work, if it's agony, do me a favor. Quit. We don't need this job—"

"Oh, I like office work. I love office work," she said, weeping. "The Dean is a very sweet man." She raised Paul's handkerchief to her nose.

"*Please*," he said, "blow it in the kerchief, will you, honey? Libby, don't we have enough doctor bills? Please leave *something* to cover your head—"

"Well, don't be *exasperated* with me!"

"Libby, maybe if you stayed home this winter you could shake—"

"I don't want to stay home." She pulled the kerchief from her coat and ran it under her nose.

"Maybe if you take that paper-marking job," Paul said. "If you want to work, you can mark papers at home."

She bent over to buckle her galoshes. "I don't want to stay at home. I'm too damn dumb to mark papers. I don't even have a degree."

"Then just read. Cook. Keep house."

"I don't want to stay at home! What's at home? What's at home but a lot of crappy furniture!"

There was no answer to that. And after a second, Libby was clearly humiliated with herself. She tilted her head, and put her hands on her hips, and tears slid from her eyes. She was saying, "Oh but I don't want to stay home though. I really don't. Oh sweetheart, there's nothing *at* home—"

"Then," said Paul in a flat voice, "do whatever you want, Libby. Whatever will make you happy."

"Whatever will make me happy."

She repeated his words with such utter hopelessness that Paul and I both moved toward her, as though she were on the very edge of collapse. He said, "Libby, what is it? *What?*"

"Oh I want a baby or something," she moaned. "I want a dog or a TV. Paulie, I can't do anything."

"Yes you can. You can do anything." His back was to me, and he was rocking her. "Yes you can, Libby." Her chin hung on his shoulder. Her eyes were closed and she shook and shook her head—saying to herself no no no, even as Paul crooned to her yes yes yes. Then her dark eyes were open and I almost believed she was going to smile. She said, looking my way, "Oh Gabe . . ."

"Yes," I said, raising a hand as though to wave to her. "You're all right, Lib."

"Oh yes, yes I am I know—" For a moment she seemed between laughter and tears. "I think I want a baby or something. I don't want to be at home, just me. I think maybe I should have a baby—" She began to weep again.

"Libby, Libby," Paul was whispering into her ear.

She rocked in her husband's arms. "A baby or a dog or a TV," she said. "Oh Paulie, what a mess, what a weary mess—"

But he went on repeating her name, over and over, as though the sound of it would remove some of her woe. She babbled and he chanted and I watched—and then I was shaking. My hands were shaking. I could not control them, or myself.

"Then give her a child! *Have a child!*"

It was only when both their heads jerked up to look at me that I knew for sure that I had spoken. The savage voice, the fierce demand, had been mine. And my hands were motionless.

Paul Herz turned and went to the window.

When I spoke again it was in hardly more than a whisper. "Perhaps if there was a baby . . ." I stopped. I had the illusion that the two figures only a few feet away were actually way off in the distance. In miniature I saw Libby's dark face and Paul's hair and their two bodies. I said no more.

But Libby did. "What are you talking about?" she demanded of me. "What are you even saying? Why don't you just not say anything for a change? What are you even saying?" she shouted hysterically. "Do you even know?"

I leaned forward to apologize. "I forgot myself," I said. "I'm terribly sorry."

"Well, why don't you *not* say anything! Why don't you just *shut up!*"

"Libby—" Paul said, but he was facing me, so that I could not even tell which one of us he was going to address.

"Why don't you mind your own business?" Libby interrupted him, looking right into my eyes.

I did not reply.

"Why don't you leave him alone for a change?" she cried in a broken voice. "He can make babies! He can make any amount of babies he wants!"

"I said I was sorry I had said anything."

"My lousy kidneys!" she cried. "I hate those kidneys. It's my kidneys, you stupid dope!"

I looked away; after a moment's confusion I turned to her husband. "I didn't know. I didn't guess."

Libby was hammering her fists on her thighs. "Then why don't you go away! Shut up, why don't you! *Mind your own business!*"

"I will," I said. "Okay," and I turned and went out the door.

But weeping, she followed me into the corridor; I heard her voice moving after me as I headed down the stairs. "How much do you expect to be told, *you dope!* You dope, Gabe, *you tease!* Oh you terrible terrible tease—"

FOUR

Three Women

1

AT DAYBREAK it was always snowing, and very late in the night too. Inside, snow blows against her bedroom window; outside, snow falls on my bleary lids; as I make a stab at navigating my car through a black antarctica to Fifty-fifth Street, snow nearly sends me up trees and down sewers. At home it pings off my own window—time ticking, *here comes dawn again*—as in my underwear and socks I dive into the disheveled bed, gather about me my rumpled sheets, and go sailing off after sleep. How my body remembers that winter. It was always tired, poor soul, and outside—beyond what body can and cannot change, where body promises nothing, annihilates no one—it was always snowing.

—

The motor thumped under me, the heater whirred; I shot nose drops up to my sinuses (I saw the cavities of my head thick with a kind of London fog), but they only burned their way down to my raw throat. The body has no loyalty—bank it with pleasure and draw out disease. Parked across from the Hawaiian House, waiting for Martha to finish work, I was getting the common cold.

My watch showed one minute after one; then two after. I had a fevered fantasy of the hands on my watch advancing toward morning, and the temperature plummeting down and down, until by daybreak Chicago would simply have cracked in two, one half to tumble in the lake, the other to be blown westward, across endless prairies and mountains, until it dropped over into the Pacific and melted away to nothing. I was dying for spring, for warmth; the weather and my pleasures were out of joint.

Three after one. Still no Martha. Mr. Spicer, the manager of the Hawaiian House, appeared in his overcoat and hat, carrying his moneybags. The police, who waited each night to take him to the deposit box, opened the door to the squad car and Spicer stepped in. A chill ran over me; I sneezed once, and then again. My head rolled down and I half slept. Mrs. Silberman was knitting a gigantic sweater for me. A workman in overalls and tennis shoes was building a box with black windows; he was my father; the box was for me to sit in.

"Hey, open up."

On the sidewalk was Martha, and someone else—a girl bundled in a coat and hat, whose face I couldn't see. "Let us in," Martha called. The air that rushed in with them penetrated my coat and moved right down to the bone.

Martha inclined her face toward me and we brushed cheeks. "Can you give Theresa a ride? Theresa, come on, this is Gabe. Can we drive her to the El, she's not feeling too fit. Theresa, close the door."

"Thank yuh."

"Don't worry about those books," I said, turning to get a look at her, "just push everything aside."

"I hardly need . . ." She blew her nose. Halfway to the El, she began to sob. Martha touched my leg, but she needn't have, for I was in no mood anyway to ask questions.

When we got to the train, Martha turned on her knees and faced the back seat. "Everything will be all right. Just try to get some sleep."

"I knew it," the girl wept. "I just knew it."

We waited until Theresa had walked up the stairway to the train and disappeared, and then I drove off.

"Poor dumb cluck," Martha said.

"Martha, I'm going to take you home. I'm going home myself—" She wasn't listening, however, and I didn't feel I had the strength to repeat myself.

"The poor jerk got herself pregnant."

"I'm sorry to hear that, but I'm going to collapse of exhaustion myself. I'm taking you home, then I'm going back to my place."

"Oh yes?"

"I'm a dying man, sweetheart. Honestly, I'm dead." She didn't answer. "You come tomorrow," I said, "to my place. Doesn't Annie LaSmith come tomorrow?"

"I promised Markie I'd take him to buy a Christmas tree tomorrow."

"Let Annie stay with him—you can come—"

"I promised him."

"Okay. I'm just too dead tonight."

In front of her building I did not even turn off the motor.

"All day I've been saying to myself: tonight I am going to have illicit relations with Gabriel Wallach."

"That makes me very proud," I said, "but my throat feels as though it's been ripped open."

"I had Abercrombie's deliver a new set of whips and thumb-screws."

"Martha, every night you roll over and go to sleep. Every night I have to go out into this weather and drive home and try to get a few hours sleep—"

She was whistling; nothing like eight hours of work to pep her up.

"I've got two classes to teach in the morning," I said. "I just haven't the strength."

"I'm not asking you to lift weights, poor baby."

I kissed her, and she said, "Come up for just an hour."

"But my body *fails* me . . ."

She took my hand and touched it to her cheek. "Why don't you just leave everything to me," she said.

"Oh sweet Martha—"

"Why don't you just come with me, all right?"

"You sound like a tart, baby."

"See? Already you're stimulating your imagination. Come."

So I followed her up the stairs; before she placed the key in the lock, she turned and put her hand on me.

"Oh," she said, "that's so nice and sweet."

"Martha, I've got to tell you that it's got no more wind in it than a choir boy's. It's spiritless, it's humbled and limp—"

"It's sweet humbled and limp."

I went into her bedroom and she continued down the hall to the children's room, where she turned off the night lamp. I heard her close the door leading to Sissy's room. Sitting on the blanket in the dark, the feel of the quilt and the sheets and the mattress under my hands filled me with awe. I waited, and then I was sinking, and then, I suppose, I was out.

When my eyes opened, it took me several minutes to see

who was moving in the dark. Beneath me and above me I felt the clean white sheets I had so desired; someone had even been kind enough to remove my clothes. I raised my head a little and saw Martha by the window; she had one foot on a stool, and was bending forward, pulling down her stockings; the way in which her breasts hung from her body sent through my mind thoughts of flowers, mermaids, cows, things female. But I did not want to possess Martha or a nasturtium or a Guernsey; I wanted only sleep.

Martha's hands were on the flesh of her hips; they ran down over her stomach and were touching her thighs. She was looking toward me in the bed, and it was as though I were waiting for some decision of hers. Even the furniture in the bedroom seemed altered, because between *us* something seemed to be being altered. Since Thanksgiving I had done the wooing, I had done the undressing, the caressing, and on the hard and serious work we had both pitched in. We had been dogged and conventional, we had proceeded step by step, until we had both clutched, and hung on, and then fallen away into sleep. To please one another we had had to do nothing at the expense of our own pleasures; we had been uncompromising and we had been lucky.

But now Martha stood by the window looking toward me for what seemed a very long time, pronouncing words I could not make out, and I was overcome with exhaustion; though I reached up to her, saying I would have to go, I don't think my head ever left the bed. I dropped away, beyond hallucination or dream, and when I did rise up, it was never to regain power or lucidity; I was simply there, and Martha's hair was down across my legs. I raised my head—such a feather, such a weight —and I saw her hands, saw her face, possessing me miles and miles away.

"Oh Gabe," she said, "my Gabe—"

I left her there alone, just lips, just hands, and was consumed not in sensation, but in a limpness so total and blinding, that I was no more than a wire of consciousness stretched across a void. Martha's hair came raking up over me; she moved over my chest, my face, and I saw her now, her jaw set, her eyes demanding, and beneath my numb exterior, I was tickled by something slatternly, some slovenliness in the heavy form that pinned me down. I reached out for it, to *touch* the slovenliness—

"Just lie still," I heard her say, "don't touch, just still—"

She showed neither mercy then, nor tenderness, nor softness, nothing she had ever shown before; and yet, dull as I was, cut off in my tent of fever and fatigue, I felt a strange and separate pleasure. I felt cared for, labored over; I felt used. Above, she was me now, and below I was her, and however I fell away from consciousness, or floated up toward light, always, beating on me, was Martha. Beating, beating, and then rising up and away, and wordlessly calling back of her delight.

Everything was right.

What I remember of that night are those three words. Out of proportion sometimes, sometimes not in sequence, but those three words bubbling through me; what I remember is my sense that a rhythm in my life was being realized, and a rhythm in Martha's too. I remember—as night went on and morning came—a greed of hers that went beyond pleasure, and on my part what I remember is the abdication of all will. For a while perhaps she was me and I her, but at some point that morning all distinctions belonged to another world. We were sexless as any tree or rock, liquid and unencumbered as a stream or a spring—and yet so connected one to the other that when I pumped within her, plunging into a final dizzying exhaustion, I might have been some inner organ of her own. Man woman mother child—all distinction melted away.

—

Later a bell rang. When I opened my eyes, Martha was at the side of the bed, wrapping herself in a robe. Outside the darkness was just beginning to lift. I knew I had to leave, that it was time again; but it was Martha who left the room, and I let myself float backwards.

Martha was pushing at me. "Gabe, Gabe—"

But I couldn't, I simply couldn't pull myself up. Martha moved into bed beside me. "Gabe," she said softly.

And then there was a knock at the bedroom door. Martha jumped up in bed, and the door opened. Limp as I was, I went even limper.

But the face in the doorway was not a child's. It was the battered face of an old Negro woman, and she was moving into the room with a cup and a saucer. "Here's your coffee, darlin'—" she began.

Then she saw me. "Oh," she said. I had been edging the sheet up around my chin, and now I lowered it an inch and, infirmly, smiled. The woman took three big strides forward and placed the cup down on the night table. When she turned and left, I tried to push out of bed, but it was as though I'd been worked on by a carpenter during the night; hammers, chisels, planes, and screwdrivers all seemed to have had a go at my body.

"I'm sick as a dog," I said.

She was sitting beside me; I couldn't see her face, for it was resting in her hands. "Are you?" she asked drily.

I leaned up on one elbow. "I'll go," I volunteered, and then my body just gave out, and I was flat on my back. "I can't seem to do it, Martha. I feel rotten. I can't move."

I listened to the snow hitting the window, and then someone knocked again on the door. "Cynthia—" Martha hissed; following a traditional impulse, I dove for the covers.

But it wasn't Cynthia at all. Annie LaSmith was in the doorway again. She came directly into the room and set a second cup of coffee down on the table beside Martha's. "Here," she said. "For him."

Martha chose not to reply; I was feigning sleep, and Annie slipped out, closing the door behind her.

"I think—" Martha began, as I crawled up from the sheet "—I really think—" but she couldn't speak for laughing.

Nor could I; tears were running down my face as I said, "I—better—go—"

"No," she said; she held my head between her hands and we looked one another right in the eye. "You're burning up—"

"I better—"

"We have to please *shhhh*! We have to stop making—please, make me stop—*laughing*—"

"I—didn't even thank her—" I said, and Martha pushed her face into my chest and kept it there until, at last, she seemed able to control herself.

"You can't go," she whispered. "You're practically on fire."

"Martha—"

"Please"—she began to giggle again—"go to sleep."

"What time is it?"

"Seven—quarter to seven. Do you think Annie *put* something in your coffee? Oh, God, I can't *stop*—just go to sleep—"

I wanted to ask some questions about Annie LaSmith— What the hell was she doing here in the middle of the night? —but I never had the chance. Martha was holding me and sporadically giggling, and then she was holding me and I was asleep.

—

Martha was gone when I awoke again, and so was her pillow. The clock said eight thirty-five—I had a class to teach in less than an hour. I made a move, but the bedroom door slowly opened, and I closed my eyes.

"He's sleeping," Markie said.

"Shhhh."

"Is he going to stay all the time?" Mark asked.

"Just till he's better."

The next voice was that of Cynthia, the skeptic. "What's the matter with him?"

"He's sick. He was visiting, and he got very sick, so I let him stay here and sleep."

"What's he sick *with*?" the little girl asked.

"He's sick," Markie explained.

"I don't know," Martha said. "We'll have to call the doctor."

"He doesn't look sick," Cynthia said.

"But he is, sweetheart."

"He doesn't look it."

"Does he have a temperature?" Mark asked.

"I don't know, love-dove. We'll have to call the doctor and find out."

"I'll bet he doesn't," Cynthia said.

"I'll bet he does," said Martha. "You have to go to school, Cyn. Let's go."

"I'll bet he doesn't have a temperature though."

"Cynthia, what's eating you? Go put your galoshes on."

"It's a waste of money to have the doctor if you don't even have a temperature," Cynthia said.

"He'll pay for his own doctor. You don't have to worry about money."

"Well," said Cynthia, "he doesn't look like he has a temperature."

"Don't you believe he's sick, Cynthia? Do you think I'm telling you a lie?"

No answer.

"Is he, Mommie?" Mark asked.

A moment followed in which I could not tell what was happening. To open my eyes, I felt, would have made Martha look like a liar. "Shhhh," I heard Martha whisper; then I heard feet moving across the floor.

A small hand was on my forehead.

Then another, even smaller.

The footsteps retreated, and once again I slept.

—

The rest of that day is bits and pieces.

Dr. Slimmer hovers over me. Temperature of 103. He leers. He gives me a shot. Martha pays. "Here's for your wife's mink, here's for your kids' summer camp, here's for gas for your Thunderbird—" "If you had a bad experience with doctors as a child, Martha, don't take it out on me." "—living off widows and children, you're a living argument for socialized medicine, Dr. Slimmer." "I have to run, I'm double-parked—"

Beyond my door, sometime during the afternoon: "You're a woman of the world, Annie—you understand. Okay?" "What you and Mr. Reganhart do is your business, darlin'." "That a girl, Annie."

Later. "Sissy—lower that damn thing! Somebody's sick!" Later. "No, honey, you can't see him sleep. He has a communicable disease. You can see him tomorrow." "What disease?" asks Markie. "A bad bad cold." "Oh," moans Cynthia, "is that all? A *cold*?" "It's serious, Cynthia—" "Did Daddy call this morning?" "Cynthia, it was the plumber, the man to fix the washing machine. I swear to you it was the plumber! Daddy's back in New Mexico, sweetheart, Arizona." "He's in New York." "Oh Cynthia, why are you so obstinate! We haven't seen your Daddy for years—what's this Daddy business? Oh baby, don't cry, oh sweet baby, I'm so sorry—" "And keep your dirty hands off my doll!" the child wails, running off.

Later. A small hand on my forehead.

"You better not get caught in here, Markie," I say, opening my eyes. "I've got a communicable disease."

"Who?"

"I'll see you tomorrow, Mark."

"Okay."

Later still.

"How do you feel?"

"What time is it?"

"It's four-thirty. I'm going to work. Are you hungry?"

"I don't think so."

"Look, take these pills. Try to take them every four hours."

"Martha, is everything all right? Is everything, you know, okay?"

"You've slept through one hell of a day."

"I'm sorry I've been—"

"Shhhh. Be sorry when you get better." She smoothed back my hair. "I just told my roomer to clear out. So I'm feeling a hundred percent better."

"Martha . . ."

"It's all right. It's not just you. I've got claims on a private life. I'm twenty-six years old. I don't like other people's moldy old sausages stinking up my refrigerator. I don't need anyone peeking over my shoulder, that's all. Good night, sick baby."

"Good night. Thank you."

"Here's a radio. Cynthia can make bouillon. I told her you might want some."

"Good night."

And then, when it was dark outside, Cynthia. One of the frilly shoulder straps on her yellow nightgown had slipped down, but she seemed unaware of it. She was staring at me, which led me to believe she had been in the doorway some time.

"Good evening," I said. "It's snowing again, isn't it?"

"Do you need any bouillon? I'm going to sleep."

"As a matter of fact, I wouldn't mind some."

She turned and left; in only a few seconds she was back. "I don't know how I'm going to get it over there. I'm not supposed to come near you."

"Tie a handkerchief around your mouth and hold your breath, and sort of slip it onto the night table, all right?"

Cynthia went off to the kitchen, and I sat up in bed. There was a murky cup of coffee on the night table; after testing it with a finger and finding it cold, I remembered how it had gotten there. I took one of my pills, and then stuck the thermometer in my mouth and settled back onto the pillows. From the bed I could look directly at the huge circus picture that Cynthia had drawn in school, and which Martha, only a week before, had had framed. It was a gay picture—although a little painstakingly crayoned—of clowns and cages and balloons and pink-faced children holding their fathers' hands; every child was connected to every other child by a parent. It made me feel that I had just lived through a very happy day. All that had happened seemed to have followed inevitably from the night before. Our lovemaking and my illness, Martha's passion and her calling the doctor—it all seemed like one event.

Cynthia appeared in the doorway; one of her mother's fancy handkerchiefs was folded in a triangle and tied bandit-fashion around her face, an eighth of an inch below her eyes. To get the cup of bouillon from the doorway to the night table took a full minute of breathless balancing.

I removed the thermometer from my mouth. "Thanks," I said.

"You're welcome," and she fled to the hallway.

"Cynthia?"

"Yes?" She turned just her head.

"Cynthia . . . Don't you want to hear if I have a temperature or not?" It was not the child's fault, of course, that she had had her juices set for her father just when I happened to come along. I had certainly been willing till now to let her take whatever attitude she chose toward me. But softened by my condition, feeling as kind as I felt weak, and suddenly lonely too, I wanted Cynthia's suspiciousness to disappear. I wanted her to fit into the orderly world of my illness.

"Well," I said, "it's almost a hundred and two. It's not good, but it's better."

Masked as she was, I couldn't make out her expression. She put in an obedient thirty seconds, then cleared her throat and told me, "I once had a hundred five."

"Yes?"

"Markie once had a hundred three."

"Cynthia, let's be friends, all right?"

"I'm friends," she said, and, shrugging her shoulders, went off to bed.

I was still sipping bouillon when Sissy came home. She went past my door, and then came back and stuck her head in.

"Wha—?" she said.

"I didn't say anything."

"I thought you said something." She leaned against the door, a trench coat covering her white hospital uniform. "I'm sorry, you know," she said. "I wish you'd tell her I'm sorry."

"What?" I said. The only opinions I had of the girl were those I had inherited from Martha.

"That I'm sorry."

"Sissy, I don't know what you're sorry about. I really don't." Sissy's appearance, my confrontation with Cynthia, and the effort of drinking the bouillon combined all at once to make me intensely fatigued. But Sissy seemed to have no idea that the reason I had been in bed all day was because I wasn't feeling well. I suppose working in a hospital produces a certain amount of insensitivity to suffering.

"Look, I didn't mean anything," said Sissy, settling in. "It's her place."

"Sis, I don't know what you're talking about."

"I'm supposed to *move*," Sissy announced, looking hurt that I hadn't known right off. I managed to recall now what Martha had told me way back in the morning.

"Well," I said vaguely. "I'm sorry."

"Some stupid thing I said I suppose. Like I don't even remember and still I've got to move."

"It must have been pretty awful."

"It was an *argument*. I don't see what I have to *move* about!"

"Sissy, you better not stay too long. Apparently I've got a communicable disease. I'm really not up to all these moral issues."

"I mean she doesn't have to jump down my throat!" And she left the room, seeing that I was no help.

And finally Martha, in her blue Hawaiian House uniform, sitting on the edge of my bed.

"Better?"

"I was . . . I don't know how I am now." I had been awakened by her presence in the room.

"You feel warm again."

"You better watch out—you'll catch it."

"I'm a mother. I'm immune by law."

"Yesterday," I said, after a moment, "was my birthday."

"Really?"

I had just thought of it. "I've just remembered," I said, "that it was."

"Happy birthday. Are you pulling my leg?"

"No."

She lay down beside me, on top of the covers. "Only for a minute," she said. "I'm sleeping with the Christmas tree. We bought a Christmas tree, Markie and I. It's a birthday tree for you, how's that? Why didn't you tell me?"

"I don't know. I've been in a fog for about a week."

"How old does it make you?"

"Twenty-eight."

"Splendid."

"Your daughter brought me bouillon. We had a little talk."

"She'll calm down," Martha said. "She'll get used to you."

"Oh, she was fine."

"Maybe you ought to go back to sleep."

"Do you want to sleep with me?"

She smiled. "I'm sore, and you'll die, and we'll both have to be buried by Dr. Slimmer. But that was nice, Gabe, so . . . Gabe, was I selfish and aggressive and thoughtless?"

"No, you weren't."

"It's a pleasure, you know, your being sick."

"This is how people decide to become invalids. Everybody just appears in doorways with soup and kisses, and the rest of the time you daydream and sleep. Except very early in the mornings—what's your maid doing here at dawn? She scared me nearly to death."

"She says she likes to travel at five because that's the only time the streets aren't dangerous. Maybe she's right. She's actually not much more misguided than anybody else I know. Gabe? Gabe, I reached some conclusions today."

"Yes?"

"No conclusions really, just a few simple truths. Just your staying—it's so nice and different. It changes us. Going to sleep with a man and not waking up with him is really pretty frightening. It stinks. I'm not a kid any more."

"I don't know how much more of that four A.M. business I could have taken anyway. I think this fever may be some psychosomatic form of surrender. When I get better, we'll have to work out some new system. There's no law that people have to make love at night—"

"There isn't, except it might not have been too genteel starting right off with afternoons. Honey, I've got a little boy running around all day."

"Then," I said wearily, "we'll have to work out something. I don't know."

"Go to sleep now," she said. "Don't worry about strategy. Take a pill."

I leaned toward Martha, for I wanted just to touch her.

"No, no, go to sleep . . . Gabe—listen, last night I said the hell with it. I said I had rights. I said this to myself. You make me feel I have rights. I do care for you. I won't be like that again."

"It wasn't bad, Martha." Then I said, "It was only strange."

"I scared myself."

"Oh, not so much," I said, smiling. "Not so much."

"A certain amount, yes."

"You didn't like it?"

"I've got to watch myself. I'm a mother of two."

"Four. There's Sissy and there's me."

"Sissy's going."

"She wants to stay. She came in and told me."

"Did she take her clothes off, the little nudist?"

"What happened?"

"I told you. I came to see some simple truths."

"She said she'd said something."

"No, she just made some smart remark to the effect that if you could stay over why couldn't Blair stay over, too. I just don't think she should hang around any more. It isn't even her, finally. It's a roomer. This is my home, you know? Did your family have roomers?"

"Not that I know of."

"Well, mine didn't either. On top of everything else, it leaves me feeling déclassée."

"Martha, I'll leave tomorrow."

"You'll leave when you're well."

"I owe you for the doctor."

"Twelve bucks, that son of a bitch." She leaned over and kissed me. "Happy birthday. Go to sleep."

I was moved by her, almost to tears. "Martha, you're a generous, competent, warm-blooded, splendid girl."

"Now if I wasn't déclassée I'd be perfect."

"I hope you realize that this sickness is a tribute to you."

"Oh, yes," she said, getting up and smoothing my blankets, "to me and our mutual loneliness—"

"That looks to be over."

"We'll see how wonderful everything is when your temperature goes down."

"It's never going down. I'm going to be fed bouillon by your daughter in her nightdress forever."

"Oh yeah?"

"Come here, Martha dear, just one minute. Come on, dearie."

"You're going to die, you know. You're going to keep this up and you're going to die."

However, I know I'm not going to die until I'm very old, and Martha trusted in my knowledge.

—

In the night the phone rang. I turned on the lamp beside the bed and looked out the window. It was four-thirty. There was not a sound in the apartment. Had I been dreaming? I dropped back into sleep, warm, protected, content.

But in the morning I knew who it was that I had been expecting to telephone. All the day before he had probably been ringing my apartment to wish me a happy birthday.

After Martha had brought me my breakfast, she plugged the phone in the bedroom, at my request. Then she started back into the kitchen, where Sissy, she told me, was crying for forgiveness. I could see she was on the verge of changing her mind about her boarder, and since I was myself preoccupied, we only touched hands, and then went about catching up on private business.

I asked the operator to give me the charges when the call
was finished, and then waited to hear my father's voice. We
had not spoken with one another since Thanksgiving, and suddenly I had a premonition that he was sick, that in fact he was
going to die.

Millie, our maid, answered.

"He's gone away," she told me.

"Where to, Millie? I didn't know."

"Grossinger's," she said, disapprovingly.

"He's all right, isn't he? He's not sick, is he?"

"Oh, he's all right."

"What's the matter, Millie?"

"Nothing."

"Did Dr. Gruber go up with him?"

"Dr. Gruber, no."

"Did she go with him, Millie?"

"I don't know who went with him."

"Okay, Millie. When will he be back? Christmas?"

"He told me not to expect them till after New Year's."

"I see . . . Okay, Millie. Look, you don't have to stay
around the apartment, you know. Get out, enjoy yourself. Go
down to Macy's, go look at all the windows. Fifth Avenue will
be full of lights."

"Hasn't he sent you a card either?" she asked. "He used to
go away, he used to send a picture post card. I suppose he has
more important things on his mind."

"I suppose so."

After a moment she said, "It's a damn shame."

"All right, Millie, you just get out and enjoy yourself."

"Happy birthday," she said to me.

While I waited for the operator to ring back with the
charges, the front door opened and I heard Sissy's voice. "You
can go to hell, Martha! You have no right!"

"I have every right and you watch your language."

"You're sexually immature—"

"Close the door, Sissy, you're letting in a draft. Close it!"

"Who cares!" Sissy cried, and the door slammed after her.

The next thing, Cynthia was at the front door, sobbing.

"Come on, Cynthia, now stop it. You don't want to go to
school with red eyes, do you?"

"I don't care. Where's Sissy *going?*"

"She's only moving, sweetheart. She's going to go to a new apartment."

"Where?"

"I don't know."

"I don't want her to move. I don't want her to move away."

"She has to . . . Now, come on—"

"*Why?*"

"Because it's too crowded here."

"Well then he's going too, isn't he?"

"Cynthia, when you're a grown woman and there's another grown woman around, and she's single— Cynthia, it's just the way it is. I'm a grown woman, my baby."

"But I'm a child, though," Cynthia said, weeping.

"Ohhhh, come on," said Martha, gently, "you hardly know Sissy. You have other friends. You have Stephanie, you have Barbie, you have Markie, you have me—"

"I don't want her moving away."

"Cyn, you have to get ready now. You have to go to school. Come on, blow your nose."

The child blew. "Will I ever see Blair again? Now where's *he* going?"

"Of course you'll see Blair again. You'll see him in Hildreth's."

"He'll go away, I know it!" For the second time that morning, the door slammed in Martha's face.

Then it opened again. "Cynthia, be careful, there's ice—"

"*I* know it," the child called back.

It was a while before Martha came in to see me. I took a pill and drank the last of my coffee, and decided it was time to dress and drive myself home and be sick there. But when I started to get out of bed, my limbs just couldn't do the job.

Martha appeared, wearing her coat, and I pretended not to notice the shape her eyes were in.

"I have to go shopping," she said. "Do you want anything?"

"You know, I feel much better. I think perhaps at noon I'll drive home."

"Slimmer said stay in bed. You can't go out in this weather; it's snowing. It's awful."

"I can't stay here forever."

"Who's talking about forever? You just can't go out now."

"Sissy doesn't have to move, Martha, because I'm staying here."

"Sissy has to move because *I'm* staying here. Please, don't mind that scene. You shouldn't be feeling guilty about anything," she said, kissing my forehead. "I mean even the things you should be, you shouldn't be. It's a privilege of the shut-in."

"But it has to do with me. I know it does."

"You only precipitated what had to be. I should be thankful to you."

"What about the rent?"

"What about it?"

"You told me Sissy helped with it."

She made a gesture with her hands that I can only characterize as hopeless. "I'll be all right."

"Martha, I feel responsible," I said. "I know I'm making Cynthia unhappy too."

"You're not making *me* unhappy! You're not making little Markie unhappy. He's out in the hall right now, just dying to take your temperature. Majority rules around here. Cynthia is going to have to start to learn the facts of life. Don't worry about her—she's going through a whining stage, that's all. It's only a battle of wills, and I can't think of any reason why I shouldn't be the winner. I'm twenty years older than she is, I earn the money around here, and I do the major part of the worrying, and she'll be fine, just fine."

"I don't want you to feel obliged to me. I'm perfectly up to being sick alone."

"You're a liar too. Gabe, don't we have some rights? It's not killing anybody, is it, you being here? Dear heart, I've been a terribly, crushingly good girl. I've been a pain in the ass to half a dozen healthy, willing, attractive men. I've been so careful it's coming out of my ears. And I was right to be, I'm not sorry a bit. But bringing Sissy in was a mistake—making love to you wasn't."

"You're sure?"

"I feel my life is right side up again." She let out a sigh then, which, in its way, thrilled me. "I'm really quite taken with you, old man."

"I'm taken with you, Martha. But I don't want you to start

chucking people out, and so forth and so on, and becoming miserable . . ."

"I'm not miserable."

"I'll admit I'm not unhappy myself."

"I didn't think so," she said, smiling.

"And now would you do me a favor, since I've set your life so straight? Would you stop by my apartment and see if there's any mail?"

"Sure."

"Take my car. The key is in my trousers. Why don't you use the car? Otherwise the battery will go dead."

It had been several years in the doing, but I had managed at last to pawn off that machine on someone.

After Martha left, Markie came in, carrying my thermometer as though it were a wand. I thanked him and he went into the living room where he said he was making Christmas cards.

I called Spigliano's office and got the departmental secretary.

"They were wondering where you were," she said accusingly.

"I'm sick, Mrs. Bamberger. I probably won't be in until the end of the week. Is Mr. Spigliano in?"

"No. I'll leave him the message."

"Would you ask somebody to pick up the papers today from my nine-thirty class?"

"Mr. Herz is in the office—shall I ask him?" Without waiting for an answer, she left the phone.

Then she was back. "Mr. Herz says he'll pick them up for you."

"Thank you."

"He says do you want him to drop them off at your apartment."

"He can just leave them in my office."

When I hung up—from a conversation that had struck me at first as only irritating—I felt strangely dependent upon Martha Reganhart. The strong attachment I had for her, I'd had almost from the very start; what was unsettling was that my needs seemed really to have begun to outdistance my feelings. And it occurred to me—a thought equally as unsettling—that she might herself be in a similar predicament. I wondered if our intimacy would have been so immediate, had it not been for the other circumstances of our lives. It seemed to me that we should try at least to slow things up a bit. I found myself hoping that when she returned she would be holding in her hand a picture post card of Grossinger's indoor swimming pool, with the words *Happy Birthday* written across the back. But she returned with an armful of bundles for herself and only a bill from the phone company for me, and I had a morbid vision of my mother's bones in the earth. Martha dumped all her gayly wrapped packages on the floor, and then because Markie was calling her, she flew out of the room to attend to his needs. And there in the bed, with no post card to read, I knew that both my father and I had been cut loose from the past.

"We going to have tuna?" Markie was asking.

"You had tuna yesterday," Martha answered. "Didn't Annie give you tuna?"

"I think eggs."

"No, Mark. You had tuna yesterday. How about a grilled cheese?"

"I'm making something. Does he have a temperature?"

She came back into the room, unbuttoning her coat; her face was rosy from the winter air. "Markie wants to know if you have a temperature."

"Only a degree and a half. How's the weather?"

"It's incredible. It's ghastly. Your car has some kind of respiratory ailment. Bronchitis—"

"Wouldn't it start?"

"Not willingly."

"There was no other mail for me?"

"Uh-uh." She began to pile her packages at the foot of the bed. "Presents," she whispered. "I have to go down to the Loop this afternoon and finish up."

"Look, why don't you wait a few days? I'll go with you."

"I thought shopping bored men."

"I might get something for Cynthia for Christmas."

"She works in subtle ways, my daughter. Are you going to neglect poor sweet Markie? And me?"

"You and Markie ought to be comforted by having your way all the time."

"Oh ought we?" She went over to the door. "I better close this. Mark?" she called. "Are you all right?"

"I'm making something," he called back.

"Mommy's right here." She closed the door and came over to sit down on the edge of the bed. "Here," she said, picking up one of the packages. "A nurse's kit for Cynthia; she thinks Sissy is a nurse. And this is for Mark—clay. He has simple pleasures. And then these soldiers, and this little chicken." She opened the lid of one of the unwrapped boxes. "Here, see? You spin this and the chicken comes out. Actually, I think I got it for myself. And then I got this book. For Cynthia." She handed it to me. "What do you think? I want your honest opinion. She's very old for her age."

"What is it?"

"It's kind of a beginner's sex book."

"Oh yes?"

"It's supposed to explain everything. Well, take a look. It has little colored drawings of people's insides, and of mother's nursing little babies . . . Well, come on, Gabe, open it. Don't kid around about this, please."

It did indeed have little colored drawings of insides, and outsides too. I flipped through, reading passages along the way.

"What do you think?" she asked.

"Listen." I read from page twenty-four a beginner's description of the sex act.

"Well," she said, "what do you think?"

"I don't know. It may make her the most popular kid in school."

"Does it strike you as too hot?"

I handed her the book. "Look."

"What are they?"

"Testicles."

"Hey, look, don't you think it's okay? Six different medical groups recommended it, thousands of psychiatrists—why can't *you* think it's okay? A few weeks ago she was walking around here talking about sexual organs. Yesterday in the co-op she began referring to these in a loud voice as my *mammaries*. Nice? She's obviously getting information from somewhere."

"Here. Look."

She looked. "Oh Gabe, *I* don't know. What should I do, store it away for five years? It's recommended for kids from eight to eleven. Oh the hell with it." She began wrapping it again. "Even after she reads it she'll get it all backwards anyway."

"Actually, if you want to hear my personal preference—"

"Go ahead. What is it actually?"

"Actually I prefer kids referring to their po-pos rather than their outer labias. Maybe I'm just old-fashioned."

"You wouldn't be so casual, jerk, if it was your little girl."

"I wouldn't be so nervous either."

"I can't help it."

"You shouldn't worry so much about her."

"She's so nutty about men—"

"She hasn't shown herself to be particularly nutty over me."

"She's *interested* in you, don't worry about that."

"Martha, she'll have a normal sex life, or abnormal, or subnormal, and this book and you—"

"I must be doing *some*thing to her. What does she think? Truly. Honestly."

"She loves you."

"You're being evasive, please don't."

"Martha, she has a will like iron. You know that. And she's intelligent and bright and pretty."

"The combination sounds like death to me."

"Well, if that's so, what's there to be done?"

"You really believe that, or are you being a polite lover?"

"You're a good mother, Martha."

"I'm a rotten crab. I lose my temper and I make them worry about money and, oh forget it—I don't know. You think I'm all right, do you?"

"Fine."

"I'll be all right, all right, as soon as that Sissy gets out of here."

I waited, and then I said, "And me."

"I don't want you to get out of here, Gabe, I really don't."

"I have to admit it, Martha—I don't think I want to go." I tried to say it playfully, but when she asked, "No?" I answered seriously, "No, I don't think so."

"Then stay sick, sweetheart. Run around the block and work up your fever. The thought of you lying here in bed, and me out shopping, it's a real pleasure. I put the key in the door of your car and I felt like a big shot. I think to myself, if the phone rings, he'll answer it. You know," she said, "we crawled into bed too quickly, though. You know that, don't you?"

"You do a lot of thinking while you shop."

"You know it though?"

"I know it."

"Okay," she said. "I don't know exactly what that establishes . . . but something. Look, I'm going to make Mark a grilled cheese sandwich. You too?"

"What are you going to do with this book?"

She turned at the door, and shrugged.

"It's an imperfect world, Martha, but you didn't make it."

"But neither did Cynthia," she said.

———

After lunch my temperature shot up, and Dr. Slimmer came to give me another shot of penicillin. We pushed him for a diagnosis of my case, but he took another twelve dollars, whispered some words about an X virus, and drove off in his Thunderbird.

"If he'd only say he didn't know! Just once. Honest to God, I'm going to start packing for England."

"Why don't you get another doctor?"

"I can't. I love that bastard. He makes me feel so *right*. You better go to sleep."

"You too," I said. "You look tired."

"I'm tired, but I'm happy. I love feeding you, do you know that? I'd like really to fatten you up. You don't happen to be losing your hair, do you?"

"Sorry."

"Because that's what I really go for, you know—nice bald old fat fellows with big sweet paunches and thick greasy beards."

"It sounds to me," I said, "as though you want to settle down."

She gave me some fruit juice and I went to sleep; but just before I slipped off I had a vision of Markie napping in his crayoned bedroom, and Martha sleeping on the sofa beside the Christmas tree, and me in my own warm bed. What peace, under one roof.

Later in the afternoon Cynthia came home from school, drank her milk, and went off with Markie to the playground to build a snowman. I lay in bed, listening to the radio, and

choosing from amongst those offered me only the most ancient of programs. I tuned in to the old ladies selling lumber
yards, and to the young girls searching, with perfect enuncia-
tion, for the love of English lords, or, later in the day, brain
surgeons with baritone voices and tweed coats. "Oh put on a
smile, Mary—here comes that young Dr. Baxter in his tweed
coat. Hi there, Doctor . . ." Yes, there harassing the air waves
were those same luckless couples who had struggled through
my childhood—for then too a radio had glowed beside my
convalescent's bed—and who turned out to be struggling still.
And recovering from a minor ailment, I discovered—being
waited upon with orange juice and aspirin, starting books
and feeling no cultural obligation to finish them, reading in
today's newspaper what the temperature had been the day
before in all major cities of the world, pouring over the
woman's page and racing results with little foothold in either
world—it was all as cocoonish and heartwarming on the south
side of Chicago as it had been fifteen years before on the west
side of New York.

At dusk, I smelled dinner being prepared in the kitchen.
Martha stuck her head in to ask if I was all right, and she must
have understood precisely the kind of pleasure I was lolling in.
I heard the back door open and close and after five minutes
had passed, I heard it swing open again. When she came into
my room, she dumped a stack of glossy magazines at the foot
of the bed.

"Go ahead," she told me, "stuff yourself. Mrs. Fletcher says
she's through, I can keep them."

"What is it?"

"*Golden Screen*, *Movieland*, *Star World*, everything."

"God bless you, Mrs. Fletcher. How did she know?"

"I managed to convey the expression on your face. How is it
up there in Pig Heaven?"

"I love it. Come here."

"I'm making dinner."

"Come here. Just for a minute."

Recuperation! Convalescence! Long live minor ailments!
Long live Pig Heaven!

—

When it was nearly dark outside, the children returned from the playground. My dinner was brought to me on a tray, and in the kitchen I could hear the others eating.

"Mother, he's swallowing without chewing."

"Chew first, Markie. You'll get a pain."

"I have a pain."

"No he doesn't, Mother."

"Eat slowly, Cynthia. Where's the fire?"

"What fire?"

"Markie, don't talk. Eat."

"When's Santa Claus?"

"On Wednesday, honey."

"Boy!" Markie exclaimed.

"There is no such person as Santa Claus."

Markie sent up a howl.

"Cynthia, that's silly. For Markie there is."

"That's right, Markie," Cynthia said, "for you there is."

"I know," the little boy said.

A wind rattled the window panes back of the drawn shades, but it was of no consequence to me. In her coat and kerchief and snow boots, Martha appeared to take my tray away.

"Good night," she said.

"Wake me when you come in."

"You better sleep through. If you are awake—"

"Please wake me. And thank you for dinner, Martha. I appreciate you for being so perfect."

She went off to work. I dozed for a while and read, while in the living room Markie and Cynthia watched television. At about eight, the front door opened.

Cynthia ran out into the hall to greet whoever had arrived. "Hi!" the child cried. "Hi, Blair!"

Mark joined in. "Blair! Blair! Tell a story!"

Sissy spoke. "Cut it out, kids. Please. We're busy."

"Are you moving away?" Cynthia asked.

Sissy started down the hall toward her room; I saw her flick by my own door.

"But *where?*" Cynthia demanded.

"You go back and watch TV, Cyn, please. Go ahead."

"Hi, Blair," Cynthia said, forlornly.

"How are you?" he asked. Then the door to Sissy's room slammed, and Mark and Cynthia's slippers padded back toward the living room.

Not much could be heard over the noise of the TV, but some fifteen minutes later there were footsteps down the corridor; then Cynthia again, running out into the hall.

"What are you doing with that, Blair?"

"Open the door, will you?"

"Where are you going?" Cynthia asked, but Blair passed down the stairs.

Cynthia walked to Sissy's room, scraping her heels; she knocked at her door, and then I couldn't hear anything.

Now Markie ran by my room; he was wearing his pajamas and his hair was slicked back from his bath. He looked in at me with half his face, then took off down the hall. I heard Sissy and Cynthia talking as they moved toward the front door.

"You can keep the phonograph here, Sis, if you want."

"Watch it, Cynthia, it's heavy. Please, honey, move—"

"You want to leave your records? I don't think Mommy would mind if you left your records."

"Mommy would mind, all right," said Sissy, and she went down the stairs. She called back from a flight below, "Don't close the door."

There were half a dozen more trips up and down the hall. Finally Blair was saying, "Why don't you burn all this crap?"

"Shhhhh."

"I got only one closet, Sister."

"Oh Blair, how can you be so selfish! I want to go with *you*! Where am I going to go?"

"You got Dave Brubeck and Gerry Mulligan, Sister—there won't even be *room* for me."

"Oh Blair," she was weeping. "You're disloyal . . ."

They went out the door again.

I heard Cynthia call, "Should I leave it open? Sissy, do you want it open? Are you gone?"

"I'll be right up," Sissy answered.

When Sissy returned, she was alone.

"Are you going now?" Cynthia asked.

"Uh-huh." Sissy had stopped crying. "I just want to check the room."

Cynthia followed her down the hall. "Where are you going? Where are you going to live? Are you going to go home?"

"I'm going to live on Kimbark."

"Oh goodie, Stephanie lives on Kimbark!" Cynthia replied. "Are you going to live with Blair? Is he your husband?"

"Cynthia, you know he's not my husband."

"Are you going to sleep in bed with him?"

"Of course not!" Sissy shot back. "Look, Cynthia—" But that was all she said; she went into her old room.

Soon they were back on the landing.

"Goodbye, Sissy," Cynthia said.

"Goodbye, Cynthia. Goodbye, Markie. I'll see you in Hildreth's."

As Sissy started down the stairs, Cynthia called, in a last attempt if not to stop what was happening, at least to slow it down, "Sissy, what's your real name? Do you have a real first name?"

Sissy stopped a moment. "Aline," she said. "My first name is Aline."

"Don't you like it?" Cynthia asked. "Don't you like people to call you that?"

"Oh, I don't mind." Outside Blair leaned on the horn of the car.

"Can I call you that?" Cynthia asked.

"Cynthia, I have to go now."

"Do you like Cynthia for a name?"

"Sure—listen, I have to—"

"I think it's horrible." Cynthia said, and she was crying. "Don't you want to stay here any more? You sure you don't want to sleep here tonight?"

"Cyn, I have to go. I don't think your mother wants me to live here any more."

"Oh," cried Cynthia, "rotten Mommy!"

The horn blew again—and Sissy was gone, having decided at the last, it seemed, to let Cynthia's judgment of her mother stand. For all the girl's hard luck and all her weakness of character, it still seemed to me a disgusting and unnecessary trick.

Soon Cynthia was bawling in the other room. Markie came to the door. "I think Cynthia's sick," he said.

I did not know what good it would do if I were the one to

go in and try to comfort her. Nevertheless, I got out of bed and put on an old bathrobe of Martha's—the pajamas that barely covered me were hers too—and started to the door. Markie, who had been watching me closely, said gravely, "You need a shave." He led me into the living room, where his sister lay face down on the floor. The Christmas tree, which I had only seen in brief glances as I went to and fro between the toilet and the bed, was so tall that its pointed top bent against the ceiling. Markie went over to the TV set and put one hand on the volume knob, as though to anchor himself to the Western he'd been watching.

I sat down on the sofa. "I'm sorry you're so upset, Cynthia. Would you like a handkerchief? Can I do anything for you?"

"You did it. You and Mommy."

"Did what?"

"Made Sissy go!"

Markie sat down on the floor, and stood up, and sat down again. I tried to give him a reassuring smile.

"How did I make Sissy go?" I asked Cynthia.

"You did."

"How?"

Cynthia wiped her eyes with her sleeve, and caught a glimpse of me from under her lashes.

"You just did."

"You'll have to tell me how I did."

"You told Mommy to do it."

"That's not so, Cynthia. I didn't tell Martha anything either way."

"Mommy stinks."

She waited for a reaction, which was not forthcoming. But it was her own grossness, rather than my silence, that made her stop crying. Some moments passed, and then in a voice a good deal less certain, she said, "She does."

"Does she?"

"Why did she have to make Sissy go? Sissy's fun. Sissy's my friend. She had no right to make her move."

"It's her house. She can ask anybody to move out, or to stay, that she likes. Don't you think adults have rights as well as children?"

"She doesn't own it."

"Yes, she does," I said.

"Ha-ha. The agency owns the house."

"She owns you, Cynthia. She owns Markie."

I looked at Markie, who was sitting on the floor now, reflecting.

"My father owns me too," Cynthia said cautiously.

I went on as best I could; though there was suspicion in her voice, there was a note of inquiry too. "Of course your father owns you too. However, right now you're living with your mother. Your mother makes your meals, and buys your clothes, and she calls the doctor, and sees you get Christmas presents, and she supports you and protects you. Do you know that, Cynthia? Your mother works to support herself, and you, and Markie."

"So does my father. He's a famous artist."

"He's a famous artist, Cynthia," I said, and then, hesitating only a moment, I added, "but he doesn't support you."

"Yes, he does."

"No," I answered, "he doesn't."

"Well, he sends presents."

He didn't; however, I said, "That's very nice, but sending presents to people isn't the same as supporting them. Supporting them is much harder. Presents are like cakes with icing, and supporting is like all the other food you eat every day. Which is more necessary, Cynthia? Which is more important?"

After a moment, in a superior tone, she said, "I don't even like cake."

"I like cake," Mark said.

I smiled, and Cynthia said to me, "He doesn't understand."

It was by no means a friendly remark but it was the result, I thought, of some conscious decision to give up the fight—it was only depressing in that it made perfectly clear that what her brother didn't understand, she did. It left me feeling that the child had much too small a back for all her burdens; I pitied her her intelligence.

Yet as a kind of tribute to her years, I said, "He's just a small boy."

"I'm her brother," Mark said.

Cynthia stood now and feigned a yawn. "I think I'm going to sleep," she said, quite formally. "I'm very tired."

"Good night then," I said.

She turned to face Mark. "I think you had better go to sleep too." With her hands on her hips, she was, in both posture and tone, as much like Martha as she could manage to be. "Come on, Markie."

Instantly Markie made known his objection.

Taking a quick look my way, she folded her arms, then glared at her brother. "That kid's going to drive me crazy," she said, and with that, made her exit.

Markie lay himself down on the floor, facing the TV set, and within minutes was asleep. I got up and turned off the television and the floor lamp, and covered him where he slept with an afghan from the sofa. Sitting back in a chair, I watched the boy's small back rise and fall; I could barely hear his breathing. I was sure that in her bed Cynthia's eyes were wide open; whatever straightening out I had attempted had to do with only the surface of her family life. How could a seven-year-old child be expected to understand her mother's troubles? How could I begin to understand the child's? I felt now that it would have been wiser of me had I remained in bed, and let her cry over whatever it was hers to cry over. I did not begin to know all that had happened over the last seven years, and it almost seemed a mistaken sense of duty—and also a decided uneasiness about my presence, where Cynthia was concerned —that had led me to defend Martha against her daughter. Yet all that had been said in the hallway between Sissy and Cynthia had seemed to me totally unjust; Martha was not rotten for a moment, and she did not stink, and I believed that I had fallen in love with her.

Having had my scene with Martha's daughter, however, I was sure that I was not falling in love with Martha's predicament. Her life was complicated in ways that would not uncomplicate themselves by a mere lapse of time. There were these two small children to consider; loving her, must I not love them too? Was I up to it? Did I really want to?

I looked blankly into the lights of the Christmas tree for a long while. *Did I want to?* I wondered what Markie and Markie's older sister could ever be to me? Was this what I wanted for my life?

When I awoke, Markie was asleep in my lap, where he must

have crawled some time during the night. Martha was standing over the two of us, her coat slung over one shoulder.

"What time is it?" I asked.

"After one. One fifteen."

"You better lift him off. I hope I didn't give him anything."

But she did not take the child immediately; she stood where she was, looking down. Then she bent so close that I could feel the cold of her skin, and lifted Markie from me.

When she came back into the living room, she was still carrying her coat. "Hadn't you better be going back to bed?" she asked.

"Not for a little while."

She spread her coat over me and sat down at my feet with her arms around my legs. I began to take the pins from her hair.

"It's been so nice," she said. "So comfortable and nice. And I'm so tired."

"Just rest."

After a while she asked if Sissy had gone.

"She's gone."

"Was there any kind of scene?"

"Cynthia got a little upset. But she's all right."

"And she never really liked Sissy. Do you know? They never really got along."

"Well then, she'll probably mourn my passing too."

"Me too," Martha said.

"I think I'll go tomorrow, Martha. I don't have a fever any more."

"You're still weak."

"I can be weak at home, I suppose."

"Who'll make your meals?"

"I will."

She said nothing then, nor did I.

"Martha," I said, some minutes later, "I can't stay here. It would get terribly complicated."

"I know."

"You seem so tired. Maybe you should go to sleep."

"Theresa Haug became hysterical in the kitchen. I had her station and mine."

"Who's Theresa Haug?"

"The girl we drove to the El."

"That seems a year ago."

"Two nights," Martha said. "Just two nights."

I remembered the girl now, sobbing into her handkerchief in the back seat of my car. "It's too bad," I said.

"It's awful," Martha said.

"Who's her boy friend?"

"He's become shy; he's married, he won't have anything to do with it."

She said that, and because it was dark, and because I was tired, and because we were becoming blue—and doubtless for other reasons as well—I was reminded of the several people it seemed I had disappointed in my life.

Martha shrugged her shoulders and said, "Gabe."

"What's the matter?" I asked.

"Nothing. I guess pleasure depresses me too. Do you know what we should do?"

"Go ahead, tell me."

"Whatever we want. Simple as that."

"And what's that, Martha?"

"You should just keep staying here," she said. "Isn't that what you want?"

"Yes," I said.

"It's what I want . . . So can't we do it?"

"I really don't know," I said.

"I think it's about time," she said. "I have rights in this world too, don't I? The whole situation isn't normal to begin with—being twenty-six and having these kids and working every night. That's not normal, so how can I even pretend to have a normal love life? My life is cockeyed and different, and my daughter is just going to have to learn that. Is that asking way too much? I can't keep going around and around with these two little psyches in my pocket. I had an alcoholic old man, and that's the way it is—nobody can go around protecting you from everything. Oh Gabe, aren't they on their own a little bit too? I'll do my best, I promise, but can't I have a lover like anybody else? Every goofy girl in the street has someone who can stay all night, but mine has to leave at three in the morning. Does that seem fair?" She turned on her knees then and took my face in her hands. "Gabe, just tell me, do I seem selfish and mean? There's them, but then there's still me, isn't there?" she asked. "Is there?" She buried her head in my lap. "Please stay with me, Gabe. Stay and live with me."

I closed my eyes a moment, hoping that what I ought to do and what I wanted to do would be one. When I opened them and looked down at Martha's face, I believed they were.

In bed, where Martha came to be with me a while, she said, "It isn't marriage, you know. You don't have to think about that—nobody has to marry me. Do you understand? Nobody ever has to feel obliged to marry me. Please don't worry about my babies, they'll be all right. They're nobody else's worry but my own. Nobody has to take them off my hands, Gabe. I don't need a husband, sweetheart—just a lover, Gabe, just someone to plain and simple love me."

———

In the morning I lay in bed until I figured that everyone was through in the bathroom. Cynthia and Markie had already held some sort of relay race in the hallway, but it was silent now, and I assumed that breakfast had begun. I wanted to surprise Martha—and to lighten her load—and before she brought my tray to me, I thought I would appear at the table, shaved and groomed, showing myself to everyone in my re-covered condition. That morning I understood what people mean when they talk about feeling like a bigger person. With the cheery disposition not only of a physical convalescent, but a moral one as well, I put my bare feet into my shoes and moved as quietly as I could across the hall and into the bathroom.

Martha's bathroom walls were covered with travel posters, two to mask windows opening onto the outside stairwell, and another to hide a crack in the plaster, which ran from the ceiling down to the toilet. *Visit Switzerland! Visit France! Visit Holland!* Brushing my teeth, I felt magnanimous about all three countries, especially little Holland, whose porcelain-faced girls in traditional garb would forever be tending tulips within the direct line of vision of whoever was sitting on the can. I picked up a brush that was on the sink; no sooner did I run it through my hair than my forehead and ears were draped with Martha's long blond strands. I didn't even feel a ripple of annoyance. Why should I?

I looked for a razor and found one in the soap dish of the

bathtub; the blade was dull and I set out looking for a new one, feeling, as one can while engaged in trivial works, at one with the world. Perhaps it was because my spirits were so high that they were able to tumble so low when I opened the medicine chest. Capless bottles, squeezed-out tubes, open jars, toothless combs, a cracked orange stick, three wilted old toothbrushes, hairpins, pills and capsules scattered everywhere. Perhaps there was a blade, but in that square foot of chaos, who could tell? Curiously, the sight of that mess was a knife sunk right down into the apple of my well-being. Nevertheless, I stuck my head into the hallway and called out, in an unexasperated voice, "Honey! Do you have a razor blade?"

The conversational mumblings in the kitchen continued.

"*Martha!* Have you got a new blade? I want to *shave!*"

No answer. I took another poke at the medicine cabinet. About the only thing one could get one's hands on—without everything falling after—was a bottle on the bottom shelf with a skull-and-crossbones label. I put my feet back into my shoes, and started down the hall, one of Martha's hairs floating down over my nose. Clutching her old misshapen bathrobe around me, I charged into the kitchen to behold Mark and Cynthia spooning Wheatena, and Martha talking to a man. At first he was only a tannish leather jacket and a big shock of red hair combed flat with water—and then, for an instant, an astonished toothy smile and a little courtly bow. He even stuck a hand out toward me, but I was in flight, my unlaced shoes dropping off my heels with each step, clopping my guilt and shame after me. There hadn't been much dignity in my getaway, which was perfectly evident to me as I leaned against the poster of Holland, catching my breath.

And it had only been the janitor. The janitor! The fury I began to feel was first directed at those damn shoes, then at my legs, which seemed by themselves to have carried me away before I'd even had a chance to think. But finally I was furious with myself for having thought again that I could simplify life.

My search through Martha's bathroom was now undertaken with the kind of single-mindedness one associates with the insane. I was no longer even thinking about shaving, only about the blade. I flung open the medicine chest to be confronted again by that skull and crossbones. Big as life it said:

DANGER. But *she* didn't seem to know there were children in the house! *She* apparently didn't read in the papers about all the poisoned kids! A mess! An unexcusable mess!

Next to the bathtub was a closet with two narrow doors. Till then I'd had no occasion to look into Mrs. Reganhart's closets —so there were things that I could not have known. The apartment itself had always appeared to me to be not so much chaotic as in a state of disarray, a condition I originally liked to think of as an extension of the lighter side of Martha's nature. Magazines spilled over onto the rugs; tables and chairs were turned so as to accommodate upraised feet; apple cores browned in brimming ashtrays. But all this had only seemed the sign of a relaxed life; I took it for evidence of a deep humanitarianism. But what I looked into as I swung open the doors of the bathroom closet was evidence of madness—dirty bed sheets thrown in amongst clean towels, wet wash cloths draped over torn Modess boxes, five bottles of suntan lotion (all sticky and dribbling), a stack of *National Geographics*, a beach pail not entirely empty of the beach, dish towels, blankets, a length of garden hose, several coffee cups full of pencil shavings—why go on? I sat down on the edge of the bathtub, and my hand came to rest in the little aluminum tray that was attached to the wall; several old wet hairy slivers of soap were instantly brought to my attention.

There was a knock at the bathroom door.

"Come on in," I said, and the door flew back.

"Haven't you at least got a razor blade without a little crud on it?" I demanded.

"Haven't you got a head with brains in it?"

"I was only looking for a razor. I didn't know anybody was out there."

"I thought you were sick. I thought you were too sick to get out of bed."

"I wanted to shave—I thought it might give a little lift to the general appearance of the place."

She was wearing a pair of tight red cotton slacks with some kind of abstract black and white design all over them. I wanted to ask if her husband had painted her pants for her, then I remembered he was her ex-husband, and then I remembered —with an unfortunate degree of vividness—all that we had attested to and promised the night before. Yet I hated her that instant for those circusy slacks, and hated her behind, which bloomed without mystery within, and I didn't care too much for her sweater either. Lumpy, turtlenecked, immense, it made her body seem mountainous and her head a pin. A pinhead! A dreamer!

"It would please me no end," she said, as I registered on my face precisely the amount of sympathy I felt for her outfit, "if you wouldn't flounce around this place in your nightclothes!"

"What the hell do you expect me to flounce around in? I didn't come prepared to stay."

"Then don't flounce around! You jerk!"

"*Me?* This place," I said, getting off the tub and raising my arms as though to protest to the postered walls, "this place is a mess! Look," I said, "look at this!" I flung open the medicine chest, which suddenly did not seem so hellish as it had two minutes earlier. If my sense wasn't right, however, there was something right about the general direction in which I was charging. I presented to her the bottle that said DANGER. "Is this any way to keep drugs with kids in the house? *Here,* so even Markie can reach it?"

"I'll worry about what Markie can reach, all right? You just worry about a little decorum."

"And what am I supposed to do, hide? Is that what all that sweetness and light was about, is that what it means to be Mrs. Reganhart's lover? Hole up in the latrine till the janitor leaves! What do you think I am? What the hell kind of nerve do you have telling me to be decorous anyway! Look at this place, *look* at it!" I turned and pulled back the closet door. A bottle of suntan lotion clinked obligingly out onto the tiles.

She did, I think, give a little gasp: found out at last.

"You could," she said in a more respectful tone, "have waited until he left. Was that asking too much?"

"I didn't know he was *here*. That's the point, Martha. You want to wire the place, flash lights back and forth? What are you making of me?" I considered the closet again. "Look at that!"

"Oh shut up." She pulled the cover down on the toilet and sat down. "Just shut up."

But I didn't want to, or intend to. I had moved well beyond the closet. I saw myself as having been weak and unimaginative the night before. Right at the start I should have had the sense, the courage, to go off and be ill by myself. I was old enough and wise enough. How could I live in a house where no strange man would ever live in peace?

I picked the lotion bottle up from the floor. "You ought to be ashamed," I said. It was not quite to the point, but I couldn't think of much else that was nasty to say. Bending over had made me woozy, and when the wooziness passed I still found it difficult to sustain my powers of concentration. What was it we were arguing about?

"Oh will you please . . ." she moaned.

"You don't know what you want, do you know? You don't know what in the world you want."

She had been ruminating, her turtleneck pulled over her chin. Now she looked up. "Look, if you don't want to stay here, nobody's twisting your arm. You don't have to precipitate some lousy argument to leave. Spare me that, will you? If you want to go"—she made a slow backhanded movement—"just go."

"You know," I said, leaning against the sink, "I'm beginning to have a little sympathy for your first husband, that poor bastard."

"Oh, that poor bastard. We all ought to shed tears for you *and* him. He was another one who couldn't walk out until we had a real rip-snorter that gave him the right. If you want to leave, Gabriel, just leave, all right?"

"What is it you want though? Can you tell me? Can you put it into a sentence or two? Tell me how you expect somebody who's supposed to be living here not to ever show his face in the kitchen. How can you want one thing," I said, slamming the sink, "and then not be willing to take what *follows*—"

She rose and stuck a fist under my nose. "I can take what follows, damn you! Don't tell me about consequences, you!"

"I'm sorry," I said, without any display of sorrow, "but you know what I'm talking about."

Her eyes were suddenly full of tears. "You didn't have to make a silly jerk out of me in front of him! Our kids play together—his daughter gives my daughter measles! Couldn't you at least have shaved?" she cried. "Oh you looked like such a bum!"

"*I was looking for a razor blade!* I was *trying* to shave in this pigsty! Oh this is impossible—this is ridiculous! I don't need this kind of agony, really!"

"Then go. Lower your voice, damn it, and go."

"You don't want me to be here anyway, that's pretty clear to anybody."

"Look, you don't want to be here, so don't pull that stuff."

"Maybe that's so—"

"If maybe that's so, then maybe you ought to take your left-over pills and shove off." She painted a smile on her face and inclined toward me. "If maybe that's so, all right?"

"That's fine. I don't need this kind of crap, no sir."

There was some rhythmic lapse in that last sentence, an absence of thunder, that left me feeling like something less than Winston Churchill on the floor of Parliament. I was dying to make some final crack about her slacks, but it wasn't really necessary. Everything we had set out to accomplish, we had accomplished. Henceforth and forever after, last night did not exist.

In the bedroom I had to hunt through the dresser to find some of the clothes I had been wearing three days before. It was a pleasure for me to have to open all her drawers: evidence, piles and piles of evidence in every one. My jacket and trousers were hanging in the closet, there with tennis rackets, snowboots, back issues of *Art News*, rolled-up rugs, stockpiles of red bricks, and, of course, all of Martha's clothes, which were hung from the rack, or piled on the floor, or shoved in on the overhead shelf. Naked, I stood there and allowed the sight to flood me with a deep sense of righteousness.

After I dressed, I looked at myself a moment in the mirror; my eyes were as expressive as two marbles, and my beard hid the angles of my face. It was a streaky orange color, as though tea had been strained through it. Looking at that face, it was difficult to think that I had been in the right. But I was glad I was leaving, I told myself, and before I left I wanted that fact registered upon the consciousness of this house.

This time I did not turn away from the threshold of the kitchen, but entered and stood firm. Markie had a milk mustache, and Cynthia, in her red jacket with the hood up and wearing her leggings, was ready for school—though the act was that she was casually lingering over her last drop of Ovaltine. She was about as casual, of course, as us two adults.

Martha was looking out the window, drinking coffee from a mug. On the back porch was a snowless gray ring where the garbage pail had stood; the sun was shining onto the white railing of the porch and the white window frames, and it lit up the walls of the kitchen with a fine, healthy glare.

"I think I'll be going now," I said.

She did not turn. Markie was leaning out toward me from his seat; Cynthia moved not a muscle.

"Okay," Martha said.

Everything that had happened, including this final eloquent exchange, seemed all at once rather shabby. I felt, with a touch of desperation, the desire to leave on good terms. Slowly, so that neither Cynthia nor Markie would miss a word, I said, "Thank you for letting me stay while I was sick." The little speech would not have fooled me, but then I was not a child; at least the sounds had been made, and they would live in the history of this family.

Martha turned; she made a movement with her mouth— wry, I suppose you would call it—which indicated to me that she found me incredibly predictable. I was disappointed that she did not at least understand what I had tried to do; but her understanding was only for her own troubles. I thought back to how she had made love on the night I had fallen ill, and I thought back on all she had said to me the evening before, and I did not care very much for her.

"So long, Cynthia," I said. "Goodbye, Mark." I started back down the hallway, feeling suddenly fevered and weak. But I was strong enough—I told myself—to make it down the stairs and into my car, and home.

When I was almost into the small dark foyer that led to the street, I heard the door of Martha's apartment open above me. There was Cynthia, her head within her hood, stretched over the bannister. In her red jacket, with her blue eyes, she looked as innocent and pretty as I had ever seen her.

She extended a hand over the railing. "Here," she said. "Mommy says these are the keys to your car."

I would have asked that she simply drop them down to me had I not thought there was a certain forlorn quality in her voice. I went back up the stairs, but when I took the keys she merely looked away.

"Thank you," I said.

"Uh-huh."

I hurried back down, and when, from the first floor landing, I took a quick look up, the child was still there. Her face rested sideways on her wrists, which were flat on the bannister. She may have had her father's dark hair, but the eyes were Martha's —inquisitive, lively, and not at all sure what they were after.

"Goodbye, Cynthia," I said.

"Goodbye."

I went a step further, and she called, "Aren't you coming back?"

I shook my head. "I don't think so."

She seemed, then, utterly confused. She raised her head from her hands, but then, flatly, she said, "Okay. Goodbye," and turned and went back into her house.

—

I had two pieces of mail waiting for me at my apartment. One was an invitation from the Spiglianos for cocktails late on Christmas afternoon. I contemplated the affair: John's Abruzzi dance, Pat's Liverwurst Delight, dinner afterwards with some madman like Bill Lake . . . But I would be sick anyway, I thought; I would never be rid of this fever and so didn't have to begin suffering over a Spigliano get-together.

There was also a picture post card in color from Grossinger's. I went around the apartment letting shades fly up, and prying windows open to allow passage out for the musty unused odor that hung over the place. With my joints feeling heavier than the limbs they joined, I cautiously laid myself down on my unmade bed. "Hello! This is the life!" was written on the card in a large scrawl, and it was signed, "Fay and Dad." A P.S. squeezed in at the bottom drifted over into the address. "We're here thru N. Yrs. Day so you can stay in Chi have gd. time Dad." That was it—no reference made to anything that had happened in his life, or mine, prior to the day before yesterday. I couldn't believe he had forgotten, but apparently he had. It was a great day for separations.

2

PERHAPS it is the watering-down of some racial guilt that causes the trouble, but Christmas has always been a day I don't enjoy. As unpracticed in the faith of my fathers as I am—which is about as unpracticed as my own particular father is—I am nevertheless not at peace with the culture when most of my countrymen, in the warmth and privacy of their homes, are celebrating the birth of their Saviour. The radio stations are all bells and organ music, the streets are empty, the frames of my neighbors' homes blink with colored light bulbs, and in snowy mangers on church lawns are assembled miniatures of figures in whose reality, or suprareality, I have never for a moment been able to believe. I realize the fun the Gentiles are having, and I wish them well, but for me it is as though all the long, shapeless Sundays of the year have fallen on one day, and I tap my fingers, a superfluous man, waiting for nightfall and December twenty-sixth, when I can come back into the world.

But nightfall seemed never to be coming—not even late afternoon. I marked dozens of freshman essays, and then I made myself a snack and carried it from the kitchen into the small living room. Sections of the Sunday *Times* that I had been intending to read for weeks were scattered around the apartment, whose furnishings seemed today to be exuding a special jumbo-sized portion of ugliness. The decor of the place might be designated as 1930s Modern; there was a chair of bent laminated wood that was upholstered in imitation alligator skin; several other chairs made of tubular steel, a chest of drawers of curved metal, and other icy-looking ornaments, none of them smacking much of hearth and home. It was a little like living in a supper club. The shades on the windows were still the blackout shades from the war.

I drank a little whiskey and ate my snack and lit the cigar that my colleagues Bill Lake and Mona Meyerling had given me when they had stopped by to visit a few days before. I settled down in earnest to smoke it—dragging on the wet end, then holding it off to look at as I exhaled. The good bachelor life. I tried to think of a girl I could invite over to share my dinner, but gave it up as a bad idea; I would end up overstimulated, undersatisfied, and a total alien from the day. Just relax, said I, and have a good time by yourself.

I went to the window. Since ten in the morning it had been looking like four in the afternoon, and it still did at half past two. I took a long gaze at myself in the mirror: old sweater, baggy trousers, hair uncombed, beard coming in orange again. To complete the picture, I jammed the cigar between my teeth and wondered about the future. It occurred to me that I would never marry; at about the same time I realized that I hated cigars.

The day crept on. Boredom soon began to teeter on the edge of something worse, and I put on my coat and went out to take a walk. When I returned, I tried to get back to marking papers, but at five I said the hell with it and went into the bathroom to shave. I changed my mind three times over, finished shaving, dressed, and walked over to John Spigliano's.

—

The door to the Spigliano apartment opened, and in the entryway stood two red-headed children, each with a pink party dress, black patent-leather shoes, and a stern expression.

"Hello," I said to the two of them.

Only their starched dresses creaked.

"Ooohh," came a voice from around the corner—which was followed by a tray full of hors d'oeuvres and a vast contraption of green. Pat Spigliano stepped into the doorway, and her dress, with a quantity of stiff green netting encircling the green skirt, momentarily displaced the little girls.

"Gabe!" Saying my name somehow caused Pat to swing the hoop a little exuberantly—and out of sight went the children. "I thought you wouldn't be coming. We heard you were sick. John will be so happy."

"I'm feeling better, thanks," I said. "I thought I'd come for—"

I was talking to myself. Pat was looking from one of her children to the other. "Stop hiding, girls—come on now, come on—"

The girls battled gamely against their mother's dress, while Pat looked back to me. "And these are the twins," she announced. "This is Michelle Spigliano and this is Stella Spigliano. And this is Doctor Wallach, girls, one of Daddy's teachers."

In loud hoarse voices, Michelle and Stella exclaimed: "*Merry Christmas, Mr. Wallach!*"

"Doctor," their mother corrected them.

"That's all right—"

But Stella erupted, as though one were needed in the house, "Doctor!" while her partner took the whole thing, as they say, from the top.

When they had both settled their heels back onto the floor, I said, "Merry Christmas to you, girls."

Pat winked at me, then went back to the business of shaping destinies. "Now take Doctor Wallach's things, young ladies—"

"No—it's not—" But one child was dragging at my sleeves while the other jumped up toward my chest, after either my hat or my tie. With a sense of hopelessness about the whole afternoon, I gave up all the garments asked for and came into the apartment.

Pat immediately pushed her hors d'oeuvres my way, and waited for my comment.

"They're very well-behaved," I said.

"We think so," she replied. "They're going to Radcliffe."

I refrained from asking whether they were just home now on vacation. As we came into the living room, Pat said, "Have some pâté?"

"No, thank you," I said.

"Well then, have a good time—have fun—" she instructed me.

"It was liverwurst before he rose into the hierarchy, and it'll be liverwurst till he dies, the symbol-hunting son of a bitch." It was Bill Lake who spoke, his wiry carcass twined around the back and arms of a chair in which Mona Meyerling was stiffly seated.

"Or becomes president," I said.

"Or bats fourth for the White Sox—who knows? The nice, frank, beastly opportunism in those two absolutely compels admiration," said Bill, neither raising nor lowering his voice, despite Mona's attempts to make him pipe down. "Which I don't want confused with affection," Bill added. "You ought to stop feeling sorry for yourself, Wallach. How would you like to be Associate Professor Spigliano and have to perform coitus on the hostess?"

"What makes you think I'm sorry for myself, Willie?"

"Mona," he said, lapsing into his W. C. Fields voice, "get the boy a drink. The boy needs a drink. Have you noticed Charleen's boy friend, with the liquidy eyes—over there, with the damp lips? Also, Wallach, self-concerned. A big dumb beautiful girl like Charleen, married to an introspective dermatologist—"

Mona was standing now; she was dressed up, and because I like her so much I'd rather not describe her outfit. "How are you feeling?" she asked. "Better?"

"I think I'm fine," I said.

"—all the ills and perversions of the world," Lake was saying, "sloth, *u*sura—"

"What do you want?" Mona asked. "A bourbon?"

"Look, I'll get it."

"—sodomy, pseudohermaphroditism—my God, the olisbos itself was no mystery to the Greeks—"

"Sit down," Mona said, "and keep him quiet."

She took the distance between the chair and the liquor table in six graceless shambles. Bill Lake babbled on, "—and what about the French? In 1750 two lowly little pederasts burned in the *Place de Grève*—" and I looked over the Spigliano's new apartment, which, surprisingly, turned out to be quite charming. On the top floor of an old red brick house on Woodlawn, it had white walls, slanting ceilings, leaded windows, and lots of room. Fifty or sixty people were standing in little knots around the Christmas tree and the fireplace and the liquor supply. Mixing one of his elaborate cocktails for Walker Friedland and his wife was the master of the place, John Spigliano. With his round dark face and shiny eyes, and a big smile to honor one of Walker's stories, he looked like an amiable, friendly, harmless, helpful little man—and yet I knew that, like his mate, he could not speak that you did not see a knife slipping between the shoulders of someone you liked—of someone you had thought *John* liked. Of course it is a mistake to expect academics to behave better than other people; but whether it is that I am a snob or a romantic or a naïf, or whether I was too idolatrous of the people who educated me,

I always expect that John is going to walk over to me one day and say that he has made up his mind and wants to join up with the human members of our race. Though I like to think of Spigliano emotions and Spigliano aspirations and rewards as having little to do with myself or anybody I care about, it is true nevertheless that he is a grand source of irritation to many of us who must work alongside him. Perhaps it's that we envy him the simple decision he has made to be a bastard.

Standing alongside John and facing Walker was Walker's wife, a stunning blonde with long legs, a high hairdo, A-plus posture, and a somewhat mannered approach to a cigarette that toppled her chic over into self-consciousness and produced in Bill Lake (so he said, tapping my shoulder) a desire to go over and offer her a laxative. She was, of course, only a sophomore in the College and was doing the best she could; if she had only known how Cyril Houghton—who was ostensibly talking to Swanson, the Swede—was casting glances at her rear end, she might have been able to relax a little. She had certainly as much influence as any of us, and more than most.

Mona was marching back with my drink in her hand, when directly beside me I heard Peggy Moberly speaking.

"She's absolutely marvelous," Peggy was saying to someone. "She's just the most charming person. We're going to have lunch together on Wednesday."

"Fine," a man answered.

"Really, she's lovely—"

"Thank you."

"And so gay. I'm simply crazy about her."

"Yes"—I now recognized the male voice—"she's a very sweet girl."

Suddenly Peggy had turned and put her hand on my hair. "I *thought* you were sitting there. What are you being a wallflower about? How are you feeling? I called your place—I was going to come over and make you a decent meal—and you didn't even answer. I thought, oh God, poor Gabe is dying—"

I stood up. "I just wasn't answering the phone, Peg. Hello, Paul."

Paul was wearing the nipped-in double-breasted sharkskin suit he'd worn the day of his arrival in Chicago. He looked severe and lean, and he held himself erect not so much to get

the edge on the rest of the party, as to be removed from it—
not haughty, just separate. "How are you feeling?" he asked me.

"I'm much better," I said. "Just some virus, I suppose."

It was our first exchange since the night in Libby's office
three weeks before. We had managed to see each other only at
staff meetings, and there even to find seats out of each other's
line of vision. It was a hard task at a round table.

"This man's wife," Peggy said, and without the aid of her
glasses she squinted across the room, "is the loveliest-looking
person. The most spirited girl—"

"We're old friends," I said.

"Oh yes, of course. Gabe *brought* Paul!" she announced,
girlishly, to herself. "Oh Peggy, what are you saying," this also
to herself. I took her hand and squeezed it. Peggy Moberly
was one of those people who expect everything of a party; and
if everything doesn't show up soon enough, they start dragging it in by the heels. She seemed now nearly worn out with
good intentions: the curl was gone from her hair, the straps of
her slip were visible, and her ankles looked to be giving out
too. In the end she reached into her purse for her glasses and
put them on—the final capitulation to reality. Resigned about
herself, she raised both our hands toward the other side of the
room and said, "She's quite the hit, that girl."

I saw no girl, however, only a huddle of men—Frank Tozier,
Larry Morgan, Victor Honingfeld, and now Cyril Houghton
and Swanson. Frank was moving his head—laughing—and
then when his chin flicked back I caught sight of Libby within
the center of the circle. Her cheeks were on fire, and with
one long white hand she was tapping her forehead; then the
hand shot above her head in a kind of Gallic explosion—her
lips moved, hesitated, moved, and the men leaned back and
laughed again. All at once she turned in upon herself, hung
her head and became shy. But the next moment she was tilting
an ear toward Cyril, who was stroking his mustache and
doubtless constructing some double-entendre for Libby's pleasure. Her throat and neck were bare, and her nose in profile
was a stately appendage—its elaborate bony edge, touched by
light from the Christmas tree, called out for a finger to be
drawn down along it. Her hair was parted in the middle and
pulled back off her forehead, and her dress was of red satin. I

was sure I had seen it before, but couldn't remember the occasion. Later in the afternoon I recalled that she had written about it in a letter.

"She looks fine," I said to Paul, while Peggy leaned backwards to counter some remark of Bill Lake's. "She looks very well."

"She's feeling fine," Paul said. Peggy leaned forward to rejoin us, and it was as though Paul and I had exchanged a message in code, the meaning of which I hadn't quite understood.

Across the room Frank Tozier was demonstrating a Latin-American dance step. He whipped his butt around with professional agility, and his feet went patter-patter-*wheee* on the Spigliano rug. Libby's hands were clasped together before her chest and her eyes were on Frank's speedy Italian shoes. When he went into a variation of the step, she moved to the side, tried the original little step by herself, failed, and with a hopeless shrug, abandoned a career on the stage. Almost at once Victor Honingfeld was alongside her, and, taking her elbow, he began his nervous and excited chatter. Libby suddenly looked as though bad news had just come her way. Victor made a circular motion with one hand, and then, the noise of the party dipping for a moment, Libby's voice, pleading, exasperated, came across the room:

"He's *not* a homosexual writer! How can you *say* that!"

Peggy tugged my hand. "Oh listen to him. All that has happened is Tom Sawyer shakes Huck Finn's hand, and Mark Twain is a queer!"

I said to Paul, "Victor's psychoanalysis may reshape the whole nineteenth century—"

"It makes me so damn angry," Peggy said, and she was moving across the room to join the debate.

Paul and I stood sipping our drinks, looking not at each other but around the room. Given the shape and size of the party, our silence would not have seemed unusual at all, I suppose, had we been either strangers or friends. But since it seemed that our fate was to be something in between, the silence eventually became more than I could bear. I did not see that matters might be improved, however, by my walking off. "You know," I said, "I'm sorry about that outburst. I was going to telephone—"

There was no way of sounding casual. Paul looked at me

attentively enough, but he had his amazing faculty for taciturnity to fall back on, and he seemed never to be beyond using it. I waited nevertheless, expecting that he might have some generous and forgiving word to say; I was willing again to be the one who had to be forgiven. It was a condition I seemed repeatedly to find myself in, and not only with the Herzes; I seemed to have to be forgiven even when I myself felt somehow wronged.

"I didn't know about Libby's condition," I said, seeing that he wasn't going to help me in what I had begun. "I didn't realize that her kidney disorder meant she couldn't . . ."

For a moment it seemed as though Paul would not finish my sentence for me. Then he said, "She can bear a child; the doctors"—the doctors again—"feel it wouldn't be safe for her, however, if she did." Then, significantly, he added, "That's all."

"I don't mean to interfere," I replied, "in what isn't my business."

"I understand," Paul said; while from across the room, I heard Libby saying, "But I don't care about his life—it's his *work*, Victor."

And Paul was trying to smile at me. "It's okay," he said. "We've decided anyway, you see, to adopt a baby."

"Yes?"

"So it's really all right," he said, but there his smile failed him.

"Fine." I was peculiarly bewildered by what Paul had announced. "That's wonderful."

"You won't say anything. I'd appreciate that."

"Of course not."

Silence followed. "I mean," Paul said, and now he looked very fatigued with me, as though it was we two who had been living together for years, "to Libby."

"You'll have to excuse me for whatever mistakes—"

"We all make mistakes," he said, sharply.

"I suppose," I said, "that's what helps us to be generous to one another. That all of us make them." I had to leave the room then, for I was full of emotion, and I did not know how it might express itself. It was good news I had heard—what anyone would have wanted for the Herzes—and yet it was not to good news that I seemed to be reacting. I went out into the Spigliano hallway, unable to say to Paul the very last thought that had crossed my mind: I hope this can make Libby happy.

"This is Michelle Spigliano, and this is Stella Spigliano, and this is Doctor McDougall, girls, one of Daddy's teachers."

"*Merry Christmas, Doctor McDougall!*"

From down the hall I heard Sam say, "Well, isn't that something, isn't that nice." A moment later he was slapping me on the back. "How are you, boy? I called you last week and you didn't answer. I thought, poor fella, must be sick as a dog. You need anything now? You feeling all right?"

"I'm much better, Sam."

"We old bachelors have to stick together, huh? Okay, Patricia, where's the cider—" and he and Pat went off to the living room. The Spigliano girls took their seats again, one on either side of the door. I was about to ask them to bring my coat and hat out of hiding when Libby came in from the living room.

I went up to her, and though I did not take her in my arms, my heart was beating as though I had. She looked up at me with her flushed face; I knew that she had watched me leave the room and had followed in order that we could be alone. My heart was beating so because I thought there was something very crucial she was going to say to me, or I was going to say to her.

But I told her simply that she was looking very well.

She answered, "Thank you. I hope you're better. No one ever really thinks of Gabe as being sick."

I let the remark remain unanswered. "I want to be straight with you, Libby," I said, "I've never meant to tease—"

"That? Oh, it was nothing." She wouldn't look at me.

"You should know I went to see Paul's parents in Brooklyn."

She was startled for no more than half a second; flatly she said, "Thank you very much. That was kind of you." She smiled then, as though I were Sam McDougall, or one of the Spigliano children. "Excuse me, will you?"

She went off to wherever she had been intending to go in the first place.

I behaved badly—with even less wisdom—from then on. I drank too much, and my voice carried, and finally I was putting my arm around Peggy Moberly, which one hasn't the right to do unless one intends afterwards to lift her up and carry her over a threshold.

"Why don't you ever call me?" Peggy asked. "Why do I give the impression that I'm only interested in books?"

"You don't give that impression at all, Peg."

"You're a cruel man," she said, but she took off her glasses anyway. "Don't you ever want to take me to the movies?"

"Yes."

"Do you want to take me to dinner tonight?"

"Yes."

"Where will we go?"

Bill Lake was performing a Cossack dance in the center of the room. Squatting, arms crossed, head up, he snapped his long legs in and out while the circle that had gathered around him clapped in time. "Hey! Ha! Hey! Ha!" The little Spigliano girls giggled in the doorway. In the corner, Charleen Carlisle and her fiancé were arguing . . . I should have married Charleen. I should have married Peggy.

"I should marry you, Peg."

"Oh don't be cruel with me, will you, Gabe?"

"I'm not being cruel. I'm being nice. Can't anybody tell the difference?"

"You know, if you haven't been feeling well, you shouldn't drink too much."

To that I shook my head. "Not so."

"Maybe we should go to have dinner now."

"Maybe we should get married."

"Gabe, you're being awful! What's the *matter* with you!" She shook a fist at me—spectacles poked out at either end—and left.

Of course, there was no excuse. We all put in a few good reprehensible days in life—exclusive, that is, of the long-range cruelties—and this I suppose was one of mine. Later on, the party had thinned out—John had performed *his* folk dance, and we were out of liverwurst and down to plain rye rounds—and I was dancing with Peggy. I kissed her neck, a sheer piece of son-of-a-bitchery.

"Gabe," she said, "don't you be mean to me. Be good to me, Gabe."

I held her tight, crushing what little she had against me, and we spun past Pat Spigliano, who was saying to her partner, Larry Morgan—

"Women are much more sexually excitable *over* thirty-five, of course—"

We danced on, two close bodies, two distant spirits. I shall catalogue no further my various indecencies, except to add that after a while I began to sing the particularly weighty lines of certain popular songs into Peggy's lonely ear.

We settled finally in a chair near the Christmas tree. Peggy was saying, "I've always been interested in Judaism, even in the seventh grade—"

As Peggy spoke, I saw my few adult years as a series of miscalculations, insincerities, and postures; either that, or I was unforgivably innocent.

"Oh where," I sang, "are all the nice Gentile boys."

"Gabe, shhhh—what are you talking about? Stop narrowing your eyes like that."

"You're after our men."

"Oh Gabe, please cut it out. *Please* . . ." For Peggy's purposes, I had to be either romantic or intelligent.

"I should have married Doris Horvitz," I said.

"Now I'm not kidding—"

I slid into a grumpy silence—Peggy, damn sweet fool, took my hand and stroked it—and listened to snatches of conversation from back of the Christmas tree. Could you believe it? He was talking about structure.

"But," answered Paul Herz, "the point is, John, that the student goes around thinking writing is like tapestry-weaving; a kind of construction work. As far as he can make out, it doesn't have anything to do with life, with being human—"

"I don't"—John was chuckling—"know if it's our duty to be teaching them, as you like to put it, to be human. I know it's nice to be *engagé*—" he said facetiously, and I lost the rest in the crash of a glass on the far side of the room.

Paul was saying, "—talk about form is an *evasion*—"

"—as a critical method has a long history, I suppose, but for myself—"

"—not talking about impressionism at *all*, for God's sake!"

"What else then?" John asked. "One has to do more than come into class and tell the student, Oh isn't this wonderful, oh isn't your heart all aquiver. I suppose to be a creative writer—"

"Could you do me a favor and stop calling him that?" It was Libby speaking now.

"I'm sorry. I thought he identified himself—"

"Do you call Melville 'a creative writer'?" she demanded. "Is that what you call Dostoevsky?"

"I meant only to differentiate between those of us who are engaged in criticism—"

"Well, the difference is obvious!" Libby said. "You don't have to bother."

"Let's go, Gabe," Peggy was saying. "You need some food in your stomach. I'm going to get our coats."

"You take care of me, Peg, my coat's a—"

"I know which is yours," she said, smiling.

I remained in my chair a moment, then rose and stretched and tried to clear my head. Back of the Christmas tree, through the branches and the tinsel and the lights, I saw Paul and Libby in profile.

She was saying, "Paul, *don't* fight with him."

"Let's go home. Let's get out of this fucking place."

"But I was having such a good *time*—"

His hand went up and smoothed her cheek; then it passed down, still touching her. I saw his fingers move inside the neckline of her red dress. "Let's go home, Libby."

I turned away. Scanning the room for a friend, I waved at Mona Meyerling, who saluted. Behind me, I heard Libby speak. "Yes yes—oh Paul—" Then she was racing right by me, one hand up to her fiery cheek, a very excited girl.

And I was in the clutches of Pat Spigliano.

"—yes, I have to," I was saying.

"And we didn't even get a chance to talk."

"We'll all get together soon," I said.

"We must. I keep telling John we have to get together with Gabe—we must have him over for a meal one night. Ahh, did you ever get together with that sweet Mrs. . . . you know, John's older student. The waitress."

"Yes, I did."

"Wouldn't it be nice if we could all get together again. She seemed like a very nice person. A very *fine* person. How is she doing?"

"She's fine," I said. "Thanks for the party, Pat. It was a regular Spigliano party."

"We love giving them, Gabe," she said, as John came over to us and Peggy appeared with our coats. Behind her was Libby, already in her familiar polo coat and kerchief. She was carrying Paul's coat on her arm.

"Goodbye," Libby said from the doorway, where Paul now joined her. "Thank you, Mrs. Spigliano."

"Goodbye," we all said, and the Herzes went out the door.

Peggy couldn't be discouraged from helping me into my coat. I had the feeling that all the people around me were winking at one another. John said, "Feeling sharp enough to drive?"

"I'm going to leave that to the taxi driver," I said. Everyone laughed heartily.

"We love having you, Gabe," Pat said. "We have to see more of Gabe," she said to her husband, "and more of Peggy, too."

"Absolutely," I said. There was no need to go on, but I did. "I have to see more of Peggy myself."

Everyone smiled, and for the first time, because I was being allowed all the prerogatives of a drunk, I felt like one.

"And we loved your friends," Pat said. "The creative writer and his wife. They seem like a very nice bohemian couple. I think it's beneficial for all of us to have a young couple like that around. Though she's a very bohemian-looking girl, isn't she? I said to John when he hired them, I'll bet they're beatniks, and well," she said, raising a finger, "I wasn't far from wrong. I wish they hadn't felt so out of place."

"I guess they didn't know everybody," said Peggy, confused.

"He's a very off-beat fellow," John said.

"I suppose so," I said, when everyone turned to me.

"However," Pat put in, "they seemed very nice." We all agreed to that, and said our thank yous again. At the door the Spigliano little girls sped us on our way with a choral good night.

Between the two high holly bushes that flanked the downstairs door, I slipped on the snow. My hat fell over my eyes and

Peggy began to laugh. While she helped me to my feet, I saw Paul and Libby again. They were standing in front of the house next door; Paul was stopped in his tracks, and Libby was in front of him, but turned around and facing him. His hands were down in his pockets and his head inclined toward the walk.

The night was cold and empty, and their voices carried. "What is it?" Libby was saying. "What is it? I thought—"

"I do," he said. "I do."

"What *is* it then?"

"I'm all right." He started walking.

"Oh, your moods," Libby said. Then, each with hands in pockets, they moved down the street and out of sight.

Peggy and I had dinner at a little restaurant on the Near North Side, where there were shaded lamps on every table and the young man at the piano drank Schweppes water and played very softly songs like "Imagination" and "Long Ago and Far Away." I continued drinking and Peggy's eyes glistened just from intimacy alone. When the wine came, I caused a disproportionate amount of trouble over its temperature, which launched Peggy into apologizing for me to the waiter, the cigarette girl, and the people at the next table. Later we took a taxi back to the South Side. She held her glasses in her gloves all the way down the Outer Drive, and on the front porch of her rooming house I pushed into her lips with painless, moribund abandon.

"Oh Gabe," she moaned into my cold ear, "let's not go too fast. Don't make me fall for you too fast."

"Okay," I said, and stumbled home.

I waited as long as I could bear to, and then sometime after one o'clock I called.

"Martha, it's me. Martha, I've missed the hell out of you. I made a damn weak, silly error. I let everyone down, myself included. I'm not flying in the face of my instincts any more, Martha. I'm not turning off my fires any more. I'll follow what I have to follow—I'm stopping being anxious, Martha—we make the laws, we do. I can't keep being what I've been. I want to be happy, Martha. I want to be with you."

I stopped, and heard what I thought for a moment was something as noncommittal as a cough. But it was the beginning of tears. She said, "Oh, you're drunk, baby—but come, come anyway."

—

"What about Daddy?" Cynthia asked.

"Daddy has decided to live in Arizona. He decided that a long time ago. I don't think that Daddy is a consideration here. He doesn't have anything to do with what I'm saying, Cynthia."

"Is Gabe our new Daddy?" Markie asked.

"He's mother's dearest dearest friend. He's your dearest friend."

"Yes," Markie said.

"Okay?"

"Will he sleep in bed with you?" Cynthia asked.

In the kitchen I sat at the uncleared table, drinking my coffee; in the children's room I heard Martha say that I would.

"Where's Arizona again?" Mark asked.

"In the southwest of the United States. I showed you on the map."

Cynthia spoke next, her words a surprise. I did not expect that she would choose so quickly to be distracted. "What's the capital?" she asked.

"Tucson. Phoenix," Martha said. "I'm not sure."

"What's the capital of Illinois?" Cynthia asked.

"Springfield."

"Why don't they make it Chicago?" asked Cynthia.

"I don't know, sweetheart."

"Gabe knows," Markie said.

"He probably does," Martha said.

"I'll bet he doesn't," Cynthia said.

"Well, it's not important."

But it was; I pushed my chair away from the kitchen table and went into the children's room, where the little lamp between the beds illuminated the wall upon which Martha's kids had poured out all their talent and aspirations. In a dim light, the crayoned stick figures, the stick horses, and round radiant suns and gloomy moons had about them a charm and gaiety that at this particular moment had no effect upon the seriousness of my mood or mission. Cynthia was sitting up in bed, wearing over her pajamas one of her Christmas presents—a red

Angora sweater; she was surrounded by her nurse's kit, her Spanish doll, and the Monopoly set, upon which the first game had been played that afternoon by Martha, me, Cynthia, and Cynthia's friend Stephanie. Mark's head was on his pillow and his hands were tucked under his crisp sheets. He was looking very happy about being in bed. A wad of clay sat on the pillow beside his head, there because he had "made" it in the morning, and had bawled loud and long throughout the day whenever separation had been suggested. It had fallen into his soup at dinner, but now that was all forgotten.

Martha stood by the window, hefty in a pair of faded dungarees, with her hair pulled into one long dramatic braid down her back. She was rocking on the outer edges of her blue sneakers, and her body was arranged in what I had come to think of as *her* posture: right hand on the chin, left hand just below the hip, fingers spread down and out over the can. Though she had earlier requested that I not be present for this scene—and though I had willingly agreed—she looked in my direction with a face upon which worry turned to relief, relief to hope. She smiled, a what-do-we-do-next smile, and sighed.

"Do I or don't I know what?" I asked.

Cynthia said, "Why isn't Chicago the capital?"

"Of America?"

"Of Illinois."

"That's a tough question." I looked over to where Markie lay in his neat little bed. "Probably," I said, "because it gets too cold for a capital here. Capitals are where the big shots live; I suppose they like it warm. What do you think, Mark? Does it look warm outside to you?"

He propped himself up on his elbows. "I can't see. Mommy's by the window."

Martha moved to the side; she looked at me as though I had announced I would now pull a rabbit from a hat, without even having a hat, let alone the rabbit.

Snowflakes were tapping against the pane. "Does it?" I asked.

"No," Markie said, though he looked up at me willing to be corrected.

"Does it to you?" I asked Cynthia.

With a lofty sophistication, she said, "It's snowing." But for a flicker of a second she had almost smiled.

"All right," I said. "Who in his right mind would make this place a capital?"

After a moment Cynthia spoke again. "Where are you going to sleep?"

"With Martha," I said.

"Maybe," said Martha, moving now between their beds, "you should close your eyes, sweethearts. You had a very tiring day. Come on, Cyn, take off your sweater."

"I think I want to wear it."

"Honey, it's brand new. You can wear it tomorrow."

"*I want to wear it now!*"

Martha took my hand. "Wear it, Cynthia," she said. "And go to sleep." She leaned over and kissed each child. "Good night."

"Can Gabe kiss us?" Markie asked.

"Sure," his mother said.

I leaned down and kissed Markie, who stuck his lips directly into mine. I put my lips to the cheek that Cynthia had turned toward me.

"Good night, Cynthia," I said. "You'll have fuzzy dreams in that sweater."

"I'll be all right," Cynthia said; and Martha turned off the light.

3

"I LOANED her a hundred," Martha said.

"And so is that what all this irritation with me is about?"

"I'm not irritated with you."

"Because we can call them up, Martha. We can tell them not to come."

"What's that have to do with anything? The roast is in the oven. We invited them. Let's leave it that way."

"Then what is it, Martha?"

"Nothing."

"What is she going to do with the money? Are you going to get that money back?"

"I suppose so."

"Martha, sit down and forget those potatoes a minute."

"Your friends will be coming—"

"And what's this 'my friends' business? We discussed whom we would have. You went through all your friends, and you said you didn't want any of them."

"Divorced women depress me. Please," she said, "I have to finish here."

"What's eating you? Sit down. What is it?"

At last she looked directly at me. "Oh hell—I don't have any money for the January rent."

"Sit down. You gave what's-her-name, Theresa, the rent money?"

She moved into a chair opposite me at the kitchen table, holding a spatula in her hand.

"Most of it," she answered.

"Including what I gave you?"

"Are you going to cause a fuss about that?"

"I'm not causing a fuss over anything."

"Well, you only gave me forty bucks," she said, "so obviously the other sixty was mine. And the rent's a hundred and thirty, so I mean forty bucks doesn't get me very far."

"We've been through all this. Didn't Sissy give you forty a month."

"I didn't ask you to give me that money. You don't have to give me a penny."

"Who said you asked me?"

"Well, I didn't."

"All right, fine. I told you I'd pay Sissy's share."

"Thanks," she said, and got up and went over to the sink. "Sissy only lived in one room," she informed me.

"Then I'll pay *half* the rent. If that's what you want to do, why don't you say so?"

She turned and faced me. "You've still got your other apartment."

"Don't worry about my other apartment. If I want to be a hot shot and have one and a half apartments, that's my business."

"Why do you have to keep the other one?" she asked. "Isn't it silly, isn't it a waste?"

"It's eighty-five bucks a month—I do it for the sake of my colleagues. He that filches from me my good name, and so on. Please, if I don't mind the eighty-five . . . Please, don't fret, Martha. If you're upset, if you don't want people for dinner—"

"Who said I didn't want people? Who mentioned people?"

"—because it's not too late. I can call them and cancel the whole thing. We can eat the roast ourselves."

"They're as good as anybody else," she mumbled, and plowed into the breakfast and lunch dishes that were still stacked in the sink.

"What kind of attitude is that? Turn that damn water off, please. I thought you were enthusiastic about having somebody for dinner. I thought you thought it would be a great pleasure for us, very domestic."

"Everything's domestic enough, thank you."

"Look, it was your idea to have somebody for dinner. What are you being so bitchy about? *You* said it would be a pleasure."

"It probably will be."

"Martha, I'm going to make out a check. We'll split the rent."

"You don't have to pay anything, really. You don't even have to pay Sissy's forty."

"I want to."

"Her moving had nothing to do with you. I told you that."

"I'll split the rent. I'll give you a check for twenty-five dollars more, is that agreeable with you?"

". . . I suppose so."

"Well, what's the matter now? Do you want me to pay the whole rent?"

"Oh forget it."

"Excuse me if I'm being obtuse. What is it you want to say to me?"

"Nothing."

"What is it?"

"Well"—she raised her hands, as though she had done everything possible to spare me—"honestly, Gabe, all this dividing in half is pretty damn silly. I mean we divide the grocery bill, and *you've* got an appetite like a horse."

"What?"

"Last night you ate *all* the green beans, you ate two-thirds of the tuna yesterday afternoon—"

"What's going on here? Cynthia ate all the ice cream, every last drop, just this afternoon, and did I start shouting about dividing the bills? What's the matter with you?"

"Why don't you just leave Cynthia out of it? There's no need to be so hard on that poor kid. At least she can have some vanilla ice cream out of this deal, for God's sake."

"I haven't been so hard on Cynthia, let's get that straightened out. Nobody's been hard on Cynthia, and least of all me. The truth of it—since we're going to speak truths—is that I'm paying half the groceries and feeding one mouth, and you're paying half and feeding three mouths. So I'm entitled to a few God damned green beans, all right?"

"Well, you're living here for practically nothing."

"I *paid* you forty bucks."

"Half of a hundred and thirty ain't forty."

"I'll pay sixty-five. I *said* I'd pay sixty-five."

"What about the other apartment?"

"Let me worry about my other apartment, will you?"

"I mean if you've moved in here, you might as well move all the way in."

"I have moved all the way in."

"Not with another apartment, you haven't."

"I've explained to you, Martha. It's simply a matter of the University, my position, a matter of appearances and dignity—"

"It's not dignified enough, is it, living with me?"

"Oh the hell with it. You're just being contrary, so the hell with it."

I went into the living room, where the table that Martha and I had pulled onto the middle of the rug was being set by Cynthia. With a painstaking concern for symmetry, the child was aligning and realigning the dinner plates between their appropriately squadroned knives, forks, and spoons. She might just as well have been defusing a bomb, for the expression on her face. As she circled the table, she smoothed out the tiniest wrinkles in the white cloth.

Markie was not around, having gone off to the playground with Stephanie and her grandmother; Cynthia had begged that she be allowed to stay at home and help with the preparations. Already she had vacuumed rugs and gone around emptying ash trays, and for one optimistic moment I believed that since she knew it was friends of mine who were coming to dine, that with these labors she was making a bid for an end to hostilities between us. Not that she hadn't been deferential to me for the two weeks I had been in her house, but it was Cynthia's kind of deference. At dinnertime, for example, she would *shove* the bread my way before I had even asked. She had not made the smallest offer of lips or face—neither a kiss or a smile—nor did she now. Watching her labor over the table, I concluded that all her dogged helpfulness was actually designed to ally herself with her mother *against* me. Martha and I had been sniping at each other for two days now, and Cynthia, a worldly and attentive baby, probably wanted only to make clear whose side she would be on, in the event of a full-scale war.

I left her posing in aesthetic contemplation over an arrangement of serving dishes she had made in the center of the table-cloth. In the kitchen I sat down at the table, pushed aside a coffee cup, and wrote out a check.

"This is for you," I said.

"I don't need any checks."

"You've got to pay the rent, so don't be silly."

"I'll explain that I'm broke. I'll pay double next month."

"Here's a hundred and twenty-five dollars. Stop being an ass. Twenty-five I owe you, the hundred is a loan. When your friend Theresa pays you back, you pay me back." I went up to where she stood, leaning against the sink, and put the check in the pocket of her apron. "What did she need the hundred for?" I asked.

"I don't know. I didn't inquire. A down payment on an abortion is probably a damn good guess. Look, I'm sorry. I've been being nervous about the rent."

"Then why didn't you tell me? If you feel rushed and upset, if you want me to—if you're feeling harried—I'll just call and say you're not feeling well."

"Listen, if you want to call because you don't want them, then go right ahead. Don't try to slough it all off on me. I made dinner, and I'm ready, so it's fine with me. I thought they were your friends. I thought you thought we'd all enjoy ourselves."

"I thought you might like them, yes. I thought they would like to meet you."

"Then let's stop calling on the phone and telling them I'm sick. I'm not sick."

"Martha, please don't worry about that hundred dollars. If that girl just takes off, if she's going to buy a ticket for a train somewhere, you just forget it."

"I didn't bring you here to support me."

"I didn't *come* here to support you! All I'm saying is, don't worry about the hundred. What the hell are we arguing about? All right? Just say all right, *all right?*"

"All right."

When the roast was nearly finished and Martha was dressing in the bathroom, the phone rang. She ran to it and spoke for some ten minutes, standing in her slip and bare feet.

"Who was that?" I asked.

"It's not important."

"That Theresa girl," I said. "How did you get so involved with her? Why didn't you tell me about this?"

"There's nothing to tell."

"She needs more money, doesn't she?"

"Well, I don't have any more!" Martha shouted, and went back into the bathroom.

—

Certainly there were others we could have invited. Anyone at all, really, could have sat down with us, eaten our food, sipped our coffee, and then gone off to carry into the streets the news of our unabashed, forthright, and impractical union. We needed only one couple—married preferably—to stand for the world and its opinions, one pair of outsiders to whom we could display our fundamental decency and good intentions, to whose judgment we could submit evidence of an ordered carnality and a restrained domestic life. Just one couple to give us society's approval, if not the rubber stamp . . . For it must have been all of this that we were after when one sunny morning a week after I had moved in, Martha woke up and said, "Let's have somebody for dinner!" and I said, "What a splendid idea!"

That the couple we chose—I chose—was Libby and Paul was not really as thoughtless and unimaginative as it may seem. If anything, it was too imaginative, too thoughtful—or too thought out. Only a moment after our evening together began, I knew how it was going to end. I still maintain, however, that for every reason one can think of why all these people would never have liked one another, there was a perfectly good one why they should have. Paul Herz could be a witty man, certainly a pensive and attentive man. Libby could be lively and gay. Martha could always laugh. And as for me, I was more than willing to be any sort of middleman in order to bring to an unbloody conclusion a painful chapter in my life. But certain chapters and pains are best left unconcluded. They can't be concluded—all one needs is to know that at the time.

The first disappointment was Martha; she wore the wrong clothes. I had thought she had been planning to don her purple wool suit, toward which I had both a sentimental and aesthetic attachment, or at least the skirt to the suit and her white silk blouse. But when she rushed past me to answer the knock at the front door, it was not a woman that moved by but a circus—a burst of color and a clattering of ornaments. She had managed to tart herself up in a full orange skirt, an off-the-shoulder blouse with a ruffled neck, strands of multi-colored beads, and on her feet what I shall refer to in the language of the streets (the streets around the University) as her Humanities II sandals. So that none of us would miss the point, she had neither braided her hair nor put it up. It was combed straight out, and when she tossed her head, the heavy blond mane draped down her back and almost brushed her bottom. Somehow her outfit managed to call into question the very thing we wished (or I wished) to impress upon Libby and upon Paul—the seriousness of our relationship. That the Herzes' lives were often more threatened than my own had led me on occasion to believe that their lives were also more serious than my own; whatever the mixture of insight and bafflement that had produced in me such an idea, it contributed also to the quality of my affections and anxieties where these two needy people were concerned.

The visitors peered out of the stairway; they were Paul and Libby Herz, they said, but was this Mrs. Reganhart's apartment? Apparently Martha looked to them as though she could not be a Mrs. anything, which may indeed have been what was in her head as she had dressed herself before her bedroom mirror. Perhaps what she had wanted to look precisely like was a free spirit, someone unworried and without cares—for a change, nobody's mother. But what she resembled finally— what I was sure the Herzes thought she looked like—was some tootsie with whom I had decided to pass my frivolous days. Through the early stages of their visit I felt some circumstantial link between myself and a gigolo or pimp. Despite several energetic attempts to govern my unconscious, I began during dinner to make a series of disconnected remarks all of which turned out to have a decidedly smutty air. "So I laid it on the line to the Chancellor's secretary—" "Remember Charlotte Foster from Iowa City? Well, she turned up in Chicago and blew me to a meal—" And so on, through the pimento and anchovies and into the roast itself. All I had to do really was shut up; we would then have been bathed in a silence that could probably have been no more destructive of pleasure than was my banal chatter.

To make matters worse—to make my Martha brassier—

Libby that day was the child saint about to be lifted onto the cross. There was even in her very flat-chestedness something that lent her an ethereal and martyred air. She was buttoned up to her white throat in a pale green cardigan sweater whose sleeves reached nearly into the palms of her hands; and her hands were just small half-closed fists in her lap. Every time a serving dish was passed to Paul he would lean over to ask Libby if she would have some. If she shook her head, he urged half a spoonful on her anyway, whispering words I couldn't hear into those ears of hers, which stuck poignantly out just where the hair was pulled back above them. If she parted her unpainted lips and consented to be fed, he would croon *fine, good* and arrange a portion of food for her on her plate. His behavior engaged Martha instantly, and the attention she showed him was almost embarrassing in its openness. After a while she looked to me not so much disgusted—though there was that in it all right—as offended by this demonstration of nutritional billing and cooing.

I had never seen Paul so solicitous toward his wife, and it would have made me uneasy too, had I not my own private source of uneasiness sitting directly in the center of the table —the roast. When it appeared and I had sunk my knife down into its pink center, a new wave of silence, deeper and more significant, went around the table (granted, this may have been my imagination again). It was as though a particularly gross display of wealth had been flaunted; we were about to dine on some mysterious incarnation of rubies and gold. Then I opened a bottle of Gevrey Chambertin (1951) and with the classy *thhhppp* of the cork, we were all reminded once again of the superfluity that characterized my particular sojourn on this earth. In short, I felt that Paul and Libby—in different degrees, for different reasons—resented me for Martha's gaudy voluptuousness and for the meal as well. I told myself that they would never understand my life, and that I shouldn't allow them to upset me. But then I thought that if all their suspicion and resentment was merely of my own imagining, it was perhaps I myself who would never understand it.

When the children came in to be appreciated in their clean pajamas, they were introduced to the guests.

"And this is Cynthia," I said, "and this is Mark."

Markie immediately went for Martha; Cynthia said, "How do you do?"

Libby looked up from her food—in which she had all of a sudden taken an interest—but only for a second. She had already returned to separating something on her plate when she commented, "Aren't they nice."

Martha ignored the remark, though not the person who had made it; she glared at Libby, then, taking a hand of each of her children, said, "Good night, dears."

"You going to come kiss us good night?" Mark asked.

"As soon as dinner is over," Martha said. "You go off to bed now."

"You going to come?" Markie asked me.

They left, Cynthia turning at the door to say that it had been a pleasure to meet the Herzes; she skipped off, her behind like a little piece of fruit, and nobody at the table seemed charmed. We ate in silence until at last Paul asked Martha how old they were, and she didn't answer.

"Cynthia is seven," I said, "and Mark is—how old, Martha? Four?"

I passed the information on to Paul. "Four," I said. "Look, would anyone care for more meat?"

"No, thank you," Paul said.

"How about some wine, Libby?" I asked.

She shook her head. Paul said, "She can't drink too much alcohol."

Some few minutes later, Paul said, "We've had a very tiring day. You'll have to excuse us."

I thought for a moment they were going to get up and leave without even finishing. He was only apologizing, however, for his wife's silence. I suppose he never felt a need to apologize for his own.

"That's all right," Martha said. "I'm tired myself."

"Do you know?" I rushed in. "It's very interesting about this wine. Now 1951 was supposedly a good year, so I procured—" Procured? Bought, damn it, bought! I babbled on, explaining how I had come to purchase the wine, while Martha began making offerings of food to Libby, calling her Mrs. Herz. Paul sat listening so silently to what I said that I went on and on and on, waiting as it were for some signal from him that I had spoken enough and could stop. But it was like sending one's voice down a well.

When we had finally finished the one bottle of wine—which everyone had been sipping parsimoniously—I ran off to the kitchen to get the other. I returned to the living room to find that the Herzes had retired to the sofa and Martha had begun to clear the table.

"We'll have coffee over there," she said, carrying the dishes away.

I sat down in a sling chair opposite the Herzes. Libby had picked up a book from the sofa.

"It's a very funny book," I said. "Martha reads the children a little every night, and they laugh . . ."

Libby set it down. "That must be nice."

"Yes," I said. And I thought, Then why did you come? Why did you accept my invitation? Why won't you let this be ended! Why won't I?

The three of us sat facing one another, and the gloom came rolling in. I said, "Excuse me, I better go say good night to the children."

In the kitchen Martha was standing over the stove, fiddling with her beads and waiting for the coffee to be ready.

"Come on," I whispered. "It's like a wake in there."

"I'll be in in a minute."

I put my hands on her bare arms, and she moved away. "Hurry up, will you?" I said. "Nobody's willing to say anything. Everyone's a little stiff."

"Oh, just a little."

"Why did you have to rush them away from the table?"

"They weren't eating anything, what was the difference?"

"I was going to open another bottle of wine."

"They weren't drinking either."

"Well, I'm going to bring in the Armagnac," I said, "the hell with it."

"What!"

"The Armagnac. What's the matter?"

"Nothing."

"Don't tell me nothing—what's the matter now?"

"That Armagnac happens to date from before I saw your smiling face."

"Martha, we'll all *die* out there."

"So we'll die. That bottle costs seven bucks. If you wanted some why didn't you think to buy it this afternoon?"

"Because you've hardly started the bottle that's here. What's gotten into you?"

"Don't people drink beer any more?"

"Look, I'll give you a check for seven dollars! Be *quiet!*"

"You and your checks." She turned back to the coffee. "I saved nickels and dimes, and bought that as a special gift for myself, but the hell with it, just take the stuff and pour—"

"This is some party! This is marvelous! Are you coming back in there tonight or aren't you?"

"I'll be in," she mumbled. "Just go ahead."

"Well, I'm taking the Armagnac." And I went back into the living room, choking the bottle around the neck. I poured four glasses of brandy without asking whether anybody wanted some. I sat back with my glass, sipped from it, and said—innocently, absolutely innocently, just in order to say something—"How's the adoption going?"

Paul turned immediately to Libby, who turned to him. He said, "I mentioned it to Gabe, you know." He looked back at me, and I felt no need to apologize; since the beginning of the evening surely it was I who had been the most burdened member of our party. We stared, Paul and I, wordlessly at one another while Libby said, "Oh did you?"

"I thought he would like to know," he said.

Libby looked down into her lap.

I said, "I think it's a fine idea, Libby."

"What is?" The question came from Martha, who had entered the room with a trayful of coffee cups. Apparently she had decided to make an effort to be gracious; it was simply the wrong moment to have chosen.

"Nothing," I said, leaning back.

"I'm sorry I interrupted."

I saw her face harden, and Paul must have seen it too. "Libby and I are adopting a baby," he said. "That's all."

"Oh yes?" She looked at Libby, and for the first time since the Herzes' arrival, she smiled. "A boy or a girl?"

The question had an astonishing effect upon Libby at first; she seemed frightened, then insulted.

Paul said, "We don't know yet. We're still in the inquiring stage."

Martha set down the tray and poured the coffee. Libby looked over to me. "We have to adopt a Jewish baby anyway," she said.

"Yes? I didn't know."

"The Catholic orphanages are crawling with kids," explained Libby in an emotionless voice, "but that doesn't help us. With the Jewish agencies there's over a three-year waiting list. Then we're a mixed marriage as far as anybody's concerned."

"But you converted—" I said.

Suddenly she said, "So what?"

I did not press for more information; Martha sat down and the four of us drank our coffee. Paul said, "You see, today we called long distance to New York. Thinking we could work something out with an agency there." He stopped explaining, and what was left unsaid was clear enough from the look on his face.

Martha said to him, "That's too bad."

"It'll work out," he assured her.

"Oh sure," Libby said.

Some moments later, Libby spoke again. When her mouth opened the words that came out were connected to none that had previously been spoken in the room. Her body was lifeless and her voice vacant, and it seemed that she might say just about anything. This girl had aroused numerous emotions in me in the past, but never before had she made me feel as I did now—afraid. Looking at me again, she said, "Paul was called in to see the Dean today."

"Libby—" her husband said.

"That Spigliano," she said, "is really going to try to get him fired."

"You're kidding," I said. "What happened?"

"Nothing." Paul inclined his head toward his cup after he had spoken, so that his face was in shadows. "I ran into the

Dean," he said softly, "I wasn't called in anywhere, Libby. I just ran into him."

"You said he as much as told you they weren't happy with you."

"Libby's exaggerating," Paul said.

"Mommy!"

We all looked toward the doorway, where Cynthia stood, rubbing her eyes.

"What's the matter, honey?" Martha said, getting up.

Cynthia's eyes landed on each of us in turn. "You're all talking too loud. I can't sleep."

Martha set down her cup. "We're hardly talking at all," she said, and chaperoned Cynthia back to her room.

Libby extended her neck its full length. "Maybe we had better go. I don't want to wake up anybody who's trying to sleep."

"Libby, Paul—please stay. Let's not run off. Why don't we all relax," I suggested, and went off to the kitchen. The door to the back porch was ajar, and Martha stood in the opening leaning against the wall and looking outside.

"Martha," I said, coming up to her and feeling the cold from outside, "what the hell is going on here? I invited them over, you invited them over. Let's not *throw* them out. I feel as though I'm in the middle of an earthquake. Let's all at least try to be civil. Let's get through this thing like human beings."

"I'm all right," she said.

"Don't mind Libby. If it's any solace to you, she's really quite miserable."

"If it's any solace to her, so am I. So we're even."

"So am I, damn it! Just control yourself. Turn around, Martha. Tell me what the trouble is."

"Married people depress me," she said, not turning.

"I thought it was divorced people."

"Why don't you go back into the living room and entertain your friends?"

And I went, but before I had even sat down again, Libby said to me, "I've been saying something ought to be done about that John Spigliano. Somebody should hit him in the jaw."

"He's a pain in the ass, Libby," I said, making a hopeless gesture, "nobody will argue that. There's really nobody who can stand him. But you've really only got to ignore him."

"Suppose," she said, "you have principles."

I smiled. "Still ignore him."

"Well," she said, "maybe you can . . ."

I tried now to ignore her. I looked over at her husband, who was leaning back against the sofa, his face marked slightly by a frown. "It isn't a matter of me, Libby," I said, "it's simply the most sensible thing to do."

Paul leaned forward. "Oh but, Jesus, the circular symbols in *Tom Sawyer*." He looked to Libby, who nodded in agreement. "What incredible horseshit," said Paul.

"Of course," I told him. "I know."

"Then," said Libby, no longer in a flat voice, "why don't you say something?"

I was puzzled for a moment, until I imagined again all the conversations that this couple—my old Libby—must have had about me. "Look, Libby, I was through all this last year. I shared your feelings exactly. But the best thing is to ignore Spigliano and do your job."

"We certainly didn't have anybody like him at Reading," she said.

"So?" I answered. "That doesn't prove anything here or there."

"It proves something," she said.

"Oh hell, Libby, you didn't have to come here if you didn't want to. I was led to believe it was so awful in Reading."

"Nobody's blaming you," Paul said now.

"Well," I replied, "isn't that nice."

"Actually, we were probably better off in Reading," Libby said, "where there weren't all these phoney and ambitious people."

"Well, you could have chosen to stay there."

Paul was standing. "Libby's not feeling well, Gabe—"

"Oh balls," I said, standing now myself, "Libby's never feeling well."

"I don't think there's any need for that kind of remark," he said, growing fierce.

"There's no need for anything," I said. "You've got some appreciation of generosity—"

"I told you Libby's not feeling well—"

"Well, I'm talking to both of you."

Suddenly Martha was in the room. "Could all of you stop shouting! Could my kids get some sleep, please!"

Libby stood up and faced her. "We're going, Mrs. Regan-hart."

"Yes," Paul said, taking his wife's elbow. "I think we'd better."

—

I took a walk that night, by myself. I pulled up my collar and went all the way down to the lake, where the waters were behaving like an ocean, breaking onto the dark rock barrier, then rushing out with the sound of violent tugging. I could not distinguish where the black water ended and where the black sky began. What I saw—actually, what I could not see—frightened me, but I hung on as long as I could, looking straight out onto it, as though fear might run through me like a cathartic, and leave me a less cautious man. Finally I broke away and dashed across the deserted park and onto the lighted streets. Walking back to Martha's apartment very slowly, I did not do a great deal of thinking because I could not figure out what to think about.

The table had been cleared and pushed back to the wall; the coffee cups, brandy glasses, and bottle had all been put away. I turned off the hall light and in the bedroom got into my pajamas, while Martha lay there with her eyes open, smoking. The bedside lamp was on, but her gaze was focused only on the smoke that rose above her head.

I sat down by the window, pushed back a corner of the shade, and peered outside. I said, "What a night."

Martha only pushed herself up a little, as though my remark had caused her some postural discomfort. Her hair was still down over her shoulders, and from time to time her eyes twittered from the smoke; that was all that moved.

"It was stupid of me to have chosen to invite those people," I said. "I should surely have realized what was going to happen beforehand." She said nothing. "I don't know why I felt the necessity to extend something that is really quite over. I should never—"

"Gabe," she said, "we have to do something about the money situation."

I rose, and I paced until I could contain myself.

"I told you," I said, "that I'll pay for the bottle. If you want,

I'll make out a check right now. Or give you cash, if you object so strenuously to my checks."

"What about the groceries?"

"Oh hell!"

She went on smoking in that contemplative, bitchy, distracted way.

"What's come over you?" I asked. "What did I say? We've been through all this, over and over it, as a matter of fact. Okay, money is a problem, and I'm willing to work it out. But what is it you want me to do, Martha, pay for everything? Is that what you think will work better? Are you sure about that?"

"Well, I prepare the food," she said. "You don't pay for that. The gas I cook with I happen to pay for. The same goes for the electric lights in the kitchen. Be reasonable, please."

I leaned toward her over the foot of the bed. "You're kidding me or something, aren't you? Look at me—aren't you? What do you want me to do—hire you as a cook?"

"You treat me like one, why not?"

"Do I? Look at me, damn it! Do I? Do you think," I demanded, "I'd hire a cook with two kids?"

She pushed her cigarette into the ash tray beside the bed. "I don't know if this is working out."

I tried deep breathing—a metaphoric way, I suppose, of pumping up the will. "Martha, if you're willing, we ought to wait until tomorrow. We'll both feel more ourselves in the morning. This has been a bad day from the start. The money mix-up, and Theresa, and the Herzes. Paul Herz is a strange fellow, impossible to get to, and Libby—Libby's very tough to figure out."

"Not so tough."

"Maybe not. I suppose she got very screwed up seeing your kids. Two handsome children getting ready for bed, Cynthia's book . . . It probably upset her."

"Those two handsome children seem to have the remarkable ability of upsetting everybody."

"I can't be responsible for her, Martha." I went back to the window and found myself staring into the drawn shade.

"That's your type though, isn't it?" Martha said. "The svelte, skinny Mediterranean ones."

"Christ, why don't you go to sleep and take your rotten temper with you."

"What—did you have an affair with her? Is that what she was up to with all that pecking away at you? Why didn't she look at me, I'd like to know? Can't anybody talk directly to me? Am I just the new lay—do you do this often, old man, so everybody's in on it except the dumb blowsy mistress herself?"

"I'm going to turn the lights off. You're not jealous, which you know, and you're not making sense. I don't go for those midnight accusations."

"You don't really dig us big fat Nordic slobs, though, do you?"

I looked at her. "I'm crazy about fat Nordic slobs, as a matter of fact." I went over and switched off the bedside light, but then I could not bring myself to get into the bed beside her. I sat on the edge.

"This just isn't working out," she said.

"*What* isn't working out?"

"Cynthia is very upset."

"Cynthia was upset before I got here."

"Not the same way."

"All right then," I said, rising. "Then I'll move out. We'll break it off. This is ridiculous, Martha. What is it you want anyway?"

"I don't want you to move out!" she said.

"*Then what do you want?*"

Suddenly she had flipped on the light and was squatting on the blanket. Her nightgown was hiked up to her knees upon which were planted her fists. "Stop raising your voice!" she demanded. "Everybody just hates for those kids to get some sleep! What do you mean you'll move out? What do you think this is, a hotel? You'll move in one week and out the next? I've got kids to think about. This is no flophouse, you!"

"Why didn't you think about your kids when I moved in?"

"Why didn't *you*?"

"I did," I said. "I thought about it plenty!"

"Well then, keep thinking about them, buddy. Don't be so fast to pack your bags." Her hair had fallen over her face, and she shook it back, showing a face puffy with rage. She stood up, violently grabbed a cigarette from the night table, and lit it. She began to tramp around the room, all her pounds and inches coming down through her bare feet onto the floor. She puffed at the cigarette, giving no thought to the flutter of ashes onto her nightgown.

I said nothing for several minutes. Then calmly: "You were the one who said it wasn't working out, Martha. Not me. I came back here tonight prepared to forget that stupid Armagnac fuss, dedicated to barreling through this miserable night, and starting in again tomorrow. You suggested I leave."

"The hell I did," she said. "Can't you remember from one minute to the next? Nobody told you to leave—you volunteered to pack your bags."

"And what do you expect somebody to do if you tell them a hundred times that it isn't working out? Don't you think tonight's been a mess and a trial for me too? Do you think you can just go around telling people it isn't working out and that they're going to *stand* there? What a night! What a *day*! You, that lousy Armagnac, Theresa whatever the hell her name is—"

"Haug. And that's my affair, not yours."

"That's fine with me. Frankly I'm sick of other people's troubles. Libby Herz, sitting there with those brooding sullen eyes, and why? Because I didn't steal her away from Paul back in Iowa? Well, don't look at me as though I'm nuts—I don't know either. I'm really finding it difficult to keep up with what certain people want of me. As a matter of fact I *didn't* sleep with her, Martha, and I didn't have an affair, though one night about three or four years ago, I don't even remember any more, I kissed her. I admit to the crime: I kissed the girl. But I never got her down in bed—though you might want to know it crossed my mind. I don't have a pure and rarefied soul, and I'm not without base instincts—but I'll also tell you that I didn't do it, and that's a fact. But you see, now apparently she *wanted* me to. I was supposed to come along and rescue her!"

Martha looked immeasurably skeptical. "Why didn't you?"

"Because she was married to her husband, Martha. To that big skinny silent prick, Paul."

"I see."

"You don't see anything. For some reason that makes me a beast in your eyes, and a coward. I've been going around for

years thinking I acted honorably, and now it's my *fault* I
didn't put it to her."

"Nobody said that."

"Well, I'm no social worker. I'm tired of meddling in people's lives!"

"It isn't meddling, I shouldn't think, when people are in
trouble."

"What is it you want me to come out for, adultery?"

"Don't sound moralistic, please. Not you. The minute you
see a stray female you take her to the hardware store to have
duplicate keys made to her apartment."

"That's right. I have no feelings. It was heartless of me to
have you cook a roast for dinner, because it made the Herzes
feel shame and dismay. I shouldn't have talked about the wine,
because that made Herz unhappy too. I can assure you he's
home now hating my guts for that damn roast beef."

"He ought to hate me too," she said, "I paid half!"

"We should have had smelts then! Smelts and stale bread
and, I don't know—orange pop! And you shouldn't have
worn those jazzy gypsy clothes either—you should have worn
something gray and washed-out, something with a rip in it."

"I've got plenty of washed-out numbers with rips in them,
thank you."

"Ah, don't start in on me with the poverty business,
Martha, because I'm not in a charitable mood."

"Poverty hell. I'm only asking you to pay your way."

"Well, what is it—do you want me to leave a ten-dollar bill
on the dresser every morning? Is that what's going on here?"

She turned and walked away at last, her head back, dragging
on her cigarette. "Watch yourself, Gabe. Please watch yourself.
I'm not a stone wall."

"I'm sorry. I'm just not a stone wall myself."

"Nobody is—let's *assume* that!"

"And maybe you ought to stop raising your voice too. Mark
gets up and peeks in the door enough as it is."

"What can I do about that?" she said.

"I don't know."

"I don't either. The child's interested. He has a natural curiosity. He never had so many doors closed in his face before.

We ought to at least have given him a little breaking-in period."

"Come on, Martha, will you—you choose to close the door as much as I do. Suddenly even sex looks one-sided to you. Please don't start switching it around so that I'm responsible for any confusions your kids might have. I haven't been here long enough. I'm not Dick Reganhart. I didn't do it. Just as it's my fault Libby's kidneys went bad on her, as though I have something to do with the fact that there are no Jewish babies. Did you see that that was addressed to me? Jewish girls don't get knocked up as often—what are we all supposed to do about that!"

Martha blew out a mouthful of smoke before she'd even had a chance to inhale it. "And what's that supposed to mean, Stonewall?"

"*What* supposed to mean?"

"You think it was easy quitting school, do you? You think it was easy marrying him? When that prissy little minister pronounced us abstract expressionist and wife I saw the whole black future, and kept my mouth shut. I got knocked up all right, but I acted like a woman about it. I'm *glad* I had Cynthia. She's a fine child, a fine lovely bright child, even if it takes her a year to warm up to you. Ten years! What do you think she is, a chameleon? She's loyal to her father—which happens to be admirable. She happens to be an admirable child, and don't you forget it."

"I didn't mean anything about you and Dick, Martha, and I'm sorry if you misunderstood."

"Well, you sure as hell go out of your way not to mean anything. I don't have such a lousy record, you know. I *had* that child, I didn't have it scraped down some drain somewhere, back in some dark alley. And then I woke up one morning and that son of a bitch was on top of me again, and I didn't have an abortion then either. These are *lives*, for God's sake. I love those kids. I'm glad I've got them, overwhelmingly glad. I work nights and I hate it—you don't *know* how I hate it. But I'm glad I've got those kids. They're *something*, damn it. At least they don't go packing their bags all the time. Men are a great big pain in the ass. Somebody ought to take all their luggage away and burn it. Then where would they be! I'll tell you something about feelings, my friend—nobody's got any any more. All they've got is suitcases! And stay the hell away from me with your big tit-holding hands—I have a right to cry. Don't soothe me, damn it!" She sat down in the chair by the window, and without covering her face, she wept.

"Martha, hang on. Try to hang on. Somehow Theresa Haug, the Herzes—"

"Oh Gabe," she wept, "the hell with Theresa Haug. The hell with all that Armagnac. I want you to marry me or give me up. I'm too old to screw around like this."

4

THE FIRST knowledge she had that day was that their room was swelling with a gleaming gray January light, but she kept her eyes closed to it and she waited. Eyes closed there was no crippled chest of drawers across the way, no half-painted dresser, no smelly rug rolled up in the corner, no curled paint petals flaking off the ceiling onto the pillow; there was only the knowledge that it was morning, a new day, and with it all the possibilities. Some mornings he touched her. Most mornings she touched him and then he touched her. This morning she was willing to wait. She would wait. She made a *hmmm* sound to let him know she was awake. But she sensed nothing new against her skin, nothing but sheets and blanket and the frail sun. She rolled over, making another sound, a slow moan of lust and comfort, a request for a simple pleasure. She continued to keep her eyes closed. Then she thought (after a decent interval): There are compromises to be made in life. One can't expect everything. He is a faithful, hard-working, dear, terribly talented, intelligent, hard-luck man. It isn't his fault . . . She moved her head an inch closer to his pillow, and then her whole body, but casually, as though she were only being tossed toward him by the oceanic process of awakening. The sun caught her full in the face. Good. She had to go all the way to the Near North Side and at least it wouldn't be miserably cold. If, however, he touched her, if his mouth slid over her breasts, if his body pressed her down, then she would not have to go at all. She didn't want to really, even if it was sunny. He need only reach out . . . But the compromises—she must compromise a little. One must begin to, certainly, at twenty-five. One couldn't go through life whining and demanding, day in and day out. She knew certain things about herself that she did not like: she cried too much; she was envious, she was always sick —she was a hopeless hypochondriac, in fact. She knew she had the wrong values. She thought about money all the time. She thought about nice clothes. She thought about nice furniture. She had always imagined that when she was married she would have a dinner service for twelve of Spode china. Spode. The word, like sun on the skin, warmed her, had a dreamy happy glow about it—she would be married, and her husband would be tall (as he was), and he would be kind and soft-spoken and strong and full of integrity (as he was), and dark (as he was), and there would be a long dinner table with a white cloth and candles, and the Spode, and weekend guests to whom she would call out, "Extra bath towels are in the linen closet just outside your room," and beyond the kitchen would be a garden of her own, with chrysanthemums and nasturtiums and petunias and fresh herbs, which she would cut with scissors for their salad. In the early evenings, when her husband had turned off the lamp in his study (and he did have a study, and in it he was writing a book), she would take him out through the kitchen door into the garden, and in the blending of the earth's dusk and their contentment, they would hold hands and smell her flowers . . . But at the age of twenty-five one had to begin to understand about compromise. Though she was not proud of herself for very many things (she would have to admit that too when she went downtown: that she was not proud of herself, which made her feel terrible) still she might have reason to become proud were she able to learn to compromise, and to like it. Yes, the second half as well, for surely if one didn't like it, if one couldn't *stand* it . . . But one must stand it. And it was simple. She had only to take it upon herself to move an inch and another inch and then—her eyes still closed—another inch and one more, and now reach out with her fingers, and now lay her hand, softly, lovingly . . . He was not there. She opened her eyes. No Paul. Only his pajamas lying on the floor. She heard him making breakfast in the kitchen. Make *me*! Make love to *me*! *I'll* make breakfast!

To the sun, filtering through the grimy windows, she said, "Why can't he just kiss me on the lips?"

She got out of bed, thinking: I want everything.

Over her nightgown she put on a robe, the same blue flannel one her parents had given her when she'd gone off to Cornell ages ago. In the kitchen he was standing over the stove, waiting for the coffee; he was already dressed in his suit and tie, and his briefcase was on the chair. The table was set neatly for two, knife on the right, fork on the left. This

morning he had cut her orange in quarters and there were two
pills beside her bread plate. Dutiful man, he had even folded
the paper napkins in half. She did not know of any other husband who so served his wife. He had always worked so hard—
at first, before their marriage, for himself, to make money for
school, to get good grades; then after their marriage for the
two of them. But from the back she saw that his shoulders
were still unbent. She came up behind him on her toes and
put her arms around his spindly body, her face in the faintly
odorous material of his jacket. For some reason their closets
smelled the way closets might in which very old maids kept
their belongings. And there was nothing to be done about it;
she had already tried air-wick and cologne and moth spray, but
apparently it was something in the very plaster of the house.

Paul jumped. "Oh Jesus—you scared me."

"I'm sorry. Good morning. It's me—sunshine." She intended her merry words to be at once winning and self-critical,
a reference to the night before.

"Honey, please put on slippers," Paul said. "The floors are
cold."

That simple remark of his almost drove her mad. "Good
morning, though . . . first."

"Good morning, Libby."

She looked up into his eyes and found nothing there to
make her doubt that he was a generous man. And she loved
him! He was so much more adult and genuine, more in contact with life's realities, than she could ever hope to be.

"Please," he said, kissing her above the eye, when she lingered beside him, "go put on slippers. I've got a class in half
an hour."

"Yes," she said; she fled toward the hall on her toes, and then
she turned, and with her face lifted, with her heart beating, she
said, "Paul, isn't it a wonderful day? It's sunny for a change. It
seems like a very significant day—" That was as much as she
could manage to tell him.

She went into their bedroom and from beneath the dresser
kicked out her slippers. While she was there she thought she
would quickly make the bed. It will please him to see me
peppy and active; it will make this dreary room orderly, if not

beautiful. But the whole day was before her, no job to go to any longer, no night classes to prepare for, nothing she really had to read, so it might even be a good thing to save the bed for a little later in the morning. She could begin painting those chairs in the kitchen—then she remembered she hadn't the whole day after all. She had to go downtown. She ran into the kitchen then to be near her husband. If anything significant was going to happen today, it was going to have to happen between them, and in less than thirty minutes. There was no time to waste making beds or worrying over painting chairs. Paint wouldn't make them look any better anyway. There was no way of cheering this place up. Only Paul.

But back in the kitchen she could not think what he could really do or say that she should allow to dissuade her from what she had planned. Her decision had come much too hard —it had been a week of dialing the number one minute and hanging up the next. She would not permit herself to be tricked by a pleasant breakfast; she wouldn't let him get away with that. It wasn't as though all their troubles had begun yesterday.

She remembered yesterday—specifically, the dinner of the night before. Paul had said nothing all the way home, though she knew he had disapproved of her behavior. Wherever they went lately she wound up arguing with people. But it was not her fault! Everyone else had been awful—that son of a bitch Gabe, that woman . . . But what had they done? What had they said to her? Why did she hate people? She would have to admit that too when she went downtown—that she couldn't control her responses, that out of the clear blue sky she began to hate people.

"I think I'm going to go out this afternoon," Libby said, picking at her orange.

"Just dress warmly."

"Don't you want to know where I'm going?"

"Out. For a walk . . ." he said. "I thought you said you were going out."

"If you're not interested . . ."

"Libby, don't be petulant first thing in the morning."

"Well, don't be angry at me for last night."

"Who said anything about last night?"

"That's the whole thing—you won't even bring it up. Well, I didn't behave so badly, and don't think I did."

"That's over and done with. You were provoked. That's all right. That's finished."

She did not then ask him who had provoked her; she just began cloudily to accept that she had been.

"Where are you going?" he asked.

"When?" Now she *was* petulant, perhaps because she no longer considered it necessary for her to feel guilty about last night.

She saw Paul losing patience. "This afternoon. You said you were going out, and then I didn't ask you where, you remember . . . so now where is it you're going?"

"Just out. For a walk."

Paul closed his eyes, and touched his palms together, as though he were praying. "Look"—his eyes opened—"you can't allow yourself to get too upset. We're doing all we can."

"I don't even know what you're talking about."

"That adoption business is what I'm talking about. It seems confused now and a little hopeless. But it won't be. Things will get sorted out. We've only just begun—you can't allow it to get to you so soon."

"I wasn't even talking about that," she said, thinking: *I wasn't even talking about that!*

"No," Paul said, "but anyway, try to relax. I'm going to call that Greek orphan place today."

"Paul, I don't mean to be hopeless, but that particular setup sounds *so*—"

"We'll just look into it," he said sharply.

Adopting a baby had been her idea in the first place, hadn't it? She could no longer keep perfectly straight in her mind who had said and done what. "Okay," she said.

"And the Jewish agency is going to send somebody next week."

"What good will that do?"

"Libby, it's an interview. It's part of adopting a baby."

"Other people just get pregnant—"

"Forget other people!"

"Don't shout at me."

"I don't shout at you."

"Not outside you don't," she said bitterly. "If I made you angry last night, why didn't you shout at me there? Why do you only quarrel with me at home?"

"You're not making any sense."

"Well . . ." she said, trying to think of something sensible to say, some simple fact. "Well, that Jewish agency, I don't see what good it is anyway. They have a three-year waiting list. Who can wait three years? I could have had a baby a long time ago—"

"That's enough."

"Well, I could have."

"So you could have," he said, raising his hands, then dropping them.

And how bald he had become, she thought, since that time I could have had my baby. How old. She felt suddenly as though they had been married a hundred years. A harsh laugh rang in her ears, and it was only herself laughing to think that it had not even been the abortion that had knocked out her reproductive powers—just her own two kidneys. How much easier for her if it had been something Paul had put his hands to, or that doctor, or her parents. Anyone. But it was only what had always lived inside her. How can he bear me? she thought. I deserve sick kidneys. Why doesn't he just leave me?

But he, unlike her, had no illusions; she knew him to be too good and too patient. She was the nut in the family, and he was the one with his hands full. She let that serve as an accurate description of their life.

"Paul, I won't be falsely pessimistic if you won't be falsely optimistic."

"It's not being falsely optimistic to say that we'll work something out. Besides, the waiting list is only two years."

"No," she said, nodding, "that's not falsely optimistic. People adopt babies . . ."

"Why don't you go downtown, Libby? Why don't you go to the Art Institute today? It's a beautiful day. Get out. Just put on that little tan hat—"

"It's a beautiful day, I don't need a hat."

He set down his coffee cup as though suddenly it weighed too much. "I only thought you looked pretty in that hat." He left it at that.

She was crushed for having crushed him, especially when he had only been suggesting that she was pretty. Still, if he found her so damned attractive . . . Everything between them was hopelessly confused.

"I thought I *would* go downtown."

He rose. "Fine."

"So I probably won't be here when you get back."

He only leaned down and finished the last of his coffee.

"Don't you want to talk about last night?" she said.

"I don't think so."

What she wanted to ask him was who had provoked her. Often when she tried to puzzle out the circumstances of her life, her mind was a blank. Last night seemed beyond understanding, and yet it was probably so simple. "I behaved rudely—" she began.

"Everybody behaved badly. Shouldn't we leave it at that?"

"I guess so."

—

After Paul left she put the breakfast dishes in the sink, on top of the lunch dishes from the day before. In the bedroom she decided once again to save the bedmaking until later. Her appointment was not until one, so there was plenty of time.

She sat down gingerly upon the sofa in the living room. She still had trouble easing her head back onto the pillows, though she had brushed and brushed them with a whisk broom and been over them many times with a damp sponge. The trouble with their furniture was that it had all been bought one afternoon at Catholic Salvage, a place she could not forget. How Paul had discovered it she still did not know, but one day after they had found the apartment, a bleak but moderately priced four rooms on Drexel, they had taken a bus, and then changed to another bus, to the brick warehouse on South Michigan. They had been the only two white people there—except in the first floor clothing section, where two spinsters, with skin the color and texture of pie crust, stood around a table full of second-hand underwear, fingering and discarding numerous foundation garments. They had already started up the metal stairs to the furniture section when Paul had turned and gone back down to a pipe rack he had spotted in men's wear; it was then Libby had seen the two pathetic old ladies holding up faded corset after faded corset, and then dropping them from crippled fingers back onto the heap. She turned away from them, tears already in her eyes, to see Paul picking out a blue pin-striped suit from amongst a half dozen limp garments strung along the rack. When she saw that the jacket fitted—with a little give and take here and there—she drew in her breath. Though she knew it didn't matter, that it was what a person was and not what he wore that counted, she nevertheless had begun to pray: "Mary, Mother of God, please don't let him buy that thing." And her prayer had been answered. He came clanging up the stairs in his Army-Navy Store shoes to tell her that the two suits he already had were plenty.

They then proceeded up one more flight and around the vast cement floor, where they picked out a kitchen table, four chairs, a desk, a sofa, a bedstead, springs, a mattress, a chest of drawers, a dresser, a mirror, three lamps, and a rug. Marching up another flight, they chose their dishes and pots and pans. And Paul walked right up and touched everything. In his coat and shoes he had stretched out on half a dozen second-hand mattresses until he had found one with enough life left in it.

"Watch out you don't fall asleep now, son," said a Negro man who walked by carrying an old console-model radio.

Paul looked up and smiled; Libby smiled too. She was full of admiration for her husband, not to mention wonder: *How can he put his head down there?* Ever since grade school she had defended the rights of all men, regardless of race; she had willingly (deliberately?) married a Jew; she had always spoken up for the underprivileged (and this even before she had become one herself). Yet she stood looking down at her husband and thinking: *These mattresses have belonged to colored people. I don't want any* . . . She had only sympathy and tenderness for the sick (and this, too, dating from before she had joined the ranks), but she thought: *They have been slept upon by sick people, dying people—*I DON'T WANT ANY! To her husband, however, she said nothing; all the while that Paul went around rapping, knocking, testing, she kept her hands in the pockets of her raincoat. She managed to get away without having had to touch anything.

"What do you think?" Paul had asked. "Do we need something else?"

There were blankets and sheets, but she did not choose to mention either until they were home. "That seems like everything to me," she said.

"Whatever else we need then, we can pick up along the way."

"Yes—if anything turns up . . ."

All together what they bought had cost $103, including the rug, which they never unrolled. "I just don't like the pattern," Libby said.

"Then why didn't you say so when we were there?"

"Maybe later I'll get used to it. Can't we keep it rolled up a little longer? I don't mind the floors, really, if you don't."

He had let her have her way, though she did not forget that the rug had cost them eight dollars—two of her visits to a doctor.

So with all of this behind her (the knowledge she had of her weaknesses, the decision to overcome the weaknesses), she took the bull by the horns and put her head all the way back onto the sofa. One could come to grips with life if only one used a little reason and a little will power. That was what she admired in Paul: his will.

In her blue flannel robe, with her head held rigidly back (she was not going to give in to her worst side), she watched the sun on the bare floor. What to do until one o'clock? She could, of course, decide the hell with one o'clock and then go ahead and do anything. But she could go ahead and do anything anyway. She could paint the kitchen chairs. However, still unfinished was the dresser, which she had begun to paint a bright yellow some six weeks ago. It seemed now to have been a mistaken bit of economy to have bought such cheap paint, for instead of being bright and gay—brightness and gaiety was what she had told Paul the apartment lacked when she had pleaded with him for money for the paint—the piece was coming out a mean, mustardy color because of the stain beneath. Well, she could go ahead and make the bed then . . . No, she would save their bed for last. And not out of laziness; she suddenly had a motive: she wanted those sheets and blankets firmly in her mind when she went downtown. What could she do now?

She could read. But the trouble with her reading was that it was too casual; it did not satisfy. She had already decided that to remedy the situation she would have to try to read the works of one writer straight through, in chronological order. Then all of another writer, and so on. She planned to start with Faulkner but she did not have the books yet. So this was no morning then to begin that project—and to start another book would not make sense, since that would delay her entry into Faulkner when she did get a chance to go over to the library. She could do something practical then. She could make out the grocery list; she could—

She could write a poem.

The idea pleased her. She would write a poem. Why not? If she could write a poem about the night before—

She grabbed a yellow pad that was on the floor beside the books and ran off with it to the kitchen; she sat down so excited with her project, that she simply swept her hand across the table, brushing away the breakfast crumbs. She would attend to them later—they were unimportant. She had never written a poem before (though sick and in bed in Reading she had tried a story), but the idea of poetry had always stirred her. Toward certain poems she had particularly tender feelings. She liked "To His Coy Mistress" and she loved "Ode to a Nightingale," "Ode to Melancholy," too. She liked all of Keats, in fact; at least the ones that were anthologized.

She wrote on the pad:

Already with thee! Tender is the night

She liked *Tender Is the Night*, which, of course, wasn't a poem. She identified with Nicole; in college she had identified with Rosemary. She would have to read it over again. After Faulkner she would read all of Fitzgerald, even the books she had read before. But poetry . . . What other poems did she like?

She wrote:

Come live with me and be my love,
And we will all the pleasures prove.

Then directly below:

The expense of spirit in a waste of shame
Is lust in action—and till action, lust
Is perjured, murderous . . .

She could not remember the rest. Those few lines had always filled her with a headlong passion, even though she had to admit never having come precisely to grips with the meaning. Still, the sound . . .

She wrote, with recollections of her three years of college, with her heart heaving and sighing appropriately.

> *Sabrina fair*
> *Listen where thou art sitting*
> *Under the glassy wave—*
> *And I am black but o my soul is white*
> *How sweetly flows*
> *The liquefaction of her clothes*
> *At last he rose, and twitch'd his mantle blue*
> *Tomorrow to fresh woods and pastures new.*
> *I am! Yet what I am none cares or knows,*
> *My friends forsake me like a memory lost,*
> *I am the self-consumer of my woes.*

And who had written those last lines? Keats again? What was the difference who had written them? She hadn't.

If she could sculpt, if she could paint, if she could write something! Anything—

The door bell rang.

A *friend*! She ran to the door, pulling her belt tight around her. All I need is a friend to take my mind off myself and tell me how silly I'm being. A girl friend with whom I can go shopping and have coffee, in whom I can confide. Why didn't Gabe take up with someone I could befriend? Why did he choose her?

She opened the door. It was not a friend; she had had little opportunity, what with her job, her night classes, and generally watching out for herself, to make any friends since coming to Chicago. In the doorway was a pleasant-looking fellow of thirty or thirty-five—and simply from the thinness of his hair, the fragile swelling of his brown eyes, the narrowness of his body, the neatness of his clothes, she knew he would have a kind and modest manner. One was supposed to be leery of opening the door all the way in this neighborhood; Paul cautioned her to peer out over the latch first, but she was not sorry now that she had forgotten. You just couldn't distrust everybody and remain human.

His hat in one hand, a briefcase in the other, the fellow asked, "Are you Mrs. Herz?"

"Yes." All at once she was feeling solid and necessary; perhaps it was simply his having called her "Mrs. Herz." She had, of course, a great talent for spiritual resurrection; when her fortunes finally changed, she knew they would change overnight. She did not really believe in unhappiness and privation and never would; it was an opinion, unfortunately, that did not make life any easier for her.

"I'm Marty Rosen," the young man said. "I wonder if I can come in. I'm from the Jewish Children's League."

Her moods came and went in flashes; now elation faded. Rosen smiled in what seemed to Libby both an easygoing and powerful way; clearly he was not on his first mission for a non-profit organization. Intimidated, she stepped back and let him in, thinking: One *should* look over the latch first. Not only was she in her bathrobe (which hadn't been dry-cleaned for two years), but she was barefoot. "We didn't think you were coming," Libby said, "until next week. My husband isn't here. I'm sorry—didn't we get the date right? We've been busy, I didn't check the calendar—"

"That's all right," Rosen said. He looked down a moment, and there was nowhere she could possibly stick her feet. Oh they should at least have laid the rug. So *what* if it was somebody else's! Now the floor stretched, bare and cold, clear to the walls. "I will be coming around again next week," Rosen said. "I thought I'd drop in this morning for a few minutes, just to say hello."

"If you'd have called, my husband might have been able to be here."

"If we can work it out," Rosen was saying, "we do like to have sort of an informal session anyway, before the formal scheduled meeting—"

"Oh yes," said Libby, and her thoughts turned to her bedroom.

"—see the prospective parents"—he smiled—"in their natural habitat."

"Definitely, yes." The whole world was in conspiracy, even against her pettiest plans. "Let's sit down. Here." She pointed to the sofa. "Let me take your things."

"I hope I didn't wake you," he said.

"God, no," she said, realizing it was almost ten. "I've been up for hours." After these words were out, they didn't seem right either.

With his coat over her arm, she went off to the bedroom by way of the sofa, where she slid into her slippers as glidingly as she could manage. She walked down the hall, shut the bedroom door, and then, having flung Mr. Rosen's stuff across a chair, she frantically set about whipping the sheets and blankets into some kind of shape. The clock on the half-painted dresser said not ten o'clock but quarter to eleven. Up for hours! Still in her nightclothes! She yanked the sheets, hoisted the mattress (which seemed to outweigh her), and caught her fingernail in the springs. She ran to the other side, tugged on the blankets, but alas, too hard—they came slithering over at her and landed on the floor. Oh Christ! She threw them back on the bed and raced around again—but five whole minutes had elapsed. At the dresser she pulled a comb through her hair and came back into the living room, having slammed shut the bedroom door behind her. Mr. Rosen was standing before the Utrillo print; beside him their books were piled on the floor. "We're getting some bricks and boards for the books." He did not answer. "That's Utrillo," she said.

He did not answer again.

Of course it was Utrillo. Everybody knew Utrillo—that was the trouble. "It's corny, I suppose," said Libby. "My husband doesn't like the impressionists that much either—but we've had it, I've had it, since college—and we carry it around and I guess we hang it whenever we move—not that we move that much, but, you know."

Turning, he said, "I suppose you like it, well, for sentimental reasons." He seemed terribly interested to hear her reply.

"Well . . . I just like it. Yes, sentiment—but aesthetics, of course, too."

She did not know what more to say. They both were smiling. He seemed like a perfectly agreeable man, and there was no reason for her to be giving him so frozen an expression. But apparently the smile she wore she was going to have to live with for a while longer; the muscles of her face were working on their own.

"Yes," she said. "And, this is our apartment. Please, sit down. I'll make some coffee."

"It's a very big apartment," he said, coming back to the sofa. "Spacious."

What did he mean—they didn't have enough furniture? "Well, yes . . . no," replied Libby. "There's this room and then down the hall is the kitchen. And my husband's study—"

Rosen, having already taken his trouser creases in hand, now rose and asked pleasantly, "May I look around?"

She did not believe that the idea had simply popped into his head. But he was so smooth-faced and soft-spoken and well-groomed that she was not yet prepared to believe him a sneak. He inclined slightly toward her whenever she spoke and, though it unnerved her, she preferred to think of it as a kind of sympathetic lean.

"Oh do," Libby said. "You'll have to excuse us, though; we went out to dinner last night. Not that we go out to dinner that much—however we were out to dinner"—they proceeded down the hall and were in the kitchen—"and," she confessed, "I didn't get around to the dishes . . . But," she said, cognizant of the sympathetic lean, though doing her best to avoid the sympathetic eyes, "this is the kitchen."

"Nice," he said. "Very nice."

There were the breakfast crumbs on the floor around the table. All she could think to say was, "It needs a paint job, of course."

"Very nice."

He sounded genuine enough. She went on. "We have plenty of hot water, of course, and everything."

"Does the owner live on the premises?"

"Pardon?"

"Does the owner of the building live on the premises?" he asked.

"It's an agency that manages the place," she said nervously.

"I was only wondering." He walked to the rear of the kitchen, crunching toast particles. Out the back window through which he paused to look, there was, of course, no green yard. "There was just"—he lifted a hand to indicate that it was nothing—"a light bulb out in the hallway, coming up. I wondered if the owner . . ."

He dwindled off, and again she didn't know what to say. The bulb had been out since their arrival; she had never even questioned it; it came with the house. "You see," Libby said, "there are two Negro families in the building and—" And *what*! I don't have anything against Negroes! But the agency does— the agency— Why do I keep bringing up Negroes all the time! "And," she said, blindly, "the bulb went out last night, you see. My husband's going to pick one up today. Right now he's teaching. We don't like to bother the agency for little things. You know . . ." But she could not tell whether he knew or not; he was leaning her way, but what of it? He turned and started back down the hall. Libby shut her eyes. I must stop lying. I must not lie again. He will be able to tell when I lie. They don't want liars for mothers, and they're perfectly right. Tell the truth. You have nothing to be ashamed of.

"My husband is a writer, aside from being a teacher," she said, running down the hall and slithering by Rosen, "and this"—she turned the knob to Paul's room, praying—"is his study."

Thank God. It was orderly; though there was not much that could be disordered. In the entire room, whose two tall winter-stained windows were set no further than ten feet from the apartment building next door, there was only a desk and a desk lamp, a chair and a typewriter, and a wastepaper basket. But the window shades were even and all the papers on the desk were piled neatly. God bless Paul.

"My husband works in here." She flipped on the overhead light, but the room seemed to get no brighter; it anything, it was dingier. But it wasn't their fault that the sun couldn't get around that way. *They* hadn't constructed the building next door. "He's writing a novel."

Rosen took quite an interest in that, too. "Oh yes? That must be some undertaking."

"Well, it's not finished yet. It is an undertaking, all right. But he's working on it. He works very hard. However this," she said quickly, "this, of course, would be the baby's room. Will be the baby's room." She blushed. "Well, when we have a baby, this will be—" Even while she spoke she was oppressed by the barren feebleness of the room. Where would a baby sleep? From what window would the lovely, healthy, natural light fall onto a baby's cheek? Where would they get the baby's crib, Catholic Salvage?

"Where will your husband work on his novel then?"

"I"—she wouldn't lie—"I don't know. We haven't talked about it. This has all happened very quickly. Our decision to have a baby."

"Of course."

"Not that we haven't thought about it—you see, it's not a problem. He can work anywhere. The bedroom. Anywhere. I'll discuss it with him tonight, if you like."

Rosen was quite taken aback; he made a self-effacing gesture with his hands. "Oh, look, I don't care. That's all up to you folks." Even if there was something professional about his gentleness, she liked him for trying to put her at her ease. (Though that meant he knew about her nervousness; later he would mull over motives and behavior.) She had no real reason to be uneasy or overexcited or ashamed. Marty Rosen wouldn't kill her, wouldn't insult her, he wasn't even that much older than she—but what right, damn it, did he have to come unannounced! *That* was the trouble! What kind of business was this natural habitat business! *They have no right to trick people*, she was thinking, and then she was opening the door to their own bedroom, and there was the bed, and the disheveled linens, and the half-painted dresser, and there were Paul's pajamas on the floor. There, in fact, was Rosen's coat, half on the floor. She closed the door and they went back into the living room.

"Actually," she said, addressing the back of his neat little suit as they moved toward the sofa, "I was trying to write a poem . . ."

"Really? A poem?" He sat down, and then instantly was leaning forward, his arms on his legs and his hands clasped, smiling. It was as though nothing he had seen up until now meant a thing; as though there was an entirely different set of rules called into play when the prospective mother turned out to be a poet. "You write, too, do you?"

"Well," said Libby, "no." Then she did not so much sit down into their one easy chair as capitulate into it. Why had she told Rosen about the poem? What did that explain to anybody— did writing poetry excuse crumbs on the floor? It was the truth, but that was all it was. They may want poets for mothers, she thought, buy they sure as hell don't want slobs.

"Well," said Rosen cheerily, "it's a nice-sized apartment." It seemed impossible to disappoint him. "How long have you been here, would you say?"

"Not long," the girl answered. "A few months. Since October."

Rosen was opening his briefcase. "Do you mind if I take down a few things?"

"Oh no, go right ahead." But her heart sank. "We're going to paint, of course, as soon as . . . soon." Stop saying of course! "When everything's settled. When I get some time, I'll begin." The remark did not serve to make her any less conscious of her bathrobe and slippers. "You see," she went on, for Rosen had a way of listening even when no one was speaking, "I was working. I worked at the University. However I wasn't feeling well. Paul said I had better quit."

"That's too bad. Are you better now?"

"I'm fine. I feel fine—" she assured him. "I'm not pale, or sick, I just have very white skin." Even as she spoke the white skin turned red.

Rosen smiled his smile. "I hope it wasn't serious."

"It wasn't anything really. I might have gotten quite sick—" *Why isn't Paul home? What good is he if he isn't here now?* "I had a kidney condition," she explained, starting in again. "It's why the doctors say I shouldn't have a baby. It would be too strong a risk. You see, I'm the one who can't have a baby. Not my husband."

"Well, there are many many couples that can't have babies, believe me."

His remark was probably intended to brace her, but tears came to her eyes when she said, "Isn't that too bad . . ."

He took a long sheet of paper from his briefcase and pushed out the tip of a ball point pen. The click sounded to Libby very official. She pulled herself up straight in her chair and waited for the questions. But Rosen only jotted some words on the paper. She waited. Finally he glanced up. "Just the number of rooms and so forth," he said.

"Certainly. Go right ahead. I've just been having"—she

yawned—"my lazy morning, you know—" She tried to stretch but stifled the impulse halfway. She certainly did not want for a moment to appear in any way loose or provocative. "Not making the bed or anything, just taking the day off, just doing nothing. With a baby, of course, it would be different."

"Oh yes." His brow furrowed, even as he wrote. "Children are a responsibility."

"There's no doubt about that." And she could not help it—she did not care if that was so much simple ass-kissing. At least, at last, she'd said the right thing. All she had to do was to keep saying the right thing and get him out of here, and the next time Paul would be home. There were so many Jewish families wanting babies, and so few Jewish babies, and so what if she was obsequious. As long as: one, she didn't lie; and two, she said the right thing. "They are a responsibility, " she said. "We certainly know that."

"Your husband's an instructor then, isn't that right, in the College?"

"He teaches English and he teaches Humanities."

"And he's got a Ph.D?"

He seemed to take it so for granted—was he writing it down already?—that she suffered a moment of temptation. "An M.A. He's working on his Ph.D. Actually, he's just finishing up on it. He'll have it very soon, of course. Don't worry about that. Excuse me—I'm sorry, I don't mean to sound so instructive. I suppose I'm a little nervous." She smiled, sweetly and spontaneously. A second later she thought that she must have charmed him; at least if he were someone else, if he were Gabe say, he would have been charmed. But this fellow seemed only to become more attentive. "I only meant," Libby said, "that I think Paul has a splendid career before him. Even if I am his wife." And didn't that have the ring of truth about it? Hadn't her words conveyed all the respect and admiration she had for Paul, and all the love she still felt for him, and would feel forever? It had been a nice wifely remark uttered in a nice wifely way—why then wasn't Rosen *moved* by it? Didn't he see what a dedicated, doting, loving mother she would be?

"I'm sure he has," Rosen said, and he might just as well have been attesting to a belief in the process of evolution.

But one had to remember that he was here in an official capacity; you couldn't expect him to gush and sigh. He must see dozens of families every day and hear dozens of wives attest to their love for their husbands. He could probably even distinguish those who meant it from those who didn't, from those who were no longer quite so sure. She tried to stifle her disappointment, though it was clear to her she probably would not be able to get off so solid a remark again.

Rosen had set his paper down now. "And so you just—well, live here," he said, tossing the remark out with a little roll of the hands, "and see your friends, and your husband teaches and writes, and you keep house—"

"As I said, today is just my lazy day—"

"—and you have a normal young people's life. That's about it then, would you say?"

"Well—" He seemed to have left something out, though she couldn't put her finger on it. "Yes. I suppose that's it."

He nodded. "And you go to the movies," he said, "and see an occasional play, and have dinner out once in a while, I suppose, and take walks"—his hands went round with each activity mentioned—"and try to put a few dollars in the bank, and have little spats, I suppose—"

She couldn't stand it, she was ready to scream. "We read, of course." Though that wasn't precisely what she felt had been omitted, it was something.

He didn't seem to mind at all having been interrupted. "Are you interested in reading?"

"Well, yes. We read."

He considered further what she had said; or perhaps he was only waiting for her to go on. He said finally, "What kind of books do you like best? Do you like fiction, do you like nonfiction, do you like biography of famous persons, do you like how-to-do-it books, do you like who-done-its? What kind of books would you say you liked to read?"

"Books." She became flustered. "All kinds."

He leaned back now. "What books have you read recently?" To this question, he gave nothing more or less than it had ever had before in the history of human conversation and its impasses.

It was her turn now to wave hands at the air. "God, I can't remember. It really slips my mind." She felt the color of her face

changing again. "We're always reading something though—
and, well, Faulkner. Of course I read *The Sound and the Fury*
in college, and *Light in August*, but I've been planning to read
all of Faulkner, you know, chronologically. To get a sense of
development. I thought I'd read all of him, right in a row . . ."

His reply was slow in coming; he might have been waiting
for her to break down and give the name of one thin little volume that she had read in the last year. "That sounds like a
wonderful project, like a very worth-while project."

In a shabby way she felt relieved.

"And your poetry," he asked, "what kind of poetry do you
write?"

"What?"

"Do you write nature poems, do you write, oh I don't
know, rhymes, do you write little jingles? What kind of poetry
would you say you write?"

Her eyes widened. "Well, I'm sorry, I don't write poetry,"
she said, as though he had stumbled into the wrong house.

"Oh *I'm* sorry," he said, leaning forward to apologize. "I
misunderstood."

"Ohhhh," Libby cried. "Oh, just this morning you mean."

Even Rosen seemed relieved; it was the first indication she
had that the interview was wearing him down too. "Yes," he
said, "this morning. Was that a nature poem, or, I don't know,
philosophical? You know, your thoughts and so forth. I don't
mean to be a nuisance, Mrs. Herz," he said, spreading his fingers over his tie. "I thought we might talk about your interests. I don't want to pry, and if you—"

"Oh yes, surely. Poetry, well, certainly," she said in a light
voice.

"And the poem this morning, for instance—"

"Oh that. I didn't know you meant that. That was—mostly
my thoughts. I guess just a poem," she said, hating him,
"about my thoughts."

"That sounds interesting." He looked down at the floor.
"It's very interesting meeting somebody who writes poetry.
Speaking for myself, I think, as a matter of fact, that there's entirely too much television and violence these days, that somebody who writes poetry would be an awfully good influence
on a child."

"Thank you," Libby said softly. Of course she didn't hate him. She closed her eyes—though not the two shiny dark ones that Rosen could see. She closed her eyes, and she was back in that garden, and it was dusk, and her husband was with her, and in her arms was a child to whom she would later, by the crib, recite some of her poetry. "I think so too," she said.

"—what makes poetry a fascinating subject," she heard Rosen saying "is that people express all kinds of things in it."

"Oh yes, it is fascinating. I'm very fond of poetry. I like Keats very much," and she spoke almost passionately now (as though her vibrancy while discussing verse would make up for the books she couldn't remember having read recently). "And I like John Donne a great deal too, though I know he's the vogue, but still, I do. And I like Yeats. I don't know a lot of Yeats, that's true, but I like some of him, what I know. I suppose they're mostly anthologized ones," she confessed, "but they're awfully good. 'The worst are full of passionate intensity, the best lack all conviction.'" A second later she said, "I'm afraid I've gotten that backwards, or wrong, but I do like that poem, when I have it in front of me."

"Hmmmm," Rosen said, listening even after she had finished. "You seem to really be able to commit them to memory. That must be a satisfaction."

"It is."

"And how about your own poems? I mean—would you say they're, oh I don't know, happy poems or unhappy poems? You know, people write all kinds of poems, happy poems, unhappy poems—what do you consider yours to be?"

"Happy poems," said Libby. "Very happy poems."

—

At the front door, while Mr. Rosen went round in a tiny circle wiggling into his little coat, he said, "I suppose you know Rabbi Kuvin."

"Rabbi who?"

He was facing her, fastening buttons. "Bernie Kuvin. He's the rabbi over in the new synagogue. Down by the lake."

She urged up into her face what she hoped was an untroubled look. "No. We don't."

Rosen put on his hat. "I thought you might know him." He looked down and over himself, as though he had something more important on his mind anyway, like whether he was wearing his shoes or not.

She understood. "No, no, we don't go around here to the synagogue. We're New Yorkers, originally that is—we go when we're in New York. We have a rabbi in New York. Rabbi Lichtman. You're right, though," she said, her voice beginning to reflect the quantity and quality of her hopelessness. "You're perfectly right"—her eyes were teary now—"religion is very important—"

"I don't know. I suppose it's up to the individual couple—"

"Oh no, oh no," Libby said, and now she was practically pushing the door shut in his face, and she was weeping. "Oh no, you're perfectly right, you're a hundred percent right, religion is very important to a child. But"—she shook and shook her tired head—"but my husband and I don't believe a God damn bit of it!"

And the door was closed, only by inches failing to chop off Rosen's coattails. She did not move away. She merely slid down, right in the draft, right on the cold floor, and oh the hell with it. She sat there with her legs outstretched and her head in her hands. She was crying again. What had she done? *Why?* How could she possibly tell Paul? Why did she cry all the time? It was all wrong—*she* was all wrong. If only the bed had been made, if only it hadn't been for that stupid poetry-writing— She had really ruined things now.

As far as she could see there was only one thing left to do.

—

Rushing up Michigan Boulevard in the unseasonable sunlight—unseasonable for this frostbound city—she realized that she was going to be late. She had gone into Saks with no intention of buying anything; she had with her only her ten-dollar bill (accumulated with pennies and nickels and hidden away for just such a crisis), and besides she knew better. She had simply not wanted to arrive at the office with fifteen minutes to spare. She did not intend to sit there, perspiring and flushing, her body's victim. If you show up so very early, it's probably not too unfair of them to assume that you are weak and needy and pathetically anxious. And she happened to know she wasn't. She had been coping with her problems for some time now, and would, if she had to, continue to cope with them in the future, until they just resolved themselves. She was by no means the most unhappy person in the world.

As a result, she had taken her time looking at sweaters. She had spent several minutes holding up in a mirror a lovely white cashmere with a little tie at the neck. She had even taken off her coat so as to have her waist measured by a salesgirl in Skirts. She had left the store (stopping for only half a minute to look at a pair of black velveteen slacks) with the clock showing that it still wasn't one o'clock. And even if it had been, she would prefer not to arrive precisely on the hour. Then they would assume you were a compulsive—which was another thing no one was simply going to *assume* about her.

But it was twelve minutes past the hour now, and even if she wasn't a compulsive, she was experiencing some of the more characteristic emotions of one. She clutched at her hat—which she had worn not to be warm, but attractive—and raced up the street. Having seriously misjudged the distance, she was still some fifty numbers south of her destination. And it was no good to be this late, no good at all; in a way it was so aggressive of her (or defensive?) and God, she wasn't either! She was . . . what?

She passed a jewelry store; a clock in the window said fourteen after. She would miss her appointment. Where would she ever find the courage to make another? Oh she *was* pathetically anxious—why hadn't she just gone ahead and been it! Why shopping? Clothes! Life was falling apart and she had to worry about velveteen slacks—and without even the money to buy them! She would miss her appointment. Then what? She could leave Paul. It was a mistake to think that he would ever take it upon himself to leave her. It must be she who says goodbye to him. Go away. To where?

She ran as fast as she could.

—

The only beard in the room was on a picture of Freud that hung on the wall beside the doctor's desk. Dr. Lumin was clean-shaven and accentless. What he had were steamrolled Midwestern vowels, hefty south-Chicago consonants, and a decidedly urban thickness in his speech; nothing, however, that was European. Not that she had hung all her hopes on something as inconsequential as a bushy beard or a foreign intonation; nevertheless neither would have shaken her confidence in his wisdom. If anything at all could have made her comfortable it might have been a little bit of an accent.

Dr. Lumin leaned across his desk and took her hand. He was a short wide man with oversized head and hands. She had imagined before she met him that he would be tall; though momentarily disappointed, she was no less intimidated. He could have been a pygmy, and her hand when it touched his would have been no warmer. He gave her a nice meaty handshake and she thought he looked like a butcher. Under his slicked-down brownish hair, his complexion was frost-bitten red, as though he spent most of the day lugging sides of beef in and out of refrigerated compartments. She knew he wouldn't take any nonsense.

"I'm sorry I'm late." There were so many explanations that she didn't give any.

"That's all right." He settled back into his chair. "I have someone coming in at two, so we won't have a full hour. Why don't you sit down?"

There was a straight-backed red leather chair facing his desk and a brownish leather couch along the wall. She did not know whether she was supposed to know enough to just go over and lie down on the couch and start right in telling him her problems . . . Who had problems anyway? She could not think of one—except, if she lay down on the couch, should she step out of her shoes first.

Her shoulders drooped. "Where?" she asked finally.

"Wherever you like," he said.

"You won't mind," she said in a thin voice, "if I just sit for today."

He extended one of his hands and said with a mild kind of force, "Why don't you sit." Oh, he was nice. A little crabby, but nice. She kept her shoes on and sat down in the straight chair.

And then her heart took up a very sturdy, martial rhythm. She looked directly across the desk into a pair of gray and impenetrable eyes. She had had no intention of becoming evasive in his presence; not when she had suffered so in making the appointment. But the room was a good deal brighter than she had thought it would be, and on top of her fear there settled a thin icing of shyness. She was alarmed at having all her pre-conceptions disappointed; and she was alarmed to think she had had so many preconceptions. She could not remember having actually thought about Dr. Lumin's height, or the decor of his office; nevertheless there was a series of small shocks for her in his white walls, his built-in bookshelves, his gold-colored carpet, and particularly in the wide window behind his desk, through which one could see past the boulevard and down to the lake. She had not been expecting to find him with his shade raised. The room was virtually ablaze with light. But of course—it was only one o'clock. One-twenty.

"I stopped off at Saks on the way up. I didn't mean to keep you."

With one of those meat-cutter's hands, he waved her apology aside. "I'm interested—look, how did you get my name? For the record." It was the second time that day that she found herself settled down across from a perfect stranger who felt it necessary to be casual with her. Dr. Lumin leaned back in his swivel chair, so that for a moment it looked as though he'd just keep on going, and fall backwards, sailing clear through the window. Go ahead, she thought, fall. *There goes Lumin* . . . "How did you find out about me?" he asked.

With no lessening of her heartbeat, she blushed. It was like living with an idiot whose behavior was unpredictable from one moment to the next: what would this body of hers do ten seconds from now? "I heard your name at a party," she said. "You see, we've just come to Chicago. A few months ago. So I didn't know anyone. I heard it at a party at the University of Chicago." She thought the last would make it all more digni-fied, less accidental. Otherwise he might take her coming to him so arbitrarily as an insult. "My husband teaches at the University of Chicago," she said.

"It says here"—the doctor was looking at a card—"Victor Honingfeld." His eyes were two nailheads. Would he turn out to be stupid? Did he read those books on the wall or were they just for public relations? She wished she could get up and go.

"Your secretary asked on the phone," she explained, "and I gave Victor's name. He's a colleague of my husband's. I—he mentioned your name in passing, and I remembered it, and when I thought I might like to—try something, I only knew you, so I called. I didn't mean to say that Victor had recommended you. It was just that I heard it—"

Why go on? Why bother? Now she had insulted him professionally, she was sure. He would start off disliking her.

"I think," she said quickly, "I'm becoming very selfish."

Swinging back in his chair, his head framed in the silver light, he didn't answer. "That's really my only big problem, I suppose," said Libby. "Perhaps it's not even a problem. I suppose you could call it a foible or something along that line. But I thought, if I am *too* selfish, I'd like to talk to somebody. If I'm not, if it turns out it is just some sort of passing thing, circumstances you know, not me, well then I won't worry about it any more. Do you see?"

"Sure," he said, fluttering his eyelashes. He tugged undaintily at one of his fleshy ears and looked down in his lap, waiting. All day people had been waiting on her words. She wished she had been born self-reliant.

"It's been very confusing," she told him. "I suppose moving, a new environment . . . It's probably a matter of getting used to things. And I'm just being impatient—" Her voice stopped, though not the rhythmic thudding in her breast. She didn't believe she had Lumin's attention. She was boring him; he seemed more interested in his necktie than in her. "Do you want me to lie down?" she asked, her voice quivering with surrender.

His big raw face—the sharp bony wedge of nose, the purplish overdefined lips, those ears, the whole huge impressive red thing—tilted up in a patient, skeptical smile. "Look, come on, stop worrying about me. Worry about yourself," he said, almost harshly. "So how long have you been in Chicago, you two?"

She was no longer simply nervous; she was frightened. *You two.* If Paul were to know what she was doing, it would be his final disappointment. "October we came."

"And your husband's a teacher?"

"He teaches English at the University. He also writes."

"What? Books, articles, plays?"

"He's writing a novel now. He's still only a young man."

"And you, what about yourself?"

"I don't write," she said firmly. She was not going to pull her punches this second time. "I don't do anything."

He did not seem astonished. How could he, with that unexpressive butcher's face? He *was* dumb. Of course—it was always a mistake to take your troubles outside your house. You had to figure things out for yourself. *How?* "I was working," she said, "I was secretary to the Dean, and I was going to school, taking some courses at night downtown. But I've had a serious kidney condition."

"Which kind?"

"Nephritis." She spoke next as a historian, not a sympathy-monger; she did not want his sympathy. "I almost died," she said.

Lumin moved his head as though he were a clock ticking; sympathy, whether she wanted it or not. "Oh nasty, a nasty thing . . ."

"Yes," she said. "I think it weakened my condition. Because I get colds, and every stray virus, and since it is really dangerous once you've had a kidney infection, Paul said I should quit my job. And the doctor, the medical doctor"—she regretted instantly having made such a distinction—"said perhaps I shouldn't take classes downtown at night, because of the winter. I suppose I started thinking about myself when I started being sick all the time. I was in bed, and I began to think of myself. Of course, I'm sure everyone thinks of himself eighty percent of the time. But truly, I was up to about eighty-five."

She looked to see if he had smiled. Wasn't anybody going to be charmed today? Were people simply going to listen? She wondered if he found her dull—not only dull, but stupid. They tried to mask their responses, one expected that; but perhaps she was no longer the delightful, bubbly girl she knew she once had been. Well, that's partly why she was here: to somehow get back to what she was. She wanted now to tell him only the truth. "I did become self-concerned, I think," she said. "Was I happy? was I this? was I that? and so forth, until I was totally self-absorbed. And it's hung on, in a way. Though I suppose what I need is an interest really, something to take my mind off myself. You simply can't go around all day saying I just had an orange, did that make me happy; I just typed a stencil, did that make me happy; because you only make yourself miserable."

The doctor rocked in his chair; he placed his hands on his belly, where it disappeared into his trousers like half a tent. "I don't know," he mumbled. "What, what does your husband think about all this?"

Her glands and pores worked faster even than her mind; in a moment her body was encased in perspiration. "I don't understand."

"About your going around all day eating oranges and asking yourself if they make you happy."

"I eat," she said, smiling, lying, "the oranges privately."

"Ah-hah." He nodded.

She found herself laughing, just a little. "Yes."

"So—go ahead. How privately? What privately?" He seemed suddenly to be having a good time.

"It's very involved," Libby said. "Complicated."

"I would imagine," Lumin said, a pleasant light in his eye. "You've got all those pits to worry about." Then he was shooting toward her—he nearly sprang from his chair. Their faces might as well have been touching, his voice some string she herself had plucked. "Come on, Libby," Lumin said, "what's the trouble?"

For the second time that day, the fiftieth that week, she was at the mercy of her tears. "Everything," she cried. "Every rotten thing. Every rotten despicable thing. Paul's the trouble— he's just a terrible terrible trouble to me."

She covered her face and for a full five minutes her forehead shook in the palms of her hands. Secretly she was waiting, but she did not hear Lumin's gruff voice nor feel upon her shoulders anyone's hands. When she finally looked up he was still there, a thick fleshy reality, nothing to be charmed, wheedled, begged, tempted, or flirted with. Not Gabe; not Paul; not an extension of herself.

She pleaded, "Please just psychoanalyze me and straighten me out. I cry too much."

He nodded and he said, "What about Paul?"

She almost rose from her seat. "He never makes love to me!

I get laid once a month!" Some muscle in her—it was her heart—suddenly relaxed. Though by no means restored to health, she felt somehow unsprung.

"Well," said Lumin, with authority, "everybody's entitled to get laid more than that. Is this light in your eyes?" He raised an arm and tapped his nail on the bright pane of glass behind him.

"No, no," she said, and for no apparent reason what she was to say next made her sob. "You can see the lake." She tried, however, to put some real effort into pulling herself together. She wanted to stop crying and make sense, but it was the crying that seemed finally to be more to the point than the explanations she began to offer him in the best of faith. "You see, I think I've been in love with somebody else for a very long time. And it isn't Paul's fault. Don't think that. It couldn't be. He's the most honest man, Paul—he's always been terribly good to me. I was a silly college girl, self-concerned and frivolous and unimportant, and *brutally* typical, and he was the first person I ever wanted to listen to. I used to go on dates, years ago this is, and never listen—just talk. But Paul gave me books to read and he told me thousands of things, and he was—well, he saved me really from being like all those other girls. And he's had the toughest life. His parents have been bastards, perfect bastards. That's true—*miserable cruel bastards!*" Though her eyes seemed hardly able to deliver up any more tears, they somehow managed. "Oh honestly," she said, "my eyeballs are going to fall out of my skull, just roll right on out. Between this and being sick . . . I never imagined everything was going to be like this, believe me . . ."

After a while she wiped her face with her fingers. "Is it time?" she asked. "Is it two?"

Lumin seemed not to hear. "What else?"

"I don't know." She sniffed to clear her nose. "Paul—" Medical degrees and other official papers hung on either side of Freud's picture. Lumin's first name was Arnold. That little bit of information made her not want to go on. But he was waiting. "I'm not really in love with this old friend," she told him. "He's an old friend, we've known him since graduate school. And he's—he's very nice, he's carefree, he's full of sympathy—"

"Isn't Paul?"

"Oh yes," she said, in what came out like a whine. "Oh *so* sympathetic. Dr. Lumin, I don't know what I want. I don't love Gabe. I really can't stand him if you want to know the truth. He's not for me, he's not Paul—he never could be. Now he's living with some woman and her two kids. Two of the most charming little children you ever saw, and those two are living together, right in front of them. She's so vulgar, I don't know what's gotten into him. We had dinner there—nobody said anything, and there was Gabe with that bitch."

"Why is she such a bitch?"

"Oh"—Libby wilted—"she's not that either. Do you want to know the bitch? Me. I was. But I *knew* it would be awful even before we got there. So, God, that didn't make it any easier."

He did not even have to bother; the next question she asked herself. "I don't *know* why. I just thought, why shouldn't we? We never go out to dinner, we hardly have been able to go out anywhere—and that's because of me too, and my health. Why shouldn't we? Do you see? And besides, I wanted to," she said. "It's as simple as that. I mean isn't that still simple—to want to? But then I went ahead and behaved worse than anybody, I know I did. Oh, Gabe was all right—even she was all right, in a way. I understand all that. She's not a bitch probably. She's probably just a sexpot, good in bed or something, and why shouldn't Gabe live with her anyway? He's single, he can do whatever he wants to do. *I'm* the one who started the argument. All I do lately is argue with people. And cry. I mean that keeps me pretty busy, you can imagine."

Lumin remained Lumin; he didn't smile. In fact he frowned. "What do you argue about? Who are you arguing with?"

She raised two hands to the ceiling. "Everybody," she said. "Everything."

"Not Paul?"

"Not Paul—that's right, not Paul. *For* Paul," she announced. "Everybody's just frustrating the hell out of him, and it makes me so angry. It makes me so *furious*! That John Spigliano! Gabe . . . Oh I haven't even *begun* to tell you what's happened."

"Well, go on."

"What?" she said helplessly. "Where?"

"Paul. Why is this Paul so frustrated?"

She leaned forward, and her two fists came hammering down on his desk. "If he wasn't, Doctor, *oh if they would just leave him alone!*" She fell back, breathless. "Isn't it two?"

At last he gave her a smile. "Almost."

"It must be. I'm so tired. I have such lousy resistance . . ."

"It's a very tiring thing, this kind of talking," Lumin said. "Everybody gets tired."

"Doctor," she said, "can I ask you a question?"

"What?"

"What's the matter with me?"

"What do you think's the matter?"

"Please, Dr. Lumin, please don't pull that stuff. Really, that'll drive me nuts."

He shook a finger at her. "C'mon, Libby, don't threaten me." The finger dropped, and she thought she saw through his smile. "It's not my habit to drive people nuts."

She backed away. "I'm nuts already anyway."

For an answer he clasped and unclasped his hands.

"Well, I am," she said. "I'm cracked as the day is long."

He groaned. "What are you talking about? Huh? I'm not saying you should make light of these problems. These are real problems. Absolutely. Certainly. You've got every reason to be upset and want to talk to somebody. But"—he made a sour face—"what's this cracked business? How far does it get us? It doesn't tell us a hell of a lot, would you agree?"

She had, of course, heard of transference, and she wondered if it could be beginning so soon. She was beaming at him; her first friend in Chicago.

"So . . ." he said peacefully.

"Really I haven't begun to tell you things."

"Sure, sure."

"When should I come again? I mean," she said more softly, with less bravado, "should I come again?"

"If you want to, of course." He looked at the appointment book on his desk. "How's the day after tomorrow? Same time."

"That's fine. I think that would be perfect. Except—" Her

heart, which had stopped its pounding earlier, started up again, like a band leaving the field. "How much will it be then?"

"Same as today—"

"I only brought," she rushed to explain, "ten dollars."

"We'll send a bill then. Don't worry about that."

"It's more than ten, for today?"

"The usual fee is twenty-five dollars."

"An hour?"

"An hour."

She had never in her life passed out, and that she didn't this time probably indicated that she never would. She lost her breath, voice, vision, all sense of feeling, but she managed to stay upright in her chair. "I—don't send a bill to the house."

"I'd rather you wouldn't," Lumin began, a kind of gaseous expression crossing his face, "worry about the money. We can talk about that too."

Libby had stood up; now she sat down. "I think I have to talk about it."

"All right. We'll talk."

"It's after two, I think."

"That's all right."

But what she meant was, would he charge for overtime? Twenty-five dollars an hour—that must be nearly fifty cents a minute. "I can't pay twenty-five dollars." She tried to cry, but couldn't. She felt very dry, very tired.

"Perhaps we can work it out at twenty."

"I can't pay twenty. I can't pay fifteen. I can't pay anything."

"Of course," said Lumin firmly, "you didn't expect it would be for nothing."

"I suppose I did. I don't know . . ." She got up to go.

"Please sit down. Sit."

She almost crept back into the chair as though it were a lap. "Don't you see, it's all my doctor's bills in the first place. Don't you see that?"

He nodded.

"Well, I can't pay!" But she couldn't cry either. "*I can't pay!*"

"Look, Libby, look here. I'm giving you an address. You go home, you give it some thought. It's right here on Michigan Avenue—the Institute. They have excellent people, the fee is less. You'll have an interview—"

"I married Paul," she said, dazed, "not Gabe—this is ridiculous—you're being ridiculous—excuse me, but you're being—"

He was writing something.

She shouted, "I don't want any Institute!"

"It's the Institute for Psychoanalysis—"

"*Why can't I have you!*"

He offered her the paper. "You can be interviewed at the Institute," he said, "and see if they'll be able to work you in right away. Come on now," he said, roughly, "why don't you think about which you might prefer, which might better suit your circumstances."

She stood up. "You don't even know they'll take me."

"It's research and training, so of course, yes, it depends—"

"I came to you, damn it!" She reached for the paper he had written on, and threw it to the floor. "I came to you and I told you all this. You listened. You just sat there, listening. And now I have to go tell somebody else all over again. Everything. I came to you—*I want you!*"

He stood up, showing his burly form, and that alone seemed to strip her of her force, though not her anger. "Of course," he said, "one can't always have everything one wants—"

"I don't want everything! I want *something!*"

He did not move, and she would not be intimidated: she had had enough for one day. Quite enough. "I want you," she said.

"Libby—"

"I'll jump out the window." She pointed over his shoulder. "I swear it."

He remained where he was, blocking her path. And Libby, run down, unwound, empty-minded suddenly, turned and went out his door. He provoked me, she thought in the elevator. He provoked me. He and that son of a bitch Gabe. They lead me on.

Ten minutes later, in Saks, she bought a sweater; not the white cashmere, but a pale blue lamb's-wool cardigan that was on sale. It was the first time in years she had spent ten dollars on herself. She left the store, walked a block south toward the I.C. train, and then turned and ran all the way back to Saks.

Because the sweater had been on sale she had to plead with two floor managers and a buyer before they would give her back her money.

—

At home later she tried several different ways of committing
suicide, but the problem was that she didn't want to die. The
problem was that she wanted to live. When she turned on the
gas, she very soon turned it off, fearing an explosion. She went
into the bedroom where she stretched out on the unmade bed
and put a pillowcase over her head. But it was hot and uncomfortable, and every few minutes she kept releasing the opening
around her neck to let air in. She remained on the bed for
nearly an hour—what she began to want was for Paul to come
home and catch her in the act. Sometimes she would put the
pillowcase off entirely, but as soon as she heard a footstep on
the stairs, or even the least little noise in the building, she
would jerk it back over her, clamp tight the bottom, and wait.
She wondered at various times (there was nothing much else
to do but think) if she should write a note and take off her
clothes and die—be caught dying—naked. Maybe he would
come in, find her unclothed, and ravish her. And she would
keep the pillowcase over her head all the while he devoured
her body. But by four-thirty he was not home. She slipped the
case, which was warm and damp from her breathing, back
onto the pillow, and made the bed.

She paced the apartment, looking—for what she did not
really know. In the living room she sat down on the floor and
began to sort through their books. When she came up with a
gayly jacketed book in her hands, she thought that perhaps
unconsciously it was this book she had been searching for.
That day she believed strongly in the guiding light of the
unconscious self; what with the conscious self doing such a
rotten job, she had to. The book she held in her hand was not
Faulkner, Fitzgerald, nor a book of verse; it was the volume
the rabbi in Ann Arbor had given her as a present after she had
been dunked in the pool at the Y, and converted. *The Wonder
of Life* it was called, and subtitled, "Suggestions for the Jewish
Homemaker." Her eye moved eagerly over the blurb on the
inside flap. ". . . creative, contemporary home life . . . traditions and ceremonies . . . how to build a Jewish record library
. . . chapters on family fun, painting, music, literature, the
community, household finances . . . the place of the woman

in a beautiful tradition . . . basic recipes . . . special holiday menus . . . how to plan a wedding, how to name a baby . . ."

When everything had ended with Paul's family, when they had slammed down the receiver at the news of Libby's conversion, this book, she remembered, had been tossed aside; it had—remembering more clearly—been *kicked* aside. But never thrown out. Books were really all they owned, and wherever they moved, from Ann Arbor to Detroit to Iowa City to Reading to Chicago, from poverty to sickness to humiliation, every single book was carried with them. Some were read, and others unread but coveted, and others just came along for the ride. That she had not even opened this one in all those years was understandable, since she was not religious or pious by nature. She was no worse a Jew, however, than she had been a Catholic—religion had always seemed to her "extra." And perhaps thinking that was her mistake. Perhaps (listen, she told herself, is this my unconscious at last making itself heard?), perhaps the adoption agencies know what they are talking about; maybe Marty Rosen's question about the rabbi had not been improper after all. Not that one could force oneself to believe—no, something else. The family . . . the home. What she had always taken for granted about Jewish life was the warm family environment. And what an irony! Look at Paul's parents; Paul himself. In the most Protestant household in America there could be no more coldness than had surrounded her first five years of marriage. But perhaps the fault was partly hers. Perhaps there was one final way out of all this mess that was not psychoanalysis, or money in the bank, or carnality, or self-pity, or madness: Religion. Not all that Christ and Mary hocus-pocus; not even a belief in God necessarily—though who could tell, maybe God Himself would come in time. But first something basic and sustaining, something to make them truly ready for, deserving of, a baby; something warm, sacred, worth while: *traditions and ceremonies, holy days and holidays and customs . . .*

Thirty minutes later she was in the kitchen. *The Wonder of Life* was spread open before her. Egg shells, peelings, onion skin and flour were all over the table and the book; there was flour on the bridge of her nose, and on her forehead where she had touched her perspiring brow. She had been grating for ten minutes, but unfortunately she had tiny wrists and was still on her first potato. Grating and grating, and oh it was so idiotic. It was insane really, the end of a disastrous day, and still she grated. And because she was Libby and she had suffered; because the more she suffered the further dignity and usefulness seemed to flee; because her right hand was pulsating, *aching*, with the effort to bring a little religion into her house; because finally she no longer believed in the restorative powers of anything or anyone, these latkes included, while she grated, she shed a few tears. Where the body found the reservoir to hold them, she could no longer imagine.

But life is full of surprises, or thought of another way, is one long one. She heard a creak in the hallway. It was not the first creak she had heard that afternoon—and she turned, not the first time for that either. There stood Gabe Wallach. *He has come for me*, she thought. *And now I'd better go. Nothing else is left.*

Then Paul was there, coming down the hallway behind Gabe, dark and shambling. Was she dreaming? Her two men. They have come for me, the two of them. All day they have followed me around and seen every stupid and selfish move. Gabe and Paul. Paul and Gabe. They are going to do something to me . . . *But I am sweet and good. I deserve as much as anybody—*

"I brought Gabe Wallach home," Paul said, moving past his silent companion into the kitchen. She recognized his shoes, and the expression on his face. Too clearly. She was not dreaming. "What are you doing? What's on your forehead?"

"Flour, nothing—"

"Libby, what are you up to?"

"Nothing! I'm just making dinner!" She tried to push everything together on the table. She shouldn't have raised her voice. But what she was doing was nobody's business but her own; at least not with Gabe so icy and hostile in the doorway. Curtly she acknowledged his presence. "How do you do?"

He gave no acknowledgment back; he waited. And for what? Paul's fired! Why else would that son of a bitch be here? He can *smell* bad news! He hates us and we hate him and that's it. Just last night . . . But the world had spun so in one day that she wondered if she might not be mixed up about the night before. Hadn't they all separated forever?

"He has—" Paul was saying, his hands way down in his coat pockets, ruining his posture, "he has some news for us. I want you to hear it."

"What is it? What's the matter?"

Paul removed a hand from his pocket and started bouncing an invisible ball with it. "All right, all right, calm down, please."

In front of Gabe, why must he treat her like a child! Who was on her side? Who was left?

To Gabe, Paul said, "You had better come in."

He only moved forward one grudging step. Paul sat down and motioned for Libby to sit too.

Wallach took a deep breath. "Look, I spoke to Paul this afternoon about a baby."

Libby listened for more, but no more was immediately forthcoming. She had a sudden sense of having been violated —shame, shock, fear attacked her. The deepest chamber of her heart had been forced open, and a secret stolen—a secret she had not even known she'd had. The two men whom she had turned against each other had come together and pooled their knowledge. They had made a decision for her about her life. She was going to have to bear a baby even if the two of them had to hold her down to do it. Oh no! *Yes!* She had ovaries and tubes, didn't she, all the necessary equipment? So what if it was a little risk—everybody had risks to take for everybody else. Hadn't Paul taken plenty for her? But that very patient doctor in Reading had carefully explained to them that child-birth might kill her. You see, Mr. Herz, she needs care, this frail girl of yours; she's hardly more than a child herself. How can she carry a foetus, bear a baby—she needs care and love, this one. *Well, stop laughing—I do! What's wrong with that? I can't have a baby! I have bad kidneys! You can't make me have a baby, either of you! I might die!*

When Gabe failed to go on, Paul said to her, "He knows of a baby. He thought we should be told about it."

"What?" Libby said. "What baby?"

Gabe remained in the doorway. "A private adoption."

"Why don't you sit down?" Paul said to him. "Would you,

please?" He suggested the chair next to his wife. "I want you to hear this," he said then to Libby. "I want you to understand it all."

Gabe came as far as the chair, but chose not to sit down. His coat had a velvet collar. The dandy! The fairy! He probably couldn't even do it himself, the cold-hearted rich bastard!

"There's nothing to hear," Gabe said. "I told you everything there is to tell. It's up to you. You can tell it to her easier than I."

Paul said, "I'd like Libby to hear it from you. Please. I don't want her to get confused."

Why was he making her out to be such a handful? I protect him—why can't he protect me! "I do not get confused," she said.

"Please, Libby, only listen. I want you to listen and decide. I asked him to come here," Paul said, "so all the terms of the thing would be straight in your mind."

"What about you . . . ?" she began, but her husband quieted her, this time with only a glance, with only the pain in his eyes.

"Somebody's pregnant," Gabe said, closing his eyes for a moment. "She doesn't want the baby. You can adopt it—" He turned to Paul and threw up his arms. "Look, that's what I told you. It's still the same. You can do with this whatever you want."

Slowly, his elbows moving through several of the ingredients on the table, Paul turned to face his wife. "You see," he explained, "it wouldn't be through an agency. I want you to understand this. It would be private. That's a little more involved; however—"

"Are they married?" she asked.

"The girl doesn't want the baby," Paul said. "She's not married."

Libby looked up at Gabe. "Who is she?"

"A girl," came the answer.

"Well, I mean, who *is* she? For you to say a girl—"

"Libby," Paul said, "she's a student, all right?"

"It's just a question," she said. "How am I supposed to know?"

"She's a student," Paul repeated.

"Where? Here?" Again she was asking Gabe.

"I don't know," he mumbled.

"Well, you're the one who's supposed to know her—"

"I didn't say I knew her," Gabe cut in.

"At the Art Institute," Paul said, hitting the table. "Does that answer the question, Libby?"

She knew then that she was being lied to. Instead of making her even angrier, the discovery soothed and comforted; it seemed to give her an advantage.

"I don't know," she said. "Who's the father? What is he? Who is he? Why doesn't he marry her? Is it her boy friend?"

"I don't know anything about the father," Gabe answered flatly. He looked over to Paul. "I gave you the girl's name. You can get in touch with her and work it out from there, if you want to. Doesn't that make sense?"

Paul didn't answer. "All right, Lib?" he asked. "What do you think? How does it seem to you?"

"We don't know anything about the father, for one thing." She had made it sound as though Gabe was responsible. "We don't even begin to know anything—"

"And I said I don't know anything about the father either," Gabe told her.

Libby looked up at his steely face. "You don't have to be rude!"

He focused on her mean, bored expression, while Paul said, "Let's just conduct this business—"

"Well, *I* am," said Libby. "You can't expect me to jump in. We don't even know anything about the father."

"He's probably a student," Paul said.

"Oh sure, he's probably a faculty member," Gabe said, as though to himself.

Oh the cruel bastard! He had no respect for what she had been through. "Well," she said to him, "it's just a matter of establishing something, if you don't mind."

"Through an agency," Gabe said, "you wouldn't know any more."

"As a matter of fact we certainly would. They try to match you up, the parents and the infant—coloring, eyes, general—" But she drifted off, for he was not listening.

"Look," he was saying to Paul, "you do with this whatever you want. May I go now?"

Paul didn't even look at him; apparently he couldn't. He shrugged, and it seemed as though he were straw, not flesh, under his coat. "You'll have to do whatever you think best," he said.

"Fine," Gabe said; he started out of the kitchen.

"Well, we have a right to *know*," Libby shouted after him. "It's our lives. You don't have to be so huffy about it."

He turned and leaned in the doorway, one hand on either wall. "Can I go?"

"Well"—she was swallowed by panic—"we don't even know anything about *her*—"

"Paul knows."

"Oh—yes?" And now she did not want to hear another word. The mother was a call girl, a dope addict—the mother was Martha Reganhart!

"May I leave now?" Gabe asked.

"Oh *go*!" Libby shot back. "If you're so impatient, go, get out of here—we don't want to keep you." She found that her husband was openly staring at her. His eyes, his kind eyes . . . Oh yes, she had been found out.

"Libby," Gabe said, "why don't you use your head—"

"Don't start insulting us," she demanded, and now she quickly turned her head and met Paul's eyes. Why didn't he protect her? Oh cruel men—cruel heartless self-absorbed bastards!

"Libby," Gabe said, softening, "I got this information and I thought you might be interested in it. And—and that's it, that's all there is to it."

"Well, isn't that nice. We've just been going through perfect hell trying to adopt a baby, so you needn't think it *terribly* generous of you to imagine we might be interested."

"Oh screw it," he said, and started down the hall.

Libby rose out of her chair, crying after him, "But we don't *know* anything!"

"We know, we know," Paul reached across with his hand.

"But what do we do?" she cried. She looked at Paul. Would he know what to do? Poor Paul? Poor trampled-on Paul? "Gabe, what do we do?"

She heard him call, "You get in touch with her. You better see her . . ."

She ran to the hallway; at the end of the apartment she saw just the paleness of his face and his hand on the knob. "No—" she said, "I won't—I can't—"

The hand on the knob turned; his feet, thank God, stayed put. "Then Paul sees her," he said. "When you get everything settled you can get a lawyer, and he'll take it from there. Maybe it would be best to get a lawyer in right at the beginning. Look, Libby, he knows all this—"

She turned back to her husband. "A lawyer," she moaned.

Paul was moving toward her with his arms extended; she could no longer read the expression on his face. "It's all right—we'll talk about it—"

"We don't know any lawyers. Lawyers cost a fortune—"

"I'll take care of it," Paul said. He took hold of her arms. "We'll take care of it. We still have the agency. They'll send somebody soon. Relax, honey, we can wait. If you prefer, if it will make you feel safer, then we'll wait and work through the agency. I thought you didn't want to wait, that's all."

"Oh no," she said, "oh no no no," but she could not tell him anything, not now, not today. "Oh it's ugly and sordid, and everything's always the same."

"Don't cry."

"I'm *not* crying! Do you see me crying? I'm just making a statement. Everything's ugly and sordid! Can't I say that?"

"Sure." His hands dropped from her arms.

"Oh Paul—"

"I'm going." It was Gabe's voice, faint, almost gone. "I'll be going now."

"Go! Just go!" she cried. "That's it—close the door and go!" But she came charging down upon him. "You just go, damn it. And thank you. Oh yes, don't think we don't appreciate everything either. We appreciate every tiny single thing you've ever done, Gabe. Oh we kiss your high and mighty ass, Gabe, don't you forget that. Thank you, thank you for this helpful hint, we thank you a million times. Kind Gabe—" she said, shaking her fist, "so kind he probably went out and impregnated a little eighteen-year-old student, especially for us—"

"Why don't you watch what you're saying, Libby."

"Why? Can't you stand a little horror in your life? I can.

Paul can." And she thought: I can't. Paul can't. Too much already. Now more. Paul will meet the mother, take her to doctors, pay her bills, listen to her sad story, watch her weep. He will remember her face and carry it with him through life. She will be the mother—I'll be the stepmother. He'll see her face, her eyes, her hair, her tears—*then who will I have!*

"—don't want your appreciation," Gabe was saying, "so don't kid yourself about that—"

"Oh but we appreciate so much," she said. "Don't you know everybody loves Gabe, all his charm and benevolence? How can any of us help ourselves? All the world loves Gabe, but who does Gabe love? We're all waiting to hear—*who?* Oh you're something, Gabriel, you really are—"

His hands were fists; that big chin of his was leaning out at her. "What is it you want, Libby? What is it you're after now?"

"Oh, I don't want anything from you!" She felt Paul's hands come down on her shoulders.

"Cut it out, Libby, control yourself—" Paul was saying.

But she was flailing her arms, to be free. "Nothing. You do what you want. People don't tell *you* what to do—"

"People tell me plenty," Gabe said. "Too God damn much!"

"Oh do they?"

"Yes!"

"Then let me tell you—" and suddenly her voice had dropped, and it was harsh, deep, pleading. "Let me tell you— *don't make Paul do it! Don't make Paul see her! Gabe, please, the last thing—*"

"I should never have come here, Libby—"

"It'll kill us. It's our baby, not hers. Ours! *Please!*"

"Libby" . . . "Libby—" Both men were calling her name, and in the dim hallway they swooped down around her and lifted her off the floor, where, on her hands and knees, she was begging.

5

ALTHOUGH Theresa Haug's pale blue uniform—the same washed-out color as her eyes—swam around her hunched shoulders and permitted a good two inches of air to circulate about her frail upper arm it had nevertheless already begun to hug her belly. She had been seduced in November; perhaps October—this was yet to be established.

I watched her clear a table and then try to take an order from one booth while she dealt with a complaint about an underdone steak from another across the way. Her helpless confusion was not a pleasant sight, but given my mood and the turnings of my mind, it was almost preferable to having to watch Mark Reganhart inhale his French fried potatoes, the last of which lay on his plate, a squad of broken-backed, tortured soldiers oozing ketchup at every fork wound. All of Markie's infantile habits, toward which I had felt kind or neutral at other times, had begun to exasperate me in the last few days. I was about to snap at him when I remembered, *I am not his father, he is not my son*, and turned away.

Again I looked at Theresa Haug, who stood a few booths from where we sat. To customers, she was mute and obliging, and efficient to the point of hysteria (or perhaps it was hysteria to the point of efficiency, it looked the same to me). In any encounter with the hostess, Mrs. Crowther—an egregious woman who was always sliding people into their seats with a melodic, "*There* you are"—Theresa's deference stopped just this side of a salute. Not that Mrs. Crowther, or anybody else, paid Theresa very much attention; there wasn't very much to attend *to*. All of her, form and features, seemed to have been designed and constructed by a committee of Baptist ministers' wives. Her stockings hung from her underdeveloped calves in a particularly heartbreaking way, her skin held no mysteries, and her mouth was just a faint-hearted dash across the blankness of her expression. Yet someone had taken the trouble to undress her and lay her down and climb on top. A seed had been dropped, and it was about its fruition that I had come to see her.

For Martha (not myself) I had spoken to Paul Herz; for Paul I had spoken to Libby; for Libby I would speak to Theresa Haug. What other way could it have been?

"Cut your potatoes," Cynthia told her brother. "Stop stuffing yourself. Stop jamming them in whole, Markie. Uh-oh for you. Here comes Mother."

Martha, who was waitress to us as well as mother and mistress, set down two glasses of chocolate milk and a cup of coffee. "How is everyone?" she asked.

"Markie's not using any manners," Cynthia said. "I don't think he should be allowed to sleep at Stephanie's."

"I want to!" Mark howled.

"Cynthia," Martha said, "don't tease him. Markie, stop whining."

"You were the one who said if he wasn't going to use manners—" began Cynthia.

Weary, quite weary of this little family group and their aggravations and struggles (*my family? mine?*), I asked Martha, "When does she get off?"

"Seven—"

"Mother—"

"I'm talking to Gabe."

I turned on Cynthia. "She's talking to me, Cynthia—how about it?"

"When's Stephanie's grandma coming?" asked Markie.

"Soon, honey."

To show that my rebuke meant nothing to her Cynthia raised her eyebrows and clicked her tongue at the violence her brother was practicing with his fork. And a feeling came over me, a rootless kind of feeling, that control over my affairs was no longer in my own hands. Something like resignation— most likely disgust, and perhaps fear too—must have shown on my face.

"You don't have to wait for Stephanie's grandmother," Martha said to me. "If it bothers you so . . . The kids can wait by themselves."

"I'm not waiting for Stephanie's grandmother. I'm waiting for your friend."

"She'll be through at seven."

"It's after seven."

"Then she'll be through soon. Look, Gabe—" A waitress came hurtling by our booth then, her tray tipping toward a disaster which might or might not overtake her before she reached the kitchen.

"There she is," I said.

Martha reached out to touch Theresa's arm. "It's seven," she said.

"Oh, look—this here—maybe some other—too *rare* he says," and with a droopy-eyed look she showed Martha a steak on her tray.

"I'll take your station," Martha said.

"But Mrs. Crowther—"

"Theresa, get dressed. I'll take your station. He's waiting."

"Yes—" She ran off down the aisle, leaving me exhausted. Martha kissed each child on the top of the head and went off toward the kitchen with Theresa's steak. "Miss . . ." someone called after her, but she was her own woman, guardian of her rights and dignity, and she just kept going.

With a newsiness altogether uncharacteristic of her, Cynthia said, "We're not sleeping at home tonight."

"That should be fun," I said. "Do you like to sleep at other people's houses?"

"Sometimes."

"Do you?" Markie asked me.

I took a napkin from the dispenser on the table and reached across and wiped the ketchup off his mouth. "You try to concentrate on eating," I said.

Cynthia pointed to where I had wiped her brother's mouth. "I think my mother wants him to learn to do that himself."

"I suppose she does."

"He should be able to teach himself to grow up a little," she said.

"He should," I agreed, "but he doesn't, and the rest of us have to look at it."

"I think my mother would prefer if you let him do that himself," she said beautifully.

"I didn't steal his mouth from him, Cynthia—I only wiped it."

Markie's dark eyes now turned up to me, his chin grazing the remains on the plate. "Are you going to marry my Mommy?"

Now I smiled. "He certainly is full of questions."

"He's only a child," Cynthia said, which in a variety of ways was a favorite line of hers.

"For a child those are pretty adult questions."

Cynthia was nonplused; finally she admitted, "Well . . . he talks to me."

My daughter. My stepdaughter. My stepson. Sitting there I continued to be visited with what ifs, and supposes.

Theresa Haug appeared in a big black-and-white checkerboard coat with saucer-sized buttons that shone. She stood beside the booth, speechless. Cynthia shrugged her shoulders, as though to indicate to me—and to the lady herself—that our visitor might be coo-coo.

"It's okay," I said, getting up from my seat, "she's a friend of your mother's."

"I don't care," answered Cynthia in a tinkly voice.

Markie had picked up the ketchup bottle, turned it on its side, and was allowing its contents to run out onto his plate. He asked, "Is that his wife?" but I don't think Theresa Haug heard.

"Ready, Miss Haug?" I asked, but got no reply. I took her arm and started to steer her toward the door.

"Bye, Gabe," I heard Markie call.

I didn't turn back; I was trying to focus all my attention on my charge and on her hardship. Nevertheless I could not really displace my own problem with hers. Martha's teary ultimatum of two short nights before still burned in my mind. As for Martha herself, it was clear that she too had not forgotten those words she had addressed to me from her bed. Surely saving Theresa Haug was not, in anything other than a metaphoric way, saving herself.

Outside the Hawaiian House, Theresa stopped. Like a poor dumb beast. I said, "I'm parked a little way off. By Dorchester . . ." I tugged at her arm, then guided her along like one blind. She kept her gaze on her coat buttons.

"It's a beautiful night for a change," I said. There was indeed a sky overhead that was purple and practically glowing. "It's getting a little warmer," I added. "That should be a help . . ."

At last we made it to the car; I unlocked the door and

helped her in. The overhead light spread like some watery dime-store paint over her plain, dull face. I closed the door for her and then walked around to the other side, in a kind of stupor too, for I was wondering if it made life more sensible, or less, to think that it was toward the alleviation of this girl's suffering that all the rest of us had been struggling—Paul, Libby, Martha, myself—these many months and years.

—

I took Theresa Haug to a restaurant on the lake shore where, to offset the sugary Muzak piped into the dining room, the walls were hung with lurid paintings of the Chicago fire. The combination of music and art impressed me as ghoulish and antisocial, but the place was quiet and close by, and it had soft lighting and a view of the lake. Theresa could have dinner and we two could accomplish our business, all by candlelight.

I had been hoping that the shadowy atmosphere might loosen her up without unhinging her, but once there she still refused to look my way. At the check room I lived through a desperate moment trying to help her out of her coat. Evidently she thought I had lost my mind and was trying to wrestle her down onto the carpet, for she uttered a forlorn hopeless little cry (her first sound) and nearly fell backwards onto me, waving her arms. "Please, please . . . your coat," I pleaded, and then she either caught on or gave herself up to still another assault, and I got what I was after, plus her limp body.

Through this confusion, the hat-check girl stood at my side tapping her lacquered nails on the metal checking tokens. She was a crooked-mouthed bitch in a black crepe dress, sporting the packed-in, boxcar variety of voluptuousness; I gave her a dirty look, and then the gaudy coat, and taking Theresa by the arm once again, led her into the dining room. Within the gentle throbbing light, underexercised, overfed merchants were enjoying dinner with their families. The specialty of the house was spareribs, and around the dim room I could see men, women, and children eating daintily with their hands, manipulating their food like Muzak's violinists their instruments. While Theresa occupied herself with a minute scrutiny of her shoes and mine, I began to believe I had made a small error of tact and taste, and out of a small and petty fearfulness. We should have gone to a drive-in hamburger joint, I thought, and sat in the car, and said what had to be said, and thereby recognized the real and unpretty dimensions of our meeting. There was an unrelentingly sedate good-natured carniverousness in the air here and it somehow led me to reflect upon the cautionary nature of all prosperous people everywhere, myself included. I had convinced myself I would be doing the girl a service by bringing her to a muted middle-class rendezvous, carpeted and melodic, when actually the only person I had set out to spare was the same old person one usually sets out to spare, no matter how complex the strategy.

Theresa carried a long plastic purse with her, about the size and shape of a loaf of bread; its insides were visible to the naked eye. Walking into the dining room, I felt it rhythmically whacking my side, and though I decided to show nothing, at one point the girl herself nearly looked up at me to apologize. But she wasn't quite able to pull it off; she merely hugged the purse to her and sank back into her pool of shame. Finally— nothing in life being endless—our crossing was over and we sat at a small corner table.

"Miss Haug . . ." I said. She was searching through her purse and, oblivious to the fact that my mouth was open, continued to search until she came up with an orange Lifesaver which she slipped secretively between her lips. I decided I had to allow her still more time to calm down, to look up. And I realized that Libby—for all I resented and suspected her manner (at the same time I responded to it), for all I had begun to hate both Herzes for the crazed and wild sparing of one another that they engaged in at the expense of others—had perhaps been prophetic in pleading that Paul be spared the job of interviewing the pregnant young woman. Not that I was myself in possession of a calm reasonableness, or even a plan of action; simply, my disappointment in seeing what Theresa was, was not the disappointment of a prospective father. Surely it is possible that Paul Herz might have wept or become angry or gotten up and walked out. I did not see any of these choices open to me. I would let her finish her Lifesaver, order a little dinner, and then begin to extract from her the information and promises necessary, and give her whatever advice she would be needing.

—

In twenty-four hours I had become a kind of authority on adoption. Leaving the Herzes' apartment I had not driven back to Martha's directly, but to the campus, where I had made my way to the law library and settled down angrily with the appropriate texts. That morning I had learned more through a telephone call Martha had made to her lawyer friend, Sid Jaffe. Jaffe had been exceedingly thorough and informative, and after she hung up, Martha told me he had even said that he would try to help her two young friends with the papers and legal work when the time came. "Free," she added. It had been generous of Jaffe, but facile I thought, and though I could not actually resent the offer, given what it would mean to Paul and Libby, I would have liked to make it clear to Martha what I believed to be her old boy friend's motive. Instead I found myself displaying a sizable amount of approval (isn't that wonderful, isn't that swell) while Martha made several statements almost punishable in the grossness of their nostalgia—statements about Sid's sweetness and reliability. Though the matter was shortly dropped, my conviction grew that I had been unfairly tested and unfairly judged. That Jaffe was sweet and reliable was perfectly all right with me, but after all, he had not been through with the Herzes what I had been. Anyway, if Jaffe was so sweet and reliable, why hadn't she taken her two kids and married him?

Of course I said nothing of the sort—though the night before, it happened that I had said something of the sort.

It should be made clear that it had been Martha and not I who had suggested that the same Libby Herz who had given us all such a monstrous evening, should become the mother of Theresa Haug's bastard child. Some time around four in the morning—this was in bed, after the Herzes' departure— Martha had no scruple about awakening me to tell me her idea. I sat up a moment, and then in a groggy fury got out of bed and came down upon the floor. I stormed around that room, round and round it; with no consideration for anyone or anything. I raised my voice, feeling in me all the ferocity of someone in a dream getting his sweet revenge. The hell with them! Fuck them—the two of them! I've had enough! Too damn much! *Let them take care of themselves!* Then I got back into bed. Through it all Martha watched me in what must have seemed a moment of pure insanity. Or maybe not; maybe it looked very sane indeed, and practical. For it occurred to me—and why not to her?—that it was not only my involvement with the Herzes that had caused me to erupt as I had. Afterwards there was silence in the bedroom, darkness and winter, and the knowledge that beside me Martha was thinking her thoughts. And I was thinking mine: My life, what is it? My life, where has it gone? One moment I knew myself to be justified and the next vindictive; one moment sensible and the next ignorant and cruel. The battle raged all night, and through it my bruised sense of righteousness, flying a big red flag reading I AM, kept rushing forward—my patriot! my defender! my own self! It cried out that I had every right to be cruel, every right to be through with the Herzes. With everybody. It raised a question that is by no means new to the species: How much, from me?

At long last morning came. Light. In the day the self does not dare fly the banners it gets away with at night. In the day there are Martha's eyes; there is Mark, visible; there is Cynthia, a brown-haired child three feet nine inches tall. There was a glimpse of Paul Herz's head as he closed the door to his Humanities class. When he has just had a haircut, the back of a man's head is where he looks most vulnerable. I am. He is. We are. What will be?

It was not willingly that I went sliding back into what I wanted to slide out of. But back I slid.

—

Theresa Haug sat up, chancing a small glance—through her small eyes—over at me.

"Miss Haug," I said once again, and without even a fight she surrendered to her gracelessness and immediately twisted one of the buttons off her blouse. The next problem seemed so large as to be facing all the diners in the room: what to do with the button? I thought, She wants me to call her Mrs. Haug—is that it? and the girl sat there dangling the button by its broken thread, spellbound by the sheer, unrelenting sweep of her misfortune. Finally I found myself extending my hand. She dropped the button into my palm and I deposited it into my coat pocket.

Her hands dove out of sight, and a strange rattling arose. I realized after a moment that its source was her skirt, a gold, luminous, bespangled garment that apparently dispatched noises upon making contact with a foreign object. Under the skirt a half-dozen crinolines were supposed to add *joie de vivre*, but the buoyant air imparted only heightened her unromantic proportions. I began feeling less and less hopeful about the chance of our exchanging two complete sentences; then my mind took a giddy turn and I could *hear* someone disrobing Theresa Haug: freeing her from her orchestral skirt, flicking open her remaining buttons, unsnapping all that seemed to hold in a piece her upper half. There was some chilling fragility about her which suggested that the elaborate network of straps and frills beneath her sheer blouse was there for unfortunate orthopedic reasons. I looked at her only with sympathy and noticed the silver cross that met the rise of her slip; the metal touching flesh made me conscious of the actuality under the clothes. It was incredible; under those layers of shiny cloth lived a woman with sexual parts. It was only a short step to wondering about the man who had seduced her. Seduction? What could the fellow have wanted? Found?

The waitress was now beside us. "How about something to eat?" I asked.

She barely opened her mouth, but nevertheless managed to say no.

I tried to slide a menu under her eyes. "Not even a sandwich? I wouldn't be hurt if you settled for a sandwich."

I smiled. She didn't. The waitress, a wall-eyed blonde in no great rapport with the world's sorrows, coughed.

"Coffee?" I asked.

"Uh-uh."

"I'm going to have coffee and a piece of apple pie. How does that sound to you?" I waited only a second more, then spoke directly into the waitress's boredom. "Would you bring us coffee and pie?"

"Two or one?"

"Two."

Theresa signaled neither pleasure nor its opposite; if you ordered her pie, she'd eat pie.

And so it turned out. When the waitress lowered our dishes

onto the tablecloth, whose soft white glow we had both been wordlessly facing for three minutes, Theresa picked up her fork, dislodged a tiny square of crust, halved it, halved the half, then pressed the back of the fork into the crumbs, a few of which attached themselves to the prongs. She carried them to her lips and finally ate in a little birdy way that I gradually realized was her conception of manners. Who had seduced her, I wondered, catching sight of her tongue? Who had wanted to?

It was an endless time before she had swallowed the few flakes of crust. "Would you like a glass of water?" I asked. "She's forgotten our water . . . Excuse me, but would you like an Alka-Seltzer?"

"Uh-uh."

"You're all right?"

She closed her eyes, then batted the lashes. "They . . . have . . . nice . . . pie," she finally articulated. "Home baked."

"Yes, it's awfully good, isn't it? Do they have home-baked pie in the Hawaiian House?"

She proceeded to deliver a series of shrugs and head-bobs to indicate yes, no, and finally that she wasn't sure. She returned to her plate, separating into pieces a crumb of pie that in itself was almost invisible.

"You don't have to eat it if you don't want to," I said.

". . . It's nice and tasty."

"But don't force yourself," I said, unnerved. "If you've already had dinner . . ."

"Is there a powder room for ladies?"

"I think so. Don't you feel well? Would you like some help?"

"I want to comb my hair." She was standing, and I wondered if she were going to pass out. In a rush, my napkin sliding to the floor, I rose and took a step toward her; the girl's face registered its first emotion: panic.

"What is it?" I asked.

Her pale face had, incredibly, paled. "Where *you* goin'?" she demanded.

"Nowhere."

"I thought you were goin'."

The people at the table beside ours looked up over their spare ribs like harmonica players. "*You* were going," I said softly.

"Uh-huh. I was goin' to wash up."

"I was just standing," I said, feeling my own color change. "Yes?"

"Why don't you just go ahead?"

She walked off, holding her purse in one hand and her table napkin in the other.

I sat down—sank down in my chair. Muzak swathed me in cotton batting and the gentle flickerings of the candles erased the flaws in the faces of the other diners. Everyone looked younger than he was, and my memory went reeling back to those first few evenings (or were they Saturday afternoons?) I had ever taken out a girl, back to all those Chinese restaurants on the upper West Side, where with a squared-off handkerchief in my breast pocket and a scented lacquer of my mother's holding fast my recalcitrant hair, I waited for my sixteen-year-old companions to return from the powder room so that we could get on with the egg roll. Later I came to interpret all those toilet trips of my first dinner partners as a sort of coquetry on a very primal level—the mysteries of the body's lower half for the anxious, throbbing adolescent boy to ponder—and it occurred to me it might be something like that for Theresa Haug as well. So far our evening had certainly been like some wearisome blind date: the boy trying bravely to live up to parental expectations of gallantry; the girl staking her all on an imbecilic shyness, which was at bottom only a misguided and sullen sort of flirtation. All that abysmal helplessness . . . all the fastening of my mind upon the word seduction. I reached into my pocket for a handkerchief and came up instead with the button off Theresa's blouse.

When she returned to the table I did not stand and so we managed to get by without incident. I noticed reddish blotches directly beneath her eyes, and then on her arms too.

"Are you sure you're all right?" I asked.

"Better," she said.

"You're not"—I went ahead, feeling guilty now for having shoved the pie upon her—"you don't happen to be allergic to apple?"

Of all things, she became coy; her hands began to flutter all over. I realized now that Theresa Haug had an age. She was no more than nineteen.

"What is it, Theresa?"

Her mouth flickered at either end; I was present at the birth of a smile. "Yes?" I said.

"Oh—I just try to bring up some color—in my face?" She ended on a high, questioning note. "In the winter I go so white . . ."

"Are you from the South?"

"Uh-*huh.*" The emphasis I took for regional pride. "You ain't," she said.

"I'm from New York."

"Mister?"

"Yes—"

"Are you the doctor? Aren't you goin' to examine me— *where?*"

"Well, look . . . I'm not the doctor. I should have made it clear."

"I thought you was the doctor."

"Well, no. I'm a friend of the people—"

"I'm supposed to see the doctor," she moaned.

"You will," I said. "Please don't worry. That's all going to be taken care of. I'm a friend of the people who are interested in adopting your baby. The baby. Martha said you were interested in giving up the child for adoption."

"Martha Lee *said* you was the doctor—"

"No, I don't think she did. There must have been a little confusion. She must have said that I'd tell you about a doctor."

Her mouth became so thin a line that I could hardly see it. "Who are *you?*"

"I'm a friend," I repeated, "of the people who are interested in the adoption. Look, you don't have to worry about a thing. I'm just an intermediary, a go-between, you see. I'll answer any questions you have, and so forth. Is that okay? Really now, you don't have to worry about a thing."

"*I'm* not worried," she said, pathetically.

"That's fine."

"I thought you was the doctor. See, I just have to get to a doctor."

"Of course . . ."

"'Cause I'm from Shelby County—Kentucky?" she said.

"And I know, you see, all this snowin' and the bad weather and all—?"

"Yes?"

"I know it's just"—she flushed—"affected my monthlies. A few warm days and I'll be myself again."

"Miss Haug, haven't you been to a doctor yet? Didn't a doctor tell you you were pregnant?"

"He weren't no specialist. Just a plain old doctor."

"Well, these people," I said, "are quite willing for you to see an obstetrician as soon as you like."

She seemed angry. "What people?"

"The people who want to adopt your baby."

"What am I supposed to do about that?"

I made believe I hadn't heard. "They're very decent people, I assure you. They're very anxious to give this baby a home. I'm sure they'll give it a good home, and all that it needs."

I could see that everything I had been saying was entirely beside the point as far as she was concerned. Nevertheless I went on. "The father—"

Here she came alive. "Oh he don't care!"

"He does," I said.

"Look, he ain't got nothin' to do with it!" It was her first display of passion and I realized that we were talking about two different people.

"Is this person in Chicago?" I asked.

"If you don't mind?" she said. "I'm not interested in talking about this person."

"You don't think he's interested in the child then?"

"I don't know—" she said, "I hardly know him."

I tried to accept that, blank-faced.

"You see," she said, leaning forward so as to whisper, "I keep, well, throwin' up—and well, now I'm really wonderin' if it couldn't be some kind of appendix condition. In the stomach?"

"I don't think so. I don't think it would be appendix."

"You're no doctor," she said.

"That's right. But neither are you."

"That don't mean nothin'. I had an aunt—my aunt? and she lived in our house, and she had an appendix, real bad? And all she was doin' was throwin' up left and right."

"That may be. How old was she?"

"She's my aunt—" Aunt had two syllables. "Seventy."

"And how old are you?"

"Twenty, next month."

"Well," I said, "there are a lot of physical conditions that can make a person nauseous. Appendicitis is certainly one, so is food poisoning—"

"I don't think I got that," she said, shaking her head.

"Pregnant women often become nauseous too, you know."

After a moment, in a small voice, she asked, "You think I'm goin' to have a baby?"

"I'm no doctor, Theresa, but I think so."

"Oh boy . . ." She rested her forehead on her hands.

"But you knew that, didn't you?"

She blurted out, "Well, what about me? What about when I quit work? What happens to me?"

"What do you mean, what happens?"

"I have to live, I have to rest. Gee whiz, mister—*money.*"

"Theresa, calm down. You have to understand that I'm only an acquaintance of the family. So I can't tell you much about money. They'll . . . look, I'm going to give you the name of a lawyer, Mr. Jaffe—"

"I can't pay no lawyer. Oh boy," she cried. "I need a doctor. Now Martha Lee *told* me—"

"You've got to calm yourself. You don't have to pay anybody anything."

"I paid somebody a hundred dollars already. And I don't know where he is at all."

"Who?"

"He was goin' to get me a doctor . . ."

"You can't find him now?"

She shook her head.

"That's too bad," I said.

She widened her eyes. "That's *awful.*"

"Look now, you don't have to worry about anything like that. You won't pay anything. The lawyer arranges the necessary papers so that it's all legal. You simply have to grant permission to the couple so that they can adopt your baby. The baby. The lawyer will speak to you about the arrangements.

His name is Sidney Jaffe. He's right here in Chicago, so there's no trouble or expense—"

"He's a Jew?" she asked, a twang in the last word.

"I think he is."

"Uh-oh."

"What's the matter?"

She shrugged. "I don't know. It just makes me sort a nervous."

"Well, don't be."

"Mister?"

"My name is Wallach. Gabriel Wallach."

"I want to go to a Catholic hospital, mister. With the sisters. I ain't goin' by no Jewish hospital, you better tell that to that lawyer."

"I will."

"I want to go by the sisters, you understand now? There was a boy, back home? And he got hit by a car, and he was just alayin' there in the road? And then they take him in the ambulance to the Jewish hospital—and they set all his bones and everything, and they gave him ether and all stuff like that, so he was knocked out good, and then counta he was a boy, they made a Jew out of him."

"I don't understand."

"You know," she said, "what they do to 'em."

"Are you sure about that?"

"Oh mister . . ." she cried, and she put her head right down on the table and let the giggles sweep in and conquer her. It took awhile, but finally she sat up and told me, "That's what they say anyway. He was a nigger, so must be. You ever been to Shelby County?"

"No."

"Well, that's my home."

"Theresa, are you a Catholic?"

"I gotta right to be anythin' I want," she said sharply. "This here is a free country."

"I was only curious. I didn't think there were many Catholics in Kentucky."

"Well, you're wrong!" she shot back. "You must be thinkin' of Republicans."

I said I supposed I was.

"At least you're a Catholic, somebody takes care of you, I'll tell you. I want to go by the sisters. Now you got to tell the lawyer—I don't want no Jewish hospital!"

"I'll tell him. I don't think there'll be any difficulty. Now Theresa"—I took a breath—"could I ask you when—"

Suddenly she was blowing out air, as though she'd just finished a race. "I don't think I feel too good. I think maybe, maybe I ought to go right on home."

"Well, if you're not well, sure—"

"I'm just a little tired out."

"Of course."

"Do you know where the train is?"

"You don't have to take the train. I'll—"

"I think maybe—" But then she wasn't thinking anymore; she ran off to the lady's room.

—

As I was driving her to Gary, Theresa said to me, "I think I need some gum."

"I'm sorry, I don't have any."

"Can't we stop?"

"I suppose so."

"See that diner up there? Could we stop there?"

I pulled off the road and onto the gravel parking area around the diner. I wondered if the girl was going to be sick again and quickly got out of the car and came around to open her door. Inside I saw Theresa running a comb through her orange hair and twisting the rear-view mirror to get a look at herself.

There was a glow in the sky, a dusty red light thrown up from the mills in Gary; directly above our heads a neon sign gave off a steady buzzing. All it said was EAT. I held the door of the diner open for her and the only verb to describe her movement then is sashay. She sashayed on through.

Inside, the counterman said, "Look who's here," but did not unfold his hairy arms. He was leaning against the sandwich counter, a fellow with a brow like a bumper. "If it ain't Miss Dixie Belle," he said.

"How are you, Fluke?" Her tone astonished me; she'd become patronizing.

"We heard you was dead," he answered.

"Well I ain't."

"No kiddin'," Fluke said.

"No—no kiddin'!" She tossed her head, then let it whirl all the way around so that she was looking over at me, where I hung back by the door. I smiled. Theresa smiled back. It was like seeing a balloon deflated—and then the next moment seeing it full of air.

Fluke, however, did not seem to expect anything else from Theresa but this display of verve and wit. He did not appear to be too crazy about her, but exhibited the deference, at any rate, that one gives to people who are always on their toes. With a less benign look in his undersized eyes, he looked at me. It was obvious that he took a particular dislike to my clothes.

"What can we do for you, Tessie?"

"I'd like some Blackjack," she said, "if you don't mind."

"Oh *I* don't mind."

"*Don't* you?"

"You're sump'n, Dixie," Fluke said, and with a groan—the groan of a man who totes around more thick dull tissue than the rest of us—Fluke raised himself off the sandwich bar and went toward the cash register.

"Five cents," he said when he came back with the gum.

Theresa took the pack and turned to me.

"Oh yes," I said, coming forward. I could not find any change in my pockets and had to give Fluke a dollar from my billfold. He didn't like the billfold any more than the coat and hat. He put my change on the counter, mostly nickels.

"Here," Theresa said to me, and handed me a stick of gum.

"Thanks," I said.

"It's your nickel," she said, significantly. Then to Fluke, "You don't look like you're workin' too hard."

"There's a recession startin'. Don't you read the papers?"

"I read plenty of papers," she retorted.

"Oh yeah?" said Fluke, and looked my way again as though I had introduced her to the pernicious habit.

"I read the *Tribune*," Theresa said. "I read the *Sun-Times*, and I read the Chicago *Maroon*, which you probably ain't even heard of down here." The last named was the University student newspaper.

"You're a big reader," Fluke said.

We stood knee-deep in the wake of that exchange for several minutes. Theresa unpeeled her gum, and we all paid undue attention to the operation.

Fluke said, "Where you workin'?"

It was the question she'd been waiting for. "No diner, I'll tell you that."

"Yeah?" said Fluke, shutting his eyes. "Where you workin'? You workin' even?"

"In Chicago," said Theresa. "The Hawaiian House."

"Big deal," Fluke said.

"At least the customers wash their hands," Theresa informed him, "after they come out of the john."

She must have had him there, for it took him a while to re-group his troops. "You're workin' up by that school," he said, "you better watch out or the Comm-uh-nists'll get you."

"So what am I supposed to do about that?" She tossed her shoulders and her coat fell open.

Fluke whistled. "Still the fashion horse, huh?"

"I do all right."

"It's gonna cost some guy a fortune just keepin' you in underwear."

"That's not funny—that's plain dirt." She turned away, and I put my hat back on.

"At least, at least"—Fluke couldn't keep a straight face for this one—"at least I didn't say 'panties,' did I?"

"That's not funny any more, Fluke," she said. "You don't know where to stop, that's your trouble." She came over and took my arm.

"Yeah?" Fluke said. "I oughta wash my mouth out with Mr. Clean."

I opened the door—Theresa was waiting for me to. Fluke called, "Watch out for those Reds, Dixie, before they kidnap you back to Russia."

She turned just her head, and that with disdain. "It so happens that people up there ain't people down here."

"You got it, kid, you got it," and Fluke mysteriously. "Take it easy, Tessie. Take it easy, sport."

Sport was me; Theresa had already swept out when I looked back to discover that Fluke had become a well-wisher; he raised a hand, and made a circle with his thumb and index-finger. Then he winked.

As I stepped out under the EAT sign, Theresa barged back across my path. She shouted in through the open doorway, "You can tell Dewey he can go straight to hell!"

———

When we were back in the car, driving south, Theresa offered me a nickel.

"That's all right," I said, and she put the nickel away.

She asked, "Can we turn the radio on?"

"Yes."

"Are you mad?" she asked.

"No."

"He's just got a dirty mind. Fluke ain't even his real name. He's just a Polock."

"I understand."

She turned on the radio. "Which you like better?" She mentioned the names of two Chicago disc jockeys.

"Whichever you want," I said.

She tuned her station in with care and patience, fiddling with the tone as well as the volume. Then, with the music pounding, she said, "See—I used to work there."

"I didn't know that."

"It's not very nice down there," she told me.

We drove on toward the outskirts of Gary where Theresa lived. As we approached, the red in the sky grew more intense, and we could see two pilot flames burning stiff above their towers.

Theresa was singing along with the record.

> "Earth angel, earth angel,
> Will you be mi-ine?
> Earth angel, earth angel,
> Will you be mi-ine?"

"You better give me directions from here on," I said, interrupting.

"Down by the next light you turn right." She went back to her singing. The disc jockey was shortly telling all us guys and gals driving home in our cars, or sitting in our living rooms, or just moping around the house missing that special someone, where to buy a used car. Then he put on a new record, the words of which were equally familiar to my companion.

"I take it you feel better," I said.

Her head was back on the seat. "I appreciate all you're doin', Mr. Wallace. Are you Martha Lee's steady?"

To save wear and tear, I said, "No, just a friend."

"Look—" she said, "you—you're not the fella who's goin' to adopt my baby?"

"I'm not. If I was I would have told you."

She considered what I had said a moment. "You better turn left now," she mumbled.

Making the turn, I said, "I told you, I'm the intermediary."

"Well, I didn't *mean* nothin' by it!"

"I didn't think you'd meant anything by it."

"You're not mad, are you?"

"Look, I'm not 'mad' about anything."

"Turn left and down the block," she said, in a voice suddenly full of disappointment.

The street—endless tiny front yards and high brick stoops—must have looked no less bleak in the daylight than at night. Trains often pass through miles of just such streets and houses upon entering and leaving our great cities. In the gutter were five or six Christmas trees still waiting for the garbage man.

"There," Theresa said, and I pulled up near the end of the block. The house she pointed to still had screens on its windows.

The radio was playing rock and roll, and Theresa asked if she could stay until the record ended. Her head moved with the beat, and when I looked over at her, I saw that her nose tugged up on her lip so that in profile you could see her two front teeth. She did not look as though she could add two and two.

"Who do you like?" she asked. "Frankie Avalon or Fabian?"

"I'm not sure which is which."

"Well, you were *listenin'* to Fabian."

I said that it seemed to me that he could carry a tune. We sat in the radio's glow for a moment, and then when the record was over, Theresa began to cry. I turned off the motor.

"Certain songs make you think of certain people," she said.

"I guess so."

She blew her nose. "Mr. Wallace?"

"What is it?"

"You been so nice. And kind."

"Everything will be all right soon," I said.

"You're the most polite man I ever met. All that standin' up and sittin' down."

"You're in an unfortunate predicament."

"You don't need to tell me," she whimpered. "Can you walk me to my door? I think I'm feelin' funny again."

She waited this time until I came around to her side and opened the door; it had all become a meaningless parody of decency. At the top of the stoop, she took out her keys and let us in. The hallway had the tomby smell of an unvacuumed place; at the rear we came to another door, which she unlocked. Inside I could see the foot of a bed and, on the linoleum floor, a pair of snappy imitation-leopard slippers.

I said, "Theresa, the next thing will be for Mr. Jaffe—"

But she had turned and was sniffling again, her frame dropped against my own.

I put my hands on her arm. "It'll be all right. Try to keep control. Mr. Jaffe—"

"Do I see you again?"

"It's best for you to see the lawyer—"

"Don't I see you again?"

"If it's necessary," I said.

Meekly: "Could you come in and talk to me, Mr. Wallace? I just feel awful." She stepped inside and pulled a string; the bulb lit up four flowered walls, the bed, a cardboard closet—a hulking thing that reminded me of Fluke—a stained little sink, and a table jammed with soaps and powders. Photographs torn from magazines, all of pudding-faced boys in open-necked shirts, were pinned to the walls.

"What'll happen about the doctor?" Theresa asked.

"I told you. It'll all be taken care of."

Her coat dropped off her, though I had not seen her undo the dollar-sized buttons. She left it where it lay on the floor, and dropped, sighing, onto the bed. The springs sang, and I could not believe in the blind willfulness of my body's parts. Theresa hit the bed—and my blood responded, as though she were some other woman; as though she *were* a woman.

"What is it you want to talk about?" I asked.

"I thought there was more *you* wanted to talk about back in the restaurant."

"For instance?"

She couldn't think of anything; not right off. "Suppose it's twins."

"That's nothing to worry about."

"What d'yuh mean? People have 'em. Ain't you never seen twins? Twin boys or somethin'?"

"Twins, triplets, or whatever, you have nothing to worry about."

"Suppose it's a moron."

"It's not going to be a moron," I said. She seemed to take this as a compliment. "Is there anything more?"

"Well," she said, "I just thought there was more *you* wanted to talk about."

"I don't think there is."

"You been a regular gentleman, Mr. Wallace. You don't see much of that in the North, you know." Then her eyes filled up again. "You been so polite and nice . . . ?"

"Goodnight, Theresa."

"Mr. Wallace?"

"What?"

"I ain't never been this way before. I don't know if I can do it alone."

"I'm sure it won't be as difficult as you imagine."

"What happens when it starts hurtin'? I'm all alone."

"But you're not alone, you see."

"I sure am."

"I meant to say we're all trying to help."

"I'm still *alone*," she said. "It ain't easy for a girl. I'm always hearin' people turnin' my doorknob and all kinds of funny things. There's always somebody behind me, you know? I don't like it alone."

"What is it your asking me, Theresa?"

"I don't know . . ."

"Are you asking that I stay with you?"

She looked away from me. "I don't understand." But then she shrugged. "I don't know."

"If you don't know, don't provoke."

"I don't understand *you*," she said in a mean, Southern drawl.

"I said don't invite trouble!"

"I don't understand what you're shoutin' for! Who said you got a right to shout at me!"

I took her blouse button out of my pocket and set it on the foot of the bed. "They'll get in touch with you," I said, and holding the door open only for myself, I left, unable to believe in my body's pulsing, unable to believe in my own temptation.

6

THE APARTMENT I returned to was not Martha's but my own—cold, musty, and unlived-in. I did not even bother to turn on the lights. The shades were drawn, making it black and to my purposes; I sat down in my bent-laminated-wood chair and tried to find sense in the lust that had so recently visited me, in the desire I had not willed, wanted, or satisfied. I contemplated the desire as though it were the act itself . . . For if in the eyes of the law there is a no man's land of innocence between the itch and the scratching of it, in the eyes of the citizen himself, who has his own problems, the one may render him just about as culpable as the other. I looked for sense; I looked for cause. I did not remain alone there in my hat and coat trying to be especially hard on myself—hardness or softness had little to do with it. I was, I think, in a state of dread. At bottom I did not feel certain about what I would say or do to the next human being I made contact with. I cannot say for sure whether, in the bedroom of that unfortunate girl, something had been hooked up inside me or disconnected, but what I knew, what I felt rather, was that within that maze of wiring that unites a man's mind, heart, and genitals, some passage of energies, some movement, vital to my being, had taken place. There are those synapses in us between sense and muscle, between blood and feeling, and at times, without understanding why, one is aware that a connection that has occurred in oneself—or that has failed to occur—has been a pure expression of one's character. And it is that which can bring on the dread.

Later, my phone rang. It was Martha and she asked me if I wanted to come home.

—

She said, opening the door, "I'm sorry I had to get you out."

"I was taking a breather, Martha."

"You were coming back?"

"I think so."

"You didn't know?"

"I didn't know for sure."

"If I'd realized that, I wouldn't have called."

"You realized," I told her, "and you called anyway."

"You might as well come all the way in," she said, and left me alone at the door; a moment followed in which I might have gone back down stairs and away. I considered it, and then moved into the apartment. It was as though I had been drawn in by that faint Hawaiian House odor that clung to Martha's uniform; it was not that I liked the odor particularly, only that I had grown used to it. In the living room she said, "You can even take your coat off." She sat down beside an ash tray thick with butts. "What were you going to do about all those classy suits?"

"I was going to leave them for the next guy."

"Who were you going to move in with now?"

"To tell the truth," I said, "I began to understand hermits."

"You mean you were going to try moving in with the fellas?"

"You're thinking of monks, Martha. I was realizing that I have some fouled-up connections, some mistaken ideas. That I'm not in tune with myself. I was understanding why ascetism was once a basic Western value."

"The old light-hearted historian," she said. "I wouldn't worry if I were you. You seem eminently in tune with yourself."

"If I am what you're trying to say I am, you ought to consider yourself lucky without me."

"I can't say I'm sure what you are."

"Then why did you want me back?"

"I think you want somebody to beat you up tonight, Gabe. I think maybe you'd better go home after all."

My coat was on my lap and my hat on my head, but I didn't move. I saw only one alternative to running away. "Why don't we get married, Martha?"

"Oh this is too romantic to bear."

"Why don't you stop crapping around?"

"Why don't you!"

"I asked you if we shouldn't get married. You want to give an answer?"

"You're the answer, you shmuck."

"Am I? I remember getting a long set of instructions when I moved in here not to propose to you."

"It's curious," she said, "what parts of the law you choose to obey and what parts you don't."

"The law isn't so uncomplicated."

"Don't be a college teacher, I couldn't stand it."

"Why don't you want to get married, Martha?"

"Is this obligation, or impulse, or what?"

"It's both, if you want to know. All three."

"You don't want to bring up love or anything, is that it?"

"You're too full of principles, Mrs. Reganhart. You're too high-minded."

"Wowee," she said.

"Why don't you face the facts?"

"Why don't you! You don't want to marry me. Isn't that a pertinent fact?"

"Wanting isn't the right word."

"Oh hell then, what is? Loving isn't the right word and wanting isn't either. Look, buddy, don't feel obligated. Oh you've got a nice fat trouble, my friend."

"Why don't you go sit in the window, Martha, and wait for Mr. Right to come along in his big shoulders and his red convertible?"

"You're damn right I'm going to wait!"

"It's great you're five nine, Martha, it's perfect you're hefty. The bigger they are the better you can enjoy the fall."

"Shut up."

"Your untrammeled, unselfish nobility is about one of the most disgustingly selfish exhibitions I've ever seen."

"Please don't you be the one to bring up words like selfish around here, all right? God might send down thunder on this whole house. Have it understood, nobody's marrying me out of a sense of loyalty. Someday somebody's going to marry me because they want to. They're going to *choose* little me."

"I'm choosing you. I'm making the choice."

"There must be some kind of noose around your neck. I can't see it, but I know it's there."

"You've got circumstances," I said. "I've got them too. Don't be an ass."

"Your circumstance is plain and simple. That isn't what I meant was invisible."

"Go ahead, Martha, you might as well go all the way."

"You don't need anybody," she said. "If you did, you wouldn't feel so obliged all the time."

"You don't know what I need—you don't begin to know!"

"Nor you, me," she said flatly.

"Then maybe that's why I was giving some thought to coming back or not. Maybe that deserves some thought."

"For instance," she said, as though I hadn't spoken, "ten minutes you're here and you haven't even asked why I called."

"I didn't think there was a specific reason."

"There is. I'm not you. I don't make phone calls out of wistful nostalgia." Her voice lost a bit of its edge. "Dick Reganhart's back in town."

For a moment the words meant nothing; all I could think was that it was the name of some third child of Martha's.

"My first love," she said. "He wants his kids. I thought you might have a suggestion," she added; whereupon she left the room.

When I found her in the kitchen she had already poured herself a cup of coffee and was drinking it standing up, looking out the back window.

"What do you mean he wants his children?"

"He wants his children. Simple as that. They're half his." She turned; in the little time it had taken to get from the living room to the kitchen her face had become pouchy with fatigue. She leaned against the window sill. "He's a great success. New York's latest fad. You can get yourself a Reganhart by plunking down a thousand bucks. He's chic, my former husband. He's grown a mustache. He's getting married to a millionairess. His new father-in-law was once Ambassador to China. How's that? A wife who can use chopsticks. All good things come to him who waits for it."

"The only trouble is he's got no rights."

"He's got rights," she said. "He's got you. You're evidence that I'm an immoral woman. He's going to take me to court and hold up your underwear as evidence."

"He knows about me?"

"There are still creeps around this neighborhood who consider it a pleasure to have smoked pot with my ex-husband. They turned me in. I'm an immoral character."

"Which isn't so."

"Which is. That's one more fact, since we're counting facts."

"You saw him then."

"I served him his dinner. He's still got the old instinct for comedy," she said. "Tomorrow he's going to come over and see his kids."

"It doesn't make any sense." I tried to engage her eyes but she looked right past me; except for the rapidity and brittleness with which she spoke, she gave no sign of falling to pieces. I asked, for lack of anything else to say, "What do you think?"

"That's what I was going to ask you." She came over and sat down at the table.

"Well, I think it's ridiculous." I sat down across from her. "As for my being evidence of your bad character, that's one of those things that's got to be proved. What the locals say, they say—it hasn't the ring of proof. It's assertion."

She did not answer; I realized that the first thing I had tried to explain was how I was not implicated.

"Well," I said, "what about *his* character? What about all those years of support payments unpaid? What about the divorce itself? You can't not be a father for six years, five years, whatever it was, and then suddenly decide you're ready. No judge is going to listen to him, Martha. You've got Jaffe still, haven't you? You've got—hell, Martha, it's an empty threat." She continued to look unconvinced. "You're not immoral," I said. "The power you've got is the fact that you know it isn't so."

"But it is," she told me when she saw that I was through. Only her jaw moved as outward evidence that she was not immune to feelings. "Because I want him to take the kids, Gabe. That's the next fact."

To which I had no ready answer. I got up and poured myself a cup of coffee. Under the sink the garbage pail was overflowing; I set down my cup and took the pail out and emptied it into the can on the back porch. When I came back in, Martha had left the kitchen and I found her in the empty children's room on Markie's bed.

"Surprised?" she said, looking at me.

"No."

"Shocked? Disgusted? Overcome? None of the above?"

"None."

"That's what she wants, isn't it?" Martha said, throwing a hopeless hand toward Cynthia's bed. "To live with her father awhile? Isn't that it, or something like it? I can't tell, I'm punch-drunk and fed up. I don't want to worry about what she wants any more. Does that make me a witch?"

"I don't think it does."

"Well, you're standing up there very big and judging," she said.

"I'll sit down," and I did, at the end of Cynthia's bed, across from Martha's feet.

"You know," she said, "I don't care. Let him come. Let him open the closets and pull out the drawers and let him find all the God damn underwear he wants. Who can care any more? All I want is to go out in the afternoon and get a cup of coffee and not have to run back and make anybody's supper. I used to wheel Markie around the campus all the time, I used to wait for the hour to be up and watch the kids changing classes. That's how I used to spend the afternoons. Right out there in front of Cobb, rocking my baby carriage. Then I got ashamed and picked myself up and went off to the playground where I belonged. But I don't have too much love for that playground, I've got to admit it. If I have to push one more swing one more time . . . This is punky of me."

"No."

"I should keep them. I should tell him to take his new life and his new wife and shove them both. Just pay up, I should say. Shouldn't I?"

"What is it, Martha? What is it you want?"

"Oh, please come here," she moaned, rolling toward me. "Please, just lie down next to me. Please, and turn off the light."

Beside her, after five minutes of silence, I asked, "How will you feel without those kids?"

"How will you?" she said.

"I'll marry you either way."

"Don't say that, will you?"

"Then I don't know what to say."

"Say I'm not immoral, all right?"

"You're not. You're not, sweetheart."

"Everything gets telescoped," she said, touching my face. "I haven't even known you two months, baby."

"What's the difference?"

"You don't have to marry me is the difference. Why does

everybody have to step up and marry me? I'm a drag on men. A strain on everybody. Oh Gabe, do you think making love would help matters? Hold me tighter, okay? Is that my whole damn downfall—hot pants? Oh let's just do it, with the doors open and all the grunts and groans and nobody tiptoeing by and nobody's neuroses blooming down the hall—nobody, nothing but our two selves."

Very early in the morning I awoke to find that Martha was no longer beside me in Markie's bed. I supposed she had gone back to her own room, but I found her barefooted in the hallway, bending over the large cedar chest in which the kids' old toys were stored. The toys, however, had been taken out and were strewn around in the hall; in their place Martha was packing away my belongings—shirts, suits, coats, underwear, ties—and hiding them out of sight.

—

The next morning Mrs. Baker ushered us into her kitchen (hers until her daughter came out of Billings' psycho ward) and in a cheery, we've-all-been-up-here-for-hours voice heralded our arrival. "Look who's come! It's Markie and Cindy's mommy, and Mr. Wallach."

The three Parrino offspring, sullen children with downy faces, took our appearance in their stride; hardly a face rose out of its cereal bowl despite their grandmother's exuberance. Cynthia, however, never without resources for drama, jumped up from the table and leaped half the length of the kitchen. She threw her arms around Martha. "Daddy's here!" she cried.

"How do you know, baby?"

"Isn't he?" she demanded. "Did he go, already?"

"No, no—he's here. I just didn't know you knew."

"He called me," she said. "Ask Mrs. Baker. Didn't my daddy call me here?"

A white-haired woman with pale hands and active fingers, who always moved around the house in full dress—weighty oxfords, fur jacket, and pink pillbox hat, veil up—Mrs. Baker gave a small birdlike reply, as though she were cracking a seed in her teeth. "That's right, dear. Last night at eleven-thirty."

"Well, I didn't know that, sweetie." Martha managed to maintain her composure in the face of Dick Reganhart's surprises and energies. "I'll bet you were excited. Does Mark know?"

"He gets confused, Mother."

Martha went to the table and smoothed back the boy's cowlick. "How are you, young man? Did you have fun sleeping over? Did you talk to Daddy?"

He looked confused all right. "I was sleeping," he said.

"You finish your breakfast now," Martha said. "Then you're going to visit with Daddy."

"Oh terrific," Cynthia said. Mark and the Parrino children said nothing.

"Hello, Stephanie," I said. "How are you?"

Mrs. Baker said, "Stephanie's daddy and Tony's daddy and Stevie's daddy is going to visit with them next month, isn't that right, honey?" She had made it sound like three people.

Stephanie nodded, and Cynthia, on the edge of her seat, said, "Do we go now?"

"Don't be impolite. You finish your breakfast," Martha said, "and we'll wait in the other room."

Mrs. Baker followed us, and when Martha and I had settled onto the sofa, she said, "Mr. Reganhart wanted to come over last night"—she had been looking only at Martha, but I now got a significant glance as well—"and I thought it over and weighed all sides and then I thought, well, it's just going to overexcite those two children. Now I hope I didn't do wrong, honey. I didn't know how you felt about it. I didn't want to call you and wake you up too. I know when Billy comes, I just think it overexcites the children." She had a very excited, anticipatory air about herself, as though there was always the possibility that she might be strung up for her last statement. She seemed to sense some acute division between herself and the general drift of life.

"Thank you," Martha said. "I think you were right."

"You don't want to disrupt their sleep," the older woman said, this time only to me. "I don't know how you folks feel, but personally eleven-thirty doesn't seem to me an hour for telephoning all around town."

"I suppose he was anxious to talk to them," Martha said.

"You're perfectly right, Martha," said Mrs. Baker. "I didn't mean that, you know. Billy certainly loves his children one hundred percent too. I didn't mean they didn't love their little ones. What kind of men would they be then?" Again the question was

for me. "Billy's certainly been very good while Bev's been re-
cuperating, I don't mean that. It's just that they're not women
and you can't expect that they're going to understand a child
the way a woman can. You men are our wage-earners and our
husbands," Mrs. Baker told me, "but there's nobody like a
mother."

I agreed. She squared the edge of a pile of magazines on top
of the TV set. "These are mine, you know—for Bev." She held
up a magazine before her, as a child will hold up something for
the entire class to see, facing each of us in turn. "These are my
genealogical journals of Illinois, Mr. Wallach. My daughter has
gotten very interested in her family history, and we think that's
a very hopeful sign. You know, Martha, Beverly never much
cared about DAR matters. But I suppose now she's had all that
time to think and so forth, and to appreciate, and well, we
think it's a good sign. I had to go all the way out to Highland
Park the other day to bring in all my books and magazines, but
I'd make a hundred trips back and forth a week if we can have
our girl back the way she was. She even asked about you,
Martha Lee."

"Did she?" Martha said. "That's very sweet."

"Oh she talks about her daddy and her brothers, and her old
old friends—little children all grown up by now—and about
you, Martha Lee, and about Richard too—that's Mr. Reganhart," Mrs. Baker informed me. "In fact, she suggested—and
it was all her suggestion, mind you—that I try to get hold of a
genealogy from Oregon. She wants to work out your family
for you, Martha Lee. Now isn't that something? I've already
written off to see what we can do. Wouldn't you call that reason to be cheered up?"

"She sounds like she's coming along," Martha said.

"Well, the doctors are encouraged, and the children are managing beautifully, and I don't meant to say that Billy hasn't
been a help. We have nothing against Billy," she said, "per se.
If a marriage doesn't work, it doesn't work, I suppose. Perhaps
we'll find out later that this was all for the best."

Neither Martha nor I responded.

"Mr. Wallach," Mrs. Baker said, "I was myself married to
two of the finest men who ever drew breath. And I lost them

both, that was God's will." She filled up instantly with tears. "But I went right ahead, and Beverly is going to go right on, and Martha Lee has gone right on, and that's the nature of a woman. To go right on, and raise her children to be strong and good, and not to be ashamed, and to respect their elders and love their country. I had two fine husbands, both of them Masons, not strong lodge men, I'll admit that, but men's men, who had the respect of their neighbors and knew their duty to their wife. After all, the husband chooses the wife, he gets down on bended knee—at least he used to—and then he's got the duty to stand by her. Wouldn't you say?"

"Yes," I said.

"I don't know what's happened to the world, Mr. Wallach. If you'll pardon me, I don't meant this personally, but I don't know what's happened to our American men. I don't understand this discontentment business and I can't say that I ever have. I don't know what men want any more. If this embarrasses Martha Lee, I'm just sorry, but heaven knows they don't make them any smarter or any prettier than you, honey. And my own Bev, they didn't make them any sweeter, you can attest to that, Martha Lee. The sweetest, kindest girl, loved animals, loved the seasons and her schoolwork, Queen of the Prom, I remember that, and a pretty girl too—and it's just not imaginable what this world has turned around and given them. Now I don't know Mr. Richard Reganhart except by name, and Billy has been very courteous through this whole ordeal, but I don't think they either of them would know a good thing if they tripped over it. If they fell over it and broke their neck, as Mr. Baker used to say."

Cynthia's voice came lancelike down the hall from the kitchen: Markie and Stevie were throwing Farina.

"Oh dear," said Mrs. Baker, and she flustered and fidgeted until Martha rose and went off to the kitchen to put down the riot. Still standing by her genealogical journals, Mrs. Baker leaned in the direction of the disturbance; when the situation seemed under control, she came over and sat down next to me, where Martha had been.

"They're two fine children," she said. "That Cindy is smart as a whip."

"She's very good at looking after Markie," I said.

"They could make a man a very nice little family," Mrs. Baker said, "believe me."

Again I nodded my head, agreeing.

"I don't know if you're a Mason or not, Mr. Wallach, and I don't want to pry."

"I'm not."

"Well," she said, "I would certainly give it some thought. I'm not going to say much more, because if a man wants to become a Mason that's up to him. You know you won't even be invited, you know that?"

"No, I didn't."

"Well, you won't, so don't sit around waiting. They don't believe in that. If a man decides he wants to be a Mason, then he's got to step forward. Now I wouldn't try to convince you of anything, Mr. Wallach. I'm only saying I think you might give it some thought. You know what they say: 'Once a Mason, always a Mason.' I was married to two men, both Masons, and both fine men, Mr. Wallach, respected in the community and in the home as well. They were stern men, and maybe they didn't wipe the dishes like some husbands do, but they knew right from wrong. You just ask over at the University—you teach, isn't that it, over at the University?"

"Yes."

"Well, you just ask around there. You talk to the top professors and you see if they're not Masons—the top professors, and deans, and so on."

"I will," I said.

At the door later, with Cynthia and Mark in their coats and the three Parrino children—hot cereal having cut through their gloom—running up and down the hallway, Mrs. Baker took my hand and whispered to me, "They'd make a man a nice fine little family, don't think they wouldn't."

—

In the back seat Martha sat beside her daughter; Mark and the little suitcase full of pajamas and comic books that the children had taken with them to the Parrinos were in front with me. After a momentary crisis on the street—Mrs. Baker all the while waving at us from upstairs—we had all submitted to Markie's seating arrangement.

"He's traveled all the way from New York to see you," Martha was saying now, "and he wants to have a good time with you, okay?"

Uncooperatively, Cynthia mumbled that she would cooperate.

Martha leaned forward, so that her hand was on my coat. "Okay?"

"Okay," Markie answered.

On Fifty-seventh Street we had to stop for the light. Martha said, "To help him have a good time, babies, I don't think he wants to hear about some things. I think he wants to hear about school, and the playground, and about your Christmas presents, and about Markie's cold that he had, and Cynthia's ballet lessons—"

"What doesn't he want to hear about?" Cynthia asked.

"I don't think, for instance, he wants to hear about Sid Jaffe, you know—or about Gabe," she said. "I don't think that's important to Daddy on such a short visit."

No one asked a question, not Mark, Cynthia, or me.

"Do you understand, Markie?"

"Okay," he said, shrugging.

"I don't think Daddy's interested that Gabe stays with us overnight. You see? If Daddy asks about Gabe you say he visits with Mother. Okay, honey?"

Mark leaned over my way. "A secret from Daddy," he whispered.

"Oh but just a small secret, that's all," Martha said. "You'll have plenty to talk about without worrying about such a little secret. Agreed, Cyn?"

We waited, and then that small guardian of truth swung her great lantern over us all. "Gabe does sleep over. Gabe's clothes are home."

"But for the time being, Gabe's clothes are put away. Cyn, Gabe sleeps over, but I think that's our private life. Your father has his private life, and we have ours. Isn't that so?"

"Okay."

"Look, Cynthia—you have a perfect right to disapprove. You go ahead and think whatever you want. Even if you want to be angry, then you be angry. You have a private life too. I'm only asking you to please do what I tell you, because I think it'll make us all happier. Baby-love, I'm sure you're not against any of us being happy, are you?"

"I'm not angry," the child said.

"That's good, Cynthia—that's a terrific girl. And this afternoon I'm going to have a talk with Daddy, and Gabe's going to take you to the Museum."

"The Aquarium," Mark demanded.

"The Museum of Science and Industry, honey," Martha said. "You can go down in the coal mine."

"We've been down in that coal mine," Cynthia said, "about a hundred times."

"I want the fish," Mark said.

"Oh hell, Markie, don't whine—*not* today—" began Martha, and then, making my first statement of the morning to the assembled Reganharts, I said sharply, "If he wants to go the Aquarium, we'll go to the Aquarium. What's so hard about that?"

To the consternation of all of us, Mark grabbed my arm and kissed it. I almost drove up on the sidewalk; and in the back seat, even Cynthia, champion of unconditional surrender, broke down and said, "Thank you." She said it softly, and when I turned my head to tell her she was welcome, I found the child, miraculously, giving me a sympathetic, almost a pitying, look.

—

After driving Martha and the children home, I drove to my office, where I spent the rest of the morning marking freshman essays. Just before I went off to lunch—and from there to pick up Martha's kids—I dialed the Herzes.

"Is she terribly upset?" asked Libby.

"I think everything's under control," I said.

"Do you have any message for Paul?"

"Whatever I tell you I would tell Paul."

"We're very appreciative," she said, "about Mr. Jaffe."

"That's fine."

"Is she young?" she asked. Then: "Is she attractive? I don't necessarily mean beautiful—"

"She's attractive, Libby. She's nineteen."

"What about the husband?"

"What?"

"The father. Is he a student?"

"No," I said.

"I thought he was a student too."

"He's an architect," I said.

She said, "And he's not going to get in the way?"

"I don't think so."

"So we can just sit back now?"

"That's right."

"Well . . . it sounds very good. I didn't realize he was an architect."

"It's all perfect," I said.

After a moment, she said, "I want to say I'm sorry for my outburst."

"That's neither here nor there, Libby."

"And how is Mrs. Reganhart?"

"She's fine."

"Do you want Paul to call you about anything?"

"Jaffe will call him."

"Of course," Libby said, "we're very appreciative."

"Of course," I said, and hung up.

—

It was like being under water, though perhaps that was some illusion I brought to the place, something to do with my sense that day of power and circumstance. At any rate, the corridors arched over, containing our movements, and the oblongs of light which gave a shape, an edge, to the darkness could have been glass-bottomed boats looking in on us; not even the noises were above-ground sounds. Everything—footfalls, laughter, parental reprimands—seemed to pulsate toward one vertically and then break under and over. Mark kept leaning across the railing and rapping on the windows of the tanks to get the attention of the fish. A guard finally told him to cut it out. "You get an angel fish excited," the guard advised me, since it was I who should have to fork over the cash, "he'll knock his head against the wall and kill himself." "I'm sorry," I said, and we walked on, up one side, past the long metallic fish of the Great Lakes, and down the other, past their rainbowed cousins of the Amazon and Nile. Long-legged Cynthia, a little Egyptian herself in an orange chemise dress and a purple pullover, seemed to pick up grace from watching the patient flutterings of the fins and the ripping gills of the baby shark, as he slid one way and then the other in his green cage.

"They eat people," Cynthia informed her brother, and then she did something on her toes that she had learned in her ballet class, and coasted on.

It was a simple enough sentence she had uttered, but I don't think the remark sank in. Mark ran off across the marble floor and disappeared around the corner; we came on him later in front of the sea horse, which he thought was a toy. I was the most permissive of adults, and followed where they led; and though other families arrived and departed, we stayed, for the mother and the father of my companions—the two unruly children, screaming and skipping up and down the echoing halls—were home having a long talk, the outcome of which none of us yet knew. Finally, tired out, I sat down on a bench in front of the hawksbill turtle, a bundle of coats and hats and scarves in my lap. The hawknose dipped and the ancient repulsive skin of the turtle's neck flashed by, and then the armored bottom went sailing past the window. He receded into the murky waters at the far reaches of the tank, and Markie settled down beside me and promptly fell asleep, his head on my arm. Cynthia approached and asked, so politely, if she could take off her shoes.

"They're very nice shoes," I said.

"They're Indian girls' shoes from Arizona," she said.

"Are they too tight?"

"No, they're perfect." Nevertheless, one beaded shoe dangled from either hand.

"Why don't you sit down and rest?" I asked. "The floor is a little cold."

"Thank you." She seated herself not beside Markie, but me.

"They are a little tight," she admitted. "That's the way the Indian children like them."

"They're very colorful and pretty," I said.

"My father brought them."

"Did he bring you the dress too?"

"And the sweater. They're from June."

"I see."

"Do you know who June is?" she asked.

"I suppose she's his new wife, who he's going to marry."

"She's very pretty," Cynthia said.

"Did you see a picture?"

"In an evening gown."

"Did Mark?" I asked.

"Mark doesn't understand everything," she said. "I think we might get to live in New York," she told me.

"Your daddy said so?"

"He asked me if I wanted to."

"I see," I said.

Cynthia pulled one foot up on the bench and began to knead her big toe. "I suppose my parents are having a talk about us," she said.

"I suppose they are."

"I'm not sure Markie wants to go live in New York."

"Why not?"

"I don't think he knows my father very well. My father has a new mustache."

"Doesn't Mark like the mustache?"

"I don't think he's used to it."

"I'll bet if you lived with him he'd probably get used to it."

She considered that. "He didn't used to have one."

"Well," I said after a moment, "people change and I guess we finally do get used to it."

"But he wouldn't be home with us, you see," Cynthia said. "He works."

"All fathers work," I said. "Most, anyway. My father works."

Her next question had a fervent, open inquisitiveness about it, and it connected in my mind with that nearly tender glance she had given me in the car, and the fact that she had chosen now to sit down beside me. On this of all days I had stopped being only her mother's property. "Is he a painter?" she asked me.

"He's a dentist."

"Ucch," said Cynthia.

"He doesn't hurt though," I said. "He's a painless dentist."

For the first time in our short and disheartening acquaintanceship she tried to please me. "Boy, I'd like him to be my dentist."

"He lives in New York too."

What she said then might at first appear to have emerged

more appropriately from the mouth of her brother; but the words belonged to Cynthia really, for she was the metaphysical one. "Is he any relation to me?" she asked.

I told her that he wasn't. We took our eyes off one another then and turned them upon that giant turtle, whose spinnings, past our gaze and back, over and over and over (endlessly, even after closing time, when no one was there), seemed nature's inspiration for the self's most urgent dreams. Chasing nothing, pursued by nothing, powerless to discontinue his own frantic rounds. The sight of him produced in me the kind of nervousness that makes some people want to scream and others get up and walk away as fast as they can.

Cynthia said, "Are you?"

"What?"

"Related to me."

"Well," I said, "I'm your friend."

"I don't think I like my father's mustache," she told me, and stood up and walked in her white anklets over to the turtle's tank. When she came back, I asked her to mind Mark, and I walked down the long corridor and found a phone booth by the tropical fish.

All Martha said was, "You can all come home now," and so we three left the Aquarium and came out, above water, into the silver light of that February afternoon, with downtown Chicago, the skyline to our right, looking as eternal as a city can.

———

In her purple suit—worn, I began to feel, only for historic occasions—and with her hair coiled up on her head, and sporting very high-heeled shoes, Martha looked solid and monumental, the type of girl who occasionally wins a beauty contest by sheer physical intimidation of the judges. Her face was lined again, as it was not in the morning but had been the night before. At the sight of the three of us, however, her manner was cheery and untrammeled. "Hi. How were the fish? Did anybody fall in?"

"Where is he?" Mark asked.

"Who?"

The boy shrugged. "Him."

"He went back to his hotel," Martha told him.

"I want milk and chocolate grahams," Mark said.

"It's in the kitchen for you, all ready. Don't spill it on your nice suit, Markie. Hi, Cynthia, you want some milk?"

In the car, driving back from the Aquarium, I had been afraid I might say the wrong words to Cynthia and turn her back into herself. But she had managed the turning on her own. "I don't want those lousy chocolate grahams, I'll tell you that. Why can't we ever have regular grahams?"

"Chocolate grahams," I said, "are supposed to be extra special." But the magic clearly had gone out of me, and I was left with only the stickiness of the remark and the vision of Cynthia, swishing her coat back over one shoulder and moving off into the kitchen with an unambiguous display of feeling. From the other room we could already hear her brother exhaling over his milk.

"How were the fish?" asked Martha, turning her back on the latest installment in The Plight of Cynthia Reganhart.

"I think they liked it."

Martha sat down on the couch and crossed her legs, so that what light filtered in through the windows caught the sheen along the meaty side of her stockings. After carefully lighting a cigarette she removed a speck of tobacco from her tongue, a gesture dense, it turned out, with sexuality. She seemed to have worked up a decided *air* about herself. Perhaps it was only that I had grown so used to seeing her in uniforms, slacks, slips, and nightgowns, that I was confusing the elegance of her costume with some heightened emotional condition; yet cross-legged, expelling smoke, sipping brandy from one of the two glasses that had been set on the floor, she seemed to be wilfully charging the place with protestations of her womanliness.

Even when she spoke, it was like one who has decided to give expression to a part of his character to which others, he feels, have not attended sufficiently in the past. The tone was artificial and vaguely defiant. "Would you like some brandy?" she asked.

"No, thanks."

"Do you mind if I . . . ?"

"Of course not."

But then Cynthia and Mark were at it in the kitchen. "Grahams!"

"Chocolate grahams!"

"Grahams!"

"*Stop it!*" Martha shouted, and the bubble in which she had been trying to sit and sip her brandy instantly burst. "*Please* stop it," she cried, "the two of you! Can't you treat each other like a brother and sister!"

"He stinks," Cynthia shouted back, and the door slammed to her bedroom. In the silence that followed, I realized that the radio that was usually in the kitchen was behind me somewhere in the living room, and that it was softly playing. It was Saturday; in New York they were performing *The Magic Flute.* Dick Reganhart and his former wife—so as to lay the ground rules of their meeting, give it the dignity of their years—had been drinking brandy and listening to the opera.

During all those years that Martha had been living her life in Oregon, I had been in New York living mine . . . This observation was pedestrian enough, but the emotion that accompanied had considerable force. So did the recollection of the long-gone Saturdays in my life, of my mother lying on the sofa, listening to the music, and of me stretched out on the rug doing my schoolwork, and at the window, his hair the color of the sunless eastern sky, my father looking down at Central Park, which was locked in the ferocity of one New York season, or turning blade by blade into another. We had had what Mrs. Baker would call a nice fine little family, and whatever my parents' aches and pains, there had nevertheless been a comforting net about the three of us, and the permanence of its disappearance suddenly set loose in me a longing that rose and rose, until my hand, as though afloat on the floodlike emotion, moved up and onto Martha's breast. But the fact that at this moment it was I who was seeking support in her flesh, was surely nothing I could expect her to appreciate.

The arc of her throat was all I saw move. "He's taking them," she said.

"Okay," I said.

"Then let's get out." She crushed her cigarette in the ash tray; she jumped up; she smoothed her skirt; she was trying to grin; perhaps without even being aware of it, she was clapping her palms together. "Well, let's go out. Let's go. Fresh air. I'll get my coat."

She went out of the room to the telephone. "You kids go down to Barbie's," I heard her say after hanging up. "Just go right down the back stairs. We'll be home in a little while."

"Where are you going?"

"Cynthia, you hold Markie's hand going down the stairs. Come on, Barbie's waiting for you."

"Mother—"

"Cynthia, let's talk later. Gabe's going to take your mother for a walk."

———

We walked in the only direction one can walk for the sake of pleasure or diversion or speculation in Chicago—toward the lake. The wind came straight into our faces, and the four-o'clock sun could barely illuminate the circle of sky around it, let alone make itself felt against our backs. We passed under the I.C. tracks and walked beyond the hotels and tennis courts and through the underpass beneath the drive. Then, still arm in arm and silent, we saw the water, which before our eyes went a color just this side of black, as though a heavy tarpaulin had been dropped over it. Private and alone, in the midst of the elements, we watched the gyrating gulls.

"There's a ship out there," Martha said.

"Where?"

"Way out—over by Michigan."

"Yes," I said, not seeing it.

"I suppose," she said, "I could go to Europe now, or stay out all night."

"If you wanted to."

"He's supposed to be changed, Gabe. He's got this big Italian mustache."

"So Cynthia said."

"How does she like it?"

"I think she likes it," I said.

"Oh sure, he's a regular image for a growing child. That's the pitch. That he's not the same old Dick. That's supposed somehow to make me heartbroken and nostalgic for all the times I got slugged."

I did not ask, and Martha did not say, whether the pitch was simply a pitch.

"I don't think I'll tell the kids for a few days. All right?"

"Sure," I said.

"Maybe I can lead into it. Maybe we can lead into it."

What could I do? Offer to marry her again? For Martha, had that ever been the issue? "I'll do whatever I can," I said.

"What he had the gall to say was that it would be a favor to all of us to get the kids out of this environment. I don't know whether he meant me or the paint flaking off the ceiling. He's gotten very fancy. You know, he came in sort of shooting his cuffs, flashing the links, and so on. And the girl looks very upper-class Bryn Mawr and horsey. Rich. Wallet-sized photos by Bachrach. He suggested that money was good for the children."

"He said that?"

"He's a very straightforward fellow. I was going to ask if he'd always known it or if his friends had been keeping it a secret from him for four years."

"Why didn't you?"

"It wasn't that kind of meeting. I even thought he was going to try to kiss me once or maybe feel me up."

"He didn't."

"He didn't."

"Did you want him to?"

"He made me very nervous. I was haughty and scared him."

"So it wasn't a mess?"

"Quite clean. He doesn't even curse any more."

"No fighting, then? No threats?"

She closed her eyes, making her admission. "What was there to fight about?"

At bedtime, Mark offered his lips as usual, and Cynthia as usual turned her cheek, but when my mouth came down to it she whispered some words that I could not understand. Because Martha was only a foot behind me, I did not ask the child to repeat whatever it was she had said. Later we went to bed ourselves, and while we each waited patiently for sleep to put an end to the day, Martha finally asked me how it had gone with Theresa Haug.

7

IN THE MIDDLE of March they left us. It had been possible during the week before to arouse Markie's interest and keep it pumped up with exotica about the Empire State Building and Coney Island, plus occasional tales from me entitled "A Manhattan Boyhood." "Gabe was a little boy in New York," says Martha, and "Oh yes," I say, "we went on the subway and we went—"

Cynthia was not so easy to manipulate, being an ace practitioner of the art herself. She began to tease. "I'll bet there aren't as many colored kids in my class," she said. In a letter on blue vellum her new stepmother had informed her that she had been accepted as a student at a private school on West Eleventh Street. She would not even lose a term. "Private school is better anyway," Cynthia said.

"Private schools are very good," Martha said.

"Which kind did you go to?"

It was not the first time that we heard the question. Martha did not even look up from the bed upon which she was separating those items of Markie's wardrobe that were in need of repair. "I couldn't afford to go to school. I delivered newspapers."

Cynthia tilted her nose and left the room; she was back minutes later, however, and addressed a statement to the woman who bore her as though that lady were Zephyr himself. "I'll bet it's not so damn windy in New York," she said.

"I'll bet it's not," Martha said. "Don't say damn."

"You do."

"I'm an adult—"

"I'm an adult, you're a child," Cynthia mimicked, and moved off with a swift swooping grace, a submarine speeding home for more torpedoes.

Martha tossed a pair of holey socks into the wastebasket at her feet. "Isn't she the brainy little saboteur," she said, a judgment, not a question, and another pair of socks followed the first.

"What's private school?" asked Mark, one eye on the diminishing pile of clothes.

"Private school is what you pay for—oh, Markie, come here, why do you wear this stuff when it's ripped? Why do you put on this underwear if it's ripped in the back?"

"Who?"

"You. Your underpants are ripped. Why didn't you say something? Do you want to show up at your father's with ripped underwear?"

The child, bewildered, slid his hand down the back of his trousers.

"And take your hand out of there," said Martha, bone weary.

Markie began to bawl. "Oh baby, it's Mommy's fault," Martha said, dropping a handful of shorts, "it's my fault, I'm a slob and oh Markie—" She smothered him with kisses while he beat on her face with his hands. "Oh it's not your fault it's ripped, baby, it's mine oh hell—"

Day after day tempers were short, tears frequent, and apologies effusive and misdirected. But finally we were driving to the airport.

"I sit in front with Mommy and Gabe," Mark said.

"I sit in front," Cynthia said—an afterthought.

"Me," the boy said.

"Look, I don't like three in front," I said. Martha said nothing at all; she had already slid in beside the driver's seat.

"I'd get to sit in front anyway," Cynthia said, "because I'm older."

"I'm older," Mark said.

"You're stupid," his sister told him.

"Stop it, will you?" I said. "Calm down, both of you."

We proceeded down Fifty-fifth Street in silence, until overhead we could hear the planes circling to land.

"We're almost there and I never sat in front yet," Cynthia said. "Just little stinky Markie."

Martha only looked at the license plate of the car in front of us. "Please, Cynthia," I said. "Let's try to be generous to each other."

"Oh sure," she said.

Martha swung around to the back, pointing a finger. "We can't all sit in front, can we? Just stop it."

The only comment was Markie's. "Ha ha," he said.

At the airport parking lot, I carried three of the suitcases; Martha, hanging a few steps behind, carried the fourth.

Inside the terminal, Cynthia displayed a considerable interest in the departure proceedings. She watched the scales to see how much each piece of luggage weighed, and she made sure that the proper tags were tied to the handles. As the suitcases joggled down the moving platform, she followed them with her eyes until they were out of sight. Then she inquired of the ticket girl if there were toilets and ice water on the plane.

"Is there someone there to pick them up?" asked the girl behind the counter.

"My father," Cynthia said.

The girl behind the counter smiled her girl-behind-the-counter smile. "*All* right then," she said, and told us which gate the plane would leave from.

In the time that remained I took Mark to the terminal bathroom, where, turning to ask me, "Hey, who owns us?" he managed to pee all over my cuff. When we came out Martha and Cynthia were standing at the newspaper stand, flipping through magazines. The angle of their heads, the way they supported themselves on their legs and moved their arms, would have indicated to anybody that they were mother and daughter. Neither of them was reading or even looking at the pictures. As I approached, Cynthia reached into her little red purse and asked the newsdealer for a copy of *Life*. She paid for it with a handful of pennies of her own, and it was then that I saw Martha's composure weaken.

"I have to sit over the wing," Cynthia told me as we started down the corridor to the departure gate. "I get sick any place else."

"I thought you never flew before."

"I know I'll get sick any place else," she said, and she ran ahead of us, catching up to her brother, who was skipping down to the gate, handsome in his new hat, coat, and suit sent from Lord & Taylor's in New York.

On the plane I had to ask several people if they would move so that Cynthia would have a place over the wing. Markie slid in beside her and immediately grabbed all the paraphernalia in the pocket before him; most of it fell to the floor. He waved the paper bag up toward Martha.

"A bag," he said.

Cynthia took it from his hand and returned it to the slot. A blond stewardess—running, it appeared, for number-one charmer of the airways—gave us a look at all her teeth. "Everything hunky-dory up here?" she asked.

"Fine," I said.

"I'm afraid you folks will have to be going now," she said.

But at this point Martha pushed past her—she had been standing aside till then, letting me do what had to be done. When she bent down across the children the jacket of her suit hiked up, showing where her slip was weakening at the seam. She had put on six or seven pounds in the last month; she was big, and not very pretty. "Goodbye, babies. Now, you write letters, hear? You've got the stamps in your suitcase and all the envelopes are addressed. You just write the letters, all right? And take care of your brother, Cyn. You listen to Cynthia, Mark. Be nice to each other, all right?"

"We're nice to each other," Cynthia insisted.

"I know," Martha said, kissing them both. She turned, and without even a glance at me, left the plane.

I leaned down one last time, and Cynthia asked if I was going to marry Martha.

"We'll see," I said. "I'm glad we two became friends, Cynthia."

She toughened instantly. "I'm always friends."

"Okay," I said. "Goodbye, Mark. Be a good boy. Send me a card from the Statue of Liberty."

Some connection was made. "Coney Island!" Markie shouted, and I started down the aisle of the plane. The blond stewardess said to me, "We'll take extra good care of them, you bet."

Minutes later we watched the plane taxi up the field, and then it was aloft, without incident. Martha said that she would just as soon not go right back to the apartment, and so we took a long ride that afternoon, all the way out to Evanston to look at the big trees and the pretty houses. Finally it was dark and we had to go home.

Children and Men

1

O F COURSE he had been miserable. Between the preten-sion and the fact, what's invented and what's given, stands one's own tortured soul. Paul Herz had been pretending all these awful years that he was of another order of men. It oc-curred to him now—as an icicle occurs to a branch, after a cold hard night of endless dripping—that, no, he was not a man of feeling; it occurred to him that if he was anything at all it was a man of duty. And that when his two selves had become confused—one self, one invention—when he had felt it his duty to be feeling, that then his heart had been a stone, and his will, instead of turning out toward action, had remained a presence in his body, a concrete setting for the rock of his heart. It all led to a very heavy sense of self—an actual sensa-tion of these last years—to a weird textual consciousness of what stood between him and others, a weighted-down feeling under the burden of underwear, tie, shirt, jacket, and coat; a sense of the volume of air itself.

Nowhere was it worse than in bed with his wife; paradoxi-cally, undressed was worse than dressed, by a long shot. Be-neath the sheets he was made particularly aware of the heaviness, the brutal materiality of his own body; his little fingers and toes, all the hard extremities of his body, were like little steel caps. The dancer has a sense of flow into the world—he felt blunt. The only hard extremity in which he felt soft was his penis. Though it rose on occasion to duty's call, and on rarer occasion to feeling's provocation, for the most part it seemed to have retired from active life. He might almost have forgotten about it had he not had reason (getting in and out of bed each day with a woman) to think about it so much. In adolescence, of course, one of his burdens had been his erection; it had seemed to him his cross to bear. Getting off buses he had tried

slouching; along the corridors at school he had covered himself with his three-ring notebook; at the urinal, one out of two
times he was peeing up in the air. But now at twenty-seven, in
a state apparently of hormonal balance, or loss, he was in need
of some stimulant. For a moment in his seat in the dark coach,
he thought about getting up and going into the rocking bathroom at the end of the car and stimulating himself. It was not
simply the movement of the train that suggested the idea; he
had entertained it, and succumbed to it, in the past, at home
when Libby was out; there had even been times with Libby
sleeping in the other room. It was not so much an act of defiance or spite, or even perversion, as of conviction: I am a man
yet. But afterwards it was not usually that of which he was convinced; afterwards it was as though the milk of life itself had
drained out of him, and he slumped onto the toilet seat a hollow thing, as though if he were to crack a bone upon the bathroom tile, the dull ringing of his body would reverberate
through the house, even to the ears of his wife.

The train was dragging to a stop. Outside it was black and
beginning to rain; they were somewhere in Ohio. Please Do Not
Masturbate While Train Is In Station. He responded to neither
duty nor feeling, just common sense. There was nothing to be
gained by making a bad thing worse. No? Then why was he
headed East?

The telegram had come to him at the University. He had
put it in his pocket and gone about his business, which, that
afternoon, was to journey down to LaSalle Street and talk to
the lawyer. He had given Jaffe a check for thirty-six dollars,
covering three visits that the girl had made to the obstetrician.
Of course, had it been Libby's own pregnancy there would
have been Blue Cross and Blue Shield to cover expenses; now,
following their uninsured crisis in Pennsylvania, he was insured
to the teeth—but now it was not his wife's hospital bills he was
going to have to pay. None of their dealings with doctors had
ever come under normal headings anyway, items the insurance
companies recognized. But then little in his life had come under normal headings: abortion, adoption, familial excommuni-
cation . . . Still, he had only recently been introduced to Jaffe
and he did not want to appear unappreciative, or self-pitying.

He had handed over the money, smiling, and Jaffe had assured him that the obstetrician had assured Jaffe that it was a perfectly normal pregnancy. But if it's a normal pregnancy *keep smiling, this is for free* why must she go to see him so often? She's nervous, Jaffe answered *impatient with me? Well, it's my money, it'll be my baby* she needs reassuring, that's all. Excuse me, Paul, I've got a client waiting *I'm a client, I came all the way down here, I'm nervous, I need reassuring—hey, how much more is this going to cost*—Thank you, Sid, thanks for everything *something for nothing, be nice, you pauper,* we appreciate, we appreciate, I'm deeply appreciative *get out, he's got a client waiting, smile and go home.*

The next day he had showed the telegram to Libby. She had begun to make a scene over something (oh yes, he never listened to her any more—which he didn't), and he had only pulled it from his pocket and tossed it on the table so as to alter the course of events. "Here! This is why I'm preoccupied. Sure, I'm preoccupied—here, read *this*!" "Oh, Paul," said Libby, reading, "what are we going to do?" "We'll do what we have to do—what I have to—"

Duty! Screw duty! *Feeling!* Aren't you a student of letters? A teacher of Dostoevsky? Puller of long faces, booster of *The Brothers K*? Enemy of Spigliano and the legions of reason? Are you not a writer of prose fiction, all heartfelt? No! Are you not the high priest of love? No! Were you ever? No! No! What an idea of himself he had constructed! What an impossible idea!

"Let me tell you what I'm going to do, Libby—*nothing!* I'm under no obligation, absolutely none. Well, what do *you* think? What are you crying about now?"

"Oh," she wept, "you have no—"

From time to time he had to do what he did then. "I've got feeling!" he roared, having smacked her. "I've got feelings that tell me he could live without me, so he can die without me too!"

With the red mark on her pale cheek, she cried less, not more, which was why, having hit her that first time some years back, he had come to do it again: it worked. In their six years he had not indulged himself on more than four or five occasions. He did not quite know what to make of this set of facts—divide five into six and compare to the national average? To get what? How was he to measure her assault upon him? Didn't he get a handicap because she had turned out to be a weakling? What about *her* handicap?

As had happened on the four or five previous occasions, he was now filled with remorse. Libby was sitting with her coffee cup, leafing through her Jewish homemaker's book; she wasn't crying, just deadly silent. "What are you looking up?" he asked softly, "a name? Does it give a list of names?" She nodded; three fingers still showed on her cheek; now two; now one.

"Well, which do you like?" Now, thank God, none. "What do you like, Lib?"

"What about Nahum?"

"For a boy," he asked, "or a girl?"

"A boy." She did more than answer—she smiled. *Oh, I'm coming back into her good graces. I need your good graces, oh yes I do, Libby.* "It means comfort," she said.

"Well, sure, Lib, if you like it. Nahum Herz? Does that sound, I don't know, perfect to you?"

"I think so."

"Well it's *nice*, honey," he said skeptically. "I suppose it's a nice old name—"

"If your father dies, do we have to name it after your father?"

"We don't have to do anything, Libby."

"I thought you might want to."

There! How many points does she get for that? He rose from the table; she was incurably—what, stupid or destructive, naïve or mean? "Libby, I want him to die! He *should* die, if there's any justice in this world. *He's ruined our life!*" But shame came in, like a rolling of waves, and carried with it the truth: I ruined it. Me.

The following day he went to see Spigliano and told him he had to go East for a few days. He waited for Spigliano to ask why. "My father's dying," answered Paul gravely. Oh gravity! What a lie. I am a man of feeling, Spigliano, and you are not. I am at one with old Fyodor and you are— Bullshit. I am you.

And that evening, at the end of the third day, he had boarded the overnight coach to New York; why, he was not certain, though the blackness of Ohio—they were moving again, heads lolling on the seats around him—and the rushing of the train, the telegram in his pocket, the knowledge of what he had left behind, the uncertainty of what he was moving into, all produced in him now a sense of the profundity of the moment. But what? How? Why was he allowing himself to be borne through space at a rapid rate on a dark night? To where?

In the morning the dawn began to lift just outside of Philadelphia. He made his way down the car to the washroom, and when he came back to his seat it was becoming day. It was as though the sky and sun held fast while the earth spun out of its darkness into light. And then he realized that this was exactly what happened. All and everything. The thought made his eyes swell. All that was natural and simple in life reduced him to tears. The dawn . . . Love . . . Libby . . .

Only when he stepped off the train in New York, dragging his bag after him, did he understand his journey. He had left his wife.

In the station he went into the coffee bar. It was nine o'clock in New York, eight in Chicago. Was she up? Sleeping? Dead? He rejected the idea, not only that Libby might be dead (wish fulfillment? no, just the old business, just guilt) but that he had left her. But the two seemed somehow to fit together: if he had *not* left her, then she couldn't be anything but living and breathing. Christ, was he trapped! It didn't even give him comfort to realize he was being irrational. He took his change in dimes and went to the phone booth; inside he sat fingering the coins. If he hadn't left Libby, it must be that he really had come East to see his father, to soothe his mother. So he made up his mind and called Brooklyn. (As he dialed he saw Libby stirring in their bed—yes, alive and breathing.) He allowed the phone to ring ten times, then an eleventh, and then—breathless—a twelfth. Then he hung up—bang! Twelve long rings because he was a dutiful man, a good son.

Good son? Dope! Jerk! Weakling! *Where's your courage?*

He remained seated in the phone booth and found some serenity in thinking that no one except Libby knew he was in New York. He might as well be anywhere. It was the first time in six years that he had been separated from his wife. This morning he had awakened—or met the day, at any rate—

without first having to feel, accidentally or on purpose, anybody's hands, feet, or hair, without having to worry first thing
in the morning about somebody else's feelings. Five and a half
years of it. Outside the booth, at nine A.M., there was no one
he knew; nobody who passed paid him any attention. Every
few minutes he heard announced the departure of another
train for another part of the East. He had only to climb aboard
and get off in Wilmington, Baltimore, or Miami Beach. Washington . . . get a little room somewhere, get a job in some
government office, and disappear. Start making a life not on
the basis of what he dreamed he was, or thought he was supposed to be, or what literature, philosophy, friends, enemies,
wife, parents told him he must be, but simply in terms of his
own possibilities.

Picking up his suitcase (the new life would be begun simply: one suit, one sport jacket, two shirts, and three pairs of
underwear) he left the booth. But in the midst of the crowds
pushing toward the tracks, he seemed not to be gaining
anonymity but losing it; and so the only train he took that
morning was the BMT, and where it carried him was back to
the place where he had been born.

There is no need to chronicle Paul Herz's feelings as he left
the subway and walked the three blocks to the Liverpool Arms.
He was anybody returning home. It was June in Brooklyn, and
he had lived seventeen Junes in Brooklyn before he had gone
off to college and a wife. Nothing was unfamiliar to his eyes.
The elevator smelled like the inside of a tin can, and the corridors smelled milky—no change there either. Upstairs the same
door was hinged on their apartment; under his feet was the
same doormat. At the age of eleven Paul had cut a sliver from
one of his father's business cards with an old razor blade and
Scotch-taped it above the doorbell: his father's name. He had
imagined at the time that it would give his saddened old man a
little lift, for Mr. Herz had just gone under for the third time
—real estate. That little sliver was still there above the bell, and
considering what the sight of it did to Paul's insides, he knew
the apartment itself would be too much. She would make unfair claims. Paul, look at this photo—remember the picnics?
Remember Uncle Nathan who died, such a young man and
the only one on your father's side with the benefits of a college

education? Paulie, Sheepshead Bay, look. You ate shrimps till they came out of your ears, you and Maury, remember? And your stamps, no one has touched a single page, and your rocks and your butterflies and your baseball glove and your report cards, still framed—oh Paul, how could you do this to your parents, a boy who got such perfect grades in Conduct—

He rang the bell for two reasons. First, if it was not for his parents' sake that he had come East, then it was for something else, and he did not want to think about that right now. (Though he could not help himself really: if he had actually left Libby, then she must be dead. Ridiculous. She was awake now in Chicago—then he had not left her. This was ridiculous reasoning!) Secondly, he rang because, having telephoned earlier, he was pretty sure no one was home. He rang again and again. Then there was only one more thing to do. He turned the door handle; to his relief he found that it was locked. He began to breathe again. Imagine having to sit in that club chair in the living room, one hand on either doily, waiting for his mother to come home. So what now? Where? Suitcase in hand, he moved past all the empty milk and sour-cream bottles to the elevator. Where? Anywhere. Start again. Last chance. Once there's a baby it's all over. To go back and become not just a husband but a father too—well, that would be that. If it had taken five and a half years to walk out on his Libby, it would take forever with some little Nahum sleeping in the other room. He got in the elevator and traveled down to the main floor. His body actually shook at the thought that if he wanted to he need no longer have any connection to anybody. Consequently he did not even leave the elevator but pushed the button marked 6 and rose once again.

"My God—Paul!"

Doris had on a gay floral apron over her slacks. Inside, instead of old lady Horvitz's oriental rugs, there was blue carpeting as far as the eye could see; instead of the meaty odor that used to waft out from the kitchen when Maury's parents were fattening their son up in this same apartment, there now floated out the pungent, domestic smell of coffee. Things had changed—everything but Doris, who seemed as stunned at seeing him as he was upon seeing her. Everyone has someone upon whose flesh and bones his first discoveries were made.

Paul had had Doris; Doris, Paul. Yes, all the inconsequentiality and fervor of their passion came back to him . . . . Doris still slouched in the shoulders and he had the old impulse to tell her to straighten up and be beautiful. But she was Maury's wife now, ten years older, and the mistress of all that carpeting. "Hello, Doris. I wondered—I was looking for my mother."

"Oh *Paul*. She's at the hospital. Maury just drove her over a few minutes ago. Paul, it's you."

"I called downstairs and she wasn't home."

"She's been living here since it happened."

Ah, *it*. Not the heart attack. Never the plane crash or the cancer or the bankruptcy. The *it*. The *tsura* one couldn't even mention.

He was home.

He looked at Doris's familiar face, and suddenly he remembered distinctly her father's voice calling out from the bedroom into the darkened living room, where the two of them had sat panting: "Doris, is that you, dolly? Is somebody with you? Tell him thank you, dolly, and tell him it's the next day already, your father has to get up and go to work soon, tell him thank you and good night, dolly—"

"How is he?" Paul asked, and waited to hear that *it* had killed his own father, that the old man's last failure was history.

"I guess," said Doris, shrugging, "I guess he's coming along. What can we expect? He's in a terrific coma. You got Maurie's telegram?"

He stood in the old hallway (waiting for Maury to finish his malted milk, waiting for Maury to finish his clarinet lesson) and was aware that somebody now knew he was in New York. All his circumstances, past and present, settled down over him. He saw Libby in the bathroom in Chicago squeezing toothpaste onto her brush. "I got the telegram," he said, and followed Doris into the apartment. "I can only stay a minute," he added.

"Just a cup of coffee. Just sit down. Paul," she said, "it's good to see you."

They came into the living room, which was nothing like the old days when every object had its coverlet, the sofa its antimacassars, the piano its Spanish shawl, the satin lamp shades their little plastic dustproof wrappings. The room now was airy and modern, all pastel shades; with no heavy drapings falling across the windows, light blazed into every corner. Avocados and gardenias flourished as though they were outdoors. There was a playpen near the window, toys all around, and in conspicuous places photographs of Maury, Doris, and a baby.

"You have a child?" Paul asked.

"Two. Jeff is in nursery school. Michael's in his crib having his bottle. Two boys—"

Before she could ask if he wanted to see Michael in his crib having his bottle, he said, "I better not stay too long, Doris."

"You look so tired."

"Traveling." He remained standing. "How's Maury?"

"He's doing wonderful—and he talks about you, Paul. He really does. We have whole conversations about you." The tinge that rose on her neck and cheeks revealed a little of the nature and spirit of those conversations. "Why don't you put down your luggage?" she suggested.

"You're looking fine, Doris, too—"

"Do I look the same?"

"Except for your hair. You wear that differently."

"Sure, well, I cut it. Not just me, everybody's wearing it short. Sit down, all right? Put down your suitcase, you make me tired standing there holding it. You like espresso? We even drink it for breakfast. You ought to see your mother drowning it with cream and sugar. You want that or you want instant?"

He decided—her silly talkativeness decided for him—to stay for a little coffee. "Either is all right."

"Sit down."

He released his suitcase with an unconscious sigh, and they smiled at one another.

"Oh Paul," she called from the kitchen, "it's so wonda-ful to see you."

Could it be? He had taken off his coat and had sat down in a chair with beautiful wooden arms; he stretched out his legs. Oh, it felt good. He even closed his eyes, even had a pure moment of thoughtlessness—his mind ceased searching out the next five minutes. Was it possible that he was happy? Had his crisis passed? Without even knowing it, had he come to some decision? Or was it only Doris and the sweet familiarity of her vowels and diphthongs? Wonda-ful, mah-velous, you could

caay faaaw me—she was humming in the kitchen. What a
good-natured girl. What a pliable simple girl. Dolly, tell him
thank you and tell him good night—Wonda-ful . . .

So was Elizabeth DeWitt Herz pliable. So was Libby simple
—oh yes, simple! And there went his happiness and his
thoughtless moment. He sat straight up, taking in the facts of
Maury's prosperity and success. Actually it didn't seem to have
been happiness he had been experiencing anyway—just relief
at Doris's not hating him. As if what Doris Horvitz did or did
not feel made any significant difference in his life. He looked at
his watch. Ten-fifteen. She is having breakfast alone. Isn't she
better off? He wanted to shout right through to where he saw
her sitting bent over the table, in that blue flannel bathrobe
with the white piping, buttering her toast. And—oh, no, no,
not crying? Libby, baby, what are you crying over now? Oh
dumbbell, look, get up, get dressed, put on that new yellow
jumper and get out. Take a nice long walk, the Midway is
green, the lake is blue, it's spring, Libby, take a train to the
Loop, have lunch, go to Stouffer's with all the ladies, go to
Field's, shop, *live*. Libby, you're alone, you see, without worries, without cares—see how wonda-ful it can be? *Free*, Libby!
Free, young, still pretty, and in Field's ten men will smile at
that face of yours—maybe, who knows, Wallach himself—

No. In Marshall Field's she will have eyes for baby clothes
and bassinets. She will bring home with her (written in her
little spiral pad purchased for just this purpose) a list of what
they will have to buy (page one); what they might have to buy
(page two); and (pages three and four) what it would be oh so
nice to have, Paul, if and when we can afford it. One short
month, darling, and we'll have our little Nahum. Our comfort.

Doris set a tray down on the coffee table in front of the
couch; Paul noticed that she had applied lipstick and eye
shadow in the kitchen. The tray settled, Doris reached behind
her and lowered the pulley lamp that extended from the wall.
She tugged at it without even looking, and the carelessness,
the at-homeness, of her movement had its effect upon him. It
led him to believe that she was very happy. She was wearing
little black sequined house slippers and they too somehow encouraged him to believe that she was happy. "Do you like

French crescents?" she asked. "You get them ready-made and you just warm them. In the oven, and that's it."

"They look very good."

"Maury likes anything European."

"Maury was always a *bon vivant*," he mumbled.

"Are you being sarcastic?" she asked. "Cause you were always sarcastic, Paul. I mean you could always cut somebody if you made up your mind to. The intellectual," she said. "You even look the same, really."

"That's very nice of you, Doris. Except I've lost half my hair."

"Oh," she said kindly, "not half." Yes, the same cuddly Doris. All right, dolly, let the young man open the door for himself and let us hear his footsteps lightly down the hallway, what do you *say*, young man—

"I'll bet Maury's got every strand."

"Maury"—she knocked on wood; that is, she looked for wood and found formica—"Maury always had a nice head of hair. With him it's in the family." She flushed again; even while she spoke, Mr. Herz lay in the hospital, a bald spot the size of a half dollar at the back of his skull. "You'd recognize him right off, Paul. You really would. Paul"—she turned serious all at once—"you know Heshy Lerner got killed in Korea. You know that?"

"I knew that," he said.

"It's hard to imagine, isn't it? He was such a good dancer, remember? And he was always, you know—you remember the type of fella Heshy was. He was very much the life of the party."

"He was a very funny guy."

"*Look*," she said, as though he had just disparaged himself, "so were you. You could really make very funny comments, Paul, when you wanted to. Paul, you were a very popular fella, and then you went away. For that matter," she rushed to say, "everybody's moving away and it's just not the same. If you don't live in the suburbs today, you don't live anywhere. Maury and I believe, however, in being individualists."

"How's my mother, Doris?"

She closed her eyes to answer. "She had to get a shot to calm her, that's how your mother is." A grave statement, intended to have a humbling effect upon the prodigal son. "Now it's a little better, but not much."

"When did it happen?" It! "His heart attack," he added.

"What's today, Saturday? Tuesday night. We were at the show and when we got back there was an ambulance and a whole crowd, and they were carrying him out on a stretcher. Maury went in the ambulance with him, and then he came back, I think it was three in the morning, maybe later, and we put your mother to sleep in Jeffrey's room, and we talked whether we should send you the telegram, and we sent it. I guess you got it, when—yesterday?"

"I got it Wednesday morning. Three days ago."

Apparently she had been expecting him to lie, or wanting him to. All she could finally do was pour coffee in his cup, from which he had as yet taken only a small sip.

"He's going to die, is that right, Doris?"

"Look, I don't *think* so . . ." It was as though she wanted, by minimizing the crisis, to excuse Paul's not running to his father's bedside.

"What do the doctors say?"

"They don't know."

"He's in a coma?"

"Since Tuesday night."

"Did he have any attacks before, recently?"

"Well, he always had heart trouble; he was never a well man, Paul, let's not kid ourselves."

"He never had heart trouble."

"He certainly did have heart trouble, I beg your pardon."

"He thought he had heart trouble, Doris."

"What do you call what he had then, a belly-ache?"

"I don't know."

She jumped up from the couch and began picking up toys from around the room and throwing them into the playpen. "You don't have to hate him, Paul," she said, "when he's in the *hospital!*"

"I don't hate him." And those few words seemed to render him helpless.

Doris apparently sensed his condition, for she rose on her toes now when she spoke. "If a man had a heart attack, and three of the biggest heart men say he had a heart attack, then I don't see how you can get here about a week later and say he *didn't* have one."

"I was talking about six years ago, Doris, seven, eight years back."

"You can have premonitions, can't you? You can have terrible troubles, believe me, that can bring things on."

"I suppose you can. I suppose you can sit around having premonitions all your life."

"You always had to believe different from everybody else. The whole world is wrong and you're right!"

It was the proper moment to get up and go. But the colorful airy apartment, Doris's bad posture and pretty face, the playpen, the scattered toys, the pulley lamp, the French crescents that you warm and serve—all of them together took most of the starch out of their argument. Even Doris's chastisements didn't seem original. The simple truth was—and it was a simple truth both must have understood, for both calmed down at the same speed—that some nice affection still lived between these two old playmates. What did any of this have to do with all that heavy breathing back when they were seventeen? On this day particularly, he was not anxious to dismiss whatever little kindnesses came his way.

Doris must have had a soft spot for kindness, for remembered affection, herself. She asked, "Another crescent?"

They ate and drank, and then they heard the baby turn in his crib and the bottle clunk onto the floor. Doris put her finger to her mouth and they were both absolutely quiet; when the crisis was over, she smiled in a motherly way.

"You're still teaching?" she asked.

"Yes."

"English?"

"That's right."

"Well, you used to read all the time, so I guess we should have guessed then . . . Oh it's really funny, Paul, talking to you. It gives me the gooseflesh. Eleven o'clock in the morning, I'm dusting my house, and I'm married, and I've just given my little boy his bottle, and my husband's just left, and I'm trying to think of shopping and a thousand things, and in walks Paul Herz. I'm sorry if I'm babbling, but that's what happens to me. Maury and I were down in Miami in January and who should we run into on Lincoln Road, just window-shopping, but Peanuts Ackerman, from Ocean Avenue, who I used to go out with for a couple months in high school. And I'm telling you, he's married, and he has this wife with him, a really terrific blonde—and three kids, and I don't know, it just gives me such a feeling whenever I see a guy I used to date, and now *I'm* married and *he's* married, and we got *fur*niture and *cars* and *kids.* I just get this feeling—"

Paul said, "I get it too."

"Are you being sarcastic again?"

He shook his head. He was no longer the sharp-tongued backseat Don Juan. Hardly. He slumped a little in his chair, for he felt there was something in this room that he had expected for himself. Never—not in Detroit, Chicago, Ann Arbor, Iowa City, not even in Brooklyn as a boy—had he felt very permanent about himself. And that was sad and ironic, for he had married early for reasons that were not really so out of the ordinary.

"I get it seeing you, Paul," Doris was telling him. "I got it seeing Peanuts and those kids, and his wife, such a terrific-looking girl. And what makes it something is that some accident, something here or there, and you might even have married the other person. I don't mean that kind of accident— I mean some quirk, anything. You think that's dumb, don't you?"

"No—I'm just not sure about the last part." He wasn't very sure about any of it, but he was not unwilling to let the girl go on and on; it was nice having a little respite from life. He had married at twenty as though to bully his way into manhood; now a little vacation from manhood was a pleasure. Everybody deserves a few minutes off now and then anyway. One deep breath, then off to the hospital . . .

"What last part?" Doris asked.

He had to think. "Marrying people by accident."

"Paul, if you want to say that you couldn't have married me because I'm not *smaaht* enough, look, go right ahead. I'll admit I don't read every book that comes out, and I'm not a bohemian or a beatnik, so if that's what you think, you're perfectly justified."

"You want to fight with me, Doris?"

"You're the one who's fighting."

"All I meant was that there probably is some real chemistry between two people who decide to marry."

"Boy, you read too many novels," she said. "It's not *all* sex."

"All right." If he could only think of a place to go, he would leave. Suddenly she filled him with the same weariness and boredom that she had in 1948. What was the name of the hospital? Where would he leave his suitcase? Where would he sleep? Why, downstairs, in his old bed, where else?

"Well, that's what you meant," she said.

"I only meant some necessary connection. Some serious service one does for the other."

"How—" she asked, pouring him another cup of coffee. "How," she asked very offhandedly, "would you explain that in terms of me and Maur?"

"I don't know you and Maury."

"You *remember* us."

"Hell, Doris"—his irritation was less with the conversation than with his own willingness to stay for yet another cup— "we've all changed."

"Well, so have you!"

"That's what I meant."

"You were a very excitable guy then, and now, I don't know, I just don't think you look so excitable any more. I suppose you matured."

"I struck you, did I, as young?"

"Well, you think it's a joke and that I'm stupid, but as a matter of fact, if you want to know the truth, at twenty Maury was much more of a man, I thought, than you. A much more settled fella, with real goals."

"Well," Paul said, raising his hands, "he seems to have reached them."

"He's doing very nicely, thank you. I can't make out if you're sarcastic or not."

"Not! Come on, Doris, ten years have gone by, what's this sarcastic business!"

"Well, I'm not ashamed of how Maury's doing. He may not be a"—at the last second she seemed to swap one word for another—"Rockefeller, but he's a very good husband to a girl.

He makes a girl very happy. It's very nice, believe me, to have somebody who's very proud of you. I know plenty of girls whose husbands never really admire them dressed up, or don't take pride in the way their wives fix their hair or in their wives' taste—which is very important to a woman—and I'm not one of them."

"You look very happy."

"Well, you do too!"

"I didn't accuse you of anything, Doris."

"Well," she rushed to say, blushing now, "you must love your wife very much to have given up everything for her."

Having stayed this long, having chosen to be unrealistic and indulgent, he should have expected it. "What did I give up?" he asked.

"I'm not criticizing."

"I only wanted to know what you thought I had to give up."

"I only meant to say that you must love your wife very much."

He had no choice. "I do," he said.

"Well . . . then . . ." But she couldn't lay off, this girl whom he had caressed and caressed. "That must make it all worth it."

"It does," he heard himself saying.

"I suppose she's an intellectual too."

"Look, Doris, it's hard to tell what you have in your mind when you say 'intellectual.'"

"Like you."

"Well, she is like me."

"Very serious," Doris suggested.

"She's quite serious. That's right."

"Well, maybe she is."

"What does that mean? She is. She's a serious girl. She's a very valuable person."

"Well," Doris said, "it's up to the individual. Personally I just don't think you happen to have liked Jewish girls. I don't think you respected them, to be frank, if you want the truth."

"My wife is Jewish."

"I meant," said Doris, not flinching, "by birth."

"I don't think that has much to do with it." Get up! Go! Why punish yourself!

"You might not think so," Doris said, "but a lot of it is in your subconscious. It's a reaction. It happens to a lot of Jewish guys. Especially smart ones." After a second, she added, "The ones who think they're smart."

"It's possible, Doris," he said, "that people choose mates for other reasons." She didn't seem to believe it; she closed her eyes once again. "Complicated reasons," he said.

"That's complicated to me, all right. You take a fella, a normal fella, and you expect he's going to first off be attracted to a girl of his own particular faith, right? Then he turns around and does the opposite. You couldn't want anything more complicated if you wrote away for it."

"As a matter of fact, you could."

Defiantly, as though she had him chained to his chair, she asked, "For instance?"

"Oh, for instance why did you marry Maury?"

"Well," she said, losing breath and coloring, "he's Jewish at least."

"Never mind, Doris. Let's forget all this."

"Why did you marry *her*?" Doris demanded. "I mean if it wasn't just a reaction, why did you?"

"Love." After he had spoken he experienced a terrible moment of confusion. But he said again, "Love."

"So then why don't you have any children?"

The question startled him further. "We don't want any children."

"I don't believe it, a Jewish fella."

"You've got too much faith, Doris, in us poor Jewish fellas."

"You're not the same fella, Paul, that's the truth. If a man and his wife have a solid relationship then they have children."

He did not wish to tell anybody in Brooklyn of Libby's kidney trouble; besides it did not seem to him that this was actually why they had no children. "Doris, that may not be so in all cases. Isn't that a possibility?"

"Listen, you make love to a girl different, if you want to know, when there are children involved. And I think I've had more experience than you! You're just not the same fella, and that's all I'm trying to say."

At last he pulled his weakened self up out of his chair. He felt he had heard just about everything that had been thought and said about him in the last five years. He set down his cup.

"You were always a lively, affectionate fella, Paul, and you know it. You were the kind of fella who you could just see someday playing with his own kids, tossing them up in the air and taking them to Ebbets Field and the whole works. You were a very affectionate fella, Paul."

"Well," he said, unable to remember where he had put his suitcase, and growing more furious by the moment, "maybe it turns out I'm a cold fish. Maybe that's my story."

But Doris was shaking her head. "You were always kissing me, Paul," she said. "That's something that if you do it, you have it all your life. *I'm* still a very affectionate person, I can tell you that. Maury says I'm sometimes too demonstrative even."

Where was the suitcase? "Doris, you don't know what you're talking about."

"And you," she said, heartbroken, her hands on her hips, "you were the smartest of any of us."

It was time to go. Go, you coward. Your suitcase is right at your feet. Go.

Where?

"Where are you going—where?" she called after him as he started down the hall. "Paul?" she called, but he had no answer. As he opened the door to the elevator she shouted to him "Paul, you're a fool. Oh Paul, you ruined your life!" It was only another voice in the chorus.

———

At home, whenever eggs were served for breakfast, he served them. It was not that Libby couldn't crack an egg properly, or even that she was unwilling to; it was simply that the way they had worked out their life together, he usually slipped from his side of the bed in the morning while she was asleep— at any rate, while her eyes were closed. Only occasionally, out of exhaustion, or a lingering sense of the fitness of things, they lay side by side in bed, wide awake; and then he was compelled —still out of a lingering sense of the fitness of things, of what was only just and right—to make the ultimate expression of that connection which husbands and wives are said to have, and which he and his wife no longer had—perhaps never had—and which therefore made the expression of it a hypocrisy beyond any hypocrisy he could ever have imagined. It was not very pleasant to start the day caught somewhere between the betrayal of your marriage—the very convention of marriage itself—and the betrayal of your own flesh. Nor to end it that way; as a result they did not often go to bed at the same hour either.

The butter melting, the eggshell splitting, the plop, the sizzle, all brought back to him (as though they ever left him) the realities of his home life.

From the far end of the room, Asher called, "Up—over? Which?"

"Up."

No longer was the El outside Asher's window, and the sun, allowed access, cast a glow on the stiff curved leaves of the potted plants that circled the room. The floors, walls, and furniture, however, hadn't gained much from the alteration in the city's landscape. As for Asher, El or no El, light or half-light, he looked the same; nose, pores, hair, belly, aroma, everything was just six years older.

"How is that weather in Chicago?" he called.

"Now it's spring," Paul answered.

"Hot, huh?"

"Yes, hot."

"There's a city that's got a climate for you. Takes all that crap from Canada, all that ice and wind, and then whshsh, those summers. My hair dropped out of my head there, Paulie, from humidity alone."

"I forget you were a Chicagoan."

"All that clamminess and police corruption," Asher called from the kitchen, "produces baldness early. Either you're perspiring into your hatband or worrying to death." He was crossing the room, the pan in one hand, the other hand drawing a bead on his nephew's hairline. "Ah, but you're not doing so bad yet yourself. In fact, you look nice, Paul. You got a nice grave expression in your face. Second violinist for the Krakow Philharmonic." He slid the egg onto the plate Paul held out to him, then sat down, the pan dangling from his hand.

Paul was feeling now the kind of relief he had felt at first at

Doris's. He was willing to accept the fact that he had made one false start this morning already. Now he understood things better; on the subway back from Brooklyn he had come to grips with the meaning of his trip. "Thanks," he said to Asher. Asher smiled; even he was a help. He had opened the door, shaken hands, and when Paul asked if there was a bed he might use for a night or two, Asher had pointed over to the sofa, no questions asked—at least not right then.

"You look in the eyes," Asher said, "like you've been having some of life's more classical experiences."

Having brought a bite of egg to his mouth, Paul set it down; he waited out the nausea that reached up from his stomach. "I didn't get much sleep on the train," he said.

"Oh, sure, well"—Asher moved out of his chair and pulled up on the high stool beside his drawing board—"that explains everything."

"But you're the same, Asher," said Paul wryly, and tried once again to eat. He told himself he had nothing to worry about. He had found a neutral bed in which to sleep; he could proceed as planned.

"Oh I manage to maintain a nice lofty attitude," said Asher.

"You've seen my father?"

Those wrinkled lids of Asher's, magnified behind his glasses, came down over his eyes, telling all. "From the hallway."

"And my mother?"

"You want me to give you a little chronicle of hysteria, or you want to go on past performances?"

"She mentions me?"

"Paul, there's nothing she won't mention. She's a dredger of polluted waters. She was never too sharp at sorting out forests from trees."

But he might as well hear it all; that too could give strength. "What does she say about me?"

"I thought you had an imaginative spirit."

He took another mouthful, and saw no reason not to confide in his uncle, not when the man wanted to be helpful. "I'm not going to see him, Asher. I can't do it. It doesn't make sense, given my life. I came all the way here to New York because . . . I don't know precisely." That much he could keep to himself. "I went over to Brooklyn this morning."

"I figured."

"It cost me a round trip from Chicago that I can't even afford. Asher, I ask you, do I owe them anything?"

Asher wasn't even willing to take the question seriously. "Nobody owes nobody nothing."

"Not when they ate my guts out," Paul said, and found appetite for his breakfast.

Asher was tapping his forehead with his fingers. "You think too much in conditions. Same old story, you miss the point."

"And I'm leaving my wife," said Paul, because he had to finally, because that was the corollary: He would not see his father. He would leave Libby. Though two sentences were needed to convey the information, he saw it as only one act, arising out of some new direction of the will. He was moving instinctively toward an unburdening. Even deciding—instinctively again—to come to Asher's seemed somehow a part of it. "It's beyond choice," he said, and felt better than at any moment in the last twenty-four hours.

Asher blinked several times, as though watching Paul's words fall into the proper slots. "No kidding," he said.

Nausea reached up a quick hand for the freshly ingested egg. Paul swallowed. "That's what it looks like," he said.

"She sleeps around?" Asher asked. "She doesn't keep the place straightened up nice?"

"You're just the same, Asher."

"You went away a few years, you think everybody went all over the place taking courses in tact, awaiting your homecoming?"

"Well, I'm not after sympathy, Asher. So never mind. I just ran into several bad breaks. The marriage hasn't worked out. Let's leave it at that."

"But the girl is still ideal, huh?"

"I'm getting out, Asher, but I'm not kidding myself where the blame lies. I was young. Things came up. I made some terrible errors of judgment that threw a pall on the thing. I didn't know a hell of a lot. And then there's the matter of one's constitution. I mean what you are; the facts about oneself."

"I don't like to tell a man over his breakfast coffee, Paul, but it's your whole philosophy that stinks bad."

"Please do me a favor, don't feel you have to spend time

cheering me up. I've arrived at my decision and I'll take the consequence. This is the consequence," he said, with a slight sense of discovery. "It hasn't been very pleasant, believe me it hasn't."

Asher was no longer giving him all his attention; he had picked up Paul's plate and was walking toward the kitchen, a frazzled outline in the sunlight. His hair needed cutting, his trousers a good pressing. "Love," he said over his shoulder, "is unnatural. Most of the guilt in the world is from cockeyed thinking." He disappeared around the flowered screen that cut off the sink from Paul's sight.

"Asher, we see life as two different things. As I remember" —and he did, which compromised his position, and smothered him in gloom—"we went over this ground a long time ago. We disagree."

"Paulie," came back a voice, "I'm going to save you a couple thousand dollars and give you a fast college education, plus a psychoanalysis thrown in." He stepped back into the light and began flicking a dish towel at the leaves of his plants.

There was the same old lack of seriousness in his uncle. He did not know if he was up to it. "You gave it to me already."

"What can I do?" Asher asked. "You don't listen."

Paul rose from the couch, which was to have been his bed. What was there left for him to do but sweat it out in some cheap hotel? But in some cheap hotel, under a bare bulb, would he survive? Better to take all the money they had left in the bank, the money they would no longer be needing for a baby, and go uptown and get a nice room that looked out on Central Park. A little class, a little comfort, might get him through. However, one does not learn to spend money overnight . . . And suppose Libby should want the baby anyway? He sat down again, as though he had only been taking a stretch to aid digestion. "Is that a condition of staying here?" he asked with a smile on his face. "Paying attention?"

"Kiddo," said Asher, "no conditions. That's what I'm telling you. I don't go in for conditions. I'm at one with life. Only guy I know."

Paul couldn't understand his uncle now any better than he had years ago. "And that little girl you had here, years and years ago—"

Asher looked up from across the room where he was watering his plants. Wasn't there water shining in his eyes as well? "My little Patricia Ann?"

"She made you happy? That's an example of oneness with life? Please, Asher, let's not make light of each other's problems."

"Ah you, you don't understand loss."

"I thought you've been telling me you're happy?"

"Putz, I'm *miserable*. What kind of issue is that? I thought we're going to have a little talk about first principles."

His suitcase wasn't far from the door. Right downstairs, Third Avenue was lined with hotels—but none of them, he knew, would be too pleasant. Then spend a dollar, he told himself, you deserve it . . . However, on that last point there must have been some inner debate; immediately he was back to thinking of himself holed up in some sleazy hotel. It seemed appropriate, yet he knew he didn't have the strength. He could get through, though, with just an ounce of companionship, someone to take a meal with and sit next to in a movie. Then, free! "Maybe later, Asher."

Asher was unhooking his sports jacket from the back of the door. "Paul, I got a new girl friend who is right up your alley. A very nifty little number with a nice pair of sloe-eyes— Washington Park is stocked with them—but gradually I'm draining out of her head all the cotton candy. See, this is a new thing for me. I don't go in for education. I prefer the thing in the pure state. You know what I've been up to for years, Paulie?" He had taken a tie from his inside pocket and was working it around his neck. "Can you take a guess? Getting the thing in its pure state. You follow me? I want to feel the precise quality of the shit against my skin. Do you get the picture? Your Uncle Asher is the child of the age. *Ecce* Asher!" His tie in place, he raised his arms. Behold! His shirt inched up out of his trousers. Realizing he was beltless, he went off toward the kitchen.

He likes being a slob, he prefers life outside the ordered world, Paul thought. One more attitude he did not share with his uncle. When *he* was sloppy it was because his mind was elsewhere. Then what did the two of them share? It was Asher he had chosen to seek out, after all; he had not even thought of Uncle Jerry and his big air-conditioned apartment.

"Anyway," Asher called back, "what troubles her is her inter-personal relationships. These are actual quotations I'm giving you: she is incapable of love. She is a destructive personality. She has never really communicated with another human being. I ask her, whatsa matter, you never lift up the phone when it rings? But she doesn't get the truth in what I'm saying. She tells me nobody can love anybody because we are all of us living in the shadow of The Bomb, and also God is dead. I want you to meet this girl, Paulie, she's got a very involved case of what you got, only you're smarter."

"I never worry about The Bomb, Asher."

"I'm talking about the disgusting load you're placing on the heart. Overworked. Misunderstood. Terrible."

He was fully dressed now, standing over Paul. "I take it, Asher, that you're in favor of emotional anarchy, separation, a with-drawal of people from people. A kind of moral isolationism."

"Very inventive," said Asher. "But what I'm in favor of is getting back in tune a little bit with nature. All this emphasis on charity and fucking. Disgusting."

"But you've always had women, Asher. You told me that too, remember? A Chinese woman and so on. That's all you talked about last time we met. You made it sound as though I was leaving a harem for marriage. Let's be serious, if we're going to have discussions."

"You misunderstood. Ass is no panacea. Not even the high-est quality."

"Then why do you pursue it?"

"One, I got needs and prefer ladies to queers. Number two, I told you, I'm the child of the age. I want to understand what all the movies and billboards are about. Three, you still haven't got what I'm talking about. I'm talking about taking a nice Oriental attitude for yourself. Pre-Chiang Kai-shek. Un-grasping. Undesperate. Tragic. Private. Proportioned. So on down the line. I only want to leave you with one thought, Paulie, because I've got to get out of here and I don't want to find you dead when I get back. Nobody owes nobody nothing. That's the slogan over the Garden of Eden. That's what's stamped on all our cells. Body cells, what makes us. There's your nature of man. The first principle you should never forget."

"To be irresponsible."

"Don't hand me that crap. I'm talking about rocks, about flowers—" He pointed across the room. "Potted plants."

"Flowers are flowers, Asher. Men are men."

"What you need is a real high enema to knock all that stuff out of you. You are the victim, my friend, of circumstantial thinking. Look at life, please, in universals. Try it. And don't commit suicide, Paul. I have to see some teamster who wants me to paint him into a beautiful picture. You think its hypocritical? It's no difference, either way. You won't commit any suicide now, okay? That also is against nature. We're on earth to take it. Hang around, you're only in your twenties. You just got your first shock from yourself. Hang around, Paulie, and I'll come back this afternoon and give you a definition of man." He whisked a canvas from beside the door. "You want to sleep here a couple months," he said, "that's okay too."

—

After Asher left, it was unclear to Paul exactly what he should do. He was where he wanted to be; he was, at any rate, in none of those places that he did not want to be. Therefore, he told himself, he should relax. But questions arose, forbidding ease. Was Asher's place to be his hideout indefinitely? Could he stand the conversation? The surroundings? He was used to less than luxury, of course, but something about Asher's kind of squalor—even sunlight couldn't elevate it out of the genus warehouse into the genus home—something in Asher's embracing of it, made him uneasy. His uncle lived with two metal chairs, a luncheonette stool, a drawing board, and various professional pieces of equipment; there was his sofa for comfort, a mattress and spring across the way for rest, a discouraging toilet, an assortment of pots and pans, and Asher's mother's old potted plants, which threw shadows all the way up the dingy walls. And around such objects Asher had built a life. What was unnerving to his nephew was the amount of self-understanding there seemed to be in the decor. Even the portion of serenity: the domicile of a man who knew what he was and was not after.

In surroundings not dissimilar, Paul was himself less at home. For all the bravado he remembered displaying at Catholic Salvage, all the plunking down on musty mattresses in order to brace up Libby, he could not say that he had ever noticed any particular metaphysical flow between himself and his furniture. Neither his home nor his condition was an expression of his self. But even if pushed, he did not think he could really tell what it was he might begin to feel at one with. And could that be, a man without satisfactions? Without serious and conscious goals? Surely there must be for him, as for others, an end in life—but if so, he could no longer with any certainty put his finger on it. Once it had been simple and clear: to lead a good life. Good in the highest sense, the oldest sense. However, it did not always seem that he had had opportunities for goodness, in the old sense—perhaps he hadn't always recognized them as they went whizzing by. Circumstances had not only been unusual, they had been fast. You went to sleep one night, woke up the next morning, and, lo and behold, you had a past. There had been circumstances, and there had been the business of maturation, the successive shock of coming face to face with one's own fallibilities. But whether it was strength he lacked, or imagination, or patience or wisdom or heart, at twenty-seven it almost looked as though the force and unexpectedness of circumstance had done him in.

Not that he had been inflexible and bullheaded. He had tried. Sometimes he had made up his mind to fight; other times he had let himself be dragged along with the tide. He had tried courage and he had tried reason; to Libby (*the* circumstance) he had been everything at different times—submissive, tyrannical, gentle, harsh, dutiful, detached, and so on. If he was no longer passionate, if that had been the first real force of his to desert him, it was because immediately following the abortion and its incumbent horrors, when the time had come to express in bed again their feeling for one another, a certain solemnity had seized them both. And though Libby, at the top of her pleasure, seemed able to fall backwards into innocence, to sever herself from their disappointments and mistakes, he found his own pleasure somewhat limited by the facts. The playfulness wasn't there any more, the agility, the carelessness —there was something didactic about the whole thing. And there was also the fear that Libby would turn up pregnant again.

If any sense at all was to be made out of the anguish they had gone through in Detroit, it was that they had been able to stave off what they had not been ready for. In the face of another pregnancy (and if there'd been one, what was to stop a second?) he did not know what they would do. So he had found himself less willing, even with all their precautions, to ejaculate. In fact, the care and attention lavished upon the precaution itself, the emotional intensity surrounding the ritual of its insertion, soon began to render the subsequent act anticlimactic. That he did, despite all his fears, continue to have orgasms, could be credited in part to the fact that Libby wanted him to; he also thought he had them coming to him. More than most young men, Paul had had some acquaintance with sacrifice, and even some power to deal with it; still, it had not really occurred to him that along with the giving up of money, security, family, and ease, he might also be called upon to give up that which was so universally awarded first place in the contest of pleasures.

Nevertheless, though he continued to believe in his rights— unable yet to relinquish the idea that there is some foundation of justice upon which this world is built—he looked forward to his own pleasure less and less. At last, even that moment toward which they both aimed (Libby particularly, with a kind of holy obsession, a marriage counselor's faith in "coming together"), that moment in which Libby showed her teeth and whimpered—her sound of ecstasy—became for him the most disheartening of all. He was afflicted with a deeper and deeper sense of consequence; at any time their life might be swallowed up by disaster and chaos.

Then, of course, Libby became sick, and out of what seemed on the surface a sheer lack of energy, her own ecstatic moments were less frequent; she seemed to pin all her hopes on him, and so he had on more than one occasion to reach a climax for two. And it was just then that his body had chosen to go into partnership with his will; what he had earlier tried to hold off, or thought to try to hold off, he no longer had to try so hard at. He had, in fact, to work and work and work until his belly ached and his wrists were locked in pain, while Libby, pale and motionless, and tiring too, would ask if he was almost there, if he would soon be there, if now he was there . . . And when at long long last, his pulses knocking, his body flooded with despair, he was able to tell her yes, yes, as misery itself seemed to be running through him and out of him, he would find her eyes riveted to the muscles of his face, measuring the joy and comfort she was able to give to her husband despite her incapacity. It was as though she had relinquished her own pleasure out of choice, so as to add hers to his and thereby overwhelm his mind's preoccupation with his body's joy. With the feverish girl already disappointed enough, he would begin the posturing: the ecstatic groan, the passionate sigh, the final collapse (I am sated!) onto her bosom, which was covered generally with a flannel nightdress to prevent her catching a chill and collapsing still further into illness.

It is a short journey from posturing to total unhappiness, shorter than one might imagine when the posturing begins, as it often does, as a stop-gap measure. And from there to a change in character—or in appearance—is not so very long either. A silence came over Paul Herz, a desire not to speak. Rather, at first, not to be heard. He found himself in the presence of others with nothing whatsoever to say. In the beginning the change troubled him—that is, when he noticed it as a change. After all, he was only a few years out of college, where he had always had a sense of himself as an energetic and frank conversationalist—hadn't he virtually talked Libby into a new girl? Perhaps so, but soon enough it was in silence that he began to find his only relief; eventually he even began to derive a kind of strength from thinking of himself as a silent person. It was his only power . . . until Chicago, where some of Libby's unconquerable belief in change (and who had inspired that in her?) rubbed off on him.

There it began to appear that perhaps in his new job lay his salvation. His students were generous and responsive—they knew nothing about him—and in the classroom he found pleasure once again in his own voice, in instruction; he could be intelligent, he could be frank, he could even be witty. He had gone off to staff meetings with a genuine desire to open up communication again with the outside world. He had thrown something off—new faces made him feel less ashamed. But one of the new faces turned into John Spigliano's. And that bastard right off threatened him more than he should have. So what if he lost his job? So plenty! He should have forced himself to stop arguing with the stupid ass—only the dispute was not simply with Spigliano. All that talk about humanity. Feeling! Who but himself was he arguing with?

Across the table from him there was not only Spigliano but Wallach too, whose new face resolved very quickly into that old and familiar face. A man who by all rights he should like, old or new; who by all rights should be his friend! Who *was* his friend! That evening they had sat in the light snowfall outside of Cobb, joking with one another, he had felt inside him a kind of unloosening. Relaxation. Remembering friendship, remembering in fact his old pal, Mush Horvitz, he had remembered that there were still the pleasures of social contact. If he and Libby could turn out to others—stop turning in to pick at one another's guts—they might rebuild marriage on a new foundation; they might not have to lean so heavily on each other. After all why was he so unhappy? When one considered unhappiness from all angles, it was ridiculous. Didn't he have a will? Couldn't he make up his mind and cease being dissatisfied? Used properly the will could set just about anything right; this he still believed. An intelligent man, certainly a young, intelligent man, could most assuredly alter the pattern of his life; the mistake was to think of it as a pattern. He had walked with Gabe Wallach down to Goodspeed, and he had even been conscious of the sympathy flowing between them; he had felt that Wallach had respect for him, and to that he could not help but respond. If Wallach had kissed Libby long ago, it was because Libby was a kissable girl. Besides, he knew that it was he himself whom Libby loved. So beneath his wife's office window he had called out to her, as years before he had called out from beneath her window in Clara Dickson Hall. In part he was trying to impress his companion: they were going to be all right, they were okay on their own now, and no longer in need of help. His singing to Libby was a kind of present to Wallach. But it was a gift to himself too, a gift of nostalgia and sentimentality. Many years had passed since he had made his girl passionate about Shakespeare, about anything. And after all they had been through together . . . "Arise fair sun, and kill the envious moon—"

And following the sentimental moment, the bottom had fallen out. His wife had informed his friend, his brand new friend, that her husband could give her plenty of babies, thank you, and like a man whose lawyer bends the truth to get him off the hook, he felt weakness, confusion, and then contempt, first for himself and then for the lawyer. From that moment on he was more willing to admit that all control over his life had gone out of his hands; perhaps he was more willing for it to be so.

Now there was a baby coming his way, and out of no real decision on his part. Events and others had decided for him: Wallach's suggestion, and Jaffe's assistance, and Libby's pounding need—and so he went along from day to day, making phone calls, paying bills, and soon would come little Nahum. Tomorrow or the next day he would have to pack his bag and go down Asher's dank stairway and step back onto the moving platform that he saw that moment as his own particular emblem. He would have to go back to what awaited him in Chicago; at the very least he had a job to return to. But why? There, in fact, was one more thing he did not have to go back to. He did not have to go to his father's sickbed; he did not have to comfort his mother; he did not have to return to Libby; he did not have to go back to his job. Anything else?

"What else is there?" he asked aloud.

Ah yes. Himself. He could take off his wedding ring (which he had not yet been quite able to do); he could leave the University. But how to divest himself of himself . . . Stretched out on Asher's sofa, fatigue helped to direct his thoughts to the precise issue at hand, self-divestment. In his drowsy state he was able to think of himself as something to be peeled back, layer after layer, until what gleamed through was some primary substance. Peeling, peeling, until what was locked up inside was out in the open. What? His Paulness. His Herzness. What he was! Or perhaps nothing. To unpeel all day and all night and wind up empty-handed. To find that all he had rid himself of was all there was. *And that?* Here his body trembled, as bodies will, overcome with grief or revelation—that he *was* Libby, *was* his job, *was* his mother and father, that all that had happened was all there was. *Or?* At the very moment that he plunged down into sleep, he soared too above all the demands and concerns he had known, beyond what he had taken for expectation, beyond what he had interpreted as need and understood as pity and love. He nearly glimpsed for himself a new and glorious possibility. But whether there was no glorious possibility, or whether sleep separated him at that moment from some truth about life's giving and taking, was impossible to say. He felt himself hovering at the edge of something; since it was sleep he next experienced, perhaps it was only that.

He did not know how long the phone had been ringing. In that first uninsulated moment his only knowledge was that they had thrown the El back up. The room was half in darkness; the other half was neither dark nor light. But outside he saw the sky; when he had got his bearings he rose and answered the phone.

"What?"

"*Maury.*"

"No—"

"This *is* Maury. It's Mush, Paul."

"Maury. Maury, I saw Doris—"

"We called everywhere—your uncle—Paul, what's happened to you?"

"I'm at my uncle's."

"When are you getting *down* here?"

"Right down—"

"You spoke to Doris, you got my telegram. Paul, are you still there?"

"I don't have the address, Maury. I walked off without the address."

"Take it down! Will you? Beth David. Ninth Floor. On Prospect—Paul, your father's going. You better get down here—your mother's in no shape to be alone."

"What's the matter with her?"

"Your father's *dying*—"

"Mush, all right—"

"I'm in the lobby. I'll wait in the lobby."

"All right, please—"

Please. Let me alone. Let me be. He turned back toward the sofa; he seemed to have just discovered the pleasure of being out of it. Neither fat Maury nor hot Doris existed as much of a force in his life. Neither could hold a candle to dear old sleep, which, if it was not the glorious possibility he had failed to catch a glimpse of earlier, was doing nicely as a substitute. He had powers of his own; he could remove himself from the scene. You cannot frustrate or overwhelm a man who isn't around. If he could drowse away the next few days . . . But, alas, this time he had the misfortune to dream, and to wake from the dream so suddenly as to believe that his symbols had been of some significance. Secrets! *What's the secret?* He pulled Asher's stool up to the drawing board and tacked on a clean white sheet. In thick black pencil strokes he wrote as fast as he could, not even bothering to snap on a bulb, afraid he would emerge from the dreamy spell and miss out on the truth.

DREAM MY MOTHER TELLS ME TO PUT CHICKEN IN REFRIGERATOR. CHICKEN IS IN PIECES AND HOLEY (WHOLLY HOLY). THERE IS COMPANY. I SHOUT THAT I AM TIRED OF TAKING DIRECTIONS. MANY MEMBERS OF FAMILY IN AUDIENCE (COMPANY—MY LIFE A SPECTACLE—BEING WATCHED). MY MOTHER HURT, WOUNDED, FLABBERGASTED, BUT I WAS HAVING A GOOD TIME. WHY SHOULD SHE INTERRUPT ME AGAIN. I GO OFF TO OTHER ROOM, MY FATHER POLISHING HIS SHOES IN BED. THEN WE GO AWAY TO SCHOOL, WHERE AS RETURNING GRADUATE I TRY TO DRESS UP LIKE GYM CLASS BUT LOOK AWKWARD, CLOWNISH AND AM TOLD BY GYM TEACHER (SPIGLIANO) WHY DON'T I GO SWIMMING IN POOL OR BOX. BEFORE OR AFTER THIS I HAVE A BROTHER (ME) AND HE AND I SEPARATE FROM COMPANY AND WE GO INTO GARAGE WHERE HE IS UPSET ABOUT WAY I HANDLED MY MOTHER. I TRY TO EXPLAIN WITH AID OF THIRD PARTY (WALLACE? WALLACH) THAT I MUST BE FREE OF HER. I AM TOO OLD. MY BROTHER CRIES. I READ (PLEAD) WITH HIM. THEN I GO UPSTAIRS WHERE I SEE MAURY AND SOME WOMAN AND MAURY'S WIFE, WHO IS LIBBY. SOME STRONG DUMB GUY STARTS TOSSING ABOUT GASOLINE (SPERM?) AND TRIES TO SET ME ON FIRE (SEX?). WHY AM I PRINTING? CHILD-EXPLAINING. DO I WANT A GOOD MARK FOR DREAM TOO? I RUN ACROSS ROOM TO PROTECT MYSELF. HE FINALLY (I THINK) DOES START FIRE. IN NEWSPAPER IT SAID HE HAD HISTORY OF POTENTIALITY FOR THIS. THIS KNOWLEDGE SOMEHOW COMFORTS ME.

CHICKEN—TO BE PUT IN REFRIG. TO BE TURNED OFF SEXUALLY. CHICKEN=SHIKSE.

IST. WHERE MOMMAS HAVE POWER. FOOD.

2ND. WET SLIMY COLD SEXUAL, LIKE A CUNT.

SHOULDN'T CUNT BE WARM? TIRED OF BEING TOLD WHAT
TO DO SO WON'T PUT CHICKEN IN REFRIG. BUT NOBODY
EVER TOLD ME WHAT TO DO. ALWAYS ON OWN. REENACT-
MENT OF EVERYBODY TELLING ME DON'T MARRY LIBBY.
EVERYBODY RIGHT. EVERYBODY WRONG. THIS IS

all beside the point. He put down Asher's drawing pencil; his
head dropped forward on the board. But now he was wide
awake. Chicken equals shikse—so what? Someone is throwing
gasoline around, so what? If he were to understand it all, right
down to his father polishing his shoes in bed—what then? The
problem, Libby, is not psychological. The problem is something else. Why did you have to go to that doctor? "Because I
couldn't take it any more." "Why didn't you at least talk it
over with me? What about this bill?" He was shaking the day's
mail in her face. "Because we don't talk *anything* over." "We
usually talk twenty-five dollars over." "I didn't know it was
twenty-five dollars when I went. I didn't do it again, did I?" "I
don't know, did you?" "No!" "What did you think an analyst
was going to tell you?" "There's something wrong with me,
Paul." "You've been sick—" "What *makes* me sick?" "Germs!
Bugs! Viruses!" "*You!*" she cried. "Then divorce me! Let's get
it over with—" Five and a half years, and it was the first time
that word had been uttered in their house. Libby's face fell,
and his own sense of failure was complete. They had all been
right, Asher, his mother, his— *Impossible!* But he had said the
word at last; it hurt very little to say it again. "Let's get a divorce then." "But you're my *husband*," Libby cried. "Maybe
then that's the trouble—" "It's *me!*" She wept. "Stop crying,
damn it, it's not you." "I don't want a divorce, I want a regular normal life—" "Libby, it's hopeless, it's awful—" "That's
why I went to the *doctor*—"

The phone rang, not back in Chicago, but in New York,
three feet from where he sat. Even before he had raised it to
his ear, he heard the voice starting in. He set it down. It
started to ring again, and he did not bother to lift it this time,
only pressed it down in its cradle. And that was how it went
throughout the afternoon: what little light there was in the
room slipped away, and the phone rang, and at Asher's
drawing board he held down the receiver as though it were a

lid beneath which all the premises of his life were melting away.

———

The next morning Asher had to empty an entire closet to get to an ironing board and an iron. He set up the board by the windows and pressed away at his suit; then he unearthed a clean white shirt and tied his black tie while looking in a mirror over the kitchen sink. Paul slid the breakfast dishes into a pan of water. Asher's reflection showed a grave turn to the mouth, but Paul made no comment; he had been able to induce in himself something that resembled serenity, which would carry him the rest of the way. Perhaps it was a good thing that the turmoil of the day before had worn him down. He had made his decisions in bed with his last ounce of energy; now, so long as he kept his mouth shut and accepted the decisions without airing them to Asher, he could coast on through.

But Asher asked, "What do you have on the agenda?"

Now that his uncle had spoken, Paul realized all the irritation he had been feeling toward the man ever since he had opened his eyes that morning and looked across the room to see Asher sleeping in his bed. He felt the emotion, however, without fully understanding it. "I'll read," he said.

"Maybe you ought to take in a movie. Keep your mind occupied."

"Reading occupies me."

"Go to the museums."

"Maybe I will."

"You don't like museums?"

"Asher, you don't have to be nervous about me."

Asher was back by the closet; he tugged and pulled and finally dove all the way in. Some tubes of paint rolled out across the floor, and Asher emerged beneath a dark hat, an honest-to-God mourner. Old man Herz was dead.

"You feel all right?" he asked, snapping the brim.

"I feel fine."

"You want to walk me to the subway? Get some fresh air? Why don't you put on a jacket and stroll over?"

"Asher, I'm not going to jump out any windows."

"That," said Asher, all dressed up and looking sinister and

pathetic, "that would be a gross misunderstanding of what I've been saying."

"You didn't influence me. You don't have to worry."

"I got the feeling I talked you into something. You walk around here like a young fellow up to no good. Look, it all comes out of the nineteenth century, Paul. It starts in the eighteenth, in fact, way back when. Reason, social progress, reform, right up to the New Deal and Point Four—it all boils down to inordinate guilt about the other fellow—"

"Please."

Asher gave up and started for the door. When he turned to face Paul again, he looked a hundred years old. "Do me a favor, will you? Stroll over with me to Astor Place, that's all. Walk me to the subway. I don't really feel all my strength this morning." It did not seem like a ploy either.

———

They walked north on Third Avenue toward the subway. There was a City Welfare Shelter on one of the cross streets, a brick building with barred windows; just as they passed, all the bums and cripples who had breakfasted there began to make their way out into the sunshine. It was such a brilliant day that some of the unfortunates seemed a little cowed by all the light. But the merciless sun also gave off merciful heat, and after squinting at it, they limped, shuffled, staggered, or trudged out the doorway; one way or another, they all headed uptown, where the money was, and the wine.

In his dark hat and creased trousers Asher must have resembled a wage-earner, for two small men approached. While one assumed a variety of postures which he must have felt to be the attitudes of humility, the other, in a soft voice, made the pitch. "Sir, Mr. Burns and me have just got out of jail, and we're a little nervous." He smiled at Paul but bore down on Asher. "Could you give us a little something, sir, for a starter?"

"Fuck off," Asher told him.

"Thank you, sir, thank you very much, sir."

"Let's cross over," Asher told Paul. Before they could reach the curb, they were accosted twice more. Mr. Burns himself, sagging in the knees, watering in the eyes, stepped forward and made a short speech dealing with his needs. Asher was filled with neither patience nor brotherly love. "Go jerk off. Get out of here you, before I get a cop."

"Yes, sir. Thank you very much, sir."

But as Asher stepped off the curb, Mr. Burns followed and —accidentally or on purpose—caught the heel of Asher's shoe under the toe of his own. Asher turned on the bum, and pointed him wickedly down with one hand. "Where's your self-respect, you dog? You're a disgrace to the poor." He tried to jam his foot back into his shoe. "Why don't you take a bath? Why don't you hide your face?"

"Up your Jewish ass," said Mr. Burns.

Paul was instantly beside Asher, but his uncle pulled away before he could be reached or reasoned with. He had the bum by the collar, shaking him. And then there was a cop and a crowd. Asher's fingers had to be pried loose from the bum by the policeman. The cop stepped on the bum's foot, while Asher straightened his tie. Paul saw tears in his uncle's eyes, as though he were already at the funeral.

"It's nothing, officer," Paul said, forcing his way forward. "It's all right, thank you. Come on, Asher."

"I ought to press charges," said Asher, breathing like a work horse.

"No, no—come on—"

Paul, Asher, the bum, and the cop were all standing inside a circle of rheumy eyes and miserable mouths. Mr. Burns' colleagues seemed torn between staying to see what would happen and getting away before they all wound up in the police wagon. It was as it had been in Paul's dream: he was surrounded by eyes. But he had to get out of this; he had to get started in doing what he was going to do, and in not doing what he wasn't going to do.

"Let's go, Asher. It doesn't matter—"

"What happened?" the cop asked.

"He was panhandling," Asher said. "Begging in the streets without a license."

The bum took issue. "Since when can't you ask for a light?"

"He called me a dirty Jew," Asher said. "The little son of a bitch. The filthy bastard."

"Sir," the bum said, pleading for a little dignity out here

under the broad blue sky. It got a rise from the crowd, and even the cop's face relaxed.

"Why don't you apologize to the man?" the cop said.

"I apologize, sir."

"Okay," Paul said. "That's fine, officer. That's okay. Isn't that all right, Asher?"

"Oh yeah." Asher slid his hat down so that Paul couldn't see his face; he turned and the crowd made room. Just then a young bum with a bowl haircut came rushing up and asked, "What are they making, a movie?"

"Some old bastard—" a shaky voice started to explain, but Paul, yanking his uncle's arm, finally maneuvered him across the street. Neither spoke for a few minutes.

"Nobody," said Asher, "usually bothers me."

"Sure."

"Usually"—there was no keeping the depression out of his voice; were the hat to be pulled down over his ears, it couldn't hide the truth—"usually I'm not so dolled up." They were passing a little concrete stoop in front of a church; Asher stopped. "I'm not used to that kind of excitement. Wait a minute." He still breathed heavily and noisily, as though he were sucking up liquid through a straw. "How about you?"

"I'm fine."

"Well, I got to sit down," Asher said, holding his side.

Paul remained standing, waiting for his uncle to regain strength. Asher looked up from where he had dropped on the church steps. "You want to hear a long story?"

"Aren't you going to be late?"

"I never told this to a soul. You want to hear it or not?"

Traffic had slowed on the street; across the way the bums they had left a block behind were passing before them. Asher dismissed them with a dirty gesture. Then he said, "This is all about how I got married and had my only child. Sit down a minute. I have to catch my wind."

Why had he not camped with his Uncle Jerry? His sympathy for Asher, worn to a frazzle, now disappeared completely. "What is this, Asher, another fairy tale?"

"What happened. Exactly *as* it happened. Fact."

"Well, I didn't know you'd been married."

"In Chicago, your wonderful Chicago. Long ago, Paulie."
Asher tilted his hat so that he could see his nephew. "Sit down.
This is when I was a student—"

"Asher, I've got business today."

But he got such a curious look for that remark that he did sit
down. What right, Asher's eyes said, do you have to give *me*
the rush act? "When I was a student, Paulie, at the Art Institute, remember? And there was a dark bushy-haired woman
taking a course there. She hadn't a grain of talent in her, this
babe, and she was one of the dumbest persons I have ever met,
before or since. But you know the way certain vulgar women
are very stirring? Do you appreciate this?"

"I suppose so."

"So I got interested in her, and got her nice and pregnant—
and I forgot to mention she was already a married lady. And to
a full-scale Chicago gangster, wanted all over, and carrying
dangerous weapons, and the works, believe me. This is 1926.
Every afternoon outside the Institute, hiding behind the lions,
he placed killers, honest to God, to wipe me out. In those days
it was nothing to wipe somebody out, of course. Just wipe
them right out and nobody raised a peep. I used to walk out
with Annette in front of me for protection. What else could I
do? This is a fact, Paul. Let's see how brave somebody else
would have been in those circumstances. I changed my place
of residence six different times, till finally she tells her husband
that she wants to marry me. That's the only way I could figure
to save my life—I proposed. And what happens then is that he
agrees, but with a couple of nice conditions thrown in. It turns
out he didn't like her any more than he liked me, so for him it
was perfect. I forgot to say, Annette, whose large foibles I was
rapidly becoming more and more aware of—this happens in a
crisis—was already the mother of four children, all under six
years of age. One of the conditions was that we take up residence in Cicero, quite a place as you know, so he can come
visit with his kiddies there every Sunday. For him it was ideal.
One day a week he fills up the tank, slaps on a couple handfuls
of after-shave lotion, and takes them for a nice ride in the
country. I took over the running of all the errands. He gave
a check for his kids, and I did the shopping, the sizing, the
wiping up after, and so on. I moved to Cicero—"

"Asher, you're making this up. I'm not in the mood. Please," he said, standing up, "not today."

"Fact!" Asher reprimanded him. "Hard fact. *My* life for a change!" He slammed his foot on the concrete. "*Please* yourself! I gave up my schooling, Paulie, and I moved into this brute's bed—you listening? He even left me an old frayed dressing gown, all gold and shoulder pads, to slip into at bedtime. And soon we had a little son of our own. Annette gave up her painting, but not much of a loss to the arts, my friend, not like me giving it up, believe me. So this brought the grand total in the house to seven, four of us with stool in our diaper regular. And Annette always in her nightie, with ashes dribbling down, breakfast, lunch, and dinner. Under a lamppost outside was posted a fellow with a sour expression to keep me strictly in line, just like in the movies. Every time I spend a penny he records it in his little notebook. How do you like that? Jot, jot, with his tongue between his teeth—he could hardly write, the dumb ox. The idea was that I shouldn't have any pocket change for myself at the end of the week. This hoodlum used to drive alongside me in his car to the A&P, Paul. He used to wait outside the shoemaker and the candy store, till we got to nod hello, how do you do, to each other. But one night I sneaked out, Paul—you want to stand there, you stand there, I'm telling *you* the facts of *my* life. One night out I sneaked, under cover of darkness, and I went to live awhile in various Western towns, and then finally I moved a little bit east at a time, by way of the south, and finally New York. A harrowing experience. But *tout passe*, you follow me? Even if we have to help it along. Out of such experiences I welded a vision of life, I came to understand the highest law of them all, that even the little animals in the forest don't even have to be told. Self-preservation!"

He stood up, shaking out his legs. "The son-of-a-bitch little bum," he mumbled, and then he and his nephew exchanged a glance. Afterwards their gaze dropped to the pavement. Any embarrassment they felt had not to do with the truth or falsity of Asher's story, but with some plot that the two of them seemed to share.

From the church steps to Astor Place they said nothing. There was a crowd around the subway entrance; businessmen hurried into banks on two corners, and Village housewives swarmed around the supermarket. The rushing and scurrying made Paul even more certain that he and Asher were somehow accomplices. They might have been about to rob the Chemical Corn Bank across the street. Asher said, "The movies on Forty-second Street are open all day."

"I told you I wouldn't jump out of any windows."

"Then what then?"

It was not out of trust or love for Asher that once again he told him a secret; it was simply that he was thrown in with him. "I'm going to look for a job."

"Is that the plan you woke up with? Does that explain the silence?"

"I suppose so."

"Because," his uncle said, reaching into his jacket, "I don't want to influence you unduly. This decision of yours." From his pocket he took a dark tie like the one he himself was wearing. "There's a little thief downstairs from me that sells everything. I bought two. You want to come?"

Paul's hand was smacking his forehead. "Asher, what are you trying to do? Tempt? Tease? What, *test me*? Haven't things been difficult enough without this? Do you consider this a helpful suggestion?"

"I only think," said Asher, not so definite about himself, "you should do what you want to do."

"What do you think—" Several shoppers turned to look at him; he lowered his voice. "What do you think I've been sweating my insides out about since I got here? Put that tie away, will you? Get it away! What's the matter with you!"

"I don't know," Asher said. "A funeral . . . I might have talked too much." He rolled the tie up into a ball. "I don't want to be responsible for your flying in the face of your real nature."

"My real nature," Paul said, exercising immense control, "is just what I'm expressing. Put the tie away, *please!*"

"It's away. Calm yourself." When he moved into the mouth of the stairway leading down to the subway, Paul didn't follow. Asher asked, "What kind of job are you getting?"

"A high-paying one."

"That's your real nature?"

"Let me map it out for you," Paul said. "You and I are different types. Let's keep that straight."

"Granted—"

"I can't preserve only myself. That's not what I want to do. I'm going to have to preserve my wife too. She's a helpless girl without a lot of strength, you understand? I took away her youth from her—don't stop me, don't interrupt. My leaving is going to be a big blow despite all the horror we have had together. She's going to need psychoanalysis—don't stop me, *please.*" But Asher had only been showing him a pair of skeptical eyes. "Whatever you think is beside the point anyway. If she thinks she needs one, then I'll give her one, and put her on her feet, and then maybe someday *I'll* be through and free and get some peace. I'll get a high-paying job and I'll send money every week, and we'll live separate lives, and that's my way of working things out. You work your life out one way—"

"What could I do with five kids?"

"I'm not *questioning* anything!" In talking they had moved down the stairs and stood now in the grim half-light. Trains rushing through the station beneath them whisked candy wrappers up against their cuffs. Paul was all but pleading. "You work your life out one way, I work mine out another. I've figured this all out, Asher, and maybe I'll be a better man for it. A happier one." But he could not help sighing. Was Asher a happy man for what he had worked out? He swallowed and tried to harden his insides. "Today is the day for acting things out. It's a crucial day and it's not gotten off to a good start. To tell you the truth, I don't know why you had to taunt that bum, for one thing—"

"I don't approve of begging," said Asher sharply. There was another rush beneath them, and until the noise passed they had to stand silently facing each other. And Paul realized that he despised this uncle of his—as much as Asher had despised that bum. An equation began to work itself out while that interminable train roared north: he was to Asher as Asher to the bum—

"—public nuisance. Shouldn't be allowed—"

"Nobody likes begging," Paul said. "I didn't think that was the point."

"We don't share the same attitude about human needs. I,

for instance, wouldn't worry about my ex-wife's psychoanalysis. I wouldn't consider that cutting the bonds."

Asher tried to move down a step, but Paul was holding on to his sleeve. Now they could both see into the change booth, where a Negro was reading a book. "It's not easy, Asher, giving birth to yourself all over again at twenty-seven. I'm cutting plenty of bonds, don't kid yourself. Plenty. Look at you," he said, holding his uncle. "Even you feel obliged still to go to my father's funeral. Isn't that right? If you were all you claim you were, or are, why bother?" That off his chest, he felt in the right; since he had watched Asher ironing his suit at eight in the morning, he had wanted to say it. "Why bother with ceremonies or institutions or anything?"

"Funerals give a sharper edge to myself. In a funeral yard I often arrive at further refinements in my quest for self-understanding."

"That isn't where people usually go to get a better grip on the objective facts."

"Another thing that separates me from people." A train had pulled into the station, and Asher was waving an arm at it and running.

Paul charged after him, and, despite the people nearby, he called, "What about your mother's plants, Asher—what about —Asher, you're going because nobody cuts all—" But Asher had slid safely behind the subway doors.

The crumb! The saboteur! The sloppy—

But he left off with condemnations, experience having taught him that what he chose to curse in others was sometimes what he was not much at home with in himself. He raced up the stairs and, in the sunlight again, headed for Cooper Union. He made another effort at hardening himself in the area between his neck and his groin. Alas, he succeeded. Jesus! He was getting better at it. What a thing—he thought, having a light philosophical moment while boarding the Madison Avenue bus—is a man.

———

In the Fifties, one could not see the sidewalk for the shoppers. While lights changed, he stood beneath a clock and tried to figure out exactly what to do. He crossed in the next swarm forward and made his way into a luncheonette, where he had a cup of coffee. When he was finished, the empty cup gave him something to stare into. There were two sets of events to contemplate: Libby waking alone in Chicago, and what was happening in Brooklyn. Absent from both he nevertheless saw both unraveling at the bottom of his cup. The counter girl came along with the Silex pot and poured, wiping out his imaginings. He rose and made his way to the telephone booth at the end of the counter.

In the Yellow Pages he found a longer list under "Employment Agencies" than he had expected. The length of the list set him back for at least two minutes. Finally he settled on writing down the names of all the agencies beginning with A and B. He also wrote down a name beginning with S, so as not to narrow his chances, then closed the book and left the store.

Neither his gait nor his expression revealed anything other than sternness and decision. As he walked he leaned forward at a sharper angle than the men around him; everybody seemed younger than himself—though that, of course, was illusion. What hair he had left, it was true, he wore longer than the others, and his suit did not come up to theirs for style and newness. He felt out of his element.

Yet within an hour he apparently had a job. It was amazing, for he had not really envisioned success. He had imagined that it was all going to be demoralizing and enervating, just as at first he had imagined himself sweating out his decision in some fetid hotel rather than on Asher's uncomfortable but unfetid sofa. He had seen the weeks ahead given over not to work but to the searching after it. But here he was back out in the reception room, while inside his office the man who had interviewed him was on the phone with a trade-magazine editor in need of somebody to write copy about the paint and wallpaper industries. He would be an associate editor. Sixty-eight hundred a year; thirty-four hundred for Libby, an equal amount for himself. All right, four thousand for Libby. There would be raises; he would manage somehow; he could live in one room. Will!

Quickly he made some plans. He would get a cheap room. He would keep a budget. Before being interviewed by the editor, he would make a quick stop at the Fifth Avenue library and look up paint and wallpaper in the encyclopedia, just to be

on the ball. He would continue to lie—he was not married, he
had been in Europe for the last year—

Sitting, waiting, in the reception room of the employment
office, he asked himself a question: Where am I?

What am I doing here, now?

At first he was only going down to the men's room to get a
grip on himself. Passing the water cooler he wished he had a
pill to pop into his mouth. He was suffering from a momentary feeling of displacement—the new-job jitters, a pheno barb
could handle it. But he had no pills with him, having no faith
in solutions of that kind. It was his wife who would try anything. He drank some water, but all he felt of it was what slid
down the pipe to his stomach; there was no draining off, no
sudden flowering of his sense of reality.

When he turned, wiping his mouth, he found that there was
a smile waiting for him from the receptionist. Are you single?
Are you romantically inclined? Do you like me? That was all
included in the smile, which he now returned. A stunning
healthy girl with a wonderful chest. What skin . . . But for all
its smoothness, the skin of the receptionist was no more solace
to him than the water. Instead of walking right up and starting
a conversation, he walked by her and into the Down elevator.
On the main floor he stepped out into the street. Fresh air. But
all it did was move over his skin. Between where the water
slid and what could be touched by a pleasant June day, he was
still in a state of disequilibrium. He was in the wrong place.
He began pacing up and down in the shadow of the office
building, exercising his legs as though they were the props of
his will. Will! *Force yourself back!* He summoned up all his
strength, once, twice, but it didn't work. Perhaps what he
should do was walk to a Western Union office and send a
telegram. What would Libby do when he didn't come home?
What had she done already? He had better telephone. Hear
her voice and hang up. So long as she was not dead.

A taxi passed just then, and he waved an arm at it. His impulse had been to do something—telegram, telephone—and
what he did was get into the cab. If there had been a phone
hanging in the middle of the street he would doubtless have
lifted it, asked for Chicago, and then waited for the voice of his

wife. But instead of a phone there was the cab. He held his head in his hands all the way to Brooklyn.

Three blocks from the cemetery he asked the driver to let him out. When he paid and tipped the fellow, the feel of the change in his palm gave him a start. He would return to the agency in the afternoon, he would say he had suddenly been taken ill. Further, he would try to make a date with the receptionist. He would even buy some pills to help him through the next week or so. What did it hurt? This was no time to be stolid. He would get a new suit with a conservative cut to it. He would wind up looking like Wallach himself. He would change over, why not? He would send Libby a telegram. A letter.

He thought and thought, short, crisp, forward-looking thoughts, while he walked toward the cemetery. After all, he did not even have to go inside the place. He wanted only to catch a glimpse of the proceedings to be convinced that it had really happened.

Yes, this was a necessary, a symbolic trip for him. He was bringing (he phrased it carefully in his mind as he slid furtively along the fence surrounding the graveyard), he was bringing the first part of his life to a formal conclusion. He would see his father lowered into the ground, covered up, and that would be that. A man's father dies only once, and regardless of their misunderstandings . . . no, that wasn't precisely what had drawn him here, though that was in it. Actually it didn't really make any difference to him, or to anybody, whether he was present or not. Staying away would, in fact, give to the event more weight than it deserved, make of his father a martyr—no, no, that wasn't precisely so. If his coming to the cemetery meant anything—he let his lids close over his eyes, for he was exhausted—it was that he wanted to go back to Libby and give it one last try . . . No! He did not want to go back to Libby! As solutions went that was the *most* unrealistic. The trouble was that she had already picked out a name for the baby, the trouble was a father dies only—

Cramped in the bushes, peering between the iron pickets, he heard the word *trouble* thumping away in his head. In the distance, midway between the fence and the railroad tracks that bound the cemetery at the far side, he saw the mourners standing in the sunlight. The day kept getting bluer and bluer, and the sun rose and rose, and around him the gravestones glittered. Behind was a long line of automobiles, none of which he recognized. Wasn't it his father being buried? Was he hiding needlessly? But time had passed—of course, everyone owned a new car. He looked back into the light. Where was the coffin? Was it over—the old man covered up? Then chapter one was history.

He tried to feel relief. He rose on stiffened legs, telling himself he would now start fresh. But inside the cemetery men were taking the arms of the women and helping them along. He couldn't be sure; were these *his* relatives? He edged along the fence, holding branches down so they would not flick back at him. He had to see just one pair of familiar eyes, and then he'd make a break for it, off and away into his new life. However, all the men were wearing hats and all the women holding handkerchiefs to their faces, and what made recognition even more difficult was the brightness, the luminosity of the day—

He was out in the open. Where was the fence? Gone! Weaving along the paths, swaying around swollen burial plots, they were headed his way. And he was in the gateway. Almost at his back—the whiff first, then the sad sight—was a hearse full of flowers. A death had taken place. The thought penetrated into him all the way.

There were several choices open to Paul that moment; it was not because all the paths of escape were blocked that, instead of moving out, he moved in. He could have run away, or simply walked away, but he moved in because *in* was the direction of his life. In and in and in, past all kinds of tombstones, fancy ones, plain ones, old ones, past memorials to cherished mothers and beloved fathers, faithful husbands and dutiful wives, and even little children, whose dates told the whole miserable story. Levine's youngster, 1900–1907. Rappaport's child, 1926–1931. Abraham's child, 1929–1940. Born the same year as Paul. Drowned? Run over? Meningitis?

Dates. Names. Flowers. Above, the sun. All came at him with sharpness and clarity. He saw now where he had misread. Not Abrahams. Abrams. Abraham's child was Isaac. Here were interred the bones of Abrams, his contemporary. The thought seized him. He moved in and in, and then up ahead he saw a figure moving out and out, toward him. But his mind was occupied with the mystery of Abrams' death and his own survival. Little Abrams catching spinal meningitis or diphtheria, himself skinning through on only German measles. Lucky him. Unlucky Abrams. *Isaac*, he thought . . . Every gravestone that he saw had a date on the right to go with the date on the left. That fact caused his knees to shake. Justice, will, order, change—the words whistled by him, windless as the day was, like spirits moving off in the opposite direction. Dates. Names. Flowers. Sky. Only facts of history and of nature had meaning. The rest was invention.

So in he moved, in, and then he saw the faces. Yes, there that wicked mouth of his father's sister, his Aunt Gertie's mouth. There a pair of sad blue eyes, more blue than sad: his simpleton cousin, the all-Brooklyn basketball star Harvey. The black hair of his beautiful cousin Clare. The soft hands of his Uncle Jerry. There in circles of fat, Maury; in black beside him, Doris. They were all clear to him; but at the center, a trick of the atmosphere, or of his senses, there was a haze, just a haze rushing toward him. He heard a cry—his name! Oh, and Asher. There was Asher. And what did Asher understand of anything? What had he understood himself? Who was the fellow in the black coat? Lichtman, who would not marry him to Libby? Who was—

No one moved, just himself, and what rushed to meet him: a figure in black. And now at last he saw who that was too, yes, and now he closed his eyes and opened his arms and what he saw next was his life—he saw it for the sacrifice that it was. Isaac under the knife, Abraham wielding it. *Both!* While his mother kissed his neck and moaned his name, he saw his place in the world. Yes. And the world itself—without admiration, without pity. Yes! Oh yes! What he saw filled him for a moment with strength. Not that in a sweep of forgiving he could kiss that face that now kissed him; it was not that which he had seen. He kissed nothing—only held out his arms, open, and stood still at last, momentarily at rest in the center of the storm through which he had been traveling all these years. For his truth was revealed to him, his final premise melted away. What he had taken for order was chaos. Justice was illusion.

Abraham and Isaac were one. His eyes opened, and in the midst of those faces—the faces of his dream, the faces of the bums, all the faces that had forever encircled him—he felt no humiliation and no shame. Their eyes no longer overpowered him. He felt himself under a wider beam.

2

U SUALLY that summer we swam off the rocks at Fifty-fifth Street. We became friendly with other couples—some married, some like ourselves—and spent long Saturdays and Sundays on the tiers of rock that led down to cool Lake Michigan, talking and sunning and offering around sandwiches and white wine out of our straw hamper. I had bought the picnic hamper at Abercrombie's as a gift for Martha, a commemoration of the Fourth of July, our first time in bathing suits together, and certainly a milestone for any American boy and his American girl.

Martha was employed now at the University as secretary to Claude Delsey, the director of the summer quarter, and, at last, had weekends off and nights free. Some months earlier she had wrapped her two waitress uniforms in brown paper, tied the package with a string and given it to her cleaning lady, Annie LaSmith. Then, with her first University pay check in her purse, she had gone off to Marshall Fields and bought three summer dresses to wear to the office: one lavender, one pale blue, and the third, my favorite, an apricot color, with a wide square neck and a pleated skirt. The following week she bought shoes, two strands of pearls, and a pair of white gloves; and then one day when Delsey was out of town, she took a few hours off in the afternoon and went up to the Near North Side, from which she returned with her hair whirled up in an intricate and elegant coiffure. She looked quite stunning, even if not entirely like herself, but in bed that night she had to wear a silk stocking over her head for protection. I complained that her headpiece had a debilitating effect upon my passions, but she said that passion was out of the question anyway—she had to lie perfectly still. Fortunately, the hairdo was beginning to sag the next day at breakfast, by lunchtime was lopsided, and by dinner beyond repair; a little after midnight she crawled in close beside me again, bareheaded.

I suppose there were times when she was really very happy, and when our life together would have seemed, to someone strolling beneath our open window on a summer night, peaceful and comfortable and serene: Martha, in shorts and a sleeveless blouse, stretched out on the sofa drinking iced coffee and reading a book; I in the chair across from her, with a yellow pad on my knee, scribbling notes for an American literature course I was to teach in the fall . . . It was a pleasant July, especially for Chicago. Whenever it threatened to turn muggy and hot, the clouds would pile up at dinnertime and a thunderstorm would clear the air and leave the city smelling like the country, and the streets perfect for a long walk over to the campus. There, with the trees damp and full and glittering in the early moonlight, the only sound was the comforting one of the night watchman going around and shaking the handles on the doors of the empty buildings. "In the fall I think I'm going to take a course," Martha told me. "Delsey said it's okay with him." "What course?" I asked. "I'm not sure yet. I went over to the Administration Building and checked—if I take one course a quarter for the next two years I can get my B.A." "Then what?" I asked. "Then," she said, "I'll have it."

On some nights the electrical storm did not come until very late, sometimes not till the early hours of the morning. Then the thunder, rumbling in and breaking over the city, would awaken the two of us, and we would lie under our thin sheet, silent but quite awake. Martha would reach over and flick the radio on, and then light a cigarette, while in the dark we listened to the dance music which crackled from time to time with the storm. When the cigarette had been smoked all the way down and the thunder had moved from over our heads, we would roll our different ways and go back to sleep.

The weekends, however, were all blue skies and sunshine, and out on the rocks we must surely have looked as cheery as the next couple. We never missed a Saturday or a Sunday; we were there by eleven in the morning, and even at sundown, with half our newspapers blown away and our books still unopened, with a hamper full of cookie crumbs and wax paper and banana skins, we generally stayed on, after the others had drifted home, to watch the rosy dusk move in over the lake. Martha was particular during these months never to allow herself to feel rushed about anything; she stayed where she felt like staying just as long as she felt like staying there—except, of course, on those Sunday nights when we packed up early and were home and by the telephone promptly at six. For it was at six, twice a month, that she placed her call to Long Island, where Cynthia and Markie were spending their summer. And late on those Sunday afternoons there would invariably be a moment—I am pulling Martha by the hand up out of the water, I am just about to pour wine into her cup—when by the lake front it would become for us as it was in bed on those nights we were awakened by the thunder: What I feel Martha feeling toward me, what I know myself to be feeling toward her, is hate.

—

On the last Saturday of July I received a letter from my father telling me that he and Fay Silberman had set a date for their wedding. It was not to be until Christmas, but Mrs. Silberman was going off in September to visit her children in California, and both the affianced had agreed that she should give some definite word to her sons and daughters-in-law out on the west coast, for they would have to begin to make plans about what to do with their children when they came East in December for the wedding. I read the letter several times that morning, and carried it in my trouser pocket when Martha and I went down to the lake. That evening, when I slipped my trousers on over my bathing suit, I took the letter out and read it again. This time I could not manage to be merely resigned; resignation became gloom.

"Will it be large and fancy?" Martha asked.

"I suppose just the family. Her children and me. He doesn't really say."

"Well, Christmas is a long way off."

"Still, it sounds definite." I looked back to the letter for some reason my father might have given to explain having decided *now* for Christmas—a reason, that is, other than Mrs. Silberman's wanting to give her family plenty of time to ready baby-sitters. But there were no reasons, only more news. "He's going to spend August out at her summer place, he says."

"You think that's what he's after—summer vacations?"

"I think he's marrying her because, one, she's pressing him, and two, he's lonely and doesn't know what else to do. But I know he's been putting it off. They've been engaged since last Thanksgiving. He's not sure himself."

"Where's her summer place?"

I turned to the letter again. For all my readings of it, it was amazing how few of the words written in that large open hand I could manage to keep in my mind. "East Hampton. He says I'm invited too. To get to know her."

Martha was putting on her shorts over her white suit. It was not until she had zipped up the side and fastened the button that she turned back to me. "Why don't you go?"

I answered as casually as she had asked. "Because I'm here."

"I thought you might want to get away for a while, that's all."

Earlier in the afternoon, Martha's lightheartedness had amused both Bill Lake and Frank Tozier, who, having stopped to visit for a few minutes, had wound up camped on our blanket for several hours, eating out of our basket. Now what could be seen of the lightheartedness was only the residue—the irritating part of the frivolity, the unconvincing part of the offhandedness. What with still trying to comprehend my father's decision, I myself had no reserves of patience and sense, and I said, "Now what's the matter?"

"Nothing." She put a towel over her shoulders and sat down and looked out across the lake where a last water-skier was flying over the surface. "I just thought that if you wanted to see your father, you should certainly feel that you can."

"Well, I feel that I can, if I want to."

"What about Theresa's baby?"

"What about it?"

"Don't you have to wait for it to come?"

"I don't understand what that has to do with anything, Martha. Did I seem to you to express a desire to go East and have a talk with my father? I didn't mean to. What would I say? What is there *to* say? Last November he bought her a nice big ring and now they've set the date, and now he's going out to the seashore with her. He's entitled to his pleasures, if those are what he thinks they are."

She took her watch from her pocket and when she put it on her wrist, I saw her look at the time.

"Would you like to leave?" I asked.

". . . No. It's lovely now."

"Martha, are you asking me why I don't go East, why I don't do something about him?"

"No."

"Because there's nothing to do."

"All I meant to say," she said, smiling, "is that if you want to see your father, or, I don't know, visit anybody, I don't want you to think that you're tied down here. That's all. If something were to come up—"

"You want me to go somewhere?"

"That isn't what I said."

"Then what's depressing you?"

"Your father's setting the date, I suppose. I suppose I'm only sharing your feelings."

"Yes," I said, "and what more?"

"Nothing." She smiled again, then shrugged. "I just felt like calling the kids. I don't any more."

"Don't be silly. We'll go home, you can call them." The idea gave me my first real lift in hours.

"It's not Sunday."

"What's the difference? It's getting chilly here anyway."

"I think I'd rather stay."

"All right. We'll stay." I put the letter back into my pocket; tonight or tomorrow I would have to write some sort of answer —send my congratulations, my approval, my *blessings*. The hell with it.

A few seconds passed before I realized that I had spoken those last few words out loud. Martha leaned her head back on the rocks so that her loose hair was spread around her. I saw her mouth move and barely restrained myself from reaching out and placing my hand across it. I did not care to be told again that I had her permission to go East if I so desired.

She said, "Is East Hampton on Long Island?"

"Yes."

"Near Springs?"

"Springs is out there too, I think." Springs was the name of the town to which she placed her phone calls twice a month. "I don't know exactly where. Do you have any idea how far out it is?"

"I'm not sure."

"I think I have a New York map in the car."

"It's not important," she said.

"Martha, if you want to call tonight, why don't you?"

She answered sharply. "Because I don't want to!"

"It was simply a suggestion," I said.

She rose then, picked up the comb that was on the blanket, and started off down along the rocks. She was pulling the comb absentmindedly through her hair as she disappeared around the edge of the cove. A little time passed, and then she was back.

She dropped the comb onto my toes. "I'm not going to give in to myself. Okay?"

"At the risk of your getting angry again, I don't think you should think of it as giving in to yourself."

"Don't you?" she asked dubiously.

"Forget it."

"I'm sorry," she said, kneeling beside me, "I'm just suddenly having a bad day." She took my hand.

"I shouldn't have brought out that letter half a dozen times either. I depressed everybody."

"You have a right to your troubles."

"They're not even new troubles—they're old ones. Whatever could have been done had to have been done a long time ago. And I don't even know what that was. The hell with it."

"You said that already."

"What is it, Martha? I thought you were happy today. You told all those jokes, you were even nice and loud, sweetheart—"

"I was. Happy, I mean. I am happy. I just thought before that today was Sunday, and then I realized it's only Saturday."

"There's no law that says you can only dial New York on Sundays."

"There is," she said. "I made it."

If that was the way she wanted it, that's the way it would have to be. But I could not escape feeling that if she did call her children, we might have a more pleasant evening in store for us. Though that was to reason directly in the face of past experience—whenever Martha put the phone back down on the hook, it took us some time before we could look each other in the eye. "Well," I said, feeling nagged at and naggy, "Sunday's tomorrow anyway."

"Right. I'll call then."

But she became bluer and bluer. "Should I get the map?" I asked. "Do you want just to see how far Springs is from East Hampton—?"

"Let's sit here and enjoy the view."

"Because you could come East *with* me. How does that sound? We'll stay with my father and Mrs. Silberman. I'm sure they'd like it. I'd like it."

"I just started work."

"Delsey wouldn't mind. Tell him you're going to visit your children."

"You don't even know whether or not Springs is close."

"The whole stretch of island is only a hundred miles."

"I'll be all right. I'll call tomorrow."

"Why don't you call tonight if you want to."

"Why don't you let me decide for myself!" She got up and jumped down two levels of rocks until she was standing at the water's edge, her back to me.

"Whatever you decided," I called down after her, "you decided for yourself!"

She turned only her head. "Oh did I?"

That was the exchange, brief but to the point.

She made her way back to the blanket later and said, "I'm just having a few bad hours." She put her hand on mine again. "It's simply a matter of keeping control."

"Would you like to have a drink?" I touched her arm, and when she moved toward me willingly, I touched her face. "Would you like to go home and take a shower and get dressed? We'll go out to dinner someplace where it's cool—"

"It's too beautiful now. I want to stay."

"Whatever you want," I said.

"Gabe, really, though," she said in a moment, "if you want to take a little trip . . . Nobody who doesn't have to stay in Chicago for a whole summer should be allowed to feel that he must."

"I don't *want* to take a trip!"

"Okay then, it's just an academic discussion. They're nice to have too," she said, but I wasn't charmed.

Or softened, or forgiving. "Though sometimes you're able to convince me that a trip wouldn't be a bad idea."

"Then—"

"Then what?" I demanded.

"Nothing . . . I didn't say it, see? The better part of wisdom is to be short on suggestions," she said, with a cold look on her face.

"Is that directed against me by any chance, that remark? I don't know that I've made any suggestions to you."

"You're a suggestion," she said, flatly.

"I'm terribly sorry about that."

"You're not."

"No, I'm not. I never made any promises."

"I said you were a suggestion, not a promise."

"Oh Christ, let's stop this. Why don't you come East with me? We'll go together—that's right, this is an outright suggestion—and you can see the kids—"

"Right now," she said, standing and patently ignoring my remarks, "you know what I'd like to do? First, I too would like us to stop being accusative—imperative, whatever it is we are. Two, I'd like to get home and take that shower; and three, I'd like to go out to dinner, some place where we can eat outside."

"We could drive East in a day."

"Delsey needs me now."

"Delsey has a big heart. Tell him why you're going."

"I don't think it would really be a good idea."

I got up too and put on my shirt. "If that's what you want."

As we started toward the car, she said, "But don't think you can't go—"

"I don't."

———

At home Martha said she wanted to pin up her hair, and she asked would I take the first shower. When I was finished I stepped onto the bath mat and opened the door an inch to let the steam out. Martha was on the phone, saying to the operator that she had been cut off again. She hung up and the phone rang; she picked it immediately off the receiver. I pushed open the door another few inches.

"Hello—hello, Dick? It's Martha again. We were cut off. I said we were cut off—we still have a lousy connection. . . . How are the kids doing? . . . And Markie? . . . Are they in, can I talk to them? . . . I know it's Saturday . . . What! . . . Well, can't you wake them up? . . . For Christ's sake, Dick, I'm their mother—what? . . . I said I'm their *mother*, I'm calling long distance . . . I *know* it's an hour later—will you please wake them up! . . . Then let them sleep late in the morning—*please*, this is costing money. . . . Okay, okay, yes. . . ." Silence. Then, "Hello—hello, Cynthia? Honey, it's Mother . . . *Mother*—what's wrong with this connection! Cynthia, baby, can you hear me? Come on, try to wake up. Rub your eyes or something—Mark, is that you? . . . Speak louder, darling. Speak into the phone . . . Cynthia, Cynthia, are you still there? Speak into the phone, darlings. Look, how are you? . . . Did you go swimming today? . . . I said, *Did you go swimming today?* Cynthia, let him talk—what? . . . Cynthia, sweetie, why don't you write? . . . Well, *ask* him for paper. . . . Of course he'll give you paper. . . . Where are all your envelopes I gave you with the address on them? . . . What? . . . Who left them where? I can't hear you if you both talk. . . . Oh children, stop arguing, please, this is long—what? . . . Of course, darling, you send it, I'd love to see it. . . . Stephanie is fine, uh-huh. . . . Cynthia, *please*, it doesn't matter if he hasn't finished it. You send it anyway. Okay, operator, fine . . . Cynthia, you write, do you hear me? And watch your brother in the water. . . . Are you both all right? Do you need anything? . . . That's fine. . . . He's here, honey. No, dear, no, no. . . . Goodbye, honey—look, let me talk to your daddy—Mark? *Markie?* Let me—hello? Is anybody there . . . ?"

She put the phone back on the hook, I turned the knob on the bathroom door and closed it.

While Martha was taking her shower the phone rang again. Later, when she came out of the shower, wrapped in a towel, I said nothing to her about my phone call, just as she had said nothing to me about hers. At first I was secretive out of a feeling that enough had happened for one day. But then sitting in the living room, waiting for her to dress, I wondered if I was not trying to spare Martha the possibility of feeling an ugly, an inappropriate emotion. Given our conversation at the lake and the phone call to Long Island, her response to my news might not be tonight what it would doubtless be in the morning.

It had become warmer all at once, and I sat without my jacket, my feet up on the window sill, watching the storm clouds begin to fill the sky over Fifty-fifth Street. Soon it started to rain and thunder, and grow darker. I sat in the dark with no light until a small lamp was flipped on behind me. I turned; Martha had come into the room, ready for dinner. The light was soft and fell in a flattering way upon the dress she was wearing; I could not remember having seen it before.

"You're looking beautiful," I said to her.

She remained standing where she was. "Thank you."

"A blond girl," I said, "with a suntan and her hair up—"

"And in a new white sharkskin dress."

"It's very lovely."

"See my shoes?"

"They're nice. It's all very lovely."

"I've never worn them before."

"Maybe we should wait until it stops raining."

"All right." She sat down across from me and put her gloves on the little end table.

After a moment I asked, "Would you like a drink?"

But she didn't seem to have heard. "This is what I wanted," she said softly.

"Yes," I said.

"And I like it—do you know that?"

"I thought you did."

"All that sun and the water and the peace, and then a man in a fresh batiste shirt and a silk tie waiting for me in the living room so we can go to dinner. Even the rain, even the thunder."

"We'll go as soon as it lets up."

After a while there was a jagged lightning streak across the sky, and a crash, and our one little lamp went out; in the kitchen the refrigerator stopped humming.

"It'll go on in a minute," I said.

"I called the kids," Martha told me.

"Did you?"

I could see only her white dress in the dark and her white shoes. "When you were in the shower," she said.

"How are they?"

"Markie left all his envelopes in the rest room of a Texaco station. But they sounded fine . . . Gabe?"

"Yes."

"I think if you go East you better go alone."

"You want me to go though?"

"A little time apart," she said, after a moment, "might not hurt."

"Will it help?"

"What's to be helped?"

"You're the one, I thought, who'd been indicating that we're at some sort of crisis."

"I don't think we are," she said.

"I didn't think so either."

"I told you I liked it. It was an agreeable day. I did laugh."

The light went on, and Martha stopped speaking; and I was moved, even made lustful in a curious self-contained way, by the cold beauty she radiated.

"You look very voluptuous and healthy in that dress," I said, "and in control."

"When we come home we'll make love. Not now."

"You're being very gallant, Martha, and very self-possessed tonight."

"Oh I know."

Suddenly she wearied me. "I think the storm's rather laid a pall on me."

"Let's go then," she said. "I'll cheer you up. Plus my suntan and my blond hair and my self-possession, I am also a lot of laughs."

"Theresa Haug had her baby," I said.

"What?"

"Libby called. Sid called her. She had a baby girl."

"When did she call?"

"While you were in the shower."

"And you weren't going to tell?"

"I thought I'd save it."

"It sounds as though the news depresses you."

"It leaves me feeling peculiarly washed-out, Martha." Which was true; I found myself having something like the reaction I had feared for Martha. I couldn't understand it.

"Aren't you happy?" she asked.

"I suppose I am. Libby was very excited. I just feel played out. That's all."

"We can sit here a while longer, if you want."

So we sat there, while outside the storm slowly rolled away. "I suppose," I said, "I should have a feeling of accomplishment."

"Do you?"

"No."

"Then what?"

"Of being unnecessary."

She did not say anything, and I could not tell if it was clear to her that the strange feeling I had was envy, envy for the Herzes.

"Just old fleeting depression," I said.

"I understand."

"This comes," I hurried to say, "on top of my father's letter—"

"Yes?"

"—and," I said, "my overhearing your conversation with the kids." So my two secrets were out. Why not?

"Oh," she said. And then, "Well, what was the difference? You were taking a shower. It was as good a time as any."

"The difference is obviously that you didn't want me to know that you wanted to call, that you *had* called. That you had broken down, given in, or however it is you choose to put it."

"You didn't want me to know the Herzes had a baby. So we're even."

Even, we sat back in our chairs. Until I asked, "How long do you think we're going to be able to keep this kind of business up?"

"I suppose something will happen some day."

"I don't know what."

She understood. "I don't care, really, if I never get married, Gabe. I've had that. I told you—I like this. Marriage is really quite beside the point. You know that."

"Do you?"

"I knew it a long time ago. I knew it the day they got on that plane. I probably knew it before then, but that was a very forceful event. I supposed that you knew it too."

"I suppose I did."

"I don't think we should worry about it then," she said. "It's still raining a little. Do you still want to make love to me?"

"Not exactly. Not now." It wasn't intentionally that I had repeated her words.

"But why don't you do it anyway?" she said. "I think we should do whatever suits our needs. My needs, all right? I would like to be seduced right now. Undressed slightly against my will, my nice new dress thrown on the floor, and bango. That'll put a little glow around dinner later."

"You want me to service you?"

"I wasn't being cynical. I meant it."

"That doesn't make it a hell of a lot less cynical, I shouldn't think."

"So I want it all," she said, musing. "If you're bothering about yourself, then the best thing is go ahead and really bother. All the way. I walked past the big shoe-bazaar place on Fifty-third yesterday and I bought another pair of sandals. They were nice and they were inexpensive, but that's not the point. The point is I have a perfectly good pair in the closet and bought these anyway."

"That doesn't seem too terribly indulgent."

"Everything adds up. I've still got my debts to pay," she said. "I am the girl who wants to be serviced. What are you?"

"He who wants to service—at least that's what I'm left with."

"Who *wants* to?"

I did not answer.

"Are you being duplicitous?" she asked. "Do you want to leave me?"

"I want the same things I've always wanted, Martha. They just get more and more illusive. I don't feel myself quite able to pull anything off."

"You got the Herzes their baby finally. Though that doesn't satisfy you either, you told me."

"I didn't make my feelings clear. It satisfied me, it's good news. Except," I confessed, "it left me feeling a little envious."

That was the truth, and it left me defenseless.

"You're just a family man at heart," she said.

"Please don't be too smart."

"How can I help it? I could have serviced *you*, you see, with a ready-made unit."

"That isn't quite what I meant, Martha. You didn't even want that yourself."

"Nor did you," she said quickly.

"We influenced one another. Can we leave it at that?"

"Would you like to leave me, Gabe?"

"If I wanted to I would. At least I'd make a stab at it."

"Would you? I'm a tough cookie, you know."

"But so am I."

"I suppose that's what we're up against. Two tough cookies like us, each getting his way. The end result will be that one of us will invite the other to take a look out the window, and then give a nice shove forward."

"Or go nuts. Or hate one another's guts. There are lots of possibilities."

"Surely we can just work out some simple way of humiliating one another," she said. "I'll screw the janitor or something."

"I'm not crazy about the turn the conversation is taking."

"I'm not either."

"It's stopped raining."

"You look very handsome," she said to me, standing up. "Did I tell you that? Put on your jacket, let me see."

"Maybe," I said, while I smoothed out my trousers and buttoned my coat, "if I do get away for a week—"

"Yes." She opened her purse and looked to see if she had the keys; she always did this, even though I had keys of my own. "Yes, and maybe you'll come back and everybody will love everybody again."

"You're much more direct than I am, Martha. And maybe smarter—"

"You just don't have to be so direct, that's all."

"No?"

"You're stronger than I am, Gabe—and it's clear what you hold against me anyway."

"It's not all that clear to me. But whatever you think it is, why don't you save it?"

We walked down the stairs, and while I held the car door open, she said to me, "Is it clear, however, the few little things I have against you?"

"I think so."

"Am I being reasonable?"

After a moment I said, "I don't think so. No."

Her eyes filled with tears. "Then is it reasonable for you to detest me for letting them go?"

"I don't detest you for letting them go."

"For involving *you* in letting them go."

"That's not true either—"

"Well, you don't feel the same, Gabe. I think you liked me noble better. But then," she said, giving me no time to reply, "I would have preferred you that way too. We have to be satisfied with what we get."

"True."

I closed the door and came around to the street side of the car. "I won't say anything," Martha told me, as I got in, "and you don't say anything, and when we get to the restaurant we'll start in fresh. Let's not ruin the night. Just look up there, how lovely it is."

———

"Martha's looking marvelous," Sid Jaffe was saying to me five days later as we drove together to pick up the Herzes.

"Yes, she is."

"She likes her job?"

"I think so. Delsey is very nice, a very amiable fellow."

"How are the kids doing, do you know?" he asked.

"She called only a few nights ago. They're out at the seashore."

"So they're all right?"

"It sounds as though they're fine."

At a red light Sid settled back into his seat, taking his hands from the wheel a moment. "Another beautiful day," he said.

"It's been a nice summer."

"I haven't been out of the office enough to find out." His smile indicated that that was generally the way things went with him.

"You ought to take a vacation," I suggested.

He sighed then, comically, but he clearly liked the picture of himself as a hard-working, industrious man. Though our meetings had been few and inconsequential, I rather admired Jaffe, admired, in fact, what he seemed to admire about himself. Generally I saw him down by the lake on Sundays; it was there that we had been introduced by Martha. He had a

long striped towel that he stretched out on when sunning,
and a portable radio in a little leather case on which he listened to the ball game; every hour or so, he would tuck his
papers under the radio, walk down to the water, dive in, and
swim long, even laps by himself, going clear out of sight for
a time. Coming up from the water, his bald head dripping
and shining, he would take a trip past our blanket at least once
during the day to stop and say hello. He never allowed himself
the pleasure of a visit, however, never once sat down—though
there were occasions during the afternoon when I would happen to look up and see him, fifty yards off on his striped towel,
glancing our way; that is, Martha's way. Late in the afternoon,
he would do a round of sit-ups, take a last swim, and then
unobtrusively leave for home.

I came to respect Jaffe on those Sundays because he seemed
to be a lonely man who had come to grips with his condition.
Watching him, I wondered what my own particular style would
be were I to wind up forty and single. There was something
orderly and methodical about him that he managed to make
attractive, though Martha had already indicated to me that it
was that same orderliness that rendered him less than exciting,
that finally—at least she had believed this in the past—made of
Sid an uninspirited, unoriginal man.

"It's amazing," Sid was saying, as the car was moving again,
"how much she looks like Cynthia."

"Who?"

"Martha. Or Cynthia like her, I suppose I should say. Now
that she's rested and suntanned . . ."

I said, "They both have the same eyes."

Sid looked sternly ahead now. "That's right."

After a long silence I asked, "You've seen Theresa?"

"I stopped by the other day."

"Did you see the baby too?"

"I did."

"And it's all right . . . ?" I asked.

"Oh sure," he said. "Has Libby been calling you too?"

I shook my head.

"I thought you meant she'd been calling. She's called my
office three times in the last day or two. Making sure the
baby's got the proper number of appendages. Actually, the

thing turns out to look a little like her. As much as it can look like anything yet."

"Did you tell Libby? I'm sure it would excite her. At least I think it would," I said.

"It did. She's a very charming girl, in her excited way."

"I'm sure this is going to make her very happy."

"It's terrific," Sid said.

"I haven't spoken to Paul, have you?"

"I spoke to him once."

"I suppose he's excited too."

"I suppose so."

"Paul's a much calmer person than Libby," I said.

"Of course, Libby tells me that his father just died. I guess that's muted his pleasure some."

I nodded. "Though," I said, a few moments later, "I don't believe they were very attached, Paul and his father."

"Apparently Paul goes to synagogue for him every day."

"He does?"

"Every morning, Libby told me. To say Kaddish."

"I didn't know that . . . I never really thought of Paul as a religious person."

"However, a death—" he began.

"Yes, I suppose you're right." There had been something in his voice that I did not like—the tone of a man who considers himself a little more upright than his neighbor.

Heading up Maryland, his mood changed, and the tone, if it had ever been present, changed too. "Well," he said, "I know someone who's going to be glad to see you."

"Who's that?"

"I take it you're Theresa's Mr. Wallace."

"Oh. Yes. She never got it right and I gave up trying."

"Well, she asked for Mr. Wallace. I think it'll help, your being there. I'm glad you could stay in town."

I did not quite understand—or rather, I thought I understood, but was a little blinded by surprise, and then by irritation. "I planned to be in town anyway," I said.

When we were within a block of the Herz apartment, he said, "So we're all straight on procedure then."

"I think so. The Herzes will wait in your car, and you'll get out with me and get a taxi."

"I'll have a taxi right by the hospital entrance."

"And I'll get Theresa, then I pay the bill—"

"You'd better pay the bill first," Sid suggested. "I think it'll be less complicated. Paul will give you the check—I called up and got the total on the bill—"

"Then I bring her downstairs," I said, "and get into the cab with her."

"I'll park the car around the corner. That way the Herzes won't have to see her. And she won't have to see them."

"That's a good idea."

"Anything else?" he asked.

"That seems about everything. I take it she hasn't seen the baby."

"That's all been taken care of."

He was not really officious, and not actually self-laudatory, and his managerial qualities were certainly to be valued, especially at this time, and yet I found myself feeling a tinge of resentment for all the little things he had thought to do. Even on the previous night, when I had told him on the phone that he could use my car, he had countered by suggesting that it might actually be better to use his—it had four doors and would make it easier getting in and out with the baby. Probably that was so, and I had acceded; but after hanging up, I had a picture of him in his bachelor apartment thinking about the number of doors my car had as compared to the number of doors his car had, and I appreciated how, after all, a certain kind of woman might find him a little dull. "I suppose that's the most sensible way," I agreed.

"Otherwise they get attached, and it could cause trouble later. With the adoption. It's better for everybody this way, the girl included."

"Absolutely."

He parked, and just as we were stepping out of the car, a window above us opened and Paul stuck his head out. "We'll be right down," he called.

Sid and I sat down on the front steps of the brick building to wait. Across the street some kids were playing in a small weedy lot; next door to us several Negro women with shopping bags in their arms were chatting on the porch; a tall thin elderly man, apparently related to one of the women, was standing down below polishing his car and occasionally tossing a remark back up toward the porch conversation. It was a restful moment, a pleasant summer moment, and there was even the smell of honeysuckle from a bush in the little scrubby yard to our left. But most pleasant of all was a pleasure I began to take in my companion's organizational abilities. As we sat there waiting for the Herzes, I looked out toward the street and counted one, two, three, four—all Sid's doors—and I told myself that everything was going to come off smoothly and easily. Why shouldn't it?

Jaffe had said something to me that I did not hear.

"I'm sorry," I said.

"—says that you're going East?"

"Martha does?"

"Yes."

It had only been at dinner that night before that I had definitely decided to go; it must have been after dinner then, between the time Martha had picked up the phone and handed it to me, that she had passed on the information to Jaffe. It was like having your decisions go out over the wire services.

"My father," I explained, "is getting married. That is, he's just set the date, and he wants me to come spend some time with him and his fiancée. My mother died a few years back, you see."

"Well, that's quite an interesting thing, for an older man like that to remarry."

"He's sixty. I imagine it is."

"How does it feel for you?" he asked pleasantly.

"Oh," I said—and wondered, as I paused, how much he really did know about my private life beyond the fact that I owned a two-door automobile— "I'm very happy for him."

"It should be pleasant."

"Yes."

"I mean your trip."

"I don't think I'll be gone more than a week."

He took that fact in. "New York?"

"They're out on Long Island. East Hampton."

"Isn't that where Dick Reganhart lives, Long Island?"

"He's in Springs."

"Oh," said Sid, "is that far?"

"As a matter of fact, it turns out to be about ten miles east."

Just then someone called down, "Hey, hi!" It was Libby. "You two—one more minute!" Her hair was hanging loose on either side of her face, and she was waving at us with her lipstick.

"Hello," I said, looking up.

"How are you?" Jaffe called.

"Terrified," she answered. "I can't get my lipstick on anything but my nose. I'm shaking all over." She ducked inside.

Jaffe turned to me. "She's really quite a spunky girl. They've had a lot of troubles apparently."

I wondered if he was trying to needle me. But his manner was agreeable, and I decided that all he had been trying to do, now as earlier, was to make conversation.

Next he said: "I suppose you'll get over to see Cynthia and Mark then."

"I'm sorry—"

"I suppose in the East you'll get over to see the kids."

"I don't really know."

"If you should, send them my love."

"Certainly."

"If they even remember me."

"Oh," I said, "I'm sure they will."

"I hope so," he said. Maybe he didn't recognize the irony; maybe he did. "I was very fond of them," he added, as though they had not departed merely from the Midwest but from his life.

A second later the door behind us opened and Libby and Paul appeared. We all greeted one another. Shaking Paul's hand, I said, "Congratulations."

By contrast to the rest of us who were suntanned—Libby included—Paul looked more haggard than ever. Of course it was only two weeks since his return from Brooklyn and his father's funeral; looking at his hair that needed cutting, and his eyes that needed sleep, I was struck again by the news of his going each day to synagogue to say the mourner's prayer. "The best of luck," I said to him.

"Thank you," he answered.

We continued to grip each other's hand. It was warming for me to believe that despite the confusions between us—even the coldness, the hostility—we could confront each other on this special day with a decent amount of respect. Suddenly I sensed Paul's helplessness in a way I never had before—that is, without even the thinnest overlay of suspicion or doubt. I thought I understood what he had felt and been made to feel toward the woman he had chosen, and by choosing, altered. *I have been searching for a Libby, and I have found myself one. I have made myself one—Martha.* A lacerating idea, but it hung on, and however it worked against me, it led me to my fullest understanding of what had happened between Paul and myself, of what his feelings had been for me. I now had an experience to go by; where Paul Herz had once had Gabriel Wallach, Gabriel Wallach now had Sid Jaffe.

"What are you going to call her?" I asked him.

"Rachel," he said.

"Because we had to wait so long." The explanation came from Libby.

"Congratulations, Lib," I said, dropping her husband's hand.

She gave me a smile, but neither extended her hand nor took a step toward me. And that was all right too, so long as everything was under control and we all coasted through the morning under the guidance of Jaffe. Sid was standing now with his hands on his hips, a soldiery posture; whenever she looked his way, Libby grinned. She held a hand out straight before her and showed him how it was shaking.

Sid said to Paul, "Well, how does it feel being a father? Have you got the shakes too?"

He had spoken just as I was about to turn back to Paul to say I was sorry to have heard of his father's death; consequently, I said nothing, for it would have been a most inappropriate comment at that moment. The best thing for me was silence. Not leading, but following. In an hour or two (I told myself this at the very same time that I simply could not believe it) the Herzes would have their baby. Getting into the front seat alongside Jaffe, I found myself remembering a day back in Iowa, the day I had driven Libby out to pick up Paul, whose old Dodge had blown a piston. I remembered having asked Libby if she had any children, and her reply, her *Oh goodness, thank God, no.* It was our first exchange face to face.

"I'm sorry we kept you waiting," Libby said, as we started off.

"That's okay," Sid said.

"We were just putting up the crib," she explained. I turned around to look at her while she spoke. "We didn't want to put it up until today," she said to me, "not until everything was sure as sure could be. It would have been awful to come home to that crib . . ."

"Well," I said, "it's only a matter now of going down and picking up the baby."

Libby became quite excited when I said that. She turned to her husband. "Isn't that something?" He took her hand in his. "Is your heart thumping?" she asked him.

He smiled. "Oh no."

"Oh I'll bet," she said.

Every time we had to stop at a traffic light, Sid turned around in his seat and teased Libby. "Well, are you still with us, Lib?"

"Still here," she sang.

"Just wanted to check. You look like you're really ready to take flight."

"Run away? Oh *no*—"

"I meant fly. Sprout wings."

"Oh," she said. "Yes, I am."

—

The hospital had not yet been landscaped. It was a huge new concrete building, one wing of which was still unfinished. The grassless, treeless ground that sloped down to the street revealed the gutted markings of trucks and tractors; the light, reflecting off the packed-in earth and the flush cement walls of the hospital, had a powdery quality, as though it were not substanceless but a film of particles that upon contact would settle over one's clothing and leave a coating on the teeth. At the sight of the hospital, the little jokes and pleasantries we had all of us been making—even Paul at the last—stopped abruptly.

The only ornament the gaunt hospital showed was a narrow-armed gold cross that hung over the central glass doorway and rose three stories high. Four nuns in flowing black habits happened to be standing under the cross as we drove by, and the cross, the flat, gray, sunlit walls and the four sisters all came together to make time seem at a standstill, nonexistent even, the illusion one is troubled by in certain anxious dreams. The surrealistic arrangement of the objects appeared to be the outward sign of a world static and impersonal, a world into which one moved with an overpowering consciousness of the sound of one's shoes, and of the slight tremulous noise of the breath, the life, in one's nostrils; where every human gesture, once made, seemed either an exaggeration or a diminution of the gesture intended; where words spoken into the boundless landscape were either inaudible or too loud—a place where one found oneself with little control over the image one wished to convey, or the effects one hoped to produce.

If no one in the car shared my several chilling illusions, they all seemed to share the solemnity that those illusions produced in me. None of us spoke as Sid continued right on past the crescent-shaped drive that led up to the hospital entrance; no one asked any questions when he turned left at the corner. Passing the unfinished wing of the hospital, on whose gently swaying scaffolds overalled workmen appeared carrying buckets and leaning into wheelbarrows, Sid proceeded halfway down the block before he pulled over to the curb and parked. We were in the shade now, and though neither nuns, nor cross, nor hard glary walls were before our eyes, my sense of imminence did not diminish. I had never been in this section of Chicago before and I had never been in a situation quite like this one either, and yet I had a very deep sense of repeating an old event. I had been through all this, precisely this, in another life.

But of course that is a feeling we all experience on occasion, and it too is illusion. If and when we allow ourselves to be convinced of other lives and other incarnations, it is to be spared the necessity of facing up to futility, of confronting the boredom and the limitation of our own predicament; for no one is particularly happy about those endless repetitions that make us predictable and contained and therefore sane—and therefore fallible, the subjects and objects of pain. Thus this event for me, this adoption we were about to set in motion, this rearrangement of people, was really not the repetition of an act in any other life; it was only a crystallization of several acts in this one. I felt the impact then of all the shufflings of parents and offspring that I had witnessed and been a part of in the last few years—the rearranging and the rearranging, as though we

could administrate anguish out of our lives. I leave my father;
the Brooklyn Herzes throw out their son; Martha cuts loose
from her children; now Libby opens her arms to Theresa
Haug's bastard child . . .

After Sid Jaffe pulled up the hand brake, no one in the car
moved, no one said a word. It lasted but a second, our collective inaction, but the uncertainty, the fear, the humility—
whatever had caused us all to take in our breath and delay for a
moment more that which we were about to do—seemed to
me a recognition by the four of us of the powers outside ourselves, a tribute to a presence, or a lack of presence, so solid,
so monumental, so stark and immeasurable, that it rendered
quite inconsequential the blankness of those hospital walls we
were about to enter. But then Sid turned a little in his seat and
said, "Well . . ." and I felt a flow of energy in me, and for all
that had failed to come out of the shufflings and separations
we had each of us been party to in the past, for all the confusion that had grown out of the rejections and the yearnings,
the demands and the hesitations and the betrayals, I put my
hand to the door and half opened it.

In the back seat Paul was leaning forward.

"I think it'll be best," Sid was saying, "if you two wait here.
It shouldn't take us too long—okay?"

"We just wait here?" Paul asked.

"That's right. And we'll bring the baby to the car, and"—he
smiled—"that'll be that."

"And the girl?" Paul asked; it seemed suddenly very important to him to hear all the details.

"She's fine," Jaffe said. "She'll just go home."

But Paul was still listening, apparently to hear what *he* had
to do; it did not quite satisfy him, it seemed, that he had to do
nothing.

Jaffe said again, almost helplessly, "And that'll be that."

A silence began to develop once more, and I rushed to fill it.
"I'll take care of her, Paul. Everything will be all right."

"Oh," he said, looking up at me. He slid his hand down into
his trouser pocket, in a gesture almost of panic, and withdrew
his wallet. He removed a check from the billfold section, examined it, and then handed it to me. I did not look at the figures as I put it in my pocket.

"Don't lose it," Libby said, pointing at my pocket.

I shook my head. "I won't."

Jaffe tried to laugh. "I guess we've *all* got Libby's shakes."

"I guess so," Paul said. "Libby included." He took one of his wife's hands, and he too worked up a smile.

"Oh, my hands are just freezing though," she said.

"Baloney," Sid said.

Libby extended one hand over the seat. "Feel."

Sid took it. "What are you talking about? They're warm as toast. Here," and he put Libby's hand in mine.

"As cold toast," I said, and everyone volunteered a little laugh, while Libby's hands were held, one by her husband, one by me. Until I let the hand go, she was not very relaxed, but sat stiffly as though a current were being conducted through her.

"Let's go," Sid said, and though his words were those of the gallant soldier leading his men over the top, he seemed, like the rest of us, to have been overcome by this last strong wave of confusion.

—

In front of the hospital was a row of yellow and black taxis in which drivers sat, reading newspapers. Sid said, "I'll meet you right down here," and went off to get a cab.

At the reception desk inside the lobby I asked for a pass to go up to the maternity ward. Then I went to the cashier's counter and paid Theresa's bill with the check that Paul had given me.

The sister behind the desk said, "Is this you, sir?"

"No."

"Who is Mr. Paul Herz?"

"He's a friend of the patient's." I did not know whether to refer to her as Miss Haug or Mrs. Haug. I could have simply said Theresa Haug, but that did not occur to me.

"And you are?" she asked.

Had Jaffe told me how to identify myself? Had I not been listening, or hadn't we really talked everything over—or didn't it matter, one way or the other? He had probably imagined that I could figure some things out for myself. What I did remember, of course, was Sid telling all of us that it was best for the hospital to know nothing of the adoption; should they find out the exact circumstances, they would most certainly bring pressure upon Theresa to give up the child to a Catholic family, or even to an orphanage. Jaffe had instructed Theresa herself not to discuss the future of the child with anyone in the hospital. If asked, she was simply to say that the infant would be raised by her own mother and father in Kentucky.

For a moment I stood silently before the nun, knowing that if there was one thing I didn't want to do, it was to go out to the car and bring in Paul to verify his check.

"You see," I said to the sister, as graciously as I could, "it's not my check."

"I understand. I wanted to know your relationship to Miss Haug."

"I'm her brother," I said.

After a second she said, "Thank you, sir." She handed me the receipt. Theresa's stay at the hospital had cost Paul $327.60. That did not include the money he had already given her to cover the pre-natal checkups and her expenses during the last two months when she had been unable to work; nor did it include the money she was to get for the next two weeks while she recuperated. As I left the cashier's counter, the only person I could think to hate was John Spigliano, who, though he had finally agreed in the Executive Committee to hire Paul for another year, had vetoed a raise for him on the grounds that Paul still had not finished his Ph.D. Walking to the elevator, I felt a disgust for him such as one feels for a scapegoat, or surrogate. One knows better but keeps hating anyway.

I took the Up elevator in the company of two young priests and a doctor who was wearing a blue surgery uniform. In soft voices they exchanged some words about a patient who was either dying or dead. When I stepped off into the corridor that led to the maternity ward, one of the priests looked up at me and smiled.

The sister behind the desk at the entrance to the ward took my pass card and led me down the aisle, between rows of beds, all white and fresh-looking. We stopped a few beds short of a large window through which the sunlight flowed. Theresa was sitting on her bed, wearing a bright-colored print dress which was decorated with pictures of burros and musical instruments and palm trees and the maps of certain South American countries. A little brown suitcase with a circular sticker that said "Carlsbad Caverns" was on the floor. When she saw me, she opened her mouth very wide, and then jumped off the bed. There was a comb in her hand, and even as she threw her arms around me, I caught the glint of a curler in her orange hair.

"You're *early*—" I felt Theresa's palms against my back, not her fingers themselves; then I smelled her nail polish. I proceeded to place my arms around her, for I realized we were being watched—which was what Theresa realized too.

"Hi. Hello," I said. In the bed just beyond Theresa's, a little woman with a big jaw and heavy bags under her eyes was giving me a friendly grin. I smiled back.

"Well . . ." I said, and finally Theresa stepped away. Now I smiled at her too. "You look fine," I said, and even while I spoke I felt the presence of the nun who had accompanied me down the corridor; Theresa's glance kept darting over my shoulder, and finally I turned to the sister. Since I had gotten by with smiles so far, I smiled at her too. She did not take to it, however. She was a woman with striking blue eyes, who was made less than handsome by a skin eruption that ran around the edge of her cowl and fringed her face. It was clear that she disapproved, but it was not clear as yet of what. I could not tell how old or young she was.

"I'll bring the baby," the sister said to me. "I'll wait by the elevator."

"Thank you," I said. "We'd appreciate it."

"Thank you," said Theresa, with both fear and devotion.

I picked up Theresa's suitcase. The woman with the baggy eyes turned on her elbow and said to me, "How was your trip?"

"Oh," I said, "fine."

"I'll bet you were surprised," she said.

"This is Mrs. Butterworth," Theresa said. "This is her *seventh*."

"Eighth," said Mrs. Butterworth.

"Imagine," Theresa said.

I offered my congratulations.

"Oh I'm used to it," Mrs. Butterworth told me. "It's you two needs congratulating."

Theresa took my hand, and I felt some of her nail polish

rubbing off on me. The hand was just about as cold as Libby's had been in the car. "Yes," I said. "Thank you."

"We live out here on the west side, right off Archer," Mrs. Butterworth said. "You know where that is?"

"I think so," I said.

"Well, you want to take a ride out on Sunday, why you just drive right out. I gave her the address. You got it, don't you, honey?"

"Uh-huh," Theresa said; she picked up her purse from the bed and waved it at her friend, indicating, I suppose, that the Butterworth address was safely locked away. It was the same plastic bag she'd been carrying that night I had met her, back in the winter.

"I think we'd better be going," I said.

"You kids take it easy now," Mrs. Butterworth called.

We started down the aisle of the ward, Theresa still with one metal curler in her hair which she must have forgotten about in the tension and excitement of leaving. Some of the women who were awake sat up in their beds and said goodbye. Theresa took hold of my arm and moved between the beds, saying goodbye and so long and see ya. At the end of the corridor I saw the nun holding a bundle in her arms. She pushed the elevator buzzer and we all stepped in. The sister did not offer to show me the baby's face within the blankets, and I did not ask to see it.

On the way down Theresa looked up at me. I tried to smile again, but she didn't have it in her to smile back.

At the main floor the nun accompanied us to the front door. A taxi immediately swung up the crescent drive; I saw first the face of the driver, a Negro, and then Sid in the back seat.

We stood out in front of the new building, where the four nuns had been standing when Sid had driven by earlier. As yet Theresa had looked neither at the sister nor at the child; either she looked at me or at no one.

I turned to the nun. "Fine," I said. "Thank you."

She only stared with her very severe eyes.

"May I have it, please?" I asked. Theresa looked straight ahead, as though she were not with us. Down below, the back door of the taxi opened.

I could see that the nun was holding her teeth together;

finally she gave me the baby, then turned and went back into the hospital. I did not know how much, or what, Theresa had told her.

"Right down there," I said to Theresa. "Mr. Jaffe's in the taxi."

She preceded me down the stairs, and I realized how strange it must look for me to be carrying the baby and Theresa to be carrying her little suitcase. But she was well ahead of me—I was making my way down like an old man, one step at a time —and there was nothing to be done about it. I looked into the blankets now, to be sure there really was a baby there, and of course there really was. All of a sudden I found myself grinning euphorically; everything was going as it should. It even seemed more sensible that it was me who was carrying the baby, not Theresa.

Down below, Sid stepped out of the cab and Theresa got in. Then he ran around the back of the cab and went in the other door. On my side the door remained ajar, and I stepped into the cab at last, easing myself and the baby through, and then I was seated beside Theresa. When I looked back to where I had begun my journey, I saw a nun standing on the top step. Suddenly she threw us a kiss—she must have thought we were another party. I smiled at her through the window. Within the blanket I felt the baby stir.

"All right," Sid said to the driver. As we started down the entryway, Theresa sighed. It was over.

"Well, how are you feeling?" Sid said to her. I saw that he had taken her hand and was patting it. Nail polish was sticking to everyone's hand now; that alone seemed to be preventing things from being absolutely perfect. I knew the thought to be an irrational one even as it passed through my mind, and yet it rather set me on edge again. After all, the girl had put the polish on for me.

"I feel fine, Mr. Jaffe. I—"

The taxi stopped, swaying us all forward. Without turning, the driver reached around with his left arm and opened the door on Sid's side; we were almost directly across the street from Sid's four-door automobile. As planned, I handed the baby to Sid; I wondered why we had not arranged for the two of us to sit side by side, so that we would not have to pass the bundle *over* Theresa. Jaffe stepped out of the car and then the driver reached around again and closed the door. It all happened very quickly.

"What . . ." Theresa said feebly. She looked at me and then out the window to follow Sid crossing the street. He stepped into the car across the way and Theresa leaned even further across me; evidently she wanted to see whom he was handing the baby to. Then she turned back to me, stunned, but not crying.

"Do you feel all right?" I asked. "Are you okay?"

"I'm okay." Looking down, she saw the nail polish on my jacket and on both our hands.

"That's all right," I said. "It's nothing at all."

The driver sat with his large hands on the wheel, while the motor ran and the meter ticked.

"But you feel all right?" I asked.

She dropped her fingers limply into her lap. "Sister Mary Frances is very strict," she said.

"That's all over."

"I don't think she liked that I said I was married."

"Well, that was silly of her."

"I said the baby was in the incubator. I said you were away on business—"

"That's all right, Theresa."

"Otherwise," the girl said, looking down still at her hands, "who would I have had to talk to?"

The driver was looking at us now in the rear-view mirror. I didn't know what more to say. "Do you have any pains? Anything at all?"

After considering an answer for a while, she said, "Uh-uh. No."

I reached into my wallet and took out a five-dollar bill which I handed across to the driver. On the other side of the street I heard Jaffe's car start up.

"Mr. Jaffe gave you the money, didn't he? For the next couple of weeks?"

She whispered so the driver would not hear. "Yes."

"Okay then."

". . . Mr. Wallace?"

"Yes."

"Are you going to take me home?"

"The driver will take you home, Theresa. Right to the door. Everything's going to be all right."

She never gave me an answer.

I said to the driver, hesitating. "Would you help her into the house?"

"Yes, sir."

For lack of anything more I could think to do, I reached into my wallet and handed the fellow another dollar.

Just before I left the cab I said, "You've been very brave, Theresa. Good luck to you," and then I was headed across the street. I saw that in the other car Jaffe's head was turned and he was speaking to the Herzes. On the street, I turned back; there was Theresa's face in the taxi window. She was saying something—she seemed to be *shouting* something. I thought the worst: she is going to push the door open, she is going to come running across the street to demand her child back. In fact, her window did begin to roll down, and I heard, or imagined I heard her calling my name. My first name. I did not remain on the street to find out. I moved around the back of Jaffe's car, opened the door and slid in beside him just as the automobile was beginning to move. When Jaffe looked over at me I saw that he was startled. I wondered if I had nail polish on my face, if I looked as though I were bleeding—if he thought that there had been some violence between Theresa and myself. Then I realized that he had not been waiting for me. But he said nothing, and we drove away.

In the back seat Libby had begun to talk softly to the baby. It sounded as though she were doing what she thought she was supposed to be doing, and it added a final pathetic note to the day's dealings. And yet, despite Libby's theatrics, despite the misunderstanding between Jaffe and myself, I knew that a series of events in which I had taken a hand had at last come to a happy ending. I turned to the back seat to appreciate the tableau of baby, mother, and father, but what I saw was out beyond the rear window: Theresa's taxi moving off in the opposite direction. I thought of the girl going back to Gary alone, and I knew that nothing had really ended. In not staying with her I had made another mistake.

No, yes, yes, no, no, yes . . . on to infinity. Had I remained in the cab, would she not have wanted me to accompany her into her little room? And once in the room, would that have been enough? Would that have been anything? If I was not to tease, or to make false promises, or to dangle before her the hope of a better or a different future, what else could I do about Theresa Haug's suffering except turn my back on it?

At the Herzes we all went upstairs and watched as Libby gently laid Rachel in her crib, which had been set up in the room that had been Paul's study. Watching Libby bend across the brand new crib, Paul was near tears. Finally he went off to the bathroom, so that I did not get a chance to say goodbye to him. When we left, his tear-filled wife kissed both Sid and me.

Jaffe drove me back to Martha's. After some three or four minutes of silence, he glanced over, and without much of an attempt at hiding his opinion of me, said, "I thought you were going to stay with her."

When I answered him, I tried to find some comfort in the fact that I had learned something; I tried to engage Jaffe's eye and let him know that I believed I meant what I was saying, but he was only waiting for me to get out of the car. "Actually," I said, "I didn't see that it made much sense."

3

I T WAS EASIER than it should have been for Dr. Wallach to imagine an old age other than this one. He set an elbow onto the sand, leaned back, and little by little he was able to bring his breathing under control. He felt encouraged by the sun's ability to dry the water on his skin, and soon his chest was moving up and down at its normal speed. He slapped his belly where it was still flat and hard; he made a fist, one hand, then the other. He had taken care of this small body of his, he had exercised it daily and fed it upon foods rich in protein and vitamins; he may have been the victim of a fad or two, but at least he had gotten through life on a minimum of fried foods. Looking down at himself in a bathing suit, he did not experience the repugnance or shame that another man sixty years of age might have felt. He looked as he had always hoped and expected he would; it was not the appearance that he could imagine to be different, it was the circumstances.

Fifty feet out from the beach, his only child continued to swim back and forth through the surf. Now and then a wave rolled in to cover the moving form, but then an arm glistened, that shock of brown hair broke the surface, and he could follow again the progress of his son, cutting effortlessly through the water. Yes, he could imagine it all to have turned out another way. He could imagine that when Gabe had returned from the Army, he had moved back into his old room in the Central Park West apartment; he could imagine that the two of them had taken up a calm and amiable life together. Gabe could have done graduate work at Columbia, and then there would have been someone with whom Dr. Wallach could have eaten his dinner in the evening and discussed the *Times* in the morning, someone with whom he could have played tennis at the club and with whom he might have gone for pleasant walks in the park when the weather was right. Someone he loved.

He had not for a moment expected that his son would live with him forever. A year, two, three, and Gabe would have found the right girl in New York—well-bred, intelligent, kind

—whom Dr. Wallach would have accepted without question as a daughter, and subsequently loved like his own child. The young couple would have been married and would have settled down in the city, Gabe teaching at Columbia, or NYU, or Hunter, or any of a dozen places. Dr. Wallach could imagine his son and his son's young wife—he could even see her, a slender girl with brown hair and a soft voice—living just across the way from him on the East Side. On Sunday afternoons he would bundle up and take an invigorating walk through the park to visit them, to stay for a light supper, and then take a taxi home. And in the summers there would have been morning swims just like this one—the son and the father (perhaps even a grandchild) coming down to the beach before breakfast and diving together into the cold blue sea, while back in the sunny white house they had all rented for the season, his daughter-in-law, a pink peignoir over her nightgown, was pouring orange juice into sparkling cut-glass goblets.

Of course at that very moment Fay was at her house preparing a nice breakfast for the three of them; and since one could by no means expect life to conform to one's fantasies—even to one's plans—he told himself that what *had* happened was not just to be endured, but to be accepted and valued. There was no reason for him not to consider himself a very lucky man for having met Fay Silberman. Without her, his last year would have been the most morbid of all. There had been Gruber in Europe with him, of course, and though the fellow was a satisfactory enough companion if one was oneself in a giddy mood, if one was not, then Gruber with his smiling and joking was worse than no one at all. In Europe Dr. Wallach had seen numerous widows and widowers traveling with friends they did not particularly care for, people to whom they had connected themselves only because they had lost those to whom they had always been connected before. He had seen them sitting opposite one another at the restaurant Tre Scalini in Rome, amidst all the old beauty of that piazza, picking at their food; he had seen them reading separate sections of the *Herald Tribune* in the lobbies of the Lotti in Paris and the Grand in Florence, waiting for the sightseeing buses to pick them up and take them away; and he did not really know who was more miserable, those who traveled with acquaintances they couldn't stand, or those who traveled, literally, by themselves. On the Queen Mary, sailing home, there had been a bosomy, bejeweled woman from Virginia, a widow of fifty-five or so, who had told him that she had gone to bed at eight o'clock every night she had been in Paris. She had pretty blue eyes behind her glasses, and powder in the creases of her neck, and she brought tears to his eyes; under the table—they were all in the lounge waiting for the horse racing to begin—he had taken Fay's hand.

Oh yes it was luck, it was good fortune indeed that had thrown him together with Fay only two days out of New York. With Fay along, so many funny little things had happened; and one warm night in Venice he had taken her for a ride in a gondola and she had lifted *his* hands and held them against her breasts. Imagine if he had had to go out with *Gruber* in a gondola! Yes, Fay had given him pleasure, and that despite all the drinking she had done—all the champagne, all the red wines and white wines and rosé wines, all the Scotch and Irish whiskies, whose consumption had added to the festive spirit, but had also helped to blur for her the image of her husband being driven, dead, around his lawn on a power mower. It had helped to erase the memory of the eight-room house in New Jersey, and of that same husband whose heart had failed him, and who—said Fay to whomever she happened to be speaking—had been very very good to her.

So Fay drank, and Dr. Wallach drank, and Gruber drank too, but then one morning they were back in America. They took a taxi from the pier to his apartment, and when he came out of the bedroom where he had changed his shoes, there she was standing in front of the fireplace with a glass in her hand. On native ground it apparently took even more alcohol than it had abroad to blur the past; at last it seemed he would have to say something before some accident, some tragedy, occurred. On Thanksgiving Day particularly he had been conscious of how much her drinking had prejudiced his son, whose approval he had been counting on (knowing all the while that he would not get it—that Fay in no way resembled the boy's mother). Eventually he had cautioned Fay, had asked her to make him a promise, and the miracle that had happened was that she had stopped. At first cut down, then actually stopped.

It was at about this time too that they had begun to talk seriously of marriage. She had acceded to a wish of his, and apparently that had soldered them one to the other. The engagement that they had announced at Thanksgiving had not actually had a great deal to do with any impending marriage; it was mostly a convenience, a way they had come upon to deal with their revitalized passions. It had been one thing, they discovered, to lie together in strange hotels in foreign lands; it was another to be back home, with Millie in the kitchen clanging pots and pans, and the bedroom door double-locked. Slowly they had come to feel a little like a pair of teen-agers, and so he had made her his fiancée.

But in only a little while, when the first excitement had faded—no one was whispering French in the hallway beyond the keyhole any more—the engagement itself seemed to matter less. There had even begun to grow in him a feeling, half sadness, half relief, that in a month or two he would be back to his single life, to the lonely meals and the smoky pinochle games with Strauss and Kirsch and Gruber.

Then one evening around Christmas time, having gone out by himself for a Chinese dinner, he returned home to find Fay, in her silver fox, collapsed on the living-room rug. In her left hand she was holding onto a gold menorah, which—she later told him—she had brought in with her from New Jersey. She had come all the way from South Orange in a cab, the nine-branched candelabra in one hand, a bottle of Scotch in the other. The taxi driver had helped her along beneath the canopy, and the doorman had supported her up to the doctor's apartment, and inside she had passed out. On the floor she hugged the candelabra to her and wept over her children in California who wrote only a post card once a month. He helped her up and brought a cold cloth for her sad eyes, and it was then that he had made her promise that she would not drink again. Later, though it was in conflict with his atheistic principles, he allowed her to light the Chanukah candles and set them up on the fireplace mantle. A few days later they went up to Grossinger's and stayed through the New Year. And now they were to be married. When they went out to dine, Mrs. Silberman would not even have a cocktail before her meal.

And the future? Well, why *wouldn't* it be pleasant? There

was a trip to the Bahamas planned for their honeymoon, and for the following spring they were talking about six weeks in South America; Fay had even called Cooks to inquire about arrangements. Nevertheless, there is no one who does not have the right to imagine what might have been—there are always the ifs. If, for instance, his son had come home to New York and given him a year or two—

He looked out to where a wave was driving in toward the shore, and he hoped that Gabe would not see it—that it would wash over him, drown him. Filled with rage, he wished that Gabe were dead. He wished that the boy had never been born. He was just like his mother—cold. He hated them both for leaving him.

But when the wave came rolling down and flowed up to the beach, he felt only remorse. His heart sank and did not rise again until he caught sight once more of his son's head. How could he hate what had been everything to him? His wife, after all, had not willed leukemia upon herself. Yet in those black months after her death, with Gabe stationed halfway across the country in Oklahoma, Dr. Wallach would sometimes think that Anna had waited until he was all alone to die to see if he had learned anything from having lived a life with her. And had he? She had been a strong-willed, polished woman; for two generations in America, and in Hamburg for generations before that, the Seligs had been professional people, lawyers and physicians, and Anna Selig Wallach had been a true enough daughter of her class. There had been a certain wisdom about her, a contemplativeness, and—for all the precious goods that had always been hers—an understanding on her part of what it was not-to-have; she knew how you were to act when everything was taken from you, without cause or warning.

It had been an education for him, watching her die. It was as though her whole life had been a training for those last three months. Not once, from fear or pain, had she cried out; not once, for all the fatigue that weighed upon her, another pound a day, had she been mean or cross. She had not lost her temper —this impressed him greatly—and even her tears, which curiously were more frequent in the early weeks of the disease than in the last, had seemed more for him than for herself. And then one evening around dinnertime she left him, and it did not really seem that he had learned very much. He cried from fear and pain for a week. One night when Millie came in with his hot milk, which he hoped would be an aid to him in falling asleep, he had had to ask her, the maid, to sit down in the chair beside his bed for a few moments. It was several months before he could sleep with the light off; she died in the early fall and not until winter did there come a morning when he awoke to find the room lit by the gray sun and not by his bed lamp.

Then Gabe had been discharged, and when he had come home, what had his father done but driven him away? He had moaned and leaned, leaned and moaned, and there was Gabe flying off to Iowa, to Chicago! God in Heaven, why had he been so clutchy? If only he had learned a *little* from her, if only he had been able to remain calm . . . But that would have been unnatural! At his age he was entitled to his feelings—why should he act happy when he was sad? Why smile each time the boy went out the front door, when each time he wanted to cry? What kind of son was it, anyway, who left his aging father!

All sons. All sons leave their fathers. Of course. He considered himself a student of psychology and he was not naïve about certain facts of life. Just the other day on the beach he had had an interesting discussion about parental problems with Abe Cole, one of New York's leading psychoanalysts, who happened to have the house next door to Fay's. He had told Abe, and four or five others sitting and chatting under their umbrella, that unhappy as he had been when his son had gone off for good, he had known in his heart that a boy does not become a man living in his father's house. In part it had been to impress Abe with his objectivity and intelligence that he had spoken so, and to impress the others too, Fay's summer friends, whom he suspected of not thinking so highly of dentists as they did of psychoanalysts. Also he had been trying to impress Fay, which he found himself doing fairly regularly of late. His desire to impress, however, had not led him to be hypocritical; he believed what he said—children grow up and go away. That was one of life's laws to which he and his son could not expect to be made exceptions. Nevertheless (and this he had not been able to say to Abe, though it was what he had hoped they might get to talk about), there *are* certain circumstances, are there not? Special predicaments people wind up in that are not of their own choosing and that both child and parent have to recognize and make accommodations for? If only his son, for instance, had had an *ounce* of patience with him; if only he himself had displayed an ounce of control . . .

However, what was was. Be philosophic. He would have to work with what he had . . . Gabe had driven straight through from Chicago in one day and had arrived at eleven-thirty the night before. They had all sat down to have a cup of coffee and a sandwich together, and no real strains had been apparent. Gabe had even said good night to her as he went off to bed, and when they were alone again, Fay had commented on what nice posture the young man had. Well, there was a certain willingness in that remark, wasn't there? And as for Gabe, he was an intelligent boy, a decent boy—so why then should there be strains? They were three grown people; if they all worked at it a little, they could have a week together that would be a foundation for their future happiness.

He reasoned and he reasoned, and still, when Gabe swam to shore, and Dr. Wallach handed a towel up to him, he found himself unable to relax. He was stiff and ill at ease, fearful of saying the wrong thing, all this in front of his own flesh and blood.

Gabe sat down beside him and they looked out at the sea. He asked if his father had gotten over his chill and Dr. Wallach assured him that he had. This enabled them to look out at the water again. The doctor checked his watch, but they were not due back for breakfast for another half hour. The beach was empty of people as far off as he could see.

"So how's teaching this year?" Dr. Wallach asked. "Still crazy about it?"

"Oh, I like it all right."

"Still like the Windy City?"

"As a matter of fact," said Gabe, rubbing his towel across his shoulders, "I'm getting a little tired of it."

He could hardly believe his ears. His heart took a long stride forward and met, head-on, the wall of his chest. Through some miracle of the will, he managed not to cry out, "Then come, come, my darling son—come back with me!"

He said instead, "Oh? No kidding." He was so proud of his self-control that he could have shaken his own hand. He looked—casually—over at his son, and saw upon his face what seemed to be depression. "So," he began again, "I suppose you won't be hanging around Chicago very much from now on."

"I don't know. I've been thinking of leaving teaching."

"Something happen?"

"It's just not quite as satisfying as it was. Maybe I'll try something else for a while."

"I see." He attempted to let more than a second elapse, but couldn't. "For instance, what? Just speaking off the cuff, you know."

"Traveling. Maybe living in Europe for a while."

"Oh. Uh-huh. Interesting . . ."

They had been speaking with their eyes toward the horizon, but now Gabe turned to the doctor and smiled. The boy had the height and carriage of his mother, but he had the doctor's long head and stern good looks. There was no doubt that he was the doctor's son. "But I'm not sure, you see, about anything," he said.

Dr. Wallach wondered if his own stern eyes looked stern enough; they were not teary, and he most assuredly did not want them to look as though they were. "When would this be?" he asked. "You know, a year, two years—"

"I don't know . . . I'm even thinking of resigning. Of not going back, except to get my belongings."

"Well, this is a surprise."

"For me too. It only occurred to me about halfway through Pennsylvania yesterday. As I said, I'm not even sure."

"Well," the doctor said—casual still—letting some sand drift slowly off his hands, "it just shows—your heart is in the East after all."

"I didn't mean to indicate that I'd decided anything—"

"Who said you decided anything? I was just making an observation." They were silent. Until Dr. Wallach said, "I mean your business is certainly your business. Europe is a beautiful and educational place, there's no doubt about that. It's too bad you didn't feel this way last year"—he was desperate with the desire to sound simply chatty—"when I was going."

"Yes—well—I thought I'd stay a little longer. I'm not so much thinking of touring as settling down there awhile."

"Well, sure, you're single. Live it up. You still like the bachelor life, huh?"

Gabe shrugged. "I'm not planning to marry anybody just yet."

"Certainly, take your time, look around. Take a walk down Fifth Avenue for yourself. The most beautiful women in the world. Let me put it this way: the Italian girl is a beautiful girl, I'll grant that, and the French girl is certainly a girl of fine qualities too. And even the English girl has got something about her, very soft skin and so forth, but for nice wholesome all-around good looks, give me an American girl, any day. If I were a young man looking for a wife, I'd look right around here. You don't even have to go very far from Central Park to find the kind of girl I'm talking about."

Gabe only nodded his head. The doctor felt his face go incandescent—how obvious he was! His son said, "Shall we go back for breakfast? I'm getting hungry."

They both got up. "No," the doctor said, "I didn't think Chicago was going to be your city forever. New York gets in a man's blood—speaking for myself, I mean. You know that song, 'Autumn in New York'—well, popular as it is, there's some truth in it."

"Of course my plans aren't definite . . ." They started off.

"Look," said Dr. Wallach, a finger on his son's arm, "nobody's plans are definite."

"I suppose that's so."

He was afraid to say more. How could he tell him he was uncertain about Mrs. Silberman when he was actually uncertain whether or not he was uncertain? Suppose he confessed to doubt and married her later anyway? Could he possibly allow himself to appear even more weak, more needy, then he had already? To his own son?

Why not! Damn it, what was a family for, if not to be weak in front of?

"Would that be a breach of contract?" he heard himself asking. "Suddenly resigning like that?"

"No, no—I don't even imagine I'll do it. It was just something impractical, really, that I thought of in a groggy state."

"After all, though, if you're not happy out there, there's no reason you should stay. You have a right to make your own decisions."

"Dad, look . . ."

"What? What's the matter now?"

"Nothing. You know, though, that when you and Mrs. Silberman marry—is this what you're getting at?"

"What?"

"Well . . . let's do get things out in the open. You know I couldn't move in with you two. I mean if I were to leave Chicago. That would be very unrealistic for you to bank on. Surely you know that as well as I do."

"Absolutely," he shot back.

"Well, okay then. I'm sorry. I just began to feel that this conversation . . ."

"Absolutely not. I was thinking about your own welfare. Now you didn't get anybody in trouble, did you?"

Gabe shook his head. "Just a change, that's all."

"Because if we're going to be open with one another—"

"Yes?"

But he owed it to everybody not to whine, not to beg. He was a sixty-year-old man earning $35,000 a year; he could not act like a child. Instead of talking about his own ambivalence, he found himself talking about his son's.

"I understand, of course, that this isn't your mother. So, believe me, I understand your feelings."

"Which feelings?"

"That you're a little skeptical where Fay is concerned."

"If I've been skeptical, it's not been my business to be. Above all I want you to be happy. If this is going to bring you contentment—"

He heard the real emotion in his son's voice, and now did indeed feel tears in his eyes. "It will," he said, interrupting. "I'm absolutely sure of that." He felt at once proud and ashamed of the strength he had displayed. Then his eyes were dry.

"Fine," Gabe said. He was even smiling. "I'm not skeptical."

"Of course. It's a psychological thing, and I understand how that is, how that comes about."

"Fine."

"Though I don't mean you're not entitled to express your

opinion. We're both grown men, and you're an intelligent person, obviously, and of course I'm always interested in your opinion on that ground alone. If you want to express an opinion to me about Fay, there's no reason for me not to hear it."

"I don't have an opinion. I only wanted to know that you wanted this."

"Well, why should you have any doubts?"

Gabe's answer was some time in coming. "I don't want to interfere. It's not my business to tell anybody how to run his life."

"No, no, go right ahead. I'm not a fragile icicle. I'd like to hear your objection. Why shouldn't I be open-minded to all points of view?"

"It's no objection."

"What is it?"

"It's only her drinking. It seemed to me—I might be wrong —a little excessive."

"Well, it isn't any more." The doctor stopped and waited. Would there be some further objection—one he had no answer to?

"You don't believe me?" the doctor asked.

"I believe you."

"Because it's a fact. She has given it up. It was only a temporary thing to begin with, a way for her to forget her husband. That's the way I analyze it."

"And now she's forgotten him?"

"You see, you're just acting psychological again. That's not a fair remark. You hardly know the woman."

"I'm sorry then. I didn't mean to sound so hard."

"Giving up something like drinking, even when it's only been a temporary relief, shows a certain strength of character."

"I agree. Maybe we ought to stop with this conversation. I only wanted to be sure, that's all."

"Sure of what?"

"That this was what you wanted."

And what more could he say? After all, Fay *had* given up drinking, and that *was* proof of some real fiber in her. What other objection could Gabe have that would carry any weight —that she was not as smart as his own mother? Well, at age sixty you come to realize that intelligence isn't everything. There are other qualities one looks for in a person. To go around expecting that he would meet in one lifetime another woman as fine and intelligent as his first wife was to go around expecting the impossible. Besides, he did not even know if that was what he wanted. Being more intelligent than Fay had turned out to be a pleasure for him—it made him feel like somebody. On the beach, for instance, he could hold his own now with a fellow like Abe Cole, rather than feeling it necessary to sit back and listen while Anna, say, conversed with the psychoanalyst.

Of course, there were moments when he was nettled slightly by the things Fay did not know or care about. Particularly since she had given up drinking, he had found her not so quick and lively a woman as he had been thinking she was. When they discussed the news events of the day, for instance, there was a certain vagueness on her part, and he had discovered that she was weak on geography. But surely that was to be preferred to a zeal and vivaciousness that had been inspired by drunkenness—which itself had been inspired by sorrow and loss. So what objection did he have? That she was not Anna? One, she couldn't be expected to be somebody else; and two, in certain ways she was a much more natural woman than Anna had ever been. When she was unhappy at least she let you know it—she got drunk. The trouble with his wife had been that she had never needed anyone. Even in dying she had been a perfect lady. But how he had wished that she would break down, how he had wished that she would ask him to close his office and stick by her bed day and night. Surely it was what he would have done had it been he who was dying of leukemia. And still, how he had revered her! How lucky to have been her husband. Her taste, her ideas, her gentility, the way she had of expressing herself . . . But then that grace and charm had been her power. He had gone through life thinking of himself as not having ideas and preferences of his own. And that was against nature; he knew now it had helped to make him, for all his wisecracking and fitfulness, a very melancholy man. With Fay he positively shone in conversation; he felt an honest-to-goodness surge within him as she sat there nodding her head and listening. If only Anna could hear him now . . .

But it was Fay's ears that listened, and Fay's eyes which, though they may not have comprehended all the fine points, at any rate revered him for speaking in their direction.

It was all too confusing; how could a man of his years and station admit to his own child that he did not know what he wanted—especially when the child was a man with whom he could no longer express his love in ways that had been available to him twenty years earlier? You could not toss a man of one hundred and seventy-five pounds up in the air and catch him in your arms. Hardly. And that too served to confuse matters—for even if the son could be persuaded, it might not be as satisfying living with him as Dr. Wallach had once imagined. The young man was occupied with his own affairs; all that brooding about leaving Chicago must have to do with people and happenings of which his father was ignorant, in which his father had no place. There was really no choice about Fay then; she was all he could hope for.

When next he spoke he was in the grips of a vertigo worse than the one that had seized him earlier when he had dived into the ocean with his son. Dizzy, numb, trembling, he had complained of a chill, and come back to the shore, sending the boy off to swim by himself. He had managed then to walk back to his towel without giving a sign of his condition, but now he actually feared that he would stagger in the middle of what he was saying.

What *was* he saying? He heard his voice but the experience of utterance did not seem to be his. "Look, this reaction isn't a reasoned one. I don't want you to feel I hold you entirely responsible." He found he was not even sure of his subject. Oh, yes—his son and Fay. "After all, it's Hamlet. Oedipus."

They were turning up through a ridge that the wind had cut in the dunes; they moved toward the street where the car was parked. "After all," the doctor said, "this is an ancient thing, very deep and imbedded in the human race, this business between children and men." His hand was on his son's shoulder, as if it were the boy he was steadying. "If I were you, I wouldn't worry about it."

—

"Now this is quite a case we're dealing with. This is strictly a case of morality . . ." The dining room, situated in a turret that extended off the old house, was alive with sunlight. The house itself had belonged, years ago, to a Sag Harbor whaling captain; it still was filled with objects from all parts of the world, many of them worn and chipped and frazzled, but as the doctor had told his fiancée, full of warmth and feeling. The pictures on the walls, old fishing scenes and nautical maps of the Sound, could hardly be seen for the strong light that bounced off the glass that encased them. Fay was holding a match to a cigarette that she had placed in her ivory holder. She looked nothing less than aristocratic in the surroundings, especially with the holder, which the doctor had bought for her because he believed it gave her substance. Gabe, in white trousers and a blue polo shirt, was settled back in his chair sipping coffee.

Breakfast had been a success—except that Dr. Wallach still had to do most of the talking. Fay, of course, had been busy serving, and Gabe had been busy eating. But now, with second cups of coffee on the table, the doctor felt the time had come to draw them out. The sparkle of the brass coffee pot, the light on the rosewood dining chairs, Fay's ivory holder between her lips, Gabe's crisp summery good looks, even the simple fact that his son's hair was still damp, made Dr. Wallach feel more optimistic about his family situation than he had in a long while. When he reached up to scratch his nose, he could smell the salt from the sea on the back of his hand; this too produced hope and excitement in him.

"Here," Dr. Wallach said, "is a man of no little education—" He was laying out his silverware as though each piece were the term in a syllogism. Hopeful as he was, he couldn't keep his hands still. "A physician, a man of the community, a respected person—no doubt a man of means. Let's say, for the sake of argument, not rich, but comfortable. He has what he wants, and then a little bit more. All that, and yet he takes his life and jeopardizes it. Now what will this poor fellow's fate be? What was he up to? Was he right or was he wrong?"

Fay nodded; he supposed she thought he would now proceed to answer his own question. She continued with her smoking.

"Fay?" he said.

"Yes?"

"What do you think about this?"

"Well . . . it's a very interesting predicament."

It did not please him to hear her use a phrase that was a favorite of his own. But agreeably he said, "It certainly is." He smoothed the edge of the white tablecloth. Then to be dramatic, to shake them up a little, he slapped the table so hard that the silverware jumped. Of late he was getting rather a kick out of thinking of himself as someone who was an unpredictable conversationalist. "What do you think, Professor?" He looked over at his son, who, thank goodness, was smiling. He could not say that the boy was not trying to be amiable. "Place yourself in the fellow's circumstances. The child is brought to you near death. I won't go into the medical nomenclature—the child simply needs a transfusion, that's the gist of it. The parents are Seventh Day Adventists. They tell you they cannot allow the child a transfusion. You tell them the child will die without it. They say they do not believe in eating blood."

There was a flicker of his son's eyes toward the window. Bored? Did he want to go already? Or was he just back to his own problems? Well, what kind of problems could they be? Young, in good health, a respected position—what kind of problem was it to be at the very *brink* of everything?

"But, Mordecai"—Fay was shaking her head—"excuse me, but the child would take the blood in the veins. That's not the same at all."

"Ah-*ha*," said Dr. Wallach. Irritation with his son faded as he felt a fish at the end of his line. Real interest had at last come swimming up out of a sea of silence—as expected. The little news item in the second section of the *Times* had caught his imagination, and he knew it could not help but do the same with the others. Though he had read it while Gabe was showering and Fay was beating the eggs, he had saved it until breakfast was over, so that they could converse without the distraction of food. Now for a good old-fashioned family discussion . . . "Ah-ha," he said, "but we are enlightened, we are students of the eighteenth century."

"Yes," Mrs. Silberman said.

"You're talking about reason, Fay, intelligence. But to them," the doctor pointed out, "a transfusion is eating blood. Now, once again, what's the answer?"

He tapped his fork on his plate. "Gabe? Fay?"

Gabe only shrugged and smiled. Something distressing moved across the doctor's consciousness: was he being patronized?

"Education," Fay announced. "There's an area where we could certainly learn something from the Russians."

Disappointed, the doctor could nevertheless not help but be braced by her good will. She was going to flatter his son. All right. At least her interest had moved beyond the question of his posture.

"Well, perhaps," Dr. Wallach said. "But I don't know that you're quite on the point. You're not a teacher, you see, you're a doctor. What do you do? Does he respect what the people want, or does he give them what they don't want, what *he* thinks is best for them? Gabe, go ahead. You're an intellectual person—this is an exercise of the intellect, I'd say. I'm interested in differing opinions on this subject."

"Yes, I'd like to hear his thinking on this too," Fay said. "The academic approach."

"Well," Gabe said.

"Your honest opinion," said the doctor, excited.

"Well, I think it could probably be explained to them—"

"You see, Mordecai," Fay said, "edu*ca*tion—"

"Shhh . . ." he said.

Gabe started again. "I think it could probably be explained to the parents. That is, the doctor could make a distinction for them—"

"Go ahead, go ahead," Dr. Wallach said, "very interesting this distinction business."

"That there are rules on the one hand, but that there's the essence of the religion too. That the rules can be suspended sometimes in the name of what's most essential. The child's life, living, is more crucial than the breaking of the commandment, or the law, not to eat blood."

Dr. Wallach saw Mrs. Silberman clicking her tongue. He did not know whether to interrupt before she said something not quite worthy of herself, or to let the conversation he had worked so to initiate, go its own way. He tried relaxing as she said, "Well, I just can't see it. I mean they are *not* eating blood.

I can't agree to that. A transfusion just isn't eating blood, not to my way of thinking."

Gabe mumbled something and turned his attention back to his coffee cup.

"Wait a minute, just a minute," the doctor rushed in. "This isn't a dispute. Actually I don't think that's quite the point Gabe was making, Fay. If I have it right, Gabe, what you're saying—"

"We just disagree, I suppose," she said with a tinkly laugh. "Because to me, you see, you can't even begin to call a blood transfusion eating blood. Our veins are one thing, and our mouths another."

Gabe simply sighed.

"Please," said Fay, waving a hand and turning to face him, "I'm not asking you to give in. Everybody's entitled to their own opinion."

"True," the young man said.

Oh no—was Fay going to carry a grudge? The boy no longer objected to her; he had made that clear on the beach. Couldn't she let by-gones be by-gones? But then she didn't know they were . . . He could not decide whether to give up on the conversation or to try to smooth things over.

"Well," he said, "I think that threw some light. I think, however, Gabriel, I think I might agree you were side-stepping a little. These, after all, aren't people who can be reasoned with."

"Of course they aren't. They're ignorant," Fay said.

She spoke so forcefully that the doctor nearly became frantic. "See, that's his approach, Fay. That's just one approach—this is an intellectual exercise, we're simply working out the kinks in our minds."

"Still—"

But he raised his palm at her, a policeman halting traffic; he could feel his eyes hardening. And it worked—she shut up. What they should do now, he thought, was get into their swim suits, take the umbrella and chairs, and go down to the beach for the rest of the day. Surely, however, the three of them could conduct an adult conversation; he was not suggesting that they should all learn to live forever in the same house. To ask for a little respect and understanding was not, to his way of thinking, to ask for too much.

Gabe had set down his empty cup on the table; he seemed waiting for permission to leave. Well, he could just stay where he was! The father was still the father, and the son the son! "So what would you *do*?" Dr. Wallach asked.

"I—" Gabe rubbed his hands along his trousers. "I'd give the child the transfusion."

"You realize the law now," said the doctor, instantly impassioned again. "You realize the law says no minor can be operated on, given a transfusion or whatever, without permission of the parents. You understand that now?"

"I'd give the child the transfusion." Gabe had spoken in a very soft voice.

"All *right*, all *right*," Dr. Wallach took his spoon and crossed it over his knife. He leaned back in his chair and tilted his head so that all the loose skin of his throat was drawn upwards. He addressed the fancy chandelier. "I wouldn't," he said.

"Mordecai!" Fay said.

He spread two hands on the tablecloth—the hands of a murderer, he thought, feeling a strange excitement—and left them there, palms down. "That's right. I wouldn't give the child a drop of blood."

"That's not a bit like you," Fay said.

How did she know? Perhaps Anna had known what he was like . . . but then having known, she had dealt with him. At least Fay didn't simply *deal* with him; she admired him. Worse —she sentimentalized him, she misunderstood and overvalued him. All of which he had encouraged. He had chosen this house for her with a taste he pretended was his own; but he knew he really had no taste. The furnishings were of a kind that his dead wife would have liked for a summer place, and so he had said to Fay, "Take it." And she had.

He kept two strong hands on the table anyway. "It's a matter of respect," he said, "that we're dealing with. You see? 'The parent is the father to the child.' Wordsworth?" he asked, turning to Gabe. Then he realized his mistake. But it was only one of several misquotations and malapropisms that had lately passed his lips. And though inaccuracy—pretension—was one thing when the audience was Fay, it was another when it was his son—or Abe Cole. It was not, he suddenly recalled, *Recollections of Things Past*, but *Remembrance!* And *Oedipus* was not by Socrates—it was by Sophocles! Christ! Under the umbrella yesterday, what an ass he must have seemed. What was he up to, passing himself off as something he wasn't? Was this his fate at the age of sixty, to be a fool?

Gabe was saying, "I think it's 'The child is the father of the man'—but I know what you mean."

It did not help the doctor's condition any to know that his son now felt the need to be kind to him. "I believe in the depth of belief," Dr. Wallach said, raising his voice. "If the other fellow's got a belief, I honor that belief. We have to have more respect for the other fellow's wish; he wants what he believes in. Who am I to tell him differently?"

"You'd let the child die?" Gabe asked.

"Absolutely!" He had not felt so sure before as he did now.

"Well," Gabe said, "I don't know . . "

"Don't know what?"

"I don't know if you really would do it, faced with the situation."

"Then you don't know me."

Apparently no one could think of what to say next. Dr. Wallach piled some silverware on his plate; then he turned and asked Fay her opinion. "Go ahead," he said, "this is still a discussion as far as I'm concerned, not a dispute."

She put out her cigarette in the ash tray. The grainy look around her dark eyes gave her an air of knowingness—until she spoke. "This is certainly a case of morals," she said, and the doctor heard his own words once again. "Morals certainly enters into it . . ."

"Exactly," he said, and quickly he turned to his son. "What do I seem to you here, Gabe, too—too Nietzschean?"

"No, no, I don't think that."

"I'm telling you, if the chips were down, if I had been this poor fellow in Texas, that's what I would have done."

Gabe seemed at last to have run out of patience. "Why? So you wouldn't lose your license?"

"Absolutely not!"

"Then it's still a mystery to me."

"You believe I'd do it though?"

"Yes, yes, I suppose I do."

"All right, all right. The why, I'll grant you, is the crux all right."

Mrs. Silberman flicked open the initialed gold case that had been her engagement present, and put a new cigarette into her holder. Since she had stopped drinking, she smoked all the time. Did that serve to blur the image of her first husband too? If it was such a difficult image to blur, if it wouldn't just *stay* blurred, then why was she even thinking of another man? Was he simply to be a convenience?

"All right, why then?" Gabe asked.

"Because," said Dr. Wallach, his thoughts turning with difficulty back to the issue at hand, "I respect people."

Mrs. Silberman momentarily withdrew the match from the end of the cigarette. "Mordecai loves people," she said, then she held very steady while she lit her cigarette.

"And I don't?"

Dr. Wallach did not know to whom Gabe had directed the question. Immediately he said, "Well, you don't respect the parents to disobey their wish that way."

"I respect the child," Gabe said.

The doctor moved one finger around in a circle just in front of his chin; he circled, he circled, then he saw the light. "Ah *that's* something, *that's* curious." He turned to his fiancée. "You see that? *That's* identification that I was telling you about. You see, he's never been a parent, so he can't understand the parent's position. But what has he been? What?"

Either she did not know, or out of respect was waiting for him to say it.

"A *child*," he announced. "So he takes the child's side in this thing."

"I see," Fay said.

"Wait a minute," Gabe said, "things are getting confused here. Maybe I wasn't clear enough. I meant I respect the child's right to *live*, and not the parent's desire to kill it. I can't have any respect for that. If you want to go ahead and be Freudian and pursue this thing all the way down—"

"Sure, sure, what?—go ahead—" Dr. Wallach said. "What?"

"Well, I don't know. You might say that the parents are using what they see as moral and religious reasons for doing away with the child. You see, I don't know anything about the case"—he motioned toward the floor, where the newspaper was—"the specifics of it, but it's even possible that for some strange reason they want to kill the child. Look, we can't begin to—"

"Now that's an awful thing to say," Fay told him, "even in jest. Parents give themselves up for their children. Look at all your father has done for you. Harvard, nice clothes, a car—"

"No, no," said Dr. Wallach, silencing her, "let's hear him. A theory is a theory. I'm very interested in his theories."

"It's not a theory," Gabe said. "I just want to rule out this identification business. You're not arguing on the issue then. You're wanting to argue with me."

Dr. Wallach pointed a finger at the boy, as though sharp thinking on his son's part had caught him out, as though his lapse had been a deliberate point of strategy, a test of the young man's alertness. "The old ad hominem—right," he said. "Well, okay, I'll give him that," he told Fay.

"Fine," Gabe said, and took a deep breath.

"Then you were saying?" Dr. Wallach asked.

"I was only asking," Gabe said, "what right, as a physician, you would have to allow the death of a child, a patient, whose life you could easily save. That's all, really."

"And I told you. People have a firm religious belief, a way of life they cherish, then I leave them alone. I myself am an atheist—"

Mrs. Silberman bestowed upon him a motherly look.

"I am, Fay, *please*, and I have a right to be. The same with these parents. Each man knows what's best for himself. You'll get older," he told Gabe, "you'll see you can't rule the world."

"Don't people trick themselves ever?"

"That's their business. What looks like a trick to you may not be a trick to them."

"Well . . ." Gabe said, and stood up.

"Well what?"

"Nothing. I just believe you're talking theoretically. If you pulled a tooth, and the patient was bleeding unduly and a transfusion was necessary—well, you'd give it. At least I think you would."

"I would not," Dr. Wallach said in a loud voice. "I absolutely would not."

"Well," said Gabe, closing his hands slowly, "okay."

"You see, this is a perfect example of an inability on your part to recognize somebody's beliefs. You don't know why people do what they do, believe me."

"True. I simply said that if one were to let somebody die needlessly, that would be wrong."

"To you what I do is wrong. Not to me!"

"I didn't say you were wrong. I said I felt the *position* was wrong!"

"*I'm* the position." Dr. Wallach was trembling. "I have my set of beliefs, you have yours—"

His son was leaning toward him, his hands on the back of a chair. "Please, I didn't mean to raise my voice. I guess we just don't agree about the transfusion. I'm willing to accept that."

Fay was trying to absorb herself in smoking, but it wasn't working. She had gone pale. "Sure, it's only a game," she said. "I know people who scream at each other over Scrabble."

"It's not a game." Dr. Wallach lifted his napkin and threw it on the table. His eyes were burning and he looked at neither of them. "This actually happened . . . in . . . in . . ." He picked a section of the paper off the rug. He cleared his throat; he found it necessary to clear it again. "In Texas. Here." He handed the paper across to Mrs. Silberman. "There, in black and white, what could happen to any of us. This man is going to lose his license, he can go to jail. It's a historical fact—go ahead, read it. I didn't make it up."

Mrs. Silberman looked at the paper, then handed it to Gabe.

Dr. Wallach began stacking the breakfast dishes. "People's lives, you don't go fooling with them. You let people be themselves—you can ruin a life like that. Your own mother, on her last night, that's what she talked about. That's what she regretted above anything else. Don't interfere—"

He set the dishes down and left the room.

—

In a few minutes the door opened and someone walked over to the bed. He did not open his eyes.

"Mordecai?"

"Yes."

"Are you all right?"

"I just became overexcited."

He felt her sit lightly down beside him. He could sense that she was afraid. She had reason to be. He wanted to open his eyes and tell her that he could not marry her. Youthful and trim as he had tried to keep himself, abreast as he had tried to stay of current affairs, he was an old man and he had had his life. Anna had been more than he could handle or understand, but he had asked her to marry him; maybe that was *why* he had asked her. He did not know. He had thought at the time and he thought still that he had loved Anna. He could no longer tell; he had never really been good at figuring people out. All he knew now was what he felt, and what he felt was no love for Fay. And no love for his son either. What was the use of loving him any more? He had sat there like a stranger, never once saying the right thing.

Fay was speaking. "Let him think what he wants, Mordecai."

"I'm not telling him what to think."

"Everybody's entitled to his own opinion," she said. "The individuals involved know what's best."

"Absolutely," he said.

There was a knock on the door. Fay got up from the bed and opened it a little. Dr. Wallach heard his son ask if everything was all right.

"He's resting," Fay answered. "I think his swim tired him out."

"Tell him I'm sorry."

"Look, young man, you're entitled to your opinions."

"Please, just tell him that I didn't mean to raise my voice."

She closed the door and came back to the bed. "When they grow up," she said, "they think they know more than their parents. He says that he's sorry. *Now* he says it."

"Fay," Dr. Wallach said, "take my hand."

"Of course, darling. He had no right, Mordecai, it was only a game—"

"Just take my hand," he said. "Please, don't say anything."

4

THAT MORNING, when Cynthia rolled over, she found that her brother had climbed the ladder of the double-decker bed and crawled into the upper bunk beside her. Barely awake, she felt she must be floating in the hollow of a bad bad dream, and suddenly, furious, confused, she pushed with violence at the sleeping little boy. He rolled only once and fell from the bed. There was the thud of his head against the wooden floor, then no further sound. It appeared the Markie was going to sleep right through it; he did not even cry.

But when Cynthia leaned out over the top bunk, she noticed something more. At first it seemed to be a red string wedged in the crack between the floor boards—only it was moving toward the wall. Trembling, she waited for her father or June to come through the door and see what she had done. When time passed and no one had entered, she thought she had just better try to fall back to sleep again. And then it became clear to her that it could not be a bad dream she was having, for if it were, she would be trying to wake herself up rather than fall asleep. She rolled toward the wall anyway and closed her eyes. It was then that she began to scream.

Later in the morning her father telephoned from Southampton Hospital. Cynthia sat in the sunny living room turning the pages of a large picture book of statues, while in the hallway June whispered into the mouthpiece. Her stepmother hung up the phone and came in to tell her to put on her bathing suit. They would go to the beach; was that all right? The child turned another page, and then June was kneeling down and holding Cynthia to her. She allowed herself to be held. Her stepmother's hair, a sunnier shade than her real mother's hair, was swept up at the back of her head; Cynthia could imagine the way it looked from the way it felt against her cheek. Soft, fine, whirled up—Markie said it was candy. She could see her brother stiffen with pleasure when he drew in his breath and lowered his face right down into the swell of June's hair. June was very thin, and when she wore a bathing suit or a summer dress, all silky and flower-smelling, Cynthia could see that she had no breasts; there was just skin over bone, like a man. All a child could really push his face into was her hair; and though Markie might amuse himself in this way, Cynthia did not think that it was suitable for her. Not that June had ever favored Markie; it was only that her hair had somehow seemed his property from the start. Certainly June had never scolded her when she spilled her milk—and she had spilled it often during the first month she had come to live in New York City. Nor had June ever once been as cross as her real mother had been to her so many times. Even now June's first impulse was not to blame Cynthia for what had happened, which was surely what her old mother would have done. No one, in fact, had had a chance to ask questions or make accusations. Only minutes after she had begun screaming, her father had carried Markie down to the car wrapped in a big towel, and driven him away in the station wagon. Though it had looked comical for a grownup to be backing a car out of a driveway wearing pajamas and a bathrobe, she had managed not to laugh. When the car swerved down into the road, there had been a flash of blood on the front side door, and then any hint of a smile had vanished completely from her face. She had walked back to the house, taken a sculpture book she liked from the shelf, and settled into a chair by the window; she pretended to be absorbed in the book, while above all she was absorbing herself in being quiet. A blind person could not have heard her turn the pages, and her respiration was as silent as the shifting of the tides of her blood—a shifting that seemed to be taking place in the hollow of her throat.

The house was quieter than it had ever been during the daytime. No child was scooting up the stairs, no friend was slamming through the front screen door, no one was arguing with anyone—and that *was* a change. Lately her father and June seemed always to be bickering at one another at breakfasttime. Ever since they had come out to Springs, there was something that June kept saying to her father in the mornings that made him angry. One morning he had become so angry that he had picked up his plate and thrown it clear across the breakfast nook to the kitchen. Markie had begun to giggle and point to where the yoke was slipping down the wallpaper onto the enamel of the sink, but she knew enough to keep her eyes on her bowl and continue spooning cereal into her dry mouth. Only June had gotten up to leave the table.

And yet that evening, when the two of them were sitting out in the white garden chairs for dinner, she had seen her father lean over and kiss June's hands and then her hair and her neck —all while Mark went circling around the house on his tricycle, pretending to be a fire engine, until it was time for him to go to bed. Earlier in the summer there had been an evening when she had been asked to go into the house for some ice from the refrigerator; when she had come onto the back steps holding the cold tray, she had seen her father open a button of June's blouse and put a hand to where her breasts should have been. June was thin, but beautiful too, and she had those perfect white teeth that Cynthia saw at that moment, as her stepmother's head went back and her father pulled her to him with his other hand. When her father hugged and kissed June, she knew it was because June was beautiful, and had been a debutante, and was rich, and had gone to Bryn Mawr College. She would be going there too now that she was rich; Martha had not gone there because she had not been rich at all. Markie was to go to Harvard College, June said, which seemed to Cynthia a ridiculous statement—Markie could not read yet, or even count successfully beyond twelve. But June and her father said ridiculous things quite often, her father particularly. In Springs he was thought of as a very funny man, though everyone agreed that Cynthia was his toughest audience. "Come on, Ed Sullivan," he would finally have to say to her, "how about just a giggle, just a little snort—just raise a *lip* even—" Whenever there were people around he would amuse them, unless, of course, he was unhappy, as he had been when June had made him throw his egg.

At night June and her father slept together in their own room in only one bed. Consequently, she knew that June would be having a baby soon. No one had spoken about it yet, but she was aware that there were happenings of which she was not warned in advance. She had figured out that the baby was coming, for she had been able to discover it was the right month. Some time earlier she had found out that a woman could only have a baby if it was the right month. She knew it was the right month because Mrs. Griffin had simply come right out and said so. She had leaned back onto her beach towel and put two wet little pieces of cotton over her eyes, and she had remarked what a perfect month it had been—*it had been just right.*

So she knew—and she did not like it either. She was not anxious to have still another brother or sister around the house. The smaller the child the more adults seemed to like it. At least the bigger she became the less people cared about her. She knew for a fact that all her father's friends in Springs liked Markie better than her. They were always picking him up and putting him down, though she herself did not really weigh that much more. She had even heard her father say to June that though Markie was the same jolly boy he had always been, Cynthia had turned into a very grave child. And whatever that meant, it was not so. She would have told June—if she had thought that June would not have been predisposed in another direction—that it was her father who had changed. Of course he called her his "special baby," and of course he swung her over his head, and whenever June kissed Markie he would march right over and kiss her. Yet whatever he did displeased her; every time she suspected he was about to do something that would make her happy, he did it, and it made her sad. Surely when he kissed her she should be happy—but she knew that June did not particularly like him to do it, and so even that finally caused discomfort.

Actually June didn't like him to kiss girls at all. That was what they had been arguing over when her father had thrown his egg. He had said that June didn't even want him to *talk* to them, to stand within ten *feet* of them; June said that wasn't so, he said it was, she said it wasn't—and then the two halves of his plate were rattling on the floor and Markie was pointing at the egg sliding into the sink. Looking steadily into her cereal bowl, Cynthia had been able to imagine how it all had happened: on the Griffins' lawn, where the party had been the night before, her father must have gone up to a girl who was there and kissed her. Cynthia was even able to imagine the girl, in a billowy dress and patent leather sandals like her own new Papagallos . . . Now whenever her father kissed her, she believed that partly it was to spite June, and she knew that would make June angry at *her*, make her cross the way her old mother used to be.

So in the Reganhart household, matters of affectionate display became complicated for a while: first June would kiss Markie, then her father would come over to kiss Cynthia, and Cynthia would have to run out of the room, or up the beach, or to the far end of the garden to get away from him. Which made her *father* angry with her. For the time being she did not want to be kissed by anyone. She had not, however, pushed Markie from her bunk because June preferred to kiss him, or because she had thought her little brother had himself wanted to kiss her. She had pushed him out because he did not belong there in the first place. He was going to do something to her. She had not had to explain to anybody why she had pushed him, because nobody as yet had asked what had happened. Nobody had scolded her and nobody so far had said what the punishment was to be.

When she was being driven to the beach in June's convertible, her stepmother asked her, "Did you see it, Cynthia?"

"See what?"

After a moment June said, "See Markie fall."

And Cynthia replied, "I was sleeping." And then she knew that what she had begun to suspect was not—as usually happened—simply what she was beginning to hope for. She knew that she was not to be punished at all. June had taken one hand from the steering wheel and put it on top of Cynthia's head, gently.

No one knew what had happened. Only Markie, and he didn't know either. He couldn't, for the same reason that he couldn't have been going to do something to her—he had been sleeping. But of course she didn't *know* that anything really had to be done. If it was the right month and a man got into bed with a lady, that was that. Her father had a penis like Markie's, and she, June, her mother, and Mrs. Griffin all had vaginas. All men had penises. They were what gave you the babies.

At Barnes Hole, where the beach was touched by an endless silver bay, she decided that she did not even want to get out of the car.

"Don't you feel well, dear?" June was asking.

"I don't want to go here." She had a sense of some new power that was hers; but now that she was at the bay, at the brink of a regular day, the familiarity of the landscape and the routine was not the comfort she had been expecting it would be.

"Where would you prefer to go?" June removed her sunglasses. While she rubbed her eyes Cynthia had to turn away —their redness embarrassed her. "Would you like to visit somebody?"

"I just don't want to go here, I'll tell you that."

"Well, how about the ocean beach?"

"I suppose so."

"Honey, where would you *like* to go?"

"Oh, the ocean beach is okay."

She did not look up to see what the effect had been of the little snarl in her voice. But looking down she saw that June's slender suntanned hand, the one with the pretty blue ring, had curled over hers again. In a moment the car had turned and they were headed for the ocean. The wind blew her hair—a delightful cool feminine feeling—and she could not help herself: she was smiling. It was because she had had to look straight into Markie's blood that she was receiving so much care and attention; she knew this, but she continued smiling anyway. The truth was that she deserved special attention; the sight of the red blood creeping down the floor boards had nearly turned her stomach. She had cried and become hysterical, and she had screamed and screamed. She remembered now what it was she had screamed: "Markie fell! Markie fell out!"

And hadn't he? Well, hadn't he? If not, then June would be punishing her now instead of rewarding her with kindnesses. If anyone at all *had* pushed Markie it was God, who had seen that it was a sin for her stupid little brother to get in bed with her when they weren't married.

They were driving along the road that led between the trees to Amagansett. "Don't you like Barnes any more?" June asked.

"The water's dirty."

"I thought it was so clean—"

"I don't like it there! I'm not going there!"

"Nobody's making you," June said, and that, she thought happily, was the case. At the edge of Springs they approached the small grocery store with the gas pump out in front. June pulled the car over and parked by the steps that led up to the store. She went inside to make a phone call, while Cynthia waited in the car and spelled out the sign over the doorway.

H. Savage—Groceries and Gas
Barnes Hole Rd, Springs

It had turned out, of course, that there was no hole at Barnes at all. She had looked for it during the first week of her stay. By herself she had walked the long stretch of beach, and then she had even enlisted Markie, but he was no help because he kept seeing holes, virtual abysses, that weren't even there. At low tide she went off alone, dragging her legs through the receding waters, but with no luck; at last she had to come back up to the blanket, her nose wet and the ends of her hair damp, and ask June where the hole was. June explained to her that it was only a name given to the place—officially it was called Barnes Landing. But all the ladies continued to smile and she realized that it was something a child wasn't supposed to know. And she was right—that same afternoon a boy with large ears had let her hang onto his tube with him, and he seemed so helpful she had decided to ask him where the hole was. He had pointed between her legs and then ducked her under the water.

She looked up the steps. Nobody in the dark store was near enough to see her; all she could make out were June's white sandals and one hand holding a Kleenex. She slid down into the crevice of the front seat of the convertible. Pushing her bathing suit aside, she put her finger a little way inside herself. So far, no baby.

Soon June emerged into the sunlight, but her expression was impossible to figure out. She had on dark glasses and was wearing her big straw coolie hat—the one Markie used to like to parade around in—and a blue jumper over the top of her bathing suit. Cynthia thought she looked like a man, but then she came down off the little porch swinging herself like a lady, and got into the car.

"May I turn the radio on?"

June nodded and they started away.

"Is it okay if I listen to music?"

"That's fine," June said.

Turning all the knobs, she asked, "Did you call the hospital?"

"I spoke to your father. Markie's resting—Cynthia, could you tune it down just a little?"

"Is he unconscious?" She had heard earlier that he was.

"That just means he's getting a good rest, Cynthia. It's the body's way of making sure we get a good rest."

"Will he be all right then?"

"Of course—" June said. "Cynthia, *please* lower the radio—"

"But then I won't be able to *hear* it—"

June did not answer. Cynthia listened to the music, her concentration not so intense that she did not notice the tears moving down June's cheeks. "Well, when he comes home," Cynthia said, her hair blowing wonderfully out behind her again, "we'll have to teach him not to fall out like that any more. He was never very careful. Even my mother will tell you that."

—

Only four other cars were parked at the end of the street leading down to the ocean beach; it was not yet noon. Cynthia raced around to help June take the blanket and folding chair out of the trunk. From the trough in which the spare tire sat, she unwedged her pail and shovel, which she had hardly played with all summer. She grabbed Markie's pail and shovel too, and dragged both pails along the pebbles of the parking area. Then she waited for June to tell her to put Markie's pail back where it belonged. Instead, her stepmother reached out and smoothed the top of the child's hair.

They spread the blanket out where the beach began its slope toward the water. A wave had rolled in a moment before, and the four or five people floundering in the sudsy wake were all laughing and calling to one another. To Cynthia the waves looked large and unfriendly. She carried her pails down to where the sand was wet and started to dig, turning regularly to see what June was doing behind her. A book was open on her stepmother's lap, though she did not seem to be reading it. She did not seem really to be doing anything.

When her sand castle had been washed away, she looked

back to see that her stepmother was talking with Mr. Siegel. Pretending to hunt for seashells, she cut a zigzag path up toward the blanket. By the time she was close enough to hear, they had stopped saying anything.

"Hi, Cindy Lou," Mr. Siegel said.

She ran to where he knelt in the sand beside June. "We saw your television program the other night, Mr. Siegel," she said.

"Well, let's hear the dark news," he said. "What's my rating, friend?" She knew that he was one of the people who liked to pick up Markie all the time. Markie, however, was in the hospital this particular morning.

"Oh I loved it!"

"Come on," he said, "you're kidding me." He tossed a handful of sand at her feet. "I understand you're a skeptic about TV. Your father tells me you're an intellectual, that you spend your mornings looking through books on Brancusi."

"I like TV though," she said. She had not quite gotten the sense of all he had said to her. "It was really funny when that old grandfather started slicing up that turkey and then it fell right in his lap. Boy, did I begin to laugh—didn't I, June?"

June smiled, barely.

"Hey, does anybody want to go in the water?" Cynthia said.

"Water?" said Mr. Siegel. "What water?"

Cynthia's laughter was uproarious.

"Not right now, honey," June said.

She knew that Mr. Siegel and June were anxious to resume their conversation, and she knew what they had been talking about. "When are you going to write another program, Mr. Siegel?"

"Now I know you're on my side, I'm going to get right home and start one this afternoon."

"For me?"

"Absolutely."

"Wow!"

"This time *two* grandfathers and *two* turkeys!"

"That's *great*!" she said, and she went skipping down to the water. She heard June calling after her, "Be careful—" with the result that she skipped right on down to the edge, as though she hadn't heard at all. A wave was rising a little way out, and the sight of it unnerved her. But she took a step directly forward, into the sea—and waited. She did not have to wait very long.

"Cynthia—*please*—"

The child turned. She had been able to get June up off the blanket; she had even been able to move her some five or six feet toward the water.

"Okay," Cynthia said, and she hopped on one leg up to where her pails lay, and flopped down in the sand beside them.

"Please, be careful, Cyn, please," June called, and just at that moment she heard Markie's head hitting the floor. A little sound came out of her mouth, but then she saw that it hadn't been Markie's head at all, only a wave collapsing onto the flat blue surf. It made her think, however. When Markie came out of the hospital he would have to wear a bandage. She decided she would be very generous to him then. She would tie his shoelaces for him and put his toys away without anybody asking.

Though the hit on the head would probably knock some sense into that kid.

She spoke these words out loud; when she tried them a second time, they made her giggle. The hit on the head will probably knock some sense into that kid. Boy, that little kid didn't know anything . . . What she knew for sure and didn't need anyone to tell her, was that she was much smarter than her brother. She was an exceptional child—that was what the teachers at her new school said. She had the mentality of a ten-year-old, which made her *five* years older than Markie. She had reason to be proud of herself. When she was an adult she would be more intelligent than others. They would all have to come to her to ask what the best thing was for them to do.

Cynthia suddenly felt herself so full of pep, so convinced that life was made for pleasure, her pleasure, that she jumped up and went racing toward her stepmother. Because she had seen Markie's blood she knew she could finally get June to agree to take her in the water. She wanted to walk right into the ocean holding June's hand. She left Markie's pail and shovel where it was and went flying to the blanket—but there was a man walking down the beach in her direction. She was momentarily stilled by the familiarity of his gait. Everything about him was so familiar, though at first she could not think

what his name was. It did not take her very long, however, to
remember, or to stop being able to forget. But where was
Mommy? Mommy had come with him to see Markie in the
hospital! Mommy would find out that she had pushed him!
Well, she hadn't—he fell! That's what he got for committing a
sin.

"June," she called, "can we go—"

But Gabe had already seen her. He had come to catch her
for her mother. All she could do now was scream and run into
her room, but they were not even in the house. They were on
the wide beach, under the bright sun, and he was so big that
wherever she fled he would find her and bring her back.

In the second before he removed his sunglasses, she wondered if she might not be mistaken. Then his hand reached out
—and yes, oh yes, oh what would happen—

"Hi, Cynthia. Hello."

June looked to see who it was. Cynthia thought of making
believe that he was a strange man, for she was not supposed
to speak to strange men. But when her mother appeared, it
would be evident to everyone that she had been lying—and
then they would know for sure that she had pushed her
brother.

"Hello," Cynthia said.

"You remember me?"

"Uh-huh. Gabe."

"Well, how are you? You look brown as a berry—you look
healthy and grown-up and—"

"I'm fine."

"Where's your little brother?"

Cynthia shrugged.

June was standing. "I'm Mrs. Reganhart."

Gabe extended his hand. "I'm Gabe Wallach. How do you
do? I'm a friend of Martha Reganhart's. From Chicago."

Now Cynthia looked up to where the cars were parked. She
recognized Gabe's car as soon as she saw it—and inside she
could make out the figure of her mother; she was crouching in
the back; spying on her. This was not the first time that the
child had had occasion to suspect her mother of spying. When
she had first arrived at her new school in New York, she had
been certain that her teacher, Mrs. Koplin, was actually her

mother in disguise. Then one rainy afternoon Mrs. Koplin's husband had come to pick her up; he had been carrying an umbrella, and Mrs. Koplin had called him Herb, and she had said that before they went home they must stop first at the A&P on Twelfth Street. And when she said that, Cynthia had known that Mrs. Koplin wasn't her mother after all. Yet she had been so certain . . . Now, however, she could actually see who the woman was, crouched in the back of the car. Cynthia started to whistle and to look up at the sky and to kick her toes into the sand. She was being watched and she did not intend to do a single thing wrong. If she could manage, she wanted it to seem as though she were having a very good time.

"—in the hospital—"

"—how long?"

"—he'll be all right, of course—"

Cynthia turned so that her mother could see only her back. Turning, she saw Markie's pail bobbling up and down at the water's edge. It was just about to be washed away, and if it was washed away who would they blame but her! They would blame her, and then they would start asking questions— Fast as she could, she started down the beach, her arms out-stretched toward the pail.

"*Cynthia—*"

"Cynthia, *what—*"

"Cyn—" Just as she got hold of the handle, somebody grabbed her arm. It was Gabe; behind him stood June, her mouth open, her hand up to her pale cheek.

"Cynthia—oh Cynthia," June said, "what are you doing? Never—"

"Getting Markie's pail." She did not know whether it would help any to cry.

"Oh . . . Oh, Cynthia, that's a good girl, that's fine—oh honey, don't go near the water alone—not today." It was June who seemed as though she were about to weep.

"I won't," she said, and she hoped her mother had seen just how much June worried about her and took care of her. They all started up the beach, and while June moved off ahead, Cynthia asked Gabe, "Why doesn't Mommy come out of the car?"

He smiled. "Martha's not in the car, Cynthia. She's in Chicago."

"What's that?" she said.

"You mean that, in the back seat? That's a beach umbrella. That's my father's beach umbrella."

"Yes?" She took another look. She felt as she had when Mrs. Koplin had called her husband Herb.

"Martha's in Chicago," he said. "She has to work. I'm visiting with my own father in East Hampton. I thought I'd come over and say hello. Your mother wanted me to."

"How did you find me?"

"Oh I just asked anybody on the streets, you know, where Cynthia Reganhart was, and they said you were down here by the ocean."

"We don't even usually come here."

"Then I suppose I was very lucky. I expected to see Mark too."

"Well, he's in the hospital."

"When you see him will you tell him I was here to visit?"

"Okay. He has to learn not to fall out of his bed, that's all."

June was standing by the blanket; she had closed her book. "Mr. Wallach," she said, "could I ask you a favor? Will you be here awhile?"

"A little while, yes—"

"Could you stay a few minutes with Cynthia? Do you mind?"

"No, no, I'd like to—"

"Do you want me to come with you?" Cynthia said.

"No, dear. You stay with Mr. Wallach. All right? I just have to phone."

But it wasn't all right! He would start to ask questions, just as her father had. When she answered, he would become angry. Her father, she remembered, had turned red in the face; she had heard him tell June that Martha was irresponsible beyond imagining, that she just had hot pans. Cynthia had wanted to say that hot pans weren't dangerous so long as you kept the handle in toward the pilot light, but she had not dared say anything. She had, in fact, liked his being angry with Martha, only it frightened her, and that made her think that perhaps she didn't like it. Finally she had asked June if she had done something to anger her father too; and June had explained. Usually, she said, you slept in bed with somebody after you were married and not before, though different people did, certainly, have different beliefs. June said she wanted it clear to Cynthia that her father was angry with her mother and not for a moment with Cynthia herself. Then she had gone on to say that this was natural too; divorced people often had differing opinions—it was what generally decided them to be divorced and live separately.

Now that Gabe had her alone, she knew that he would ask her questions too. He would ask if she had told. She wanted to go off in the car with June, but June was running up the beach, and Gabe was sitting on the blanket as though he belonged there.

"Well," he was saying, looking up at her, "how do you like New York, Cynthia? It's a big city, isn't it?"

"It's okay."

"Are you having a pleasant summer?"

"It's okay."

"Well, you really take things in your stride. Just okay?"

She took a quick look down at him. "Uh-huh." Maybe he wasn't going to ask if she had told about him and Martha sleeping in the same bed—but then she knew from experience that adults did not always ask what they wanted to know right off.

Gabe was leaning back on his elbows, and he did not say anything more. He seemed to be thinking about himself. He was wearing a blue shirt and white trousers and his feet were bare. She kept wanting to look at his feet, but she was afraid he would catch her.

"Is your father still a dentist?" she asked.

"He still is," he said. "You remember?"

"You know," she said, "my mother didn't take very good care of my teeth."

"Didn't she?"

"I had four cavities when I got here."

"All kids have cavities," Gabe said. "I used to have cavities, and my father was a dentist, with an office right in our house."

"Markie didn't have any," she said.

"Mark's too small probably. Little children his age just naturally don't get cavities. I think Martha took care of your teeth, Cynthia. Didn't she take you to Dr. Welker?"

She chose not to answer. He would take Martha's side in anything; they had slept in bed together, so he had to. "Well, it wasn't funny when they had to start drilling," she said.

"I'll bet it wasn't. Are you all right now? Let me see?"

"I suppose so," she said. She wouldn't let him look in her mouth; it was none of his business. "Except where I hurt myself this morning."

"Where?"

"My elbow. Right here."

When he leaned over to look, she knew he would see that she hadn't hurt herself at all; it was Markie who had fallen. He tried to touch her and she jumped. "Oww! Watch it."

He looked at first as though he was going to be mad at her; then he was bending his own arm up and down from the elbow. "Just move it like this," he said. "That should make it feel better."

She bent it up and down once. It did feel better; *she* felt better.

"Does that help any?" Gabe asked.

"Yes, I think so." She bent it twice more. "Oh yes," she said. "Would you like to make a sand castle?"

He looked at his watch. "I don't think so, Cynthia."

"Would you like to watch me make one?"

He smiled.

"What's the matter?" she asked. "Do you have to go home?"

To this he shrugged. "Cynthia, I really don't know."

She did not understand him. Did he or didn't he? He leaned back again and was no fun. No one was. Except sometimes Markie. She would tickle her brother until he couldn't hold it in any longer, and then, with that funny look on his face, he would give in and wet his pants—and then he'd start to cry. But he didn't even get punished for it. June would come in and pick him up and hug him, even though his legs were all wet. Cynthia would sit on the lower bunk and watch until little Mark was promised something or other that would make him stop crying. He liked to be tickled, but when it was over and his pants were changed, he would say that she had made him do it. She wondered if he had come up into her bunk this morning just to be tickled. Well, it wasn't her fault—he wasn't supposed to climb that ladder to her bed anyway. If he fell it was his own fault. She didn't want anybody in her bed with her at all. It was irresponsible. Probably Markie thought he was going to give her a baby because she wasn't married. That's what could happen, of course. June said that one of the most important reasons for getting into bed with somebody was to have a baby; that was why her father felt it was only for married people. Otherwise, her father said, it was a damnshame. And a damnshame, she knew, was the same as a sin—and a sin, for example, was leaving hot pans around on which children could burn themselves. It showed no regard for your children, that was for sure.

She turned on her belly and looked up at the parking lot. Yes, it was still a beach umbrella in the back seat. She found herself wondering if June was going to come back—not in a few minutes, but at all. It might be that all the adults were going to make a switch; maybe that was why Gabe was here. Maybe it had all been arranged beforehand, even Markie's falling out of bed. June and Markie and her father would go one way, and then she and Gabe would have to move back to Chicago and live with her real mother once again. Then she could get to see Stephanie. And Barbie. That might even be fun. And she wouldn't have to sleep in a double-decker bed any more, so there'd be no accidents to worry about. She could sleep in her old bed and her mother could read to her from that *Charlotte's Web* book. They would get to have dinner at the Hawaiian House, and her mother would bring extra-thick milk shakes to their table because she worked there and knew the cook personally. She could see Blair and Sissy in Hildreth's. She knew that Sissy was probably going to have a baby from sleeping in bed with Blair; she knew they slept in bed together because one night she had seen them, before her mother had made Sissy move out. If they were all in Chicago then Markie wouldn't be in the hospital right now. She wondered if Markie would ever stop being unconscious.

"Markie's unconscious," she said.

"Is he?" She could not tell whether or not he had known.

"He just lay there, and then I screamed and my dad came. I didn't see him fall. I was sleeping."

"Well," said Gabe, "he'll be all right, Cyn. I don't think you have to worry."

"I'm not. I think he was sleeping anyway. I don't think he was unconscious. He's not even supposed to be in my bed anyway, you know."

He looked down at the blanket. Didn't he believe her? "Well, he's not! Ask anybody!" she said. He would always take her mother's side against her father, so how could he know anything!

"I want to go in the water!" She could not think of anything else to say.

"Yes?"

"But," she said wearily, "somebody has to take me, and nobody ever will." That was a lie; her father took her—but Gabe couldn't know that either. She waited, but he did not even answer; he always seemed to be thinking about himself.

Finally he asked, "Would you like me to?"

"To what?"

"Take you into the water."

"You can't. You have pants on."

"Want to see a trick?" he said, standing.

"What?"

He began to unzip his trousers. She couldn't bear to watch; she wanted to close her eyes, to bury her head in the sand. Oh she didn't want to see! He was so big and he would have one just like Markie's, and it would look so awful. But she could not bring herself to close her eyes; she could not even move them away, let alone cover them with sand.

What she saw was a tan bathing suit. "And now I'm ready to go swimming," Gabe said. He threw his trousers onto the blanket and reached down and offered her a hand. His legs were all covered with hair, she got a good look at them as he pulled her to her feet.

"Aren't you going to take your shirt off?" she asked.

"Don't you want to just play at the edge?"

When he said that, there was a wild pounding in her chest, a surging, something akin to happiness, but more violent and sudden. "Uh-uh," she said. "I want to go all the way in—if you hold me."

"Do you usually do that? It's getting a little rough."

"I do, though. If there's a grownup."

She waited for him to take off his shirt. "Okay," he said, and when he took her hand and they started down the beach, the sea was so sparkling and blue that there seemed to be no boundary between the affection she felt for those waters and for the companion who walked beside her. Both filled her with delight. She began to wish that Gabe was her father and June was her mother—she especially wanted June to be her mother if she was going to keep touching her hair the way she had all day. Her real mother and father could have Markie, and then everything would be even; no one would be gypped.

By the time she reached the water's edge, she was not sure that she wanted to go through with it. Under the waves, which rushed toward her, it would be black and cold. But there were the people, ten or fifteen of them now, being knocked down and swept backwards, and all of them laughing and having a good time. The sunlight on all the wet heads made them look polished.

"Let's go out there," she said. "Okay?" She pointed to where the bathers were.

"Well, okay—"

"Can you carry me in? I don't like the shock."

"Of what?"

"The cold water shock. Carry me?"

Gabe put his hands under her arms. "Here we *go*—" and he lifted her up. "Now hold on," and he began to wade out.

When he stopped the first time, she said, "Hey, further."

"Wow, what a brave girl you are, Cynthia Reganhart."

"Come on, further—"

"Hang on tight."

"Okay."

"Hang on now—"

"Oh oh oh—" she yelped into his ear. "Oh—keep going—oh oh *look*—"

"Hang on—hang on—" Gabe called.

"Whooo!" she yelled.

"Ready, get set—"

"Heeeeere—"

"Wheee—"

She was looking straight up as it came curling over their heads, Gabe squeezed her to him, and she pressed her arms around his neck, and the wave was hanging over them, as though it would never break. She closed her eyes, held her breath, and *crash!* It came flowing down all over them, and she felt the two of them floating, and then their heads rose above the water, and Gabe's hair was hanging into his eyes.

"You look funny!" she shouted.

"So do you!" They were in water only as high as Gabe's knees, and the other bathers were rubbing their eyes and some were blowing their noses right into the ocean.

"I wasn't even scared," she said into his ear.

"Fine. Hang on. There's another one coming."

"This is fun—"

"Close your mouth, you dope!"

"Then I can't *taaaalk*—" she screamed, and the wave rolled in and over. Gabe held her tight and they came up right through the foam.

"Whew!" he said. "Are you all right?"

"Uh-huh." Gabe was wiping her nose off with a handful of water. Oh she didn't just like him—she loved him! She wondered when he was going to kiss her.

"Do you have to go back to Chicago?" she asked.

"I think so, Cynthia."

"To*day?*"

"No, not today—"

"Will you come play with me?"

"Well, we'll see—here comes one!"

"Oh it's a big—"

"Hang on tight!"

"Ooohhh—"

Oh she was glad Markie was unconscious! Oh what a good time! What a tall tall wave! It teetered over their heads and she pushed her face into Gabe's neck, and she waited—and then something collided with them. She felt herself and Gabe tumbling, and then Gabe was gone and she was still tumbling, but alone. Her feet were up and her head was down, and the water wouldn't let her rise. She tried to stand but there was no bottom for her feet. She was rolling, away across the sea, and she swore, oh she swore that she loved everybody. She swore it, but no hand reached down to pick her up. I love Markie Mommy Daddy June Gabe everybody—*Please, Markie, I'm sorry—*

Her head was in the sunlight. She had thought that she was way out beyond the buoys, but when she looked up she saw she was almost up on the dry beach. Sand was beneath her hands, and a big fat man was sitting in the water next to her. He was breathing very loud, and when he saw her sitting there, he said, "Some wave, kid, huh?" His belly hung over the top of his suit, and all the time he was getting up he kept saying, "Whew! Whew!" He started up the beach and then Cynthia saw Gabe running toward her through the low water.

"Are you all right?" he called. "Cynthia, hey, come here—give me your hand. What's the matter? Are you okay?"

"You let me go," she said.

"We got knocked into, honey. Come on, give me your hand. Are you all right? What is it—?"

She allowed herself to be helped up. But she refused to cry. She knew that he had let her go. She started up toward the blanket by herself.

——

Then it was dark again and she was in bed. Downstairs Mrs. Griffin was reading a book. Cynthia had not seen her father all day, and a little while ago June had gone off to the hospital too. She had left directly after dinner, when Mrs. Griffin had come to sit with Cynthia. June had said she was only going to kiss Markie good night and then would be back. The drive to the hospital was fourteen miles; for herself Cynthia did not believe that kissing anybody good night was that essential. It was mostly for babies. Gabe had used to kiss her good night in Chicago, and that was because he thought of her as some sort of baby who could be tricked by a kiss; she had never liked that. She had never liked *him*; now she remembered. He had made her mother unhappy. If it hadn't been for him, her mother would have married her father again. But he took her mother into the bedroom and closed the door and made her get into bed with him and say she wouldn't marry Cynthia's father. Whenever Gabe was nice it was only a trick. To-day was a perfect example—he had wanted to get back at her for what she had told her father. He would probably try to get his hands on Markie too, and drown him; she had better warn her little brother about that.

She leaned her head over the side of the bunk so that it

would be upside-down and make Markie laugh. "Hey, Markie
—look at me, booo-aaaa!"

His pillow was puffed up, but he wasn't there. He was still
in the hospital—how could she forget that? His bed had been
made for him and the floor had been mopped up too. The
sight of his pillow, all ready for his bleeding head, gave her the
shivers; it almost made her cry, but she wouldn't allow it to. It
wasn't her fault that he had fallen. He had no right to get in
bed with her. She did not want to marry him. She did not want
to marry anybody. When she had a baby she didn't want to
have a strange baby that she didn't even know; she wanted the
baby to be her. Little Cynthia. She would have a lot of regard
for her baby. When the baby wanted to cry she would hold it
so that it could put its head on her breasts. By then she would
have them . . . She picked up her pillow, doubled it over, and
sank her own head down into it. The pillow was a mother . . .
And then she couldn't help it, she was crying. She was all in a
jumble. She missed her mother. She really did. She wanted to
see her, to put her head right into her mother's breasts—and
yet two days later, when all the adults had returned to the
house from the funeral, Cynthia had her chance and did not
even use it. She sat beside June all through the afternoon, and
it pleased her that her mother saw when June reached out and
smoothed her hair back for her.

SIX

The Mad Crusader

1

IF SOMEONE had asked Gabe what he had been doing for the last five minutes, he could not have given a satisfactory answer. He couldn't remember—at least not until he looked around and saw where he was. His faith in his own ability to tell where and what he was about had diminished with the oncoming winter. It had already begun to diminish in the autumn, when he had returned to Chicago. Of late he was not always very lucid; however, the realization that he wasn't came to him only in moments when he was. Otherwise he did not fully sense that he was no longer observing and understanding in the ways that he was used to. In the most lucid moments, he could not decide whether that might not be a form of self-improvement. But mostly he was without irony.

The crowds weren't helping him any. He was—yes, shopping! Despite the complaints of merchants that the recession had cut Christmas trade by a third, the downtown shops were no less tumultuous than he remembered them to be at this season. Registers rang; clerks called, "Mr. M! Mr. R! Miss Gloria!"; the faces around him glowed red from the cold of the streets, from the heat of indoors. He spent the darkening hours of the afternoon walking out of one store and into another, through the blowy Loop and then straight into the wind up Michigan Boulevard—most of the time with no idea of what he was after. He opened the doors of shops that were completely inappropriate, or would have seemed so had he been able to establish what sort of gift *was* appropriate. As the day wore on, his fuzziness became indistinguishable from his apathy. Around five he pulled his car out of the garage on Wabash and found himself heading south in the murderous rush of homeward traffic.

It was snowing—or sleeting, or sooting—when he pulled

off the Outer Drive. His watch showed five-thirty. Since he did not want to go back and sit around his apartment for an hour before eating, he decided he would eat now, hungry or not, and have a long evening. He tried to relish the idea of a long evening. He had two applications to fill out later, one for a job teaching American literature in Greece, another for a position in Istanbul. Though he doubted that either was exactly the place he had been looking for, he was certain that he could not stay on much longer in Chicago; it was one of the few things he was certain of. In filling out the applications he would at least have begun to make a plan for departing. What was to be avoided was resigning and subsequently having no place to which he had to go. He might not even have returned after the summer, had it not been that there wasn't any place he could think of to which he could migrate, no place where there would be a chance of a little peace and some happiness. Of course, it was not exactly happiness he had discovered in choosing to remain amidst familiar surroundings—it was just that by staying he had avoided the onus of running. Whether sailing off to the Middle East this coming September would be any less what it might have been a year before, he could not tell in advance. He could only make out the applications and wait to see what happened.

He parked outside a delicatessen on Fifty-fifth Street. He tried hard to work up an appetite by looking at the salamis hanging in the window. The disorder that he had come to feel as an undercurrent in his life had arisen, he knew, out of just such absurdities as eating when he didn't want to. He must try to bring together his actions and his appetites. Yet there always seemed to be extra bits of time to juggle with: a stretch between classes, a dull period after lunch, the solitary hours when the sun was setting. In more pleasant weather he might have taken a walk, but they were having a miserable December —and where was there to walk *to*? He thought of phoning Bill Lake, or calling Mona, and then he remembered a pleasant-looking, slightly assertive girl he had met at the Harnaps' after a Moody lecture; but he did not know where she lived, and besides, he did not want new friends. Not now—he was leaving town. He should have left, he thought, watching his wipers deal with the sluggish precipitation, he should have left long before this. But at the end of the summer he had had strong feelings about "facing up" to what had happened, so he had returned from the East—and what was there to face up to? He had not come back for facing up's sake; he had returned to Chicago to assert his sense of his own innocence.

Forcefully he entered the delicatessen. Like someone's mother, he pushed upon himself two sandwiches and then dessert. He did his best to stretch out the meal; he ate a pickle; he asked the waitress for a newspaper to read while he downed a second cup of coffee; nevertheless he was back out on the street in time to hear the grim old church on Kimbark ring out six o'clock—and there it was before him: his long evening.

The streets of the neighborhood had a black sheen, like the backs of animals. He drove aimlessly around. Every few blocks there were washed-out-looking Christmas trees stacked up against buildings. The men trying to sell the trees stood by, hands in the pockets of their overcoats; some stirred at little fires they kept going in old paint buckets. The drizzle stopped and started, changed from rain to snow and back again. Still, he did not head home.

Where he met with one-way signs he had a stronger sense of purpose than he had at those intersections where he had a choice of directions—where he might head east, west, north or south, drive a thousand or two thousand miles to a place where nothing would suggest the past and he could turn into his old *old* self again. He remembered a self of his that was more substantial than the one he was saddled with now; he remembered being *in* the saddle. He remembered being happier. Well then, he would just take off—except there were certain practical matters to restrain him. His father's wedding was the day after Christmas. It would only add to the wear and tear to move between now and then. Directly after the wedding, however, there was nothing to stop him from taking off for Europe . . .

Except his having made up his mind to the contrary. He would not depart until he had a definite commitment about the future; he would depart in a dignified fashion, affairs in order. He was not the kind of man who could walk off a job, whatever the extremes of depression led him to believe about himself. Furthermore, there was no need for him to run away, not so long as he could continue to be realistic about what he had and had not done. He had only to distinguish for himself between the impact one had on the lives of others and the sheer momentum of fate—chance, luck, accident, for which no man who had merely crossed another's path could be held accountable.

But having a lucid moment, he was forced to contemplate the crossing of paths . . . The same impulse that had led him to want to tidy up certain messy lives had led him also to turn his back upon others that threatened to engulf his own. He had finally come to recognize in himself a certain dread of the savageness of life. Tenderness, grace, affection: they struck him now as toys with which he had set about to hammer away at mountains. He had tried to be reasonable with everyone—but the demands made upon him had been made by unreasonable people. But the demands made on *them* had not been reasonable. Still, he had tried to be true to his feelings, to what he was . . . So on the one hand he still believed himself put upon; on the other, he saw—or was willing to see—where he had not been savage enough. And he doubted that he ever could be, for it did not seem that he knew how to be; and he was not finally sure that he should be. Or *had* he been savage? Circles . . .

Fortunately the choice now was not between extremes of impotence or savagery. He had simply to get back on his feet. There were two applications to make out, a wedding present to buy for his father.

On the Midway he turned left and started for the Outer Drive. He would try it again. He should not have permitted himself to have been so indecisive all afternoon. The stores would be open late because of the holiday; he had only to go into one (which one?) and pick something out (what?). He couldn't turn up at his father's wedding empty-handed . . . though he would just as soon not turn up at all. The only reason he had wandered around all afternoon unable to make a choice was because he had not even wanted to recognize the necessity for making one.

When he reached Stoney Island, he swung the car to the right, *away* from the Drive—no, he would not fly East on Christmas Day, he would invent an excuse— Then at Sixty-third he turned left, out toward the streaming lights headed for the Loop. How could he ignore a wedding he had helped bring about?

Against his will! Almost on the Drive, he made a wild U-turn, and with cars bleating all around him he leaned over the wheel and headed into Sixty-third again, for he refused to be responsible for his father's fate. In his aggravated mood he was finding it necessary to believe either in fate, *blind* fate, as having arranged for his father's condition, or in himself as the agent of misery; himself as a kind of witch, mindless, malevolent . . . And in time past what was it he had seemed to others —Libby, Martha, his father—but an agent of deliverance? Well, he had delivered his father all right—into a lifeless, hopeless union! How could he buy a present for what was not a wedding, but a funeral? As a life went slipping away—oh how she would feed on his father's good heart!—he was to stand by in his tuxedo, smiling!

Impotence and savagery, that was precisely the choice. Either do nothing, or put his foot down and call a halt to the whole thing. Then what? The circumstances of his father's union seemed to render him impotent. When he had the rights, he did not seem able to muster the power; when he had the power, he did not know if he had the rights—which washed away what power he had.

With no plan at all—a condition no more comfortable for having become regular—he continued west on busy Sixty-third, under the iron structure of the El. A Salvation Army band, five men and two maidens, made a thin blue line across the intersection at Dorchester. "Silent Night, Holy Night" beat valiantly up into the thick wet air. A cornet lashed out at a high note, the neon lights sizzled in the rain, and then all was consumed in the roar of a train shooting by overhead. For evangelical reasons of its own, the band turned and was marching back toward the curb it had just stepped down from, missing a few beats in the change-over. Gabe slouched in his seat as horns blew behind him.

Out his side window he saw a lanky colored man hustling in and out of a flock of evergreens. Wet, dark, and limp, the branches tipped against the wall of a brick apartment building. Moving amongst them, holding her coat together under her

chin, was Martha. Parked at the curb was the little beat-up convertible that he knew she had bought for herself; the bumpers
were crusty and one door wasn't shut tight. He saw her remove her wallet from her purse. She handed a bill to the
Negro—and traffic was moving again, horns blowing down his
neck. But he did not start forward—he couldn't. A train overhead drove down on the piles of the El with all its force. An
equivalent force drove down in him. For the moment he had
been stripped of his clothing and thrown in a dark cell for a
crime he had not committed. But the bars, the blackness, the
disgrace, the humiliation—he *must* have committed it! Un-
watched, he followed Martha's face; he had not seen it since
he had stood across from her in the little graveyard near the tip
of Long Island, where Markie had been buried—and where he
had felt, with the same intensity, the confusion he felt now.

—

His second trip to the Loop was not altogether unsuccess-
ful. A small package sat on the seat beside him when he arrived
back on the South Side a little after eight. Carrying it up the
dim stairway to the Herz apartment, he could feel the muddi-
ness of the stairs under his shoes. Galoshes stood outside doorways on each landing. Beneath an exhausted bulb on the third
floor, he rubbed his feet on the welcome mat and knocked. A
slender girlish figure swung the door back; she was wearing
slacks and a sweater, and her hair was in her face. She made a
small noiseless clap with her hands. It was a gamble dropping
in on someone as unpredictable as Libby, and he was relieved
that she seemed pleased to see him.

"Hi!" She pushed her hair up with both hands. "Come in—
shhhh, though." Her fingers went up to her lips.

He whispered, "I just want to drop something off."

"What?"

He had been holding the package behind him. Coyly.
"This." They were in the living room, beside the false fireplace,
inside of which sat piles of books. Candles burned in a long tin
holder on the mantle, flitting light over half of Libby's face. A
hard glare from a gooseneck lamp fell on the frazzled uphol-
stery of the couch and chairs. The room seemed a vast and
barren place; no rug still, and little furniture—though café
curtains had been hooked on to several of the windows.

Libby rattled the gayly wrapped box. "What is it?"

He pointed down the hall, to what had formerly been Paul's study. "For the smallest Herz."

With a jerky movement of her head, she shot her hair back and flopped down on the sofa. But the hair fell forward, along the fragile line that ran from the corner of her eyes to the corner of her mouth, a line he had first appreciated long ago. "How sweet, Gabe." She held the package in her lap, fingering the ribbon. "Chanukah gelt," she said.

For a moment he was puzzled; then her suggesting that he had meant to present Rachel with a gift for the Jewish holiday disappointed him. She did not appreciate the good-natured spontaneity of the purchase—that looking for a wedding present, he had settled on a baby present. "Just a little toy," he said.

"For Chanukah—"

He interrupted, smiling. "Is it Chanukah time again?"

"You like too much to tease me about that."

"When I got up this morning I was thinking how much I felt like Purim."

"What you don't want to say is that you really brought it for Christmas."

He let the matter drop. Earlier in the year, when they all had begun to act like friends again, he had submitted to a thorough examination on the subject of his lack of faith. He was to be accused now, and only half-playfully, of celebrating the Christian heresy. Libby herself was in the clutches of another divinity. He simply smiled, again.

"May I open it for her?" Libby asked.

While she worked away at the ribbon, he asked where Paul was. But she wasn't giving him much attention; the present she was so feverishly opening might have been for herself. "He'll be back—what sweet wrapping paper—we haven't seen —ooops, I don't want to tear it—seen you for what, a month? —you have to come to dinner—though you can drop in when—aahhh—" Two sheets of tissue paper floated down around her house slippers. "Oh she'll love it," she said, lifting the dog from the box. "Gabe, it's such a charming little— Do you wind this, yes?"

"Just turn the key."

"It plays?"

"I think so."

"Gabe, thank you so much," she said, as a tune tinkled out of the animal. "She'll be crazy about it."

"I was a little afraid it might be too old for her—the key turning—"

"She happens to be a brilliant six-month-old. Would you like to see her?"

"Should you wake her?"

"We can watch her sleep. I spend hours watching her sleep."

"If that's okay with you—"

"You haven't seen her for ages," Libby whispered, as he followed her down the hall. "She's grown and grown . . ."

In Rachel's room they stood side by side over the crib. Striped curtains were pulled across the windows; a double row of framed Mother Goose pictures hung from the wall. Since his last visit—the night Libby had called the office and asked Paul to bring him home for a drink to celebrate Rachel's third month in the family—a new floor of black and white linoleum squares had been laid. When Libby brushed by the curtains, they gave off a crisp sound. The floor shone . . . She might have ruffled him earlier by muddling the reasons for his gift-bearing, but that was no longer important. It hadn't really been so spontaneous a purchase anyway. It was, in fact, for this moment that he had driven from the Loop directly to the Herzes. He waited beside the crib for those feelings that he believed he deserved to have. He waited.

"Her hair gets blacker," Libby whispered, "and her eyes get bluer . . . She's a Rachel, isn't she? Can't you see her drawing water from a well—" The infant stirred; Libby's wistfulness ceased for a moment. She resumed, in a voice barely audible, "—out of a well in what-do-you-call-it, Dan, Nineveh? Isn't she something?"

"She's a honey."

"She's our baby," Libby said.

They watched the child sleep. The "our" had not been un-intentional, of that he felt sure; it was simply Libby's final refusal to give up a claim on anyone. She kept her hold on you—for if she was not in desperate need at the moment, there was always the future. She was what she had charged him with being: the tease. He scowled at her in the dim room, remembering that letter full of sweetness she had sent to him from Reading. He believed he must still have it somewhere. He couldn't bear her, really. Our baby. Nineveh!

However, he had not dropped in unannounced, bearing an offering, to work up old grievances. He had come for the satisfactions that a new child is said to give. He had expected to be able to look down into the crib and know that all was not wrong in the world, or in himself. But no such assurance was forthcoming.

Yet he had helped to rescue Rachel, he had helped to place her in this crib . . . But nothing happened, no matter what weights he placed on his own scales. He stood beside Libby, looking down at Rachel, at the white sheet, at the wool blanket, at the incredible infant hands . . . Then he saw his solace, what it was that would set his days right. During these last few months he had been continuing to live the restricted bachelor existence—necessary, of course, to a discovery of taste, pleasures, limitations—when he was just about ready for a more expansive career. Till now everything had been by way of initiation. Bumbling toward a discovery of his nature, he had made the inevitable errors of a young man. But he was ready now to be someone's husband, someone's father. Looking down at Rachel, he was convinced that he had been feeling edgy of late only because he was on the edge of something. What else? It explained much that seemed inconclusive, uncertain, about the past.

Turning, Rachel made a weak nasal sound. It was slight, but human and penetrable; it broke through the thin skin of his reflections. What looked to be truth poured through: he was imagining in the name of the future what should have been a past; he could have left young manhood, stopped bumbling, whenever he chose . . .

When Libby put the musical dog at the end of the mattress, he was unprepared for the urge he felt to reach in and take it back. He found himself reduced to elemental emotions and passions. He had been hoping that the child would render him less culpable than he had been feeling since dinner. Now he turned from Rachel's dog. He still did not have a present for his father and Mrs. Silberman. *Nothing has changed.*

In the hallway, Libby asked, "Isn't she darling? An honest opinion now. A few unbiased words to an objective mother."

"Unbiased, I'd say she's perfect."

"For which statement you will be allowed the pleasure of being her baby-sitter some night. We prefer unbiased baby-sitters."

His desire earlier to take the toy away caused him to speak now with too much eagerness; he knew he was too eager to play her game, but he did. "That might be fun. I think I'd enjoy it."

"Are you an unbiased diaper man?"

"Well, I do have what they call a slight fecal aversion—"

"Can't use you," Libby broke in. "This enchanting child poops a blue streak." They were in the living room, speaking in normal voices, smiling with kindness at one another. "Will you stay?" Libby asked, pushing her hair back. "Stay for coffee?"

He had not come so as to leave more firmly convinced that nothing at all had changed. There was Libby smiling—wasn't that a change? And Rachel *was* a living fact, which counted for something. "I wouldn't mind some," he said.

"Let me just turn it on."

When she returned to the living room he asked her if Paul was still at his office. Alone with Libby he always felt the necessity to establish clearly Paul's whereabouts. That compulsion had a long history, and the contemplation of it momentarily fatigued him. No sooner had he decided to remain in her company to be cheered up a little, than he saw how inappropriate she was to induce in him optimism and serenity.

"He went to services," she said. "He should be home soon."

"Is tonight the holiday?"

"He's saying Kaddish."

". . . I didn't know."

"You did know it was Chanukah though—didn't you?"

"Libby—" he began, ending only with, "I'm afraid not." And he remained seated.

"Now you know what *that* is?" She pointed to the four candles flickering into extinction in the holder.

"Candles for Chanukah?"

"A menorah—oh you did know. You pretend because it

gives you some pleasure—a savage atheistic pleasure"—she smiled still—"to frustrate me about all this."

"You have certainly become a very Jewish girl, Libby," was his reply.

"Well, what are you being, Gabe—skeptical? Don't you believe it's possible? You don't see me as a very religious person? Do I strike you as unalterably secular?"

"You strike me as very religious."

"But you don't take it seriously, do you?"

"What?"

"Being Jewish. Being religious!"

"For myself or for you?"

"Either. Both!" she said, slightly leaving her seat.

"It's not an issue in my life."

"It is in mine." Clearly it was only herself that she cared to talk about anyway; though she added, "And it can't help but be in yours. You were born one."

"I can only assure you again that it isn't. At least it hasn't been yet—all right?"

"Not on the conscious level perhaps."

He made a slight whistling noise through his teeth.

"Well, you *have* an unconscious," she said.

To which he nodded.

"So how do you know what's *in* it?" she asked.

He remembered her having said something like that long ago. "How do you?" he asked.

"I"—she hesitated, and she flushed—"interpret your actions."

"Oh yes?"

"Don't you interpret mine?" Before he could answer, she spared him by opening the question out all the way. "Don't we interpret everyone's? I'm not saying all your problems have to do with your identity as a Jew—"

"You see me as a man with a lot of problems, it seems."

"I just think now that you're like the rest of us." Her gaze dropped.

Of late a drop of self-pity was coloring his life—more than a drop. It colored his answer. "You didn't always," he said.

With that, the tug he had once felt toward this girl came back to him. They still had the old impulse to flirt, it seemed. Had they been brave enough, or weak enough, or silly enough, to have gone ahead and slept with one another a certain tender curiosity would probably have died out between them long ago. But their sentimental exchange released an anchor, and sexuality moved now on the surface. He sensed the energies of Libby's body—the purr, the whininess—as he had not earlier, when they had been together beside the crib. Though there she had been conscious—he thought—of whatever energies she imagined him still to have.

Libby became at once dramatic and metaphysical; she tossed her head, not simply to deal with her hair. "We lose some things, we gain others."

"Well," he answered, smiling and appalled, "you've gained religion."

"And it makes all the difference."

"Oh does it? Between what and what?"

"Between knowing what you are and what you aren't," she said. "Knowing what's important and what's not. Go ahead and be cynical if you want. Remember Isabel Archer?"

"I do."

"Well, she didn't know what was valuable; she didn't know *who* was valuable."

"At the end I thought she came to know—"

"Now I do too."

He paused. "That statement," he said, knowing he had just been maligned, "isn't marked by much humility, for a religious person like yourself."

"Well, I *do* know more."

He only nodded; one of the energies he happened to be without was the energy to resist an attack, from himself or from another.

"I feel different about myself, Gabe. My marriage, my child." The word turned her lyrical on the spot. "Paul lights the candles and he says the prayer, in Hebrew, and I stand on the side and watch—and I'm holding Rachel—and that's a very special feeling. I've never had it before."

"You're happier?"

The reverent mood into which she had plunged herself made it impossible for her to give him a facile answer. However he was taking her, she was taking herself absolutely seriously. "We have Rachel," she said.

He had no desire to be hard on her any longer, even if she should be hard on him. What was she but a very simple girl? "She's a fine little baby," he said.

"She's a dream. I know I sound corny saying all these excessive things, but I can't help it. When I was growing up I swore I'd refrain from certain practices—one of them was boring people about my babies."

"It shows you don't have to be true to adolescent ideas, or fantasies."

"It does. I was a great enemy of religion, too, you know. I raised a lot of hell—caused a lot of hell—around our house about God and Christ and the Virgin Mother. But it's different now, Gabe. Being a Jew."

"What is?"

"You're skeptical again."

Not until she made me so, he thought. The truth was that more often than not he was willing to believe the best of her. "Do you believe in God now? Is that what you're saying?"

"I don't know whether I believe in God," came her sharp reply.

"Then we're probably a good deal closer in our theology than you think."

"You don't understand. What's important is being something. Maybe I'm not making myself clear."

"In one way you are, in one way you aren't."

"You don't understand," she told him, "the power of faith."

"Faith in what?" he demanded.

"All I'm saying is that everything's changed . . . I'm changed . . . Paul's changed." In a lower, less courageous voice, she said again, "Paul is changed."

"I didn't mean to be cavalier about your happiness," he said, after some time had passed. "Or about your conversion. I'm really not a very fierce atheist, Libby. How did all of this begin anyway?"

"I only wanted to let you know . . ." Apparently she saw no sense in going on.

". . . Of course."

"It was only a discussion. I only want to add"—she seemed

unable finally to drop the subject—"that in the end believing or disbelieving in God isn't the point."

"Not for you perhaps."

"Not for a lot of Jews."

"Not even for Paul?"

She lifted her chin—too high. "I don't know. Religion has a different meaning for a man than for a woman."

"Paul believes then?"

"You don't understand about marriage. I think that's something I've observed about you, Gabe," she said sternly.

"Who's even *talking* about marriage?"

"You don't have to believe exactly as your mate does, to be happy."

He relaxed a little, and sat back; apparently she had not been about to accuse him of anything specific.

"I don't know what Paul believes," she said.

Nothing further was said by either of them, and so Libby's final admission became laden with gravity. Suddenly she rose and left the room; alone, he found himself contemplating the hardest fact of the Herzes' life: the husband did not make love to the wife. *Still . . . ?* No sooner did the idea come into his mind than he pushed it right out. He had not been put on this earth to service the deprived, whatever the deprived themselves might think. Whatever *he* might think! He could not fathom yet his soft heart. It was an affliction! It was not soft at all! *He* was soft—the heart was hard.

He was having another bad day.

Two of the candles Paul had lit burned out. The two still wavering cast a homey light, domesticating the barren room, hypnotizing its inhabitant. He was brought around again to thinking of himself as a husband and a father.

Libby burst back into the living room. "Chanukah, Gabe, doesn't even require that you believe in God—" A small black tray, two cups and a coffee pot upon it, was thrust against her body and accentuated what little bosom she had. She stood over him ready to put the tray down. To reach out for her would require little maneuvering on his part; he believed she was aware of this. "It's the people it commemorates," she said, peering straight down at him, "what they did and so forth— and though *they* believed in God, what you're celebrating is what they *did*. You can think of it as the Jewish Fourth of July."

"Oh Libby—"

"Oh Libby what! Libby what! Doesn't that make any sense to you?" She seemed angry about something; perhaps it was what she was talking about.

"Oh Libby be quiet or you'll wake up your baby. That's all," he said softly.

"Well . . ." She set the tray down. "You're not going to win me with charm."

Silence followed. Libby sat on the sofa, the meaning of what she had said unfolded while they looked at each other's shoes. They both drank their coffee.

"You can pour yourself more," she said, "if you want more."

"I still have some, thank you."

She asked stiffly, "When will you be going East?"

"Christmas Day. I'm going to fly out that morning."

"Will it be a big formal wedding?"

"Mostly family and old friends."

"Paul's mother is coming to visit us," she said.

". . . He mentioned something about it the other day."

"I didn't know . . ."

"We had a cup of coffee at the Commons."

"I didn't know you'd talked."

"Just a chat."

After a second of what was clearly indecision, she asked, "Did he tell you how long she's going to stay?"

He shook his head.

"Well, I suppose he couldn't," she said, curling her mouth not quite all the way into a smile, "because we haven't decided. It's all a little like walking on eggs. It's the first time she's going to be seeing the baby," she said, waving her arms and nearly tipping the coffee pot, "so it'll all work out."

"It should be a thrill for her."

"That's what we think. Hope. It's her only grandchild."

"When is she coming?"

"She's taking the train—she doesn't fly. Oh—Christmas Eve." She took a sip of coffee and calmed down. "I'm not all stone and mortar, as you can see, about all this. I only think we should have established how long she'll stay, that's all. So she knows and we know . . . in case, you know. It's all had to be a little feeling-out and careful."

"I'm sure that everything will work out," he said dutifully.

"Yes—she *wanted* to come, after all. I'm simply a little unnerved. Not that I'm what I used to be. I used to be"—she lifted one hand—"impossible. But it's the adoption that's gotten to me a little. The combination of things. We're going to court right after Christmas, so there's that too. The twenty-ninth—Paul told you that?"

"No."

Relief—apparently Paul had not told him anything he had not as yet told her. "We sign the paper—and she's ours. Absolutely ours. Though I can't imagine her not being ours. You know? If she's not ours whose can she be? I'm not a total coward, Gabe, no matter what I may seem to people—but you don't know how thankful I am that we never had to see or know anybody else who was involved. When I think of how kind you and Sid and Martha Reganhart— Sid called before, in fact, and I know it's something about the court business, and I really was hoping that he wouldn't tell it to me, because I don't want to hear. I'm not a coward, but it's just—Rachel is Rachel."

"I understand."

"And he didn't tell it to me."

Sid's accession to her desire made her, of all things, gloomy. Gabe said, "Why should you have to be distracted by legal details anyway? That's not a mother's business."

"Except that I'm so neurotic. Well, I am still—somewhat," she said, though he had not raised a finger. "I was sure some catastrophe had occurred, and that that was why he wanted to speak to Paul and not me."

She waited to hear what he would tell her. "That sounds like the old neurosis coming out, all right," was what he said, moving in his chair.

"I guess I still need someone around to reassure me every fifteen minutes or so—do you mind terribly?"

"Since I'm here, I might just as well reassure you as not."

"I can pay you off in coffee. Want more?"

"I don't think so. I'd better go."

"Don't. Do wait till Paul comes. We hardly ever see you—"

Suddenly she was cheery and full of energy. "I think we should all do something together. I don't know—go out to dinner. You know those Greek places, where they dance and have the old Greek music—wouldn't you like to go? I want to, Paul wants to, I think—and why don't you come? We could go any place really, just have dinner, or go to the ballet when it comes, or the opera. I've been clipping things to do out of the Sunday paper all winter long. We have a good baby-sitter I really trust, and we can go if you want to. Any night. It would be fun."

"It sounds as though it would."

"You see, Gabe? Everything looks so much better. We're halfway out of debt; we've even paid off most of the co-op loan, which I thought we wouldn't pay till we were dead, and I've gained two whole pounds. I don't know if it's noticeable or not, but I have, and the doctor says I'm a veritable Tarzan. And then there's Rachel—and she's always there. Isn't that something? I'm in the kitchen and she's in the other room, and I'm in the living room, and she's—well—there. Though sometimes I'm in the kitchen—this is my nuttiness again—and I think, Oh Christ she's *not* there. And I zoom into her room, and she *is* there, tight asleep—or awake and gurgling to herself. I know I swore I'd never be a bore about my baby, but I can't help it. Really, even Paul's mother doesn't unnerve me that much. What can she do? What can anybody do?" Tilting her head, she made herself look a little younger, a little more innocent, than she was. "If I could apologize, Gabe, for that terrible night when I said those awful things to you—I really want to apologize with all my heart."

"You've apologized already."

"It was just so awful—" She was close to tears. "I can't apologize enough."

"So long as everything's worked out."

"You've never been anything but kind to me, Gabe." Unable to control her emotions, she left the room. In the few minutes while she was gone, he put on his coat.

"I didn't mean to drive you out," she said, coming down the hall.

"I have to go home and fill out an application anyway." He did not take the hand which she was holding a little way out from her side. "I only dropped by for a minute."

"What are you applying for?"

"For a job in Istanbul—exotic, don't you think?"

"Paul said you might not be staying next year."

"I'm thinking of going abroad for a year or two."

"We're going to miss you. If *we're* still here. Paul has given up on his Ph.D."

"I didn't know."

"He's given up writing, I think. Now he says he might want to teach in a high school. That's okay with me—I don't care where he teaches, so long as he stays happy."

"Of course."

"By the end of next year," said Libby, moving rapidly on, "we'll all be scattered all over the place again." She had taken a step backwards into the hall. "Would you like to get a last look at Rachel?"

"No, I'd better—"

"Wait one second—" She ran off, leaving him to stand in his coat. What was she up to?

She reappeared just as abruptly. "There are just those little catches on the side of the crib. I couldn't remember closing them. I'd put new sheets on, and then I couldn't remember— As I said, I'm still the old nut I always was."

To smile seemed inappropriate, but that was what he did. "It's natural to worry, Libby."

"I want to tell you something, Gabe."

This girl! This girl!

"I want to tell you because I think you would want to know."

"And what is that?"

"Sid, tonight when he called, told me that he was going to get married."

He'd had no idea what she might be going to say. Even after she had spoken, he did not immediately see what the news had to do with him. "I didn't know that," he said.

"I wasn't sure . . ."

"No, I didn't know."

"And I thought you would want to."

Only now was he stunned. "Certainly, why not . . ."

"I saw her the other day, Gabe. Outside the co-op. I had Rachel in the carriage, and suddenly I turned and started pushing it the other way. I was actually running, and I knew it was noticeable, but I couldn't help it. Remember that warm day we had? Well, that was it. I think she saw me, but I couldn't stop myself. If she had looked into the carriage and seen Rachel, I knew it would break her heart. It would break mine. I go to bed and I lie awake, ever since that happened, and I think: Rachel's going to smother under the blanket. I think I haven't snapped those damn snaps, the ones that lower the bars on the side. I even thought of asking Paul to send this crib back for another model. Truly, I get up four and five times a night. I get up and I check—and then I wind up in bed, thinking about her. Every time I go down to the basement to hang up my wash, I somehow think of her little boy. I was probably rude and impolite again, and awful, but I just had to turn the carriage around and get away. Then when Sid told me he thought he was going to be married pretty soon . . . Well, I didn't know if you knew or not—I don't want to seem a gossip, but I thought you would want to hear."

"I'm glad you told me."

"I feel I'm talking about things that are none of my business—"

"It was a horrible thing, Libby. I suppose that makes it everybody's business."

She did not understand that he was trying to shut her up, but it was not entirely her obtuseness that was responsible—his tone had been vague. He realized that he wanted to hear even more. So did Libby.

"What—what does she . . . say about it? How does she feel now?" she asked him.

"I don't know."

"I thought perhaps you run into her. At the University."

"We even manage not to run into one another."

"I'm sorry, Gabe. It's a hard thing to forget. It's a hard thing *not* to talk about. I keep wondering what it's like for her. I nearly called her once—I feel now how rotten I was with her, when I was being rotten and crazy with everyone. I almost called her one evening to come over for coffee. But I don't even know what to say. You become somehow afraid of a person when something like that happens to him."

"The best thing for all of us is to let the past be. There's nothing anybody can do about it."

"I feel terrible that she saw me and I kept running."

She waited; he nodded. "I was going to say something to Sid," she said. "He's been so kind to us, he hasn't charged a penny, and he's been so concerned, so decent. I was going to ask him to explain for me to her . . . That's it, you see, it would all have taken so much explanation."

—

Despite his inability to keep his mind precisely on what he was about, by ten o'clock he had managed to complete both applications. He typed the address on each envelope, then settled back in his chair. It was done. By March he would hear, and by June he would be gone. There was really nothing more for him to do in the way of planning.

Except call Jaffe.

At first he could not explain why the idea had occurred to him. Then he remembered Libby saying that Jaffe had called *her*, and the nervousness she had expressed over the lawyer not giving her his message directly—at the same time that she had expressed gratitude for his reticence. What a girl! She still had the power to present her anxieties in such a way that they came to seem your anxieties. It did not appear to be an unconscious talent either—it never had. Doubtless what she had been hoping was that Gabe would volunteer on the spot to call Jaffe for her and to work out whatever little problem had arisen. But, of course, no problem of which she didn't know the details beforehand could be imagined by Libby to be "little." If Sid had called, what else but catastrophe! Theresa wanting Rachel for her own—or worse.

Was that even a legal possibility? He did not know the final ins and outs of the adoption. He had not even realized that Theresa would have to do any signing. *Had* Jaffe called to say Theresa wouldn't sign? Was the natural father to sign too? Did he have to be dug up now? Would he meet the Herzes?

No, it probably wasn't even necessary for the father to appear in the court at all. Whatever the necessities, Jaffe would take care of them; he was a capable man, he would see to it that everything was tight and binding; the Herzes would be protected. It was not his business to brood over the last-minute details; he had his own applications to mail. The Herzes were Rachel's parents and they would have to work out matters for themselves.

With Jaffe's help.

Why not? Surely he was better equipped than a layman to deal with whatever problem might have arisen; that he did not charge them for his services was his own affair . . . Not that if some last-minute help were needed, he himself wouldn't step forward. If there *was* some foul-up concerning Theresa Haug, he felt he could solve it as well as anybody. Better, in fact. What he would have liked was for Jaffe to call him and *ask* that he be of assistance. He had no reason to believe, however, that Jaffe would ever again seek his help . . . which was precisely why *he* should call him. Call him. Yes, he would really like to do that. Jaffe should know that he was quite willing, and quite able, to play his part in this adoption right down to the end.

Martha should know that too. Surely she would if he were to sit down and call Jaffe right now. Where else had she been going with that Christmas tree?

. . . Some things Gabe surmised about her now; some things he knew. He knew, for instance, that she had moved. One day on the co-op bulletin board he had seen an index card announcing a sale of furniture; he had recognized the handwriting even before recognizing the address. Then one day he had seen her, just her back, moving through the doorway of a little rooming house on Kenwood. That night, driving down Kenwood—it was not too far out of his way, one cross street was as good as another really—he had seen Jaffe's car parked outside. That was how he had learned about the convertible too. He had seen it in front of the rooming house, and on another night, when he happened to be driving by Jaffe's apartment on Dorchester, he had seen it again. The following week he saw it parked outside of Jaffe's apartment on three different nights. The week after, only two. But probably it was parked there now; they would be up in Jaffe's apartment decorating that tree.

Leaning forward again in his chair, he set about checking what he had written. Reviewing the facts of his birth, education, and professional experience, a conviction began to grow in him that bad news awaited the Herzes. He had only Libby's

insane anxieties to go on, but surprisingly, the application before him, with its listing of accomplishments, of degrees at-
tained and works completed, led him further and further into
pessimism. He was reminded (not that he had to be) of all that
was unrecorded there—what he had not been prepared for,
the unaccomplished. Having failed to imagine in the past what
calamities there might be, he began imagining present calamities for which he had no real evidence.

Still, nothing was to be lost in giving Jaffe a ring. He would
like to catch Martha in the lawyer's apartment anyway. To be
sure, she was under no further obligation to him; however, for
him to find her with Jaffe now would perhaps make her aware
of the suspicions he had about times past—that he had come
to suspect that as soon as he had driven off to Long Island in
August, she had gone to bed with her old suitor. Of course,
concrete evidence was slight—only that when he had called
Chicago to tell her that Markie was in a coma in the Southampton Hospital, Sid Jaffe had picked up the phone.

At the funeral nothing had been said about the phone call,
about anything, in fact. He had watched her suntanned, ex-
pressionless face looking down into the grave. Afterwards the
only words spoken between them had been hers. "Please, let
me start from scratch." He had thought then that she had said
little out of grief and fatigue—and out of her desire to end the
affair. It was a desire he saw fit to obey. No, to honor. But in
the months that followed he was more and more convinced
that she had said so little out of shame as well as sorrow. Now
when he needed it, he summoned up the image of Martha receiving the tragic news in bed.

And he happened now to need it. He did not feel he was
deceiving himself by continuing to believe that he was not an
irresponsible man. Even his decision to call Jaffe about the
adoption was evidence in his own behalf. Chances were it was
only Libby's morbid imagination to which he was bending;
nevertheless, he did not want it said by others—or by himself
to himself—that he had gone less than all the way once again.
If that *was* what he had done in earlier days, surely it had to be
chalked up partly to inexperience; youth, he told himself. But
now he was older. He would simply pick up the phone and
have a talk with Jaffe. He would like Martha to be reminded,

should it happen that she was once again in Jaffe's bed, that in the end it was she who had been unfaithful to him, and not the other way around.

For the moment he believed this. For the moment he believed more. Standing over the phone, he reasoned that even if he had married her, there was no guarantee that one morning a child of hers might not have rolled from his bed (or tripped down the stairs, or slipped in the bathtub, or stepped in front of a car, or swallowed a bottle full of iodine) and died.

2

Dear Mr. Jaffe—
I am not able to come to your office about that baby or ever.
I have not told you all the truth. I am a married woman. My
real name is Mrs. Harry Bigoness the other name I made up
though my first name is Theresa really. Haug isn't my Maiden
name it is just something I made up because I suppose I liked the
sound of it. I am only a housewife in Gary Ind. and I went
astray and now I am back with my husband Mr. Bigoness and we
both do not want me mixed-up in any of that business. That is all
my "shameful" past and was a big big mistake. Harry knows what
is best for our family especially with this "recession" on. I don't
think I should get mixed-up again. I had done all I can. I hope I
am not cauzing trouble but it was a shock to me and Mr. Bigoness
and now it is over and done, with. Harry says it is absolutely
done, with. Excuse me.

Yours Very Truly,
Theresa Bigoness (Theresa "Haug")
12/16/57

Gabe:
Here is the letter I told you about—let me know what happens.
Sid Jaffe
P.S. Please save the letter for my files. Thanks for your interest.
—

The mills were dark and nearly smokeless; for all the mass
and solidity, without purpose. High up on concrete foundations, the wooden houses—two stories each, set fifteen feet
apart—brought to mind prehistoric lake villages, dank shacks
on stilts. The dwellings went on and on, as did the aerials
hooked to the roofs, until blocks away the weather blurred the
wires and rods, leaving what might have been ancient writing,
hieroglyphics, illegible markings in the unpleasant winter sky.
It was a day of dampness, of heaviness, a day without color; a
haze like cold steam moved forward in puffs. Stuck to a few
front doors were clumps of holly; those Christmas trees visible
behind lace curtains were not aglow—there was no wasting of

electricity, no sign anywhere of comfort or luxury. The big soiled cars lining both sides of the street indicated that, though it was a Tuesday and not yet four in the afternoon, men were at home. The day itself felt grainy to the skin.

Twisting the key in the door of his car, Gabe had numerous shooting thoughts, but only one that was strong and recurrent. *I am in it again.*

There was nothing of value in the car, yet he came around to check the far door too. His stray thoughts turned on theft, assault, violence . . . He informed himself that his life didn't depend on this little trip. Yet the mills, the houses, the fact that Harry Bigoness was probably a steel worker, served to intimidate him. The man's name could itself have been a word having to do with the atmospheric conditions, the haze, the chill, the shadows. *The weather will be mostly bigoness through the late afternoon and evening. Big business. Big onus. By gones—let them be—*

Bigoness. Over one of the four bells he found the name. Each time he rang the bell he cleared his throat. He looked at his clothing. The smell he smelled was not himself; it was the house exuding its odor—wet surfaces and old carpeting, a dusty weightiness in his nostrils. The varnished baseboards looked sticky. In the pebbled glass that cupped the electric bulb over his head, last summer's bugs showed through as dirty spots. He stopped clearing his throat when he became conscious that he had been doing it. His hand shot up to his pocket. Theresa's letter was still there; he hadn't dropped it anywhere.

He rang again, and again nothing happened. He did not know what to do next. Though in it now, he had only to walk down the stairs and get in the car to be out of it. After all, if the snarl was legal—a matter of signatures, identities—then it was only sensible to leave it to a lawyer to untangle . . . Only he did not see that he could give up so easily. He would talk to Theresa; when her husband came home, he would talk to him—and that would be that. They were probably no more than nervous. *He* was probably no more than nervous.

No one seemed to be at home. He tried not to pay any attention to the emotion he felt; however, he could not help but recognize it as relief. He marched three steps forward and twisted the knob of the glass-paned door leading to the inner stairway. When it opened, his heart did not know how to respond; it was no longer entirely clear as to what was in its own interest. It rose and sank simultaneously, like two hearts. He rushed up three landings to Apartment C; without hesitating very long, he knocked. He had only taken time to count the number of milk bottles lined up on the doormat. Six. He heard a creaking, but when no one answered, he decided it was only his weight on the floor boards. He knocked again, then took out his billfold, hunting for a blank scrap of paper, and he came upon a business card of his father's. Crossing out the printed name and number, he began to phrase a message. He was reminded that he had only eight days in which to buy that present. A child's cry came faintly through the door.

"Hello?"

The crying had already stopped.

He knocked. "Is anyone home?"

Feet moved. "Hello? Theresa? Mrs. Bigoness?"

He knocked again. "Is any . . . ? Theresa, it's only Mr. Wallace." Mispronouncing his own name had its effect—it made sharp the feeling that he had erred in taking this trip upon himself. He should simply have washed his hands of . . . "Hello?"

Inside something dropped, someone spoke; footsteps crossed the floor. Then the door opened, a crack; a blue-eyed little girl, no more than four or five, stood before him in red pajamas.

"Close it, Melinda—get back—"

The child was looking at him. From behind her came a brief barrage of sobs. Then the man's voice again.

"Oh hell—*Melinda!*"

The little girl turned away and the door eased slowly shut. Gabe reached for the knob, pushed it, and the door went flying backwards into the wall.

"Hey!"

A slender dark man, in need of a shave, was standing over an ironing board, a plastic basket full of wash beside him on a wildly yellow living-room rug. The first thing he noticed—even before he noticed that the man was wearing an apron—was that the fellow was not, as he had imagined he would be, older than himself. "Hey—what's the matter with you—get out!" The small boy who was crawling on the floor began to wail.

"Are you Mr. Harry Bigoness? My name is—" He could not say Wallace again, though he hadn't the chance to say anything.

"Just get out of here, that's all!" Rubbing madly at his chin, plucking at the apron, the man came around from behind the iron. Big mahogany furniture lined all the walls; the panels of a chest before which Bigoness now stood were designed to give the illusion of depth. "Close the door, get out of here, will you!"

The little girl was pulling at her father's blue work trousers. "I want my sandwich."

"Mr. Bigoness, I'm representing Sid—"

"Get your hand off my door—don't you understand?"

"I want my sandwich."

"—the lawyer who has been in correspondence with you people—"

Not too gently, Bigoness uncurled the little girl's hand from his leg and advanced upon him. The man's chest curved in toward its center, but out to beefy shoulders; his arms were ridiculously long. It was his build more than his face that made him look stupid. "Now did I ask you, get your hand—"

"You don't even know who I am."

"You woke up that kid—"

"If you'd have answered when I rang—"

"Who do you think you are, invading people—" A crash, then a shattering, then a whimper, came from another part of the house. "*Get*, before I call the police!"

"Daddy!" The little girl had disappeared and was calling from behind some door. "My Daddy!"

"Mister, I'll give you three—"

He might then have turned, stepped back. Bigoness's face was not very far from his own. "Is your wife home—may I speak—"

"Oh—oh—everything fell! It fell on me! I didn't—" As the little girl cried in the other room, the small boy on the floor continued to whimper. Bigoness tried to fill his lungs; he rose up on his toes; his head moved. His visitor held fast—and Bigoness broke for another part of the house.

"Oh hell." His moan was deep, pitiful.

"It just fell," the little girl was explaining.

"Oh Melinda—"

By the time Bigoness had returned to the living room, with a sponge in one hand, the front door was shut, and Gabe was standing inside, hat in hand. "Mr. Bigoness, I'm here representing Sid Jaffe, the lawyer. He's been writing to you about this adoption case. He's written four letters since he received a letter from your wife about a month ago. He's tried to call you on the phone, but it's been disconnected—"

"Did I say come in here, you?"

"Haven't you received Mr. Jaffe's letters?"

"You're trespassing on private property that don't belong to you!"

"He's sent the letters to this address."

"Where does he come off sending letters to my address? Where's he get my address?"

"From the phone book."

"I never received any letters. I never got 'em, and I don't want 'em. I'm asking you to go, Mister. I'm asking you nice—"

"Mr. Bigoness, I don't want anything from you. Is your wife home?"

"My wife's my business."

The little girl had returned to the living room. She began asking again for her sandwich. All the while the two men talked, she pulled at her father's trousers.

"I've come down from Chicago—"

"I'm busy—"

"All we would like is for you to sign a paper, and for your wife—"

"I'm busy, she's busy, we're all busy! Now—"

"—a consent form, and that's it. There's nothing for you—"

"I said three times, *Get out!*"

"Will you please listen to me?"

"I want my sandwich."

"It's a simple procedure. It'll take five minutes—perhaps if I speak to Theresa—"

"My wife's my business."

"She had a child—"

"I want my sand—"

"I don't care *what* she had, she don't have time to go—"

"I only want a word with the two of you."

"*Listen*—"

"I want my sandwich."

"Bigoness, simply let me—"

"*I want my sandwich!*" The little girl threw herself upon the floor. "*I want to eat!*"

Instantly another howl went up. What she had thrown herself upon was her little brother.

"Christ," groaned the harassed father. "*Ohhh*—"

Gabe held his words, and Bigoness dropped back on the sofa. "Oh man," he said, "what are you *bothering* me, huh? It's Christmas time, don't you know that? What are you bothering me about?"

"I only want to talk to you, Mr. Bigoness, and to Mrs. Bigoness."

Two dark, distrustful eyes took him in, head to toe. "Your name Wallace?" the man asked.

"That's right."

Bigoness nodded, his lashes dropping halfway over his eyes. Softly he said, "You son of a bitch."

"Daddy! My *sandwich*—"

"You want a sandwich, go make it."

"I can't reach the peanut butter."

"Ain't that too bad."

"*Daddy!*"

"Oh man . . ." His feet swung down; Gabe saw only obstinacy in the thick dark workman's shoes. Bigoness was heading out of the room. The solemn little girl did not smile with victory; she followed on her father's heels, whimpering. "I'm the new nigger around here," Bigoness said.

Alone, he took quick glances around the room—as though Theresa might pop up from behind a chair or emerge from back of the curtains. The decor was Chinese modern—the yellow rug swam with pop-eyed dragons; the walls were papered with rickshaws and coolies and junks. There was nothing that was not immense, no object, no design. The two lamps at either end of the sofa were the size of small people—they *were* small people, one a yellow woman, the other a yellow man, each in kimono, each with hands up sleeves, each with bulb screwed in top of head. All the upholstery was silky, Oriental;

only the TV set made a forthright concession to the Occidental world of Indiana. The room seemed to be expanding and narrowing by the moment. There was no chair in which one could sit without sinking. He instructed himself to remain standing—let Bigoness sit. He felt himself becoming excited. He went over what had to be accomplished; he was excited because he felt that something already had been. He had not fallen back—no matter how close he might have come. What he did counted, not what he thought.

Jaffe had indicated on the phone that if the signing of the consent forms could not be worked out, he might have to take a chance and appear in court without any signatures at all. He would report to the court that the child had been abandoned. The danger, however, was that a social agency of the court might be called into the case at the request of the judge; the adoption could then be delayed for months and months, with any number of complications arising. The social agencies of the courts were not very sophisticated—nor, said Jaffe, were the courts themselves, which frowned upon private adoptions anyway. If it was necessary for him to claim abandonment in court, there might even be religious trouble. The infant had been born in a Catholic hospital of a mother who claimed to be Catholic—if the judge sitting in County Court that day also happened to be Catholic, it might eventually be suggested that the child be turned over to a Catholic adoption agency to be placed in a Catholic family, or, for the meantime, in a Catholic orphanage.

Further, since the court presumed the offspring of a married woman to be the offspring too of her lawful husband, it was quite impossible—Jaffe had explained, countering a suggestion of Gabe's—to go into court with Theresa alone. Whether the husband was or was not the natural father was inconsequential; the child was simply not his wife's to give away. He had to sign. Also—it was here that Gabe had stopped listening —there were matters of inheritance, insurance benefits . . . He had stopped listening because he had begun to wonder how this could be anybody's business but Jaffe's . . . Then Jaffe was saying that he was going to have to start charging the Herzes for his time. Since he would now have to go down to Gary, track down the Bigonesses, talk with them—

Here Gabe had butted in. Jaffe had been thorough till then, but certainly not friendly; he had been clipped and to the point and even impatient. So Gabe had *leaped* in—he could himself do the tracking down, if that was all right with Jaffe. He could do the initial consulting, if that was okay . . . "And I'd rather," he had said, "that you wouldn't tell the Herzes—"

But he had not bothered to instruct Jaffe not to tell Martha, if he chose to. He had been sure she was in Jaffe's apartment while the two of them had spoken, while he had informed Jaffe of his willingness and persuaded him finally—how pleasant!—of his usefulness. Waiting for Bigoness to return now, he had a full-blown daydream: he saw himself being reconciled with Martha. He dreamed of stealing her back from Jaffe. He saw himself on the brink of many changes. He was not sorry now that he had come, nor that his trip was a secret from the Herzes. It gave him strength, knowing that he did not want or expect their gratitude.

Bigoness had removed his apron; he was eating a sandwich. He had taken up a leaning position in the door and had the air of someone who has just completed some serious thinking. His beard was blue, as were his eyes, and his part seemed chopped into his hair. His face sloped almost straight back from his nose, as if the brain within was tubular in shape. "Now who is it you represent again, Mr. Wallace?"

"The lawyer who's written you about this adoption. Sid Jaffe."

Bigoness thought that over while he chomped away at the sandwich.

"Have you read Mr. Jaffe's letters?"

No answer.

"I asked if you've read Mr. Jaffe's letters."

"You know," Bigoness said, making much of the unhurried ease with which he continued to eat, "I'm in the union, Mister"—he swallowed—"and we got a lawyer too, a pretty smart cookie. So I know what questions I got to answer and I know which ones I don't have to answer. It's in the Constitution of this country that I only have to answer what I want. If you want to keep talking, that's all right with me, you go ahead. I got to eat my sandwich anyway. But don't try to tell me what I've *got* to answer, and what it says in the Constitution I don't have to answer if I don't want to." Secure in his rights, he ambled over and plunged into the upholstery of a wing chair near the window. Spreading the blinds with two fingers, he looked outside, a new man, a bored man, a defiant man.

"I wonder if I could speak to your wife."

"You spoke to my wife, buddy."

"She's not at home?"

"Maybe she is, maybe she isn't."

"Mr. Bigoness," he began again, "nobody wants anything of you. Or of your wife. Mr. Jaffe has only asked—you know this if you've read his letters—he only wants you to come down to the court on the twenty-ninth and sign a consent form saying that you want your child adopted by another family. This was all arranged months back, between Mr. Jaffe and your wife. It's simply a matter of signing the papers. At the time we didn't even know she was your wife, you see."

"Whatever happened months back, I don't care about neither."

"Doesn't your wife care?"

"My wife cares about what I care about. I've got nothing to do with any paper-signing."

"I don't think you understand what kind of paper it is. It doesn't make you responsible for the child. Just the opposite, in fact. It will free you of any responsibility at all where this child is concerned."

"Well, I don't have no responsibility, Mister. I've got kids of my own."

"That's what I'm saying."

"Shit, that ain't what you said. What do you think I am? Why don't you go back to Chicago and tell Mr. Jaffe to sign his own papers? Cause Theresa ain't signing nothing. I mean her name ain't even Haug, for crying out loud."

"She's obliged to, however."

"Oh yeah?"

"She's legally responsible for that child, until she signs a paper which releases her from that responsibility."

Bigoness tried eating again.

"And so are you," Gabe said.

"Oh is that so?"

"You're her husband."

"I ain't the father." He did not seem delighted to have had to make the statement. He mumbled, "Why don't you go see him."

"Because he's not responsible—"

"Oh screw that," said Bigoness. "You ain't sticking me. See," he said, his mouth narrowing to a point, "I know what you guys are up to. I know what kind of business you guys are in."

"I'm not in any kind of business."

"Tessie told me, don't worry about that. I ain't signing any papers, so why don't you think twice and leave me alone."

"Why don't you let me talk to your wife?"

"Look, why don't you leave us *both* alone! I'm not signing any papers, don't you understand me? I've been signing papers all my life. Five papers to get this here sofa carried up those stairs, you understand that? I signed a paper for my car. I signed a paper for my Hollywood bed that's right there in the bedroom—where it's going to stay! I signed for plenty, and I paid for plenty and nobody's going to stick me. We got a lawyer in the union, Mister. I can get advice whenever I need it, don't kid yourself about that."

"Any lawyer will tell you that if you want to be sure that nobody does stick you where this baby is concerned—"

"Look," he said, standing, "the only way you don't get stuck is you don't sign."

"What I'm trying to explain—"

"I understand what you're trying to explain."

"You don't seem to."

"You think you're so smart and I'm so stupid?"

"Why don't you just listen to me?"

"I listened plenty. I listen to what Tessie tells me you guys—"

"I want to speak with Theresa myself."

"You *can't* speak to her! Why don't you leave us alone? I got a lot of bills, Mr. Wallace. Maybe you don't know what that is. I've been out of work for five months. I've been taking care of this house here for five rotten months, and now my wife's home with me and she's out working, and that's that. You got a paper," he said, "well you leave it here. I'll take a look at it for you, okay? We got nothing else to talk about."

"You'll have to sign in court, however."

"Oh sure." He dropped his lids again, moved his shoulders, shifted on his heavy shoes. His entire body said, *Listen to this guy, will you?*

"A judge has to witness the adoption. That protects you as well as the people who are adopting the baby."

"I told you, didn't I, that I got a lot of bills—don't you *listen*? I'm going to pay them, you hear, don't you worry about that either. But I just ain't stepping up to some judge, see, and saying, here I am, your honor, go ahead and stick my ass in the workhouse."

"This has nothing to do with any work or workhouse, or with any bills you may have."

"I've been married already before this, buddy. I've been married, I've been divorced. I've been around. I've lived in six different states in my life, you understand? I've been involved with your kinds of lawyers, believe me."

"What kind is that?"

"I ain't got no prejudice. I just been involved, so I know what I'm talking about. You guys got some kind of deal going, that's all right with me. Tessie got confused, made a little mi—"

"Daddy—" His little girl had stepped back into the living room. He pointed to the small boy who had been sitting in the center of the rug all the while they had been talking.

The little girl said, "Walter's still making a tinkle."

It took a moment for the words to register on Bigoness. "Oh Jesus!" Again he fled.

A second later a door opened; a child cried; the toilet flushed; Bigoness moaned. He came back to the living room with still another child in his arms.

"C'mon, cut it out, boy," Bigoness was saying, as he paced the rug; the diaperless child in his arms rolled back his head and howled. The little girl followed her father as he walked. "C'mon, Walter boy, you're all right. Ah come on now, stop crying, will you? You going to be a big man or you going to be a little sissy boy?" The little boy continued to weep. "Oh man," groaned Bigoness, "look, why don't you leave me alone?" At that moment he did not appear to be anything but pitiful. "This little kid's been strapped to that toilet seat for about a hour—and it's on account of *you* butting in around here. You come in here and you dis-repp everything, and I forget all about him. Why don't you go away and stop breaking up my house? I don't know whether you trying to stick me, or you in the black market—you guys that sell babies, I don't know which—but why don't you just get out?"

"I've explained to you who I am."

"Tessie told me about you, Wallace—"

"Well, I don't know what she could have said."

"You guys care about one thing, and that's the buck."

"*What* guys?"

"You *got* the baby, why don't you just leave us alone?"

"Because you're responsible for that baby—until you sign that paper—"

"The hell I am! What do you want from me, Mister!"

"I want you to come into court with your wife, and sign" —his weariness almost overwhelmed him—"a little paper. Mr. Jaffe's office will pay your travel expenses, we'll get you a baby-sitter—"

"Where is this court, Africa? Man, I've had a rough time— I'm waiting on a phone call for a job—"

"The court is in Chicago."

"I don't live in Chicago."

"I *said* we'll pay your expenses; it'll take a couple of hours. You're not working anyway—"

"My wife is."

"We'll pay *her* a day's salary! Stop being contrary!"

"I'm not getting mixed up in no black market."

"*This isn't the black market!*"

"Don't you raise your voice in my house, hear? *This is my house!*"

"I won't raise my voice—I'll get you hauled into *court* if you keep this up!"

"Yeah? For what?"

"You're going to have more trouble than you bargained for, Mr. Bigoness!"

"You go ahead, you tell me what for, huh?"

"You want to support a fourth child?" He had spoken desperately—had he gone *too* far? Either too far or not far enough . . . Suppose Bigoness said *yes*.

"It's not my kid—"

"It's your wife's!"

"It ain't hers either. You want to stick somebody, you go stick old Dewey, he's the son of a bitch knocked her up. He's the son of a bitch took her away from here. When she married me, Mister, she married my three kids too. She ain't running out again, you understand that? I had one old lady run away already. She thought life was a bowl of cherries, see. One day she just takes our little portable phonograph and all her Ricky Nelson records and so long, honey. I was left with them three kids—and I didn't run out on them neither. Her son-of-a-bitchin' family wouldn't take them—okay, I didn't run out on them. I went and found them another mama. Don't tell me what I'm going to support! I *got* three kids, and I didn't set them out in the street, neither. I'm a nursemaid around here, and scrub lady, but pretty soon they're going to open that mill up and then old Tessie's going to get her ass back in this kitchen, and this here family's going to get shaped up around here. You just leave us alone, Wallace, and I'll work everything out all right. Don't you worry about me!"

"What does Theresa make in a day?"

"What she makes is my business."

"You tell me what she makes, and we'll make good her salary for the morning, she has to be up in Chicago. We'll cover both your travel expenses."

He had to wait a long time for a very short answer.

"Yeah?"

"That's right."

He waited again; he could not tell what might or might not push Bigoness the wrong way.

"What about a baby-sitter?" Bigoness asked.

"And a baby-sitter."

"Well, she makes . . ." He looked up at the ceiling for a figure—and found one. "She makes herself about sixteen, seventeen bucks a day, that's about what she makes."

"That's good pay for a waitress."

"Well, that's what she makes. Who the hell said she was a waitress? Maybe she's a waitress, maybe she's isn't."

"And how much are travel expenses?"

Bigoness hardly hesitated. "About fifteen bucks."

"For one person, fifteen dollars?"

"I'm talking about round trip."

"So am I."

"What are you saying? I'm a liar? Jesus!"

"I'm only saying that it's about four or five, from Gary to Chicago and back."

"Well, what about lunch, huh? Meals? What"—he searched —"what about the general inconvenience?" He seemed to feel he had hold of something with that last phrase. "What about that?"

"Look, someone is trying to adopt a baby; somebody, whether you appreciate it or not, Bigoness, is finally doing you a favor. *Did* you a favor. Don't try to turn this into a business venture—"

"Oh man, oh man! Look what's talking about business!"

"Bigoness, this is not the black—"

"And Jesus, what did I ask for, a million dollars? A brand new washing machine? A TV? Je*sus!* I'm asking for ten lousy bucks more for fare."

"For two—"

"Well, I'm busted, damn it! I'll tell you that—I ain't ashamed. *I* didn't do it. Old Wanda pulled her ass out of here over a year ago, when this one was just born." He pointed to docile, sleepy Walter, on the sofa. "She just took off, and she took the checkbook with her. I raced down to the bank, but it was too late—she'd wiped me out, the son of a bitch. And now this fuckin' recession. The bastards are *hounding* me, Mister. Don't worry, I get letters all right, I get plenty of letters. I never got so much mail in my whole life. They're all lining up outside to take my furniture away—take my bed away, my TV away—but I'll tell you, I didn't make this recession, and I didn't ask for it neither. I like nice things too"—he was pointing down at Gabe's shoes—"I like nice sofas and I like nice big beds to roll around in, just like everybody else. I got a new Plymouth, and that there's a guaranteed orthopedic mattress on that bed, that's the best money can buy. I gave that little bitch Wanda the best money can buy. Don't think I don't like nice things—don't worry about that!"

He let Bigoness finish. He let him feel that he was finished. He let him stand there empty-handed. "I'll give you ten dollars each for the train," he said finally. "And seven and a half

dollars for a half day of your wife's wages. And four dollars so
you can pay a baby-sitter for four hours. That's thirty-one fifty.
Mr. Jaffe will write and tell you the place and the time. Is there
a phone where he can reach you?"

"I'm doing business with you. I ain't doing business with no
shyster lawyer."

"I'm acting for Mr. Jaffe. *He's* acting for the family."

"What kind of jerk you think you're dealing with?"

"I don't know what it is that's bothering you now—"

"Don't think I ain't got you figured out, Wallace. You ain't
just spreading cash around for your own fun, don't kid me.
Now you're a pretty smart fella, all right. I see the way you
come in here and act tough and hard, and all the time being
fancy and ritzy, sort of like Lepke—I've seen all about him on
the TV, don't worry about that. Oh, you're going to keep me
in my place and all that. Well, I'll tell you one thing—I may be
out of work, but nobody's going to make shit out of me while
I'm standing around. You ain't the first one that's tried it, and
you ain't getting away with it neither. You want that kid—
okay, you take the kid. But don't come around here thinking
you're going to make shit out of me. That's what old Wanda
thought, you see, but she got it all wrong. And old Tessie
thought she's going to do it too, but she come back for her
Thanksgiving dinner, Mister, she come crawling back here for
turkey stuffing and candied sweets all right, and now she's
going to be a good mama to those kids, you hear? I'll take fifteen bucks for the train, like I said—fifteen for me, and fifteen
for Tessie. Don't talk to me about no ten-dollar train rides."

"You should disabuse yourself of the notion that this is the
black market."

Bigoness nodded and nodded. "Yeah, I'm going to do just
that. That's still going to cost you another ten bucks, Mr.
Wallace, even if it's the red-white-and-blue market." He was
amusing himself, which did not mean that he was not in dead
earnest. He was fully alive to the possibilities of the moment.
"That's going to cost you exactly forty-one dollars and fifty
cents. Don't think I don't know how to add up a row of figures either."

Gabe reached into his jacket. Bigoness whitened; did he
think Gabe had a gun? Only a moment earlier Gabe had been

wondering if Bigoness had one . . . He took out his billfold. "Let's make it forty-five," he said. "Four and a half dollars for the general inconvenience. You forget the general inconvenience." He set three bills, two twenties and a five, into the groove of a small floral ash tray. He set them down just out of Bigoness's reach. And the fellow could not wait; he took a hurried, desperate walk to the cash, and nearly stumbled on the rug.

—

There had been moments when he could have backed away. He had not. He had humbled Bigoness—raising the ante had done it, finally. He had remained stern, unmovable; that was his accomplishment. In the flush of success, he tried to think of a single mistake he might have made, and halfway home he came up with one. Whether the train was five, ten, or fifteen dollars made no real difference to a man who owned a new Plymouth. Bigoness would drive into Chicago, as he himself was driving now; Bigoness had known he would all along.

Conned . . . Really? He made himself relax. Forty-five dollars, fifty or even sixty, wasn't much when one considered what had been accomplished . . . by him. Though toe to toe with Bigoness—in that second when, shouting at one another, he had believed himself about to be hit, or shot—he had seen his usurpation of Jaffe's offices as the most selfish and stupid act of all; he had seen himself seeing only himself. But he'd been mistaken.

When he reached Chicago, he drove directly up Kenwood. Why Kenwood? Why not? Old energies began rising to the surface. He slowed the car; behind Martha's windows were the lights of a Christmas tree. Ah, *she* had it . . . She must be home from work; her car was parked in front. He contemplated his solitude, the injustice of his isolation, and found no reason whatsoever for his having to eat dinner alone again tonight. He did not have to wash his hands of anything. He parked the car. One of the doors of her car was slightly ajar; before heading up the stairs, he slammed it shut. It wouldn't stay; it slipped and was ajar again.

Everything she has is broken . . . But the thought no longer filled him with fear and distrust. It was not that which had been building in him in the long ride up from Gary. Forgiving himself, he forgave her.

3

MARTHA'S head poked out just beyond the bannister at the top of the short stairway. "Yes?"

He did not know whether she could see him, but he felt he could not advance another step without being invited to do so. He leaned his head into the shaft of light, feet in place. "Martha? It's Gabe . . . Wallach."

When she moved to the head of the stairs, he was surprised to find her fully dressed. He had imagined her in a robe; he had even imagined her having a visitor. But all that was missing were her shoes; she wore a white blouse and a narrow red skirt. He waited for her to speak, to move, to turn and walk away.

She said, "Why, hello."

"Are you busy?"

"No."

". . . I thought you might be free to have a bite with me."

"I was just eating."

"Oh, I see."

He would not have been surprised, really, if that moment his enterprise had fallen through; but neither of them moved.

He asked, "How are you?"

"I'm fine . . . How are *you*?"

"Fine."

Up in the shadows, she crossed her arms and leaned one shoulder against the wall. He would not believe that she was so blatantly registering impatience. He couldn't really be sure that she wasn't standing up there smiling.

"I see you're an automobile owner," he said.

"Oh yes."

"Would you mind very much if I advanced out of the doorway here?"

"If you like—"

"You see, I came to ask if you wanted to have dinner with me."

"Well, I've begun, you see—"

"Oh, I didn't know."

"Yes." Then: "But you're welcome to come up the stairs."

"I'd like to," he said, without advancing.

"Well—why don't you then."

"I don't want to interrupt your dinner." He started up toward her.

"One doesn't really think in terms of interrupting a plate full of raw vegetables." God, she *was* smiling.

"Well—would you like to go out then?"

"No, no, I like raw vegetables—"

He was beside her. Her hair was pulled back, her lipstick was paler, but that seemed the extent of the change. It had really been only a few months. "How are you?"

"I'm pretty well," she said. "*You* look well."

"It's good to see you, Martha."

"I live just down here."

She turned away—but the *way* she had turned . . . He heard instantly the openness, the pleading in his last words. He had spoken too softly—not that he could have helped it. His desire to be tender was almost more than he could manage. It seemed to be affecting him as far down as his muscles; the weakness in his fingers was such that he could not even have made a fist, had there been any reason for his wanting to. The sternness Bigoness had been witness to was nowhere to be seen. He followed after her, neither too close nor too far. It was like having endured a long rainy spell; and now, no clouds —and soon, the sun.

At least she was not what he had been dreading as he had rung her bell. Actually he should be feeling energetic, not limp. For down below he had awaited a face hard, grudging, foul, a witch's face. And what had she been to him in that awkward moment on the stairs but kind? Whose face had he seen but hers? Not until he stepped into her room did it occur to him that her kindness could have arisen out of the simple fact that she was about to marry another man. It cost her nothing to be nice; why fight *him* any longer? Inside the door, which remained ajar, he looked when he could at her hands. At least it was not the kind of engagement that is spoken of as formal. There were no rings.

He was gripped by shyness. "Well, well," was what he said.

"May I take your coat?"

"Well—it's a pleasant little room."

"Well, it's a little room."

"But pleasant . . ." A blue India print covered a small bed pushed against the far wall; the print hung an even half inch from the floor, all around an even half inch. There were two red throw cushions at the head of the bed. An old oak table was set in the center of the room, two candlesticks upon it; before the chair in which Martha had been sitting was a plate full of raw vegetables: a carrot, some lettuce, a stick of celery, slices of a green pepper. Against the walls were a chest and a washstand, and hanging untilted above the bed was Cynthia's large circus picture. It was the first object he recognized from the old life. Then the sight of some paperbacks on a bookshelf by the window touched him nearly as much as the picture; they might have been real, palpable human things. The throw cushions on the bed, the little red rug, and the stumps of two lavender candles on the table helped to save the room from austerity. A tissue-thin Chinese shade ballooned over the ceiling bulb, releasing a thin gold light onto the table top. There were three bulbs strung around the tree, fewer than there had seemed to be from outside. He commented on the comfort of the place.

"Oh I suppose so," she said, not unpleased. "There are six women in the house and only one bath. *That's* not entirely comfortable."

"Do you all share that refrigerator?" He motioned to a big old Westinghouse purring in the hallway.

"Discomfort number two."

"Still—"

"It's not too bad, no. Oh there's an Indian girl, or Pakistani, and she leaves her little footprints on the toilet seat—"

"Yes? Both feet?"

"Both. I think you're thinking of dogs. Truly, she squats up there . . . Life is very international here. There's a silent little Korean girl, and a noisy dyke, and a chesty young thing who's an assistant associate copywriter on the Near North Side but lives down here for the culture. And there's a terribly heavy pathetic German girl who types theses for people, and there's one of those guitar players without make-up, who I believe squats too. And there's me. I seem to represent the old sturdy bourgeoisie. What do you think of that? May I take your coat?"

"You sound as though you like being the delegate from the middle classes. You sound—you look—at ease, Martha."

She hung his coat in the closet, and while her back was turned he peeked into it. He found no resemblance to any closet of her past. There were even empty hangers. She seemed —so nice. It turned out she wasn't at all bad bourgeois. Had he not allowed full play to his morbid imaginings, had he not such a weak-minded sense of causality, he would have come back to her months ago. He would have come back had he not been sure that she no longer had any use for him; he would have come back had it not been for Jaffe's car parked outside here, and her car parked outside there; he would have come back if his mind had been clearer. At least he was certain she was pleased that he was here now; believing this to be so, he was so excited that for a moment he actually trembled.

"I suppose I am," Martha said.

"That's fine."

Conversation was exhausted.

She reached for the shoebag hanging inside the closet and, hardly raising her knees, stepped into a pair of slippers.

He looked around the room, having seen everything twice already. "I notice," he said finally, "that you have a car."

"That seems to have impressed you all right."

"Well, it's rather a snappy number. Though your front door doesn't close all the way, I notice—"

"Oh, but I think that adds dash."

"Absolutely."

They both worked a little at grinning. "I just got it back," she said, sitting down at the table.

"From being fixed?"

"From being stolen. Would you like to sit down? Do you want a carrot? I'm afraid that's all I can offer. The dyke made free with my leftover salmon. She's very aggressive about canned foods. Would you like some sherry? There's a bottle in the closet."

"I'll just sit." He pulled out a chair opposite her; on its seat rested a lavender cushion. Everything was so—careful. Suddenly the order of the place—everything matching—was no longer becoming; it was chilling—though that passed too. "Who stole your car?"

"Some poor dishonest boys, I suppose. The police found it three days ago. It was in a junk yard. They'd sold it. Though a friend of mine says it went there on its own; you know, out of some deep knowledge of its own essence."

He said, "Oh yes," and smiled. The words of this friend of hers served to settle his emotions. He did not tremble; he was not chilled. That he did not feel distant from her, that he could see this day as an extension of their first days almost a year before, did not mean that she was not conscious of all that had intervened. Of course he was conscious of all that too; it was just that he was willing to forget it. She was probably only being nice. She had a friend who said such-and-such. He had an impulse to ask her if she was really going to marry this friend; he had every reason to believe she was, except the reasons he had not to . . .

She had given him an opening, so he went ahead and made talk. "How did it get stolen? Did you leave the key in?"

She frowned, looking up from her plate. "No, I didn't leave the key in."

He had somehow offended her. "Well—how then?"

"Well . . . as a matter of fact," she said, having decided, it seemed, to go on, "I saw them stealing it. I was working a little late one night—reading *The Princess Casamassima* in my office —and when I came out to the Midway, there was my car being pushed away, out toward Cottage Grove."

"Being pushed?"

"Yes. I started running after them, and felt like Barbara Stanwyck or someone, shouting, 'Stop, thief! Help!' and so on, and waving my handbag—and then I was out of breath, and they were pushing it faster than I could run, so I turned and came back to the office and called the police. I called the operator, and I told *her* I wanted the police." She cut a piece of lettuce and ate it. Footsteps were mounting the stairs; he restrained himself from looking over his shoulder. Martha went on as though she were expecting no one. Her desire to be witty and gay, an ingénue, made him uneasy, but he made it his business to look interested.

"And the operator," Martha said, "—this is the Chicago part of the story—the operator asked me what I wanted them for, and I told her my car was being pushed away, being stolen, and she said oh no, it was probably the snow-removal people."

"She did?"

"It hadn't snowed for nearly a week—which I managed to convince her of finally—and then she asked me where I was calling from, and she gave me the police. The Hyde Park district police, and I told *him* that my car was being stolen, right *then*, and that if they just sent a squad car around they could intercept it, but he began to ask me what kind of car it was and where I lived, and I told him, look, they're stealing it *right now*. You just have to go there *now*. And he asked me where exactly it had been parked before it was pushed, and I told him across the Midway, and he said, Oh then it was being stolen really in the Woodlawn district, and I said, but the operator connected me with you, and he said that was because I was *calling* from Hyde Park—and then there was a lot of clicking and a terrible dreadful dead line, and I was pulling my clothes and stomping the floor, and then I was talking to another Sergeant O'Somebody with a lilting voice from the Woodlawn district—whom I proceeded to tell that my car was being stolen, right then. That was the idea I kept trying to push to the front, you see, that it was being stolen at that very moment. But he took my name and my home address, and he asked where I was calling from, and I told him, and then— well, this goes on and on, you know, from one sweet sergeant to the next. Apparently if I had been able to arrange to call directly from the car while it was being pushed, I could have worked something out with the authorities. Finally I just sat in my office sort of awestruck, and two hours later two policemen showed up at my house, right here, and stood in the doorway and asked what the trouble was."

"Then how did you get it back?"

"Sid called somebody in the department—you remember Sid?—yes, well"—she was no longer so interested in the telling, but pushed hurriedly on to the end—"and some plain-clothes men came around, and then they—well, they called me at the office three days ago and said they'd located it. I drove down in the police car to a depressing little junk yard on the west side, and honestly, the junk dealer, who'd paid something like ten bucks for it, had tears in his eyes when I got in and the policemen towed me away. The battery had been taken out, and for some obscure reason, the little ash tray."

"But now you've got a battery—"

"Oh it's in perfect condition."

"One can see that all right."

"Oh yes? Wait'll you see me driving around with my top down and my hair blowing in May. Then you'll be brimming with envy, and I'll just *shoot* by, nose in the cool air."

"Yes."

She turned back to her slender dinner—ah, slenderizing for somebody, he thought. What was wrong with the way she had always been?

He waited to see what the effect would be of her gay anecdote. But it had been too gay; it had no effect. He was already beginning to regret having come, though only slightly. "I wouldn't mind that glass of sherry now," he said.

"It's in the closet, if you want to help yourself."

He poured the sherry and set the bottle on the table. He understood what she had told him: Go ahead, pal, get a look at the closet . . . at the new me. He could not keep his mind out of her mind. He remained standing and walked around the room while Martha continued with her meal. He pushed aside a branch of the tree and looked over the tinsel at their two automobiles on the street. To make the visit inoffensive, he supposed it was now his turn to be jocular. It was his turn to say that he too was getting along just fine. But what he wanted to pour forth was only the truth. His energies, born again this day, were spinning down.

"I saw you buying this the other night," he said.

"The tree?"

They were not facing one another. "I was on Sixty-third and I happened to see you."

"Oh, yes?"

"—smaller than I thought it was." It was nearly impossible to think of what to say.

"It's smaller than *I* thought it was," she answered. "I'm afraid it was my money's worth, however."

Without much heart, he laughed. "It's a good sherry," he said.

"Are you sure I can't offer you something? A celery?"

"Thank you, no." He came around to the chair facing her; he saw no sense in being anything but serious. "Well, Martha, how are you getting on?" It had not been his intention to sound fatherly, but he could not dissolve his feelings into words; he simply couldn't find the right tone.

She shrugged. "I'm getting on."

"Are you taking a course still? You said—"

"As a matter of fact I am."

"What in?"

"Well, Henry James as a matter of fact." Making her admission, she used her hands in a way that was not very natural to her, or to anyone.

"How do you like him?"

She hesitated; then sat on both his eagerness and her embarrassment. "Not very well, I don't think."

If she was going to be offhanded, he would be more offhanded. Tapping his glass, he said, "That's too bad. I believe I once encouraged you to read some James."

"Oh, that's right . . . Well, his conscience gives me a pain, frankly. Oh—and do you want to know a phrase I'm not too crazy about? 'To put a fine point on it.' Do you really like to hear about people going around putting fine points on it? Oh, and the other one—'She hung fire'—what is that anyway? I hung fire, you hung fire, we hung fire. The girls at my school all hung fire. He writes a little bit like a virgin, don't you think? I mean I think he has a very virginal mind, to put it mildly."

"That strikes me as an extraordinarily virginal remark."

"Well," she said, standing and walking around the table to the door, "you should know that it isn't." In the hallway she opened the refrigerator; then back in the room she asked, "Would you like to share my yogurt?"

"I meant critically virginal."

"I asked if you were interested in some yogurt."

"I have the sherry, thank you. Martha, it's no blow to me if you don't care for James."

"I didn't intend it to be. You asked what I thought, so I told you."

"At least we continue to fight our battles," he said, with a mild display of anger, "on the headiest of planes."

She turned, apparently thought one thing, and then said another. "Who's fighting?"

"I'm not."

Sitting down across from him again, she said, "I'm not either." She looked at him for a moment. "I'm hanging fire. Have I got it right?"

"You're still a semi-cheery girl—"

"Why shouldn't I be? There's nothing for me in gloom, Gabe. I'm getting married, you know."

"No, I didn't . . . Yes, I did."

"Which?"

"I just did hear about it, that is. Sid told Libby Herz."

"Yes? How is *she*?"

"The baby will be legally theirs next week."

"So Sid said . . . It seems Theresa was married—"

"Yes."

"You've heard about it?"

"Yes." Dying to say more, he said nothing.

"Apparently it's gotten a little complicated."

"So I heard," he said. "When will you be getting married?"

"We haven't set a date. There are some other matters."

"Of course."

Silence.

". . . How is Cynthia?"

"Are you asking if she's the other matter?"

"Well—"

"Because she is."

"How is she?"

"She's living in Paris with her father."

"I didn't know that."

"Neither did very many of us, till recently."

"I see."

"Apparently she's all right, Gabe. I don't mean to be sounding secretive. We just learned a few weeks ago that Dick's divorced again. *He* was going to arrange to keep it a secret from us."

"I'm sorry to hear that."

"It'll all work out," Martha said. "You know . . ."

"How did you find out?"

"June Reganhart stopped off here, on her way to Hawaii or some place—to convalesce from him."

"And to tell you?"

"We had lunch together. She wasn't a bad girl, you know. She wasn't silly."

"I thought she seemed decent."

"Too decent for that son of a bitch. He finally hit her too. But she's a higher class girl than I am. He only had to smack her once. But in front of that poor baby."

He thought: she does not mention Markie at all.

"By the time she grows up," Martha said, "she'll have seen quite enough, don't you think?" She carried her dishes over to the small marble washstand and stood there longer than was necessary to rinse the two plates. Her pose was so familiar—her weight on one leg, her head bowed—and so much did he desire her, so much was his desire to touch her and his desire to blot out the past one single yearning, that he walked to where she stood and put a hand to her hair.

She told him no. He put his hand down. The stirring within him was not just lust; lust was subsumed within it. He had to undo all that had been done, do what had not been done. He walked off and sat down again behind his glass. She had suffered most; she still suffered most; he would respect what she wanted of him. He would go slow; to go slow and to be immovable were not mutually exclusive. He thought of Cynthia in Paris. He thought of Markie dead. He thought of it squarely.

"So what happens with him in Paris?" he asked.

She turned, as though having recovered herself. "It'll be worked out. We can only do what we can."

"Do you want him to send her back then?"

She closed her eyes a moment. "Yes. We do."

"I see."

"Do you? You've been saying that since you came in."

He could not believe that she really wanted to be callous. But perhaps that was only self-deception on his part. He did not answer.

"I'm marrying him," she said, "because I want to."

"I can only offer my congratulations."

"I'm not asking for your approval." She brought a glass with her from the sink and sat down opposite him. "How about you pouring me a little sherry?"

"To the second Mrs. Reganhart," she said, with feeble witty intentions. "To her recovery in Hawaii. That's my last duchess hanging on the wall, et cetera."

They drank. Then Martha moved across the room, onto the India print, placing a throw pillow between her head and the wall. "And what about you, Gabriel?" she asked. "What are your plans?"

Apparently she had only gotten up to be more comfortable. Having sparred, were they now going to talk, at last? "Well" —he turned his chair to face her—"I'm leaving Chicago. In May."

"Forever?"

"I think so. I've applied for a job in Turkey—a lectureship in Istanbul. And also one in Greece."

"You've obviously got your heart set on Turkey, I can see."

"I've got my heart set on leaving, in a way."

"Well, to Turkey," she said, and sipped at her glass. "How is your father?"

"He's getting married, you know, next week."

"I remember. It's still going to happen?"

"Oh yes."

"You don't sound as though you've suffered a conversion to Silbermanism. Isn't that . . ."

"I think of it as Fayism myself. No, no conversion."

"Why don't you just fly to the wedding and storm through the church doors and say, 'No! I, I—' What's his name? Ulysses' son?"

"Telemachus."

"I—well, you get the idea."

Of course, he had had the thought himself. "You're full of literary allusions these days."

"I'm the oldest kid in my class. I have to set an example. Oh Gabe—"

"Yes?"

"I was only teasing, partially, about Henry James." Again he felt that she had not said what had first come to her. "I was being, specifically, not to put too fine a point on it, a sort of, what could be called an, though not entirely, aesthetic bitch."

She had her knees up under her; leaning forward she nearly toppled off the bed as she placed her glass on the floor. "I think he makes a lot of sense."

"That's swell. The whole department will be relieved."

"Now you're going to be the bitch?"

How could he help it? He was imagining her married to Jaffe—and resenting Jaffe too, for not even having mentioned to her his trip to the Bigonesses. Of course, it might be that Jaffe had not spoken with her since the day before . . . Nevertheless, he still would not tell anyone himself!

Unfortunately, this time there was no strength to be derived from the decision.

"—is virginal."

"What?"

"Pull your chair up if you can't hear."

"Yes." He dragged his chair over to where Martha sat. She was smiling at him.

"The fat girl who types theses lives next door," she whispered, "and she puts an empty water glass to the wall. To hear."

"To hear?"

"Yes."

"And what," he said, not amused, "does she get to hear?"

"Oh. Discussions. About Henry James. A little Browning."

"And that excites her?"

"Well, she's terribly fat." He did not know what to make of her girlishness or what to do with it. He did not know if she was up to what he began to believe she was up to. "No, look— I was saying, when your eyes fogged over, that you do get the feeling that old James, for all he does know, doesn't really know what goes on when the bedroom door snaps shut. It seems to me that people live more openly with their passions."

"More openly than what?"

"Aren't you following me? Than in James—"

"All people?"

"Well, no, of course not . . . I suppose I live more openly with mine . . ."

"Yes?"

"Than you, I suppose—for one."

"I see."

"You see still again?"

"I'm never quite sure, Martha." It was not meant to be a summation of his way of life; she took advantage nevertheless.

"That's what I mean," she said. "I've done what I've felt strongly about."

"I thought you were going to talk about James this time without being a bitch. I thought, in fact, you were going to talk about James."

"I'm talking about passions. I've gone out on a limb once or twice, is all I said—"

"And now?"

"Right now, or now?"

"Both."

"I don't know, Gabe—"

He kissed her; she said, "Let's not, no," but he had managed to twist her about and force her backwards. His passion for her was so intense, had so much to do with the alteration he had believed his life to have begun to undergo in the last twenty-four hours, that it overrode his other powers. He could not talk; he could not reason. His weight upon her, he forced his hands onto her body, and she thrust him away. It was all very clumsy . . . "Please," she said, "the door is open—"

He went to close the door; when he turned, Martha was standing. He tried to kiss her again. "What do you think you're doing?" she said.

Compromised by his having been *pushed* from the bed, compromised further by the adolescent ring to her words, his pride beat once, beat twice, but could not really sustain itself. "Are you going to put me on the spot, Martha? Are you going to make me explain myself?"

"I don't want to sleep with you."

"With whom else then?"

"Please, don't put on that you've been cuckolded—"

"Is that what you'd call putting too fine a point on it?"

"I suppose that's what he means."

They kissed again. Martha's feet slowly gave way; they were backed onto the bed, face to face. He held back none of his weight, none of his passion. Then she pulled away; she reached up and caught him with a stiff open palm squarely on the side of the head.

He sat up at the foot of the bed, his elbows on his knees, his face hidden.

"I can't afford this," she said, and stood.

"I thought the first thing you might say," he told her, not quite looking up, "would be apologetic."

"I take my life more seriously than that." He heard the faucet begin to run at the other end of the room. He tried not to speak again until he had himself mostly under control, but he could not wait that long.

He asked, "Did you plan on that?"

"Did you?"

"No."

"Well, that's the only thing you're ever overcome with then, my friend—desire. Aside from that you're a perfectly prudent man."

His jaw tingled, and his eye too, where a fingernail had nicked it. He pulled himself up. The dampness at the edge of his lash was not a tear, so it must be a drop of blood. On the floor before him was a shoe of his, on its side. He tried to put it on standing up, but finally he had to sit down to manage, and he was humiliated. He went to the closet for his coat, while Martha said nothing.

"You might have sat in your chair, Martha," he said, "and saved us this. You might not have talked so fetchingly about your passions. You have a long finger, Martha, and you beckon with it. Prudent is not the word to describe you—"

"Why don't you please go?"

He felt totally dislocated; with his coat on and buttoned he still could not believe in the last three minutes.

Martha was lighting the two candles on the table just to be doing something. "I can't afford to sleep with you. I hope you at least understand that."

"You can with him?"

"That's right." She spoke stiffly. "I think I can."

"Even when you were supposedly committed to me?"

She walked to the Christmas tree. "Who are you to talk about commitment?"

"I know, Martha—"

"You don't know a God damn thing." Then, caught, she lost control, or gained it. "I've had a penchant for jelly-filled men, but I've gotten over it. I've spent my life associating with the wrong kind of men, one way or the other."

"You only get in bed with whomever you want—"

"That's exactly the case—"

"—when you want."

"Shut up. Please go. You can't make me feel rotten over something I couldn't even help. I've given up being self-destructive. That's right, I'm going to bring some order into my life. There's order in this world, and I'm due for my share of it."

"I hope you get it."

"Why shouldn't someone else aside from you? Why should it be only you who get away unscathed?"

"That's another virginal opinion, Martha. Nice and narrow."

"Are you going to tell me about your fine conscience? Those little pains don't even *begin* to count. Don't kid yourself—your conscience and James's conscience both give me a pain in the ass, if you want the truth."

"And your own?" he asked viciously.

"Mine's fine! Sid Jaffe happens to be a fine man. He's not jelly either. He's going to get me my baby back, do you know that? If he has to fly to Paris and get that son of a bitch guillotined, he's going to get her back here. And then I'm going to have an orderly life—do you hear? Don't ever try to get me in bed again, you! And don't worry about my conscience. Worry about your own. I'm not playing it safe. I'm using some sense for once. I've let go and let go and let go—I've let go plenty. I've had a wilder history than you, by a long shot. I've got a right to hang on now. Don't ever get in bed with me again. Ever!"

All he could think to say, as an answer, a defense, was to tell her what had happened that afternoon in Gary. But of course that was no answer. He could say nothing. His hour with Bigoness—after all, what was he going to build it into? That puny little exchange—the humbling of a stupid man—was not enough to elevate his life. He lived a little life, an insignificant life. Puny . . . Nothing at this point seemed able to give him proportion or dignity. It was not even out of anything so weighty as jealousy that this woman's intended had not mentioned to her his phone call. What he had done, what he had forced Jaffe to let him do, counted for nothing. He turned to leave, and then—because he was so unwilling, so incredulous —he turned back for a final instant. And what his eyes saw in her eyes—could it be? Uncertainty? She knows she is fooling herself. She is in pain! *Now* he must take her in his arms! But he could no longer deceive himself with what he wanted to believe were her feelings.

4

Puny?

Fury! Fury was what he was feeling! He had made plans of his own for the afternoon. The sun was high, the streets clear and brilliant. He had told himself to make plans and he had made them. He had seen a handsome quilt advertised in the Sunday papers—which took care of his present. He would buy it. He had a date for drinks in the Loop at five with the girl he had met at the Harnaps'. She had sounded pleasant and genuine on the phone, and not so assertive this time, he preferred to believe, as eager. He would have dinner with her too. She was assistant to the curator at the Art Institute. Fine. His humiliation was two nights past; it no longer was going to get him down. Nothing was going to get him down . . . Except that he was so damned angry. He was going to have to miss his penicillin shot too. He drove with no regard for the law—though he had justice on his mind—changing lanes, leaning on his horn, braking sharply, speeding, speeding down to Gary. There were still those applications to mail. He had rushed so, that he'd forgotten again to put them in his pocket. He couldn't keep everything on his mind, with the result that he sometimes couldn't keep anything on it.

Thirty minutes later he was threading his way in and out of monotonous, endless streets; the glare of the sun made them no less dreary. He saw only lusterless houses, insulated from light, life, the seasons. In the muddy little squares of front yard —snow-filled on his last visit—children sat and shivered, or hopelessly slid their tricycles through the soft earth. Some men were in the streets washing their cars, arms moving mechanically up and down, water ringing on hub caps, steam twirling off roofs. He peered at every street sign, while slowly the blue sky and white sun drew away, restoring a proper and wintery distance between heaven and earth. Even the stinking weather was against him. His anger and disgust burned steadily away. That he had not stopped to think of his other affairs—he had rushed down the stairs, into the car, and off—did not decrease his passion any; his fury had many causes. For one thing (this dawned slowly) he was lost.

A half-dozen men in faded field jackets and heavy shoes were congregated around the pumps of a gas station; he pulled off the road and up beside them. When he leaned toward them to speak, a whizzing sensation fanned out from his eye through the left half of his skull. Under the gaze of these idle men he grew conscious of his small bandage. The wound throbbed; leaving Martha's, he should have driven directly home and washed the cut. He could not even remember the name of the movie he had gone to see instead; he had not really seen it.

He wasn't thinking. *He had to start to think.* Yet he did not want to calm down, if that's what thinking would accomplish. If he wasn't being prudent, that was all right with him.

He asked directions—his foot all the while tapping the gas —and received a curt reply from a short man with a not very high opinion of him. But he had asked curtly in the first place. He listened, then drove off—some words having to do with his bandage following after him. While he was swinging away, a foot kicked the rear fender. Sons of bitches. As though nobody else had troubles.

But he had only gone off the curb. He felt himself not permitting himself to calm down.

Today? The nineteenth. Six days before he was to go East; four shopping days, sang the radio, till Christmas. Carefully he had planned this day. Lovingly. Resurrectingly! Looking himself over in the mirror as he was about to depart—for his shot first, then the Loop—he had only decided to phone on the chance that Theresa herself might be home, just to make certain, to check up. And the nerve of that dumb bastard! Who the hell did he think he was!

He pulled up behind a two-toned Plymouth, tan and white. Woolly tassels framed the rear window, and two tailpipes stuck out from the car's underside. The machine had a high polish. He looked the automobile over, tried a door and found it locked. The urge he had was undefined, but destructive. Before starting up the stairs he thought of getting back in his car and driving around Gary, from one diner to another, until he found Theresa. He could deal with her, then *she* would deal with her husband.

Breezing out of the alley on a tricycle came the blue-eyed Bigoness girl. She looked flatly up at him, where he stood at the top of the stairs. He went into the house, working out in his mind the blood relationship between this child and Rachel. There was none. He rang the bell once, then leaned all his weight against it until he heard shoes galloping down the stairs.

"Vic? Yo, Vic?" Bigoness beat down one flight, then another, until he was confronted with the enemy. He came to a powerful halt, practically rearing backwards.

"You—"

"That's right—"

Outrage: "Where were you! Around the corner?"

"I telephoned from Chicago. I think we'd better have a talk. Right now."

"Right now I got other things."

"Well, you're going to have to have this thing too."

"You don't tell me what I got to have or don't—"

He had an official tone. "It's now three o'clock. I have to be back in Chicago—"

"Nobody told you to come down here in the first place."

"I told myself. You told me."

"The hell I—"

"We had better move our conversation upstairs. I take it your wife isn't home?"

"Look, I told you—I spent it. Little Walter got sick as a dog. What do you expect, I'd let him die? Let a little kid run a hundred and *four*—"

"I think we should be talking in private." A door had opened on the next landing. His eye released a small crack of pain. He should have gone first for his shot.

"—let the kid die?" Bigoness was shouting, dramatically. "You got a sick kid, man, you call a doctor, you buy medicines—"

"Nevertheless, I gave you the money for a purpose."

"I didn't sign anything, did I?"

"Just your word."

His what? Bigoness gaped.

"A promise, Bigoness. An agreement."

"I said I'd think about it. Don't tell me I signed something!"

"You said you'd do it."

"You're thinking of some other customer, Jack. Something came up . . . Look, I'm waiting on a phone call, will you—" Bigoness reached for the door.

His eye gave him another ten seconds of pain. He would get blood poisoning. A movie? Why a movie? He was doing things backwards, today too. He should have gone first for the shot, *then* come here. "Let's," he said calmly, wedging his foot in the door, "talk a minute upstairs. Maybe we can still reach some sort of agreement."

"I don't think so."

"We'd better try." He would be out of here by four, meet the girl at five . . . His date now seemed even more crucial to his life than his shot. Dropping his head, he stepped through the door. He had an immediate and overwhelming sense of the vulnerability of his back. Why had he dropped his head— so Bigoness wouldn't strike him on the chin, on the eye?

Upstairs he paused momentarily at Bigoness's door; his heart struck, like a clock hitting the hour; he moved through.

"*Hey*—"

The TV set was on; the place smelled of furniture polish. He pictured Bigoness rubbing down the living room suite and watching give-away shows all day. To his own astonishment, he stepped forward and turned off the sound.

"I'm busy—"

"I see your car's been washed," Gabe said. "You can't be that busy."

"Me washing my car is none of your business."

"My business is that you have a car."

"Oh man, everything is your business."

"You have a car, yet you took money for train fare—"

"I never said I didn't have a car. I like to take trains, that's all." He had no intention of being comic.

"You like to take money apparently."

"God damn you, I never stole in my life!"

He saw with relief that Bigoness had not shut the door behind him; it became easier to get his words out. "I'm saying that you had no right to take all that money in the first place.

In the second place, you had no right to spend it and then tell me you and your wife can't come up to Chicago a week from Monday because you can't afford to. That money was so you could afford to."

"I said I had—"

"Just let me finish. Third—you see—you had no right to go back on your word."

"You done now?"

"For the moment."

"I ain't signing any papers."

So much weariness and so much rage rose within him that the one canceled out the other.

"I don't want to get mixed up in anybody else's troubles." It was Bigoness who had spoken.

"You are mixed up in them."

"No, sir," said Bigoness, shaking his head.

"Your wife's mixed up in them."

"Uh-uh."

"Bigoness, what is it you want?" But what he expected to hear, he did not. Bigoness's finger slid in under his belt. The man had no grand schemes; he had no grand mind. It was victory enough for him to walk cockily to the window, slightly bowlegged, his fingers hooked in his trousers. It was enough for him to have suddenly become a cowboy. God! Gabe wished himself the owner of a pistol, a knife. But what did he have, outside of his will, and his intelligence, and whatever strength was in his body? And that strength was probably not as great as his opponent's. He sat behind a desk all day. Still, he had ten or twelve pounds on the fellow, at least two inches . . . The vision he had was of himself leaping upon the man's back and pummeling him until he agreed to show up a week from Monday. The back he saw himself pummeling was, in fact, turned to him now. If he was going to jump, this was his chance.

Of course he did not even begin to take it. "I think," he said to the back, "you're allowing the situation to run away with you. Perhaps I've made it sound like a larger issue than it really is."

The back—at least it might just as well have been the back—spoke. "Man, you don't go around laying out cash for small issues. I'm getting out while the getting's good."

"That cash was for train fare and expenses."

"I got a right to change my mind." He turned to show his face: stolid. Not till then did Gabe realize that he was himself sitting on the sofa, that he had sat down.

"Let's forget the forty-five," Gabe said.

Bigoness's lashes fluttered; only half his eyes showed. "What do you mean, forget it?

"Forget it. That's all. You had a doctor bill—"

"You don't believe me?"

"Whatever you had is okay with me. Let's simply forget it."

"Well," said Bigoness, coming around to turn up the sound of the television, "all right, I'm willing."

Bigoness was willing.

Gabe ignored everything he could possibly ignore. "Now we can start from scratch," he said.

"We sure can."

"I want to assure you"—repeating and repeating and re-peating—"that neither of these papers that you sign will bind you to anything whatsoever. In fact, it's precisely the opposite that you're going to bring about. Signing these papers will free you from any responsibility where Theresa's baby is con-cerned. Do you see that? Isn't that clear yet?"

"I ain't signing any papers."

"But aren't you listening to me?"

"I just told you, Mister," said Bigoness, as though ad-dressing one demented, "that I don't want to get involved. Understand? Get it? You're willing to forget the forty-five bucks, I'm willing to forget it. Why don't we call it quits, be-fore we get angry at each other."

"Bigoness"—he was barely able to prevent his head from dropping into his hands—"there's a child's life involved here. A child can have a decent family and a good life and a good education, and all it takes from you is a short little trip into Chicago . . ."

"You hand me a laugh, you know?" He had not interrupted Gabe; he had only waited for exhaustion to overtake him. "You think you can come out here and just push people around because they're having hard times, don't you? Just tell people what to say and where to sign on the dotted line. You think nobody's got anything to think about but you and your business. But I'll tell you, buddy"—pointing—"people have been thinking they're going to tell me what to do all my life. Now you're working, now you ain't; now you're making a buck eighty an hour, now you're making a buck eighty-five; now you're a man, now you're nothing but a nursemaid. And now you're going to tell me I'm going to sign those papers, and I'm telling you"—tapping his chest—"I'm not. I make up my mind about things—nobody makes it up for me. Not you, not Tessie, not that bitch Wanda, not anybody but Harry Bigoness! And don't you go telling me about decent families, you hear? What the hell you mean? I ain't been out of this place for six weeks—I could've run out on those kids too, you understand? But I got guts, you understand that? I could say just like Wanda—screw 'em, and just take off too. But I'm no bum, Mister. Nobody's ruining my life for me. I work in a factory and you walk around in a tie all day, but at least I earn an honest living. You think I'm some kind of lower kind of person, but I didn't run out on those kids, did I? I got 'em a new mama, didn't I? I always held a job, since I'm sixteen years old, and I read a couple books too, in case you want to know, and I didn't make this recession—understand?—and don't think you're going to shove anybody around because of it!"

"You're telling me then that you won't do it?"

"Jesus, you're a slow learner, ain't you? I told you that on the phone. You could have saved yourself the gas."

"What does your wife think of this?"

"She knows what's good for her."

"I'd like to see her."

"Hey, I just asked you, who do you think you're shoving around?"

Again the image of himself leaping upon Bigoness, dragging him down by the throat, crossed his mind, even as he was thinking that he should never have come. He was only matching pride against pride. Dumb pride against dumb pride.

"Then what do you propose to do about this child your wife brought into the world?"

"I don't think I get you, Wallace."

"As far as the law is concerned, it's you who's responsible for this child. Look, I told you all this last time."

"And what is it you're asking?"

"I'm asking what you propose to do about it."

"—you take me for stupid—"

He rose; he could not bear one more minute of it. "*I take you—*"

There was a banging beneath him, a thumping, as though his heart was beating upwards in him. A broom handle whacked against the ceiling below, then a voice, "Phone!" Bigoness was darting past him, through the doorway—

"Right there!" he called, tearing down the stairs. "Hold it!"

Gabe stood where he was, each shoe planted on a dragon. Beneath him were the grotesque designs; around, hemming him in, were the heavily oiled surfaces of the elaborate furnishings. When he finally made a move it was only mildly defiant; he switched off the television set. Then he looked around. Where was the phone? He was not sure whom he wanted to call; it was simply that there were other people whose business was more properly the Bigonesses than was his own.

In the dark corridor that led to the bedrooms, the phone sat on a small table. He picked it up to find it dead. Of course—he was not thinking. His eye throbbed, opportunely. He could leave because he needed his shot. He could leave because he had an appointment in the Loop at five. Instead he moved further in the apartment, at first aimlessly, then after some clue to Theresa's whereabouts. The search began to seem rational.

He entered a room where the shades were drawn; the mattress was furled with sheets and the carpet littered with cups and saucers. He pulled at the tangle of bedding and a man's pajama top slipped onto the floor. He groveled under the blankets with one hand, and pulled forth what turned out to be a thin blue nightgown. He rushed to the closet. Suits, trousers—a dress! Skirts! Hanging before him was Theresa's gold skirt. She did live here! He turned a pocket inside out, heard a noise—and made a break for it.

The noise came from back of one of the doors leading off the hall. It was only the whine of a kitten or a puppy. He went into the kitchen and began to open all the drawers. He could leave because nothing was working out. Nothing was in these drawers but silverware, playing cards, and green stamps.

The noise again. A child, a little boy, somewhere in the apartment. And with him his mother, hiding? His stepmother?

He followed after the sound, located the door, and opened it. He really should go; this was insane.

The boy was strapped to the toilet seat. When he saw Gabe he let out an agonized scream. He strained to release himself from the seat; his face went from red to white to red again; the odor of the child's feces was overpowering. Gabe's eye throbbed. He closed the door, then opened it and was in the bathroom, leaning over the miserable child. The odor was of sickness. He slid the boy's shirt up and looked for whatever was holding him down. The child began to pull and yank, his arms straining upwards as he screamed and wept.

Wallace!

No one was calling him. But his head grew dark and heavy, as though a blow had been struck upon it. His stomach was turning. He was himself, but this life was another's. The room was pink; so was the toilet paper; so were the dirty linens stuffed into the bathtub. His fingers worked along the tape that crisscrossed the child's middle. Minutes passed before he came to a small knot at the side of the seat. He worked at it with what he thought was all his attention. But he had no luck. He kneeled on the floor before the child, and at last he gave in and held his head in his hands. *I am here.*

Go! Go away!

Suddenly he was flooded with sympathy for Bigoness. He worked helplessly at the tape, feeling only sorrow for the stupid bastard. The law that held him accountable was absurd. Him meaning Bigoness. He heard Bigoness saying that he was not involved. So why didn't he leave the man alone? *Go home.* But in that same instant he saw himself strangling Bigoness, squeezing his throat till the face turned colors—and then was no color. He was holding a gun to Bigoness's head— At that moment the child shot forward, arms and legs whirling. A pain shot through Gabe's whole body—he had been caught on the side of the head by the little boy's shoe. *His eye!* He howled; the child screamed hysterically.

"Shhhh," he said, shaking. "Quiet, shhhhh . . " He wiped the child's brow, then his own. He hunched over the tape, as though working against time. He should look through all of Theresa's pockets. He should never have left her alone in that taxi. Why not. *How* not? His arms were hanging at his sides, three times their own weight. He couldn't do it. He couldn't handle it. Alone he would only complicate matters further. Call Jaffe. He was at a point with Bigoness where he could save nothing. There was a point beyond which it made no sense to go. That was called prudence—

. . . She had wanted to smack him. She had planned it, right there on the steps. She had led him on. Always she had led him on, made use of him, tried to rope him—

The child wept, actual suffering, actual tears. Gabe's fingers were no longer of any use. They were stiff. Revolted suddenly, his stomach turned and turned. He rushed to the window and flung it open. Down in the alleyway below, the little Bigoness girl pedaled back and forth. Call Jaffe.

"Shhhhh, please—just a minute . . . you'll be all right." He had turned back to the boy, a nondescript dark-haired child. He touched the damp hair. He felt sorry again for Bigoness, a man who had stuck by his children. He forced himself to get control, to think straight. He would have taken his coat off, but it did not seem to him that he had time. He searched (telling himself: I am an educated man, I am a decent man) and he searched for the little hook that held the child down— and discovered instead the toilet handle. An educated man, he finally flushed it. The water rushed, the child howled, the smell rose, and diving down one final time, he found the attachment that bound the child, and ripped it open.

He had to pick up the boy. He had to clean him. Flushing the toilet a second time, he carried him from the bathroom. He moved under weights that were only his clothes, his shirt and jacket and coat. All right, he had been imprudent—*now* was he happy? But there was no backing out, not if he had gone too far. But when had he begun going *too* far? He told himself, *I am here*, and it meant nothing.

"What the hell—you crazy— *Put that kid down!*" Bigoness was flying at him, his arms making great circles.

"I just took him off—"

"Put him down! I know where you got him, you son of a bitch!"

"You left him tied—"

"You son of a bitch! *Give him to me!*" The child out-howled his father, as he was wrenched away.

"I wasn't stealing your baby! God damn it, let's keep this straight—!"

"Get out! Get out, Wallace, before I call the police!"

"Call the police and you'll make the biggest—"

"—no mistake to throw a guy like you in jail." He rocked the weeping child in his arms.

"You're letting your imagination run away with you."

"I'm calling the cops. I'll give you three."

Quickly Gabe said, "You'll bring your creditors right down on your head."

"I'll bring them down on yours, you crook!"

"Look—*look*, this is absurd! You know it is! I'm not connected—listen to me, will you? You'd better calm down and think over what's best for you."

"I know what's best . . . Ah quiet down, Walter honey—oh you son of a bitch, I know what's— Come on now, Walter, willya? You'll be all right, boy . . ." He paced the floor with his child, a worried parent.

"Why don't we make some kind of deal, please—"

"Why don't you bug off!"

"Why don't we make a cash deal?" He put himself in Bigoness's line of vision. "I want a favor and you need money."

"I don't need your money. I got a deal coming up with Vic, my buddy. I'm going to have myself some work in just about two weeks. Three weeks."

"Your phone call didn't work out, did it?"

"Why don't you keep your nose out of my business, you wheedling son of a bitch." He placed his child, who had howled himself almost to sleep, down on the sofa.

"I'll give you"—he reached for a figure—"fifty dollars more."

Bigoness turned; Gabe had a second thought. "A week from Monday, as soon as you and Theresa have signed the papers, fifty dollars more."

"And this ain't the black market, huh? What are you trying to do, get me all fucked up with the union?"

"Fifty dollars for an hour's work. Yes or no?"

". . . That's no big offer, is it, for me taking such a big chance?"

"You've already *taken* forty-five dollars."

"I didn't take—you gave. You tried bribing me already."

"Well—" he said, uncertainly, having still a third thought, "it was just as big a chance then."

"And that's why I don't want nothing to do with it, you understand?"

"Look, yes or no? Fifty dollars." He had nearly said a hundred.

"Twenty-five now, and twenty-five then?"

"Nothing now."

"Nothing now never helped nobody's troubles."

"You've *had* forty-five already."

"Jesus! I thought we were going to forget about that. Boy oh boy! First you tell me you're going to forget it, and I say I'm even willing—and now you keep bringing it up again!"

In the morning Gabe had cashed a check so as to have money for the weekend, for the present, for dinner that evening. He had with him a little under a hundred dollars. What prevented him from handing it all over to Bigoness was only the word *bribe*. But fifty was surely not less of a bribe— and a hundred might do the trick. A hundred right now. No!

Nevertheless, he saw one door closing, saw it shut. Jaffe could no longer go into court and claim abandonment; a subsequent investigation would uncover Bigoness, uncover this moment. Deep, he had to go deeper. He could not now give Bigoness nothing; of course he couldn't.

"—want to be surer, then fifty later too."

"I don't follow you." He had to pretend an inability to comprehend, when in fact their two minds—one moving down, one moving up—had apparently met.

"—what I suppose is the best thing, for you to feel safe and me to feel safe, that we ain't either going to get screwed, is you give me fifty now and then you hold out another fifty for then, see, and then . . ."

"I still don't follow you."

"More when it's over," Bigoness was saying. But his voice had dropped.

Gabe used Bigoness's own phrase. "Are you done now?"

"Well . . . yeah, I'm done."

"Didn't you get a letter today, from Mr. Jaffe?"

"I don't get no mail."

"You got a letter telling you when and where to show up."

"What do you think, that's all I got to worry about?"

"What I'm asking is, do you know what's wanted of you exactly—the place and the time?"

"I don't know nothing."

He took out his billfold. Bigoness sat up. Gabe took from it an old dry-cleaning receipt and wrote on the back the necessary information. He offered the slip of paper to Bigoness, continuing to hold his billfold in the other hand. "Take it," he said. He pushed it in Bigoness's direction; Bigoness extended his hand—and then it was fluttering to the rug. Gabe had opened his hand, but Bigoness had not closed his. Very faintly, Bigoness grinned.

"Pick that up."

"Shit, that ain't a fifty-dollar bill. Don't look like it to me."

"You know what it is. Pick it up."

"Hey, what am I, a carpet sweeper to you? Huh? Your slave?" Bigoness sat down on the sofa beside his child, who moaned now in his sleep. He started tapping his fingers together before his mouth; inspired, he whistled "Here Comes the Bride."

"Twice I've asked you to pick that paper up."

Nothing.

"I thought you were concerned about your family." Bigoness's eyes were on his billfold; deliberately he had not put it away; had that been a mistake? "I thought you were a man who worried about the doctor's bills."

"All dressed in white . . . da-da da-*da*-da . . ."

This stubbornness! This thick head! To think that he had *put* the idea of a bribe into this dumb ox's head!

"Look, what kind of bastard are you—"

"Watch—" Bigoness began.

"We're talking about a baby. *Pick that money up!*"

"It ain't money."

"Paper! *Pick it*—"

"I didn't ask for this recession, Wallace, before you blow a gut. I never asked for hard times."

"What kind of—"

"Ah shit, what kind are you? Huh? I'm taking the big risk, while you guys make thousands."

"Can't I get it into your head—"

Bigoness waved one hand. "Okay, you're the happy father then, what do I care? I'm giving you a kid for the rest of your life. Don't you appreciate that, Poppa? A little—what? Boy? Girl?"

"—beside the point."

"Well, I got a right to know what it is. Here you keep telling me that kid really belongs to me, I got a right at least to know what it is." He waited.

"A girl."

". . . Well, maybe I'd like another little girl around here. Just to even things up. Man, you give me a hard enough time, in the end I might just as well move the little bastard right in here with the rest of 'em."

Gabe said nothing; no muscle moved.

"At least that'd be the legal thing, right? You got to consider that, don't you?"

"Adoption is perfectly legal. Don't be sly."

Bigoness shook his head as though he knew better. "That may be and then it might not be, given the way things are. But if I'm willing to give up a little baby, seems to me you ought to have a little more respect. A hundred dollars more for a whole little baby—man, that's not bad."

"Either you pick up that paper or I leave. I didn't make this recession either, don't be a God damn fool. I didn't give you your hard times. I'm sorry about all your marital difficulties, I'm sorry you're out of a job—"

"Oh yeah, you're sorry."

"Either you pick it up—" He felt silly, picky, quibbling; he felt he was missing the point himself. Was everything to come down to this—his having his way? "Or I leave and you get nothing."

No response.

"I mean that." No word from Bigoness, no movement at all. No whistling. Without any clear impression of what would follow, Gabe took a step toward the door. And Bigoness ducked down; his hand swooped across the rug; he twisted the paper around in his fingers, then shoved it into his shirt pocket.

They were silent, however, as though it were not quite over. Bigoness said, "You're getting me cheap, Mister. When a man is down," he said sourly, "you sure do know how to make him crawl around for you."

But even as Bigoness spoke, Gabe felt moved to thrust the entire billfold at him. Everything. Go all out. What was the difference? He just wanted it *over*! He looked at Bigoness, Bigoness at the billfold. Gabe thought: he only wants what I put in his head to want.

Bigoness whined, "What about expenses?"

"I gave you forty-five—"

"Oh shit—"

"*Here.*" He did not think, did not reason. He jammed a bill into Bigoness's hand. He hoped it would be a ten; it turned out to be a twenty. What difference? "The rest you get after you sign."

"You ain't going to subtract—"

"No. No!"

He turned, just as the little boy rolled over and woke up. Of course Bigoness had known that he had not been stealing the child. Yes, Bigoness was smarter than he was, smarter under pressure. *Why shouldn't he be?* He moved through the door, so weary that he could not have put up much resistance had the extortionist, the thief, the miserable bastard chosen that moment to attack him from behind for the rest of the money. But no one laid a finger on him as he passed out the door and down the stairway. All the violent thoughts had been his own.

He emerged from the front door as a woman with a shopping bag was struggling up the porch steps, one at a time. He held the door open for her.

"Oh, how is little Walter?" she asked.

"Oh—I—"

"Aren't you . . . ?"

"No."

"I'm sorry, I saw you going in . . ."

"Yes?"

"I thought you were Harry's doctor." She giggled. "You *look* like a doctor."

"I'm just—"

"Well, isn't it something?"

"Yes."

"We never cared for her, you know. Not a bit. I've never myself liked Southerners. And my husband, well, he spotted her right off."

"Well, yes—"

"Harry, on the other hand, is good to those children as gold."

"Yes—I have to be going—" He showed her that he was about to release the door.

"It's a shame, a hard-working boy like that, and, well, I won't even say the sort she is. Maybe she'll work out this time, but she's no proper stepmother even," she said hopelessly. "Just running off—"

"Excuse me, I have to go—be going—"

"—better off without her, if you want my opinion. Don't you believe—"

"I think—" said Gabe, and breaking away, he let fly the door.

He drove back to Chicago as madly as he had left it. He went immediately to the doctor's office, and by the time he got to the Loop for drinks it was nearly six. A slender, dark-haired girl had sat alone at a table for half an hour, the waitress told him, then paid for her drink and left. He drove home; not till he was there did he remember that he had forgotten the quilt. At nine Libby called. She asked if he would fill in for their baby-sitter on Christmas Eve; their regular girl had gone for the holidays. He said yes. It would give him something to do the night before he left. It would please Libby and it would please him—if not now, then. He said yes, and then he did not let Libby hang up. He talked and talked; he said more words to her than he had in years. He told her he had gone to the doctor in the afternoon and gotten the second of three penicillin shots. He told her how he had leaned over in a movie and hit his head on the corner of the seat. He had dropped his billfold, tried to pick it up, and whack. He should have gone off instantly to wash it out but had neglected to. He hadn't realized he had broken the skin. However, had he not gone to the doctor the next day, he might well have wound up with a serious case of blood poisoning. So near the brain . . . He did not ask to speak to Paul. He saw no way of getting around to it, no cool, calm way even of his making the request that might not send Libby screaming down the hall. And he did not call Jaffe. He had called a day or two before to say that everything was fine, just perfect. There was no sense in calling again. After all, there was nothing for Jaffe to do; he had himself done everything.

He went to bed earlier than he should have, with the result that he slept badly. His head ached all through the night. The doctor had assured him that he would not expire in his sleep; the doctor was a humorous man who took minor ailments lightly. Of course, Gabe had only raised the question lightly— he did not really expect to die. Nevertheless, for long stretches he did not sleep because he would not allow himself to. It was as though his illness might overpower him were he not awake to protect himself. But dozing, he had dreams of struggle and loss, dreams of falling. He was wrestling with Bigoness over a pit alive with monsters. They rolled and rolled, arms locked about one another, and then they fell, onto Bigoness's rug.

He awoke. The room was dark. He set his mind a task. He tried to figure out the amount of money that would have been appropriate—safe—wise—binding—*right*—to have promised Harry Bigoness.

5

Gabe:
   We will be at the Cape Cod Room (splurge! our sixth an-niversary!) of the Hotel Drake (AM 3–4582) from 7–8:30. At Surf Theater (AM 4–9724) till 10:20. Meet train at LaSalle St. Station 10:45. Home by 11:15 thereabouts. Be charming to Mrs. Herz when we bring her home. Very charming. I am nervous—but have not been so expectant in years. Oh brave new world and so on. If Rachel wakes up (she will), expect you to read to her. Bottle may help.

L.

On her way out she handed the note to him. "Here's where we'll be," she had said. At seven-thirty, while they were still at the Drake he wrote a memorandum to himself on the back of Libby's note:

> *1. Have plane ticket.*
> *2. Take quilt.*
> *3. Call taxi by ten.*
> *4. Call airport first, check etc.*
> *5. Mail applications!*
> *6. Enough cash.*
> *7. Call Jaffe.*
> *8. Call Bigo*

Number eight was crossed out. It was then written in again. The process was repeated three times over.

—

At eight—the Herzes were still enjoying dinner at the Cape Cod Room—Rachel woke up and cried briefly. He gave her a bottle. He stood by the crib, thinking over and over all that he had been thinking over and over for days. There were no new thoughts for him to have. He referred to his list of things to do. At eight-fifteen he telephoned Gary.

"I'd like to speak"—yes, this was safe, this was wise—"to Theresa Bigoness, please."

He heard the broom bang against the ceiling.

"Hello?"

"Theresa?"

"Uh-huh."

"This is Gabe Wallach."

"Who?"

"Martha's friend . . . Mr. Wallace."

"You want to speak to Harry?"

"I wanted to speak with you. Privately. To say hello . . . Just to make sure everything is all right. Is everything . . . ?"

". . . I'm okay."

"I was sorry I couldn't get to see you—"

"Uh-huh."

"—when I came to talk to your husband."

"Maybe you better talk to him."

"I wanted to tell you that Mr. Jaffe's looking forward to seeing you on the twenty-ninth, you know. You remember Sid Jaffe—he got your letter, of course."

"Uh-huh."

"Everything's all right then?"

"I feel okay."

"And we'll be seeing you on the twenty-ninth?"

"I've got a job."

"I know. The twenty-ninth, of course, has been taken care of."

"The mill's all closed up, I have to work—"

"Hasn't your husband told you that you're coming into town on the twenty-ninth?"

Silence.

"Theresa, you're coming, right? You have to, you know. That was all made clear to you by Mr. Jaffe."

"I have to work."

". . . I've paid your salary for that day, more than your salary already."

"Uh-huh."

"Theresa, are you listening to me? You do remember me?"

"I have to go upstairs now."

"When you were in trouble, Theresa, everybody up here was very kind to you. You were taken care of—weren't you?"

Again she did not see fit to answer immediately.

"Well, isn't that so?"

"No."

"It is so, Theresa. Don't you remember how unhappy you were?"

"Not everybody was nice to me."

"Who wasn't?"

"Not everybody," she whispered.

"Your husband has agreed to come up to Chicago. Hasn't he told you that?"

"I didn't have to be treated like that."

"What are you talking about? Like what?"

"I have to hang up now. I can't talk long, count of it's Mr. Phelp's phone, not mine."

"Theresa—"

———

Time passed. The Herzes were finishing up at the Cape Cod Room AM 3–4582; Rachel lay on a blanket on the living room floor, where her sitter had carried her—where, for some fifteen minutes, he had been looking at her. Once again he called Gary.

"I'd like to speak to Harry Bigoness, please."

The broom.

"Hullo?"

"This is Wallace, I'm calling from Chicago."

"Look, you just call my wife?"

"No."

"What do you want anyway?"

"I wanted to give you a ring, to make sure everything was all right."

"Yeah?"

"Yes, that's all."

No answer now from the husband.

"Everything's okay then, about the twenty-ninth?"

"My kid was in the hospital."

"Who?"

"Walter."

"What's the matter?"

"Something with his insides. They don't know."

"I'm sorry to hear that."

"—won't be able to . . ."

"What?"

This round the words were sharp and clear; Bigoness took his time with them. "I said I don't think I can make it."

It was Gabe's turn to be silent.

And Bigoness's to lose his temper. "Did you try to talk to Tessie before?"

"I've promised you your money, Mr. Bigoness—"

"My kid is sick!"

"Well, that costs money—"

"God damn right it costs money. What do you think it costs, nothing?"

He said nothing—and not out of strategy; he had no strategy, only confusion.

"Look," said Bigoness carefully, "I ain't got time to talk. I'm meeting with a friend. I got some business . . ."

"You just can't change your mind like this."

"I'm too busy."

"What are you going to do then?"

"I told you."

". . . What do you want, Bigoness—more?"

"You asking?"

"I asked you a question, that's right."

"You want to talk about money?"

"How much do you want—don't be coy, God damn it."

"I've been talking to the lawyer down the union. I'm talking to a friend here—he knows something too."

"So? What?"

"I know my rights, Wallace."

"No one's tried to deprive you of your rights."

"I know what you been full of crap about, and what you ain't."

"How much money do you want?"

"If I wasn't hard up I wouldn't ask a guy like you for a God damn penny."

"I understand."

"Five hundred bucks."

"That's ridiculous."

"I ain't the doctors, Mister—" Bigoness began rapidly. "I ain't the President of the United States. I ain't Khrushchev or any of those guys. I didn't give my kid bad inside troubles. I need five hundred bucks. Take it," and there was a tremor in his voice, "or you know what."

"And what'll it be next?"

"What next?"

"Tomorrow. What will it be then, another five hundred? What'll it be by the twenty-ninth? This is crazy, Bigoness. Whoever you're talking to is giving you the wrong information. You can't go around extorting money from people; that's against the law. Why don't you follow your own instincts?"

"See," said Bigoness, "you don't trust me."

"*What?*"

"You son of a bitch." It was said for what seemed to be the simple pleasure of saying it.

"What's going on with you, Bigoness? You're ashamed of asking for this money yourself. Bigoness—don't hang up—"

"I got business upstairs."

"Bigoness, you're a father yourself—"

But the phone clicked.

—

He removed his jacket from the closet, where Libby had neatly hung it beside his coat. He opened his checkbook and wrote out a check. Then he came back into the living room and tried to play with Rachel. He was able to make her smile. He checked the time; the Herzes were entering the movie. He could drive down in forty minutes, back in forty minutes, allowing himself at least an hour in Gary. He would hand the check over to Bigoness and this time be given proper assurance. But he could never be properly assured. Nor could he leave Rachel alone . . . He would mail the check tonight, and fly to New York tomorrow—

Nothing would work. He was rocking Rachel now, to get her back to sleep. It's all become too abstract, he thought, holding the child. Bigoness did not believe Rachel was as real as Walter. He had to be put in touch with the simplest of human facts. He was stupid, but he had feelings. If he could meet Paul, see Libby—see Rachel. If he could be Gabe, rocking her. In one way it was all so simple.

—

He asked the operator for Gary again.

"May I speak to Harry Bigoness?"

"What is this, a joke?"

"Please, I'm calling from Chicago."

"So what!"

"Can you get Harry Bigoness to the phone?"

"You the guy's been calling all night?"

"I'm sorry, please, I'd like—"

"A little peace and quiet, that's what we'd like!"

The phone was dropped; he waited to hear the broom beat on the ceiling.

"Yeah?"

"Mr. Bigoness—this is Wallace."

"You son of a bitch, I told you not to talk to my wife, didn't I?"

"I felt it was important to speak to her."

"How about what other people feel, huh?"

"I want to talk to you now—"

"What were you going to tell her to do, that's what I want to talk about!"

"I wanted to find out whether you were still coming."

"Then what?"

"That was all."

"You're trying to screw up my life for me—"

"That's absurd—"

"Everything's that way to you! Not to me! You leave off Tessie, you hear?"

"I've written out a check for five hundred dollars."

". . . Oh yeah, is that right?"

"That's right."

"I got to see it," Bigoness said, He was not managing to sound as cool as he intended. "Before I believe it," he added.

"I've got to be sure about you too."

"I'm plenty reliable, don't worry about me. You're the one don't strike me as a safe bet."

"What is that supposed to mean?"

"It means I want to see that check before I make any promises. I want to make sure it don't bounce, to put it blunt."

"I can assure you it won't."

"Maybe you better bring cash."

"*Bigoness*—look, I want you to realize, I don't want you to forget—a child—"

"Look—"

"A child, like Walter—"

"You don't believe Walter was in the hospital. I'll tell you whose fault it is too; that kid ain't never recovered from the shock of you, Mister—"

"All I'm saying, all I want to make clear—" he broke in, "is that the child, the parents . . . Bigoness, is this clear to you? They're all as real as you and I. They've got feelings—"

"*I* got feelings, damn it! Who don't have feelings! You just stay away from my wife, do you hear? She's home now and she's staying home. Soon as I get work she's going to start learning to be a good mama—"

"Nobody's *trying* to get her away from you."

"If I catch her ass down that Fluke's place—"

"Why don't you *listen*—"

"I'm listening all right. We're talking about whether that check of yours is going to bounce."

"Do you understand about this child?"

"Oh yeah, I know. She's my responsibility and she's my legal problem. Don't worry, Wallace, I got some advice about that too. I told you what I'd do if you keep bugging me now—"

"You won't understand."

"It's you," Bigoness said maliciously, "won't understand."

"Bigoness—you're at home tonight?"

"I told you, I got business—"

"You stay where you are. Don't you move!"

—

He took what was his from the closet. His watch showed that the movie had just begun. No one would ever know; he would set it right; the knowledge of how close he had pushed them all to failure would be his own—as would the knowledge of his final success. That was fair. He carried Rachel into her bedroom and dressed her in a red snowsuit and a pair of white shoes; he dressed her right over her woolen pajamas. He lined a wicker laundry basket that he found in the kitchen with a double thickness of blanket; then he wrapped the child in still another blanket and carried her in the basket down the stairs of the building.

Up till now he had stopped before the end. Now with the basket beside him on the front seat, he started the car.

Someone was to get what he wanted! Someone was to be satisfied! *Something was to be completed!*

Finish! Go all the way!

He began to tremble. But why? What had he to bring to Bigoness's attention but the very simplest facts of life? Bigoness would have to see the child to believe it, to stop bargaining over it. A life! A life! What was there left to appeal to, but the man's human feelings?

He tucked Rachel securely in the basket. Then with the motor rocking beneath him, he picked her up and held her to him. And it was not out of pity or love that he found himself clutching her; the mystery of her circumstances was not what was weighing him down. He clutched her to himself as though she *were* himself. It was as though the child embraced the man, not the man the child. He ground his teeth, locked his arms: if only he could be as convinced as he was determined; if only he could tell which he was being, prudent, imprudent, brave, sentimental . . . A bleeding heart, a cold heart, a soft heart, a hard, a cautious . . . which? Oh if he could only break down and give in and weep. But there was no comfort for him in tears, or in reason. He had passed beyond what he had taken for the normal round of life, beyond what had been kept normal by fortune and by strategy. Tears would only roll off the shell of him. And every reason had its mate. Whichever way he turned, there was a kind of horror.

SEVEN

Letting Go

1

T HE WAITER boned her fish for her, then left them to themselves. Libby said, "I don't feel very much like a mother tonight."

"And what do you feel like instead?"

"A—the girl in *The Tempest*. What's her name? I don't mean to be too precious, but since you're asking . . ." she said, preciously.

"Prospero's daughter—" But he could not give undivided attention to the task of remembering the daughter's name. His eyes, unable to come to rest on the face opposite his own, kept moving off to a table very near the wooden booth in which they sat. A woman in the party of four dining only a few feet away struck him as familiar; yet neither she nor her companions looked like anyone he might know. She had blond hair and a pointed chin, and a topaz pin clipped to her dark suit. Though she seemed to be engaged by every syllable spoken at her table, she had the air of someone who knows she is being looked at.

But he did not care to have the air of someone who is staring, and he tried to stop. Because of what this evening meant to Libby, because he had promised before they had left the house (promised himself, while Gabe was shown the bottles, the warming pan, the baby powder) that he would do nothing to spoil these few hours, he pretended to think of the name of Shakespeare's heroine, all the while trying to give a name to the woman at the next table. Eventually she looked over and their eyes met. He swung rapidly back to Libby—catching *her* eye with equal embarrassment. It was not, however, the same embarrassment that had been settling and resettling over their table since they had entered the restaurant; it was not shared.

"—easier than imagining yourself Hamlet, don't you think?"

"Yes."

"Or maybe that's because I'm a woman."

"I don't know," he said, trying to get the drift of her words.

"I wonder if it's not a theory at all, but a failure of my own mind. That's always a possibility."

"You're too hard on that mind of yours."

"Oh, darling Paul, I know what I am. Well—truly—*you* can probably understand what it's like to be Desdemona, can't you, as *well* as Othello?"

"That question has a slight drunken lilt to it."

"Are these silly questions?"

"Well, no."

But his response had apparently not been quick enough, gentle enough, loving enough, reassuring enough; apparently not, for her brow was instantly furrowed. "I think," he said, gentle, loving, reassuring, "I missed what you started to say at the beginning . . ."

"Aren't you listening?" she asked, directly.

"I am."

"I said it's easier to identify with Shakespeare's— Are you really at all interested in this?"

"Yes." He had no right to disappoint her tonight. "We used to talk about Shakespeare all the time."

"I know."

He realized that his remark had done nothing to reassure her about the present. Without exactly feeling shame, he felt disloyal to their earliest days. Then he did not even have to glance over: he knew who the woman with the topaz pin was. He remembered the name of the Shakespearean heroine too, but did not choose to interrupt again whatever it was that Libby wanted to get on to.

"Go ahead—I'm sorry," he said.

"I didn't think—I thought I was boring—"

"I was thinking about my mother's coming. Excuse me. Go on . . . do."

Out of respect for his troubles, she looked apologetic; he knew what would make her forgiving. Yes, he had learned how to move her about as he wanted. "It's not important," she was saying. "Now that I consider it—turn upon it," she said, smiling, bubbling up instantly, "the broad beam of my intelligence, I don't even think it holds water. The fact is you can't really believe in Ophelia either. I was being morbidly romantic. I was being high."

"You said you could identify with Ophelia?"

"I said one could. *Then*"—she flushed—"I said I could. Easier than Hamlet, I meant though, whom I find incredible. Is this heresy?"

"No—"

"Miranda!"

"Oh—yes."

"Prospero's daughter."

"Oh yes, that's it."

"Oh brave new world—isn't that *The Tempest* too?"

"I think so."

"Isn't that funny . . ." She went back to eating. "Though Miranda is quite incredible too. If it's fair to Shakespeare to talk about credibility in terms of that play— How are your frog's legs?"

"Fine. How is the sole?"

"I love sole. I forget until I eat it how fond of it I am. I'm feeling absolutely exuberant."

"On one martini," he said, and wished he could stop himself from sounding paternal. It was an impulse that seemed to grow in proportion to Libby's desire to converse with him.

"It's true, you know. Something about my kidneys makes me drunk much faster than normal people."

"So you don't feel normal either?"

"The day I strike people as normal . . ."

His response was so immediate that he had not even time to ask himself whether it might not, in fact, be true. "You strike me as normal tonight."

"Oh good. But I feel different." Leadingly: "I don't know if you do . . ."

"Yes. Of course."

"Happy?" She spoke the word so girlishly as to diminish the risk; she might have been asking nothing more than if he liked his food.

"Yes," again without hesitation.

"I'm so . . . happy isn't the word."

"I don't think it is for me either," he admitted.

She went right on. "I'm trembling inside. Way inside, *beneath* the martini."

"You look very composed."

"Never as composed as you. Do you mind if I speak under the influence of alcohol?"

He could not have felt more sober himself, which accounted in part for the trouble he was having keeping up with her decision to be gay. He had grown so used to her fidgety that he did not really remember her animated. But tonight she managed to be full of excitement, and still to look as though under her red dress all her limbs were securely attached to her slight frame. If he was not able to look directly at her, it was only partly because she struck him as unfamiliar. It was also that he could not be sure what she was going to say to him, or ask of him, next. Probably she was not too sure either—which doubtless explained why the embarrassment was shared. At first he had believed that their discomfort tonight had only to do with their not being used to extravagances. He had difficulty recalling the last time they had gone out for the purpose of "having fun." He had to go far back—and in going far back, he concluded that he was mistaken about the identity of the woman at the other table. At precisely the same moment he felt more disposed than ever to protect Libby. He would concentrate only on her. He felt her continuing to concentrate only on him. She had been concentrating on him, barreling down on him, for days; and for just as many days he had been doing his best to look the other way, to slide out from under her gaze by treating her like his child. Her total attention had gotten to him—

No. It was his mother's arrival that was causing the trouble. He had already figured out Libby's place in his life; consequently, he did not believe she could rattle him. "When we came in," Libby was saying, "and everyone was waiting in line for a table—when you went up and said, 'My name is Herz, I have a reservation,' it was one of those moments when I just felt terribly married."

"And you liked that?" Again, fatherly, as though he knew all there was to know about her—and at the moment when he was not sure, suddenly, quite what he did know.

"It was a small thrill," she said. "Tonight's a larger thrill." He did not respond, and she rushed to say, "Unless—are we going to spend too much?"

He had to reassure the two of them; if Libby could not rattle him any longer, money could. "But we have so many things to celebrate, Lib."

"I did have a little qualm when we came in here."

"When I said my name is Herz?"

"About three seconds after that." She put her hand on the table and he knew enough to cover it with his own. "I won't have any dessert, darling," she whispered.

Embarrassment settled over them. They returned to their food. He was finding this altogether different from any dinner they had ever eaten at home. Was it two or three times now that she had called him "darling"?

"Do you know what I discussed with Gabe last week?"

He looked up to see that her face had subsided to its every-day shade. Her lovely skin . . . "What?"

"I didn't tell you. The night he brought the present for the baby—don't you think he's changed, Paul?"

"Who? I'm having trouble keeping up with you martini-ized."

"He seems very crushed, Gabe does. He's lost a lot of his, I don't know . . . air."

"He's had some bad luck with his father."

A moment passed. "Did he tell you that?" Libby asked.

"You told me that."

"Oh yes . . ." she said. "You forget about other people's troubles when you have your own." For a moment he felt as though she were judging *him*. Until she added, "Suddenly I'm aware of him in a new way. I asked him to baby-sit out of sympathy, really."

"Glenda didn't go home to Milwaukee then?"

"Yes, she did go away. But I needn't have thought of Gabe, you see."

"I wondered . . ." He did not mean to sound like Othello, never having felt like him before. "I wondered how you decided on him."

"Then—why didn't you ask?"

"I thought you'd arranged it," he began to explain, somewhat flustered, "arranged it all beforehand."

"Well, you should have asked. I think he gets a lot of pleasure out of Rachel. He asked if you believed in God."

He was not jealous; he was annoyed. "How did that come up?" He had never in his life been jealous, a fact of his character which he had long ago absorbed. It contributed to his picture of himself as a man who did not have all the human fires. He had come to think of himself as less special than he once had.

Nevertheless, it seemed that what he had just tried was to make Libby think that he *was* jealous! He wondered if he could be feeling under attack only because of the woman at the other table, who brought to his mind old failures, misunderstandings of his youth. It was a youth that he himself saw as long past; having ceased to excuse himself for what he was, he no longer needed it as a crutch. It was a help to him too that others, seeing that he was half bald and wore old clothes, did not even mistake him for a young man.

"We were talking about religion," his wife said. "His family, you know, was very German Jewish and removed. I would have liked to have met his mother—you know, I once—I think she had a great effect on him."

"You once what?"

"We were talking about Chanukah. I didn't know what to say, Paul. There are some things we haven't discussed a lot lately. You and I."

"I think we've probably become a little used to each other by now." Smiling.

"We just don't talk as much, though. That's a fact. That's all. We do hardly talk."

"I think if we feed you a martini every night—"

"And you?" she said quickly.

"You see, it doesn't take on me."

"I know," she said lugubriously.

Dinner might have been finished and the check paid without any further conversation, had not the blond woman and her party walked over to their booth. "Excuse me, aren't you Paul Herz?"

"Yes—" Trying to rise, he got caught between the table and the seat. Half standing, taller than Libby but shorter than his visitor, he said, "Yes—you look very familiar—"

"My name"—he saw Libby looking back and forth as the woman spoke—"is Frankland. I'm Marge—Howells."

"I thought that's who you might be—" And then both rushed so to introduce their mates that no one heard anyone else's name, and they all had to be introduced a second time. The other couple, friends of the Franklands', stood back and watched. Slowly Marge Howells began to look like herself, or as much of her as he could remember. He had never really taken a long look at her, even back in Iowa; that had not been the nature of their meeting. Here, across the room, she had looked older, haughtier. Paul asked Marge, and Marge Paul, what each was doing in Chicago. It turned out that the Franklands lived in Evanston.

"I'm teaching," Paul said, answering her next question.

Tim Frankland, a physician, had a habit of extending his lower lip beyond his upper lip; he combined this now with a brief nod. "No kidding," he said.

"At the University," Libby said.

Frankland paid his first bit of attention to her. "Down on the South Side," he said, pointing at the floor.

"That's right," Paul said.

"Tim is doing research this year," Marge told them. "We've been in Evanston for three or four years." She turned, but only half looked at her husband. "Isn't that right, darling?"

At the very same moment that he heard Marge say "darling" —and disbelieved it—Paul felt himself powerfully married to his wife. "We've been in Chicago for a year, a little more than a year."

The other couple with the Franklands now moved out of the dining room, saying they would meet Tim and Marge in the lobby. Silence followed their departure.

"Well, it's been three or four years," Marge said, "since we've met, I think."

Dr. Frankland gave a very stiff, very polite grin to everyone.

"Where is it we met before?" Libby asked.

"Iowa City," Marge said.

"Do you have children?" Paul asked.

"One. A girl."

"We have a girl too," Libby said. "Six months."

"Jocelyn is three," Marge said to Paul.

"Time flies," Dr. Frankland said to Libby, as though she might not have known. "Yours will be three before you realize it."

"Do you ever see your friend?" Marge asked. "You remember—"

"Gabe Wallach."

"Yes. How's he doing? Do you ever hear from him?"

"He's teaching at Chicago too," Paul said.

"No kidding," Tim Frankland said.

"Oh," said Marge, "Tim has heard all these names." She did not smile with much confidence.

"That was when Marge was revolting against her family. Your bohemian period, dear." But the remark was meant for the edification of the crowd; there were obviously certain areas of the past with which Dr. Frankland didn't have too much sympathy.

"Gabe's baby-sitting for us tonight, as a matter of fact," said Libby.

"I thought he'd be married—"

Libby made the announcement as though it gave her pleasure. "No, he isn't."

"Still knocking the girls over." The words were spoken by Dr. Frankland.

"I suppose so," Paul said.

Apropos of nothing, or so it seemed, Libby said, "He's a very generous person."

"It's a coincidence," Marge said, "all of us being in Chicago, isn't it?"

"We were in Pennsylvania for a while," Paul said.

"We should all get together," Marge answered.

"Yes," Paul said, when no one else did, "that would be fine."

"Yes . . . It was nice running into you," Dr. Frankland said. "We're in the book, of course."

"So are we," Libby said, as though that tied the score.

"What do you call your daughter, Paul?"

"Rachel," Libby said.

At this the two women were called upon to take a sudden interest in one another. Marge was the one who smiled.

Frankland felt called upon to be magnanimous. "That's a nice old-fashioned European name."

"Whom does she resemble?" Marge asked.

"Paul," said Libby.

"I'm afraid Jocelyn looks like me."

"Well, we have to be going," Tim Frankland said. "I'm afraid the Hodges are waiting—"

"Oh yes—"

"Goodbye. Say hello to Gabe Wallach—"

"Oh yes—"

Libby waited until they were barely out of earshot. "I'm afraid the Hodges are waiting," she said, in a fair imitation.

"I had a feeling you didn't like them."

"I didn't mean to be too obvious, but that man's a horror. And she—I don't know. At the end I suddenly thought she wasn't so bad. Who is she? I don't remember her at all. I thought we'd met her at Cornell."

"She was a friend of Gabe's."

"That's what I thought, after I found out it was Iowa. Gabe certainly has catholic tastes."

"Of course, it was a long time ago."

"She couldn't have been any— Well, she didn't strike me as very genuine. Did she you?"

"She's all right, I suppose."

"Well, she chose old Tim—I wouldn't be so sure. 'I'm afraid the Hodges are waiting.' Hey, that's not too bad, is it?" She did it again. "Did we know her well?" she asked suddenly.

"I met her once with Gabe. I don't think you did."

"*Oh*," she said, "this isn't the girl friend of his you once helped move, is it, when I was sick? The girl he dropped, ker-plunk."

"I think," Paul said, "that was somebody else."

"The more I learn about Gabe," Libby said, "the stranger he seems. I don't know if he has any substance or what."

"There are girls like her in everybody's past, I suppose."

"Well, sweetheart, who was there in yours?"

After a moment, he said, "Doris. I've told you about Doris . . ."

"But you were in high school. Gabe was a man."

"Well . . ."

"Gabe knows a lot about some things," said Libby, "but then he seems to have so little imagination about others. He didn't even begin to know what I was saying when I spoke about religion, for instance."

"You said . . ." He was looking directly at his wife now; he had forced himself to while she spoke of Gabe's past, and he for some reason made references—veiled, to be sure—to his own. "You said you didn't know what to tell him."

She was surprised. "I didn't say that."

"You said that you didn't know what I thought."

"Well, I *don't* know what you think . . ."

"Well . . ." He had led himself into this. "What do you want to know?"

"What?"

Marge Howells had come and gone, and nothing had happened to him. It was not shame that was filling him with the incredible desire to answer questions. "I'm not hiding anything," he said, and indeed he did feel perfectly innocent.

"Paul . . . no?"

The moment passed, though it left its mark. "Well, no." He was not sure he could believe himself—though he was not completely unsure. Marge had come and gone and nothing had happened to him. "So what do you want to know?" he asked jokingly.

". . . I don't know. What do you do when you go to the synagogue?" she asked, shrugging her shoulders.

"I sit there." She might as well be told that. He was afraid, however, of other questions she might ask, though he could not really inform himself as to what they might be. He continued to close back upon himself. "I sit there," he said again.

"You say the prayer."

"No."

"Don't you?"

"No, I don't."

"You did that Friday I went—"

"I did that Friday. I knew you expected certain things. I don't when I'm alone."

"You see—now there's something I didn't know that . . ."

"Well, we're married, Libby, but we're separate too."

"I know that."

"I don't think that's too unusual."

"I don't know," she said, looking defeated. "I don't know what's usual and unusual. I'm still trying to figure marriage out. Excuse me—I don't want to keep embarrassing you by being naïve. I didn't mean to embarrass you by saying Rachel resembled you either—"

"I don't think that's what's embarrassing us."

"I keep blushing tonight, Paul. And you're my *husband*."

"We're just both excited about this whole week."

"Yes . . . I'm not saying I'm not happy."

"We're just not used to things working out." He wondered if that could be it. "It's something we'll have to become adjusted to."

"I'm a little drunken, darling, but you're sober, and you mean that, don't you? I keep having the strange feeling that our troubles are over. That I've been being born and born for years and years, and now I'm out. That's a weak statement from a woman who's supposed to be somebody else's mother, I know it probably makes me sound ill-equipped . . . What I mean is that if things will calm down for a while, I *will* be equipped. I'm embarrassed about the past. I keep saying 'embarrassed' only because it's the only damn word I can think of. I really want to talk to you, Paul. The last few days I've thought and thought, because they seem so significant . . . Can't we begin to talk a little?"

"Sure."

"I want you to tell me sometimes what you're thinking. That'll make all the difference—"

"Yes, but, Libby, you understand—" He knew he had opened this floodgate himself; he had allowed himself the pleasure of optimism, and now he was paying. It would all wind up, tonight or tomorrow or next week, with Libby crying.

"I don't expect to know everything. If I can know . . . If I don't have to stay home all day imagining it. Everything else is all right now—now it's simply you and me that needs working out." She was trying to grin; he was trying to collect himself. But he couldn't; some inroad had been made. "I tell people about what you think," Libby said, "and I don't even know what you *do* think. Are we religious or aren't we?" With that question she looked quite beaten again. "There—that's one simple little thing—"

"You see, we're not one person. We're two."

"—because we have to communicate *somehow*."

"Of course—"

"I don't think every marriage has to be lustful. I understand that differently now. I've made myself understand it differently. But if it's not that, then it's going to have to be something else."

"Libby—you've had a lot of patience . . ."

Near tears, she answered, "Thank you."

"I can only ask for a little more." Another woman would, at this moment, have struck him, or left him; knowing this made him feel no more noble about his plea.

"Everything seems to be changing," said Libby, "but you."

"Then I must be changing too, Lib. I have changed."

"How?"

He did not ever think of such easy solutions as Marge Howells; he did not think of solutions. "I don't know," was all he said.

"You still don't love me, do you?"

"That's an unfair . . . an inexact way to put it, for both of us."

"I don't know what that means."

His responses were not satisfying either of them; he might just as well be silent. Libby asked, "Am I ruining our evening? Oh hell—"

They finished up what food remained on their plates.

"If you did believe in God," she said, sliding her fork on the empty plate, "I wouldn't feel it was an important question at all. You know that?"

"Because you do?"

"I don't. I can't. I don't even want to. But you're different. I don't even know what you are—but I love you, Paul. And I don't care that you don't love me. I know you're a good man."

"I didn't say I didn't love you," he began.

"I don't care. Let's pay the bill—let's take a walk. I feel chaotic inside. I'm sorry if I've ruined our ten-dollar dinner."

—

"Please," she said, as they walked west toward the theater, "I can't keep one foot in each camp any longer."

She waited, but did not hear him ask that she explain. It was difficult to tell whether he was not listening, or was thinking, or had chosen simply to ignore her.

"I can't keep provoking other men, Paul. I'm just spilling out everything—and I'm sorry. How much was dinner, eleven dollars? I know I'm responsible for wasting it. When I was a child I always wound up crying on my birthday—there would always be an argument, somehow or other. I had a way, I have a way, of ruining significant days. I suppose I shouldn't have had that drink what with these kidneys inside me. I was just edgy enough, and now I'm just drunk enough—and I want you to talk to me. Please, we'll walk all the way to the movie, and please, you just talk. Up at Cornell you could persuade me of anything. Persuade me now."

"About what?"

"About you. I keep thinking that either you believe in God or you love me. It's not something I've given a lot of thought to, but it comes into my head, and I might as well say it. Weak as I am, Paul, I've always said things. Blurted them out. It's our sixth anniversary," she said after a moment. "Persuade me, will you? You just can't cut me out of your life!"

The air was cold; they were walking directly into a light wind. Neither looked at the other. "I can't give you positive answers," he said. "I'm not sure either way, about either."

"Stop sparing me too, all right?"

"Libby, since my father's death, since that trip, it's been me who's felt as though he's been being born. Perhaps you have, but so have I. And I've not come out yet."

"When—?"

"I don't know." He raised his hands impatiently. "I'm trying to speak indirectly . . ."

"Why do you go to the synagogue then? Why do we stay married? I keep thinking, Well he believes—"

"Faith is private; why do you have to feel so impassioned about mine?"

"When you came back from New York I thought everything was going to change. I thought religion—"

"I'm not so sure any more about the religion I came back with from New York. Things have gotten better. That's precisely it."

"Don't think," she said gloomily, "they've gotten that much better."

"And that's why I still go to synagogue. They haven't gotten that much better."

"I don't think I'm understanding everything you're saying. Are you saying that if we were both perfectly happy, then you wouldn't go at all?"

"I suppose, in a way, that's what I'm saying."

"Well, what do you *do* there—do you pray? Why do you even go there? Are you praying for things to get better, so you can just forget all about it?"

"Things won't get 'better,' Libby."

"That's not so! They have gotten better. If you would just give yourself up to *us*!"

"First you told me not to spare you—"

"But you're being unreasonable. You don't try to make things better. You're distracted from me!"

"I'm never not thinking of you, Libby; that's not so."

"I'm not talking about *thinking* about me."

"Look, I don't understand my actions any more than anybody else. I'm not going to try to defend myself for not having the feelings you want me to."

"I don't want you to have any feelings but the normal ones."

"If I can't feel what I have to, I *do* what I have to."

"I don't see how you can do them then."

"I force myself."

"Oh Paul, I hate you for saying that."

"I go and sit in the synagogue, Libby—"

"Yes—now tell me why, damn it?"

"Because I don't feel complete about myself. Everything seems . . . incomplete."

"Yes?"

"And I don't go because I expect to be completed either."

"I don't understand your God," she said, heartbroken.

"I've been mystified lately by things looking as though they're getting better. It's shaken my faith."

"Is that supposed to be a joke? Are you going to toy with me, *tonight*? Lately I feel indulged—I don't even mean indulged; I mean too underestimated even for me."

"I'm not making jokes."

"Well, I don't believe in doom! You believe in doom—that's what you're saying. Don't you love Rachel at least? Don't you feel anything toward her?"

"I love Rachel."

"So? *And?*"

"And what?"

"Well, can't you believe in pleasure? Can't we have a pleasant life together? Is that so hard? I don't think you have any right to justify your—whatever it is, concerning me and our marriage—"

"I haven't tried to justify—"

"Let me finish—it's a very involved thought and I'm a lousy thinker. Please, Paul. What you're saying—I don't even know if I've got it—but you're saying that you and I are supposed to be unhappy because that's in the nature of things. Well, it may be in the nature of things, but it's not in *my* nature! I'm just dying to be happy, I just can't wait very much longer. I wish you'd stop dragging your heels about it, too. Please, Paul, if you'd just relax."

"Oh, Libby . . ."

"Well, what?"

"I can't make myself be what I'm not."

"Oh that's an excuse! That's—philosophy! I've made myself be what I'm not—don't you know that? You can't act this way, Paul, you're stronger than I am. You'll just have to be!"

Whatever his next thoughts were, he kept them to himself.

"What kind of God is that anyway!" she demanded.

"I can only believe as much as I can manage to believe for what must appear to somebody else—even my wife, Libby—to be very private reasons. I didn't believe they were so eccentric, however."

"I think you just go to the synagogue to get away from me."

"Please . . . I go there to say the mourner's prayer."

"You said you *don't* pray."

"That's right. I don't pray."

"Oh Paul—"

"I mourn, all right? You see, this is difficult to talk about."

"Well—but don't mourn: *fix things up!*"

"Certain things I have to accept."

"But then *I* have to accept the things *you* have to! That's what's unfair, don't you see? You're being," she said hopelessly, "terribly unfair . . . and pompous," she added faintly.

"You see, are we getting anywhere with this conversation?"

"I'm getting confused. You're going at things upside down. You've given up," she said, incredulously.

"I've perhaps given in."

"Well, that's the same damn thing. That's *worse*."

"We're not going to understand one another—" But when she stopped walking, when she closed her eyes, he took her hand and added, "Tonight."

"I don't think so," she said. "I don't think you know what you believe."

"I don't know *all* I believe."

"Well," she said weakly, "I hope you see that's not making me very happy."

"You think too much about being happy."

"But that's all there is, Paul."

—

When they emerged later from the movie, she took her husband's arm. The push and hurry of the crowd behind them reminded her that it was Christmas Eve. How very far she had come . . .

"Did you think it was funny?" she asked.

"I thought the first half was. I thought the second half was lousy."

"That's exactly what I thought."

To her surprise, his fingers were touching her face. Did she have a smudge on her cheek? For a moment she could not believe that he was only touching her. And when she could, she was afraid to speak. She hung on to his arm, treating her treat as though it were an everyday occurrence; praying.

"We'd better take a cab," he said, leading her to the curb.

"Oh darling, this night is costing a fortune."

"Gabe isn't going to charge us, is he?"

"Well, no."

"Then we've saved all that."

The movie seemed to have cheered him up; she hesitated to believe that it was she who might have helped initiate some change—though, God knows, she had not spoken so openly to him in years. Could it possibly be so easy? Probably he had only made up his mind to please her. But what she was asking of him was not much more, really, than that. She had only to make it clear to him now what exactly she knew to be necessary for her pleasure . . .

To be kissed. In the back of the taxi, driving to the station, she wanted to be kissed. Recognizing the desire as sentimental did not decrease its poignancy a bit. Everything she wanted tonight she wanted poignantly. After some minutes had passed, she felt that she might have to settle for just being in the cab beside him, driving through the rush of the holiday streets to the station.

And so she settled for it. A taxi, after all, was a treat in itself. She had not ridden in one since the night five years before when they had left that doctor's office in Detroit. And that was all so distant that she might never have stepped foot in a cab before tonight. She had difficulty, anyway, associating herself with any of those other Libbies, the young, stupid, helpless Libbies . . . though Libby Herz was always and forever sloughing off old Libby Herzes—bidding a fond farewell sometimes to what she had been as little as twenty-four hours earlier. Still she couldn't help feeling that this night was truly different. This *week* had been truly different. New strength had flowed into her simply from a decision to have new strength flow into her. At least it seemed as simple as that, driving in the cab, her coat pushed up against her husband's, her hand finding his. The news from Gabe's own mouth that he was going abroad must have something to do with it too, if Paul had in the past been distracted from her, she could not deny that she had had certain distractions of her own. But she knew that no matter what was dealt out to them in the future —and she did happen to see only good things coming their way now —she would never write to him, as she had in Pennsylvania, or dream about him, as she had in Iowa, or see him as being any more than he was, which was what she had always done, of course. She was even pained with herself for that damn charming little note she had slipped into his hands as she and Paul had been about to go off for dinner. However, it was not easy for one as passionate as she was, she thought, to be cured overnight of an old and crucial attachment. Nor for someone as needy as she had been.

But she did not need Gabe any longer. She could not afford to, especially when he was not at all as powerful as he had led her, or she had led him to lead her, to imagine. She herself had a family that needed her. She was going to help Paul to love her. Now that they were already entering what she had begun to see as the first settled period of their life, she would dedicate herself to destroying her husband's isolation. He did not have to be separate any longer. She would convince him of happiness.

But when they left the cab her mood altered. She supposed she *was* a little disappointed at having traveled three miles in the back of a dark cab unkissed. But aside from that, Paul had actually said or done nothing to weaken her hope in him. When he paid for the cab, in fact, she felt as she had when he had addressed the headwaiter—very wifely. The sight of her husband taking his change from the driver convinced her that they would never be divorced. No, it was not Paul . . . It only seemed that she had ridden as far as she could on the crest of that single martini. Buoyancy left her, she knew she was that girl who had driven in the other cab five years back, and that she would be the same girl five years hence. And she knew that Paul knew it.

When they settled on a bench in the busy waiting room of the train station, it was ten thirty-five.

"I'd better call Gabe," she said.

Paul had picked up a newspaper off the bench; he sat there rattling it, not reading it. "About what?" he asked.

"To see if everything is all right." Uncontrollably she had begun to worry.

"I'll call."

She must, suddenly, be looking so frightened that he felt duty bound to be nice to her; she imagined that he himself was so upset now that he couldn't sit still . . . until he leaned over and kissed her.

"Paul . . ." It was no longer necessary to call. She was absolutely *bouncing* from mood to mood.

But he was already moving away, toward an arrow which pointed to the phone booths. Having soared upward a moment earlier, she now plunged down, as she had two moments before. She understood his touching her face outside the movie theater, and his kissing her just now, as being linked up with some defense he was building against the appearance of his mother. The big clock overhead showed that Mrs. Herz was only seven or eight minutes away . . . But if he felt stronger by way of kissing her, wasn't that something? No? The trouble with his moments of affection was that that's all they were, *moments*. One hug didn't have any connection with the next kiss. She closed her eyes. She did not understand everything that was happening. Was anything even happening? On the street she had asked a few questions, and he had agreed to give a few answers. Though in the restaurant he had practically knocked her over by asking, "What do you want to know, Libby?" Then a moment later, as she struggled to think of what it was she wanted to be told, she had seen him becoming Paul again. To think that she had pried him open for good—or even for more than ten seconds—was to overestimate her own meager powers.

Only one of her powers was not so meager. It was no small ability to be able to forget the past. *I will forget the past. I will make Paul forget the past. I will convince him of happiness.*

When he returned he sat down and checked his watch against the clock on the wall.

"Well, how is he doing?" She smiled.

"Oh—he's doing all right."

"You sound as though he's not doing all right at all. Don't you think he can really change a diaper?"

"Well, he's doing all right," he said.

"Is the baby sleeping?"

"Yes."

"Has she gotten up for a bottle?"

"He didn't say."

"Well, darling, didn't you ask. Maybe Gabe forgot where—"

"He didn't forget."

"Paul, don't be nervous about your mother."

"I suppose I am."

"Don't be. That's all past."

"I know . . ."

"We'll indulge her every whim. We won't allow her to wash a dish. I'm nervous, but I don't feel uncertain."

He was standing. "I'm going to the men's room, Lib."

"Honey, don't you feel well?" Her love for him was so intense, she could have wept for his discomfort.

"I just want to go to the men's room before the train arrives." He went off in the direction he had gone before.

She loved him; they would begin again—he could be made to want to. She was feeling more influential than she ever had in her life. It must come of being a mother. It must come of moving out from under pressure, from their crisis having passed. Oh she would help him now! Her Paul!

Then he was running toward her, just as the loudspeaker filled the waiting room with news of the arrival of the New York train. She raced to meet him—*my Paul!*—and together they raced to the track. He was saying something to her which she could not hear in the rush of people—and then Mrs. Herz was upon them. The old woman was clinging to her son. An arm flew out, Libby slipped within it, and both women were sobbing into Paul's coat. She felt Paul's hand on her back; his thin straight body was a support for her head. No other hand touched her, but she was old enough now—yes!—not to expect everything. She did not expect everything; only what was coming to her. She had been patient.

They took another taxi all the way home. Mrs. Herz talked about the train ride, and Libby asked her questions that had only to do with the trip. Paul was virtually silent.

—

They climbed the stairs and came into the apartment to find what Paul already knew, but for which he had found no way whatsoever to prepare his companions. Though he was not a man to believe in miracles, though he trusted his senses, he had not been able to believe that it would be the way it was when they walked through the door. If he could not understand it, it would not be. But though he could not understand it, it was.

Libby began to run from room to room. His mother stood where she was. When Libby came back into the living room

there were a few moments in which no one spoke a complete
sentence, though everyone spoke. Then Mrs. Herz had picked
up her suitcase and stood holding it. The two women began to
scream. Paul said, "Please sit. Both of you, sit. Sit down!"

2

THERESA had been told to stay in the bedroom. Harry had said it was none of her business.

And that was true. She had just forgotten everything that had happened. She was too busy to think about anything. All she ever did was iron clothes, and wash dishes, and sew on patches, and darn socks, and change diapers, and listen to what Harry told her to do—like to keep her ass out of Fluke's place. But he needn't have—when did she ever have a minute for herself?

Everything was for *them*. What about me? she thought, and tears came to her eyes. She was only twenty. She'd never had any fun. Only with Dewey, and then right off she'd gotten caught. And Dewey hadn't even cared about her. Did Harry? He said he loved her. That was why he had married her. That was why he had asked her to come back to him. Oh yeah?

She wondered if it was too late for her to become a nun. Would they allow you to be a sister if first you'd been a Baptist? At least if you were a sister you weren't the slave of any damn man! Or any kids! What that little Walter deserved was a good crack. Otherwise he'd never learn to do it in the bowl. She'd told Harry that, but he just told her to go to the bedroom. He and Vic were going to go into the trucking business. Oh yeah. On what? He couldn't even afford a Christmas tree. Some Christmas Eve! Locked in a room. She was not to leave her room if Wallace came.

She thought about Mr. Wallace. She hated his guts. Talking to him on the phone, she had been unable to stop her heart from pounding away. She tried to remember what he looked like. Every time she heard "Earth Angel" she thought of him. It was almost like their song. In the past when she heard it, she had thought of Dewey.

She went to the closet and looked at her clothes. When was she ever going to get to wear anything but an apron? She never had a chance to dress up. Harry never took her any place; all she'd done since Thanksgiving was change diapers. That Wanda was smart to get out when the getting was good. But she had

gotten out too. The trouble was she should have *stayed* out.
She tried to remember why she had come back. Because she
missed a nice family Thanksgiving! Everybody in America
had been eating candied sweets and turkey and dressing and
cranberries—except her. She loved candied sweets more than
anything, and when she had called Harry, he had said that that
was just what he was having. So she'd come back, and there
hadn't even been any damn candied sweets at all! Just the
same, she thought then that he really loved her. He said he
loved her when she asked him. Then why did he make her stay
in her room? She had a right to see Mr. Wallace if he came.
Gabe.

She thought about sex all the time.

Harry didn't. At least not with her, she thought, moving
from the closet and flopping down across the bed. She had
heard people say that men only want women for one thing.
Well, the only thing Harry wanted *her* for was to be a maid to
him and those kids. And they weren't even her kids! She began to whimper. She had only become twenty on November
nineteenth!

It was just too bad Dewey had been married—otherwise he
would have had to marry her. But of course *she* was already
married. The only one who wasn't married was Mr. Wallace.
Boy, she had really told him off on the phone. Harry had been
good and mad when she had finally repeated to him what he
had said to her. Who the hell did he think he was! Who was
he, breaking up families! He was nothing but a goddam Jew,
making a dollar on somebody else's troubles! Vic said he
wouldn't be surprised if the Jews had made the recession.

She wondered what it was like to do it with a Jew. She remembered the story of the little nigger boy they had taken to
the hospital back home. She began to giggle and then she was
crying, really crying this time. Harry just got on top, most
times when she wasn't even ready. The only warning she had
was that he would get up and pull down the shades all the way,
then draw the curtains across and close the door tight. They
couldn't even see each other's face. She knew he made believe
he was doing it to Wanda. Well, she could make believe she
was doing it to somebody else, too! She had, many times—
even with Dewey she had made believe she was doing it with

somebody else. But that was because she knew that Dewey was making believe *he* was doing it with somebody else. Nobody who did it to her ever made believe he was doing it to her.

Well, she might not be a beauty queen, but at least she was clean and she had nice clothes.

But when could she ever wear them?

—

She put her ear to the door. She could hear hardly any of what was being said. Apparently he had been there for some time now, even while she had been on the bed, thinking things over. Little by little the voices were getting louder, and more frightening, and she was afraid to open the door. Harry had told her it was none of her business.

Why did she have to listen to him? She wasn't his slave!

But she wasn't going to run away again. Harry took care of her.

She thought of how she could get out of the room. Quietly she opened the door, and then tiptoed down the hallway to the room where the children slept. Once inside the children's room, she quickly closed the door, but then she couldn't hear anything again. Though in the corridor she had heard Mr. Wallace's voice, and then some terrible thing that Harry was saying. When he got mad, he could really get mad.

Melinda was sleeping; the little baby, George, was sleeping too. And Walter was pretending to sleep. He was trying to trick her again. Her excuse for coming in was to make sure none of them had kicked off a blanket, but she wasn't going to do anything for Walter if he was going to try to trick her. She stood over his bed.

"All right, Walter, why are you actin' like you're sleepin'?"

He did not answer.

"That's just like you act like you can't do it in the bowl. I'm goin' to take your diaper away from you, then what you goin' to do, huh?"

She shook him. "Don't you pretend you're sleepin', Walter." She shook him again.

The child's eyes opened.

She gave him a good crack across the face.

He began to howl. "Well, that's what you deserve," she

said, but he only howled louder. She knew he hated her. She would have cracked him again, just for good measure, but he was howling like an animal.

The door swung open. "What's going on in here!" Harry shouted.

She could hear Vic and Gabe arguing in the other room. "He spit at me—so I hit him, to teach him—"

"He don't spit at nobody!" Harry said. His face was red; he was shaking a finger at her.

"Well, he spits at me! So I gave him a good crack."

"You don't give nobody a good crack! I'll give *you* a crack!"

"I got a right to come out in the living room. It's my house too."

"I'll tell you whether to come out in the living room or not!"

"I'm not your slave—"

"You get back in your bedroom!"

"I got a right to see Mr. Wallace, if I want—"

But Mr. Wallace was in the doorway, with Vic. Melinda was sitting up in bed, and now George was crying too. And she was only twenty years old! What were any of these strangers to her? Christmas Eve without even a tree!

From the doorway Mr. Wallace was shouting—at *her*. "—you agreed, Theresa—" His face was red too. Vic had his hand on Mr. Wallace's shoulder.

"Yes—"

"—extortion—"

"—back in your own room and *stay*—"

"—money already! months ago—"

"—baby—"

"*It's my living room too!*" she screamed, and raced into it.

On the sofa was a laundry basket, and there was a small baby in it. She heard the men shouting—heading back to where she stood.

Nobody would hit a woman with a child. Her child! She picked it up and held it in her arms. *It was her child!* She looked at its face.

"It's my baby—I'm holdin' my baby—" she screamed, as they came at her.

"Put that baby down!"

"Theresa—" Wallace said.

"It's mine! I ain't goin' to sign nothin'!"

"It's not yours!" Mr. Wallace was moving his arms. "It's not yours!"

"—it's not yours—" Harry was saying, but not to her.

Mr. Wallace was screaming, "*I'll kill you!*"

"*Hey*—"

Vic had grabbed Mr. Wallace's shoulder. Mr. Wallace's mouth was open, and his face was huge and red, almost as though it would pop. God, he wasn't really handsome at all. "*That baby*—" he roared, but Harry was lunging toward her. She broke for the bedroom.

But she couldn't lock the door in time; he barged through. What was she doing?

"You nuts—*crazy*?"

"Walter spit at me!"

"Put that baby down, God damn you. Put it down!"

"You ain't goin' to order—"

"I got five hundred bucks! I'm going to get two hundred more, you miserable little bitch! You give me that baby!"

"You can't sell my baby!"

"Oh it's not your damn—"

"I'm only twenty—"

He was coming at her. "You want to go out in the cold? You don't want me to go in a business? You want to *starve*?"

She thrust the baby at him. "I just want you to know, Harry," she said, "that I just ain't no—"

But he wasn't listening. He was heading back to the living room with the baby in his arms. "You got to know, Harry," she said, following after, mumbling, "I want to get dressed up and go out every once in a while, I want, every once in a while—"

A few minutes earlier there had been all that screaming in the living room; now no one was speaking. Vic was standing, and Mr. Wallace was on the floor. On his knees. His forehead was touching the rug, his arms were over his ears. He was not moving.

Harry said, "Hey, did you hit . . . ? She knew right off how scared he was.

"Uh-uh," Vic said. "He just crumpled up. You all run out—and he fell down. Like that."

No one spoke. Vic was scared; she was scared too.

"You didn't hit him?"

"He just crumpled up."

Harry walked around Mr. Wallace. His face was no longer red. "Hey, Mr. Wallace?"

A very thin sound rose from the figure on the floor.

"He said telephone," Vic said. "He said something."

"He wants to use the telephone," she said.

"It ain't connected."

"Downstairs," she said. She was shivering. She wished Mr. Wallace would get up off the floor.

Harry was still holding that baby. It was a good baby—it didn't even cry. But she didn't want an extra baby anyway.

"Better take him to the phone," Harry said finally.

She said, "Me?"

"Who's he going to call?" asked Vic.

"He's gotta call somebody. Sombody gotta get him . . ."

Mr. Wallace was rising off the floor. He did not take his arms from his ears. He did not look up. He did not smile—she thought he might; that it might be a joke he had pulled to make them all quiet down.

Vic and Harry were whispering. She led Mr. Wallace down the stairs. When Mr. Phelps opened the door, she said, "Something's happened to this man . . ." She couldn't look at him, and neither could Mr. Phelps, who stepped aside.

At the phone she watched his fingers dialing. But he was not able to speak very well. He handed her the phone—but she didn't want it either. Mr. and Mrs. Phelps were standing back, watching; when she turned to pass the phone on to them, neither of them stepped forward.

She had to speak into it. "Hello?" she said. ". . . That was Mr. Wallace. Somebody better come help him . . . He had some kind of attack."

The man on the other end asked where she was calling from; in terror, she gave him the address. Had he dialed the police?

She whispered, "Are you the man who's got a little baby?"

He said that he was.

"Come get it then!" she pleaded. "We don't want it!" and hung up. She turned to the Phelpses. "Don't tell Harry—"

But all of a sudden she felt gypped. While she had been holding that baby she should have made Harry promise her something. She should have made him promise to take her out some place nice to eat on Sundays. She should at least have made him promise that! But she had missed her chance. And she was only twenty. Tears came to her eyes again. She could not believe that her good times were all gone.

*D*ear Libby,

Only just a moment ago I opened the envelope from you. I should tell you that I thought I had thrown it away, unopened, months ago. But today it is rainy, and I am about to leave for Italy, and my bags are packed—I am sitting in the hotel lobby, in fact, in the midst of my luggage, waiting before I take a taxi to the airport. Fishing around in my raincoat pocket for my tickets I discovered your letter. I suppose I would have come upon it earlier if it had not been such a fine, dry fall here. Coming upon it another day, I might have thrown it away a second time, despite the numerous forwarding addresses on its face, which give to it an air of earnestness something like your own. It may be that I choose to sit down and answer you now because I am all packed and ready to go. It may be that I have not changed too much, or at all. Nevertheless, I have tried to find enjoyment in traveling, and I think mostly about what I see.

I cannot, of course, come to Rachel's first birthday celebration, what with four months having elapsed since it was held. However, had I been in America in July, near you and your family, I don't believe I would have come then either. I am not even sure what to make of your having asked me. Nor am I entirely certain why, once having decided to send me an invitation, you sent only *the invitation*, and no other word, no further remark.

Sitting here, my first thought as to your motive was not pleasant. I saw you standing above me, saying: We have survived, not you. But I can't hold that image in my mind—nor the image of you fastening the envelope and slipping it into the box for no other reason than to be arrogant. I may be deceiving myself, but I believe what you hoped was that your invitation would catch up with me and inform me, wherever I was, that Rachel was now one year old, and yours—still and for good. That would have been kindness enough, surely, considering how close I brought all of you to an awful end. But your kindness is even larger, is it not? Knowing you, I think: why wouldn't it be?

However, if this little card you sent is an invitation to be forgiven—for me to feel free to accept your forgiveness—I must say that I am unable to accept. Because I don't know that I'm properly penitent. And I feel, perhaps wrongly, that this attitude might qualify your forgiveness.

I can't bring myself yet to ask forgiveness for that night. If you've lived for a long while as an indecisive man, you can't simply forget, obliterate, bury, your one decisive moment. I can't—in the name of the future, perhaps—accept forgiveness for my time of strength, even if that time was so very brief, and was followed so quickly and humiliatingly by the dissolution of character, of everything. Others—you—may see my decisiveness—my doing something—anything—that!—as born only of desperation, and therefore without value. I, nevertheless, have to wonder about it a little more. You see, I thought at the time that I was sacrificing myself. Whatever broken explanations I offered to others in the days that followed, whatever—I find I cannot finish this sentence.

The rain has slackened and I must go. I don't believe that for you and me to correspond, on this matter or others, would be beneficial to either of us. But, of course, you are the one who knows that. I take it now that that was why you thought to have your card say nothing, just the time and the place of the event, and its nature. Thank you. It is only kind of you, Libby, to feel that I would want to know that I am off the hook. But I'm not, I can't be, I don't even want to be—not until I make some sense of the larger hook I'm on.

Yours,
Gabe

CHRONOLOGY

NOTE ON THE TEXTS

NOTES

Chronology

1933 Born Philip Roth on March 19 in Newark, New Jersey,
second child of Herman Roth and Bess Finkel. (Bess
Finkel, the second child of five, was born in 1904 in Elizabeth, New Jersey, to Philip and Dora Finkel, Jewish immigrants from near Kiev. Herman Roth was born in 1901
in Newark, New Jersey, the middle child of seven born to
Sender and Bertha Roth, Jewish immigrants from Polish
Galicia. They were married in Newark on February 21,
1926, and shortly afterward opened a small family-run
shoe store. Their son Sanford ["Sandy"] was born December 26, 1927. Following the bankruptcy of the shoe
store and a briefly held position as city marshal, Herman
Roth took a job as agent with the Newark district office
of the Metropolitan Life Insurance Company, and would
remain with the company until his retirement as district
manager in 1966.) Family moves into second-floor flat of
two-and-a-half-family house (with five-room apartments
on each of the first two floors and a three-room apartment on the top floor) at 81 Summit Avenue in Newark.
Summit Avenue was a lower-middle-class residential street
in the Weequahic section, a twenty-minute bus ride from
commercial downtown Newark and less than a block
from Chancellor Avenue School and from Weequahic
High School, then considered the state's best academic
public high school. These were the two schools that
Sandy and Philip attended. Between 1910 and 1920, Weequahic had been developed as a new city neighborhood at
the southwest corner of Newark, some three miles from
the edge of industrial Newark and from the international
shipping facilities at Port Newark on Newark Bay. In the
first half of the twentieth century Newark was a prosperous working-class city of approximately 420,000, the majority of its citizens of German, Italian, Slavic, and Irish
extraction. Blacks and Jews composed two of the smallest
groups in the city. From the 1930s to the 1950s, the Jews
lived mainly in the predominantly Jewish Weequahic
section.

1938   Philip enters kindergarten at Chancellor Avenue School in January.

1942   Roth family moves to second-floor flat of two-and-a-half-family house at 359 Leslie Street, three blocks west of Summit Avenue, still within the Weequahic neighborhood but nearer to semi-industrial boundary with Irvington.

1946   Philip graduates from elementary school in January, having skipped a year. Brother graduates from high school and chooses to enter U.S. Navy for two years rather than be drafted into the peacetime army.

1947   Family moves to first-floor flat of two-and-a-half-family house at 385 Leslie Street, just a few doors from commercial Chancellor Avenue, the neighborhood's main artery. Philip turns from reading sports fiction by John R. Tunis and adventure fiction by Howard Pease to reading the left-leaning historical novels of Howard Fast.

1948   Brother is discharged from navy and, with the aid of G.I. Bill, enrolls as commercial art student at Pratt Institute, Brooklyn. Philip takes strong interest in politics during the four-way U.S. presidential election in which the Republican Dewey loses to the Democrat Truman despite a segregationist Dixiecrat Party and a left-wing Progressive Party drawing away traditionally Democratic voters.

1950   Graduates from high school in January. Works as stock clerk at S. Klein department store in downtown Newark. Reads Thomas Wolfe; discovers Sherwood Anderson, Ring Lardner, Erskine Caldwell, and Theodore Dreiser. In September enters Newark College of Rutgers as pre-law student while continuing to live at home. (Newark Rutgers was at this time a newly formed college housed in two small converted downtown buildings, one formerly a bank, the other formerly a brewery.)

1951   Still a pre-law student, transfers in September to Bucknell University in Lewisburg, Pennsylvania. Brother graduates from Pratt Institute and moves to New York City to work for advertising agency. Parents move to Moorestown, New Jersey, approximately seventy miles southwest of Newark; father takes job as manager of Metropolitan Life's south Jersey district after having previously managed several north Jersey district offices.

1952   Roth decides to study English literature. With two friends, founds Bucknell literary magazine, *Et Cetera*, and becomes its first editor. Writes first short stories. Strongly influenced in his literary studies by English professor Mildred Martin, under whose tutelage he reads extensively, and with whom he will maintain lifelong friendship.

1954   Is elected to Phi Beta Kappa and graduates from Bucknell magna cum laude in English. Accepts scholarship to study English at the University of Chicago graduate school, beginning in September. Reads Saul Bellow's *The Adventures of Augie March*, and under its influence explores Chicago.

1955   In June receives M.A. with Honors in English. In September, rather than wait to be drafted, enlists in U.S. Army for two years. Suffers spinal injury during basic training at Fort Dix. In November, is assigned to Public Information Office at Walter Reed Army Hospital, Washington, D.C. Begins to write short stories "The Conversion of the Jews" and "Epstein." *Epoch*, a Cornell University literary quarterly, publishes "The Contest for Aaron Gold," which is reprinted in Martha Foley's *Best American Short Stories 1956*.

1956   Is hospitalized in June for complications from spinal injury. After two-month hospital stay receives honorable discharge for medical reasons and a disability pension. In September returns to University of Chicago as instructor in the liberal arts college, teaching freshman composition. Begins course work for Ph.D. but drops out after one term. Meets Ted Solotaroff, who is also a graduate student, and they become friends.

1957   Publishes in *Commentary* "You Can't Tell a Man by the Song He Sings." Writes novella "Goodbye, Columbus." Meets Saul Bellow at University of Chicago when Bellow is a classroom guest of Roth's friend and colleague, the writer Richard Stern. Begins to review movies and television for *The New Republic* after magazine publishes "Positive Thinking on Pennsylvania Avenue," a humor piece satirizing President Eisenhower's religious beliefs.

1958   Publishes "The Conversion of the Jews" and "Epstein" in *The Paris Review*; "Epstein" wins *Paris Review* Aga Khan Prize, presented to Roth in Paris in July. Spends first summer abroad, mainly in Paris. Houghton Mifflin awards Roth the Houghton Mifflin Literary Fellowship to publish the novella and five stories in one volume; George Starbuck, a poet and friend from Chicago, is his editor. Resigns from teaching position at University of Chicago. Moves to two-room basement apartment on Manhattan's Lower East Side. Becomes friendly with *Paris Review* editors George Plimpton and Robert Silvers and *Commentary* editor Martin Greenberg.

1959   Marries Margaret Martinson Williams. Publishes "Defender of the Faith" in *The New Yorker*, causing consternation among Jewish organizations and rabbis who attack magazine and condemn author as anti-Semitic; story collected in *Goodbye, Columbus* and included in *Best American Short Stories 1960* and *Prize Stories 1960: The O. Henry Awards*, where it wins second prize. *Goodbye, Columbus* is published in May. Roth receives Guggenheim fellowship and award from the American Academy of Arts and Letters. *Goodbye, Columbus* gains highly favorable reviews from Bellow, Alfred Kazin, Leslie Fiedler, and Irving Howe; influential rabbis denounce Roth in their sermons as "a self-hating Jew." Roth and wife leave U.S. to spend seven months in Italy, where he works on his first novel, *Letting Go*; he meets William Styron, who is living in Rome and who becomes a lifelong friend. Styron introduces Roth to his publisher, Donald Klopfer of Random House; when George Starbuck leaves Houghton Mifflin, Roth moves to Random House.

1960   *Goodbye, Columbus and Five Short Stories* wins National Book Award. The collection also wins Daroff Award of the Jewish Book Council of America. Roth returns to America to teach at the Writers' Workshop of the University of Iowa, Iowa City. Meets drama professor Howard Stein (later dean of the Columbia University Drama School), who becomes lifelong friend. Continues working on *Letting Go*. Travels in Midwest. Participates in *Esquire* magazine symposium at Stanford University; his speech "Writing American Fiction," published in *Commentary* in March 1961, is widely discussed. After a speaking engagement in Oregon, meets Bernard Malamud, whose fiction he admires.

1962   After two years at Iowa, accepts two-year position as writer-in-residence at Princeton. Separates from Margaret Roth. Moves to New York City and commutes to Princeton classes. (Lives at various Manhattan locations until 1970.) Meets Princeton sociologist Melvin Tumin, a Newark native who becomes a friend. Random House publishes *Letting Go.*

1963   Receives Ford Foundation grant to write plays in affiliation with American Place Theater in New York. Is legally separated from Margaret Roth. Becomes close friend of Aaron Asher, a University of Chicago graduate and editor at Meridian Books, original paperback publisher of *Goodbye, Columbus.* In June takes part in American Jewish Congress symposium in Tel Aviv, Israel, along with American writers Leslie Fiedler, Max Lerner, and literary critic David Boroff. Travels in Israel for a month.

1964   Teaches at State University of New York at Stony Brook, Long Island. Reviews plays by James Baldwin, LeRoi Jones, and Edward Albee for newly founded *New York Review of Books.* Spends a month at Yaddo, writers' retreat in Saratoga Springs, New York, that provides free room and board. (Will work at Yaddo for several months at a time throughout the 1960s.) Meets and establishes friendships there with novelist Alison Lurie and painter Julius Goldstein.

1965   Begins to teach comparative literature at University of Pennsylvania one semester each year more or less annually until the mid-1970s. Meets professor Joel Conarroe, who becomes a close friend. Begins work on *When She Was Good* after abandoning another novel, begun in 1962.

1966   Publishes section of *When She Was Good* in *Harper's.* Is increasingly troubled by Vietnam War and in ensuing years takes part in marches and demonstrations against it.

1967   Publishes *When She Was Good.* Begins work on *Portnoy's Complaint* of which he publishes excerpts in *Esquire, Partisan Review,* and *New American Review,* where Ted Solotaroff is editor.

1968   Margaret Roth dies in an automobile accident. Roth spends two months at Yaddo completing *Portnoy's Complaint.*

1969   *Portnoy's Complaint* published in February. Within weeks becomes number-one fiction best-seller and a widely discussed cultural phenomenon. Roth makes no public appearances and retreats for several months to Yaddo. Rents house in Woodstock, New York, and meets the painter Philip Guston, who lives nearby. They remain close friends and see each other regularly until Guston's death in 1980. Renews friendship with Bernard Malamud, who like Roth is serving as a member of The Corporation of Yaddo.

1970   Spends March traveling in Thailand, Burma, Cambodia, and Hong Kong. Begins work on *My Life as a Man* and publishes excerpt in *Modern Occasions.* Is elected to National Institute of Arts and Letters and is its youngest member. Commutes to his classes at University of Pennsylvania and lives mainly in Woodstock until 1972.

1971   Excerpts of *Our Gang*, satire of the Nixon administration, appear in *New York Review of Books* and *Modern Occasions;* the book is published by Random House in the fall. Continues work on *My Life as a Man;* writes *The Breast* and *The Great American Novel.* Begins teaching a Kafka course at University of Pennsylvania.

1972   *The Breast,* first book of three featuring protagonist David Kepesh, published by Holt, Rinehart, Winston, where Aaron Asher is his editor. Roth buys old farmhouse and forty acres in northwest Connecticut, one hundred miles from New York City, and moves there from Woodstock. In May travels to Venice, Vienna, and, for the first time, Prague. Meets his translators there, Luba and Rudolph Pilar, and they describe to him the impact of the political situation on Czech writers. In U.S., arranges to meet exiled Czech editor Antonin Liehm in New York; attends Liehm's weekly classes in Czech history, literature, and film at College of Staten Island, City University of New York. Through friendship with Liehm meets numerous Czech exiles, including film directors Ivan Passer and Jiří Weiss, who become friends. Is elected to the American Academy of Arts and Sciences.

1973   Publishes *The Great American Novel* and the essay "Looking at Kafka" in *New American Review.* Returns to Prague and meets novelists Milan Kundera, Ivan Klíma, Ludvik Vaculik, the poet Miroslav Holub, and other writers blacklisted and persecuted by the Soviet-backed Communist regime; becomes friendly with Rita Klímová, a blacklisted translator and academic, who will serve as Czechoslovakia's first ambassador to U.S. following the 1989 "Velvet Revolution." (Will make annual spring trips to Prague to visit his writer friends until he is denied an entry visa in 1977.) Writes "Country Report" on Czechoslovakia for American PEN. Proposes paperback series, "Writers from the Other Europe," to Penguin Books USA; becomes general editor of the series, selecting titles, commissioning introductions, and overseeing publication of Eastern European writers relatively unknown to American readers. Beginning in 1974, series publishes fiction by Polish writers Jerzy Andrzejewski, Tadeusz Borowski, Tadeusz Konwicki, Witold Gombrowicz, and Bruno Schulz; Hungarian writers György Konrád and Géza Csáth; Yugoslav writer Danilo Kiš; and Czech writers Bohumil Hrabal, Milan Kundera, and Ludvik Vaculik; series ends in 1989. "Watergate Edition" of *Our Gang* published, which includes a new preface by Roth.

1974 Roth publishes *My Life as a Man*. Visits Budapest as well as Prague and meets Budapest writers through Hungarian PEN and the *Hungarian Quarterly*. In Prague meets Vaclav Havel. Through friend Professor Zdenek Strybyrny, visits and becomes friend of the niece of Franz Kafka, Vera Saudkova, who shows him Kafka family photographs and family belongings; subsequently becomes friendly in London with Marianne Steiner, daughter of Kafka's sister Valli. Also through Strybyrny meets the widow of Jiří Weil; upon his return to America arranges for translation and publication of Weil's novel *Life with a Star* as well as publication of several Weil short stories in *American Poetry Review*, for which he provides an introduction. In Princeton meets Joanna Rostropowicz Clark, wife of friend Blair Clark; she becomes close friend and introduces Roth to contemporary Polish writing and to Polish writers visiting America, including Konwicki and Kazimierz Brandys. Publishes "Imagining Jews" in *New York Review of Books*; essay prompts letter from university professor, editor, writer, and former Jesuit Jack Miles. Correspondence ensues and the two establish a lasting intellectual friendship.

1975   Aaron Asher leaves Holt and becomes editor in chief at Farrar, Straus and Giroux; Roth moves to FSG with Asher for publication of *Reading Myself and Others*, a collection of interviews and critical essays. Meets British actress Claire Bloom.

1976   Interviews Isaac Bashevis Singer about Bruno Schulz for *New York Times Book Review* article to coincide with publication of Schulz's *Street of Crocodiles* in "Writers from the Other Europe" series. Moves with Claire Bloom to London, where they live six to seven months a year for the next twelve years. Spends the remaining months in Connecticut, where Bloom joins him when she is not acting in films, television, or stage productions. In London resumes an old friendship with British critic A. Alvarez and, a few years later, begins a friendship with American writer Michael Herr (author of *Dispatches*, which Roth admires) and with the American painter R. B. Kitaj. Also meets critic and biographer Hermione Lee, who becomes a friend, as does novelist Edna O'Brien. Begins regular visits to France to see Milan Kundera and another new friend, French writer-critic Alain Finkielkraut. Visits Israel for the first time since 1963 and returns there regularly, keeping a journal that eventually provides ideas and material for novels *The Counterlife* and *Operation Shylock*. Meets the writer Aharon Appelfeld in Jerusalem and they become close friends.

1977   Publishes *The Professor of Desire*, second book of Kepesh trilogy. Beginning in 1977 and continuing over the next few years, writes series of TV dramas for Claire Bloom: adaptations of *The Name-Day Party*, a short story by Chekhov; *Journey into the Whirlwind*, the gulag autobiography of Eugenia Ginzburg; and, with David Plante, *It Isn't Fair*, Plante's memoir of Jean Rhys. At request of Chichester Festival director, modernizes the David Magarshack translation of Chekhov's *The Cherry Orchard* for Claire Bloom's 1981 performance at the festival as Madame Ranyevskaya.

1979   *The Ghost Writer*, first novel featuring novelist Nathan Zuckerman as protagonist, is published in its entirety in *The New Yorker*, then published by Farrar, Straus and

Giroux. Bucknell awards Roth his first honorary degree; eventually receives honorary degrees from Amherst, Brown, Columbia, Dartmouth, Harvard, Pennsylvania, and Rutgers, among others.

1980   *A Philip Roth Reader* published, edited by Martin Green. Milan and Vera Kundera visit Connecticut on first trip to U.S.; Roth introduces Kundera to friend and *New Yorker* editor Veronica Geng, who also becomes Kundera's editor at the magazine. Conversation with Milan Kundera, in London and Connecticut, published in *New York Times Book Review*.

1981   Mother dies of a sudden heart attack in Elizabeth, New Jersey. *Zuckerman Unbound* published.

1982   Corresponds with Judith Thurman after reading her biography of Isak Dinesen, and they begin a friendship.

1983   Roth's physician and Litchfield County neighbor, Dr. C. H. Huvelle, retires from his Connecticut practice and the two become close friends.

1984   *The Anatomy Lesson* published. Aaron Asher leaves FSG and David Rieff becomes Roth's editor; the two soon become close friends. Conversation with Edna O'Brien in London published in *New York Times Book Review*. With BBC director Tristram Powell, adapts *The Ghost Writer* for television drama, featuring Claire Bloom; program is aired in U.S. and U.K. Meets University of Connecticut professor Ross Miller and the two forge strong literary friendship.

1985   *Zuckerman Bound*, a compilation of *The Ghost Writer*, *Zuckerman Unbound*, *The Anatomy Lesson*, with epilogue *The Prague Orgy*, published.

1986   Spends several days in Turin with Primo Levi. Conversation with Levi published in *New York Times Book Review*, which also asks that Roth write a memoir about Bernard Malamud upon Malamud's death at age 72.

1987   *The Counterlife* published; wins National Book Critics Circle Award for fiction. Corresponds with exiled Romanian writer Norman Manea, who is living in Berlin, and encourages him to come to live in U.S; Manea arrives the next year, and the two become close friends.

1988 *The Facts* published. Travels to Jerusalem for Aharon Appelfeld interview, which is published in *New York Times Book Review*. In Jerusalem, attends daily the trial of Ivan Demjanjuk, the alleged Treblinka guard "Ivan the Terrible." Returns to America to live year-round. Becomes Distinguished Professor of Literature at Hunter College of the City University of New York, where he will teach one semester each year until 1991.

1989 Father dies of brain tumor after yearlong illness. David Reiff leaves Farrar, Straus. For the first time since 1970, acquires a literary agent, Andrew Wylie of Wylie, Aitken, and Stone. Leaves FSG for Simon and Schuster. Writes a memoir of Philip Guston which is published in *Vanity Fair* and subsequently reprinted in Guston catalogs.

1990 *Deception* published by Simon and Schuster. Roth marries Claire Bloom in New York.

1991 Travels to post-Communist Prague for conversation with Ivan Klíma, published in *New York Review of Books.*

1991 *Patrimony* published; wins National Book Critics Circle Award for biography. Renews strong friendship with Saul Bellow.

1992 Reads from *Patrimony* for nationwide reading tour, extending into 1993. Publishes brief profile of Norman Manea in *New York Times Book Review.*

1993 *Operation Shylock* published; wins PEN/Faulkner Award for fiction. Separates from Claire Bloom. Writes *Dr. Huvelle: A Biographical Sketch*, which he publishes privately as a 34-page booklet for local distribution.

1994 Divorces Claire Bloom.

1995 Returns to Houghton Mifflin, where John Sterling is his editor. *Sabbath's Theater* is published and wins National Book Award for fiction.

1997 John Sterling leaves Houghton Mifflin and Wendy Strothman becomes Roth's editor. *American Pastoral*, first book of the "American trilogy," is published and wins Pulitzer Prize for fiction.

1998 *I Married a Communist*, the second book of the trilogy, is published and wins Ambassador Book Award of the English-Speaking Union. In October Roth attends three-day international literary program honoring his work in Aix-en-Provence. In November receives National Medal of Arts at the White House.

2000   Publishes *The Human Stain*, final book of American trilogy, which wins PEN/Faulkner Award in U.S., the W. H. Smith Award for best book of the year in the U.K., and the Prix Medicis for the best foreign book of the year in France. Publishes "Rereading Saul Bellow" in *The New Yorker*.

2001   Publishes *The Dying Animal*, final book of the Kepesh trilogy, and *Shop Talk*, a collection of interviews with and essays on Primo Levi, Aharon Appelfeld, I. B. Singer, Edna O'Brien, Milan Kundera, Ivan Klíma, Philip Guston, Bernard Malamud, and Saul Bellow, and an exchange with Mary McCarthy. Receives highest award of the American Academy of Arts and Letters, the Gold Medal in fiction, given every six years "for the entire work of the recipient," previously awarded to Willa Cather, Edith Wharton, John Dos Passos, William Faulkner, Saul Bellow, and Isaac Bashevis Singer, among others.

2002   Wins the National Book Foundation's Medal for Distinguished Contribution to American Letters.

2003   Receives honorary degrees at Harvard University and University of Pennsylvania. Roth's work now appears in 31 languages.

2004   Publishes novel *The Plot Against America*, which becomes a best-seller and wins the W. H. Smith Award for best book of the year in the U.K.; Roth is the first writer in the 46-year history of the prize to win it twice.

2005   *The Plot Against America* wins the Society of American Historians' James Fenimore Cooper Prize as the outstanding historical novel on an American theme for 2003–04.

Note on the Texts

This volume contains the first two books published by Philip Roth: *Goodbye, Columbus and Five Short Stories* (1959) and *Letting Go* (1962).

The novella and five short stories in *Goodbye, Columbus and Five Short Stories* were published between fall 1957 and spring 1959 in the following magazines: "You Can't Tell a Man by the Song He Sings": *Commentary*, November 1957; "Conversion of the Jews": *Paris Review*, Spring 1958; "Epstein": *Paris Review*, Summer 1958; "Goodbye, Columbus": *Paris Review*, Autumn–Winter 1958–1959; "Defender of the Faith": *The New Yorker*, March 14, 1959; "Eli, the Fanatic": *Commentary*, April 1959. Houghton Mifflin awarded Roth a Literary Fellowship in 1958 and agreed to publish the six works in a collection that was brought out in 1959. An English edition of "Goodbye, Columbus," without the short stories, was published in 1959 by Andre Deutsch. Roth did not subsequently revise the book. The text printed here is taken from the 1959 Houghton, Mifflin edition of *Goodbye, Columbus and Five Short Stories.*

Letting Go was published by Random House in 1962. Excerpts from the novel were published in *Cosmopolitan* (May 1960), *Esquire* (January 1962), *Mademoiselle* (May 1962), and *Harper's* (June 1962). Andre Deutsch also brought out an edition in England in 1962. The novel was not subsequently revised by Roth, and the text of the 1962 Random House edition of *Letting Go* is the one printed here.

This volume presents the texts of the original printings chosen for inclusion here, but it does not attempt to reproduce nontextual features of their typographic design. The texts are presented without change, except for the correction of typographical errors. Spelling, punctuation, and capitalization are often expressive features and are not altered, even when inconsistent or irregular. The following is a list of typographical errors corrected, cited by page and line number: 12.30, Katherine; 22.12, BRENDA: (*to me*); 22.13, (the choir boy again); 28.27, policeman; 44.31, shivered,; 49.18, then; 54.17, said; 63.23, even, if as; 68.30, Sometimes.; 72.16, ushing; 107.15, things?; 107.29, the Harvard; 116.7, on the; 118.31, Yes,; 146.15, going?"I; 158.5, You; 195.17, Lagerhans; 219.11, *please*"; 219.12, as as; 220.33, said; 222.29, Mrs?"; 234.25, envelopes; 239.10, Touchett's; 240.30, peoples'; 272.19, paste,; 277.9, worlds; 295.29, *D*; 299.36, thin," I suppose,; 301.30, *Reganhart*; 315.19, friends; 350.12, here, he; 375.37, Michigan,; 386.9,

Brittanica; 395.5, *times*; 402.32, Boboli."; 425.2, of father's; 439.2, upon?; 439.20, question?; 448.27, anway; 452.24, girl scout; 453.29, stops; 455.2, Beverley; 472.24, old old; 478.10, poet,; 504.21, in,; 518.30, Jerry; 546.16, Shweppes; 560.12, nickles; 596.25, then; 740.12, me; 742.16, pegnoir; 743.31, then; 749.21, "Autumn . . . York"; 762.12, positon; 767.35, Griffen's; 776.3, umbrella.; 825.19, effecting.

Notes

In the notes below, the reference numbers denote page and line of this volume (the line count includes chapter headings). No note is made for material included in standard desk references. Quotations from Shakespeare are keyed to *The Riverside Shakespeare*, ed. G. Blakemore Evans (Boston: Houghton Mifflin, 1974).

GOODBYE, COLUMBUS AND FIVE SHORT STORIES

9.19–20   Galen Drake]   Radio personality and talk-show host.

16.15–17   Prince Andrey's . . . Princess Liza]   Characters in *War and Peace*.

17.5   Lowell House]   Harvard residential college.

35.33   Brownie Reflex]   Kodak snapshot camera.

35.35   *tallas*]   Prayer shawl.

41.35   Hadassah]   Zionist women's organization.

53.22–23   Andre Kostelanetz . . . Mantovani]   Trained as a classical musician in czarist Russia, Andre Kostelanetz (1901–1980) adapted classical compositions to a simplified popular form and orchestrated popular standards; composer and arranger Annunzio Paolo Mantovani (1905–1980) pioneered "easy listening" music.

59.5   Bob Mathias]   Track and field athlete (b. 1930) who won the gold medal in the decathlon at the 1948 Olympics.

74.7   *jahrzeit*]   Yiddish, "year's time." On the anniversary of a person's death, a memorial candle set in a small glass jar is lit in remembrance.

84.15   Billy May]   Music arranger (1916–2004) who worked with the Glenn Miller Band and Bing Crosby.

87.2–3   Aly Khan . . . marrying movie stars]   Prince Aly Khan (1911–1960) married American actress Rita Hayworth in 1949. He was the son of Aga Khan, spiritual leader of millions of Asian and African Muslims and self-proclaimed descendant of the Prophet Mohammed.

90.20   *shtarke*]   Strong, brave, big shot.

91.31   *poilishehs*]   Poles.

93.22–23   Mogen David]   Sweet kosher red wine.

113.15   Hank Greenberg]   Baseball's first Jewish superstar (1911–1986).

119.21   Fier und tsvansik . . . finf und tsvantsik]   Twenty-four . . . twenty-
five.

128.31   P.T.]   Army physical fitness test.

131.27   Good *shabbus*]   Good (happy) Sabbath. Salutation on the day of
rest.

133.25   *trafe*]   Not kosher.

133.36   "Ain Kelohainu"]   Prayer chanted in praise of the one God.

135.10   *leben*]   Literally "life," here a term of endearment.

140.18   *ballabusta*]   Mistress of the household, a fine housekeeper.

144.29   *chrain*]   Horseradish root served at the Passover seder.

149.4   *tsimmes*]   A big deal made out of nothing (slang).

155.11   Howard Fast]   Left-wing American writer (1914–2003), author of
popular historical novels such as *Citizen Tom Paine* (1943) and *Spartacus*
(1951).

163.5   *Vus far*]   Yiddish question words: What's for?

168.22   *oysgamitched*]   Completely exhausted.

185.8–9   Kefauver Committee]   Estes Kefauver (1903–1963), Democratic
senator from Tennessee, headed a committee to investigate the infiltration
of organized crime into interstate commerce (1950–51).

185.30   (to alter an Ancient's text)]   Cf. Heraclitus (c. 540 BCE–c. 480 BCE):
"A man's character is his fate."

193.27   DP]   Designation for displaced persons after World War II.

195.14   island of Langerhans]   Islets of Langerhans, endocrine cells within
the pancreas that secrete insulin, named for the German anatomist, Paul
Langerhans (1847–1888), who discovered them.

214.4–5   Food and Drug Act]   The Pure Food and Drug Act of 1906 (the
"Wiley Act") gave the federal government the authority to test and evaluate
food and drugs for safety and efficacy.

LETTING GO

277.5–6   Henry Wallace]   Henry Agard Wallace (1888–1965) served as Secretary of Agriculture (1933–40) in Roosevelt's cabinet and as Vice-President
(1941–45). He was the Progressive candidate for President in 1948.

309.22   Riker's]   The prison at Riker's Island on the East River.

310.29   *shaifele*]   Daughter.

367.3   *yiddishe maydele*] Jewish maiden, affectionate phrase for a little girl.

369.18   *shmekele*] A little shmuck (penis), a really stupid person.

378.23   *gonifs*] Thieves.

390.24   *mamza*] Bastard; an untrustworthy man.

415.15   *Marjorie Morningstar*] Bestselling novel (1955) by Herman Wouk (b. 1915), the story of a beautiful, intelligent young woman who rebels against her middle-class Jewish parents.

423.19   *Kirby Higbe*] Walter Kirby Higbe (1915–1985), hard-throwing pitcher notorious for his colorful life off the field.

424.34   Dore Schary] Newark-born screenwriter, director, and producer (1905–1980) who was president of MGM studios from 1951 to 1956; also an activist, he served as chairman of B'nai B'rith's Anti-Defamation League.

428.33   *haymishe*] Warm, friendly.

445.14   de Staël] Russian-born painter Nicolas de Stael (1914–1955).

477.31–32   slipping a note to Enrico Fermi] Italian physicist Enrico Fermi (1901–1954) directed work on the first controlled nuclear chain reaction, which took place at the University of Chicago on December 2, 1942.

477.33   Quiz Kid] NBC's "Quiz Kids" radio show premiered on June 28, 1940, and ran for thirteen years (in its later years on television as well). Children with IQs ranging from average to above 200 were asked questions like, "Divide the number of Ali Baba's thieves by the number of quints, add the horsemen of the Apocalypse, and subtract the number of days it took to make the world."

478.10   Barnaby Googe] English poet and translator (1540–1594).

478.11   Breadloaf] Writers' colony in Middlebury, Vermont.

478.12–13   rejection slips . . . hand] Poet and critic John Crowe Ransom (1888–1974) long served as editor of *The Kenyon Review*, an influential journal based at Kenyon College in Ohio.

487.3–4   arise . . . moon!"] *Romeo and Juliet*, II.ii.4.

527.17   Modess] Sanitary napkins.

551.18   He that filches . . . name] *Othello*, III.iii.159.

580.25   *Already . . . night*] John Keats, "Ode to a Nightingale."

580.32–33   *Come live . . . prove.*] The opening lines of Christopher Marlowe's "The Passionate Shepherd to His Love."

580.35–37   *The expense . . . murderous*]   The opening lines of Shakespeare's Sonnet 129.

581.7–9   *Sabrina fair . . . wave*—]   Cf. Milton, *Comus*, lines 859–61.

581.10   *And I . . . white*]   Cf. Blake, "The Little Black Boy," line 2.

581.11–12   *How sweetly . . . clothes*]   Cf. Robert Herrick, "Upon Julia's Clothes," lines 2–3.

581.13–14   *At last. . . pastures new.*]   Milton, *Lycidas*, lines 192–93.

581.15–17   *I am! . . . woes.*]   The opening lines of John Clare, "I Am."

591.17–19   "The worst . . . backwards, or wrong]   Cf. Yeats, "The Second Coming," lines 7–8: "The best lack all convictions, while the worst / Are full of passionate intensity."

668.12   *tsura*]   Trouble, misery.

822.14   Lepke]   Louis "Lepke" Buchalter (1897–1944), New York labor racketeer and leader of the gang of hired killers popularly known as "Murder, Incorporated." Lepke was executed at Sing Sing prison in 1944.

828.23   *The Princess Casamassima*]   1888 novel by Henry James.

Library of Congress Cataloging-in-Publication Data

Roth, Philip.
    [Selections. 2005]
    Novels & stories, 1959–1962 / Philip Roth.
        p. cm. — (The Library of America ; 157)
    Includes bibliographical references.
    Contents: Goodbye, Columbus and five short stories—Letting
go.
    ISBN 1–931082–79–0 (alk. paper)
        I. Title: Novels and stories, 1959–1962. II. Title: Goodbye,
Columbus. III. Title: Letting go. IV. Series.

PS3568.O855A6   2005
813'.54—dc22   2005040916

*This book is set in 10 point Linotron Galliard,
a face designed for photocomposition by Matthew Carter
and based on the sixteenth-century face Granjon. The paper
is acid-free Domtar Literary Opaque and meets the requirements
for permanence of the American National Standards Institute. The
binding material is Brillianta, a woven rayon cloth made by
Van Heek-Scholco Textielfabrieken, Holland. Composition by Dedicated Business Services. Printing by
Malloy Incorporated. Binding by Dekker Book-
binding. Designed by Bruce Campbell.*